Danielle Steel
THREE-IN-ONE

Danielle Steel
THREE-IN-ONE

BCA

LONDON NEW YORK SYDNEY TORONTO

This edition published 1992
by BCA by arrangement with
PIATKUS BOOKS LTD

Reprinted 1992, 1993

*A catalogue record for this book is available
from the British Library*

CN 5674

Printed and bound in Great Britain by
Mackays of Chatham PLC, Chatham, Kent

A PERFECT STRANGER

Danielle Steel

To Nicholas,

May you find what you want in life,
know it when you see it, and
have the good luck to get it –
and keep it ! ! !

With all my love,
D.S.

Chapter 1

The garage door opened eerily, its mouth yawning expectantly, a large dark toad about to gobble an unsuspecting fly. From across the street a little boy watched it, fascinated. He loved watching the door open like that, knowing that the beautiful sports car would be around the corner in an instant. He waited, counting . . . five . . . six . . . seven . . . Unknown to the man who had pressed the remote control device on his dashboard, the little boy watched him come home every night. It was a favourite ritual and the boy was disappointed when the man in the black Porsche came home late or not at all. The boy stood there, in the shadows, counting . . . eleven . . . twelve . . . and then he saw it, a sleek black shadow speeding around the bend, and then in a smooth manoeuvre sliding into the garage. The unseen child stared hungrily at the beautiful black car for one more moment and then slowly went home, with visions of the black Porsche still dancing in his eyes.

Inside the garage, Alexander Hale turned off the motor, and then sat there for a moment staring into the familiar darkness of his garage. For the hundredth time that day, his mind drifted once again to Rachel. For the hundredth time he pushed the thought of her away from his mind. He sighed softly, picked up his briefcase and got out of the car. A moment later the electronic device would automatically close the garage door. He let himself into the house through a back door in his garden, and he stood in the downstairs hall of the pretty little Victorian townhouse, staring into the emptiness of the once cosy kitchen. There were copper pots hanging from a wrought iron rack near the stove, but the cleaning lady hadn't shined them in ages, and there was no one else to give a damn. The plants which hung thickly in front of the windows were looking dry and lifeless, and he noticed, as he switched on the lights in the kitchen, that some of them had already died. He turned away then, glancing only briefly into the small wood-panelled dining-room across the hall, and then walked slowly upstairs.

Now when he came home, he always used the garden entrance. It was less depressing than coming in through the main hall. Whenever he came through the front door in the evening, he somehow still expected her to be there. He expected to see her with the luscious pile of thick blonde hair knotted on top of her head, and the deceptively prim suits she wore to court. Rachel . . . dazzling lawyer . . . noble friend . . . intriguing female . . . until she hurt him . . . until she left . . . until their divorce, exactly two years before, to the day.

He had wondered on his way home from the office if he would always remember the day so exactly. Would some part of him call out in remembered pain on a given morning in October, for the rest of time? Would he always be reminded? It was strange really how both of their anniversaries had fallen on the same day. The anniversary of their marriage, and that of their divorce. Coincidence, Rachel had called it matter of factly. Ironic, he had said. How awful, his mother had said when she called him the night the papers came. He had been blind drunk and laughing, because he didn't want to cry.

Rachel. The thought of her still disturbed him. He knew it shouldn't after two years, but it did . . . The golden hair and the eyes the colour of the Atlantic Ocean just before a storm, dark grey, tinged with blue and green. The first time he had seen her had been as the attorney for the opposition in a case which had settled out of court. It had been a mighty battle, though, and Joan of Arc couldn't have pleaded the case with more enthusiasm and flair. Alexander had watched her throughout the proceedings, fascinated and amused, and more attracted to her than he had been to any woman in his life. He had invited her to dinner that night, and she had insisted on paying her half of the cheque. She didn't 'corrupt professional relationships' she had told him, with an arch little smile that half made him want to slap her, and half made him want to tear off her clothes. She had been so goddamn beautiful, and so goddamn smart.

The memory of her made him knit his brows as he walked

2

past the empty living-room. She had taken all the living-room furniture with her to New York. She had left the rest of their furniture to Alex, but the big double parlour on the main floor of the pretty little Victorian house they had bought together had been stripped bare. Sometimes he wondered if he hadn't bought new furniture just so he could remember, so he could resent her, each time he walked past the empty living-room to the front door. But now, as he walked upstairs, he didn't see the emptiness around him. His mind was a million miles away, thinking back to the days before she left him, thinking about what they had and had not shared. They had shared hope and wit and laughter and their professions, their bed, this house and very little else.

Alex had wanted children, to fill the bedrooms on the top floor with noise and laughter. Rachel had wanted to go into politics or get a job with an important law firm in New York. The politics she had mentioned vaguely when she met him. It would have been natural for her. Her father was a powerful man in Washington, and had once been Governor of their home state. It was something else she had in common with Alex, whose sister was a Congresswoman in New York. Rachel always admired her greatly, and she and Alex' sister Kay had rapidly become fast friends. But it wasn't politics which took Rachel away from Alex. It was the other half of her dream, the law firm in New York. In the end, it had taken her two years to pick up stakes and leave him. He ran the finger of his mind over the wound now. It no longer smarted as it once had. But at first, it had hurt him more than anything in his life.

She was beautiful, brilliant, successful, dynamic, amusing ... but there had always been something missing, something tender and gentle and kind. Those were not words one used to describe Rachel. And she had wanted more out of life than just loving Alexander, more than just being an attorney in San Francisco and someone's wife. She had been exactly twenty-nine years old when they met, and she had never been married. She'd been too busy for that, she told him, too busy chasing her life's goals. She had promised herself when she left law school that by the time she was thirty she would have made it 'big'. What does that mean,

3

he had asked her. A hundred thousand a year was the answer, and she didn't even blink. For an instant, he had laughed at her. Until he saw the look in her eyes. She meant it. And she'd get it. Her whole life was geared to that kind of success. Success measured by that kind of yardstick, dollar bills and important cases, no matter who was destroyed in the process. Before she left for New York, Rachel had walked over half of San Francisco, and even Alex had finally let himself see what she was. She was cold and ruthless and ambitious and she stopped at nothing to reach her goals.

Four months after they were married, a spot opened up in one of the most prestigious law firms in town. At first, Alex was impressed that she was even being considered. She was, after all, a fairly young woman, and a young attorney, but it didn't take long to figure out that she was willing to use every ugly manoeuvre she could to get the job. And she did, and she got it. For two years, Alex tried to forget what he'd seen her pull to get the job. He told himself that she only used tactics like that in business, and then the final crunch came. She was made a full partner and offered a spot in the New York office. This time it was more than a hundred thousand dollar a year job. And Rachel Hale was only thirty-one. Alexander watched with horror and fascination as she wrestled with the choice. The choice was simple, and as far as Alex was concerned, it shouldn't have been a choice at all. New York or San Francisco. Alexander, or not. In the end, she told him gently, it was just too good an opportunity to pass up. 'But it didn't have to change their relationship.' She could still fly home to San Francisco almost every weekend, or of course if Alex wanted to . . . he could give up his own law practice and come East with her.

'And do what? Prepare your briefs?' He had stared at her in hurt and fury. 'So where does that leave me, Rachel?' He had stared at her after she had announced her decision to take the job in New York. He had wanted it to be different, wanted her to tell him that she wouldn't take it, that he mattered more. But that hadn't been Rachel's style, any more than it would have been Alex's sister's. Once he was willing to face it, he realised that he had known one other woman like Rachel before. His sister Kay had pushed her

4

way to what she wanted, storming over obstacles, and devouring or destroying those who inadvertently crossed her path. The only difference was that Kay did it in politics and Rachel in law.

It was easier to understand, and respect, a woman like his mother. Charlotte Brandon had somehow successfully managed both children and a career. For twenty-five years she had been one of the country's best-selling authors, yet she had managed Alex and his sister, stayed close to them, loved them, and given them her all. When her husband had died when Alex was a baby, she had taken a part-time job doing research for a newspaper column, and eventually ghost-written it completely, while in whatever spare time she had, she sat up until the small hours writing her first book. The rest was history, chronicled on the book jackets of the nineteen books she had written and sold in millions over the years. Her career had been an accident created by need. But whatever her reasons, she had always somehow managed to treat what had happened as a special gift, as something she could share and enjoy with her children, not as something she loved more than she loved them. Charlotte Brandon was truly a remarkable woman, but her daughter was different; angry, jealous, compulsive, she had none of her mother's gentleness or warmth or ability to give. And in time, Alex learned that neither did his wife.

When Rachel left for New York, she had insisted that she didn't want to divorce him. For a while, she had even tried to commute, but with their separate work loads at opposite ends of the country, their weekends together became less and less frequent. It was hopeless, as she eventually admitted to Alex, and for two endless weeks he had actually considered closing his own lucrative practice and moving to New York. Hell, what did it mean to him? Maybe it wasn't worth hanging on to, if it meant losing his wife. At four o'clock one morning, he made the decision, he would close his practice and go. Exhausted, but feeling hopeful, he reached for the phone to call her. It was seven in the morning in New York. But it wasn't Rachel who answered. It was a man with a deep honey-smooth voice. 'Mrs Hale?' He sounded blank for a moment, 'Oh, Miss Patterson.' Rachel Patterson. Alex

5

hadn't realised that she had begun her new life in New York under her old name. But he hadn't realised either that along with the new job, she had begun a whole new way of life. There was very little she could say to him that morning, and he listened to her voice at the other end with tears in his eyes. She called him back later that morning from her office.

'What can I say, Alex? I'm sorry . . .?' Sorry? For leaving? For having an affair? What was she sorry for? Or was she just sorry for him, poor pathetic bastard that he was, sitting alone out in San Francisco.

'Is there any point trying to work it out?' He had been willing to try, but at least this time she was honest.

'No, Alex, I'm afraid not.' They had talked for a few more minutes and then finally hung up the phone. There was nothing left to say, except to their own attorneys. The following week Alex filed for divorce. It all went smoothly. 'Perfectly civilised,' as Rachel had said. There had been no problems at all, yet it had shaken Alex to the very roots of his being.

And for an entire year he had felt as though someone near and dear to him had died.

Possibly it was himself he mourned. He felt as though part of him had been put away in crates and boxes, like the living-room furniture that had been shipped to New York. He functioned perfectly normally, he ate, he slept, he went on dates, he swam, he played tennis, racquet ball, squash, went to parties, travelled, and his law practice boomed. But some essential part of him was missing. And he knew it, even if no one else did. He had had nothing, except his body, to give to a woman in more than two years.

As he walked upstairs to his study, the silence in the house became suddenly unbearable, and all he wanted was to run. Lately, it was something that happened to him often, that overpowering urge to get out, to get away from the emptiness and the silence. It was only now after more than two years without her that the numbness was wearing off. It was as though the bandages were finally peeling away, and what was left beneath was lonely and raw.

Alex changed into jeans, sneakers and an old parka, and thumped rapidly back downstairs, one long powerful hand

6

lightly touching the banister, his dark hair slightly rumpled, his blue eyes intense as he slammed the door behind him and turned right until he reached Divisadero, where he began running slowly up the steep hill to Broadway, where at last he stopped and turned to look at the breathtaking view. Beneath him, the bay shone like satin in the twilight, the hills were veiled in mist and the lights of Marin sparkled like diamonds and rubies and emeralds just across the bay.

When he reached the stately mansions on Broadway, he turned right and began to walk toward the Presidio, glancing alternately at the huge impressive houses and the tranquil beauty of the Bay. The houses themselves were among the finest in San Francisco. These were the two or three most expensive residential blocks in the city, boasting brick palaces and Tudor mansions, remarkable gardens, breathtaking views, and towering trees. One saw not a soul walking, and heard not a sound from the neat row of houses, though one could easily imagine the tinkle of crystal, the ring of fine silver, the liveried servants and gentlemen and ladies in dinner jackets and dresses of satin or silk. Alex always smiled to himself at the images he painted. Somehow they made him less lonely than what he imagined as he drifted past the smaller houses or the less impressive streets he frequently walked. There he always envisioned men with their arms around their women, with smiling children and puppies playing in the kitchen, or stretched out in front of warm, crackling fires. In the big houses there was nothing that he wanted. That was a world he did not aspire to, though he had often been in houses like those. What Alex wanted for himself was something very different, something that he and Rachel had never had.

It was difficult to imagine being in love anymore, caring about someone deeply, difficult to imagine looking into someone's eyes and wanting to explode with joy. There had been none of that for Alex in so long that he had almost forgotten what it could feel like, and sometimes he wasn't even sure that he wanted that any more. He was tired of the bustling career women, more interested in their salaries and how quickly they'd get their next promotion, than in getting married and having kids. He wanted an old-fashioned

7

woman, a miracle, a rarity, a gem. And there were none. There had been nothing but expensive fakes in Alex's life for almost two years. And what he wanted was the real thing, a perfect flawless remarkable diamond, and he doubted very seriously that there were any around. But one thing he did know and that was that he wasn't going to settle for anything less than his dream. And he didn't want another woman like Rachel. That much he knew too.

He put her out of his thoughts again now and he stood there, looking at the view from the Baker Street stairs. They were carved steeply into the hillside joining Broadway to Vallejo Street below, and he enjoyed the view and the cool breeze as he decided to go no farther and sat down on the top step. As he unravelled his long legs beneath him, he smiled at the city he had adopted. Maybe he'd never find the right woman. Maybe he'd never marry again. So what? He had a good life, a nice house, a law practice that was both enjoyable and successful. Maybe he didn't need more than that. Maybe he had no right to ask for more.

He let his gaze take in the pastel coloured houses of the Marina, the little Gingerbread Victorians in Cow Hollow, not unlike his own, the rounded Grecian splendour of the Palace of Fine Arts well below him, and then as his eyes left the dome Maybeck had created half a century earlier, he found himself looking down at the rooftops below him, and then suddenly there she was. A woman sitting huddled at the bottom of the steps, almost as though she were carved there, a statue like those on the Palace of Fine Arts, only this one far more delicate, with her head bowed, and her profile silhouetted by the light across the street. He found himself sitting very still and staring, as though she were a sculpture, a statue, a work of art which someone had abandoned there, a handsome marble in the form of a woman, so artfully fashioned that it almost seemed real.

She did not move for almost five minutes, and then sitting up very straight she took a long, deep breath of the fresh night air, and exhaled it slowly as though she had had a very hard day. There was a cloud of pale fur coat around her and Alex could see her face and her features come clear in the dark. There was something unusual about her which made

8

him want to see more. He found himself sitting there, unable to look away. It was the oddest feeling Alex could remember, sitting there, staring down at her in the dim light from the street lamps, feeling pulled by her. Who was she? What was she doing there? Her presence seemed to touch him to the very core of his being as he sat very still, wanting to know more.

Her skin looked very white in the darkness, and her hair was shiny and dark, swept softly into a knot at the nape of her neck. Her hair gave the impression of being very long, and held in place perhaps by only one or two well-placed pins. For a moment, he had an insane desire to run down the steps, towards her, to touch her, and take her in his arms, and loosen the dark hair. And almost as though she sensed what he was thinking, she looked up suddenly from her reverie, as though pulled back from a very great distance by a firm hand. She turned towards him, and stared. And what he saw as he looked down at her was the most beautiful face he had ever seen. A face, as he had first suspected, with the perfect proportions of a work of art, tiny, delicate features, a flawless face filled with enormous dark eyes, and a gently curving mouth. But her eyes were what captivated him as they looked at each other, eyes which seemed to fill her entire face, eyes which seemed to be filled with im-measurable sorrow, and in the lamplight now he could see two shining rivers of tears on the white marble cheeks. For one endless instant, their eyes met, and Alex felt as though every ounce of his being reached out to the unknown beauty with the big eyes and dark hair. She looked so vulnerable and so lost as she sat there, and then as though embarrassed by what she had let him see even briefly, she quickly bowed her head. For an instant, Alex didn't move, and then suddenly he felt pulled towards her again, as though he had to go to her. And then as he watched her, trying to decide what to do, in an instant she stood up, enveloped in fur. It was a lynx coat that drifted about her like a cloud. Her eyes flew to Alex's again, but this time for only an instant, and then as though she had been only an apparition, she seemed to walk into a hedge and disappear. For a long moment, Alex stared at where she had been, rooted to the spot where

9

he sat. It had all happened so quickly. Then suddenly he stood and ran quickly down the steps towards where she had sat. He saw then a narrow pathway leading to a heavy door. He could only guess at a garden beyond it, and there was no way of knowing to which house it belonged. It could have been any one of several. So the mystery ended there. For an impotent moment, Alex found himself wanting to knock on the door she had entered. Perhaps she was sitting in the hidden garden behind the locked door. There was an instant of desperation, knowing that he would never see her again. And then, feeling foolish, he reminded himself that she was only a stranger. He stared at the door for a long pensive moment, and then turned slowly and walked back up the stairs.

Chapter 2

Even as Alex put the key in his front door, he was haunted by the face of the crying woman. Who was she? Why had she been crying? From which house had she come? He sat on the narrow circular staircase in his front hallway staring into the empty living-room and watching the moonlight reflected on the bare wood floor. He had never seen a woman so lovely. It was a face that could easily haunt one for a lifetime and he realised as he sat there without moving that, if not for a lifetime, he would certainly remember her for a very long time. He didn't even hear the phone when it rang a few minutes later. He was still lost in thought, pondering the vision he had seen. But when he finally heard the phone, he ran to the first landing with a few quick bounds and into his den in time to dig the phone out from beneath a stack of papers on his desk.

'Hello, Alex.' Instantly, there was a moment of silent tension between them. It was his sister, Kay.

'What's up?' Which meant what did she want. She never called anyone unless she wanted or needed something.

'Nothing special. Where were you? I've been calling for the last half hour. The girl working late in your office told me you were going straight home.' She was always like that. She wanted what she wanted when she wanted it, whether it suited anyone else or not.

'I was out for a walk.'

'At this hour?' She sounded suspicious. 'Why? Something wrong?' He sighed softly to himself. For years now, his sister had exhausted him. There was so little give, so little softness to her. It was all cold and hard and sharp. She reminded him sometimes of a very sharp crystal object one would put on a desk. Pretty to look at, but not something one would ever want to pick up or touch. And it had been obvious for years that her husband felt the same way.

'No, nothing's wrong, Kay.' But he also had to admit that

11

for a woman as indifferent as she was to other people's feelings, she had an uncanny knack for sensing when he was down or out of sorts. 'I just needed some air. I had a long day.' And then, attempting to soften the conversation and turn her attention slightly away from him, 'Don't you ever go for a walk, Kay?'

'In New York? You must be crazy. You could die here just from breathing.'

'Not to mention mugging and rape.' He smiled gently into the phone and he could sense her smile too. Kay Willard wasn't a woman who smiled often. She was too intense, too hurried, too harassed, and too seldom amused. 'To what do I owe the honour of this phone call?' He sat back in his chair and looked at the view, as he waited patiently for an answer.

For a long time, Kay would call about Rachel. Kay had stayed in touch with her ex-sister-in-law for obvious reasons. The old Governor was someone she wanted to keep in her court. And if she could have talked Alex into going back to Rachel, the old man would have loved it. Provided, of course, that she could have convinced Rachel of how desperately unhappy Alex was without her, and how much it would mean to him if she'd only give it another try. And Kay wasn't above that kind of pushing. She had already tried to manoeuvre a meeting between them several times when Alex had come to New York. But even if Rachel had been willing, of which Kay was never entirely sure, it had become clear over the years, that Alex was not. 'So, Congresswoman Willard?'

'Nothing special. I just wondered when you were coming to New York.'

'Why?'

'Don't be so blunt for chrissake. I just thought I'd have a few people over for dinner.'

'Like who?' Alex saw her coming and he grinned. She was amazing, his sister the steam roller. You had to say one thing for her, she never quit.

'All right, Alex, don't get so defensive.'

'Who's defensive? I just wanted to know with whom you want to have me to dinner. What's wrong with that, unless of course there happens to be someone on your guest list who might just make us all a little uncomfortable? Should I guess initials, Kay, would that make it easier?'

She had to laugh in spite of herself. 'All right, all right, I get the message. But for chrissake, Alex, I ran into her the other day on a plane back from D.C. and she looks just great.'

'She should. On her salary, so would you.'

'Thank you, dear.'

'Any time.'

'Did you know that she's been asked to run for office?'

'No.' There was a long silence. 'But I'm not really surprised. Are you?'

'No.' And then his sister sighed loudly. 'Sometimes I wonder if you realise what you gave up there.'

'I certainly do, and I'm grateful every day of my life. I don't want to be married to a politician, Kay. That's an honour that should be reserved only for men like George.'

'What the hell does that mean?'

'He's so busy with his practice, I'm sure he doesn't even notice when you're in Washington for three weeks. Me, I'd notice.' And he didn't tell her that her daughter noticed too. He knew because he talked to Amanda at great length whenever he went to New York. He took her out to lunch, or dinner, or for long walks. He knew her better than her own parents, not that Kay gave a damn. 'By the way, how's Amanda?'

'All right, I guess.'

'What do you mean, "you guess"?' The criticism in his tone was easy to read. 'Haven't you seen her?'

'Jesus Christ. I just got off the fucking plane from D.C. What do you want from me, Alex?'

'Not much. What you do is none of my business. What you do to her is something else.'

'That's none of your business either.'

'Isn't it? Then whose business is it, Kay? George's? Does he notice that you never spend ten minutes with your daughter? Does he make up for it?'

'She's sixteen years old for chrissake, she doesn't need a babysitter any more, Alex.'

'No, but she needs a mother and a father.'

'I can't help that. I'm in politics. You know how demanding that is.'

'Yeah.' He shook his head slowly, and that was what she wanted to wish on him. A life with Rachel 'Patterson'. 'Anything else?' He didn't want to talk to her any more. He'd had enough of listening to her in just five minutes.

'I'm running for the Senate next year.'

'Congratulations.' His voice was flat.

'Don't get too excited.'

'I'm not. I was thinking about Mandy, and what that might mean for her.'

If I win, it'll mean she's a Senator's daughter, that's what.' Kay sounded suddenly vicious, and Alex wanted to slap her face.

'Do you think she really cares about that, Kay?'

'Probably not. the kid has her head so high in the clouds, she probably wouldn't give a shit if I ran for President.' For a moment Kay sounded sad and Alex shook his head.

'That's not what matters, Kay. We're all proud of you, we love you, but there's more than that . . .' How could he tell her? How could he explain? She cared about nothing except her career, her work.

'I don't think any of you understand what this means to me, Alex, how hard I've worked for it, how far I've come. It's been killing, and I've made it, and all you do is bitch about what kind of mother I am. And our dear mother is worse, and George is too busy cutting people open to remember if I'm Congresswoman or Mayor. It's a little discouraging, kiddo, to say the least.'

'I'm sure it is. But sometimes people get hurt by careers like yours.'

'That's to be expected.'

'Is it? Is that what it's all about?'

'Maybe.' She sounded tired. 'I don't have all the answers. I wish I did. And what about you? What's happening in your life these days?'

'Nothing much. Work.'

'Are you happy?'

'Sometimes.'

14

'You ought to go back to Rachel.'

'At least you get to the point quickly. I don't want to, Kay. Besides, what makes you think she'd want me?'

'She said she'd like to see you.'

'Oh Christ.' He sighed into the phone. 'You never give up, do you? Why don't you just marry her father and leave me in peace, that would get you the same results, wouldn't it?'

This time Kay laughed. 'Maybe.'

'Do you really expect me to marry to further your career?' The very idea amused him, but underneath the outrageousness of it, he knew there was a grain of truth. 'I think what I love best about you, big sister, is your unlimited nerve.'

'It gets me where I want to go, little brother.'

'I'm sure it does, but not this time, love.'

'No little dinner with Rachel?'

'Nope. But if you see her again, give her my best.' Something in his guts tugged again at the mention of her name. He didn't love her anymore, but now and then just hearing about her still hurt.

'I'll do that. And think about it. I can always throw something together when you're in New York.'

'With any luck at all, you'll be in Washington and too busy to see me.'

'Could be. When are you coming East?'

'Probably in a couple of weeks. I've got a client to see in New York. I'm co-counsel for him on a fairly big case out here.'

'I'm impressed.'

'Are you?' His eyes narrowed as he glanced out at the view. 'Why? Will it sound good in your campaign material? I think Mother's readers will get you more votes than I will, don't you?' There was a touch of irony in his voice. 'Unless of course, I have the good sense to remarry Rachel.'

'Just don't get into any trouble.'

'Have I ever?' He sounded amused.

'No, but if I run for the Senate, it'll be a tight race. I'm running against that morality maniac, and if anyone even remotely related to me does something unsavoury, I'll be up shit creek.'

'Be sure you tell Mother.' He said it in jest but she responded immediately with a serious voice.

'I already have.'

'Are you kidding?' He laughed at the very thought of his elegant long-legged, couture-clad white-haired mother doing anything unsuitable which might jeopardise Kay's bid for a seat in the Senate, or anywhere else.

'I am not kidding, I mean it. I can't afford any problems right now. No nonsense, no scandal.'

'What a shame.'

'What does that mean?'

'I don't know . . . I was thinking of having an affair with this ex-hooker who just got out of jail.'

'Very funny. I'm serious.'

'Unfortunately, I think you are. Anyway, you can give me my list of instructions when I come to New York. I'll try to behave myself until then.'

'Do that, and let me know when you're going to be here.'

'Why? So you can arrange a blind date with Rachel? I'm afraid, Congresswoman Willard, that even for the sake of your career, I wouldn't do that.'

'You're a fool.'

'Maybe so.' But he didn't think so any more. He didn't think so at all, and after that phone call with Kay ended, he found himself staring out the window and thinking not of Rachel, but of the woman he had seen on the steps. With his eyes closed, he could still see her, the perfectly carved profile, the huge eyes and the delicate mouth. He had never seen a woman so beautiful or so haunting. And he sat there at his desk, with his eyes closed, thinking of her, and then with a sigh, he shook his head and opened his eyes again and stood up. It was ridiculous to be dreaming of a total stranger. And then feeling foolish, he laughed softly, and brushed her from his mind. There was no point falling in love with a perfect stranger. But he found, as he went downstairs to make something for dinner, that he had to remind himself of that again and again.

16

Chapter 3

Sunlight flooded into the room and shimmered on the beige silk bedspread and identically upholstered chairs. It was a large handsome room with long French windows that looked out over the Bay. From the boudoir which adjoined the bedroom, one could see the Golden Gate Bridge. There was a white marble fireplace in each room, and there were carefully selected French paintings, and a priceless Chinese vase stood in a corner, in a Louis XV inlaid vitrine. In front of the windows was a handsome Louis XV desk, which would have dwarfed any room except this one. It was beautiful and enormous and sterile and cold. There was also a small wood-panelled room which adjoined it, filled with books in English and Spanish and French. The books were the soul of her existence, and it was here that Raphaella stood quietly for a moment, looking out at the Bay. It was nine o'clock in the morning and she was wearing a perfectly sculptured black suit moulded to her form, showing off its graceful perfection subtly yet with immense style. The suit had been made for her in Paris, like most of her clothes, except those she bought in Spain. She rarely bought clothes in San Francisco. She almost never went out. In San Francisco, she was an invisible person, a name people rarely mentioned and never saw. For most of them it would have been difficult to associate a face with the name of Mrs John Henry Phillips, and certainly not this face. It would have been difficult to imagine this perfect snow white beauty with the huge black eyes. When she had married John Henry, one reporter had written that she looked like a fairy tale princess, and had then gone on to explain that in many ways she was. But the eyes which gazed out at the Bay on an October morning were not those of a fairy tale princess, they were those of a very lonely young woman, locked in a very lonely world.

'Your breakfast is ready, Mrs Phillips.' A maid in a crisp

white uniform stood in the doorway, her announcement more like a command, Raphaella thought, but she always felt that way about John Henry's servants. She had felt that way too in her father's house in Paris, her grandfather's house in Spain. It always seemed to her that it was the servants who gave the orders, when to get up, when to get ready, when to eat lunch, when to eat dinner. 'Madam is served' announced dinner in her father's house in Paris. But what if Madam didn't want to be served? What if Madam only wanted a sandwich sitting on the floor in front of the fire? Or a dish of ice-cream for breakfast instead of toast and poached eggs? The very idea made her smile as she walked back to her bedroom and looked around. Everything was ready. Her bags were stacked neatly in the corner, they were all glove soft in a chocolate-coloured suede, and there was a large tote bag in which Raphaella could carry some gifts for her mother and aunt and cousins, her jewellery, and something to read on the plane.

As she looked at her luggage, she felt no thrill of pleasure to be going on a trip. She almost never felt a thrill of pleasure anymore. There was none left in her life. There was an endless strip of highway, heading towards a destination both unseen and unknown, and about which Raphaella no longer cared. She knew that each day would be just like the day before. Each day she would do exactly what she had for almost seven years, except for the four weeks in the summer when she went to Spain, and the few days before that when she went to Paris to see her father. And there were occasional trips to join her Spanish relatives for a few days in New York. It seemed years now since she had last been there, since she had left Europe, since she had become John Henry's wife. It was all so different now than it had been at first. It had all happened like a fairy tale. Or a merger. There was a little bit of both in the tale. The marriage of the Banque Malle in Paris, Milan, Madrid, and Barcelona to the Phillips Bank of California and New York, both empires consisting of investment banks of major international proportions. And her father's first gargantuan business deal with John Henry had won them, jointly, the cover of *Time*. It was also what had brought her father and John Henry together so often that spring, and as their plans began to prosper, so had John Henry's suit with Antoine's only child.

Raphaella had never met anyone like John Henry. He was tall, handsome, impressive, powerful, yet gentle, kind, softspoken, with a constant glimmer of laughter in his eyes. There was mischief there somewhere, and in time, Raphaella had learned how much he liked to tease and play. He was a man of extraordinary imagination and creativity, a man of great wit, a man of great eloquence, great style. He had everything that she or any other girl could ever want.

The only thing that John Henry Phillips had lacked was youth. Even that was difficult to believe as one looked into the lean handsome face, or watched the powerful arms when he played tennis or swam. He had a long, beautiful body which men half his age would have envied. His age had, at first, discouraged him from pursuing Raphaella, yet as time when on, and the frequency of his trips to Paris increased, he found her more charming, more open, more delightful on each occasion. And despite the rigidity of his ideas about his daughter, Antoine de Mornay-Malle did not resist the prospect of seeing his old friend marry his only child. He himself was aware of his daughter's beauty, her gentleness and openness, and her innocent charm. And he was also aware of what a rare catch John Henry Phillips would be for any woman, despite the difference in years. He was also not blind to what it would mean to the future of his bank, a consideration which had weighed with him at least once before. His own marriage had been based on affection, and good business sense as well. The ageing Marquis de Quadral had been the reigning financial genius of Madrid but his sons had not inherited his passion for the world of finance and had, for the most part, gone into other fields. For years, the elderly Marquis had had an eye out for someone to succeed him in the banks he had founded over the years. What happened instead was that he met Antoine, and eventually, after a great deal of fancy footwork, the Banque Malle joined forces on numerous deals with the Banco Quadral. The union rapidly quadrupled Antoine's power and fortune, delighted the Marquis, and brought along with it the Marquis's daughter, Alejandra, Marquesa de Santos y

Quadral. Antoine had been instantly taken with the flaxen-haired, blue-eyed Spanish beauty, and at the time he had been thinking for some time that it was time he married and produced an heir. At thirty-five, he had been too busy building his family's banking business into an empire, but now other considerations had begun to weigh with him as well. Alejandra was the perfect solution to the problem, and a very handsome solution at that. At nineteen, she was a startling beauty, with the most devastatingly exquisite face Antoine had ever seen. It was he who looked like the Spaniard beside her, with his black hair and dark eyes. And together they made an extraordinary pair.

Seven months after they met, their wedding was the main event of the social season, after which they honeymooned for a month in the South of France. Immediately thereafter, they dutifully appeared at the Marquis's country estate, Santa Eugenia, on the Coast of Spain. The estate was palatial, and it was here that Antoine began to understand what marriage to Alejandra would mean. He was a member of the family now, yet another son of the elderly Marquis. He was expected to make frequent appearances at Santa Eugenia, and come as often as possible to Madrid. It was certainly what Alejandra planned to do, and when it was time to return to Paris, she implored her husband to let her stay at Santa Eugenia for a few more weeks. And when at last she returned to him in Paris, six weeks later than she had promised, Antoine fully understood what was going to happen after that. Alejandra was going to spend most of her time as she always had, surrounded by her family, on their estates in Spain. She had spent all of the war years sequestered there and now, even after the war, and married, she wanted to continue to live in those familiar surroundings.

Predictably, on their first anniversary, Alejandra gave birth to their first child, a son named Julien, and Antoine was well pleased. He had an heir for his own empire now, and he and the Marquis strolled quietly for hours on the grounds of Santa Eugenia when the child was a month old, discussing all of Antoine's future plans for the banks and his son. He had his father-in-law's full endorsement, and in the year since he had married Alejandra, both the Banque Malle and the Banco Quadral had grown.

Alejandra remained at Santa Eugenia for the summer with her brothers and sisters, their children, cousins, nieces, and friends. And when Antoine returned to Paris, Alejandra had already conceived again. This time Alejandra suffered a miscarriage, and the next time she delivered twins, born prematurely and dead at birth. There was then a brief hiatus when she spent six months resting, with her family, in Madrid. When she returned to Paris to her husband, she conceived yet again. This fourth pregnancy yielded Raphaella, two years younger than Julien. There were then two more miscarriages and another stillbirth, after which the ravishingly beautiful Alejandra announced that it was the climate in Paris which did not agree with her, and her sisters felt she would be healthier in Spain. Having seen her inevitable return to Spain coming throughout their marriage, Antoine quietly acquiesced. It was the way of women of her country, and it was a battle which he never could have won.

From then on he was content to see her at Santa Eugenia, or in Madrid, surrounded by female cousins, sisters, and duennas, perfectly content to be always in the company of her relatives, assorted women friends, and a handful of their unmarried brothers who squired them to concerts, operas and plays. Alejandra was still one of Spain's great beauties, and in Spain she led an exceedingly pleasant life of indolence and opulence, with which she was well pleased. It was no great problem for Antoine to fly back and forth to Spain, when he could get away from the bank, which he did less and less. In time he induced her to let the children come back to Paris to attend school, on the condition of course that they flew to Santa Eugenia for every possible vacation and four months in the summer. And now and then she consented to visit him in Paris, despite what she constantly referred to as the detrimental effects of the French weather on her health. After the last stillbirth, there were no more babies, in fact after that there was only a platonic affection between Alejandra and her husband, which she knew from her sisters was perfectly normal.

Antoine was perfectly content to leave things as they were, and when the Marquis died, the marriage paid off. No one was surprised at the arrangement. Alejandra and Antoine had jointly inherited the Banco Quadral. Her brothers were amply compensated, but to Antoine went the empire he so desperately wanted to add to his own. Now it was of his son that he thought as he continued to build it, but Antoine's only son was not destined to be his heir. At sixteen, Julien de Mornay-Malle died in an accident, in Buenos Aires, playing polo, leaving his mother stunned, his father bereft, and Raphaella Antoine's only child.

And it was Raphaella who consoled her father, who flew with him to Buenos Aires to bring the boy's body back to France. It was she who held her father's hand during those endless hours, and as they watched the casket being lowered solemnly on to the runway at Orly, Alejandra flew back to Paris separately, surrounded by sisters, and cousins, one of her brothers and several close friends, but always surrounded, protected, as she had lived her entire life. And hours after the funeral, they urged her to go back to Spain with them, and acquiescing tearfully, she allowed them to take her away. Alejandra had a veritable army to protect her, and Antoine had no one, only a fourteen year old child.

But later, the tragedy provided a strange bond between them. It was something they never spoke of, but which was always there. The tragedy also provided a strange bond between her father and John Henry, as the two men discovered that they had shared a similar loss, the deaths of their only sons. John Henry's boy had died in a plane crash. At twenty-one, the young man had been flying his own plane. John Henry's wife had also died, five years later. But it was the loss of their sons which for each had been an intolerable blow. Antoine had had Raphaella to console him, but John Henry had no other children, and after his wife died, he had never married again.

At the start of their business association, each time John Henry came to Paris, Raphaella was in Spain. He began to tease Antoine about his imaginary daughter. It became a standing joke between them until a day when the butler

22

ushered John Henry into Antoine's study, but instead of
Antoine, he found himself staring into the dark brown eyes
of a ravishingly beautiful young girl who looked at him
tremulously like a frightened doe. She gazed up almost in
terror at the sight of a strange man in the room. She had
been going over some papers for school and checking
through some reference books her father kept there, and her
long black hair poured over her shoulders in long straight
streams of black silk punctured by cascades of soft curls. For
a moment he had stood there, silent, awed. And then
quickly, he had recovered, and the warm light in his eyes
reached out to her, reassuring her that he was a friend. But
during her months of study in Paris she saw few people, and
in Spain she was so well guarded and protected that it was
rare for her to be alone anywhere with a strange man. She
had no idea what to say to him at first, but after a few
moments of easy banter, she met the twinkle in his eyes and
laughed. It was half an hour later when Antoine found
them, apologising profusely for a delay at the bank. On the
way home in the car he had wondered if John Henry had
finally met her, and he had to admit to himself later that he
had hoped he had.

Raphaella had withdrawn a few moments after her
father's arrival, her cheeks blushing to a delicate pink on the
perfectly creamy skin.

'My God, Antoine, she's a beauty.' He looked at his
French friend with an odd expression, and Antoine smiled.

'So you like my imaginary daughter, do you? She wasn't
too impossibly shy? Her mother has convinced her that all
men who attempt to talk to a young girl alone are murderers
or at least rapists. Sometimes I worry about that look of
terror in her eyes.'

'What do you expect? All her life she has been totally
protected. It's hardly surprising after all if she's shy.'

'No, but she's almost eighteen now, and it's going to be a
real problem for her, unless she spends the rest of her life in
Spain. In Paris she ought to be able to at least talk to a man
without half a dozen women standing in the room, most if
not all of them related to her.' He said it in a tone of
amusement, but there was also something very serious in his

eyes. He was looking long and hard at John Henry, sizing up the expression he still saw lingering in the American's eyes. 'She is lovely, isn't she? It's immodest of me to say it about my own daughter, but . . .' He spread his hands helplessly and smiled.

And this time John Henry met his smile fully. 'Lovely isn't quite the right word.' And then in an almost boyish way he had asked a question which brought a smile to Antoine's eyes. 'Will she dine with us this evening?'

'If you don't mind very much. I thought we'd dine here, and then we can stop in at my club. Matthieu de Bourgeon will be there this evening, and I've been promising him for months that I'd introduce you the next time you're here.'

'That sounds fine.' But it wasn't Matthieu Bourgeon that John Henry was thinking of when he smiled.

He had managed to draw Raphaella out successfully that evening and yet again two days later when he had come to the house for tea. He had come especially to see her, and brought her two books he had told her about at dinner two days before. She had blushed again, and fallen once more into silence, but this time he was able to tease her back into chatting with him, and by the end of the afternoon, they were almost friends. Over the next six months, she came to regard him as a personage almost as revered and cherished as her father, and it was in the light of an uncle of sorts that she explained him to her mother when she went to Spain.

It was during that trip that John Henry appeared at Santa Eugenia with her father. They stayed for only one brief weekend, during which John Henry successfully charmed Alejandra and the armies of others staying at Santa Eugenia that spring. It was then that Alejandra understood John Henry's intentions, but Raphaella didn't come to learn of them until later that summer. It was the first week of her vacation, and she was due to fly to Madrid in a few days. In the meantime she was enjoying the last of her days in Paris, and when John Henry arrived, she urged him to come out with her for a walk along the Seine. They talked about the street artists and the children, and her face lit up when she told him about all of her cousins in Spain.

She seemed to have a passion for the children, and she looked infinitely beautiful as she looked up at him with her huge dark eyes.

'And how many do you want when you grow up, Raphaella?' He always said her name so deliberately. It pleased her. For an American, it was a difficult name.

'I am grown up.'

'Are you? At eighteen?' He looked at her in amusement, and there was something odd in his eyes which she didn't understand. Something tired and old and wise, and sad, as though for an instant he had thought of his son. They had talked about him too. And she had told him about her brother.

'Yes, I am grown up. I'm going to the Sorbonne in the Fall.' They had smiled at each other, and he had had to fight himself to keep from kissing her then and there.

All the while, as they walked, he was wondering how he was going to ask her, and if he had gone totally mad for wanting to ask her at all. 'Raphaella, have you ever thought about going to college in the States?' They were walking slowly along the Seine, dodging children, and she was gently pulling the petals off a flower. But she looked up at him and shook her head.

'I don't think I could.'

'Why not? Your English is excellent.'

She shook her head slowly and when she looked up at him again her eyes were sad. 'My mother would never let me. It's just . . . it's just too different from her way of life. And it's so far.'

'But is that what you want? Your father's life is different from hers too. Would you be happy with that life in Spain?'

'I don't think so.' She said it matter of factly. 'But I don't think I have much choice. I think Papa always meant to take Julien into the bank with him, and it was understood that I'd go to Spain with my mother.' The thought of her surrounded by duennas for the rest of her life appalled him. Even as her friend, he wanted more for her than that. He wanted to see her free and alive and laughing and independent, but not buried at Santa Eugenia, like her mother. It wasn't right for this girl. He felt it in his soul.

'I don't think you should have to do that, if that's not what you want to do.'

She smiled up at him with resignation mingled with wisdom in her eighteen year old eyes. 'There are duties in life, Mr Phillips.'

'Not at your age, little one. Not yet. Some duties, yes. Like school. And listening to your parents to a certain extent, but you don't have to take on a whole way of life, if you don't want it.'

'What else then? I don't know anything else.'

'That's no excuse. Are you happy at Santa Eugenia?'

'Sometimes. And sometimes not. Sometimes I find all those women very boring. My mother loves it though. She even goes on trips with them. They travel in great bunches, they go to Rio and Buenos Aires and Uruguay and New York, and even when she comes to Paris, she brings them with her. They always remind me of girls in boarding school, they seem so . . . so . . .' The huge eyes looked up at him apologetically '. . . so silly. Don't they?' She looked at him and he nodded.

'Maybe a little. Raphaella . . .' But as he said it, she stopped walking suddenly and swung around to face him, ingenuous, totally unaware of her beauty, her long graceful body leaned towards him and she looked into his eyes with such trust that he was afraid to say more.

'Yes?'

And then he couldn't stop it any more. He couldn't. He had to . . . 'Raphaella, darling. I love you.' The words were the merest whisper in the soft Paris air, and his lined handsome face hovered next to hers for a moment before he kissed her. His lips were gentle and soft, his tongue probing her mouth as though his hunger for her knew no bounds, but her mouth was pressed hard against his now too, her arms around his neck, pressing her body into his, and then just as gently he pulled away from her, not wanting her to sense the urgency that had sprung up in his loins. 'Raphaella . . . I've wanted to kiss you for so long.' He kissed her again, more gently this time, and she smiled with a womanly pleasure he had never before seen in her face.

'So have I.' She hung her head then, like a schoolgirl. 'I've

26

had a crush on you since we first met.' And then she smiled up at him bravely. 'You're so beautiful.' And this time she kissed him. She took his hand then as though to lead him farther down the Seine, but he shook his head and took her hand in his.

'We have something to talk about first. Do you want to sit down?' He motioned to a bench and she followed him.

She looked at him questioningly, and saw something in his eyes that puzzled her. 'Is something wrong?' Slowly, he grinned. 'No. But if you think I just brought you out here this afternoon to "spoon", as they said in my day, you're mistaken, little one. There's something I want to ask you, and I've been afraid to all day.'

'What is it?' But suddenly her heart was pounding, and her voice was very soft.

He looked at her for an endless moment, his face close to hers and her hand held tightly in his own. 'Will you marry me, Raphaella?' He heard her sharp intake of breath, and then closed his eyes and kissed her again, and when he pulled slowly away there were tears in her eyes and she was smiling as he had never seen her smile before and slowly, the smile broadening, she nodded.

'Yes . . . I will . . .'

The wedding of Raphaella de Mornay-Malle y de Santos y Quadral and John Henry Phillips IV was one of a magnitude seldom seen. It took place in Paris and there was a luncheon for two hundred on the day of the civil ceremony, a dinner for a hundred and fifty family members and 'intimate friends' that night and a crowd of more than six hundred at Notre Dame for the wedding the next day. Antoine had taken over the entire Polo Club and everyone agreed that both the wedding and the reception were the most beautiful they had ever seen. Remarkably, they had also managed to strike up a bargain with the press so that if Raphaella and John Henry would pose for photographs for half an hour, and answer whatever questions arose, they would be left in peace after that.

The wedding stories were featured in *Vogue*, *Women's Wear*, and the following week's *Time*. Throughout the press interviews, Raphaella had clutched John Henry's hand almost desperately, and her eyes seemed larger and darker than ever before in the snow white face. It was then that he vowed to keep her shielded from the prying eyes of the press in the future. He didn't want her having to cope with anything that made her uncomfortable or unhappy, and he was well aware of how carefully protected she had been during her early years. The problem was that John Henry was a man who attracted the attention of the press with alarming frequency, and when he took a bride forty-four years his junior, then his wife became an object of fascination too. Fortunes of the magnitude of John Henry's were almost unheard of, and an eighteen year old girl, born of a Marquisa and an illustrious French banker was almost too good to be true. It was all very much like a fairy tale, and no fairy tale was complete without a fairy princess. But thanks to John Henry's efforts, she never was. Together, they maintained an anonymity no one would have thought possible over the years. Raphaella even managed to attend two years of school at the University of California in Berkeley and it went very smoothly. No one had any idea who she was during the entire two years. She had also refused to be driven to Berkeley by the chauffeur, and John Henry bought her a little car which she drove to school.

It was exciting too to be among the students, and to have a secret and a man she adored. Because she did love John Henry, and he was gentle and loving in every way. He felt as though he had been given a gift so precious he barely dared to touch it, so grateful was he for the new life he shared with this ravishingly beautiful, delicate young girl. In many ways, she was childlike, and she trusted him with her entire soul. It was perhaps because of that that it was such a bitter disappointment to him when he discovered that he had become sterile presumably from a severe kidney infection he'd had ten years before. He knew how desperately she had wanted children, and he felt the burden of guilt for depriving her of something she wanted so much. She insisted, when he told her, that it didn't matter, that she had all the children at Santa Eugenia whom she could spoil, and amuse and love. She loved to tell them stories, and buy them presents. She kept endless lists of their birthdays and was always going downtown to send some fabulous new toy off to Spain.

But even his failure to father children could not sever the bond which held them together over the years. It was a marriage in which she worshipped him and he adored her, and if the differences in their ages caused comment among others, it never bothered either of them. They played tennis together almost every morning, sometimes John Henry ran in the Presidio or along the beach, and Raphaella ran along beside him, like a puppy dog at his heels, laughing and teasing and sometimes just walking along in silence afterwards, holding his hand. Her life was filled with John Henry, and her studies, and her letters to her family in Paris and Spain. She led a very protected, old-fashioned existence, and she was a happy woman, truly more of a happy girl, until she was twenty-five.

Two days before John Henry's sixty-ninth birthday, he was to fly to Chicago to close a major deal. He had been talking about retiring for several years now, but like her father, there was no real end in sight. He had too much passion for the world of high finance, for the running of banks, the acquiring of new corporations and the buying and selling of huge blocks of stock. He loved putting together mammoth real estate deals like the first one he had done with her father. Retirement just wasn't for him. But when he left for Chicago he had a headache, and despite the pills Raphaella had pressed on him that morning, the headache had grew steadily worse.

In terror, his assistant had chartered a plane and flown him back with him from Chicago that evening, arriving with John Henry barely conscious. Raphaella looked down into the pale grey face as they brought him off the plane on a stretcher. He was in so much pain he could barely speak to her, yet he pressed her hand several times on their way to the hospital in the ambulance, and as she looked at him in terror and despair, fighting back the tears that had clogged her throat she suddenly noticed something odd about his mouth. An hour later his face looked strangely distorted, and shortly thereafter he fell into a coma from which he did not rouse for several days. John Henry Phillips had had a stroke, it was explained on the news that evening. It was his office which had prepared the press release, keeping Raphaella, as always, from the prying eyes of the news.

John Henry stayed in the hospital for almost four months, and had two more, smaller strokes before he left. When they brought him home he had permanently lost the use of his right arm and leg, the youthful handsome face sagged pitifully on one side, and the aura of strength and power was gone. John Henry Phillips was suddenly an old man. He was broken in body and spirit from that moment, yet for another seven years his life had dwindled on.

He never left his home again. The nurse wheeled him into the garden for some sunshine and Raphaella sat with him for hours at a time, but his mind wasn't always clear any more, and his life, once so vital, so busy, so full, had changed radically. There was nothing more than a shell of the man left. And it was this shell that Raphaella lived with, faithfully, devotedly, lovingly, reading to him, talking to him, comforting him. As the nurses who tended him around the clock cared for the broken body, she attempted to console the spirit. But his spirit was broken, and at times she wondered if hers was as well. It had been seven years since the first series of strokes. There had been two more strokes since, which had reduced him still further, until he was unable to do much more than sit in his wheelchair, and most of the time he stared into space, thinking back, to what was no more. He was still able to speak, though with difficulty, but much of the time he seemed to have nothing more to say. It was a cruel joke that a man who had been so alive should be rendered so small and so useless. When Antoine had flown over from Paris to see him, he had left John Henry's room with tears streaming unashamedly down his cheeks, and his words to his daughter had been quite clear. She was to stand by this man who had loved her, and whom she had loved and married, until he died. There was to be no nonsense, no whimpering, no shrinking from her duties, no complaining. Her duty was clear. And so it had remained, and Raphaella had not shrunk or whispered or complained for seven long years.

Her only respite from the grim reality of her existence was when she went to Spain in the summers. She only went for two weeks now, instead of four. But John Henry absolutely insisted. It tortured him to realise that the girl he had married was as much a prisoner of his infirmities as he was himself. It was one thing to keep her from the prying eyes of the world, while amusing her himself night and day. It was quite another to lock her in the house with him, as his body decayed slowly around him. If he could have found the means, he would have killed himself, he said often to his doctor, if only to set both of them free. He had mentioned it once to Antoine, who had been outraged at the very idea.

'The girl adores you!' He had thundered in his old friend's sick room. 'You owe it to her not to do anything crazy like that!'

'Not like this.' The words had been garbled but comprehensible. 'It's a crime to do this to her. I have no right.' He had choked on his own tears.

'You have no right to deprive her of you. She loves you. She loved you for seven years before this happened. That doesn't change overnight. It doesn't change because you are ill. What if she were ill? Would you love her any the less?' John Henry shook his head.

'She should be married to a young man, she should have children.'

'She needs you, John. She belongs with you. She has grown up with you. She'll be lost without you. How can you think of leaving her a moment sooner than you must? You could have years left!' He had meant to be encouraging, but John Henry had faced him with despair. Years . . . and by then how old would Raphaella be? Thirty-five? Forty? Forty-two? She would be so totally unprepared to start looking for a new life. These were the thoughts that rambled agonisingly through his mind, that left him filled with silence and his eyes glazed with anguish and grief, not so much for himself, but for her. He insisted that she go away as often as possible but she felt guilty for leaving him, and going away wasn't a relief.

It was John Henry who repeatedly urged her to break out of her prison. Whenever he learned from Raphaella that her mother was going to New York for a few days, with the usual crowd of sisters and cousins, on her way to Buenos Aires or Mexico City, or wherever else, he was quick to urge Raphaella to join them. Whether it was for two days or ten, he always wanted her to join them, to get out into the world if only for a moment, and he knew that in that crowd, she would always be safe, well protected, heavily escorted. The only moments in which she was alone were on the flights to Europe or New York. His chauffeur always put her on the plane in San Francisco, and there was always a rented limousine waiting for her at the other end. The life of a fairy-tale princess was still Raphaella's, but the fairy tale had considerably changed. Her eyes were larger and quieter than ever now, she would sit silent and pensive for hours, looking into the fire, or staring out at the bay. The sound of her laughter was barely more than a memory and when it rang out for a moment, it somehow seemed like a mistake.

Even when she joined her family for their few day visits to New York or wherever, it was as though she weren't really there. In the years since John Henry's illness, Raphaella had increasingly withdrawn, until she was scarcely different from John Henry. Her life seemed as much over as his. The only difference was that hers had never really begun. It was only in Santa Eugenia that she seemed to come alive again, with a child on her lap, and another teetering on her knees, three or four more clustered around, as she told them wonderful tales that kept them staring at her in rapture and awe. It was with the children that she forgot the pain of what had happened, and her own loneliness, and her overwhelming sense of loss. With the grown-ups, she was always reticent and quiet, as though there were nothing left to say, and joining in their merriment seemed obscene. For Raphaella, it was like a funeral that had gone on for half a lifetime, or more precisely for seven years. But she knew only too well how much he suffered, and how much guilt he felt for his invalid state over the last year. So when she was with him, there was only tenderness and compassion in her voice, a gentle tone, and a still gentler hand. But what he saw in her eyes cut him to the very core of his being. It was not so much that he was dying, but that he had killed a very young girl, and left in her place this sad, lonely young woman with the exquisite face and the huge, haunted eyes. This was the woman he had created. This was what he had done to the girl he had once loved.

As Raphaella walked swiftly down the thickly carpeted steps on to the next landing, she glanced quickly down the hall and saw the staff already dusting the long antique tables that stretched down the endless halls. The house they lived in was one that John Henry's grandfather had built when he first came to San Francisco after the Civil War. It had survived the earthquake in 1906 and was now one of the most important architectural landmarks in San Francisco, with its sweeping lines and five stories perched next to the Presidio and looking out at the Bay. It was unusual also because it had some of the finest stained glass skylights in the city, and because it was still in the hands of the family that had originally owned it, which was very rare. But it was not a house in which Raphaella could be happy now. It seemed like a museum or a mausoleum to her than a home. It seemed cold and unfriendly, as did the staff, all of whom John Henry had had when she arrived. And she had never had the chance to redecorate any of the rooms. The house stood now, as it had then. For fourteen years it had been her home, and yet each time she left it, she felt like an orphan with her suitcase.

'More coffee, Mrs Phillips?' The elderly woman who had been the downstairs maid for thirty-six years gazed into Raphaella's face as she did each morning. Raphaella had seen that face five days a week for the last fourteen years, and still the woman was a stranger to her, and always would be. Her name was Marie.

But this time Raphaella shook her head. 'Not this morning. I'm in a hurry, thank you.' She glanced at the plain gold watch on her wrist, put down her napkin and stood up. The flowered Spode dishes had belonged to John Henry's first wife. There were a lot of things like that in the house. Everything seemed to be someone else's. 'The first Mrs Phillips' as the servants put it, or John Henry's mother's, or grandmother's, or . . . there was nothing that was

Raphaella's. Sometimes she felt that if a stranger were to walk through the house enquiring about artifacts and paintings and even small unimportant objects, there was not a single thing about which someone would say, 'Oh, that's Raphaella's.' Nothing was Raphaella's, except her clothes and her books, and the huge collection of letters from the children in Spain which she kept in boxes.

Raphaella's heels clicked briefly across the black and white marble floor of the pantry. She picked up a phone there and buzzed softly on an inside line. A moment later, it was picked up on the third floor, by the morning nurse.

'Good morning. Is Mr Phillips awake yet?'

'Yes, but he's not quite ready.' Ready. Ready for what? Raphaella felt an odd tug in her soul as she stood there. How could she resent him for what wasn't his fault? And yet, how could this have happened to her? For those first seven years it had been so wonderful, so perfect . . . so . . .

'I'd like to come up for a moment, before I leave.'

'Oh dear, you're leaving this morning?'

Raphaella glanced at her watch again. 'In half an hour.'

'All right. Then give us fifteen or twenty minutes. You can stop in for a few minutes on your way out.' Poor John Henry. Ten minutes, and then nothing. There would be no one to visit him while she was gone. She would only be gone for four or five days, but still she wondered if maybe she shouldn't leave him. What if something happened? What if the nurses didn't pay attention to what they were doing? She always felt that way when she left him. Troubled, tormented, guilty, as though she had no right to a few days of her own. It was always John Henry who convinced her, who insisted, emerging from his reverie to force her away from this nightmare that they shared for so long. It wasn't even a nightmare any more. It was just an emptiness, a limbo, a comatose state while their lives continued to drone on.

This time she took the elevator to the second floor and then walked to her bedroom after telling the nurse that she would be in to see her husband in fifteen minutes. She looked long and hard in the mirror then smoothed the silky black hair and ran a hand over the tight heavy knot of it at the nape of her neck. She took a hat out of her closet then. It was

34

a beautiful creation she had bought in Paris the year before, as hats returned to the world of high style. As she put it on carefully, tilting it to just the right angle, she wondered for a moment why she had bothered to buy it at all. It had a whisper of black veiling which lent further mystery to her large almond shaped eyes, and with the contrast of the black hat, and her hair and the little veil, the creamy white of her skin seemed to stand out even more than before. She carefully applied a thin gloss of bright lipstick and clipped pearls on her ears. She ran a hand over her suit, straightened her stockings and looked in her handbag, to ascertain that the cash she always carried on trips was concealed in a side pocket of the black lizard bag her mother had sent her from Spain. She looked, when she stood in front of the mirror, like a woman of incredible elegance, beauty and style. This was a woman who dined at Maxim's, and went to the races at Longchamps, this was a woman who partied in Venice and Rome and Vienna and New York. This was a woman who went to the theatre in London. This wasn't the face or the body or the look of a girl who had slipped into womanhood unnoticed, and who was now married to a crippled and dying seventy-six-year-old man. As she saw herself, and the truth, all too clearly, Raphaella picked up her bag and her clothes and and grinned ruefully to herself, knowing more than ever how appearances can lie.

She shrugged to herself as she left her bedroom, tossing a long handsome dark mink coat over one arm as she made her way once more to the stairs. The elevator had been put in for John Henry, but most of the time she still preferred to walk. She did so now, up to the third floor, where a suite had long since been set up for her husband, with three rooms adjoining it, for each of the nurses who cared for him in shifts. They were three matronly women, content with their quarters, their patient, and the job. They were handsomely paid for their services, and like the woman who had served Raphaella breakfast, they had somehow managed to remain unobtrusive and faceless over the years. Often she found herself missing the passionate and often impossible servants of Santa Eugenia. They were servile on the most part, yet often rebellious and childlike, having served her mother's family sometimes for generations, or at least for many years. They were warlike and childlike and loving and giving. They were filled with laughter and outrage and devotion for the people they worked for, not like these cool professionals who worked for John Henry.

Raphaella knocked softly on the door to her husband's suite of rooms, and a face appeared rapidly at the door. 'Good Morning, Mrs Phillips. We're all ready.' Are *we*? Raphaella nodded and stepped inside, down a short hall into a bedroom, which like her own room downstairs, had both a boudoir and a small library. Now, John Henry was tucked into his bed, staring across the room at the fire already burning in the grate. She advanced towards him slowly, and he seemed not to hear her, until at last she sat down in a chair next to his bed and took his hand.

'John Henry . . .' After fourteen years in San Francisco, her accent was still evident when she said his name, but her English was perfect now, and had been for many years. 'John Henry . . .' He turned his eyes slowly towards her without moving his head, and then slowly, he moved himself so that he could look at her, and then the lined, tired face contorted into a half smile.

'Hello, little one.' His speech was slurred but she could understand him, and the agony of his crooked smile since the stroke always tore at her heart. 'You look very pretty.' And then after another pause, 'My mother had a hat like that a long time ago.'

'I think on me it is very silly, but . . .' She shrugged suddenly looking very French as she smiled a hesitant little smile. It was her mouth that smiled now. Her eyes seldom did. And his never did any more except on rare occasions, when he was looking at her.

'You're going today?' He looked worried, and again she wondered if she should cancel her trip.

'Yes. But, darling, do you want me to stay?'

He shook his head and smiled again. 'No. Never. I wish you would go away more often. It does you good. You're meeting . . .' He looked vague for a moment, searching his memory for something obviously no longer there.

'My mother, and my aunt, and two of my cousins.'

36

He nodded and closed his eyes. 'Then I know you'll be safe.'

'I'm always safe.' He nodded again, as though he were very tired, and she stood up, bent to kiss his cheek, and then ever so gently let go of his hand. She thought for a moment that he was going to sleep, but suddenly he opened his eyes as she stood staring down at his face.

'Be careful, Raphaella.'

'I promise. And I'll call you.'

'You don't have to. Why don't you forget about all this, and have some fun.' With whom? Her mother? Her aunt? A sigh fought its way through her, but she didn't let it escape.

'I'll be back very soon, and everyone here knows where I'll be, if you need me.'

'I don't need you . . .' He grinned for a moment, 'Not like that. Not enough to spoil your fun.'

'You never have.' She whispered the words to him, and bent to kiss him again. 'I'll miss you.'

This time he shook his head and turned away from her. 'Don't.'

'Darling . . .' She had to leave him to go to the airport, but somehow she didn't feel right leaving him like this. She never did. Was it right to leave him? Should she stay?

'John Henry . . .' She touched his hand and he turned to face her again. 'I must go now.'

'It's all right, little one. It's all right.' The look in his eyes absolved her, and this time he took her firm young hand in his gnarled worn fingers that had once seemed so gentle and so young. 'Have a good trip.' He tried to fill the words with every ounce of meaning he could give them, and he shook his head when he saw her eyes fill with tears. He knew what she was thinking.

'Just go, I'll be fine.'

'You promise?' Her eyes were filled with tears now, and his smile was very gentle as he kissed her hand.

'I promise. Now be a good girl and go, and have a good time. Promise me you'll buy yourself something outrageous and absolutely beautiful in New York.'

'Like what?'

'A fur coat or a wonderful piece of jewellery.' He looked

wistful for a moment. 'Something you would have liked me to buy you.' And then he looked into her eyes and smiled.

She shook her head as the tears rolled down her cheeks. It only made her look more beautiful, as the little black veil added further mystery to her eyes. 'I'm never as generous as you are, John Henry.'

'Then try harder.' He tried to bellow it at her, and this time they both laughed. 'Promise?'

'All right. I promise. But not another fur.'

'Then something that sparkles.'

'I'll see.' But where would she wear it? At home in San Francisco, sitting by the fire? The futility of it all almost overwhelmed her as she smiled at him from the doorway and waved at him for the last time.

Chapter 4

The chauffeur slid the car to the kerb at the section marked
'Departing Flights' at the airport, and showed the
policeman his special pass. John Henry's drivers had gotten
special passes from the governor's office, and they were
renewed every year. It allowed them to park where they
wanted to, and now it would allow the chauffeur to leave the
limousine at the kerb while he took Raphaella inside, to put
her on the plane. The airline was always warned that she
was coming, and she was always allowed to board the plane
before everyone else.

Now as they walked sedately down the huge bustling
hallway, the chauffeur carrying her tote bag, strangers
glanced at the startlingly beautiful woman in the mink coat
and the veil. The hat added an aura of drama and there
were gaunt hollows beneath the perfectly carved ivory
cheekbones that framed her splendid dark eyes.

'Tom, would you wait here for me for a minute, please?'
She had touched his arm gently to stop him as he marched
dutifully along the airport corridor beside her, bent on
getting her to the plane as quickly as he could. Mr Phillips
didn't like her lingering in airports, not that reporters or
photographers had bothered them for years. Raphaella had
been so totally kept away from public attention that even
the newspapers no longer knew who she was.

She left the chauffeur standing near a pillar and walked
rapidly into the bookstore, glancing around as the driver
took up his post against the wall, holding her large leather
tote bag tightly in one hand. From where he stood, he could
admire her striking beauty, as she wandered between the
shelves of magazines and books and candy, looking very
different from the other travellers wandering past in parkas
and car coats and old jeans. Here and there you'd see an
attractive woman, or maybe a well-dressed man, but
nothing to compare with Mrs Phillips. Tom watched her

take a hardcover book off a shelf, walk to the cash register, and reach into her bag.

It was then that Alex Hale came hurrying through the airport, his briefcase in his hand, and a suit bag draped over the other arm. He was distracted. It was early, but he still had to call his office before he got on the plane. He stopped at a bank of telephones just outside the book shop, put down his bags and dug into his trouser pocket for a dime. He dialled his office number quickly and inserted the extra coins the operator requested as their receptionist picked up the phone. He had several last-minute messages to leave for his partners, there was a memo he wanted to explain to his secretary before leaving, and he was anxious to know if the call he was expecting from London had come, and just as he asked the last question, he happened to turn around and with amusement he saw a copy of his mother's latest book changing hands at the counter of the bookstore. A woman was buying it, wearing a mink coat, and a black hat with a veil. He stared at her with fascination, as the secretary on the other end put him on hold while she took another call. And it was then that Raphaella began to walk towards him, her eyes only slightly concealed by the veil, and the book carried in her gloved hand. As she passed near him, he was suddenly aware of the lure of her perfume, and then suddenly it dawned on him that this was not the first time he had seen those eyes.

'Oh my God.' The words were a whisper as he stood there staring. It was the woman on the steps. Suddenly there she was, disappearing into the crowd at the airport, with his mother's latest book in her hand. For an insane moment, he wanted to shout 'Wait!', but he was trapped on hold and couldn't move until the secretary returned with the answer to his question, as his eyes desperately combed the constantly moving crowd. In a moment, despite his attempts not to lose sight of her, she had passed beyond him, and once again vanished. The secretary came back on the line a moment later, only to give him an unsatisfactory answer to his question, and tell him that she had to return to another call. 'And for this I waited on the phone all this time, Barbara?' For the first time in a long time, the receptionist noted that

40

he sounded angry, but she only had time to mutter 'sorry' and then had to answer two more calls.

And then, as though he could still find her if he hurried, he found himself rushing through the crowd looking for the fur coat and the black hat with the veil. But it was obvious within a few moments that she was nowhere in sight. But what the hell difference did it make anyway? Who was she? No one. A stranger.

He chided himself for the romanticism that made him chase some mystery woman halfway through an airport. It was like looking for the white rabbit in Alice in Wonderland only in this case he was looking for a beautiful woman with dark eyes, wearing a mink coat and a black hat with a veil and of course carrying *Lovers and Lies* by Charlotte Brandon. 'Cool it.' He told himself softly as he passed through the crowd to the airport desk, where people were already lining up for their seat assignments and boarding cards. There seemed to be mobs ahead of him, and when at last he got to the counter, the only seats they had left were in the last two rows of the plane.

'Why not just put me in the bathroom while you're at it?' He looked ruefully at the young man at the counter, who only smiled.

'Believe me, whoever gets here after you will be put in there, and after that we'll be sticking them in the cargo hold. This one is filled to the gills.'

'That ought to be charming.'

The airlines representative smiled disarmingly and held out both hands. 'Can we help it if we're popular?' And then they both laughed. Suddenly Alex found himself looking around for her again, and once more to no avail. For an insane moment, he wanted to ask the man waiting on him at the counter if he had seen her, but he recognised that that temptation was more than a little mad.

The airline rep. handed him his ticket, and a moment later he took his place on line at the gate. He had enough on his mind as he stood there, the client he was planning to see in New York, his mother, his sister, Amanda, his niece. Still, the woman in the mink coat once more began to haunt him, just as she had the night he had seen her crying on the stairs.

41

Or was he totally crazy and it wasn't the same woman at all? He grinned to himself, his fantasies even bought his mother's books. Maybe it was all very psychotic and he was finally losing his mind. But the prospect seemed to amuse him as the line moved slowly forward, and he pulled his boarding pass out of his pocket, and once more pushed his thoughts ahead to what he had to do in New York.

Raphaella took her seat quickly as Tom stowed the tote bag under her seat, and the stewardess quietly took the beautifully-cut dark mink coat. All of the personnel on board had been warned that morning that they would be carrying a VIP on the trip to New York, but she would be travelling in coach instead of first class, which was apparently her standard choice. For years she had insisted to John Henry that it was much more 'discreet'. Lost among the housewives and secretaries and salesmen and babies in the coach section, no one would expect to find the wife of one of the richest men in the world. When they pre-boarded her as they always did, she settled quickly into the next to the last row, where she always sat. It was discreet almost to the point of being invisible. Raphaella also knew that the airlines personnel would make every effort not to place any other passengers in the seat beside her, so that it was almost certain that she would sit alone for the entire flight. And after she thanked Tom for his help, she watched him leave the plane just as the first passengers came on board.

Chapter 5

Alex stood with the throng of others, inching his way along the narrow gangway to the door of the plane, where one by one they were funnelled into the mammoth aircraft, their boarding passes checked and taken, their seats pointed out by the flock of smiling stewardesses who stood ready to greet them. The passengers in first class had already been seated, and they sat hidden in their private world, two curtains drawn to protect them from any curious gaze. In the main body of the plane, the masses were already settling in, shoving too big pieces of hand baggage into the aisle, or stuffing briefcases and packages into the overhead racks, so that the stewardesses were rapidly obliged to cruise up and down, urging passengers to put everything except hats and coats beneath their seats. It was an old litany for Alex who searched for his seat mechanically, knowing already where it was. He had already surrendered his suit bag to a stewardess at the entrance, and his briefcase he would slide beneath his seat after selecting one or two files that he wanted to read during the first part of the trip. It was of this that he was thinking as he made his way towards the rear of the plane, attempting not to bump other passengers or their children, as he moved along. For an instant he had thought again about the woman, but it was futile to wonder about her here. She had been nowhere in the crowd that had waited to board the aircraft, so he knew that she would be nowhere on this plane.

He reached the seat they had assigned him, and quietly stowed his briefcase underneath it, preparing to sit down. He noticed with only mild annoyance that there was already a small piece of luggage stowed under one of the seats beside him, and he realised with dismay that he would not be sitting alone for the flight.

He hoped it would be someone with as much work to do as he had. He didn't want to be bothered with conversation on

43

the trip. He settled himself quickly, pulled the briefcase back out from under his seat, extricated the two files he wanted, glad that his seatmate had, momentarily, disappeared. It was several moments later when he felt a stir beside him and he instinctively shifted his gaze from the page he was reading to the floor. And as he did so, he found himself staring down at a pair of very graceful and expensive black lizard shoes. Gucci, he registered without thinking, the little gold clips embedded in the throat of the shoe. He then noticed, all in a split second, that the ankles were even more attractive than the shoes. Feeling faintly like a schoolboy, he found himself looking slowly up the long elegant legs to the hem of the black skirt, and then up, the interminable expanse of fine French suit to the face looking down at him, her head cocked slightly to one side. She looked as though she were going to ask him a question, and as though she were perfectly aware that he had just looked her over from her shoes to the top of her head. But as he looked up to see her, a look of total astonishment overtook Alex and without thinking, he stood up beside her and said, 'My God, it's you.'

She looked equally startled as he said it, and only stared at him wondering what he had meant and who he was. He seemed to think he knew her, and for a terrified instant she wondered if it was someone who had long ago seen her photograph somewhere, or read of her in the press. Perhaps it was even a member of the press, and for a long moment she had the urge to turn and run away. But on the plane she would be his prisoner for hours. Anxious, she began to back away from him, her eyes wide and frightened, her handbag clutched beneath her arm, she was going to find the stewardess, and insist that this time she had to be moved to first class. Or perhaps it was not too late for them to deplane her. She could make the next flight to New York. 'I . . . no . . .' She murmured softly as she turned away, but before she could take one step, from him she felt his hand on her arm. He had seen the terror in her eyes and was horrified at what he'd done.

'No, don't.'

She turned to face him then, not quite sure why she did it. All her instincts were still telling her to flee. 'Who are you?'

'Alex Hale. I just . . . it's that . . .' He smiled gently at her, pained at what he saw in the beautiful woman's eyes. They were eyes filled with sorrow and terror. Perhaps injured too, but that he did not know yet. All he knew was that he didn't want her to run away, not again. 'I saw you buy that in the airport.' He glanced towards the book which still lay in her seat, and to Raphaella it was a *non sequitur* which made no sense, '. . . and I, I saw you once on the steps, at Broderick and Broadway about a week ago. You were . . .' How could he tell her now that she had been crying? It would only make her flee from him again. But his words seemed to jar her, as she looked at him long and hard this time. She seemed to be remembering, and slowly a faint blush overtook her face.

'I . . .' She nodded and looked away. Perhaps he was not a papparazzi. Perhaps he was only a madman or a fool. But she didn't want to travel five hours sitting beside him, wondering why he had held her arm or said 'My God, it's you.' But as she stared at him, immobile, wondering, as his eyes held her tightly, standing where she was, the final announcement to take their seats came over the loudspeaker in the aeroplane, and he moved slowly around her, to clear the way for her to her seat.

'Why don't you sit down?' He stood, looking very strong and tall and handsome, and as though unable to escape him, she silently walked past him, and took her seat. She had put the hat in the overhead rack above her before Alex had found his seat, and now her hair shone like black silk as she bowed her head and turned away. She seemed to be looking out the window, and Alex said nothing further to her, as he sat down in his own seat leaving a vacant seat between them.

He felt his heart hammering inside him. She was as beautiful as he had at first thought, the night he saw her sitting on the steps, surrounded by the cloud of lynx, her haunting black eyes looking up towards him, and the rivers of tears pouring silently down her face. This was the same woman, sitting only inches away from him, and every fibre of his being wanted to reach out to her, to touch her, to take her in his arms. It was madness and he knew it. She was a

45

perfect stranger. And then he smiled to himself. The words were apt. She seemed perfect in every way. As he gazed at her neck, her hands, the way she sat, all he could see was her perfection and when he saw her profile for an instant, he could not tear his eyes away from her face. And then aware of how uncomfortable it made her, he suddenly grabbed the two files and stared into them blindly, hoping to make her think that he had forgotten his fascination with her, and had turned his mind to something else. It wasn't until after take-off that he saw her glance towards him, and from the corner of his eye he saw her stare at him long and hard.

Unable to play the game any longer then, he turned towards her, his eyes gentle on her, his smile hesitant but warm. 'I'm sorry if I frightened you before. It's just . . . I don't usually do things like this . . .' The smile broadened, but she didn't smile in return. 'I, I don't know how to explain it.' For a moment, he felt like a true madman trying to explain it all to her, as she sat there staring, with no expression on her face other than the look in her eyes which had so touched him when he first saw it. 'When I saw you that night on the steps, when you . . .' He decided to go ahead and say it, 'when you were crying, I felt so helpless when you looked up at me, and then you disappeared. Just like that. You just vanished. And for days it bothered me. I keep thinking of the way you looked, with the tears running down your face.' As he spoke to her, he thought he saw something soften in her eyes, but there was no trace of anything different in her face. He smiled again and shrugged softly, 'Maybe I just can't resist damsels in distress. But you've bothered me all this week. And this morning there you were. I was watching some woman buy a book, while I called my office,' he grinned at the familiar book jacket, without telling her just how familiar it was, 'and then I realised it was you. It was crazy, like something in a movie. For a week I'm haunted by a vision of you, as you sit crying on the stairs, and then suddenly there you are, looking just as beautiful.'

This time she smiled in answer, he was so sweet and he seemed so young, in a funny way he suddenly reminded her of her brother, who had been in love every other week when he was fifteen, 'and then you disappeared again,' he went on despairingly, 'I hung up the phone and you had vanished into thin air.' She didn't want to tell him that she had stepped into a private office, and was taken by several secluded corridors to the plane. But he looked puzzled for a moment. 'I didn't even see you board the plane.' And then he lowered his voice conspiratorially. 'Tell me the truth, are you magic?' He looked like an overgrown child and she couldn't surpress a grin.

Her eyes began to dance as she looked at him, no longer angry, no longer afraid. He was a little mad, a little young, and a lot romantic, and she could sense that he didn't wish her any harm. He was just sweet, and somewhat foolish. And now she nodded to him with a small smile. 'Yes, I am.'

'Aha! I thought so. A magic lady. That's terrific.' He sat back in his seat with a broad smile and she smiled back. It was an amusing game. And no harm could come to her after all, she was on the plane. He was a stranger, and she would never see him again. The stewardesses would whisk her away almost instantly when the plane reached New York and she would be safe again, in familiar hands. But just this once it was amusing to play this game with a stranger. And she did remember him now, from the night when she had been so desperately lonely, and she had fled the house and sat, crying on the long stone steps that led down the hillside. She had looked up and seen him, and before he could approach her she had fled through the garden roof. But as she thought of it, she noticed that Alex was smiling at her again. 'Is it difficult being a magic lady?'

'Sometimes.' He thought he heard an accent as he listened but he wasn't sure. And then, lulled by the safety of the game he decided to ask her.

'Are you an American magic lady?'

Still smiling at him in return, she shook her head. 'No, I'm not.' Although she had married John Henry, she had remained a citizen of both France and Spain. She didn't see what harm could come to talking to Alex who seemed to be staring at the collection of rings on both her hands. She knew what he was wondering, and knew also that he would have a hard time finding out what he wanted to know.

47

Suddenly she didn't want to tell him, didn't want to be Mrs John Henry Phillips, just for a while. For a little while she wanted to be just Raphaella, a very young girl.

'You haven't told me where you're from, Magic Lady.' His gaze tore itself away from her hands, He had decided that whoever she was, she was successful, and he had been relieved not to find a solid band of gold on her left hand. He had decided for some reason that she probably had a wealthy father and maybe her old man had been giving her a hard time, maybe that was why she had been crying on the steps when he first saw her. Or maybe she was divorced. But the truth of it was that he didn't even care. All he cared about were her hands, her eyes, her smile, and the power he felt that drew him to her. He had felt it even at a distance, and it made him want to reach out to her again. And now he was much closer, but he knew he couldn't touch her. All he could do was play the game.

But she smiled at him openly now. For an instant, they had become almost friends. 'I'm from France.'

'Are you? Do you still live there?'

She shook her head in answer, suddenly more sober. 'No. I live in San Francisco.'

'I thought so.'

'Did you?' She looked up at him in surprise and amusement. 'How did you know?' There was something very innocent about her as she said it. And yet at the same time the eyes were wise. Her way of speaking to him suggested that she had not been much exposed to the big bad world. 'Do I look like a San Franciscan?'

'No, you don't. But I just had a feeling that you live here. Do you like it?'

She nodded slowly, but the bottomless sadness had come back to her eyes. Talking to her was like sailing a boat through difficult waters, he was never quite sure when he was about to run aground, or when he was safe and could sail free. 'I like it. I don't see very much of San Francisco any more.'

'Don't you?' He was afraid to ask a serious question, like why she didn't see much any more. 'What do you do instead?' His voice was so soft that it caressed her, and she

48

turned to him with the largest eyes he thought he'd ever seen.

'I read. A great deal.' She smiled at him then and shrugged, as though embarrassed. And then blushing faintly, she looked away and then back at him to ask a question. 'And you?' She felt very brave, asking something so personal of this strange man.

'I'm an attorney.'

She nodded quietly, and smiled. She had liked his answer. She had always found the law intriguing, and somehow it seemed a suitable occupation for this man. She had guessed that he was around her own age. In truth, he was six years older than she. 'Do you like it?'

'Very much. And you? What do you do, Magic Lady, other than read?'

For a moment, with a touch of irony, she was going to tell him that she was a nurse. But that seemed an unwonted cruelty to John Henry, so she said nothing for a moment and only shook her head. 'Nothing,' she looked up at Alex frankly. 'Nothing at all.'

He wondered again what her story was, what her life was like, what she did all day long, and why had she been crying that night? Suddenly, it bothered him more than ever. 'Do you travel a great deal?'

'Now and then. Just for a few days.' She looked down at her hands, her eyes fixing on the large gold knot on her left hand.

'Are you going back to France now?' He had assumed Paris, and was, of course, right. But she shook her head.

'New York. I only go back to Paris once a year, in the summer.'

He nodded slowly and smiled. 'It's a beautiful city. I spent six months there once, and I loved it.'

'Did you?' Raphaella looked pleased. 'Do you speak French then?'

'Not really.' The broad boyish grin returned. 'Certainly not as well as you speak English.' She laughed softly then and fingered the book she had bought at the airport. Alex noticed it with a twinkle in his eye. 'Do you read a lot of her?'

49

'Who?'

'Charlotte Brandon.'

Raphaella nodded. 'I love her. I've read every book she ever wrote.' And then she glanced at him apologetically. 'I know, it's not very serious reading, but it's a wonderful escape. I open her books and I am instantly absorbed into the world she describes. I think that kind of reading seems silly to a man, but it . . .' she couldn't tell him that the books had saved her sanity over the last seven years, he would think she was crazy. '. . . it's just very enjoyable.'

He smiled more deeply. 'I know, I've read her too.'

'Have you?' Raphaella looked at him in nothing less than amazement. Charlotte Brandon's books did not seem like the sort of thing a man would read. John Henry certainly never would have. Or her father. They read non-fiction books about economics, or world wars. 'Do you like them?'

'Very much.' And then he decided to play with her for a little longer. 'I've read them all.'

'Really?' Her huge eyes widened further. To her, it seemed an odd thing for an attorney to do. And then struggling, she smiled at him again and held the book towards him. 'Have you read this one? It's the new one.' Maybe she had found a friend after all.

He nodded as he glanced at the book. 'I think it's her best. You'll like it. It's more serious than some of her others. More thoughtful. She deals very heavily with death, it isn't just a pretty story. She's saying a lot.' He knew that his mother had written it the previous year, before she'd had some fairly important surgery, and she had been afraid it would be her last book. She had tried to say something important with it, and she had. And Alex's face was more serious as he looked at Raphaella. 'This one means a lot to her.'

Raphaella looked at him strangely. 'How do you know? Have you met her?'

There was a moment's pause as the broad smile returned to his face, and he leaned over and whispered to Raphaella. 'She's my Mom.' But this time, Raphaella laughed at him, the sound was that of a silvery bell and it pleased his ears. 'No, really, she is.'

50

'You know, for a lawyer, you're really very silly.'

'Silly?' He tried to look outraged. 'I'm serious. Charlotte Brandon is my mother.'

'And the President of the United States is my father.'

'Congratulations.' He held out a hand to shake hers, and she slid her cool hand gently into his they shook firmly. 'By the way, I'm Alex Hale.'

'You see!' She said, laughing again. 'Your name isn't Brandon!'

'That's her maiden name. She is Charlotte Brandon Hale.'

'Absolutely.' Raphaella couldn't stop laughing now as she stared at him and laughed more. 'Do you always tell stories like this?'

'Only to total strangers. By the way, Magic Lady, what's your name?' He knew it was a little pushy, but he desperately wanted to know who she was. He wanted to lose their mutual anonymity. He wanted to know who she was, where she lived, where he could find her, so if she disappeared again into thin air, he'd be able to track her down.

But she hesitated in answer to his question, only for an instant, and then she smiled, 'Raphaella.'

He shook his head dubiously with a small smile. 'Now that sounds like a story to me. Raphaella. That's not a French name.'

'No, it's Spanish. I'm only half French.'

'And half Spanish?' Her colouring told him that it was true, the raven-black hair and black eyes and porcelain-white skin were what he would have expected from Spain. Little did he know that she got her colouring from her French father.

'Yes, I'm half Spanish.'

'Which half? Your mind or your heart?' It was a serious question and she frowned as she considered the answer.

'That's a difficult question. I'm not sure. I suppose that my heart is French, and my mind is Spanish. I think like a Spaniard, not because I want to so much, but mostly out of habit. Somehow that whole way of life pervades everything that you are.'

51

Alex looked over his shoulder suspiciously and then leaned towards her to whisper, 'I don't see a duenna.'

She rolled her eyes and laughed. 'Ah no, but you will!'

'Really?'

'Very much so. The only place I'm ever alone is on a plane.'

'How strange, and rather intriguing.' He wanted to ask her then how old she was. He guessed twenty-five or six, and would be surprised to learn she was thirty-two. 'Do you mind it?'

'Sometimes. But without that, it would probably seem very strange. I'm used to it. Sometimes I think it would be frightening not to be so protected.'

'Why?' She intrigued him more than ever. She was different from every woman he had ever known.

'Then one would have no protection.' She said it with great seriousness.

'From what?'

She paused for a long moment and then smiled at him and said gently. 'People like you.' He could only smile in answer, and for a long moment they sat together, with their own thoughts and questions each about the other's life. She turned to him after a little while, and her eyes were curious and happier than they had seemed before. 'Why did you tell me that story about Charlotte Brandon?' She couldn't figure him out, but she liked him, he seemed honest and kind and funny and bright, as best as she could judge.

But he was smiling at her now in answer. 'Because it's true. She is my mother, Raphaella. Tell me, is that really your name?'

She nodded soberly in answer. 'It is.' But she had offered no other, no last name. Just Raphaella. And he liked that name a great deal.

'In any case, she's really my mother.' He pointed to the picture at the back of the book and then looked quietly at Raphaella still holding the book in her hand. 'You'd like her a lot. She's a remarkable woman.'

'I'm sure she is.' But it was obvious that she still didn't believe Alex's tale, and then with an expression of amusement, he reached into his jacket and withdrew the narrow black wallet Kay had given him for his birthday the year before. It bore the same interlocking G as Raphaella's black lizard bag. Gucci. He pulled out two dog-eared photographs, and silently he handed them to her across the empty seat. She gazed at them for an instant, and then her eyes grew wide. One of the photographs was a miniature of the one on the back of the book, and the other was one of his mother laughing as he held an arm around her, and his sister stood at her other side with George.

'Family portrait. We took it last year. My sister, my brother-in-law, and my mother. Now what do you think?'

Raphaella was smiling and looking at Alex with sudden awe. 'Oh, you must tell me about her! Is she wonderful?'

'Very much so. And as a matter of fact, Magic Lady,' he stood up to his full height, slipped the two files into the pocket in the seat in front of them, and sat down again in the empty seat next to hers, 'I think you're pretty wonderful too. Now, before I tell you all about my mother, can I interest you in a drink before lunch?' It was the first time he had used his mother to woo a woman, but he didn't care. He wanted to know Raphaella as well as he could by the time the plane landed in New York.

They talked for the next four and a half hours, over two glasses of white wine, and then over a fairly inedible lunch which neither of them noticed, as they talked about Paris and Rome and Madrid, and life in San Francisco, and writing and people and children and law. She learned that he had a beautiful little Victorian house that he loved. He knew about her life in Spain at Santa Eugenia, and listened with rapt fascination at her tales of a world that dated back centuries and was like nothing he had ever known. She told him of the children she loved so much, of the stories she told them, of her cousins, of ridiculous gossip about that kind of life in Spain. She told him about everything but John Henry and the life she led now. But it was no life, it was a dark, empty void, a non-life. It wasn't that she wanted to conceal it from him, it was that she didn't want to think about it herself.

When at last the stewardess asked them to fasten their seat belts, they both looked like two children who had been told that the party was over and it was time to go home.

'What will you do now?' He already knew that she was meeting her mother, her aunt, and two female cousins, in true Spanish fashion, and that she would be staying at the hotel with them in New York.

'Now? I will meet my mother at the hotel. They should already be there.'

'Can I give you a ride in a cab?'

She shook her head slowly. 'I'll be picked up. In fact,' she looked at him regretfully, 'I will be doing my disappearing act as soon as I arrive.'

'At least I can help you pick up your luggage.' He sounded as if he were pleading.

But she shook her head again. 'No. You'll see, I'll be escorted right off the plane.'

He tried to smile at her then. 'Are you sure you're not a jailbird, and you're travelling in custody or something?'

'I might as well be.' Her voice was as sad as her eyes. Suddenly the gaiety of the last five hours had faded for both of them. The real world was about to intrude on their little game. 'I'm sorry.'

'So am I.' And then he looked at her seriously. 'Raphaella ... could I see you while we're in New York? I know you'll be busy, but maybe for a drink, a . . .' She was already shaking her head. 'Why not?'

'It's impossible. My family would never understand.'

'Why not for God's sake, you're a grown woman.'

'Precisely. And women from that world don't run around having drinks with strange men.'

'I'm not strange.' He looked boyish again and she laughed. 'All right, so I am. Will you have lunch with me and my mother? Tomorrow?' He was improvising but he'd drag his mother to lunch if he had to haul her out of an editorial meeting by the hair. If Charlotte Brandon was required as a duenna in order to convince Raphaella to come to lunch with him, then that was who they would have. 'Will you? The Four Seasons. One o'clock.'

'Alex, I don't know. I'm sure I'll be . . .'

'Try. You don't even have to promise. We'll be there. If you can make it, fine. If you don't show, I'll understand. Just

54

see.' The plane had touched the runway and there was a sudden urgency in his voice.

'I don't see how . . .' She looked distressed as her eyes met his.

'Never mind. Just remember how much you want to meet my mother. The Four Seasons. One o'clock. You'll remember.'

'Yes, but . . .'

'Shhh . . .' He put a finger to her lips, and her eyes held his for a long time. He leaned suddenly closer to her and was desperately aware of how much he wanted to kiss her. Maybe if he did, he would never see her again, and if he didn't, perhaps he would see her again. Instead, he talked over the roar of the motors as they taxied towards the terminal. 'Where are you staying?'

Her eyes were enormous as she looked at him, hesitating, unsure. In effect, he was asking her to trust him, and she wanted to, but she wasn't sure if she should. But the words were out of her mouth almost as though she couldn't control them as the plane jolted to a sudden stop. 'The Carlyle.' And then as though by a prearranged signal, two stewardesses stood in the aisle, one held her mink coat, the other pulled her tote bag from beneath her seat, and like an obedient child, she asked Alex to hand her her hat from the overhead compartment, and without saying a word she put it on, unfastened her seat belt and stood up. She stood there, as he had first seen her in the airport, swathed in mink, her eyes veiled by the little black hat, her book and her handbag clutched in her hand. She looked at him, and then held out a black kid gloved hand. 'Thank you.' The words were for the five hours he had given her, for the cherished moment, the flight from reality, for a taste of what her life might have been, could have been, and was not. And then, her eyes lingering on his for only a moment, she turned away.

The two stewardesses who had come for Raphaella had been joined by a steward who stood firmly behind her now, and one of the spare exits was opened at the rear of the plane, near where she and Alex had sat, as the stewardesses announced on the PA system that passengers would be deplaning up front. The door at the rear opened briefly, and

Raphaella and the three crew members stepped quickly out. The door was immediately shut again, and only a few of the passengers in the rear wondered what had happened and why the woman in the dark mink had been taken out. But they were busy with their own lives, their own plans, and only Alex stood there for a long moment, watching the door through which she had fled. Once more, she had escaped him. Once more, the woman of the dark, haunting beauty was gone. But now he knew that her name was Raphaella, and that she would be staying at the Carlyle. Until suddenly, with a sinking feeling, he realised that he didn't know her last name. Raphaella. Raphaella what? How could he ask for her at the hotel? Now his only hope was to see her the next day at lunch. If she showed up, if she could get away from her relatives . . . if . . . He felt like a small, terrified schoolboy as he picked up his coat and his briefcase and began to make his way towards the front of the plane.

Chapter 6

The waiter at the Four Seasons escorted the tall, attractive woman across the floor to her usual table near the bar. The stark modern decor served as the perfect backdrop for the colourful people who populated the restaurant night and day. As she made her way to the table, the woman smiled, nodded, acknowledged a friend who stopped a conversation just long enough to wave. Charlotte Brandon was a regular here. For her, it was like having lunch at her club, and her tall, thin frame moved with ease in the familiar surroundings, her snow-coloured hair peeking out from beneath a very becoming dark-mink hat, which perfectly matched the beautiful mink coat she wore over a navy blue dress. In her ears were sapphires and diamonds, and around her neck three strands of large, beautiful pearls, and on her left hand a single sapphire, which she had bought herself for her fiftieth birthday, after she had sold her fifteenth book. The previous book had sold over five million copies in paperback, and she had decided to splurge and buy the ring. It still amazed her to realise that it had all started with the death of her husband when his plane crashed, and she had taken her first job, doing research for a very boring column she had never really enjoyed. But what she had enjoyed, she discovered quickly, was writing, and when she sat down to write her first novel, she felt as though she had come home at last. The first book had done nicely, and the second had done better, but the third book was a bestseller right off the bat, and from then on it was hard work but smooth sailing, and she loved her work more every year, with each book. For years now, all that had really mattered to her were her books and her children and her grandchild Amanda.

There had never really been anyone important in her life after her husband died, but eventually she had forced herself to go out with other men. There had been half a lifetime now of close friends, warm relationships, but never anyone she wanted to marry. For twenty years the children had been her excuse, and now it was always her work. 'I'm too difficult to live with. My hours are impossible. I write all night and sleep all day. It would drive you crazy! You'd hate it!!' Her excuses were numerous and not very valid. She was a well-organised, well-disciplined woman who was able to schedule her working hours like an army battalion going on a march. The truth was that she didn't want to get married again. She had never really loved anyone since Arthur Hale. He had been the bright light in her heaven, he had been the model for half a dozen heroes in her books. And Alexander looked so much like him, it always brought a lump to her throat just to see him, so dark, so tall, so long and lean and handsome. It filled her with pride to realise that this extraordinarily beautiful, intelligent, warm human being was also her son. It was a very different feeling than she had when she saw her daughter. Kay always filled her with some secret guilt over what she had done wrong. Why had Kay turned out so bitter, so cold, and so angry? What could have made her that way? Was it her mother's long work hours? The death of her father? Sibling rivalry? For Charlotte, there was always a sense of failure, of sorrow and misgiving, when looking into those cold eyes so much like her own, yet seeing nothing happy reflected there.

She was so different from Alex, who stood to his full height now as he saw his mother, with genuine glee in his eyes, and a warm happy smile.

'My God, Mother, you look gorgeous!' He stooped slightly to kiss her and she gave him a quick hug. It was the first time in several months that he'd come to New York from San Francisco, but she never really felt that they were very far apart. He called her often, to see how she was, to tell her some story, to enquire about her latest book, or explain his most recent case. She had an ongoing sense of belonging in his life, yet with neither of them clinging too tight. It was a relationship which in every way she cherished and as she sat down across the table from her son, her joy to be seeing him showed in her eyes. 'You look better than ever!' He smiled at her with obvious pride.

'Flattery, my darling, is wicked but delightful. Thank you.' Her eyes danced into his and he grinned at her. At sixty-two she was still a beautiful woman, tall, graceful, elegant, with the smooth skin of a woman almost half her age. Cosmetic surgery had assisted her in maintaining the beautiful face and smooth complexion, but she had been a beautiful woman from the first. And as involved as she was in the promotion and publicity of her works, it wasn't surprising that she was anxious to stay young. Over the years, Charlotte Brandon had become a large business. As the woman behind the pen, her face was an important part of her image, as was her warmth and her vitality. She was a woman whom other women respected and who had won the devotion of her readers over three decades. 'So what have you been up to? You look wonderful too, I might add.'

'I've been busy. Non-stop in fact since I last saw you.' But as he said it, his eyes strayed suddenly to the door. For an instant, he had thought that he'd seen Raphaella, a dark head in a mink coat had come up the stairs, but he saw that it was a different woman, and his eyes returned rapidly to his mother's face.

'Expecting someone, Alex?' She was quick to see the look in his eyes and she smiled. 'Or just tired of California women?'

'Who has time to meet any? I've been working night and day.'

'You shouldn't do that.' For a moment she looked at him sadly. She wanted more for him than just a half life. She wanted more than that for both her children, but so far neither had seemed to find what they wanted. Alex had had the abortive marriage to Rachel, and Kay was devoured by her passion for politics and the ambition which obscured everything else in her life. Sometimes Charlotte thought that she didn't understand them. She had managed to have both after all, a family and a career, but they told her that times were different, that careers could no longer be run as genteely as hers had been. Were they right or just kidding themselves about their own failures? She wondered now as she watched her son, questioning if he was happy with his solitary existence, or if he wanted something very different.

She wondered if he had a serious relationship with a woman, someone he truly loved.

'Don't look so worried, Mother.' He patted her hand with a smile and waved to the waiter. 'Drink?' She nodded, and he ordered Bloody Marys for both of them, and then he sat back with a grin. He had to tell her. Now, in case Raphaella arrived on time. He had told her one o'clock, and he had met his mother at twelve-thirty. Then again there was the chance that Raphaella wouldn't come at all. His brow clouded for an instant, and then he looked into his mother's deep blue eyes. 'I invited a friend to join us. I'm not sure she can make it.' And then, looking boyish and embarrassed, he looked down for a moment and then back into the blue eyes. 'I hope you don't mind.' But Charlotte Brandon was already laughing, a youthful happy sound that filled the air and it always made her smile. 'Stop laughing at me, Mother.' But her laughter was always contagious, and he found himself grinning as she wiped the tears from her eyes.

'You look about fourteen years old, Alex. I'm sorry. Who in God's name did you invite to lunch?'

'Just a friend. Oh dammit. A woman.' He almost added, 'I picked her up on a plane.'

'Is she a friend of yours here in New York?' The questions weren't prying, they were friendly, as Charlotte continued to smile at her son.

'No. She lives in San Francisco. She's just here for a few days. We flew in on the same plane.'

'That's nice. What does she do?' She took the first sip of her drink, wondering if she shouldn't ask, but she was always curious about his friends. Sometimes it was hard not to sound like a mother, but when she pushed too hard, he always told her gently to stop. She looked at him enquiringly now, but he didn't seem to mind. He looked happier than she'd seen him look in a long time, and there was something wonderfully warm and gentle about his eyes. He had never looked that way with Rachel, he had always looked so uncomfortable then and so worried. She suddenly found herself wondering if Alex had some kind of surprise in store.

But he was only grinning at her in amusement, in answer to her question. 'You may find this difficult to believe,

Famous Author Charlotte Brandon, but she doesn't seem to do a damn thing.'

'My, my. How decadent.' But Charlotte did not look disturbed, only curious at what she read in the eyes of her son. 'Is she very young?' That would explain it. Very young people had a right to take some time to figure out what to do. But when they were a little older, Charlotte expected them to have found their way, at least to some kind of job.

'No. I mean, not that young. She's about thirty. But she's European.'

'Ah.' His mother said, understanding. 'Now I see.'

'It's strange though.' He looked pensive for a moment. 'I've never known anyone who's led that kind of life. Her father is French, and her mother is Spanish, and she has spent most of her life locked up, surrounded, escorted, besieged by relatives and duennas. It seems like an incredible life.'

'How did you ever get her away from them all long enough to get to know her?' Charlotte was intrigued and took her attention away only long enough to wave vaguely at a friend halfway across the room.

'I haven't yet. But I plan to. That was one of the reasons why I invited her to lunch today. She adores your books.'

'Oh God, Alex, not one of those. For God's sake, how can I eat with people asking me questions about how long I've written and how many months it took to write each one of my books?' But her tone of reproach was playful, and she still wore a half-hearted smile. 'Why can't you play with girls who prefer other authors? Some nice girl who likes to read Proust or Balzac or Camus, or adores reading the memoirs of Winston Churchill. Someone sensible.'

He chuckled at the earnest look she wore and then suddenly over her shoulder he saw a vision enter the Four Seasons and Charlotte Brandon thought she actually heard him catch his breath. Seeing the direction in which he was staring, she turned to see a remarkably beautiful, tall, dark-haired young woman standing at the top of the stairs, looking tremendously fragile and yet at the same time entirely self-possessed. She was a most beautiful woman and all eyes were turned towards her in frank admiration as they stared. Her posture was perfect, her head held high, her hair gleaming in a carefully woven knot of what looked like black silk. She wore a narrow dress of dark chocolate brown cashmere which was almost the same colour as the rich fur. She had a creamy silk Hermes scarf knotted loosely around her neck, there were pearls and diamonds in her ears. Her legs looked endless and graceful in a pair of chocolate coloured stockings and brown suede shoes. The bag she wore was in the same rich brown leather, and this time it was not Gucci but Hermes. She was the most beautiful creature that Charlotte had seen in years, and she suddenly understood the rapt expression of her son. What also struck her, as Alex excused himself from the table and approached her, was that there was something very familiar about the girl. It was a face which Charlotte had seen somewhere, or maybe it was only that she was so typical of the aristocracy of Spain. She had a grace and a presence as she moved towards the table which suggested the bearing of a young queen, yet at the same time from the look in her eyes one could sense a gentleness, a shyness, which were remarkable given her striking good looks. This time it was Charlotte who almost uttered an exclamation as she watched her. The girl was so beautiful that one could only observe her with awe. And it was easy to understand Alex's fascination. This was a very, very rare gem.

'Mother, I'd like to introduce you to Raphaella. Raphaella, my mother, Charlotte Brandon.' For an instant, Charlotte wondered at the absence of a surname, but the question was forgotten as she looked into the dark haunted eyes of the girl. At close range, one could see that she was almost frightened, and she was a little out of breath, as though she had run. She shook hands very properly with Charlotte, and let Alex take her coat as she sat down.

'I am so terribly sorry to be late, Mrs Brandon.' She looked Charlotte squarely in the eye, a faint blush on her creamy cheeks. 'I was engaged. It was difficult to . . . get free.' Her eyelashes veiled her eyes as she settled back in her seat, and Alex felt for an instant as though he would melt watching her. She was the most incredible woman he had ever seen. And as she looked at them side by side, Charlotte couldn't help thinking that they made a remarkable pair. Their dark heads close together, the big eyes, the splendid young limbs, the graceful hands. They looked like two young gods of mythology destined to make a pair. Charlotte had to force herself back into the conversation with a pleasant smile.

'Not at all, dear. Don't worry. Alex and I were just catching up. He tells me that you flew in from San Francisco last night also. To visit friends?'

'To meet my mother.' Raphaella began to relax slowly, although she had declined a drink when she sat down.

'Does she live here?'

'No, in Madrid. She is passing through on her way to Buenos Aires. And she thought that . . . well, it gives me a chance to come to New York for a few days.'

'She's lucky to see you. I always feel that way when Alex comes to town.' All three of them smiled then, and Alex induced them to order lunch before they went on. It was after that that Raphaella confessed to Charlotte how much her books had meant to her over the years.

'I will admit that I used to read them in Spanish, and now and then in French, but when I first came to this country, my . . .' she blushed and lowered her eyes for a moment. She had been about to tell them that her husband had bought some of Charlotte's books for her in English, but suddenly she had stopped. It seemed dishonest, but she didn't want to talk about John Henry now. 'I bought them in English, and now I read them all in English all the time,' and then her eyes grew slowly sad again as she looked at Charlotte, 'you don't know how much your work has meant to me. Sometimes I think it's what has . . .' Her voice was so soft it was almost inaudible. '. . . sometimes it's what has kept me alive.' The agony in her voice was plainly apparent as Charlotte watched her, and Alex was reminded of the first time he had seen her, crying on the stairs. Now in the splendour of the New York restaurant, he found himself wondering what was the secret that weighed so heavily on her soul. But she only looked up at his mother, with a small smile of thanks, and without thinking, Charlotte reached out and touched her hand.

63

'They mean a lot to me when I write them. But the important thing is that they mean something to people like you. Thank you, Raphaella. It's a beautiful compliment, and in a sense, it makes my life worthwhile.' And then as though she sensed something hidden, some distant wish, some dream, she looked hard at Raphaella. 'Do you write too?'

But Raphaella only smiled and shook her head, looking very young and childlike and not as sophisticated as she had seemed at first. 'Oh no!' And then she laughed. 'But I am a storyteller.'

'That's the first step.' In silence, Alex watched them. He loved seeing them together, the richness of the contrast, two beautiful women, yet one so young and so fragile, the other so mature and so strong, one with white hair and one with black, one he knew so well and the other not at all. Yet he wanted to know her. He wanted to know her better than he had ever known anyone before. As he watched them, he listened to his mother go on. 'What kind of a storyteller are you, Raphaella?'

'I tell stories to children. In the summer. All my little cousins. We spend the summer together in our family house in Spain.' But Charlotte's knowledge of such family 'houses' told her that it was something more than that. 'There are dozens of them, we are a very large family, and I always love to take the children in hand. And I tell them stories,' and she smiled happily, 'and they listen, and giggle, and laugh. It's wonderful, it does something good to the soul.'

Charlotte smiled at the younger woman's expression as she nodded, and then as she gazed at her, it was as though everything came into focus in her head. Raphaella . . . Raphaella . . . Spain . . . a family estate there . . . and Paris . . . a bank . . . She had to fight an impulse to say something aloud. Instead, she let Alex carry on the conversation as she looked again and again at the face of the girl. And as she looked, she wondered if Alex knew the whole story. Something told her that he did not.

Only an hour after she had joined them, Raphaella looked regretfully but nervously at her watch. 'I am so sorry . . . I'm afraid I must go back to my mother and my aunt, and my cousins. They will probably think that I've run away.' She didn't tell Alex's mother that she had feigned a headache to escape lunch with her own entourage.

She had desperately wanted to meet Charlotte Brandon, and to see Alex again, if only once. He offered now to escort her to a taxi, and leaving his mother with a fresh pot of *café filtre,* he promised to return immediately, and left with his ravishing friend on his arm. Before she left, Raphaella had said everything proper to Charlotte, and for a single moment, their eyes had met and held. It was as though Raphaella were telling her the whole story, and as though Charlotte were telling her that she already knew. It was one of those silent communications that happen between women, and for as long as their eyes held, Charlotte felt her heart go out to this lovely young girl. She had remembered the whole story as she sat there, only now it was no longer a tragic item in the news, she had seen the living, breathing, lonely young woman to whom the tragedy had occurred. For an instant, she had wanted to put her arms around her, but instead she had only shaken the cool slender hand and watched them go, her son so handsome and the girl so startlingly lovely as they disappeared down the stairs.

Alex was gazing at her with obvious pleasure as they emerged on to the street and stood there for a moment, inhaling the cool autumn air and feeling happy and young. His eyes danced and he couldn't help smiling, as she looked up at him with something sad and wise and yet also something happy lurking in her eyes. 'My mother adored you, you know.'

'I don't know why she would. But I also adored her. What a lovely woman she is, Alex. She has all the qualities a woman should have.'

'Yeah, she's a pretty nice old girl.' He said it in teasing fashion, but he wasn't thinking of his mother as he looked into Raphaella's eyes. 'When am I going to see you again?'

But she looked away nervously before she answered, glancing into the street to see if there was a passing cab. And then she looked back at Alex, her eyes dark and troubled, her face suddenly inexplicably sad. 'I can't Alex. I'm sorry. I must be with my mother . . . and . . .'

65

'You can't be with them day and night.' He sounded stubborn and she smiled. There was no way that he could understand it. He had never lived a life like hers.

'But I am. Every moment. And then I must go home.'

'So must I. Then I'll see you there. Which reminds me, young lady, there was something you forgot to tell me when you told me you were staying at the Carlyle.'

'What?' She looked suddenly troubled.

'Your last name.'

'Did I do that?' It was difficult to tell if her innocence was real or feigned.

'You did. If you hadn't shown up today, I would have been forced to sit in the lobby of the Carlyle for the rest of the week, waiting until you walked by, and then I'd have thrown myself at your feet in front of your mother and embarrassed you royally, begging for your name!' They were both laughing as he said it, and he gently took her hand in his own. 'Raphaella, I want to see you again.' She looked up at him, her eyes melting into his, wanting everything he wanted, but knowing that she had no right. He bent slowly towards her, wanting to kiss her, but she turned away, burying her face in his shoulder and holding tightly to the lapel of his coat with one hand.

'No, Alex, don't.' He understood that if her world were filled with duennas, then she wasn't likely to kiss a man in the street.

'All right. But I want to see you, Raphaella. What about tonight?' There was a brief chuckle in his shoulder as she moved to look at him again.

'What about my mother, and my aunt and my cousins?' He was impossible, he was so stubborn, but he was also one of the nicest men she had ever met.

'Bring them along. I'll bring my mother.' He was only teasing and she knew it, and this time she laughed out loud.

'You're impossible.'

'I know. And I also won't take no for an answer.'

'Alex, please!' She looked at her watch again and suddenly panicked. 'Oh my God, they'll kill me! By now they must be back from lunch.'

'Then promise you'll see me tonight for a drink.' He held

tightly to her arm, and then suddenly remembered. 'And what the hell is your last name?'

She flung a hand away from him and hailed a cab passing nearby. It shrieked to a stop next to them, and Alex held the one arm more tightly. 'Alex, don't. I have to . . .'

'Not until . . .' It was half a game and half in earnest and she laughed nervously and looked into his eyes again.

'All right. All right. Phillips.'

'Is that how you're registered at the Carlyle?'

'Yes, your honour.' She looked meek for a moment and then nervous again. 'But Alex, I can't see you. Not here, and not in San Francisco, and not ever. This must be goodbye.'

'For chrissake, don't be silly. This is just the beginning.'

'No, it's not.' She looked serious for a moment as she stood there and the cabbie snorted impatiently while Alex glared. 'This is not the beginning, Alex, it's the end. And I must go now.'

'Not like that!' Alex looked suddenly desperate, and then regretted that he hadn't kissed her. 'What? You just had lunch with me so you could meet my famous mother? Is that nice?' He was teasing but she looked at him in confusion and he knew that he had scored a hit.

'Oh Alex, how could you . . .'

'Will you see me later?'

'Alex . . .'

'Never mind. Eleven o'clock tonight. The Café Carlyle. We can talk and listen to Bobby Short. And if you're not there, I'll come upstairs and pound on your mother's door.' But he looked suddenly worried. 'Can you get away from them by eleven?' Even he had to admit that it was funny. She was thirty-two years old and he was asking her if she could escape her mother. In fact, it was utterly absurd.

'I'll try.' She grinned at him, looking suddenly young again, but with a hint of something guilty about her eyes. 'We shouldn't do this.'

'Why not?'

She was about to tell him, but knew that she couldn't, standing on the sidewalk with an impatient cab driver beginning to snarl. 'We'll talk about it tonight.'

'Good.' He grinned broadly. Then she'd be there. And

67

with that, he pulled open the door to the cab and swept her a bow. 'See you this evening, Miss Phillips.' He bent slightly and kissed her on the forehead and a moment later, the door was closed and the cab was speeding uptown, as Raphaella sat in the back seat furious at her own weakness. She should never have misled him from the beginning. She should have told him the truth on the plane, and she should never have gone to lunch. But just once, just once, she told herself, she had a right to do something wild and romantic and amusing. Or did she have that right at all? What gave her that right as John Henry sat dying in his wheelchair, how dare she play such games? As the cab neared the Carlyle she vowed that that night she would tell Alex that she was married. And she was not going to see him again. After tonight . . . there was still that one more meeting . . . and her heart fluttered just at the thought of seeing him one more time.

'Well?' Alex looked at his mother victoriously and sat down. She smiled at him, and as she did so she felt suddenly very old. How young he looked, how hopeful, how happy, how blind.

'Well what?' The blue eyes were gentle and sad.

'What do you mean, "Well what?" Isn't she incredible?'

'Yes.' Charlotte said it matter of factly. 'She is probably the most beautiful young woman I've ever seen. And she is charming and gentle and lovely and I like her. But Alex . . .' She hesitated for a long moment and then decided to speak her mind. 'What good is that going to do you?'

'What's that supposed to mean?' He looked suddenly annoyed as he took a sip of his cold coffee. 'She's wonderful.'

'How well do you know her?'

'Not very.' He grinned at her then. 'But I'm hoping to change that, in spite of her mother and her aunt and her cousins and her duennas.'

'What about her husband?' Alex looked suddenly as though he had been shot. His eyes flew open as he stared at her, and then they narrowed again with rare distrust.

'What do you mean, "Her husband"?'

'Alex, do you know who she is?'

68

'She is half Spanish and half French, she lives in San Francisco, she is unemployed, thirty-two years old I learned today, and her name is Raphaella Phillips. I just discovered her last name.'

'That doesn't ring a bell?'

'No, and for chrissake, stop playing games with me.' His eyes darted fire, and Charlotte Brandon sat back in her chair and sighed. She had been right then. The last name confirmed it. She wasn't sure why, but she had remembered that face, though she hadn't seen a photograph of her in the papers for years. The last time was perhaps seven or eight years ago, leaving the hospital, after John Henry Phillips had had his first stroke. 'What the hell are you trying to tell me, Mother?'

'That she's married, darling, and to a very important man. Does the name John Henry Phillips mean anything?'

For a fraction of a second, Alex closed his eyes. He was thinking that what his mother was telling him couldn't be true. 'He's dead, isn't he?'

'No, not as far as I know. He had a series of strokes several years ago, and he must be almost eighty, but I'm sure he's still alive. We'd certainly all have heard about it if he weren't.'

'But what makes you think she's his wife?' Alex looked as though an earthquake had struck him, right between the eyes.

'I remember reading the story, and seeing the photographs. She was just as beautiful then. It struck me as shocking at first that he was marrying such a young girl. I don't know, she was seventeen or eighteen, something like that. The daughter of some important French banker. But when I saw them together, at a press conference I went to with a journalist friend, and I saw some of the photographs I felt differently. You know, in his day, John Henry Phillips was an extraordinary man.'

'And now?'

'Who knows. I know that he's bedridden, and seriously impaired by his strokes, but I don't think the public knows much more than that. She has always been kept very much out of the public eye, which was why I couldn't place her at

69

first. But that face . . . one doesn't forget it easily.' Their eyes met and Alex nodded. He hadn't forgotten it easily either, and he knew that he never would. 'I take it she hasn't told you any of this.' He shook his head again. 'I hope she does.' His mother's voice was gentle. 'She ought to tell you herself. Maybe I shouldn't have . . .' Her voice trailed off and he shook his head again, and then stared miserably up at the woman who was his oldest friend.

'Why? Why should she be married to that ancient bastard? He's old enough to be her grandfather, and he's practically dead.' The injustice of it tore at everything in his heart. Why? Why should he have Raphaella?

'But he isn't dead, Alex. I don't understand what she has in mind with you. Except that I'll tell you honestly, I think that she herself is confused. She's not sure what she's doing with you. And you should keep in mind that she has led a totally sheltered life. John Henry Phillips has kept her totally concealed from the public for almost fifteen years. I don't think she's used to meeting brash young lawyers or having casual affairs. I maybe wrong about her, but I don't think I am.'

'I don't think you are either.. Christ.' He sat back in his chair with a long unhappy sigh. 'Now what?'

'Are you seeing her again?'

He nodded. 'Later tonight. She said she wanted to talk to me.' He wondered if she would tell him then. And then what?

Alex realised as he sat staring into space across from his mother, that John Henry Phillips might live for another twenty years . . . at which time Alex would be almost sixty, and Raphaella would be fifty-two. A lifetime of waiting, for an old man to die.

'What are you thinking?' His mother's voice was very soft.

Slowly he dragged his eyes back to hers. 'Nothing very pleasant. You know,' he spoke slowly, 'I saw her one night on the steps near her house. She was crying. I thought about her for days until I saw her again on the plane coming here. And we talked, and . . .' He looked up at his mother bleakly.

'Alex, you hardly know her.'

'You're wrong. I do know her. I feel as though I know her

70

better than anyone else. I know her soul and her mind and her heart. I know what she feels and how lonely she is. And now I know why. And I know something else.' he looked long and hard at his mother.

'What's that, Alex?'

'That I love her. I know that sounds crazy, but I do.'

'You don't know that. It's too soon. She's almost a complete stranger.'

'No, she isn't.' And then, he said nothing further. He put the money down for the cheque, looked at his mother and stood up. 'We'll work it out.' But Charlotte Brandon only nodded, thinking it unlikely that they would.

When Alex left her a few minutes later on Lexington Avenue, the look in his eyes told her that he was determined. And as he bowed his head in the stiff breeze and walked briskly North, he knew in his own mind that he didn't care what it would take to win Raphaella, but he would do it. He had never before wanted any woman as he wanted her. And his fight for her had just begun. It wasn't a fight which Alex Hale was willing to lose.

Chapter 7

At five minutes to eleven in the evening, after a brisk walk up Madison Avenue, Alex Hale turned right on Seventy-sixth Street, and walked into the Carlyle.

He had reserved a table for them in the Café Carlyle, with every intention of chatting with Raphaella for an hour and then enjoying Bobby Short's midnight show. He was one of the greater gifts of New York, and sharing him with Raphaella was a treat Alex had looked forward to all night. He checked his coat at the door and wove his way to the designated table, and then sat there for ten minutes, waiting for her to arrive. At eleven fifteen, he began to worry, and at eleven thirty, he wondered if he should call her room. But he realised that was impossible. Especially now that he knew about her husband. He realised that he had to wait for her quietly without creating a stir.

At twenty minutes before twelve he saw her staring through the glass door and looking as though she were poised to run. He tried to catch her eye but she didn't see him, and then after a moment of scanning the room, she disappeared. Almost without thinking, Alex rose from the table, and hurried to the door and out into the lobby in time to see her escaping down the hall. 'Raphaella!' He called out softly and she turned, her eyes huge and frightened, her face very pale. She was wearing a beautiful ivory satin evening dress that fell straight from her shoulders to its black-bordered hem at her feet. On her left shoulder she wore a huge elaborate pin with an enormous baroque pearl at its centre, surrounded by onyx and diamonds, and she wore ear-rings to match. The effect was very striking, and Alex noticed once again how incredibly beautiful she was. She had stopped when he called her, and she stood very still now as he stood in front of her, in his dark blue striped business suit with a look of great seriousness in his eyes. 'Don't run away yet. Let's have a drink and talk.' His voice was very gentle, and he wanted to reach out to her, but he didn't even dare to touch her hand.

'I . . . I shouldn't. I can't. I came to tell you that . . . I'm sorry . . . it's so late . . . I . . .'

'Raphaella, it's not even midnight. Couldn't we talk for just half an hour?'

'There are so many people . . .' She looked unhappy as they stood there, and suddenly he remembered the Bemelmans bar. He was sorry to miss out on Bobby Short with her, but it meant more to him to spend the time talking about what she had on her mind.

'There's another bar here where we'll be able to talk more quietly. Come on.' And without waiting for an answer, he tucked her hand into his arm, and led her back down the hallway to a bar across from the Café Carlyle, and here they slipped on to a banquette behind a small table, and Alex looked at her with a slow, happy smile. 'What would you like to drink? Some wine? Some sherry?' But she only shook her head in answer, and he saw that she was still very distressed. When the waiter had left them, he turned to her and spoke softly. 'Raphaella, is something wrong?' She nodded slowly, first looking down at her hands, her perfect profile etched sharply in the darkened room as he watched her, thinking that there had never been a woman as beautiful as she. And then she looked up at him, her eyes seeking his, as though that alone caused her great pain. The look of sorrow on her face was the same that he had seen that first evening, when he had found her crying on the steps. 'Why don't we talk about it?'

She took a little breath and sat back against the banquette, still keeping her eyes locked in his. 'I should have spoken to you about it earlier, Alex. I have been . . .' She hesitated on the words and then went on, 'very deceitful with you. I don't know what happened. I think I was carried away. You were so nice on the plane. Your mother was so charming. But I have been most unfair to you, my friend . . .' Her eyes were filled with sorrow and she gently touched his hand. 'I have given you the impression that I am free, I have been very wrong to do so. And I must apologise to you now.' She looked at him bleakly and withdrew her hand. 'I am

73

married, Alex. I should have told you that from the first. I don't know why I played this game with you. But it was very, very wrong. I can't see you again.'

She was a woman of honour, and he was touched to the core by the earnestness with which she looked at him now, the tears dancing on the tips of her lashes, her eyes so very big, her face so very pale.

He spoke to her carefully and with great seriousness, as he would have to Amanda, when she was a very little girl. 'Raphaella, I respect you very much for what you have just done. But must that affect our . . . our friendship? I can accept your situation. Couldn't we go on seeing each other in spite of that?' It was an honest question, and he wasn't about to let go.

She shook her head sadly. 'I would like to see you . . . if . . . if I were free. But I am a married woman. It's not possible. It wouldn't be right.'

'Why?'

'It would not be fair to my husband. And he is such . . .' She faltered on the words. '. . . such a good man. He has been . . . so fair . . . so kind to me . . .' She turned her face away and Alex saw a tear roll swiftly down one delicate ivory cheek. He reached out a hand to smooth his fingertips across the satiny softness of her face, and suddenly he wanted to cry too. She couldn't mean it. She couldn't mean to be faithful to her husband for the rest of his life. The horror of that began to dawn on him as he watched her face.

'But Raphaella . . . you can't be . . . the night I saw you on the steps . . . you're not happy. I know that. Why can't we see each other and just enjoy what we have?'

'Because I have no right to that. I'm not free.'

'For God's sake . . .' He was about to tell her that he knew everything, but she stopped him with one hand held out as though to defend herself from an aggressor, and with one swift movement she stood up and looked down at him with the tears still running down her face.

'No, Alex, No! I can't. I'm married. And I'm very, very sorry for letting it go this far. I shouldn't have. I was dishonest to come to lunch with your mother . . .'

'Stop confessing, and sit down.' He reached out gently for

74

her arm and pulled her towards him, back on to the seat, and for reasons which she herself did not understand, she let him, and then he wiped the tears from her cheeks with his hand. 'Raphaella,' he spoke very softly so that no one else could here, 'I love you. I know that sounds crazy. We hardly know each other, but I love you. I've been looking for you for years and years. You can't walk out on that now. Not for what you have with . . . with your husband.'

'What do you mean?'

'I mean that from what I understand from my mother, your husband is very old, and very ill, and has been for years. I have to admit, I had no idea who you were when I met you, it was my mother who recognised you, she told me who you were and about . . . about your husband.'

'Then she knew. She must think I'm awful.' Raphaella looked deeply ashamed.

'No.' He was definite and then his voice sounded urgent as he leaned towards her. He could almost feel the warmth of her silky flesh next to his and he had never been as filled with desire as he was right then, but this was no time for passion. He had to talk to her, make sense to her, make her see. 'How could anyone think you awful? You've been faithful to him, haven't you, all these years?' It was almost a rhetorical question and she nodded her head slowly and then sighed.

'I have. But there is no reason to stop now. I have no right to behave as though I'm free, Alex. I'm not. And I have no right to confuse your life, or touch it with the sorrow of mine.'

'The reason your life is so lonely is because that is how you are living it. Lonely and alone with a very sick, elderly man. You have a right to so much more than that.'

'Yes. But it's not his fault things turned out as they did.'

'Nor is it yours. Must you punish yourself?'

'No, but I cannot punish him.' The way she said it told him that he was losing the battle again, and he felt a desperate sinking in his heart. And as he did, she stood beside him.

Chapter 8

Alex and his niece stood side by side for a long moment, watching the skaters circling gracefully below them in Rockefeller Center. They had just finished an early dinner at the Café Français, and he had to get her home by eight o'clock if he was going to catch his plane.

'I wish I could spend my life like that, Uncle Alex.' The small delicate blonde girl with the china blue eyes and soft halo of curls looked up at her uncle with a smile.

'What? Skating?' He smiled, as much at what she had said as at the tiny figure she was beside him. They had shared a pleasant evening, and as always the loneliness of the pretty teenager tore at his heart: She was like no one else in her family. Not her mother or father, not even her grandmother, or Alex himself. She was quiet and devoted, gentle and lonely and loyal. She reminded him in fact of Raphaella as they stood in the chill air. Perhaps they were both people who had suffered at the hands of life, and he wondered if they were almost equally lonely as he looked down at the young girl. He had also been wondering all evening what was on her mind. She had seemed quiet and troubled and now she watched the skaters with a look of longing, like a very hungry child. He wished suddenly that he weren't taking the night flight to San Francisco, and that he had more time to spend with her, maybe they could even have rented skates. But he already had his reservation, and had given up his room at the hotel. 'Next time I'm in town, we'll come do this.'

She grinned up at him. 'I'm real good now, you know.'

'Oh yeah?' His look was teasing. 'How come?'

'I go skating all the time.'

'Here?' He glanced down at the graceful girl with pleasure. And he was sorry again that he didn't have time to let her show him how 'real good' she was.

But she was shaking her head in answer. 'Not here. I can't

afford this on my allowance.' That in itself seemed to him absurd. Her father was one of the leading surgeons in Manhattan, and Kay certainly had a decent sum of her own money by now. 'I skate in the park, Uncle Alex.' It was only now and then that she still called him that.

'By yourself?' He looked horrified and she smiled at him with hauteur.

'Sometimes. I'm a big girl now, you know.'

'Big enough not to get mugged?' He looked angry as they stood there and she shook her head and laughed.

'You sound just like Grandma.'

'Does she know you go skating in Central Park alone? Come to think of it, does your mother?' In the end, Kay had gone back to Washington before he got there and he hadn't seen her this trip at all.

'They both know. And I'm careful. If I skate at night, I leave the park with other people, so I don't have to walk alone.'

'And how do you know those "other people" won't hurt you?'

'Why should they?'

'Oh for chrissake, Mandy, you know what it's like here. You've lived in New York all your life. Do I have to explain to you what one doesn't do here?'

'It's not the same for a kid. Why would someone mug me? What would they get? Two rolls of Lifesavers, three bucks, and my keys?'

'Maybe. Or . . .' He hated even to say it. 'Or maybe something much more precious. They could hurt you.' He didn't want to say rape. Not to the innocent little face looking up at him with the funny smile. 'Look, just do me a favour. Don't do it.' And then, with a frown between his eyes, he reached into his pocket and pulled out his wallet, whence he took out a single brand new hundred dollar bill. He handed it to Amanda with a serious expression, and her eyes grew wide in surprise.

'What are you doing?'

'That is your skating fund. I want you to come here from now on. And when you run out, I want you to tell me and I'll send you some more. That's just between you and me, young lady, but I don't want you skating in Central Park any more. Is that clear?'

'Yes, sir. But Alex, you're crazy! A hundred dollars!' And then she grinned broadly and looked again about ten years old. 'Wow!' And without further ado she stood on tiptoe, threw her arms around her uncle, kissed him soundly on the cheek and stuffed the hundred dollar bill into her little denim bag. The fact that she had taken it made him feel better, but what he didn't know and would have worried about severely was that as often as she skated, the money would only last for a few weeks. And she would have been embarrassed to ask him to send her more money. She just wasn't that kind of girl. She wasn't demanding. And she was always grateful for whatever she got without asking for more.

Reluctantly, he looked at his watch, and then down at Amanda. His regret was instantly mirrored in her face. 'I'm afraid, young lady, that we're going to have to leave.' She nodded and said nothing, wondering how soon she would see him again. His visits were always like a burst of sunshine for her. That and the time that she spent with her grandmother made her life a little more bearable and a lot more worhwile. They walked slowly up the sloping promenade towards Fifth Avenue, and when they reached the street he hailed a cab.

'Do you know how soon you'll be back, Alex?'

'I don't know. It won't be too long.' He always had the same feeling of pain and remorse when he left her. As though he should have done more for her, and reproaching himself that he had not. But how much could one do? How could one replace one blind parent and another who was unfeeling? How could one give a child what she had not had for almost seventeen years? And despite her diminutive size, she was no longer a child, even Alex could no longer ignore that. She was a singularly beautiful young girl. It was only amazing that she had not yet discovered that herself.

'Will you be back for Thanksgiving?'

'Maybe.' He saw the imploring look in her eyes. 'All right. I'll try. But I won't promise.' They had by then reached her building, and Alex left her with a hug and a kiss on the cheek and a long hard squeeze. He could see that there were tears sparkling in her eyes as she left him, but her wave as he drove away in the taxi was a gallant one, and her smile filled with all the promise of her sixteen and a half years. It always made him sad to leave her. Somehow she always reminded him of the opportunities he had missed, the children that he himself didn't have. He would have loved it if Amanda had been his daughter. And that thought in itself always made him angry. His sister didn't deserve a child as lovely as that.

He gave the driver the address of his hotel, where he picked up his luggage from the doorman and then settled back in the seat with another glance at his watch and a long tired sigh. 'Kennedy Airport, please. United.' He realised then that it would be good to get home. He had only been in New York for two days but they had drained him. The exchange with Raphaella the night before had left him feeling bleak and lonely. His business had gone well, but it seemed eclipsed by the emotional turmoil he felt as they drove slowly uptown. He found himself thinking less and less of Amanda and more and more of Raphaella as he sat there. He was sorry for her, and yet at the same time angry. Why did she insist on being faithful to a husband who was old enough to be her grandfather and already half dead? It didn't make any sense. It was crazy ... He remembered the look on her face as she had walked away from him the night before. Yesterday. He had seen her only yesterday. And then suddenly, with an inexplicable surge of rage he asked himself why he had to be understanding, why he had to accept what she said. 'Go away' was in effect what she had told him. But he had decided not to. All of a sudden. Just like that. 'Driver . . .' Alex looked around him as though he had suddenly awoken. They were on Ninety-ninth Street on the East River Drive. 'Take me to the Carlyle.'

'Now?'

Alex nodded emphatically. 'Now.'

'Not the airport?'

'No.' To hell with it. He could always stay at his mother's apartment if he missed the plane back to San Francisco. She had gone to Boston for the weekend, to do some promotional appearances for her new book. It was worth one more try, just to see her. If she was there. If she would come downstairs to see him. If . . .

In her room at the Carlyle, Raphaella was stretched out on the large double bed in a pink satin bathrobe, wearing cream coloured lace underwear underneath. For the first time in what seemed like centuries, she was alone. She had just said goodbye to her mother, and her aunt and her cousins, who were by now at the airport, boarding the plane for Buenos Aires. She was going back to San Francisco in the morning, but for tonight, she could relax at the Carlyle, and do absolutely nothing. She didn't have to be charming, pleasant, patient. She didn't have to translate for her family in a dozen elegant stores. She didn't have to order meals for them, or run around the city shopping. She could just lie there with a book and relax, and in a few moments, room service would bring her dinner to her room. She would eat it in solitary splendour in the living-room of the suite she always stayed in, and she looked around as she lay there feeling a mixture of exhaustion and delight. It was so good not to hear them chattering, not to have to feign amusement, or pretend to be happy every moment any more. She hadn't had a minute to herself since she'd gotten there. Not that she ever did. That was the whole point. She wasn't supposed to be alone. Never. That was not the role of a woman. A woman had to be surrounded, protected, guarded. Except of course if it was just a matter of being alone overnight at the hotel as she was now, before going back to San Francisco in the morning. She would keep to her room, order room service, and in the morning leave for the airport in a limousine.

After all, one had to be careful, she reminded herself cynically in her room, if she wasn't, look what happened. As they had a thousand times in the last forty-eight hours, her thoughts flew to Alex, to the shape of his face, the look in his eyes, the broad shoulders, the softness of his hair . . . that was what happened. One got accosted by strangers on aeroplanes. One went to lunch with them. One went out for drinks. One forgot one's obligations and one fell in love.

She reminded herself once more of her decision, consoled

herself that it was the right thing to do, and forced her mind back to other things. There was no reason to think about Alex Hale anymore, she told herself. No reason at all. She would never see him again. She would never know him any better. And his declaration to her the night before in the hotel lobby was only the infatuation of a very foolish man. Foolish and foolhardy. How could he expect her to see him again? What made him think that she was willing to have an affair? But then as her thoughts lingered over his face one more time as she lay there, she found herself wondering if her mother had ever done anything like that. Had she ever met anyone like Alex? Had any of the women whom she knew in Spain? They seemed perfectly satisfied to lead sequestered lives, lives in which they constantly spent money, bought jewellery and furs and dresses and went to parties, but lived surrounded by other women, behind carefully guarded walls. What was wrong with her? Why was she suddenly chafing at those traditions? The other women she knew in Paris and Madrid and Barcelona, they had the parties, and the amusements, and the gala events which made the years drift by. And they had children . . . children . . . her heart always ached when she thought of babies. For years she had been unable to see a pregnant woman walk by her without wanting to burst into tears. She had never told John Henry how bereft she felt for the lack of children. But she always suspected that he knew. It was why he was always so lavish, why he spoiled her so much, and always seemed to love her so much more.

Raphaella forced her eyes shut and sat up on bed in her bathrobe, angry at herself for letting her thoughts take the turn they just had. She was free of that life for one more night, one day. She didn't have to think of John Henry, of his pain, of his strokes, of what would happen to her until he died. She didn't have to think of what she was missing, and what she had already missed. There was no point thinking of parties she would never go to, of people she wouldn't meet, and children she would never have. Her life was cut out for her. It was her destiny, her path, her obligation.

With the back of her hand, she wiped a tear from her cheek now, and forced herself to pick up the book which lay beside her on the bed. It was the Charlotte Brandon she had bought at the airport, and it was these thoughts that her books always kept her from. For as long as the books lasted, they kept everything but their intricate stories from her mind. They were her only haven, and they had been for years. With a comfortable sigh, she opened the book again, grateful that Charlotte Brandon was still able to write two a year. Sometimes Raphaella read them over. She had read most of her books at least two or three times each. Sometimes she read them in different languages. But she had read only two or three pages, when the phone rang and broke into the world into which she had fled.

'Hello?' It seemed odd that someone should call her. Her mother was already supposed to be on the plane. And they never called her from San Francisco, unless something had gone terribly wrong. And she had called John Henry that morning, and the nurse had said that he was doing fine.

'Raphaella?' At first the voice was not familiar, and then suddenly her heart began to pound.

'Yes?' He could barely hear her.

'I . . . I'm sorry . . . I . . . I was wondering if I could see you. I know you explained it all to me last night, but I just thought that maybe we could talk about it more calmly, and . . . well, maybe we could just be friends.' His heart was pounding as hard as hers. What if she said she didn't want to see him? He couldn't bear the thought suddenly that he might never see her again. 'I . . . Raphaella . . .' She hadn't answered, and he was instantly terrified that she might have hung up the phone. 'Are you there?'

'Yes.' It was as though she could barely speak now. Why did he have to do this? Why did he have to call her now? She was resigned to her obligations, to her duty, why did he have to taunt her in this terribly cruel way? 'I am here.'

'Could I . . . could we . . . could I see you? I . . . I'm leaving for the airport in a few minutes. I just thought I'd stop and see if I could see you.' It was all he had wanted to do. First talk to her, once more, before catching the last plane.

'Where are you?' A frown crossed her face as she wondered.

'I'm downstairs.' He said it with such an abashed tone of apology that she laughed.

'Here? In the hotel?' She was smiling. He was ridiculous really. Like a very small boy.

'What do you say?'

'Alex, I'm not dressed.' But it was a minor detail. And suddenly they both knew he had won. Even if only for a few minutes. But he had won.

'So what? I don't care if you wear a towel . . . Raphaella . . .?' There was a long silence between them. And then he heard the doorbell of the suite in the distance. 'Is that your mother?' 'Not very likely. She just left for Buenos Aires. I think it's my dinner.' A second later the door to the suite opened slowly and the waiter rolled the cumbersome table into the room. She signalled that she would sign it, and did so as she returned her attention to the phone.

'So what are we going to do? Will you come downstairs, or do I have to come up and bang on the door of your room. Or I could masquerade as a waiter from room service . . . how about that?'

'Alex, stop it.' And then she sounded serious again. 'I said everything there is to say last night.'

'No, you didn't. You didn't explain to me why you feel the way you do.'

'Because I love my husband.' She squeezed her eyes shut, denying what she also felt for him. 'And I have no choice.'

'That's not true. You have a lot of choices. We all do. Sometimes we don't want them, but they're there. And I understand how you feel, and I respect it. But can't we at least talk to each other? Look, I'll stand in the doorway. I won't touch you. I promise. I just want to see you. Raphaella . . . please . . .'

There were tears in her eyes and she took a deep breath to tell him that he had to go away, that he couldn't do this to her, that it wasn't fair, and then suddenly, not knowing why she did it, she nodded. 'All right. Come up. But just for a few minutes.' And when she hung up the phone, her hand was trembling and she felt so dizzy that she had to close her eyes.

She didn't even have time to slip into some clothes before

he rang the doorbell. She just tightened her robe around her and smoothed down her hair. It was hanging long and heavy down her back, and she looked much younger than she did when she wore it in the heavy knot. She hesitated for an endless moment in front of the door before she opened it, reminding herself that she could still refuse to let him in. But instead, she unlocked it and turned the doorknob and then she stood there, staring up at the remarkably handsome man who stood waiting on the other side. He stood as silent as she did for a moment, and then she took a step backwards and gestured inside. But there was no smile on her face now, only a very serious expression as her eyes followed him into the room.

'Hello.' He sounded nervous and looked boyish and stood staring at her for a long moment from across the room. 'Thank you for letting me come up here like this. I know it's a little crazy, but I had to see you.' And as he looked at her, he wondered why he had come. What was he going to tell her? What could he possibly tell her except that every time he saw her, he was more in love with her than he had been the time before. And when he didn't see her, she haunted him like a ghost he couldn't live without. Instead he just looked at her and nodded. 'Thank you.'

'It's all right.' Her voice was very quiet. 'Would you like something to eat?' She waved vaguely at the enormous rolling table and he shook his head.

'Thank you. I already had dinner with my niece. I didn't mean to interrupt your dinner. Why don't you sit down and start.' But she only shook her head and smiled at him.

'It can wait.' And then after a moment's pause, she sighed and walked slowly across the room. She looked out into the street with a distracted expression, and then slowly back at him. 'Alex, I'm sorry. I am deeply touched by what you feel, but there is nothing I can do.' The voice that spoke to him was that of a lonely princess, aware always of her royal obligations, and regretful that there was nothing more she could do. Everything about her was aristocratic, her posture, her expression, the way she stood there, even in the pink satin bathrobe Raphaella Phillips was regal to the very soles of her feet. The only thing that told him that she was human was the look of intense pain which could be hidden in her eyes.

'What about what *you* feel, Raphaella. What about you?'

'What about me? I am who I am. I can't change that. I am the wife of John Henry Phillips. I have been for almost fifteen years. I have to live up to that, Alex. I always will.'

'And for how many of those years has he been . . . the way he is now?'

'More than seven.'

'Is that enough for you? Telling yourself that you are fulfilling an obligation? Does that console you for your lost youth? How old are you now? Thirty-two? You've lived like this since you were twenty-five, Raphaella. How can you? How can you go on?'

Slowly she shook her head in answer, her eyes brimming with tears. 'I have to. That's all. It doesn't matter.'

'Of course it matters. How can you say that.' He walked to her side and looked down at her gently, 'Raphaella, we are talking about your life.'

'But there are no choices, Alex. That is what you don't understand. Perhaps that is why the way my mother lives is better. Maybe that's why all of that makes sense. That way, there are no temptations. No one ever gets close enough to force you to make a choice. There are no choices then.'

'I'm sorry that this is so painful. But why must it be a choice? Why must we talk about all that now? Why can't we just be friends, you and I? I won't ask anything of you. But we could meet as friends, maybe just for lunch.' It was a dream and he knew it, and Raphaella did too as she shook her head.

'How long do you think that would last, Alex? I know how you feel. And I think that you know I feel the same way too.' Something in his heart soared as she said it, and he wanted to take her in his arms, but he didn't dare.

'Can we forget that? Can we pretend it doesn't exist?' The look on his face said it was not possible.

'I think we have to.' And then, with a small brave smile 'Perhaps in a few years, we'll meet again.'

'Where? At your family's home in Spain, after they lock you up again? Who are you kidding? Raphaella.' He walked to where she stood, and put his hands gently on her shoulders as she looked up at him with those enormous troubled black eyes that he already loved so much. 'Raphaella, people spend a lifetime looking for love, wanting it, needing it, seeking it, and most of the time they don't find it. But once in a while, once in a great while, it comes to you, it throws itself in your lap, pounds on your door and says "Here I am, take me, I'm yours". When it comes, how can you turn away from it? How can you say "not now, maybe later"? How can you take that chance, knowing that the opportunity may never come again?'

'Sometimes taking that opportunity is a luxury, a luxury one can't afford. I can't afford it right now. It wouldn't be right and you know that.'

'I don't know that. Would letting yourself love me really take something away from your husband? Would it really make any difference to him in the condition he's in?'

'It might.' Her eyes didn't waver from Alex's and he hadn't taken his hands from her shoulders as they stood facing each other in the centre of the room. 'It might make a very big difference if I grew indifferent to his needs, if I was never around to see that he was properly cared for, if I became involved with you, and forgot about him. Something like that could kill him. It might make the difference for him between life and death. I could never fail him like that.'

'I would never ask you to. Never. Don't you understand that? I told you, I respect your relationship with him, I respect what you do and are and feel. I understand that. I'm just telling you that you have a right to something more, and so do I. And it doesn't have to change anything for you with your husband. I swear it, Raphaella. I just want to share something with you that neither of us have, maybe that we've never had. From what I can gather, you live in a vacuum. And so do I. In some ways I have for a long time.'

Raphaella looked up at him with the painful look of decision still in her eyes. 'How do you know we would even have anything, Alex? Perhaps what you feel is all an illusion, a dream. You don't know me. Everything you think of me is a fantasy.'

But this time he only shook his head and lowered his mouth gently on to hers. For an instant he felt her stiffen, but his arms circled her so quickly and so firmly that she could not pull away, and moments later she didn't want to. She clung to him as though he were the last man left on earth, and her entire body began to pulse with a passion she had never known before. And then, breathlessly, she pulled herself from him and shook her head, turning away.

'No, Alex. No!' She turned to face him with a look of fire in her eyes. 'No! Don't do this! Don't tempt me with what I cannot have. I can't have it, and you know that!' And then she turned away, her shoulders bent, her eyes filled with tears. 'Please go.'

'Raphaella . . .' She turned slowly to face him then, her face distraught, her eyes huge in the sharply etched face. And then it was as though he saw her melt in front of his eyes, the fire went out of her eyes and she closed them for an instant and then walked towards him, her hands going around him, her mouth hungrily reaching for his.

'Oh darling, I love you . . . I love you . . .' His words were gentle yet urgent, and she held him and kissed him with all the pent up loving of more than seven years. And then, without thinking, he slipped the pink satin bathrobe from her shoulders, and knelt to kiss her body as she stood before him, a goddess he had revered from the moment he had first seen her crying on the steps. This was the woman he had longed for, the woman he had needed, and almost instantly loved. And as he held her and caressed her, Raphaella knew that she was giving herself to him with all of her heart. It seemed hours before they stopped kissing and touching and holding and reaching out, and running their hands over each other's skin. She felt her legs tremble beneath her and then suddenly he swept her into his arms, the pink satin robe left behind them on the carpet, and slowly he walked into the bedroom and deposited her on the bed. 'Raphaella?' His mouth formed her name as a question and she nodded slowly, with a small hesitant smile, as he turned the light off and slipped his clothes off quickly until he lay beside her. He touched her hungrily again with his mouth and his hands. She felt now as though she were dreaming, as though this couldn't be happening, as though it couldn't possibly be real, and with an abandon she had never before known, she gave herself to him, her body arching and pulsing and throbbing with a desire she had never even dreamed of. And with the same fervour, Alex pressed himself to her, his body reaching deep inside her to her very soul, their arms intertwined, their legs part of one body, their mouths holding tight in one endless kiss until suddenly the final moment of their pleasure burst from them, as together they seemed to soar.

Then they lay quietly together, in the soft lamplight, as Alex looked at the woman he knew that he loved. For an instant, he was suddenly frightened. What had he done, and what would she do now? Would she hate him? Would it be over? But as he saw the warmth dawning in her eyes he knew that this was not the end, but the beginning, and as he watched her, she leaned closer to him, kissed him softly on the lips, and ran a hand ever so slowly down his spine. His whole body began to tingle, and he kissed her again, and then lay on his side and watched her smile.

'I love you, Raphaella.' The words were spoken so softly that only she could have heard him, and she nodded slowly, the smile spreading to her eyes. 'I love you.' He said it again, and her smile broadened.

'I know. And I love you too.' She spoke as softly as he did, and suddenly he pulled her closer again, tightly into his arms, so she could never leave him. And as though she understood, she held him closer. 'It's all right, Alex . . . sshhh . . . it's all right.'

He turned off the light again then and they lay there. A few minutes later his hands began to caress her again.

Chapter 9

'Raphaella?' It was only a whisper, as he lay on one elbow looking at her. He wasn't sure if she was awake. But now her eyes fluttered slowly open in the first light of morning, and the first thing she saw was Alex, looking down at her with his eyes full of love. 'Good morning, my darling.' He kissed her then, and smoothed the long silky black hair so much like his own. And then suddenly she saw him grinning, and she smiled in return.

'What are you laughing about, so early in the morning?'

'I was just thinking that if we ever had children and they ever had anything but jet black hair, you'd be in big trouble.'

'Oh would I?' She looked at him in amusement as he nodded.

'Yes, you would.' And then he looked at her pensively, a single finger tracing a line around her breasts and down the centre of her body to where her legs joined, and then lazily he brought the finger back up again to circle her breasts. He stopped for a moment, a question in his eyes. 'Don't you want children, Raphaella?'

'Now?'

'No. I mean ever. I was just wondering if . . .' He hesitated and then decided to ask her. 'Can you?'

'I think so.' She didn't want to betray John Henry's weakness, so she said no more, as he watched her face.

'Because you didn't want to, or because . . . for other reasons?' He had somehow sensed that she was being discreet.

'Other reasons.'

He nodded quietly. 'I wondered.' She leaned towards him then, and kissed him softly on the mouth. And then suddenly she sat up in bed with a look of terror, glanced at the clock and stared at Alex with a hand over her mouth.

'What's the matter?'

'My God . . . I just missed my plane.'

He grinned at her, looking unimpressed. 'I missed mine last night. 'In fact', the grin grew slowly, 'I never even retrieved my luggage from the doorman.'

But she wasn't listening to him. 'What'll I do? I have to call the airline . . . I'm sure they have another . . . my God, when Tom goes to meet me at the airport . . .'

Alex's brow clouded as soon as she said the words. 'Who is Tom?'

This time it was Raphaella who was smiling. 'The chauffeur, silly.'

'Good. Anyway, you can call home and tell them you missed the flight. Just tell them you'll catch . . .' He had been about to say 'The next one', but suddenly he had a thought. 'Raphaella . . . what if . . .' He was almost afraid to say it, and slowly he reached for her hand. 'What if we don't go home until tomorrow, and we spend the weekend here together? We could.'

'No, we couldn't. They expect me . . . I have to . . .'

'Why? You don't have anything to do at home. You said so yourself, and one day, or even two, can't make that much difference now. We won't be this free again for a long time. We're here, we're alone, we're together . . . how about it? Until tomorrow?' He pulled her into his arms as he asked her, praying she'd say yes. But she pulled away again slowly, her face thoughtful, but unsure.

'I'd have to lie to them, Alex. And if . . .'

'If anything happens,' they both knew he meant to John Henry, 'you can get the next plane back. It's no different than it was all week while you were here with your mother. The only difference is that now you'll be here with me. Please.' He looked gentle and boyish, and she wanted nothing more than to be in New York with him, but what about her obligations . . . John Henry . . . but suddenly she knew that she had to do something for herself this time. She looked up at Alex and nodded. She looked frightened, but excited, and he let out a whoop of joy. 'Darling, I love you!'

'You're crazy!'

'We both are. I'll go take a shower, you order breakfast, and then we'll go out for a walk.' But the awkwardness of ordering breakfast for two hadn't occurred to either of them, so she ordered an enormous breakfast from room service, and when they asked for how many, she promptly answered 'service for one'. She reported to him as he stood in the shower, and she found herself looking at his body with longing and admiration once again. He was so tall and strong and handsome, he looked like a statue of a Greek god. 'What are you looking at, Madam?' He peeked out at her with water running down his face.

'You. You're so beautiful, Alex.'

'Now I know that you're crazy.' And then he looked at her soberly for a moment. 'Did you call home?' She shook her head like a recalcitrant schoolgirl and he stood very still in the shower, and the water running over his body made her want to follow it with her tongue. She couldn't think about home now. Home was not real. All she could think about was him. 'Why don't you go do that now, babe.' She nodded slowly, and left the room. As she sat beside the telephone, the beauty of his body seemed to fade. Suddenly she felt like Mrs John Henry Phillips again. What lie would she tell them? The operator answered too quickly and she put the call through to San Francisco right away. It was only a moment later when she had the nurse on the line and was told that John Henry was sleeping, it was one o'clock in the afternoon in San Francisco, and he had already had lunch and was taking a nap.

'Is he all right?' She was terrified. Perhaps she would be punished. Maybe he'd be worse now and it would be her fault. But the nurse's cheerful voice came across the line quickly.

'He's just fine. We had him in the chair for an hour this morning. And I think he enjoyed it. I read the paper to him for a little while after lunch, and he went right to sleep.' Then nothing was different, it all sounded the same as it had been when she left. She explained that she had been delayed in New York with her mother. And she would be flying back to San Francisco the next day. She waited for an instant, almost expecting the nurse to call her a liar and a whore, but nothing happened, and she knew that her mother would never call from Argentina, so there was no reason to think that she would be found out. But she felt so terribly guilty, it seemed impossible that they wouldn't know. She asked the woman to tell Tom not to pick her up at the airport that day, and told her that she would call the next morning to tell them what plane she'd be on. It occurred to her that she could take a cab from the airport with Alex, but if she did something like that then they would wonder what she was up to. She had never taken a cab from an airport in her entire life. She thanked the nurse then, asked her to tell Mr Phillips that she had called and to tell him that everything was fine, and then she hung up, her eyes quiet, her face grave.

'Something wrong?' Alex emerged from the bathroom, his hair combed and with a towel around his waist. She looked different than she had a few minutes before when he had told her to go and call home. 'What happened?'

'Nothing. I . . . I just called them.' She lowered her eyes.

'Is something . . . something with . . .' There was an obvious question in his voice and he looked worried but she quickly shook her head.

'No, no. He's fine. I just . . .' She looked up at him miserably then, 'I just feel so guilty. Alex, I should go home.' It was an anguished whisper as he sat down beside her. He sat very still for a moment, and then put an arm around her shoulders and held her tight.

'That's okay, if that's what you want to do. I told you. I understand. I always will.' She looked at him then with eyes full of confusion, and he pulled her close to him again. 'It's okay, darling. Everything is fine.'

'Why are you being so kind to me?' She buried her face in the bare flesh of his shoulder as she asked him.

'Because I love you. I told you that last night too.' He smiled and kissed the top of her head.

'But you barely know me.'

'Bullshit. I know you right down to the tips of your toes.' She blushed then, but she also knew that he had meant it in another sense, a more important one. And oddly, though she had known him for such a short time, she believed him. He did know her. Better than anyone ever had. Even her husband.

'Will you be very angry if I go back today?' She sounded regretful and let out a long quiet sigh.

'No, I'll be very sorry. But not angry. If that's what you have to do, then it's okay.'

'What will you do? Go back to see your mother or your sister?'

'No, my mother's in Boston, Kay is in Washington, and my niece has lots of plans for the weekend. I'll go home. Probably on the same flight with you, if we can get seats together. Would that be all right with you?' She nodded. 'Good.' He stood up slowly. 'Then call the airline. I'll go shave.' He sauntered back into the bathroom, and closed the door as she sat there, feeling as though she had just given up the only thing she wanted in the world. Time with Alex. Together. Just the two of them. Alone. She sat there for a long moment, and then walked to the closed door and knocked softly. 'Yes?'

'May I come in?' He opened the door and looked down at her with a smile that told her again that he loved her. 'Of course you can, silly. You don't have to ask. Did you call the airline?'

She shook her head sheepishly. 'I don't want to.'

'Why not?' He felt his heart pound as he waited.

'Because I don't want to go back yet.' She looked like a little girl as she stood there, her long hair falling over her shoulders, still tousled from the night before. 'I want to stay here with you.'

'You do, do you?' He couldn't keep the smile off his face, as he put down his razor and grabbed her with one hand, using the other to grab a towel to wipe the soap from his face. 'Well, I'd like nothing better.' He kissed her long and hard then, and took her back to bed. It was half an hour before they had ended their lovemaking and the waiter from room service arrived.

They sat down to breakfast together after the waiter had left them, she in the pink satin robe and he in a towel, the two of them happy and smiling and making plans for the day. It was as though they had always been together, as they divided up the scrambled eggs.

'And then I want to go to the top of the Empire State

Building, and I want to eat hot chestnuts, and I want to go skating . . .'

He laughed at her. 'You sound just like my niece. She loves to skate too.'

'Then we can go together. But first I want to go to the Empire State Building.'

'Raphaella!' He groaned as he finished his coffee. 'Do you mean it?'

'I certainly do. I never get to do things like that!'

'Oh, baby.' He leaned across the table to kiss her. 'You are the most beautiful woman I have ever seen, Raphaella.'

'Then you are blind and crazy and I love you.' But she was wondering if she was the crazy one. This was absolute madness. And the maddest thing of all was that she felt as though she had known him all of her life.

Together, they devised a scenario whereby Raphaella could retrieve Alex's luggage from the doorman, and when the bellboy brought it upstairs, Alex got dressed, as Raphaella took a bath. They stood side by side in the huge closet arranging their things and chatting, and it was very much like a honeymoon, as she remarked to him on their way downtown. He dutifully took her to the top of the Empire State Building, to lunch at the Plaza, and then for a hansom carriage ride in the park. They spent two hours wandering through the wonders in the Metropolitan Museum, and they wandered into Parke-Bernet to watch an auction of French antiques in full swing. And then, happy and relaxed and more than a little tired, they crossed the street to the Carlyle, and rode the elevator back up to her room. She was yawning as she took off her coat and hung it up in the closet, and Alex was already lying on the bed with his jacket and shoes off, holding out his arms to her.

'I don't know about you, lady, but I'm exhausted. I don't think I've done that much in one day since I was a kid.'

'Me too.' She found herself suddenly wishing then that she could take him to Paris, and to Barcelona and Madrid, where she could show him all her favourite things there. And then she wanted to take him to Santa Eugenia, to see the place where she had spent all her summers, and where they could visit with all of the children whom she loved so much.

It was strange to think of them sometimes. The children she had told stories to when she had first married, were getting married and having babies of their own now. Sometimes it made her feel very old, as though an important part of life had passed her by.

'What were you thinking just then?' For an instant, he had seen the old sorrow lingering in her eyes.

'I was thinking about Santa Eugenia.'

'What about it?' He probed further.

'I was thinking about the children there . . . oh Alex . . . you don't know how I love them.'

In a firm, quiet voice, he spoke to her and reached for her hand. 'One day we'll have children of our own.' She said nothing, it was a subject she didn't like to discuss. She had put it away from her fourteen years before.

'It doesn't matter.'

'Yes it does. Very much. To both of us. I wanted children very much with my wife.'

'Could she not have them?' Raphaella looked hopefuly and curious as she asked him, as though they would have that in common, as though they had both been robbed by the same turn of fate.

'No.' He shook his head and looked pensive. 'She could have had them. But she didn't like children. Funny, how you look at things different as time moves on. If I met a woman who felt that way now, I don't think I could love her. I thought I could talk Rachel into it. But I couldn't. She was too involved in her work. Looking back, I guess it's just as well we didn't have kids.'

'What did she do?'

'She was an attorney.' Raphaella looked impressed and he kissed her softly on the lips. 'But she wasn't much of a woman, Raphaella, don't look like that.'

'Did you leave her?'

He shook his head again. 'No. She left me.'

'For a man?'

'No.' He smiled now, and there was no bitterness as he did so. 'For a job. That's all that mattered to her. Ever. It's just as well things worked out as they did.' They lay side by side like old friends and seasoned lovers, and Alex smiled.

'Is she very successful?'

'Probably.'

She nodded slowly. 'Sometimes I wish I were. The one thing I think I would have been good at was denied me, and everything else . . . well . . . there's nothing much I can do.'

'You tell stories to children.'

She smiled and looked embarrassed. 'That's hardly a life's work.'

He was studying her quietly, remembering something his mother had said. 'Why don't you write down the stories? You could write children's books, Raphaella.' Her eyes shone for a moment as she considered the suggestion, but then he went to her and took her in his arms, 'I hope that you know that if you never do a damn thing except love me, that will be enough.'

'Will it? Won't you be bored?' She actually looked worried.

'Never. It's funny. All my life I've been surrounded by ambitious women, professional women, women with all kinds of careers. I never thought I could understand a woman who was any different. And suddenly I realised that what I've wanted all along was someone like you. I don't want to wrestle and compete, and fight over who makes the bigger living. I just want to be myself with someone I care about, someone warm and kind and intelligent and nice to be with . . .' He nuzzled her neck. 'You know, that sounds kind of like you.'

She looked at him for a long moment and then tilted her head to one side. 'You know what's strange? Right now, I feel as though this is my life. Here. With you. As though nothing else ever existed, as though my life in San Francisco isn't even real. Isn't that odd?' She looked puzzled and he touched her face gently before kissing her on the mouth. And then he pulled away from her slowly with a small smile.

'No. As a matter of fact, I don't find it odd at all.' His arms were around her again then, and he kissed her hungrily as her hands drifted slowly to the growing mountain between his legs.

Chapter 10

The stewardess's voice droned on endlessly announcing their arrival in San Francisco, and Alex was aware of a feeling of depression stealing over him as the plane descended slowly towards the ground. Their two days together had been so perfect, so idyllic. They had gone to dinner the night before, and then gone to listen to Bobby Short as he had originally planned. And she had loved it. After that they had sat up and talked until almost four o'clock. Alternately discovering each other's bodies, and then lying side by side telling each other about their respective lives. When the sun came up on Sunday morning, she knew all about Rachel, his mother, her father, Julien, the brother who had died at sixteen playing polo, and her marriage to John Henry, in the beginning, and now. It was as though they had always been together, as though they had always been meant to be. And now, they were coming back to San Francisco, and he was going to have to let her go, at least for a while. And he would have to content himself with what little time she could spare him, as she stole away from her other life in her husband's house. At least that was what they had discussed the night before.

'What are you thinking? You look awfully serious.' He looked at her gently as they prepared to land. He sensed easily that she was feeling the same sadness he was. Their few days together had seemed like a lifetime, and now once again, everything was going to change. 'Are you all right?'

She looked at him sadly and nodded. 'I was just thinking . . .'

'What about?'

'Us. About how things will be now.'

'It'll be all right.' He spoke near to her ear, in a quiet intimate way which thrilled her, but now she shook her head.

'No, it won't.'

He took her hand in his own and held it, searching her eyes and suddenly not liking what he saw. He suspected that she was being besieged by guilt again, but that was to be expected after all, they were nearing home turf. It would be harder to put aside her obligations here. But she didn't really have to. There would be room for both men in her life.

'Alex . . .' Her voice faltered on the words. 'I can't do it.' As her eyes met his they filled with tears.

'What do you mean?' He tried to fight his own panic and maintain at least an outward appearance of calm in the face of what he thought she had just said.

'I can't.'

'You don't have to do anything right now, except relax.' It was his best professional voice, but it didn't seem to soothe her as the tears spilled on to her cheeks and rolled slowly until they fell on to their clasped hands. 'We can work all of this out later, as we go along.'

But again she shook her head, and her next word was only a whisper. 'No . . . I was wrong . . . I can't do it, Alex . . . not here. Not in the same town with him. It's just not right.'

'Raphaella, don't . . . just give yourself a little time to adjust.'

'To what?' For an instant she looked angry. 'Betraying my husband?'

'Is that all it is?'

She shook her head again, her eyes begging him to understand. 'What can I do?'

'Wait. Try to live with the joy we have. Be fair to him and to yourself. That's all I want for all of us . . .' She nodded slowly and he squeezed her hand tightly in his own. 'Will you give it a chance?'

It seemed an eternity before she answered. 'I'll try.'

The plane landed a moment later and when it stopped at the gate, two stewardesses appeared, one carrying her fur coat, and Raphaella stood up quietly and put it on, giving no sign that the man she'd been seated next to had been anyone important to her at all. She picked up her tote bag, buttoned her coat, and then nodded. Only her eyes said 'I love you' as she walked away and disappeared out of the rear exit in the plane as she had done before. The exit was closed

98

again after she'd gone through it, and Alex felt a loneliness engulf him the like of which he'd never known. He suddenly felt as though everything he cared about had been stolen from him, and a wave of terror swept through him . . . what if he never saw her again? He had to fight panic as he waited to deplane with the others, and then walked zombie-like to the baggage claim to pick up his bag. He spotted the long black limousine waiting at the kerb outside the building and the chauffeur who stood with the others, still waiting for her bags. Alex left the terminal quickly, and stood for a moment looking at the long black car. The reflection of the bright lights on the window hid her from his vision but he couldn't bring himself to move away, and as though Raphaella had sensed this, one of the rear windows rolled down slowly as she pressed the little button with one finger. She looked anxiously out at him, wanting in some way to touch him again. Their eyes held for an endless moment and then as though the sun had just risen for them again, he smiled gently at her, and then turned and walked towards the garage. In his heart he was whispering 'tomorrow', and wishing it were tonight.

Chapter 11

It was almost eight fifteen as he sat there, his foot tapping gently as he sat in his den. The wine was standing open next to the cheese and fruit he had set out on the table, the fire was crackling brightly, the music was playing, and he was a nervous wreck. She had said any time after seven-thirty, but he had not heard from her all day, and now he wondered if for some reason she had been unable to get out. She had sounded as lonely as he had when she had called him the previous evening, and his whole body had ached with the longing of wanting to take her in his arms. And now as he stood frowning down at the fire, wondering if anything had happened, he jumped at the sound of the phone.

'Alex?' His heart pounded and then skipped a beat of disappointment. It wasn't Raphaella, it was Kay.

'Oh. Hi.'

'Something wrong? You sound uptight.'

'No, I'm just busy.' And he wasn't in the mood to talk to her.

'Working?'

'Sort of . . . no . . . nothing . . . never mind. What's up?'

'Jesus. Talk about the bum's rush. I wanted to talk to you about Amanda.'

'Something wrong?'

'Not yet, thank God. Fortunately I know more about teenagers than you do. That hundred dollars you gave her, Alex. No go.'

'What do you mean?' His face tightened as he listened to his sister.

'I mean that she's sixteen years old, and the only thing kids that age do with money is buy drugs.'

'Did she tell you why I gave it to her? And by the way, how did you find out, I thought that was just between the two of us.'

'Never mind how I found it. I was going through some of her things, and it turned up.'

'Christ, what do you do to the kid, Kay, frisk her?'

'Hardly. But you forget how delicate my position is, Alex. I don't want her keeping dope in my house.'

'You make her sound like a goddam junkie.'

'Horseshit. But if I'd let her, she'd keep a box of joints around, like you and I would keep scotch.'

'Have you ever just simply asked her not to?'

'Sure. You really think kids do what you say?' Her total disrespect for her daughter drove him crazy and he felt the urge to explode as he listened to the innuendoes in his sister's voice.

'I think your attitude about her is disgusting. I think she is one kid you can trust. And the reason I gave her the money is so that she could go skating at Rockefeller Center. She tells me that she goes skating a lot, and she skates at Wollman Rink, in the park. I don't know if you're aware of it, but that kid could get murdered going in and out of Central Park. As her uncle, I'd like to treat her to the skating sessions. I had no idea you'd take the money away from her though or I'd have arranged it some other way.'

'Why don't you just let me handle my own daughter, Alex?'

'Why don't you admit that as a mother you stink?' His voice bellowed across the room as he stood there, wishing that there were something he could do for the child. 'I want you to let Amanda keep that money.'

'I don't give a damn what you want. I sent you a cheque in that amount today.'

'I'll take this up myself with Amanda.'

'Don't bother, Alex.' Kay's voice was like ice. 'I check her mail.' His own sense of frustration only mirrored what he knew Amanda must have felt in dealing with Kay.

'You are a vicious bitch, do you know that? And you have no right to harass that child.'

'And where do you come off judging how I treat my daughter? You have no children, damn you. What the hell do you know?'

'Maybe nothing, Sis. Maybe nothing at all. And I may

not have children, dear Congresswoman Willard. But you dear lady, have no heart.'

She hung up on him then and at the same moment he heard the doorbell ring, and he felt a rush of emotions swirl around him like a riptide. It was Raphaella, he knew it. She had come after all. And suddenly his heart was soaring, but he had not yet forgotten the exchange with his sister about Amanda, and he also knew that he wanted to speak to the girl himself. He ran down the flight of stairs from his den to the front door, and pulled it open, and stood looking at Raphaella for a moment, happy, confused, and slightly harassed.

'I was worried that something had happened.' She shook her head and said not a word, but the smile that she wore spoke for her, and then carefully she stepped inside. And then as he closed the door behind her, Alex swept her into his arms and held her very tight. 'Oh baby, how I missed you . . . are you all right?'

'Yes.' It was a tiny word buried beneath the fur coat she wore and his own body as he hugged her. She was wearing the lynx coat that she had worn that night on the steps. And then she hugged him again, under her own steam this time, and when she did he saw that there was something tired and sad in her eyes. She had left a note in her bedroom saying only that she was going for a walk to visit friends, just in case they came to find her. That way none of the servants would panic and call the police when she didn't come back immediately from her walk. They were always uneasy about her evening strolls anyway, and John Henry would have had a fit if he knew. 'I thought today would go on forever. I waited and I waited, and I waited, and every hour felt like two days.'

'That's how I felt today at the office. Come on,' he took her by the hand and walked her to the stairway. 'I want to show you around upstairs.' As they made their way through the house, she was aware of the emptiness of the living-room, yet in contrast she was overwhelmed by the warmth of his bedroom and the den. The two rooms were filled with creamy wools and soft leathers, huge plants and endless shelves of books. There was a fire burning brightly in his bedroom and Raphaella felt instantly at home.

'Oh Alex, it's so pretty! And so comfortable and so warm.' She rapidly shed the heavy fur coat and curled up on the floor beside him in front of the fire, the thick white rug beneath them, and before them on a low glass table were the wine and the cheese and the pâté he had stopped to buy for her on the way home.

'Do you like it?' He looked happily around him. He had put together the decor himself when he bought the house.

'I love it.' She smiled, but she was oddly quiet, and he sensed again that something was wrong.

'What is it, Raphaella?' His voice was so gentle that it brought tears to her eyes. For all the pleasant patter about his house, he had sensed from the first moment that she was deeply upset. 'What's wrong?'

She closed her eyes for a moment, and then opened them again, as she reached out instinctively for Alex's hand. 'I can't do this, Alex . . . I just can't. I meant to . . . I was going to . . . I had it all planned, how every day I could spend with John Henry, and every night I could slip out for a "walk" and then come here to be with you. And when I thought of it,' she smiled sadly again, 'my heart flew. I felt young and excited and happy, like . . .' she faltered, her voice barely audible, her eyes damp, '. . . like a bride . . .' Her eyes roved slowly towards the fire, but she left her hand in his. 'But I'm not any of those things, Alex. I'm not young any more, at least not that young. And I have no right to that kind of happiness, not with you. And I'm not a bride. I'm a married woman. And I have a responsibility to a very sick man.' Her voice grew stronger and she pulled her hand away from his. 'I can't come here any more, Alex. Not after tonight.' Now when she faced him, her voice was resolute.

'What made you change your mind?'

'Coming home. Seeing him. Remembering who I am.'

'Did you forget me in all that?' It sounded pathetic to his own ears and he was angry at himself for saying it, but it was what he felt. Life had just dealt him a cruel blow. A woman he wanted desperately, and was not destined to have.

But she brought his hand gently to her lips and kissed it as she shook her head. 'I didn't forget you, Alex.' And then, 'I

103

never will.' And then, almost as she said it, she rose to go. He sat there watching her for a long moment, wanting to stop her, to fight her, yet knowing that there was nothing he could do. He had wanted to make love to her again, to talk to her, to spend the night with her . . . to spend his life with her. Slowly, he got to his feet.

'I want you to know something, Raphaella.' He reached out and pulled her into his arms. 'I love you. We barely know each other, and yet I know that I love you. I want you to go home and think about what you're doing, and if you change your mind, even for a moment, I want you to come back. Next week, next month, next year. I'll be here.' He held her tight for a long, long time, wondering how long it would be before he would see her again. He couldn't bear the thought that perhaps he never would. 'I love you. Don't forget that.'

'I won't.' There were tears streaming from her eyes now. 'I love you too.'

They walked downstairs then, as though they both knew that there was no point staying in the house any more, it would be too painful for them both. And with an arm around her shoulders, and her eyes filled with tears, he walked her home. She turned only once on her doorstep, waved once, and then disappeared.

Chapter 12

For the next two months, Raphaella moved as though underwater. Her every step seemed to be weighted, heavy, slow. She couldn't move, she couldn't think, she couldn't walk, she could barely even talk to her husband, who puzzled at length over what might have happened in New York. Some ghastly episode of hostility with her mother, some kind of family argument or feud. It was weeks before he decided to broach the subject, but when he did, Raphaella seemed almost not to hear.

'Did something happen with your mother, little one? Was she insisting that you start to spend more time in Spain?' In vain, he sought an answer, unable to imagine what could have brought such pain to Raphaella's eyes.

'No, no . . . it was nothing.' There had been something then. But what?

'Is anyone ill?'

'No.' She smiled bravely. 'Not at all. I'm only very tired, John Henry. But you mustn't trouble yourself. I should take more air.' But even the endless walks didn't help her. In vain she walked from one end of the Presidio to the other, down to the little pond at the Palace of Fine Arts and even to the edge of the Bay, then struggling back up the hill. But no matter how tired or how breathless or how exhausted or how much she pressed herself, she couldn't forget him. She found herself wondering day and night what he was doing, if he was well, or happy, if he was working, or in the pretty little house on Vallejo. It seemed as though every hour of the day, she wanted to know where he was. And yet she knew that in all likelihood she would never see him again, never touch him, never hold him. The realisation of that made her ache to her very core, until at last she had felt so much pain that she was numb, and her eyes were almost glazed.

After two months of it, she spent Thanksgiving Day with

John Henry, moving like a robot, her eyes distant and dull. 'More turkey, Raphaella?'

'Mm?' She stared at him in answer, seeming not to understand what he had just said. One of the maids had been standing by with the platter attempting in vain to catch her attention, until John Henry finally spoke up. They were sharing Thanksgiving Dinner in his bedroom, served on trays, so that he could remain in bed. His health had failed again slightly in the past two months.

'Raphaella?'

'Yes? . . . oh . . . no . . . I'm sorry . . .' She looked away and shook her head, and then she sat there, trying to make conversation with him, but tonight he was too tired. A half hour after dinner, his chin nodded down gently on to his chest, his eyelids closed and he let out a soft snore. The nurse who had been standing by gently lifted the tray away from him and lowered him farther into the bed, signalling to Raphaella that she might as well go. And then slowly, slowly, Raphaella walked down the endless hall to her own rooms, her mind filled with thoughts of Alex, and then as though mesmerised, she walked to the phone. It was wrong, and she knew it. But she could call to wish him a Happy Thanksgiving after all. What was wrong with that? Everything, if what she had to do was avoid him, and she knew that she did. She knew that even the sound of his voice, the look in his eyes, his touch, all of it could weave her into the same delicious web again, and she had tried so hard to flee. Out of honour, out of a sense of duty, she had desperately tried, and now, as she dialled his number, she knew that she had failed. She didn't want to stay away from him for a moment longer. She couldn't. She just couldn't. Her heart pounded as she dialled the phone. It seemed an eternity before he answered, but now that she had dialled, she would not hang up.

'Hello?' She closed her eyes when she heard it, relief and pain and excitement sweeping over her all at once.

'Hello.' He didn't recognise her for a moment, and then suddenly his eyes widened, and at his end he looked as though he might go into shock.

'Oh my God.'

'No.' She smiled softly. 'It's only me. I called to wish you a Happy Thanksgiving.'

There was a pause. 'Thank you.' He sounded strained. 'How are you?'

'I . . . I'm fine . . .' And then suddenly, she decided to tell him. No matter if he had changed his mind, if he no longer loved her, if he had met someone else. She had to tell him. Even if only just this once. 'I'm not fine . . . it's been awful . . . I can't . . .' She almost gasped with the remembered pain and emptiness of the last two months. 'I can't live like this any longer. I can't bear it . . . Oh Alex . . .' Without meaning to, she had begun to cry, from sorrow as much as from relief. At least she was speaking to him again. She didn't give a damn if the world ended then and there. She was happier than she had been in months.

'Where are you?' His voice sounded tense.

'I'm at home.'

'I'll meet you on the corner in five minutes.'

She was going to say no, she was going to tell him, that she couldn't do that, but she didn't have the strength to fight it anymore. She didn't want to. Silently, she nodded her head, and then, 'I'll be there.'

She ran into the bathroom then, splashed cold water on her face, and then dried it hurriedly in one of the huge Porthault towels, ran a comb through her dark hair, pulled open her closet, grabbed her lynx coat, and then literally ran from her room, down the stairs and out the door. This time she had left no message, no explanation, and she didn't know how long she would be gone. Maybe five minutes, maybe an hour. But John Henry didn't need her just now. He was sleeping, he had his nurses, his servants, his doctors, and just this once, she wanted something more, much, much more. She found it as she ran hastily towards the corner, her dark hair flying behind her, the coat open, her lips suddenly caught in a half smile, as a sparkle came to her eyes which hadn't been there in months, and as she rounded the corner, suddenly she saw him there, in dark slacks and thick sweater, his hair tousled, his eyes bright, and slightly out of breath. He ran towards her so quickly and pulled her into his arms with such force that they almost collided and could easily have knocked each other out. Instead, he crushed his mouth down on hers, and they seemed to stand there that way forever. It was an outrageous chance to take, there on the corner, but fortunately no one saw them, and for once in her life, Raphaella didn't really care.

As though by silent agreement, they began to walk slowly towards his house a few minutes later, and as he closed the door quietly behind them, Raphaella looked around her and let out a long sigh.

'Welcome home.' He didn't tell her then how much he had missed her. He saved that until they lay side by side in his bed. It was as though for two months they had both lived in limbo, barely alive, barely existing between numbness and constant pain. The two months they had just endured were among the worst moments Raphaella could remember. For Alex they had been much the same, yet now it was as though none of it had ever happened, as though they had never been apart and never would be again. He wanted to ask her what would happen, but he didn't quite dare. He decided simply to cherish the moment, and pray that she was ready now for something more than they had had in the past two months.

'Happy Thanksgiving, my darling . . .' He pulled her once more into his arms, and they made love yet again. It was after ten o'clock when he finally remembered the turkey he had left cooking in the oven. It was an hour overcooked, but when they went down to the kitchen to find it, neither of them cared. Raphaella wore his bathrobe, and Alex wore blue jeans and a shirt, and together they ate and they talked and they laughed. It was indeed a homecoming, and unlike her first Thanksgiving dinner earlier that evening, this time Raphaella ate as though she hadn't seen food in years.

'And your work? It's going well?' She looked so happy as they sat there, she was smiling like a relaxed happy child.

'I wouldn't say that.' he looked sheepish, 'If I worked for someone else, I'd probably have lost my job in the last two months.'

'I don't believe that, Alex.'

'It's true. I haven't been able to keep my mind on anything.'

She looked momentarily sobered. 'Neither have I . . .' And then she looked at him again and her eyes gentled. 'Except you. It was like a kind of madness which took me and just wouldn't let me go.'

'Did you want it to?'

'Yes. If only to stop the pain. It was . . .' She looked away, embarrassed, 'it was a very difficult time for me, Alex. I have been wrestling with my conscience since the last time I saw you.'

'And what happened tonight? What made you call?'

'I couldn't bear it any longer. I felt as though I might die if I didn't speak to you right then.' He nodded, knowing the feeling only too well. And then he leaned across the table to kiss her.

'Thank God you called. I don't think I could have stood it much longer. I wanted to call you so badly. A hundred times I had the phone in my hand. Twice I even called, but you didn't answer, so I just hung up. God, I thought I'd go nuts.' She nodded in silent understanding, and as he watched her, he decided to take the next step. 'And now?' They were terrifying words, but he had to ask her. He had to know sooner or later, and he wanted to know now. 'Do you know what you want to do now, Raphaella?' He was leaving it to her, but he had already decided that he wouldn't let her go as easily this time. Not after what they had both been through. But this time he didn't have to fight her. She smiled softly at him and touched his hand with her own.

'We'll do what we have to . . . to be together as much as we can.'

He sat watching her for a moment, as though he was afraid to believe what she had just told him. 'Do you mean that?'

'Yes. Do you still want me? I mean the way you did before?'

But what he did next answered her question. He pulled her from her seat and took her in his arms with such force and passion that she could barely breathe. 'Alex . . .!'

'Does that answer your question?' There was fire and joy and excitement suddenly in his eyes. 'My God, woman, how I love you. Yes, I want you. I love you, I need you.

And I'll accept any way we have to work things out, so we can be together as much as we can, without hurting you, or . . . or . . .' She nodded. He didn't want to say John Henry's name. 'In fact,' he stood up suddenly again and strode across the kitchen, pulling open a drawer and fishing out a single key. He walked back to where he sat, reached for her hand, and carefully put the key in it, 'That's the key to this house, my darling and I want you to be here whenever you can, as much as you want to, whether I'm here or not.' Her eyes filled with tears then, and he pulled her gently into his arms, and then a few moments later, they wandered slowly upstairs again. She had the key to the house in the dressing gown pocket, and there was a smile in her eyes that had never been there before. She had never been happier in her life.

They spent the next three hours making love to each other again and again, and at last, as they lay side by side, still not totally sated, yet infinitely content, Raphaella jumped in surprise as she heard the phone. Alex frowned as he listened, shrugged and then picked it up, sitting up slowly in the bed. And then as he listened, the frown deepened, and without thinking, he stood up, still holding the phone, with an expression of horror on his face. 'What . . . when . . . oh my God. How is she?' He knit his brows and his hand trembled as he grabbed a pen. The conversation went on in garbled mono-syllables for a few more minutes and then he hung up and dropped his head into his hands with a soft moan. Raphaella stared at him in horror. All she could think of was his mother.

'Alex . . .' Her voice was fearful and gentle. 'Darling . . . what is it? What happened . . . darling . . . tell me . . . please . . .' Her hands were gentle on his shoulders, and then softly she stroked his head and his neck as he began to cry. It seemed like hours before he looked up at her.

'It's Amanda, my niece.' The words were a hoarse croak as she sat there. And then, with enormous effort, he told her the rest. 'She's been raped. They just found her.' He took a deep breath and closed his eyes for a moment before opening them again and going on. 'After Thanksgiving dinner this

afternoon, she went skating... alone... in the park, and...'
His voice faltered. 'She was beaten, Raphaella. Her arms
are broken, and my mother said...' He cried openly again
as he spoke, 'They beat up her face, and... and...' His
voice dropped to a whisper, 'they raped her... little Mandy
...' He couldn't go on then and Raphaella took him in her
arms with tears flooding her eyes.

It was an hour later before they caught their breath and she
went to get him a cup of coffee. He sat in bed sipping it
slowly, smoking a cigarette. Raphaella looked over at him
worriedly with a small frown between her eyes. 'Can you still
catch a plane tonight?' Her eyes were large and dark and
damp, and her face was lit as though with some magical light
from within. It was as though suddenly her face took away
his anger, as though all the fury drained from his being, just
from being with her. Without answering her question he
moved towards her, and pulled her into his arms, where he
held her tightly, as though he might never let go. They lay
like that for a long moment, as Raphaella stroked his back,
with one graceful hand. They said nothing and then, pulling
carefully away from her he looked down into her face again.
'Will you come to New York with me, Raphaella?'

'Now?' She looked stunned. In the middle of the night?
What would she say to her household, to John Henry? How
could she go with him? She had had no time to prepare
anyone. Her mind raced. But no one had prepared Amanda
either, the poor child. There was a look of despair in her eyes
as she looked up to answer his question. 'Alex... I want
to... I'd like to. But I can't.' She had taken such a big step
tonight. She wasn't yet ready for more. And she couldn't just
leave John Henry.

He nodded slowly. 'I understand.' He turned to look
again at this woman that he borrowed, who was someone
else's, not his, and yet whom he loved so much. 'I may be
gone for a while.' She nodded slowly. She wanted
desperately to go with him, but they both knew she could
not. Instead she held him tightly in her arms, wordlessly,
and offered whatever comfort she could.

'I'm sorry, Alex.'

'So am I.' He was more composed now. 'My sister should be horse whipped for the way she takes care of the child.'

'It can't be her fault.' Raphaella looked shocked. 'Why was the child alone? Where *was* her mother, dammit? Her father . . .' He began to cry again and Raphaella held him tight.

They called the hospital three more times that evening, and Amanda was still listed as critical when at last Raphaella went home. It was by then a little after four thirty, and they were both exhausted, but they had done the little they could do, and Raphaella had helped pack his bags. They had sat and talked for hours, staring into the fire as Alex told her what Amanda had been like as a little girl. What had come clear to Raphaella was how he loved her, and how much it pleased him that her parents had never taken time with her as a child.

'Alex? . . .' She looked at him pensively in the firelight. It was the only light which had remained in the dark room. 'Why don't you bring her back here when she's better?'

'To San Francisco?' He looked startled. 'How could I do that? I'm not prepared . . . I don't have . . .' He sighed softly. 'I'm at my office all day. I'm busy.'

'So is her mother, and the difference is that you love her.' Raphaella smiled softly in the glow from the embers, and he thought that he had never seen her look as beautiful as she did now. 'When my brother died, and my mother went back to Santa Eugenia with her sisters . . . all my father and I had were each other.' She looked very far away for a long moment. 'And I think we helped each other a lot.'

Alex looked pensive as he watched her. 'I doubt very much that her parents would let me bring her out.'

Raphaella looked at him quietly. 'After what happened, do they really have a choice? Isn't it a little bit their fault that they weren't taking better care of their daughter, that they let her go there, that maybe they didn't even know where she was?'

Silently he nodded. It was what he had been thinking all evening. He blamed it all on his sister. And her insane ambition that had long since blocked everyone else from her view. 'I'll think it over.' And then he looked at her pensively.

'We could fix up the third floor for her, couldn't we?'

She grinned at him then, 'Yes, "we" could. I could easily get it all ready in a few days. But Alex . . .'

There was an unspoken question in her eyes now, and this time it was Alex who smiled. 'She'd love you. You're everything her mother has refused to give her.'

'But her mother may not like it, Alex . . . after all, I'm . . . we're not . . .' She faltered and he shook his head.

'So? Does it really make a difference? Does it to us?' She shook her head.'

'But to other people, people who matter to Kay, it would seem wrong.'

'I don't care.' His voice was harsh now. It was then that he had looked wistfully once more at Raphaella, thinking of his family, and the trip to New York. 'I wish you were coming with me.' He said it yet again as he had watched her dress to go home that morning, and now he whispered it one last time as she prepared to leave him and walk the last block to her house alone.

Her eyes were damp now in the grey before the morning, and she wasn't sure but she thought that his were too. In their own way, they had been keeping a vigil for Amanda, staying awake, keeping her alive in their thoughts and their conversation, reaching out to the child who lay so bruised and battered so far away in New York. But it wasn't of Amanda that Raphaella was thinking as she kissed Alex again and touched his face for a last time. 'I wish that I were coming too.' She felt once again the cruelty of her situation, the push and pull of obligations she had to fulfill for John Henry, yet she was so grateful to have Alex back in her life again, to be sharing even a night or a moment with him. All that she really regretted was not being able to help him make the difficult journey to New York. 'Will you be all right there?' He nodded, but he wasn't smiling. He would be all right. But would Amanda? They had talked of bringing her home to San Francisco, but what if she didn't survive? The thought crossed both their minds now as Raphaella's lips gently touched his eyes. 'May I call you?' He nodded, this time with a smile.

They both knew that a great deal had changed between

them in one evening. It was a leap that they had made together, hand in hand.

'I'm going to be staying at my mother's.'

'Give her my love.' Their eyes met and held for a long moment as she kissed him for a last time. 'And don't forget how much I love you.'

He kissed her long and hard then, and finally with a last move she was gone. The heavy oak door closed a block away a few minutes later, and Alex walked quickly back to his house to shower and dress before catching the seven o'clock flight to New York.

Chapter 13

Charlotte Brandon waited nervously downstairs in the hospital lobby, staring at the reception desk and the vending machines that sold candy and coffee, as Alex went upstairs to see Amanda for the first time. The last report he had had when he called from the Carlyle was that she was doing better, and she was a little less sedated, but now she was in great pain. Visits were not encouraged, but since Alex had come so far to see her, they would let him into the intensive care unit, on the hour, for five or ten minutes but no more.

And now, Alex had vanished into the elevator, as his mother sat numbly, watching the passersby. But the faces were all blank and unfamiliar as they hurried in and out of the lobby, carrying flowers, presents, shopping bags with slippers and bedjackets. Twice she had watched hugely pregnant women amble in slowly with tense faces, holding on tightly to their husbands who clutched little overnight bags in their hands. Charlotte remembered moments like that in her own life with tenderness but tonight she felt very old and tired, and all she could think of was her grandchild, lying in a bed on another floor. And Kay had not yet been to see her. She was due in from Washington in a few hours. George had come in, of course, but he only checked the charts and offered little comfort to the child.

George was really not the right man to be a father to his daughter in this circumstance. He was too uncomfortable with her feelings.

'Mother?' She jumped at the sound of Alex's voice speaking her name, and turned to see the look of grief in his eyes. It struck fresh terror in her heart.

'How is she?'

'The same. And where the hell is Kay?'

'I told you, she's in Washington, Alex. George called her immediately after the police called him, but she couldn't get away until tonight.' It had been more than twenty-four hours since the nightmare had occurred. And Alex's eyes blazed.

'She should be goddam shot. And George, where the hell is he? The nurse up there says he keeps coming and going, just to check the charts.'

'Well, there isn't much else he can do, is there?'

'What do you think?' They both fell silent. He didn't tell her that Amanda had been sobbing so hysterically when he'd gotten there that they'd had to give her another shot. But at least she had recognised him, and she had clung so desperately to his hand. Just looking at him now, Charlotte Brandon's eyes filled with tears once again, and she sat down in one of the orange vinyl lobby chairs and blew her nose.

'Oh Alex, how do things like this happen?'

'Because there are crazy people out there, Mother. And because Amanda has two parents who don't give a damn.'

Charlotte spoke softly as Alex sat down in the chair next to hers. 'Do you really believe that, Alex?'

'I don't know what I believe. But I do know one thing. Whatever Kay feels for her child, in her heart, she still has no right to be the one to bring her up. Even if she thinks she loves her, and I'm not even convinced that she does, she still has absolutely no idea of what's involved, no idea of what she owes that child as her mother. And George is just as bad.' Charlotte nodded her head slowly. She had thought so before, but she had never anticipated anything like this. She looked into Alex's eyes, and she saw something there she had never seen before.

'Are you going to do something about this, Alex?' She had suddenly sensed it. It was as though she knew.

'I am.' He spoke with quiet determination.

'What do you have in mind?' Whatever it was, she knew it would be radical, and for Amanda's best interest. She had a great deal of faith in her only son.

'I'm taking her back with me.'

'To San Francisco?' Charlotte Brandon looked momentarily stunned. 'Can you do that?'

'I'm going to. Just let them try to stop me. I'll make the biggest stink you've ever seen, and see how my darling political sister enjoys that.' He had Kay over a barrel and they both knew it. His mother nodded her head.

'Do you think you can take care of her out there, Alex? It isn't as though she's had a skating accident. There are going to be emotional repercussions from all this as well.'

'I'll do my best. I'll get her a good shrink and give her all the loving I can. It can't hurt. And it's more than she has here.'

'I could keep her with me, you know.'

'No, you couldn't.' He looked at her honestly. 'You're no match for Kay. She'd threaten you into letting her come back to them in a week.'

'I'm not sure of that.' Charlotte looked only slightly miffed.

'Why risk it? Why not make a nice clean break? San Francisco is a long way off.'

'But you'll be alone out there with her, Alex . . .' And then, as she said the words, she suddenly understood, and her eyes bore into her son's, asking a silent question, as slowly he began to smile. He knew his mother well.

'Yes?' He had nothing to hide from his mother. He never had before. They were friends, and he trusted her, even with the secret of Raphaella.

This time Charlotte smiled too. 'I'm not quite sure how to phrase what I'm thinking. Your . . . er . . . young friend . . . the . . . uh . . .'

'Good God, Mother!' He chuckled softly. 'If you mean Raphaella, yes, I'm still seeing her.' He didn't want to admit that she had just returned to him after two months of agonising separation. He didn't want his mother, or anyone, to know that Raphaella had ever had doubts. It hurt his pride as much as his soul, but the fact that he was involved with a married woman, and one as well known as Raphaella, was not a secret he would keep from Charlotte Brandon. His face sobered as he looked at his mother. 'We talked about all this last night, before I left. I think she could give a great deal to Amanda.'

'I don't doubt it,' Charlotte sighed softly, 'But Alex, she has . . . other responsibilities . . . her husband is a very sick man.'

'I know that. But they have nurses. She won't be able to

be with Amanda day and night, but she'll be with us some of the time,' at least he prayed that she would, 'and regardless of Raphaella, Mother, this is something I have to do for Amanda, and for myself. I won't be able to live with myself if I leave that child here with Kay gone all the time, and George lost in the clouds. She's withering from the lack of attention. She needs more than they have to give her.'

'And you think you can?'

'I'm sure as hell going to try.'

'Well,' she took a deep breath and looked at her son, 'I wish you well, darling. 'I think what you're doing is probably right.'

'Thank you.' There was a mist in his eyes as he kissed her cheek and stood up. 'Come on, I'll take you home, and then I'll come back for the next visiting round on the hour.'

'You must be exhausted after the trip.' She looked at him worriedly and there were dark circles under his eyes.

'I'm fine.' And he was even more so a few minutes later as his mother opened the door of the apartment, and the phone was ringing determinedly. Without asking permission to answer it, Alex pounced on it and then instantly beamed. It was Raphaella.

'How is she?'

The smile faded slowly as his thoughts reverted again to his niece. 'About the same.'

'Have you seen your sister?'

'Not yet.' His voice hardened on the words. 'She's not coming in from Washington until tonight.' At her end, Raphaella looked shocked, but Alex couldn't see.

'But you're all right?'

'I'm well. And I love you.'

Raphaella smiled. 'So do I.' She had missed him unbearably all day, and had gone on several long walks. She had already been to his house twice. And it did not feel like intruding into the house of a stranger, it felt like coming home. She had carefully cleaned up all the debris from the Thanksgiving dinner and watered all his plants. It was amazing how naturally she felt herself fit into his life. 'How's your mother?'

'Fine.'

'Give her my love.' they talked on for a few moments and then Alex told her that he had decided to bring Amanda home.

'What do you think?'

'What do I think?' She sounded a little surprised to be asked. 'I think it's wonderful. You're her uncle and you love her.' And then, shyly, 'Alex . . . could I . . . could I fix up her room?' He nodded slowly, thinking. He wanted to tell her to wait, until they knew if Amanda would make it, but he couldn't bring himself to say the words. Instead he only nodded again, as though wanting to force the fates.

'Go ahead.' And with that, he looked at his watch and realised that he had to get back to the hospital. 'Call me later, if you can. I have to go back.' It was wonderful, her presence in his life now. No more silence, no more waiting, no more agony, or ghastly sense of loss. She was there as though she had always been and always would be. 'I love you.'

'I love you too, darling. Take good care.'

He gently put the phone back in its cradle, and with a soft smile, his mother quietly disappeared into the kitchen to make tea. And when she returned a few minutes later with two steaming cups, she saw that Alex was already wearing his coat.

'You're going back now?' He nodded soberly and without saying more, she picked up her coat again. But Alex instantly stopped her. She had been at the hospital all night the previous night.

'I want you to get some rest.'

'I can't, Alex.' And when he saw the look in her eyes, he said nothing more. They each took a sip of their tea and went outside to hail a cab.

Chapter 14

He was looking down at Amanda from the doorway, and all he could see was the narrow bundle, huddled in the white sheets and blue blankets on the bed. From the angle at which she was lying, Charlotte could still not see her face. But as she walked around the bed to stand next to Alex, she had to fight her own reactions so that they wouldn't show in her face. She had felt the same way again and again the night before.

What she saw before her was a tiny young girl who looked more like nine than sixteen, but only by her shape and the size of her hands and arms could one even distinguish vaguely what was her sex and age. Her arms were mostly encased in plaster, her hands lay exposed and immobile like two small sleeping birds, and the face which they looked at on the pillow was only a mass of swelling and bruises in purples and blues. Her hair framed her face like a soft curly halo, and the eyes which opened were of a clean bright blue. They looked a little like Charlotte's, and a little bit like Alex's, but it was hard to tell now, they looked so anguished, and rapidly filled with tears.

'Mandy?' His voice was a whisper, and he didn't dare touch even her hand now, for fear that it would hurt. She nodded slowly in answer, not saying a word. 'I'm back, and I brought Grandma with me.' Amanda's eyes went to her grandmother, as two steady rivers of tears flowed into the pillow beneath her head. There was no sound for a long moment as the heart-rending blue eyes looked at the familiar faces, and then once again there were the sobs as Alex gently stroked her hair. There was a communication between them which went beyond words, and Alex only stood there, his eyes gentle, his hand soft and smooth on the girl's hair. And in a moment Amanda closed her eyes again and fell asleep. A nurse signalled to them a moment later, and Charlotte and Alex left the room. They both looked exhausted and desperately worried, but in Alex's eyes there was a growing seed of fury for his sister Kay. It didn't explode from him until they reached Charlotte's apartment and when they did he was almost too angry for words.

'I know what you're thinking, Alex.' His mother's voice was gentle. 'But right now it won't help.'

'Why not?'

'Why don't you take it easy until you can talk to Kay? You can get it all out of your system then.'

'And when will that be? When do you suppose Her Majesty will finally turn up?'

'I wish I knew, Alex.'

As it turned out, it was the next day.

Alex was sipping a styrofoam cup of coffee, and Charlotte had gone home for a few hours to have a nap. They had moved Amanda that morning, out of intensive care, into a brightly painted little pink room. And now she lay looking just as battered and broken, but there was something a little bit more lively in her eyes. Alex had been talking to her about San Francisco, and once or twice she had almost looked as though she cared.

It was at the end of the day that she finally spoke of her fears to her uncle.

'What am I going to tell people? How can I explain what happened? I know my face is all messed up. One of the nurses aids said so.' They hadn't allowed her a mirror. 'And look at my arms.' She looked at the two cumbersome plaster casts moulded around her elbows, and Alex glanced at them but failed to look impressed.

'You're going to tell them that you had a car accident on Thanksgiving. That's all. It's perfectly plausible.' And then with a look of intense meaning, he looked straight at Amanda, and put a hand on her shoulder. 'Darling, no one ever has to know. Not unless you tell them, and that's up to you. But other than that, no one knows. Only your parents, your grandmother, and I.'

'And whoever reads the papers.' Then with another look of despair at Alex, 'Was I on the news?'

He shook his head in answer. 'No, you were not. I told you. No one has to know. You haven't been shamed. You're

121

no different than you were before you came in here. You're the same Amanda. You had a terrible accident, a horrible experience, but that's all it was. It didn't change *you*. It wasn't *your* fault. People won't respond to you differently, Amanda. You haven't changed.' It was what the therapist had stressed to him that morning, that they had to insist to Amanda that she was not different now, and that it was not in any way her fault. Apparently it was common among rape victims to think that they were in some way responsible for what had happened, and afterwards to think that they had been altered in some major way. Admittedly, in Mandy's case she was perhaps more altered than others. She had lost her virginity to a rapist in the park at sixteen. There was no doubt that the experience would affect her severely, but with treatment and a great deal of understanding, the psychiatrists felt that she had a good chance of coming out of it whole. His only regret, he had mentioned to them that morning, was that he had not been able to meet with Amanda's mother, and unfortunately Dr Willard didn't have time for a consultation either, but his secretary had called to tell the psychiatrist to go ahead and meet with the girl.

'But it's not just the victim in these cases who needs help,' he had stressed to Alex. 'It's the family who need help as well. Their outlook, their view of what happened will colour the victim's attitude about herself forever.' And then he had looked at him with a small smile. 'But I'm awfully glad that you could talk to me this morning. And I'm seeing Amanda's grandmother this afternoon.' And then he had added sheepishly the rejoinder that Alex had heard for most of his life. 'You know, my wife reads all her books.'

But right now his mother's books were not foremost on his mind. He had also asked Amanda's doctor how soon she could go home, and he had said that he felt certain that she could be released by the end of the week. Which meant Friday, if not before, which suited him perfectly. The sooner he got Amanda back to San Francisco, the happier he would be. And it was that that he was thinking of as Kay walked into the room, looking lanky and chic in a brown suede pantsuit trimmed with red fox.

Their eyes met and held for a long moment, and Kay said not a word. They had suddenly become opponents in the ring, and each one was aware of just how lethal the other could be.

'Hello, Kay.' Alex spoke first. He wanted to ask her how she could explain how long it had taken her to show up at the hospital, but he didn't want to make a scene in front of his niece. He didn't really have to. Everything he felt, all his fury, was easy to read in his eyes.

'Hello, Alex. Nice of you to come East.'

'Nice of you to come up from Washington.' Round one. 'You must be very busy.' Amanda was watching them, and Alex saw her face go pale. He hesitated for only a moment and then he left the room. When Kay emerged again a few moments later, he was waiting for her in an alcove down the hall. 'I want to talk to you for a minute.'

She looked at him with mocking amusement. 'I figured you would. Such a nervous little uncle, coming all the way to New York.'

'Are you aware, Kay, that your child almost died?'

'Perfectly. George checked her charts three times a day. If things had gotten worse, I'd have come home. As it was, if it's any of your goddamn business, I couldn't.'

'Why not?'

'I had two meetings with the President. Satisfied?'

'Not really. On Thanksgiving?'

'That's right. At Camp David.'

'Do you expect me to be impressed?'

'That's your business. But my daughter is mine.'

'Not when you totally abdicate your responsibilities, Kay. She needs a hell of a lot more than just George looking at her charts. She needs love, for chrissake, and tenderness, and interest, and understanding. My God, you're a woman, Kay. She's just a child. And she's been beaten and raped. Can't you even conceive of what that means?'

'Perfectly. But nothing I do now will change that. And two days didn't make any difference. She's going to have to live with this for a lifetime.'

'And how much of that time are you going to devote to her?'

'That's none of your fucking business.'

'I've decided otherwise.' His eyes were like steel.

'And just what exactly does that mean?'

'I'm taking her back with me. They said she could travel by Friday.'

'The hell you are.' Kay Willard's eyes blazed. 'You take that child anywhere and I'll have you in jail for kidnapping.'

'You filthy little bitch.' His eyes narrowed as he looked down at her. 'As a matter of fact, my dear, unless you are fully prepared to answer to charges of child abuse, I wouldn't do a damn thing if I were you. Kidnapping, my ass.'

'What do you mean, "child abuse"?'

'Just that, and criminal negligence.'

'You really think you'd have a chance of making that stick? My husband is one of the most prominent surgeons in New York, a great humanitarian, dear Alex.'

'Fine. Prove it in court. You'd love that, wouldn't you? It would look sensational in the papers.'

'You sonofabitch.' She had finally begun to realise that he meant it. 'Just what exactly do you have in mind?'

'Nothing elaborate. Amanda is coming to California with me. Permanently. And if you need something to tell your constituents, you can explain that she had a severe accident, and needs extensive rest in a warm climate. That ought to do the trick.'

'And what do I tell George?'

'That's your problem.'

She looked at him with fascination. 'You really mean it, don't you?'

'I do.'

'Why?'

'Because I care about her a great deal.'

'And you think I don't?' She didn't even look hurt, just annoyed.

Alex sighed softly. 'I don't think you have time to care about anyone, Kay. Except maybe the voters, and whether or not they'll cast their lot with you. I don't know what makes you tick any more, and I don't really care. All I do know is that it's destroying that child, and I won't let it . . . I won't let you.'

'And you're going to save her? How touching. Don't you think it would be a little healthier for you to use your spare emotional energy on a grown woman and not a sixteen-year-old girl? You realise that all of this is a little sick, don't you?' But she didn't look genuinely worried and he knew she wasn't. She was just mad as hell, and she had no way out.

'Why don't you keep your seamy little insinuations to yourself, along with your ambitions in regard to my ex-wife.'

'That has nothing to do with it.' But it was obvious that she was lying.

'That's a refreshing switch. And in case you're worried, believe me, my interest in Amanda is only that of an uncle. Not that I think you're worried.'

'I think you're an ass, Alex. And you're playing games, just like Amanda.'

'You think getting raped was a game?'

'Maybe. I'm not too clear on the details yet. Maybe this is what she wanted. To be rescued by her big handsome uncle. Maybe this is all her little plot.'

'I think you're sick.'

'Do you? Well, Alex, it doesn't worry me what you think. And I'll let you play your little game for a while. It might do her good. But I'm coming out to get her in a month or two, and that's the end of it. So if you think you're going to hang on to her, you're crazy.'

'Am I? Are you willing to face those charges I mentioned?'

'You wouldn't.'

'Don't try me.' They stood there for a moment, equal in their antagonism, Alex having won, for the moment. 'Unless something back here changes radically, she's staying with me. Besides which, the girl is sixteen, Kay, she's old enough to speak her own mind.'

'Have you told her that you're planning to save her from me?'

'Not yet. She was hysterical until this morning.' Kay said nothing, and then with a last venomous look she started to walk away. She stopped for a moment, and levelled a vicious look into her brother's eyes.

'Don't think you can play your games with me, Alex. You can have her out there for now, but when I want her home she's coming. Is that clear?'

'I don't think you understand my position.'

'I don't think you understand mine. It's a dangerous one. What you're doing could affect me politically, and that's something I won't tolerate, not from my own brother.'

'Then you'd better keep your ass in line, lady, and stay out of my hair. And that's a warning.' She wanted to laugh at him then, but she couldn't. For the first time in her life she was afraid of her younger brother.

'I don't understand why you're doing this.'

'You wouldn't. But I do. And so will Amanda.'

'Remember what I said, Alex. When I need her to come home, she comes back here.'

'Why? To impress the voters with what a great mother you are? That's a crock of shit.' But as he said it, she took a step towards him as though to slap him. He grabbed her wrist first and the look in his eyes was terrifying. 'Don't do it, Kay.'

'Then get the hell out of my life.'

'With pleasure.' His eyes glinted with victory, and she turned on her heel and walked away as quickly as she could, disappearing a moment later around a bend and into the elevator, and only moments after that into the limousine which waited for her at the kerb.

When Alex walked back into Amanda's room, she was sleeping and he gently stroked her hair on the pillow, picked up his coat and left. But as he walked quietly through the lobby, he decided that he couldn't wait until he got to his mother's apartment to call. It was taking a chance to call her, but he had to. He had to share it with someone, and he only wanted to share it with her. With a businesslike voice, he asked to speak to Mrs Phillips. And she came on the line a moment later.

'Raphaella?'

'Yes . . .' And then a sharp intake of breath as she realised who it was. 'Oh. Is . . .? . . .' She sounded frightened, as though she thought it meant that Amanda had died.

'No, no, everything's fine. But I had to let you know that my niece and I will be coming to San Francisco at the end of the week, and your father wanted me to say hello when I reached the States.' If anyone was listening, it sounded like a perfectly respectable call. And Raphaella had fully caught his meaning. She was beaming from ear to ear.

'Will your niece be with you for long?'

'I . . . uh . . . believe so. Yes,' he grinned. 'I do.'

'Oh . . .' She had almost said his name in her excitement. 'I'm so pleased!' And then she thought of the room she had promised to put together for him. 'I'll take care of the accommodation as quickly as I can.'

'Wonderful. I'd be very grateful. And of course I'll reimburse you as soon as I get to San Francisco.'

'Oh shut up.' She was grinning into the phone, and a few minutes later, they both hung up. Friday, he had finally told her, or maybe Saturday. It didn't give her much time.

Chapter 15

The next two days were a kind of frenzy for Raphaella. She spent the mornings reading quietly to John Henry and holding his hand as he drifted off to sleep, and then she would hurry downtown to go shopping, telling the chauffeur not to wait. She would prefer to go home in a cab. And if Tom found her behaviour a trifle eccentric, he was too well trained to mention it as she raced into the nearest store. Each afternoon she emerged carrying enormous bundles, and the bigger items she had sent directly to the house. She was buying floor samples and pieces in funny little thrift shops, like a wonderful old wash stand from a decorator, and a whole set of Victorian wicker from a garage sale she'd passed on the street as she raced home in a cab. By the end of the second day she had created total chaos, and she almost cried with relief when Alex apologetically told her on the phone that he wouldn't be back until Sunday night, but he had very good news. He had seen George that morning and everything had gone smoothly. George had agreed that it would do Amanda good to get away. They hadn't discussed the length of her visit, but once she was in California it would be easy to extend it, she would already be away. For the moment, he had casually mentioned 'a few months' and George hadn't demurred. Alex had called the best of the private high schools in San Francisco, and having explained the severity of her 'accident', read them a transcript of her grades, and explained who her mother and grandmother were, it had not been very difficult to get her into the school. She was to start after the first of the year. In the meantime, she would rest at home, go for walks, get her health back, and do whatever she had to, to get over the shock of the rape. She had a month to recuperate slowly before going back to school. And when Raphaella asked how Kay had taken it, Alex sounded strained. 'It was less pleasant with her than with George.'

'What does that mean, Alex?'

'It means I didn't give her any choice.'

'Is she very angry?'

'More or less.' He changed the subject quickly then and as Raphaella hung up the phone, her thoughts were filled with the young girl, wondering what she was like, if she would like her.

It was as though Raphaella had suddenly acquired not just a new man, but a new family as well. And there was Kay to consider. Alex had mentioned that his sister would be coming out to San Francisco at some point to check on Amanda. And Raphaella hoped that eventually they could all become friends. They were, after all, civilised people. Kay was undoubtedly an intelligent woman, and Raphaella was sorry that she and Alex were at odds. Perhaps, eventually, she could do something to still the troubled waters. In the meantime, after the phone call, she bustled about setting everything right on the third floor of Alex's house. She had told him that he could reach her there while she worked on the room for Amanda, and when she was through with her labour of love, she sat down on the bed with a broad, happy grin. In a few days, she had wrought a minor miracle, and she was very pleased.

She had turned the bedroom into an airy haven, a room filled with pink flowered fabrics and Victorian wicker, a huge flowered rug she had bought right off the floor at Macy's, and the antique washstand with the white marble top. She had put a large pink azalea in the old sink, and there were delicate flowered prints in gold frames on the walls. The bed was a four-poster with a white canopy and pink bows, that they had delivered only that morning. There was a huge pink satin quilt on the bed, and a little fur throw rug over a nearby chair. There was more of the flowered fabric and the wicker in the little study beyond. She had even found a small pretty desk which sat in front of the windows, and the bathroom had also been filled with pretty feminine things. The fact that she had been able to do it at all in so few days was nothing less than extraordinary, and that she had been able to bribe and cajole everyone into making deliveries still amazed her.

She had bought all of her purchases with the huge roll of cash she had gotten at the bank on Wednesday morning; she didn't want her cheques to record any of those purchases. All of her accounts were balanced at John Henry's old office, and it would have been impossible to explain what the cheques had been for. This way she only had a single sum that had been withdrawn, and she would find some way to explain it, like a shopping spree, or perhaps in time the secretary wouldn't remember if it had been before or after her trip to New York.

The only one she had to account to now was Alex, and she was a little bit nervous about what he would say. In truth she had not spent a great deal of money, and he had asked her if she could see if she could order a bed. She had of course done a great deal more than that in the upstairs bedroom, but much of it was in fact simple. It was just done with a great deal of caring and style and good taste. The lavish profusion of flowers, the little white curtains she had sewn and trimmed with pink ribbons, the cushions she had thrown here and there, and the wicker she herself had spray painted late one night made the difference. The extra touches that now looked so expensive in fact were not. But she hoped that Alex would not be angry at the extent of the decorating, she had just found as she went along that she couldn't stop until she had turned it into the perfect room for the battered young girl. After the horror of what had happened to her, Raphaella wanted to help provide the girl with something special, a home she could sink into with a long happy sigh, a place where she would be loved and could relax. She closed the door softly now, and went back downstairs to Alex's bedroom, looked around, straightened the bedspread, picked up her coat, and walked down the stairs and out the front door.

With a sigh Raphaella opened the door to John Henry's mansion, and walked slowly upstairs with a thoughtful look and a slow step. She looked around her at the velvet hangings, the medieval tapestries, the chandeliers, the grand piano in the foyer, and she realised once again that this was her home. Not the cosy little house on Vallejo, not the place where she had just spent almost a week like a crazy woman decorating a room for a young girl who also was not her own.

'Mrs Phillips?'

'Mmm?' Raphaella looked up startled as she turned to go down the hall to her room. It was almost time for dinner and she still had to dress. 'Yes?' The nurse from the second shift was smiling at her.

'Mr Phillips has been asking for you for the last hour. Perhaps you'd like to spend a moment with him before you change.'

Raphaella nodded quietly and murmured, 'Yes.' She walked slowly to the door of his room, knocked once, turned the knob and walked in, without waiting for him to bid her to enter. The knock was only a formality, like so many others in their lives. He was lying tucked into bed, with a blanket over him, his eyes were closed and the light in the room was very dim. 'John Henry?' Her voice was only a whisper as she stared at the broken old man who lay in his bed. This was the room that had once been their bedroom, the room he had also long ago shared with his first wife. At first it had bothered Raphaella, but John Henry was a man of tradition, and he had wanted to bring her here. And somehow the ghosts had all faded as they had lain there. It was only now that she thought of them all again. Now that he almost seemed to be one of them. 'John Henry . . .' She whispered his name again and he opened his eyes. When he saw her, he opened them fully, smiled his crooked smile and patted a place next to him on the bed.

'Hello, little one. I asked for you earlier but they said you were out. Where were you?' It was not an interrogation, only a friendly question, but something inside her flinched nonetheless.

'I was out . . . shopping . . .' She smiled at him. 'For Christmas.' He didn't know that her packages for Paris and Spain had all been shipped a month before.

'Did you buy anything pretty?' She nodded. Oh yes, she had. She had bought lovely things . . . for Amanda . . . her lover's niece. The realisation of what she was doing struck her once again like a physical blow. 'Anything pretty for you?' She shook her head slowly, her eyes very wide.

'I didn't have time.'

'Then I want you to go shopping tomorrow, and get something for yourself.' She looked at the long angular frame of the man who was her husband, she was once more devoured by her own guilt.

'I'd rather spend the day here with you. I . . . I haven't seen you very much lately . . .' She looked apologetic and he shook his head and waved a tired hand.

'I don't expect you to sit here with me, Raphaella.' He shook his head again, closed his eyes for a moment and then opened them again. There was something infinitely wise in the eyes that gazed out at the young woman. 'I never expected you to sit here with me waiting, little one . . . never . . . I am only sorry that it is so long in coming.' For a moment she wondered if his mind were wandering, and she looked at him with sudden concern in her eyes. But he only smiled, 'Death, my darling . . . Death . . . It has been a long wait for the final moment. And you have been a very brave girl. I will never forgive myself for what I've done.'

'How can you say that?' She looked at him in horror. 'I love you. I wouldn't be anywhere else.' But was it true now? Wouldn't she rather be with Alex, she asked herself as she reached for John Henry's hand and took it very gently in her own. 'I have never regretted anything, my darling, except . . .' She felt a lump rise in her throat as she watched him, '. . . that this has happened to you.'

'I should have died when I had the first stroke. I would have, if life were a little more fair, and if you and that young fool doctor you hired had let me go.'

'You're being crazy.'

'No, I'm not, and you know it. This is no life for anyone, not for me and not for you. I keep you here year after year as my prisoner, you're still almost a child, and I am wasting your best years. My own are long gone. I was . . .' He closed his eyes briefly as though he were in pain and the frown on Raphaella's face deepened as she watched him. He very quickly reopened his eyes and looked at her again. 'I was wrong to marry you, Raphaella. I was too old.'

'John Henry, stop it.' It frightened her when he spoke like that, and he didn't do it often, but she suspected that many of his thoughts centred on this theme. She kissed him gently and looked at him closely as he leaned forward. He looked deathly pale as he lay in the huge double bed. 'Have they had you out in the garden for any air this week, darling? Or on the terrace?'

He shook his head with a crooked little smile.

'No, Miss Nightingale, they haven't. And I don't want to go. I'm happier here in my bed.'

'Don't be silly. The air does you good, and you like going out in the garden.' She sounded quietly desperate, thinking that if she hadn't been spending so much time away from him she would have been aware of what the nurse was doing for him. They should have been taking him out. It was important that they keep him moving, that they keep him as alive and interested as they could. Without that, she knew that he would stop trying, and sooner or later he would just simply give up. The doctor had told her as much many years earlier, and she could see now that he had come to a very bad spot. 'I'll take you out tomorrow.'

'I don't want you to.' He looked querulous for a moment. 'I told you, I want to stay in bed.'

'Well, you can't. So how's that?'

'Pesty child.' He glared at her, but he smiled then, and raised her hand to brush them with his lips. 'I still love you. So much more than I can tell you . . . so much more than you know.' His eyes looked faintly misty. 'Do you remember those first days in Paris . . .' He smiled to himself and she smiled with him. '. . . when I proposed to you, Raphaella.' He looked at her clearly. 'My God, you were only a child.' They looked at each other tenderly for a moment, and she leaned forward to kiss his cheek once again.

'Well, I'm an old woman now, my darling, and I'm lucky you still love me.' And then she stood up, still smiling. 'But I'd best change for dinner, or you may throw me out and find yourself another girl!' He chuckled at this and when she left the room with a kiss and a wave, he felt better, and she berated herself all the way back to her room for having neglected him so terribly for the past week and a half. What had she been doing, running around buying furniture and fabric and curtains and carpets for almost a whole week? But as she closed the door to her bedroom, she knew what she had been doing. She had been thinking of Alex, of his niece and of setting up her bedroom, of the other life that she wanted so badly. As she stared into the mirror for a long moment, tormenting herself for having neglected her husband for almost ten days, she wondered if she had a right to what she had with Alex. This was her destiny, with John Henry. She really had no right to ask for anything more. But could she give it up now? After two months she was no longer sure that she could.

With a deep sigh she opened her closet, and pulled out a grey silk dress she had bought with her mother in Madrid. Black pumps, the exquisite necklace of grey pearls that had belonged to John Henry's mother, matching ear-rings, and a delicate grey slip. She threw it all on the bed and walked into her bathroom, lost in thought over what she'd been doing, thinking of the man she had almost forgotten, and the one that she never could, yet knowing that both men needed her. John Henry more than Alex of course, but they both needed her, and more than that, she knew that she needed them both.

Half an hour later, she stood in front of her mirror, a vision of elegance and grace in the pale grey silk dress. Her hair smoothly combed into the knot she wore at the nape of her neck, the pearls on her ears and lighting up her face. And as she looked into the mirror, she had no answers. There was no way to see the end of the story. All she could hope for was that no one would get hurt. But as she closed the door to her bedroom, she felt a tremor of fear run through her, knowing that that was almost too much to ask.

Chapter 16

On Sunday evening, the nurse put John Henry to bed at eight-thirty, and Raphaella walked slowly and thoughtfully to her room. She had been thinking about Alex and Amanda all evening, making a mental note of when they would be leaving the city, boarding the plane. Now they were only two hours from San Francisco, but she felt for the first time in ages that they might have been in another world. She had spent the day with John Henry, gotten him out to the garden in the morning, carefully wrapped in blankets and wearing a warm scarf and a hat as well as a black cashmere coat over his silk robe. In the afternoon, she had pushed the wheelchair out on the terrace, and by the end of the day, she had to admit to herself that he looked better, and he was relaxed and tired that evening when they put him to bed. This was what she was supposed to be doing, this was her duty, he was her husband. 'For better or worse.' But again and again, her mind wandered back to Alex and to Amanda. And more and more as she sat in the brick palace, she felt as though she lay buried in a tomb. But she was shocked at her own feelings, and suddenly the evil of what she was doing had risen to haunt her. She was no longer sure it was right.

At ten o'clock, she sat staring sadly, knowing that their plane had just landed, that they would be collecting their luggage and looking for a cab. At ten fifteen she knew they were on their way to the city, and with every ounce of her being she found herself wishing that she could be there. But suddenly the fact that she had fallen in love with Alex seemed wrong to her, and she was afraid that in the long run John Henry would pay the price, in lack of attention, lack of her company, lack of a certain feeling, and without that, she knew that John Henry would not stay alive. But can't you do both, she found herself silently asking? She wasn't sure that she could. When she was with Alex it was as if no one else in the world existed, and all that she wanted was to be with him and forget everyone else. But she couldn't afford to forget John Henry. If she forgot him, she might as well put a gun to his head.

She sat there staring silently out the window, and eventually she got up and turned off the light. She still sat there in her grey silk dress from dinner, which she had eaten on a tray in his room while they talked and he dozed between bites. He had been exhausted from all the fresh air. But now she sat very still, as though she were watching, looking for someone, for something, as though Alex would suddenly appear outside. It was eleven o'clock when she heard the phone ring, and she started and picked it up, knowing that all of the servants would be in bed except for John Henry's nurse. She couldn't imagine who would call. But when she picked it up it was Alex, and she trembled at the sound of his voice.

'Raphaella?' It frightened her to be talking to him here, but she wanted desperately to reach out to him. After their two month separation after New York, and then his trip to see about Amanda, now suddenly she ached to be with him again.

'The room for Amanda is incredible.' He spoke softly and for a moment she was frightened that someone might hear, but there was such joy in his voice that she couldn't resist.

'Does she like it?'

'She's in seventh heaven. It's the first time in years I've seen her look like that.'

'Good.' Raphaella looked pleased as she tried to imagine the young girl discovering the pink and white room. 'Is she all right?'

He sighed in answer. 'I don't know, Raphaella. I suppose so. But how all right could she be after what happened? Her mother made an outrageous scene before we left. She tried to make her feel guilty for leaving. And then, of course, she admitted that she's afraid of what it will look like to the voters if her daughter is living with an uncle instead of with her.'

'If she handles it right, it could just seem that she's very busy.'

'I said pretty much the same thing. Anyway, it got ugly, and Mandy was so exhausted that she slept all the way out here on the plane. Seeing that beautiful room you put together for her was the happiest thing that happened to her all day.'

'I'm glad.' But as she said the words, Raphaella felt unbearably lonely. She would have liked to see Amanda's face as she walked into the room. She would have liked to have been there at the airport, to have come home with them in the car, and walked into the house with them, to share each moment, to see their smiles, to help make Amanda feel welcome in the house which Raphaella had been in and out of a dozen times in the past week. Suddenly she felt left out and as she listened to Alex's voice on the telephone, she felt desperately alone. It was an almost crushing burden, and she was reminded of the night when she had cried in a similar loneliness on the steps near the house . . . the night she had first seen Alex . . . it seemed a century ago as she thought of it now.

'You've got very quiet. Is something wrong?' His voice was deep and alluring as Raphaella closed her eyes and shook her head.

'I was just thinking of something . . . I'm sorry . . .'

'What was it?'

She hesitated for a moment. 'That night on the stairs . . . the first time I saw you.'

He smiled. 'You didn't see me in the beginning though. I saw you first.' But as they reminisced about their first meeting, Raphaella began to get nervous again about the phone. If any of the servants were awake, they could pick it up at any moment, and she was worried about what they might hear, or think.

'Perhaps we should talk about this tomorrow.'

He understood her. 'Will we see you then?'

'I'd like that.' The prospect warmed her, and for an instant the loneliness dimmed.

'What would be a good time for you?'

She laughed softly, she had nothing to do, now that the room for Amanda was done. It had been her only project in years. 'Just tell me when. I'll come over. Or would it be better if . . .' She suddenly worried about Amanda. Perhaps it was too soon to meet the girl. Perhaps she would resent meeting Alex's lover, maybe she wanted her beloved uncle all to herself.

'Don't be silly, Raphaella. If I could talk you into it, I'd love it if you'd come over now.' But they both knew that Amanda was tired, and it was too late. 'Why don't you join us for breakfast? Can you come over that early?'

Raphaella smiled. 'How about six? Five fifteen? four thirty.'

'That sounds great.' He laughed as he closed his eyes, he could envision every detail of her face. He was aching to see her again, to touch her, to hold her, to let their bodies entwine as though they had always been one. 'As a matter of fact, with the time difference, I probably will be up at six. Why don't you just plan on coming over when you get up. You don't even have to call. I'm not going into the office tomorrow morning. I want to make sure that the woman who's coming to help Amanda is okay.' With two broken arms, the girl was virtually helpless, and he had had his secretary make arrangements for a combination light housekeeper-practical nurse. And then after a moment, 'I'll be waiting for you.' The longing in his voice was as clear as the hunger in Raphaella's own.

'I'll come early.' And then forgetting her anxiety about who might be listening in on the phone. 'I've missed you, Alex . . .'

'Oh baby,' the sound of his voice said it all. 'If you only knew how I've missed you.'

They hung up a few moments later, and Raphaella sat for a long time, staring at the phone with a radiant smile. She glanced at her watch as she stood up to undress. It was after midnight and in six or seven or eight hours she would be with him again. The very thought of it made her eyes dance and her heart race.

Chapter 17

Raphaella had set her alarm for six-thirty, and an hour later she slipped quietly out the front door. She had already spoken to one of John Henry's nurses, and had explained to her that she was going to an early Mass and then for a long walk. It seemed like a wholesome explanation for what would undoubtedly be an absence of several hours. At least she hoped it would be as she hurried along the street in the December fog and the early morning chill, with her coat pulled tight around her, and a pearly grey light bathing everything she could see. She reached the cosy little house on Vallejo in a matter of moments, and was pleased to see that most of the lights were already on. That meant that Alex was awake then, and she hesitated for a moment, facing the big brass knocker, wondering if she should knock, ring the doorbell, or use her key. In the end, she opted for a quick ring, and then stood there, breathless, excited, waiting, a smile dawning on her face, before his hand even touched the door, and then suddenly there he was, so tall and handsome, with a smile on his own lips, his eyes bright. Without saying a word, he pulled her quickly inside, closed the door and folded her tightly into his arms. They said nothing for a long moment, but his lips found hers and they clung together that way for what seemed like a very long time. Afterwards he just held her, sharing the warmth of his body, and letting one hand stroke her shining black hair. He looked down at her almost with amazement, as though he still found it remarkable that he knew her at all.

'Hello, Alex.' She looked up at him happily with a twinkle in her eyes.

'Hello.' And then as he stood back just a little. 'My God, you look lovely.'

'Not at this hour.' But she did. She looked absolutely radiant. Her eyes were big and bright like onyx flecked with diamonds, and her face was pink from the brisk walk. She had worn a pale peach coloured silk shirt and beige slacks with the lynx coat. And beneath the slacks he could just see cinammon suede Gucci shoes. 'How is Amanda?' Raphaella glanced towards the upstairs, and Alex smiled again.

'Still asleep.' But he wasn't thinking of Amanda. The only thing he could think of this morning was the incredibly beautiful woman who stood before him in the front hall, and as he looked at her, he wasn't sure whether to take her downstairs to the kitchen and offer her coffee or rush her upstairs with far less social pursuits in mind.

But as she watched him struggle with the decision, Raphaella grinned. 'You look positively wicked this morning, Alex.' With a spark of mischief of her own, she took off the heavy lynx coat and dropped it on the newel post at the foot of the stairs.

'Do I?' He feigned innocence. 'I wonder why.'

'I can't imagine. Can I make you coffee?'

'I was just thinking about doing that.' But he obviously looked disappointed and she laughed.

'But?'

'Never mind . . . never mind . . .' He began to usher her downstairs, but they didn't get past the first step when he turned to kiss her, and they dawdled there for a long time, as he held her tightly in his arms. It was thus that Amanda found them, as she wandered sleepily down the stairs in a blue flowered nightgown, her blonde hair a halo around the pretty young face, and the bruises fading slightly around her eyes.

'Oh.' It was a single sound of surprise, but Raphaella heard it instantly, and almost jumped out of Alex's arms. She turned, blushing slightly, to see Amanda looking at her with a host of questions in her eyes. She glanced at Alex then, as though there she would find an explanation. As she watched them, Raphaella thought that she looked very much like a little girl.

Raphaella turned and walked towards her with a soft smile, and held out her hand, only to gently touch the fingers exposed at the end of Amanda's casts. 'I'm sorry to intrude on you so early in the morning. I . . . I wanted to see how you were.' She was mortified to have been caught necking on the stairs, and suddenly all her fears about meeting Amanda surged up in her again, but the girl looked so fragile and guileless that it was impossible to imagine her as any kind of threat. It was Raphaella who felt threatening, afraid that she might have upset the girl.

But Amanda smiled then, a soft blush creeping into her cheeks. 'It's okay, I'm sorry, I didn't mean to walk in on you and Uncle Alex.' It had pleased her to see them kissing. She never saw any warmth in her own home. 'I didn't know anyone was here.'

'I don't usually go visiting this early, but . . .

Alex cut in quickly, he wanted Amanda to know who Raphaella was, and just how important she was to him. She was old enough to understand that at sixteen. 'This is the fairy godmother who put together your room, Mandy.' His voice was tender, and so were his eyes as he looked at them both, while the three of them hovered near the stairs.

'You are? You did?'

Raphaella laughed at the amazement in the girl's eyes. 'More or less. I'm not much of a decorator, but it had been fun to put together the pretty pink and white room.'

'How did you do it so quickly? Alex said there was nothing in it at all when he left.'

'I stole everything.' They laughed and she grinned. 'Do you like it?'

'Are you kidding? It's terrif!' This time it was Raphaella who laughed at both the excitement and the slang.

'I'm so glad.' She wanted to hug her then, but she didn't quite dare.

'Can I offer both of you ladies breakfast?' Alex was beaming down at them both.

'I'll help you.' Raphaella volunteered as she followed him down the stairs.

'Me too.' Amanda seemed happily engaged for the first time since the tragedy. And she looked even happier an hour later, as the three of them sat around the kitchen table, chuckling over the remains of fried eggs and bacon and toast. Mandy had even managed to butter the toast with her casts on, Raphaella had made the coffee, and Alex had seen to the rest.

'Excellent teamwork!' He commended the two women, as they teased him again about being a very imperious chef. But what was evident above all as Raphaella cleared the table was that the three of them were comfortable together, and she felt as though she had just been given a priceless gift.

'Can I help you get dressed, Mandy?'

'Sure.' The girl's eyes lit up, and half an hour later, with Raphaella's help, she was dressed. It was only when the new housekeeper came at nine, that Alex and Raphaella were once again alone.

'What a wonderful girl she is, Alex.'

He beamed at her. 'Isn't she? And . . . God, Raphaella, it's amazing how she's recovering from the . . . from what happened to her. It's only been a week.' His face had sobered as he remembered.

Raphaella nodded slowly, thinking back over the past week. 'I think she'll be fine. Thanks to you.'

'Maybe thanks to both of us.' He hadn't been oblivious to the gentle, loving way she had of handling the girl. He had been touched by her obvious warmth, and the way she had reached out to Amanda, and he hoped that it meant good times for the three of them in days to come. Amanda was part of his life now, but so was Raphaella, and it meant a great deal to him for the three of them to be close.

Chapter 18

'What do you mean you don't like the angel?' Alex looked at her with a crooked grin as he perched on the top of a ladder in the empty living-room. Raphaella and Mandy were standing beneath him, and Mandy had just told him that the angel looked dumb.

'Look at him, he's grinning. He looks silly.'

'If you ask me, you guys look pretty silly too.' They were both lying on the floor playing with the trains Alex had brought up from the basement. They had been his father's and now his.

Alex clambered down the ladder and observed the fruit of his labours. He had already strung the lights and Mandy and Raphaella had done most of the decorating while he had gotten things started, assembling the trains. It was the day before Christmas, and his mother had promised to come out for a visit in two days. In the meantime, it was just he and Amanda and Raphaella. She had been spending as much time as she could with him, but she had her own things to do.

She had been attempting to make things a little bit festive for John Henry, and Alex had even gone with her to pick out a small tree. And she had spent a week planning a party for the servants, wrapping gifts and putting up funny red stockings with their names. They were always amused by her thoughtful gestures, and the gifts she had bought them were always useful as well as expensive, gifts they were happy to get and would enjoy for many long years. Every thing was done with a kind of generous fervour, a seal all her own. The presents were beautifully wrapped, carefully selected, the house looked lovely, filled with poinsettias and pine cones, little pine plants, and there was a huge handsome wreath on the front door. Just that morning she had taken John Henry around the house in his wheelchair, and afterwards she had disappeared and returned with a bottle of champagne. But this year she noticed that he viewed it all with less interest. He seemed far removed from any Christmas joy.

'I'm too old for all this, Raphaella. I've seen it too often. It doesn't matter anymore.' He seemed even to struggle with the words.

'Don't be silly. You're just tired. Besides, you don't know what I bought you.' But she knew even that wouldn't bring him around. He was increasingly lethargic, increasingly morbid, and had been this way for months now, as though he no longer cared.

But with Alex she found the Christmas spirit, and in Amanda she saw the childlike joy she loved so much in her little cousins in Spain. For Amanda there were long strands of red berries, arrangements of holly, long strings of popcorn they made for the tree, there were decorations they baked and cut out and painted. There were gifts that they made as well as the ones they bought. For weeks it had been an exhausting proposition and now it culminated with the decoration of the tree. Just before midnight they were finished, and the presents were stacked in little piles all over the floor. In the empty parlour the tree looked gigantic, the lights splendid, and the little train tooted freely around the floor.

'Happy?' Alex smiled lazily at her as they stretched out in front of the fireplace in his room, as he burned a stack of logs.

'Very. Do you think Mandy will like her present?'

'She'd better or I'm sending her back to Kay.' He had bought her a little lamb jacket like Raphaella's, and had promised her driving lessons as soon as the casts were off her arms. They were due off in another two weeks. Raphaella was giving her ski boots which she had begged for, a bright blue cashmere sweater and a whole stack of books.

'You know,' Raphaella smiled happily up at him. 'It's not like buying for my cousins. It feels like . . .' She hesitated to say it, feeling foolish, '. . . like having a daughter, for the first time in my life.'

He grinned down at her with a sheepish smile. 'I feel the

same way. It's nice, isn't it? Now I realise how empty the house was. It's so different now.' And as though to prove it, the impish little face poked through the door. The bruises were gone now, and the look of devastation was fading slowly from her eyes. In the month that she'd been in San Francisco, she had rested, gone for long walks and talked almost daily to a psychiatrist who was helping her to live with the fact that she had been raped.

'Hi, you guys. What are you up to?'

'Nothing special.' Her uncle looked at her happily. 'How come you're not in bed?'

'I'm too excited.' And with that, she walked into the room and took two large cumbersome packages from behind her back. 'I wanted to give you both these.' Raphaella and Alex looked at her with surprise and pleasure, and sat up on the floor as she held out the gifts. She looked as though she were going to explode with the excitement, and she sat down on the edge of the bed, swinging her long blonde hair away from her face.

'Should we open them now,' Alex was teasing, 'or should we wait? What do you think, Raphaella?' But she was already opening hers, with a smile, until she pulled away the paper, and then she caught her breath and let out a little gasp.

'Oh Mandy . . .' She looked at the young girl with amazement. 'I had no idea you had a camera!' But she shielded the gift from Alexander, suspecting that his gift was the mate to hers, and a moment later she saw that she was right. 'Oh, they're so lovely. Mandy . . . thank you!' Her pleasure was written all over her face as she embraced the girl she had come to love, and for a long startled moment, Alex just sat and stared at his gift. Mandy had photographed them without their realising it. The pictures were stunning both in composition and attitude. Then she had them framed, and had given the one of Alex to Raphaella and the one of her to Alex. It was at a perfect reflection of Raphaella that he now stared. And it wasn't only accurate in detail and feature, but in the spirit she had caught, the warmth and the sorrow and the loving of the rich black eyes, the softness of the face, the creaminess of her complexion.

One had a sense of precisely how the woman thought and breathed and moved. And she had done just as good a job with Alex, catching him when he wasn't aware. Raphaella had been harder because she was around Mandy less often, and Amanda hadn't wanted to press herself on them when they had so little time alone. But it was clear from the awed faces of the recipients that her gifts were an enormous success.

Raphaella jumped up to kiss her and hug her tightly, and a moment later Alex did the same, and after that the three of them sat on the floor by the fire and talked for hours. They talked about ˜people, about life, about dreams and disappointments, Amanda talked openly now about the pain inflicted by her parents. Alex nodded and tried to explain what Kay had been like as a young girl. They talked about Charlotte and what it had been like to have her for a mother, and Raphaella had talked about the rigidity of her father, and how little suited she had felt for the life imposed on her with her mother in Spain. In the end, they even talked about her and Alex, speaking openly to Amanda about how grateful they were for whatever they could have of each other, in whatever little bits of time. It surprised them both that she understood it, that she wasn't shocked by Raphaella's marriage, and Raphaella herself was startled to realise that Amanda thought her something of a hero for sticking by John Henry until the end.

'But that's what I'm supposed to be doing. He's my husband, even if . . . even if everything is changed.'

'Maybe, but I don't think many women would do that. They'd go off with Alex just because he's young and handsome and they loved him. It must be hard to stay with your husband like that, day after day.' It was the first time they'd discussed it openly and for a moment, Raphaella had to force herself not to change the subject, but to face it with these two people she loved.

'It is hard.' She sounded very soft and very sad as she thought of her husband's worn face. 'Very hard sometimes. He's so tired. It's as though I'm the only thing that makes him want to go on. Sometimes I'm not sure I can carry the burden of that another step. What if something were to happen to me, what if I had to go away, what if . . .?' She looked mutely at Alex and he understood. She shook her head slowly, 'I think then he would die.'

Amanda was looking at her face, as though searching for an answer to a question, as though seeking to understand this woman she had come to admire and love so much. 'But what if he did die, Raphaella? Maybe he doesn't want to live any more. Is it right to force him?' It was a question as old as the ages, and not one which could be answered in one night.

'I don't know, darling. I just know that I have to do whatever I can.'

Amanda looked at her in open admiration as Alex watched them both with pride. 'But you do so much for us too.'

'Don't be silly.' Raphaella's embarrassment was obvious. 'I don't do anything. I just turn up here every evening like a bad fairy, peering over your shoulders, asking if you did the laundry,' then she grinned at Alex, 'telling you to clean up your room.'

'Yup, that's all she does, folks.' Alex was teasing as he stepped in. 'In fact, she doesn't do a damn thing, except eat our food, hang around in our bedrooms, decorate the house, occasionally feed us, polish the copper, read the briefs I sweat over, teach Amanda to knit, weed the garden, bring us flowers, buy us presents.' He looked at her, prepared to go on.

'It really isn't very much.' Raphaella was blushing, and he tugged at a lock of the jet black hair.

'Well, if it isn't, pretty lady, I'd hate to see you at full speed.' They kissed softly for a moment, and Amanda tiptoed to the door.

Amanda smiled at them from the doorway. 'Good night, you two.'

'Hey, wait a minute,' Alex stretched out a hand to pull her back. 'Don't you want your presents now too?' She giggled in answer and he stood up and pulled Raphaella to her feet. 'Come on, you guys, it's Christmas.' He knew that Raphaella wouldn't be with them the next day until late.

The three of them trooped downstairs laughing and

talking and pounced on the presents with their names on them, with obvious glee. Alex had a beautiful Irish sweater from his mother, a set of pens from Amanda, in addition to the photograph she'd given him upstairs, a bottle of wine from his brother-in-law, nothing at all from his sister, and a Gucci briefcase from Raphaella, along with a tie, and a beautifully bound old leather book, which was a book of poems he had told her about a month before.

'My God, woman, you're crazy!' But his reproaches were interrupted by Amanda's squeals as she opened her gifts. But then it was Raphaella's turn. She had a little bottle of perfume from Amanda, and a pretty scarf from Charlotte Brandon which touched her a great deal, and then there was a small flat box which Alex handed her with a mysterious smile and a kiss. 'Go on, open it.'

'I'm afraid to.' Her voice was a whisper and he saw her hands tremble as she pulled off the paper and stared at the dark green velvet box. Inside, there was a creamy satin lining and on it nestled an exquisitely simple circle of black onyx and ivory banded in gold. She saw instantly that it was a bracelet, and then noticed in amazement that there were earrings and a beautiful onyx and ivory ring to match. She slipped the whole set on and looked in the mirror at herself in stupefaction. It all fitted perfectly, even the black and white ring. 'Alex, you're the one who's crazy! How could you?' But they were so lovely, she could hardly reproach him for the expensive gift. 'Darling, I love them.' She kissed him long and hard on the mouth, as Amanda smiled and started the little train.

'Did you look inside the ring?' She shook her head slowly and he took it off her right hand. 'It says something.' Quickly she held the ring up, and looked at the engraving on the gold band which lined the ring, and she looked up at him with tears standing in her eyes. It said 'Someday'. Only that. Just one word. His eyes pierced into hers now, filled with meaning. It meant that someday they would be together, for always. Someday she would be his, and he would be hers.

She stayed until three o'clock that morning, an hour after Amanda finally went to bed. It had been a beautiful evening, a wonderful Christmas, and as Alex and Raphaella lay side by side on the bed, staring into the fire, he looked at her and whispered it again. 'Someday, Raphaella, someday.' The echo of his words still rang in her head as she walked the last block home, and disappeared through the garden door.

Chapter 19

'Well, children, if old age doesn't kill me, undoubtedly my own behaviour will. I must have eaten enough for ten people.' Charlotte Brandon stared around the table with a look of happy exhaustion, and the other three looked much the same. They had devoured a mountain of cracked crab for dinner, and Raphaella was serving espresso in little gold and white cups. They were among the few nice things that Rachel had forgotten when she'd left for New York.

Raphaella put the cup of coffee in front of Alex's mother and the two women exchanged a smile. There was a quiet understanding between them, based on a compatible sharing of someone they both loved a great deal. And now they had two such bonds to bring them closer. There was Amanda as well.

'I hate to ask, Mother, but how's Kay doing?' Alex looked only slightly tense as he enquired. But Charlotte looked at him frankly, and then at her only grandchild.

'I think she's still very upset that Amanda's out here. And I don't think she's given up hope that Amanda will come back.' Charlotte's audience immediately wore tense faces, but she was quick to reassure them on that head. 'I don't think she's going to do anything about it, but I think she realises now what she's lost.' Amanda hadn't yet heard from her mother in the four weeks since she'd left New York. 'But I don't really think she has time to pursue it. The campaign is beginning to get underway.' She fell silent and Alex nodded, glancing at Raphaella, who wore a worried smile.

'Don't look so uptight, pretty lady.' He spoke to her softly. 'The wicked witch of the East isn't going to hurt you.'

'Oh, Alex.' The four of them laughed, but Raphaella was always uneasy about her. She had an odd sense that if she had to, Kay would do anything to get what she wanted out of life. And if what she wanted was to separate Alex from Raphaella, perhaps she would find a way to do just that.

Which is why they made sure she knew nothing about them and they led a totally hidden life. They never went out in public. They only met in the house. And there was no one who knew about them, except Charlotte, and now Amanda.

'Do you think she'll win the election, Mother?' Alex looked searchingly at his mother as he lit one of his rare cigars. He only smoked Havanas when he could get them, long narrow pungent aromatic wonders, which he got from a friend who flew in and out of Switzerland, where he bought the Cuban cigars from another old friend.

'No, Alex, I don't. I think this time Kay has bitten off more than she can chew. The incumbent is a great deal stronger than she is. But she's certainly trying to make up for it with a lot of hard work and a great many tough speeches. She's also fighting for an endorsement from every powerful politician she can find.'

Alex looked at his mother oddly. 'Including my ex-father-in-law?'

'Of course.'

'God bless her. She's incredible. She's got more goddamn nerve than anyone I know.' And then he turned to Raphaella. 'He's a powerful man in politics, and he's one of the reasons Kay was so pissed off when I got divorced from Rachel. She was afraid that the old man would be mad. And he was.'

He grinned at Raphaella in amusement. 'He sure as hell was.' Then he looked at his mother again. 'Is she seeing Rachel?'

'Probably.' Charlotte sighed. Her daughter would stop at nothing to get what she wanted. She never had.

Alex turned to Raphaella again and took her hand in his. 'See what an interesting family I come from. And you think your father is peculiar. You should only know some of my cousins and uncles. Christ, at least half of them are nuts.'

Even Charlotte laughed in amusement, and Amanda slipped into the kitchen and began to clean up. Alex noticed it after a moment, and raised an eyebrow in Raphaella's direction. 'Something's wrong?'

She whispered softly. 'I think it upsets her to talk about her mother. It brings back some difficult memories.'

For an instant Charlotte Brandon looked worried, and then she gave them both the news. 'I hate to tell you this, now, children, but Kay said she was going to try to be here. By the end of the week. She wanted to see Amanda around Christmas.'

'Oh shit.' Alex sat back in his chair with a slump and a groan. 'Why now? What the hell does she want?'

His mother looked at him bluntly. 'Amanda. What do you think? She thinks it's hurting her politically to have Mandy out here. She is afraid that people think there's a secret, maybe the girl's pregnant, or she's coming off drugs.'

'Oh, for chrissakes.' As he said it, Raphaella disappeared into the kitchen, to chat with Mandy as they cleared. She could see that the child was distressed by the conversation, and at last she put an arm around her shoulders, and decided to tell her, so that she too would be prepared.

'Amanda, your mother is coming out here.'

'What?' The girl's eyes flew wide. 'Why? She can't take me back with her. I won't go . . . I'll . . . she can't . . .' Her eyes filled instantly with tears and she clung to Raphaella who held her tight.

'You don't have to go anywhere, but you should see her.'

'I don't want to.'

'She's your mother.'

'No, she's not.' Amanda's eyes went cold and Raphaella looked shocked.

'Amanda!'

'I mean it. Giving birth to a baby doesn't make a woman a mother, Raphaella. Loving that child and caring for it and about it, sitting with it when it's sick, and making it happy and being its friend, that's what makes a mother. Not getting votes and winning elections. Christ, you're more my mother than she ever was.' Raphaella was touched but she didn't want to come between them. She was always careful about that. In her own way, she couldn't be more than an invisible partner in their lives, not for her or for Alex. She had no right to take Kay's place.

'Maybe you're not being fair to her, Amanda.'

'No? Do you have any idea how often I see her? Do you know when I see her, Raphaella? When some newspaper

152

wants to take pictures of her at home, when she's going to some goddamn youth group and needs me as a prop, when I make her look good somewhere, that's when I see her. That's the only time I see her.' And then the final damnation. 'Has she called me here?'

But Raphaella knew better. 'Would you have wanted her to?'

Amanda was honest. 'No, I would not.'

'Maybe she sensed that.'

'Only if it suited her purposes . . .' And then, with a shake of her head, she turned away, suddenly no longer a perceptive, angry young woman, but once more a child. 'You don't understand.'

'Yes, I do.' More than she wanted to admit to Amanda. 'I'm sure she's not an easy woman, darling, but . . .'

'It's not that.' Amanda turned to face her with tears in her eyes. 'It's not that she's difficult. It's that she doesn't give a damn about me. She never did.'

'You didn't know that.' Raphaella's voice was gentle. 'You will never know what's happening inside her head. She may feel a great deal more than you think.'

'I don't think so.' The young girl's eyes were bleak, and Raphaella shared her pain. She walked over to her and held her for a long moment.

'I love you, darling. And so does Alex, and so does your Grandma. You have all of us.'

Amanda nodded, fighting back tears. 'I wish she weren't coming.'

'Why? She can't hurt you. You're perfectly safe here.'

'It doesn't matter. She scares me. She'll try to take me away.'

'Not if you don't want to go. You're too old to be forced to go anywhere. And besides, Alex won't let that happen.'

Amanda nodded sadly, but when she was alone in her bedroom she sobbed for two hours. The prospect of seeing her mother again filled her with dread. And after Alex left for the office the next morning, she sat staring mournfully out at the fog hanging over the bay. It looked like an omen of dreadful things coming, and suddenly, as she watched it, she knew that she had to do something, before her mother came.

It took her half an hour to find her, and when she did, her mother sounded curt on the phone. 'To what do I owe this honour, Amanda? I haven't heard from you in a month.'

She didn't remind her mother that she hadn't called or written either. 'Grandma says you're coming out.'

'That's right.'

'Why?' Amanda's voice trembled. 'I mean . . .'

'Just what do you mean, Amanda?' Kay's voice was like ice. 'Is there some reason why you don't want me to come out there?'

'You don't need to. Everything is just fine.'

'Good. I'll be happy to see that.'

'Why? Dammit, why?' Without meaning to, Amanda started to cry. 'I don't want you to come out here.'

'How touching, Amanda. It's always nice to know that you're just thrilled.'

'It's not that, it's just . . .'

'What?'

'I don't know.' Amanda's voice was barely more than a whisper. 'It'll just remind me of New York.' Or her loneliness there, of how little time her parents gave her, of how empty the apartment always was, of the Thanksgiving she had spent alone . . . and then been raped.

'Don't be childish. I'm not asking you to come here. I'm coming to see you out there. Why should that remind you of New York?'

'I don't know. But it will.'

'That's nonsense. And I want to see for myself how you are. Your uncle has hardly gone out of his way to let me know.'

'He's busy.'

'Oh really? Since when?' Her voice rang with contempt and Amanda bristled instantly at the words.

'He's always been busy.'

'That was Rachel, darling, not Alex.'

'Don't be a bitch, Mother.'

'Stop it, Amanda! You may not speak to me like that. As it so happens, you're so goddamn blind about your Uncle Alex, that you wouldn't notice his shortcomings. It's no wonder he wants you around. After all, what else does he

154

have to do! Rachel tells me he's so stuck on himself, he has no friends. Except now of course, he's got you.'

'What a stinking thing to say.' As always when she was confronted by her mother, she began to seethe with rage. 'He has a damn good law practice, he works very hard, and he has lots of things in his life.'

'And how would *you* know, Amanda?' There was a vicious implication in the words, which made Amanda catch her breath.

'Mother!' She sounded very young and very shocked.

'Well?' Kay pressed in for the kill. 'It's true isn't it? Once you're back with me – he'll be alone again. No-wonder he hangs on so tight.'

'You make me sick. He happens to be involved with a perfectly wonderful woman, who is worth ten of you, and is a better mother to me than you've ever been or ever will be.'

'Really?' Kay began to sound intrigued and suddenly Mandy's heart raced. She knew she shouldn't have told her, but she couldn't stand the implications her mother was making. It had just been too much. 'And who is she?'

'That's none of your business.'

'Is that right? I'm afraid I don't agree with you, my dear. Is she living with the two of you?'

'No,' Amanda sounded nervous. 'No, she's not.' Oh God, what had she done. She instinctively sensed that telling her mother had been a terrible thing to do, and she was suddenly frightened, for Raphaella and Alex, as much as for herself, 'It doesn't matter. I shouldn't have said anything.'

'Why not? Is it a secret?'

'No, of course not. For God's sake, Mother, ask Alex. Don't pump me.'

'I will. Of course, I'll see for myself when I'm out there.' And so she did. The following evening, at nine-thirty, with no prior warning, the doorbell rang, and Alex bounded up the stairs. He couldn't imagine who it could be that late in the evening, and Raphaella was downstairs chatting over tea and cookies with Amanda and his mother. They were in no way prepared for the vision which appeared only a moment later, at the foot of the stairs. Amanda's mother stood in the kitchen doorway, watching them with considerable interest, her red hair freshly coiffed, in a dark grey mohair coat with a matching skirt. It was a perfect outfit for a politician. It looked serious and somehow managed to make her look both competent and feminine all at the same time. But it was her eyes which intrigued Raphaella as she stood for the introduction and held out a graceful hand.

'Good evening, Mrs Willard. How do you do?' Kay greeted her mother curtly with a peck on the cheek before taking the proffered hand, which she shook hard and then moving away from the perfectly etched cameo face. It was a face which she somehow thought she remembered, it was familiar yet not a face she had met before, at least she didn't think so. Had she seen her somewhere? Seen her picture somewhere? It troubled her as she walked slowly to where her daughter stood. Amanda had not come towards her, and as far as anyone knew thay had had no contact since Amanda left New York. She hadn't had the heart to admit to anyone that she had called her mother the day before, and spilled the beans about Raphaella.

'Amanda?' Kay looked at her questioningly, as though she were asking if Amanda would say hello.

'Hello, Mother.' Reluctantly she forced herself to approach her and then stood looking uncomfortable and unhappy only a foot away.

'You look very well.' She gave her a perfunctory kiss on the forehead, and looked over her shoulder. It was obvious that her interest in Raphaella was greater than her interest in anyone else in the room. There was an air of distinction and of elegance about Raphaella that intrigued Alex's older sister more than anyone knew.

'Would you like coffee?' Alex poured her a cup, and Raphaella forced herself not to move. She had grown so used to playing lady of the house in the past month that she had to remind herself now not to anything which might give her away. She sat quietly at the table, like any other guest.

The conversation went on inanely for another half hour, and then after a private word with Alex, Raphaella excused herself and left, explaining that it was getting late. It was shortly after ten o'clock. And as soon as the door closed behind her, Kay's narrowed eyes fell on her brother, and she wore a tight little smile.

'Very interesting, Alex. Who is she?'

'A friend. I introduced you.' He looked intentionally vague, and he didn't see that Amanda blushed.

'Not really. All you told me was her first name. What's her last name? Is she anyone important?'

'Why? Are you soliciting campaign funds out here? She doesn't vote in this country, Kay. Save your energy for someone else.' His mother looked amused and coughed over her cup of tea.

'Something tells me that something about her isn't kosher.' Just the way she said it annoyed Alex, and he looked up with an irritated glance. He was also uncomfortable about not having escorted Raphaella back to her house, but he agreed with Raphaella that it was best not to make a big show of their relationship to his sister. The less she knew the better off they'd all be.

'That's a stupid thing to say, Kay.'

'Is it?' Christ, she'd been in his house for less than an hour and she was already driving him nuts. He tried not to let it show, but it did. 'Then what's the big secret about her? What's her name.'

'Phillips. Her ex-husband was American.'

'She's divorced?'

'Yes.' He lied. 'Anything else you want to know? Her criminal record, job references, scholastic achievements?'

'Does she have any?'

'Does it matter?' As their eyes met, they each knew that they were almost at war. What Kay wondered was why. The purpose of her trip, and her alleged interest in her daughter was forgotten as she ferreted for information about her brother's intriguing friend. 'And more importantly, Kay, is it any of your business?'

'I think so, if she's hanging around my daughter, I'd like to know who and what she is.' The perfect excuse. The virtues of motherhood. It covered her like an umbrella as Alex sneered.

'You never change, do you, Kay?'

'Neither do you.' In neither case was it a compliment.

'She looks empty to me.' He fought himself not to react. 'Does she work?'

'No.' But he hated himself instantly for answering. What business was it of hers, dammit? It wasn't, and she had no right to ask.

'I suppose you think that's terribly feminine, not working, I mean.'

'I don't think about it one way or the other. It's her business. Not mine. Or yours.' And with that, he rose with his cup of coffee, and looked pointedly at the three women in the room. 'I assume, Kay, that you came to visit your daughter, so I'll leave you two together, much as I hate to leave the child alone with you. Mother, do you want to come upstairs with your cup of tea?' Charlotte Brandon nodded quietly, looked searchingly at her daughter and then her grandchild and followed her son out of the room. It wasn't until they got upstairs that she saw him relax again. 'Christ, Mother, what the hell does she think she's doing with that inquisition of hers?'

'Don't let it bother you. She's just checking you out.'

'Christ, she's a bitch.' Charlotte Brandon said nothing in answer, but she was clearly upset.

'I hope she isn't too hard on Mandy. I thought she looked terribly upset when Kay came into the room.'

'Didn't we all.' He stared into the fire with a distant look in his eyes. He was thinking of Raphaella, and wished she hadn't left when she did. But in the face of Kay's interrogation, he was just as glad she was gone.

It was fully an hour later, when Amanda knocked on the door of her uncle's den. Her eyes were damp and she looked exhausted as she sat down heavily in a chair.

'How'd it go, sweetheart?' He patted her hand and her eyes filled with tears.

'The way it always goes with her. Shitty.' And then with another desperate sigh. 'She just left. She said she'd call us tomorrow.'

'I can hardly wait.' Alex looked rueful, and reached out to rumple his niece's hair. 'Don't let her get to you, love. You know how she is, and there isn't a damn thing she can do to you here.'

158

'Oh no?' Amanda looked suddenly irate. 'She told me that if I didn't come home by the beginning of March, she was going to have me put away in some kind of institution, and claim that I was out of my mind and had run away.'

'What's happening in March?' Alex looked troubled, but not as much as his niece thought he should.

'She's going to start campaigning around the colleges after that. She wants me to come along. She thinks that if they think she can relate to a sixteen-year-old, then she can relate to them. They should only know! Christ, I'd rather be locked up in an institution.' But when she turned to him, her eyes looked ten years old. 'Do you really think she'd do that, Alex?'

'Of course not.' He smiled at his niece. 'How do you think that would look in the papers? Hell, it looks a lot better to have you out here.'

'I didn't think about that.'

'That's what she counted on. She's just trying to scare you.'

'Well, she did.' She thought then about telling Alex that she had told her Mother on the phone about Raphaella, but for some reason she just couldn't bring herself to broach the subject, and maybe the fact that she'd thrown Raphaella in her mother's teeth wouldn't matter that much after all.

As it happened, it didn't. Until five o'clock that morning, when Kay woke up slowly in her bed at the Fairmont Hotel. It was eight o'clock in the morning, by Eastern time, and she awoke as she always did, out of habit, only to realise that in San Francisco it was only five a.m. She lay there quietly, thinking about Amanda and her brother, and then thinking back over the half hour she had spent with Raphaella ... the dark eyes ... the black hair ... that face. And suddenly, as though someone had put the photograph before her, she suddenly remembered the face she had seen the night before. 'My God,' she said it aloud, and sat up brusquely, staring at the far wall, and then lying down again, with narrowed eyes. 'Could it ... it couldn't ... but it could ... Her husband had come to address some special Congressional Committee. It had been years before, and he had already been a very old man, but one of the most respected financiers in the country, and she remembered distinctly now that he had made San Francisco his home. She had spoken to him only briefly, and had been introduced, for only a moment, to his remarkably beautiful young wife. She had been scarcely more than a child bride then, and Kay had been fairly young herself. She hadn't been particularly impressed with the dark-eyed young beauty, but she had been overwhelmed by the power and intensity of the man. John Henry Phillips ... Phillips ... Raphaella Phillips, Alex had told her ... her ex-husband, he had said. And if that was the case, the girl was probably worth a bundle. If she had divorced John Henry Phillips, she could be worth millions. Or could she? Had she divorced him? Kay found herself suddenly wondering. She hadn't heard about a divorce. She waited an hour then, and called her secretary in Washington.

It would be easy to get the information, she figured. And she was right. Her secretary called her back half an hour later. As far as anyone knew, and she had spoken to several people who should have had the information, John Henry Phillips was still alive and had never been divorced. He had been a widower for several years, and was married to a Frenchwoman now, by the name of Raphaella, the daughter of an important French banker named Antoine de Mornay-Malle. She was thought to be in her early thirties, and the couple lived in seclusion on the West Coast. Mr Phillips had been very ill for several years. So he had, echoed Kay as she hung up the phone in her darkened hotel room in San Francisco, but as far as she was concerned so was her brother. As she felt her own rage blaze within her, she decided that her brother had been raving mad for years. And it was precisely what she told him the next morning.

Chapter 20

'Are you totally out of your goddamn mind, you incredible ass?' Kay had raged into his office only moments after he'd arrived himself.

'My, my, aren't we charming this morning.' He was in no mood for his sister, and particularly not for the performance she was delivering on the other side of his desk. 'May I ask what you're referring to?'

'The married woman you're involved with, Alex. That's what I'm referring to.'

'I would say you've made two fairly presumptuous assumptions. Wouldn't you?' He looked cool but angry as he sat there and watched her storm around the room until she finally stopped and stood facing him across his desk.

'Is that right? Can you tell me that that was not Mrs John Henry Phillips I met last night? And that you are involved with her?'

'I don't have to tell you a damn thing.' But he was stunned by the accuracy of his sister's information.

'Don't you? And you don't have to tell her husband either?'

'Her husband, and she, and I, are none of your goddamn business, Kay. The only thing out here that is your business is your daughter, and that's it!' He stood up to face her now. But he knew that she had a score to even. She had lost her daughter to him, probably for good, and he had threatened to reveal her publicly as the next best thing to a child abuser. That was not going to win him her friendship now. But he didn't give a damn. He didn't want her friendship. But he did want to know what she knew about Raphaella and how she had found out. 'Just what exactly are you referring to, in all this?'

'I'm referring to the fact that my daughter tells me there's a woman in your life, who is "worth ten of me", as she puts it, and I want to know who the hell she is. Because I have a right to know that, Alex. I have a right to know who's around her. I'm her mother, no matter what you think of me. And George isn't going to put up with your keeping her forever either. She's his daughter, too.'

'I'd be surprised to hear that he remembered that.'

'Oh shut up for chrissake. You and your smartass pious comment, it's easy for you to come in and pick up the pieces. You haven't had to take care of her for sixteen years.'

'Neither have you.'

'Bull. The point is, Alex, just exactly who do you have around her now? That was something I wanted to know when I got out here.'

'And you found Mrs Phillips unsuitable?' He almost laughed in his sister's face.

'That's not the point either. The point, my dear, is that you seem to be shacking up with the wife of one of the most influential men in this country, and if anyone finds out, I am going to be politically dead. Not because of anything I've done, but by association, because of you and your lousy scandal and I have no intention of letting you ruin me politically for one lousy piece of ass.'

But what she had just said was too much for Alex. Without thinking, he leaned across the desk and grabbed her arm. 'Now, listen here, you lousy political slut. That woman is worth not ten of you, but ten thousand. She is a lady from the top of her head to the soles of her feet, and my involvement with her is none of your goddamn business. In what affects your child, she is nothing but wonderful to her, and as for me, I'll do what I goddamn well want to do. It is none of your goddamn business. I don't give a shit about your political career and I never have. You would like it one hell of a lot better if I had stayed married to Rachel and done you some good. Well tough shit, big sister, tough shit. I didn't stay married to her, and I am never going back to her, and she is almost as big a bitch as you are, my dear. But the woman I am currently involved with is an extraordinary human being, and she happens to be married to a bedridden old man who is damn close to eighty. Any day he is going to die, and I'm going to marry that woman you met last night, and if you don't like it, old girl, you can bloody well shove it.'

162

'How adorable, Alex, and how fluent.' She tried to wrench her arm free, but he didn't let her go. He only tightened his grip as his eyes hardened still more. 'The fact is, my dear, that the old boy is not dead yet, and if anyone finds out what you're up to, it'll be the biggest scandal in the country.'

'I doubt that. And I don't really give a shit, Kay, except for Raphaella.'

'Then you better start thinking,' her eyes glinted evilly at him, 'Because I may take care of the matter for you myself.'

'And commit political suicide?' He laughed bitterly at her, and let go of her arm to walk around the desk to where she stood. 'I'm not worried about that.'

'Maybe you should be, Alex. Maybe all I'd have to do to take care of it for you is to tell the old man myself.'

'You couldn't get near him.'

'Don't be so sure. If I want to, I'll get to him. Or to her.' She stood there, measuring her brother, and he had to fight himself not to slap her face.

'Get out of my office.'

'With pleasure.' She started towards the door. 'But if I were you, I'd think twice about what I were doing. You're playing a big game, for high stakes, and you won't win this one, Alex, not if it could cost me my ass. I've got too much riding on this next election to let you play with dynamite over some little French whore.'

'Get out of my office!' This time he roared at her, and she flinched as he grabbed her arm again, almost dragged her to the door and threw it open. 'And stay out. Stay away from all of us, damn you! You're nothing better than filth!'

'Good-bye, Alex.' She looked him squarely in the eye as she stood in the doorway. 'Remember what I said. I'll get to him if I have to. Remember that.'

'Get out.' This time he lowered his voice, and she turned on her heel and left. And he found that he was shaking violently when he sat down at his desk. For the first time in his life, he had actually wanted to kill someone. He had wanted to throttle her for every lousy word she had said. It made him sick to remember that she was his sister. And as he sat there, he began to worry about Amanda, thinking that perhaps Kay might try to force her to go back to New York with her. After half an hour of intense deliberation, he told his secretary that he was leaving for the day. And just as he left his office, in her house, Raphaella was picking up the phone. It was a call from Alex's sister, and Raphaella frowned as she took the call.

'No, nothing's wrong. I thought maybe we could meet for coffee. Could I perhaps come over on my way to see Mandy later . . .' Raphaella blanched.

'I'm afraid not, my . . .' She had been about to tell her that her husband was ill. 'My mother isn't well. She's staying with me just now.' And how had she gotten the number? From Alex? From Mandy? From Charlotte? The frown on Raphaella's face deepened still more.

'I see. Then could we meet somewhere?'

Raphaella suggested the bar at the Fairmont, and met Kay there shortly before lunchtime, where they both ordered drinks. But Kay didn't wait until the drinks arrived before explaining her purpose in seeing Raphaella. She made no bones at all about why she had come.

'I want you to stop seeing my brother, Mrs Phillips.'

Raphaella looked stunned as she sat there, awed by the sheer nerve of the woman. 'May I ask why?'

'Do you really have to? You're married, for God's sake, and to a very important man. If your involvement with Alex became known, it would be a scandal for all of us, wouldn't it?' It was Raphaella's first taste of the true evil in the woman's eyes. She was hateful to her very core.

'I imagine it would be quite a scandal for you. That's it, isn't it?' She spoke politely and with a delicate smile.

But when Kay answered, she smiled too. 'I would think the greatest scandal would be for you. I can't imagine that your husband, or your family in Europe, would be terribly pleased with the news.'

Raphaella paused for a moment, trying to catch her breath as their drinks arrived, and the waiter disappeared once again. 'No, I wouldn't enjoy that, Mrs Willard.' Her eyes sought Kay's now, as one woman reaching out to another, 'I don't enter into this lightly. I didn't want to get involved with Alex, as much for his sake, as for my own.

There is very little I can give him. My life belongs entirely to my husband, and he is a very sick man.' Her voice was weighted down with sorrow as she spoke, and her eyes were full. 'But I'm in love with your brother. I love him very much. I love my husband, too, but . . .' She sighed and looked immensely European and lovelier than ever, strong and at the same time very frail. Kay hated everything about her. Because she was everything that Kay would never be. 'I can't explain what happened with Alex, or why. It just did. And we're trying to work it out as best we can. I can assure you, Mrs Willard, we are above all discreet. No one will ever know.'

'That's nonsense. My mother knows. Mandy knows. Other people do and will find out. You can't control that. And you're not playing with fire. You're playing with the atom bomb. At least as far as I'm concerned.'

'So you expect us to end it?' Raphaella looked tired and annoyed. What a dreadful selfish woman she was. Amanda was right. She thought only of herself.

'Yes, I do. And if he isn't strong enough to, then you do it. But it has to end. Not just for my sake, but for yours, too. You can't afford to get found out, and if I have to, I'll tell your husband.' Raphaella looked at her, shocked.

'Are you mad? He's paralysed, bedridden, attended by nurses, you would tell him something like this? You'd kill him!' She was outraged that Kay would dare to make such a threat, and she looked like the kind of woman to do it.

'Then you'd better think of that. If it would kill him, he would in effect die by your hand. It's in your power to stop this, now, before anyone finds out. Besides which, think of what you're doing to my brother. He wants children, he needs a wife, he's lonely. What can you give him? A few hours now and then? A roll in the sack? Shit, lady, your husband could live for another ten or fifteen years. Is that what you're offering Alex? An illicit affair for the next ten years? And you claim that you love him? If you loved him, you'd let him go. You have no right to hang on to him, and ruin his life.' What she was saying cut Raphaella to the quick. It didn't occur to her at that precise moment that Kay Willard's interest was not in Alex's life, but her own.

'I don't know what to say to you, Mrs Willard. It has never been my intention to hurt your brother.'

'Then don't.' Raphaella nodded dumbly, and Kay reached for the check, signed her name and the number of her room and stood up, 'I think we've finished our business with each other. Don't you?' Raphaella nodded again, and without saying another word, she walked away, and hurried past the doorman with tears streaming from her eyes.

Kay went to see Mandy that morning. Alex was already back from the office, and he and Mandy were sitting quietly in the den when she arrived. There was no way she could take Mandy back with her now. Her interest in her daughter had already waned. She had decided that she had to get back to Washington. She reminded her only to think about March, said good-bye stiffly to Alex, and told her mother she would see her in New York. Charlotte was leaving the following afternoon.

And it was obvious that there was a sense of relief in the house as Kay's rented limousine pulled away. It was only as Alex realised that Raphaella hadn't called him all afternoon that the relief began to ebb. And then suddenly, he understood what had happened, and he called her house instead.

'I . . . I'm sorry . . . I was busy . . . I couldn't call . . . I . . .' He knew it for sure then, from the sound of her voice.

'I need to see you right away.'

'I'm afraid I . . .' Tears streamed down her cheeks as she fought to keep her voice normal.

'I'm sorry, Raphaella. I must see you . . . it's Mandy . . .'

'Oh my God . . . what happened?'

'I can't explain it till I see you.'

She was at the house twenty minutes later, and he apologised profusely for the deception, but he had known that it was imperative that he get to her right away, before she pulled away again, before she cut herself off from what they both needed so much. He told her honestly what happened with his sister, and he forced from her a description of Raphaella's hour with Kay at the Fairmont bar.

'And you believe her? Do you really think you're

166

depriving me? Hell, darling, I haven't been this happy in years.'

'But do you think she would?' She was still worried about the threat to John Henry.

'No, I don't. She's a bitch. But she's not completely crazy. There's no way she could get to him.'

'She could, you know. I have no control over his mail, for instance. His secretaries bring it to the house and give it directly to him.'

'She's not going to put something like that in a letter, for God's sake. She's too concerned with her own neck.'

'I suppose that's true.' Raphaella sighed lengthily and let herself melt into his arms. 'My God, what an incredible woman she is.'

'No,' he said softly, 'what an incredible woman you are.' He looked down at her carefully then. 'Shall we forget that any part of the last two days ever happened.'

'I'd like that, Alex. But should we? How do we know that all of her threats are idle?'

'Because there's only one thing my sister cares about, Raphaella, and that is her career. In the end, that's the only thing that matters to her, and to get at us, she would have to jeopardise that, and she won't. Believe me, darling. I know she won't.' But Raphaella was never quite as sure. She and Alex and Amanda went on with their lives, but the threats of Kay Willard seemed to ring in Raphaella's ears like an echo for months. She only hoped that Alex was right in believing that Kay's threats were empty.

Chapter 21

'Amanda?' Raphaella's voice rang out in the house as she closed the door behind her. It was four o'clock but she knew that Amanda was due from school. In the months since Amanda had settled into living with Alex, Raphaella had taken to dropping by in the afternoons, sometimes before Mandy got home from her classes, to tidy up the house, fix her a snack, and sit peacefully in the sunshine in the garden, waiting for the young girl to come home. They would have long talks sometimes about whatever they thought was important, now and then Mandy told a funny story about Alex, and lately Raphaella had been showing her drafts of the children's book she had started after Christmas. She had worked on it for five months now, and she hoped to have it in final draft form when she left for Spain in July.

But today it wasn't her manuscript she had brought with her, but a copy of *Time* magazine. On the cover was a photograph of Kay Willard, and beneath it the caption, 'The White House in 1992 . . . '96 . . . 2000?' Raphaella had read the article thoughtfully and then brought it with her when she came to see if Mandy was home from school. Her daytime visits to the house on Vallejo had begun to happen slowly, and now Mandy expected her to be there every day. She usually came when John Henry slept in the afternoon. And lately he had been sleeping longer and longer, until finally they had to wake him for his dinner at six.

'Amanda?' Raphaella stood silent for a long moment, her dark hair tucked into a neat little straw fedora, and she was wearing an exquisitely cut cream coloured linen suit. 'Mandy?' For a moment, she had thought that she heard a noise as she walked slowly upstairs.

It was on the third floor that Raphaella found her, sitting in one of the wicker chairs in her bedroom, her feet tucked under her and her chin on her knees as she stared sullenly at the view.

'Amanda? . . . Darling?' Raphaella sat down at the bed, the magazine and her beige lizard handbag still tucked under her arm. 'Did something happen at school?' She sat down on the bed and reached out to take the girl's hand. And then slowly Amanda turned to face her, her glance instantly taking in the magazine under Raphaella's arm.

'I see that you read it too.'

'What? The article about your mother?' The pretty sixteen-year-old nodded. 'Is that why you're upset?' It was unusual in the extreme for Mandy not to come running downstairs at the sound of her voice, laughing and smiling and filled with tales of what had happened at school. But the girl only nodded again. 'I didn't think it was a bad piece.'

'Except for the fact that none of it's true. Hell, did you read the part about my having a terrible car accident last winter, and recuperating slowly on the sunny West Coast with my uncle, while my mother comes out to see me in every spare moment she has?' She glared unhappily at Raphaella. 'Shit, I'm just glad she's never come back here since Christmas.' As it turned out, she wouldn't have had much choice. After her one explosive visit, Alex had been fully prepared to tell her to stay away, but Kay had never turned up again anyway. In fact, after the first few months, she hardly ever called. 'Christ, Raphaella. She's such a bitch and I hate her . . .'

'No, you don't. Maybe in time you'll come to understand each other better.' Raphaella didn't know what else to say. She sat peacefully with her for a few minutes and then touched her hand gently. 'Do you want to go for a walk?'

'Not really.'

'Why not?'

She shrugged her shoulders, obviously depressed, and Raphaella understood. She had her own fears about Kay Willard. Nothing more had happened between them, but Raphaella was always aware that it still could. Kay's last conversation with Alex had been filled with more ugliness but she'd agreed to leave Amanda where she was for the time being.

Half an hour later Raphaella managed to force Amanda out into the brilliant May sunshine, and arm in arm they walked back down to Union Street, and wandered in and out of all the shops, stopping at last for an iced capuccino at the Coffee Cantata, the seat next to them laden with packages filled with silly things.

'Think Alex will like the poster?' Amanda looked over her iced coffee at Raphaella, and they both grinned.

'He'll love it. We'll have to put it up in his study before he comes home.' It was a large poster of a woman on a surfboard in Hawaii, which only a teenager could have loved. But the important thing was that their shopping had completely taken Amanda's mind off her mother, and Raphaella was relieved. They didn't get back to the house until five thirty, and Raphaella hastily left Amanda, promising to return as always, later that night. Then she began the short walk to her own home, thinking of how totally her life had meshed with Mandy and Alex in the past six months. It was a balmy beautiful evening, and the sun was shooting golden lights on to all the windows as the late afternoon sky began to give off a soft glow. She was halfway home when she heard a horn behind her, and turned around, startled to see a black Porsche, and then she quickly noticed Alex at the wheel.

She stopped walking for a long moment, and just stood there, their eyes meeting and holding as though seeing each other for the first time. He pulled the car up slowly behind her, and leaned back against the red leather seat with a smile. 'Want a ride, lady?'

'I never talk to strangers.'

Neither of them spoke for a moment, as they smiled. And then his brow creased a little bit. 'How's Mandy?' It was like having a teenage daughter of their own now. She ate into their thoughts as well as their time alone. 'Did she see the piece in *Time*?' Raphaella nodded slowly, her face sobering as she came closer to the car.

'She came home from school this morning, Alex. I don't know what to tell her. She gets more violent about her mother all the time.' And then after she frowned and he nodded, she looked at him worriedly. 'What are we going to tell her about July?'

'Nothing yet. We can tell her later.'

'How much later?'

'We'll tell her in June.' But he looked worried too.

'What if she won't go?'

'She has to. At least this once.' And then he sighed. 'Just one more year until she turns eighteen, we might as well humour Kay a little. A court battle would hurt everyone now. If Mandy can put up with just this one visit, it should help keep the peace. You know, considering the fact that this is an election year for her, and that she thinks Amanda is essential to her winning the election, it's a goddamn miracle she didn't have her kidnapped and brought home. I suppose we should be grateful for small things.'

Raphaella looked at him honestly. 'Mandy wouldn't have stayed with her mother if she'd forced her to go back.'

'That's probably why she didn't try. But there isn't a damn thing we can do about this summer. She'll just have to go.' Raphaella only nodded in answer. It was something they had agreed to a month before. Amanda would go home to her mother just before the fourth of July weekend, spend a month with her at their summer home on Long Island, and then go to Europe with her grandmother for a month in August before returning to San Francisco for another year of school.

Alex had thought it a major victory to get Kay to agree to her coming back to San Francisco, but he knew that his niece would go through the roof at the prospect of going home. But he had called her psychiatrist who felt that she could handle the confrontation with her mother, and he felt that most of the psychological damage from the rape had also been put to rest. They all knew that she was going to have a fit at the idea of leaving Alex and going home to George and Kay. Raphaella planned to fly East with her, and leave her in New York, where she herself would spend a night at the Carlyle before flying on to Paris for a week, and then Spain for another two. It was her annual pilgrimage to see her parents, and to spend a little time in Santa Eugenia. And this year it meant even more to her than it had before. She was going to try out the final draft of her children's book on all her little cousins, and she could hardly wait to see how it would go. She would simply translate the stories into

Spanish as she read them. She had done it before when she brought books with her from the States. But this year was more important, because the stories were her own and if the children liked them, she was going to send the collection to Charlotte's agent and see if anyone would buy them in the fall.

When Raphaella looked at him he was grinning at her. 'What's so funny, Alexander?'

'We are.' He smiled more gently at her now, a warm light kindling in his eyes. 'Listen to us, discussing our teenage daughter.' He hesitated for a minute, and then gestured to the empty seat next to his. 'Want to get in for a minute?' She hesitated only briefly, glancing at her watch, and then absentmindedly looked around to see if anyone she knew was nearby.

'I really should get home . . .' She wanted to be with John Henry when they brought him his tray at six o'clock.

'I wouldn't push you.' But his eyes were so gentle, his face so handsome, and they hadn't had a moment alone in such a long time. It seemed as though Amanda was always with them. And when she went upstairs at midnight, they had so little time left before Raphaella had to go home.

Now she smiled and nodded. 'I'd love to.'

'Do we have time for a quick ride?'

She nodded, feeling wayward and mischievous, and he rapidly put the car in gear and sped off, heading down the hills towards the speeding traffic on Lombard Street and then into the wooded seclusion of the Presidio, sweeping down to the water until they sat next to the small fortress beneath the Golden Gate Bridge at Fort Point. Above them, traffic was hurrying across the bridge into Marin County, and there were sailboats on the water, a ferry, several small speedboats, and a brisk breeze which whipped Raphaella's hair as she took off her straw hat.

'Want to get out?' He kissed her and she nodded, and they stepped out side by side. Two dark-haired, tall, handsome people holding hands, looking out at the Bay. For a time, Raphaella felt very young as she stood there, thinking of the months they had already shared. They had grown so close, and spent so many nights together, whispering, talking, sitting by the fire, making love, running down to the kitchen at two in the morning to make omelettes or sandwiches or milk shakes. They had so much and yet so little . . . so many dreams . . . so little time . . . and such endless hope. As they stood side by side looking at the last of the sunlight shimmering on the boats, Raphaella turned to look at Alexander, wondering if they would ever have more. A few minutes, an hour, the hours before sunrise, stolen moments, and never much more than that. Even the child that they shared was only borrowed and in another year she would be gone. She was already thinking of what colleges to apply to, and Raphaella and Alex were already having pangs, feeling the loss before it hit them, wishing her there with them for many more years.

'What were you thinking just then Raphaella?' He looked down at her gently and brushed the hair from her eyes with one careful hand.

'About Amanda,' she hesitated and then kissed the hand as it brushed near her lips. 'I wish that she were ours.'

He nodded silently. 'So do I.' He wanted to tell her then that there would be others, someday, in a few years, children of their own. But he didn't say it, knowing how it hurt her not to have children. But it was a recurrent theme between them, her guilt at keeping him from marrying someone else and having children of his own.

'I hope she'll be okay this summer.' They began to walk slowly along the edge of the road, as the spray splashed up towards them stopping just short of where they stood.

He turned to her then. 'I hope you'll be okay too.' They hadn't said much about it, but in six weeks she was leaving for Spain.

'I will.' They stopped walking, and she held his hand tightly. 'I'll miss you terribly, Alex.'

He pulled her close. 'I'll miss you too. God . . .' He thought for a moment, 'I don't know what I'll do without you.' He had gotten so used to seeing her every night, and now he couldn't imagine a life without her.

'I won't be gone for more than three weeks.'

'That will feel like an eternity, especially with Mandy gone too.'

'Maybe you'll get some work done for a change.'

He grinned softly at her and with the boats passing slowly by them they kissed, and then they walked on arm in arm. They wandered along for another half hour and then regretfully got back in the car. It had been a pleasant ending to a golden afternoon, and when he dropped her off two blocks from her own home, she touched his lips softly with her fingertips and blew him a kiss before stepping out of the car.

She watched him drive away towards Vallejo, and smiled to herself as she walked the last two blocks towards home. It was extraordinary how much her life had altered in the past seven months since she'd met Alex. It had changed subtly, but it had changed a great deal. She was the mistress of a wonderful, handsome, charming young lawyer, the 'daughter in love', as Charlotte called her, of a novelist she had always admired, she was the stand-in mother for a lovely seventeen-year-old girl, and she felt as though she had a home in the house on Vallejo with the funny little overgrown garden and the brick kitchen filled with copper pots. And yet, at the same time, she was still who she always had been, Mrs John Henry Phillips, the French-born wife of a celebrated financier, the daughter of the French banker, Antoine de Mornay-Malle. She was going, as she always did, to Santa Eugenia to see her mother, she was doing everything as she always had before. Yet there was so much more to her life now, it was so much richer, so much fuller, so different, so happy. She smiled to herself as she turned the last corner before she reached the house. What she had didn't hurt John Henry, she reassured herself firmly as she put her key in the front door. She still spent several hours in the morning with him, saw to it that the nurses were attentive and careful, that his meals were as he liked them, that she read to him for at least an hour every day. But the difference was that there was so much more now.

After her mornings with John Henry, she spent two or three hours in her room working on the children's book she was going to try out on the children in Spain. And around four o'clock every afternoon, she walked slowly down to Vallejo, while John Henry took his nap. She almost always managed to be at the house before Amanda, so that the girl came home to someone who loved her, and she didn't have to be alone in the house. And often, Alex got home just before Raphaella left to go back to her own house. They would kiss and greet each other like married people, the only difference was that then Raphaella had to rush off, to spend another hour or two with John Henry, chat if he felt like talking, tell him some amusing story, or turn his wheelchair so that he could see the boats on the Bay. They always had dinner together, only now they no longer used the dining-room. John Henry ate in bed, on a tray. And once she was sure that he was comfortably settled, that the nurse was in charge, the house was quiet, she waited in her room for half an hour, and then she went out.

She was almost sure that the servants had their suspicions about where she went and how long she stayed, but no one ever dared to mention her nightly disappearance, and the sound of a door closing at four or five in the morning was something no one questioned any more. Raphaella had finally found a life she could live with, after eight years of intolerable loneliness and pain, and it was a life in which no one suffered, no one was hurt, in which she inflicted no pain. John Henry would never know about Alex, and she and Alex had something which meant a great deal to them both. The only thing which occasionally bothered her was what Kay had said so long ago, that she was keeping him away from someone who could give him more. But he said that it was what he wanted, and by now Raphaella knew that she loved him too much to give him up.

As she ran up the stairs to her bedroom, she mentally prepared what she would wear. She had just bought a turquoise silk dress at I. Magnin, and with her creamy skin and dark hair it made a sparkling impression as she put it on and clasped diamond and turquoise ear-rings to her ears.

She was only ten minutes late when she knocked on the door and opened it to see John Henry with the tray set before him, as he sat propped against pillows in his bed. As he sat there with his eyes burned deep into their sockets, his face lined, with one side of his face limply hanging down, one eye drooping, and his tall frame and lean arms so bent and so

175

frail it suddenly stopped her where she stood in the doorway. It was as though she hadn't seen him in a very long time. He looked as if he had slowly begun to lose the tenuous grip on life to which he had clung for almost eight years.

'Raphaella?' He looked at her strangely as he said the word in the garbled fashion he had said it for the past eight years, and Raphaella looked at him almost in astonishment, remembering once again to whom she was married, what were her duties, and how far she was from ever being Alex's wife.

She turned to shut the door softly behind her, brushing the tears from her eyes with one hand.

Chapter 22

Raphaella said good-bye to Alex at five o'clock in the morning, when she left him to go home to her own house. She had already packed her bags the night before, and now all she had to do was go home, leave a few memos for the servants, dress, have breakfast, and say good-bye to John Henry before she left. Her leavetaking would be simple and solemn, a kiss on the cheek, a last look, a touch on his hand, and always the vague guilt that she shouldn't be leaving. That she should be with him, and not going to Spain. But it was a ritual that they were both used to, and it was something which she had done every year for fifteen years. It was leaving Alex which was so much more painful, it was wrenching just to know that she wouldn't see him for a day. But the next weeks seemed almost unbearable, as they clung to each other before the first light of dawn. It was almost as though they were afraid that something would come between them forever, as though they would never find each other again. Raphaella clove to him like a second skin as they stood there, and she made no move to leave him at the foot of the stairs. She looked at him sorrowfully then, her eyes filled with tears, shaking her head with a small girlish smile.

'I can't make myself leave you.'

He smiled and pulled her still closer to him. 'You never leave me, Raphaella. I'm with you, always, wherever you go.'

'I wish you were coming with me to Spain.'

'Maybe someday.' Always someday . . . someday . . . but when? It was a line of thought she never liked pursuing because it always made her think that when their 'someday' came, John Henry would be dead. It was almost like killing him just to think it, so she didn't, and lived in the present instead.

'Maybe. I'll write to you.'

'May I write to you?' She nodded in answer.

'Don't forget to remind Mandy about the extra suitcase and her tennis racket.'

He smiled at her then. 'Yes, little mother. I'll tell her. What time do I have to get her up?'

'At six thirty. The plane leaves at nine.' He was going to take Mandy to the airport, but it was unlikely that he would even see Raphaella there once they arrived. She would as usual be deposited by the chauffeur, and spirited on to the plane. But they had ordered Mandy's ticket for the same flight, and at the other end, Raphaella was giving Mandy a lift to the Carlyle in her rented limousine. It was there that Charlotte would come to get her, and accompany her to Kay's apartment. Amanda had flatly stated that she wasn't going to face her mother alone. She hadn't seen her since the explosive exchange after Christmas, and she was feeling very skittish about going home at all. Typically, her father was at a medical convention in Atlanta, and he wouldn't be there to cushion the blow. 'Alex,' Raphaella looked at him longingly for a last time. 'I love you.'

'So do I, babe.' He held her close. 'Everything's going to be all right.' She nodded silently, not sure why she felt so uneasy about the trip, but she hated leaving him. She had lain awake beside him all night. 'Ready to go?' She nodded, and this time he walked her almost all the way home.

She did not see him at the airport, but it was like finding a piece of home as she saw Mandy get on the plane, wearing a wide-brimmed straw hat, a white cotton dress and white sandals they'd bought together and carrying the tennis racket Raphaella had been afraid she'd forget.

'Hi, Ma.' Mandy grinned at her and Raphaella laughed at the pretty young girl. Had she been taller and looked a little less elfin she might have looked more like a woman. But as it was, she still looked like a girl.

'It sure is good to see you. I was already getting lonely.'

'So is Alex. He burned the eggs, spilled the coffee, forgot the toast, and almost ran out of gas on the way to the airport. I don't think his mind was on what he was doing, to say the least.' The two exchanged a smile, it was comforting to Raphaella just to hear about Alex, as though it brought him

178

a little closer, as they made their way across the country to New York. Five hours later they finally got there in the heat and the confusion and the fetid furore of a New York summer. It was as though San Francisco didn't exist, and they would never find their way back. Raphaella and Mandy both looked at each other with exhaustion and longed to go home.

'I always forget what it's like here.'

Mandy looked around the airport in amazement. 'Christ, so have I. Jesus, it's awful.' But with that, the chauffeur found them, and in minutes they were ensconced in the back of the air conditioned limousine. 'Maybe it's not so bad after all.' She grinned happily at Raphaella who smiled and took her hand. She would have given anything to be riding in the Porsche with Alex, and not sitting in the back of a limousine in New York. For months now, the trappings of her life with John Henry had irked her, the servants, the protection, the enormous house. She wanted something so much simpler, like the little house on Vallejo, and her life with Amanda and him.

When they got to the Carlyle, there was a message from Charlotte that she had been delayed at a meeting with a publisher and she was going to be late. Amanda and Raphaella went up to the suite, took off their shoes and their hats, sat down on the couch and ordered lemonade.

'Do you believe how hot it is out there?' Mandy looked at her miserably and Raphaella smiled. Amanda was already finding every reason to hate New York.

'It won't be so bad on Long Island. You'll be able to to swimming every day.' It was like reconciling a child to the prospect of camp, but Amanda did not look reconciled for a moment as the bell rang at the door of the suite. 'It must be our lemonades.'

She walked quickly to the door with her handbag in her hand, the bright red silk suit she had worn on the plane only slightly wrinkled, and she looked very beautiful in the rich red with her white skin and dark hair. It always startled Amanda how beautiful Raphaella was. It was something one never quite got used to, that breathtaking face and those enormous dark eyes. Alex certainly didn't take her for granted, she had noticed, he looked nothing less than dazzled every time she walked in the door. And she was always so beautifully put together, impeccably chic. Now, as Amanda watched her, she pulled open the door with a small impersonal smile and an air of authority, prepared to see a waiter with a tray bearing two long, cool lemonades. What she saw instead was Amanda's mother, standing in the door of the suite looking hot and rumpled in an ugly green linen suit and a strange self-satisfied little grin. As though she had won. Amanda felt a ripple of fear rush through her and Raphaella looked polite but strained. The last time they had seen each other was at the Fairmont bar six months before, when she had threatened to reveal the affair with Alex to John Henry.

'My mother couldn't make it, so I thought I'd pick Mandy up instead.' She stared for a moment at Raphaella, and stepped into the suite.

Raphaella closed the door as Kay entered and watched as she crossed the room to her only child, who stood staring nervously at her mother, making no move towards her, and saying nothing, her eyes opened wide.

'Hello, Mandy.' Kay spoke to her first as she approached her, and still Amanda said nothing. Raphaella noticed that Amanda looked more than ever like a frightened child. She looked desperately unhappy as she stood there and the tall red head approached. 'You look fine. Is that a new hat?' Amanda nodded and Raphaella invited Kay to sit down just as the bell rang again and the lemonades arrived. She offered one to Kay who declined it and handed the other one to the girl who accepted it mutely, with eyes that pleaded with Raphaella, and then she lowered them into her lap as she sipped her drink. It was a strange, awkward moment, and Raphaella was quick to fill the gap with small talk about the trip. It was nonetheless an awkward half hour as they sat there, and Raphaella was relieved when Kay rose to go.

'Will you be going straight to Long Island?' Raphaella asked, wishing she could comfort Mandy.

'No. As a matter of fact, Mandy and I are going to be taking a little trip.' At this, she instantly caught her daughter's attention, as the girl watched her with hostile eyes.

'Oh really? Where?'

'To Minnesota.'

'Something to do with your campaign, Mother?' The words were her first to her mother and an accusation filled with scorn.

'More or less, it's a county fair, but there are some things I should go to. I thought you'd enjoy it.' Her face said she was angry, but she didn't dare let it show in her words. She looked then at Amanda who looked tired and miserable. All she wanted was to be back in San Francisco with Alex, and Raphaella had to admit that it would have been a lot more pleasant for her as well. Only her manners and breeding had induced her to be more than civil to Kay.

Amanda picked up her single suitcase and her tennis racket and faced Raphaella. They stood for just an insant like that, and then Raphaella folded her rapidly into her arms. She wanted to tell her to be patient, to be gentle, yet to be strong and not let her mother hurt her, she wanted to tell her a thousand things but it was no longer the place or the time. 'Have a good time, darling.' And then more softly, 'I'll miss you.'

But Amanda said it openly, with tears in her eyes. 'I'll miss you too.' She was crying silently as she fled into the hallway of the Carlyle, and Kay paused for a moment in the doorway, seeming to take stock of every inch of Raphaella's face.

'Thank you for bringing her in from the airport.' There was no mention of the rest of what Raphaella had done for her, the six months of loving and motherly care as she helped Alex with the niece they had both come to love so much. But Raphaella wanted no thanks from this woman. All she wanted was her assurance that she wouldn't hurt the girl. But there was no way to get that, no way to admonish Kay to be kind to her own child.

'I hope it's a good month for you both.'

'It will be.' Kay said it with a curious little smile as she watched Raphaella. And then, almost grinning over her shoulder she tossed back at the dark-haired beauty. 'Have a good time in Spain.' With that, she stepped into the elevator with Amanda, and Raphaella, feeling suddenly empty and bereft, found herself wondering how Kay knew that she was going to Spain. She didn't think that Alex had mentioned it to her in the brief calls that had established Mandy's plans for July. There had been something odd and evil about Kay as she had come to pick up her daughter but Raphaella decided that she was oversensitive about Kay. She had proven after all that her threats were empty ones. She had done none of the things she had threatened to the previous winter. Her worst sin seemed to be her eternal selfishness and the all-consuming political ambition which ruled her every move.

Chapter 23

The next morning as Raphaella boarded the plane to Paris she wasn't even looking forward to seeing her nephews and nieces, all she wanted was to go home. This leg of her journey only carried her further away from where her heart was and she felt tired and lonely. She closed her eyes, and tried to pretend that she was on her way to California and not to France.

It was a flight which she was certainly used to, and from sheer boredom, she slept halfway across the Atlantic. She did a little reading, ate lunch and dinner, and thought smilingly of when she had met Alex on the trip to New York the previous fall, but it seemed inconceivable now to her to speak to a stranger, as inconceivable as it had seemed to her before. She couldn't help smiling to herself as they prepared to land in Paris. He certainly wasn't a stranger any more. 'And how did you two meet?' She could imagine her father asking. 'On a plane, Papa. He picked me up.' He what? She almost laughed openly as she fastened her seatbelt and prepared to land. She was still amused at the idea as she was taken off the plane before the others, and whisked through customs, but she was no longer amused by anything as she reached the gate and saw her father's face. He looked stern and almost angry as he stood like a statue, watching her come towards him in an outfit that would have brought an appreciative smile to any man's eyes. She wore a black suit, with a white silk shirt and a little black straw hat with a veil. As she saw him, her heart suddenly fluttered. It was obvious that something had happened. He had bad news for her . . . perhaps her mother . . . or John Henry . . . or a cousin . . . or . . .

'Bonjour, Papa.' He barely unbent as she reached up to kiss him, and his substantial frame seemed more rigid than rock. His face was old and lined, and the eyes looked at her coldly, as she peered into his ice-blue eyes with a look of fear on her face. 'Has something happened?'

'We will discuss that at home.' Oh God . . . it was John Henry. And he didn't want to tell her here. Suddenly, all thought of Alex left her mind. All she could think of was the elderly man she had left in San Francisco, and as always she reproached herself for leaving him at all.

'Papa . . . please . . .' They stood in the airport looking at each other. 'Is it . . . is it . . .' Her voice sank to a whisper. 'John Henry?' He only shook his head. After not seeing her for an entire year, he had nothing to say to her. He remained a wall of granite as they climbed into his black Citroën. He nodded to the driver, and they started home.

Raphaella sat frozen in terror for the entire drive into Paris, her hands trembling when at last they stopped outside his house. The chauffeur held open the door for them, his black uniform suiting her father's expression and Raphaella's mood. There was an odd kind of feeling, as she walked into the enormous foyer filled with gilt mirrors and marble-topped Louis XV tables. There was a magnificent Aubusson tapestry hanging on one wall, and a view of the garden through the french windows beyond, but the overall feeling was one of arctic splendour and it somehow made things worse as her father glared at her in displeasure and waved in the direction of his study up a tall flight of marble stairs. It was suddenly like being a child again, and as though somehow, in some way, unbeknownst to her, she had erred.

She merely followed him up the steps, carrying her handbag and her hat in one hand, waiting until her private audience to discover in what way she had sinned. Perhaps it was after all something to do with John Henry, as she walked hurriedly up the stairs, she couldn't imagine what it could be, unless it was something that had occurred while she was in New York. Perhaps another stroke? But it didn't seem like bad news he was going to share with her. But rather some terrible censure over something she had done. She remembered that particular expression on his face from her youth.

He marched solemnly into his study, as Raphaella

followed suit. It was a room with enormously high ceilings, wood panelling, walls covered with bookcases, and a desk large enough for a President or a King. It was a handsome example of Louis XV furniture, dripping with gilt, and highly impressive as he took his chair behind the desk.

'*Alors* . . .' He glared at her, and waved to a chair across from the desk. There had been not a moment of kindness between them. Not a kind word, and barely an embrace. And although her father was not a warm man, or given to excessive demonstration, he was certainly being, even for him, excessively stern.

'Papa . . . what is it?' Her face had grown very white during the long drive from the airport, and now she seemed even more pale as she waited for him to begin.

'What is it?' His eyebrows drew together, and his face looked fierce as he stared first at his desk and then at her. 'Must we play games?'

'But Papa . . . I have no idea.'

'In that case,' he almost bellowed the words at his daughter, 'You are totally without conscience. Or perhaps very naïve, if you think you can do anything you wish, in any corner of the world, and not have it known.' He let the words sink in for a moment and Raphaella's heart began to race. 'Do you begin to understand me?' He lowered his voice and looked at her pointedly as she shook her head. 'No? Then perhaps I should be more honest with you, than you are with me, or your poor husband, lying sick at home in his bed.' His voice was filled with reproach and contempt for his only daughter, and suddenly, like a child caught in a terrible misdemeanour, she felt awash with shame. The pale cheeks were suddenly suffused with a flush and Antoine de Mornay-Malle nodded his head. 'Perhaps now you understand me.'

But her voice was clear when she answered. 'No, I do not.'

'Then, you are a liar, as well as a cheat.' The words rang out like bells in the large austere room. 'I received,' he said the words deliberately, as though he were addressing parliament instead of his only surviving child, 'several weeks ago, a letter. From an American Congresswoman, Madame

Kay Willard.' He searched Raphaella's face and she felt her heart stop.

Raphaella waited, barely able to breathe. 'It was, I must tell you, a very painful letter for me to read. Painful, for a number of reasons. But most of all because I learned things about you, my daughter, which I had never hoped to hear. Shall I go on?' Raphaella wanted to tell him not to, but she didn't dare. He went on anyway, as she knew he would. 'She not only explained to me that you are cheating on your husband. A man, may I remind you, Raphaella, who has been nothing but good to you since you were barely more than a child. A man who trusts you, who loves you, who needs your every waking moment, your every thought, every breath, to keep him alive. If you give him anything less than that, you will kill him, as I'm quite sure you are aware. So, not only are you destroying this man who has loved you, and who is my oldest and dearest friend, but you are apparently destroying as well the lives of several other people, a man who apparently had a wife who loved him and whom you have estranged, keeping him from a decent woman, as well as having children, which apparently is something dear to his heart. I also understand from Madame Willard that after a serious accident, her daughter has gone to California to recover and to live with this man you have stolen from his wife. Not only have you done that, but apparently you are corrupting this child as well, with your shocking behaviour. In addition, Madame Willard is in the Congress and from what she tells me, she will lose all chance to continue her life's work if this scandal comes out. In fact, she tells me that she is going to retire immediately if you and her brother don't stop, because she cannot face the disgrace such a scandal would bring to her, and to her husband, her ageing mother, and her child. I might add as well, that if such a matter were to become public, you would disgrace me and the Banque Malle as well, which does not even bring into consideration how your behaviour would be viewed in Spain. Not to mention what they would make you in the press.'

Raphaella felt as though she had just been crucified, and the enormity of what had happened, of the accusations, of what Kay had done, and what her father had just said to her were almost more than she could cope with as she sat there. How could she tell him? Where would she begin? The truth was that Kay was a vicious hungry politician who would stop at nothing to get what she wanted, and that she was not retiring, but running for election again, this time as senator. That Amanda had not been 'corrupted' by her and Alex but deeply loved, that he hadn't been married to Rachel when she had met him, that he didn't want Rachel back, and that she herself was still giving everything she could to John Henry, but that she loved Alex too. But her father only sat there, staring at her with disapproval and anger in his eyes. As she looked at him, feeling powerless before him, the tears spilled from her eyes and ran down her cheeks.

'I must also tell you,' he continued after a moment, 'that it is not in my character to believe the word of a total stranger. At considerable inconvenience and great expense, I hired a detective who, for the past ten days, has chronicled your activities, and seems to confirm what this woman says. You came home,' he glared at her in fury, 'no earlier than five o'clock in the morning, every single night. And even if you don't care what you are doing to those around you, Raphaella, I should think that your own reputation would matter to you more than that! Your servants must think you a slut . . . a whore! A piece of garbage!' He was roaring at her, and left his seat to pace the room. She had still said not a word. 'How can you do such a thing? How can you be so dishonoured, so disgusting, so cheap?' He turned to face her and she shook her head mutely and dropped her head into her hands. A moment later, she blew her nose in the lace handkerchief she extracted from her handbag, took a deep breath and faced her father from across the room.

'Papa . . . this woman hates me . . . what she has said . . .'

'Is all true. The reports from the man I hired say so.'

'No,' she shook her head vehemently and stood up as well. 'No, the only accurate thing is that I love her brother. But he is not married, he was divorced when I met him . . .' He instantly cut her off.

'And you are a Catholic, or had you forgotten? And a married woman, or had you forgotten that too? I don't care if he was a priest or a Zulu, the fact is that you are married to John Henry and you are not free to whore around as you choose. I will never be able to look at him again after what you have done here. I cannot face my oldest friend, because the daughter I gave him is a whore!'

'I am not a whore!' She shouted the words at him, with sobs clutching at her throat. 'And you didn't give me to him. I married him . . . because I wanted to . . . I loved him . . .' She didn't go on.

'I don't want to hear your nonsense, Raphaella. I want to hear only one thing. That you will not see this man again.' He glared at her angrily and walked slowly towards her. 'And until you do that, and give me your solemn promise, you are not welcome to be in my house. In fact,' he looked at his watch, 'your flight to Madrid is in two hours. I want you to go there, to think about this, and I will come to see you in a few days. I want to know then that you have written to this man and told him that it's over. And to assure that you keep your promise, I intend to keep the surveillance on you for an indefinite time.'

'But why, for God's sake, why?'

'Because if you have no honour, Raphaella, I do. You are breaking every promise you ever made when you married John Henry. You are disgracing me as well as yourself. And I will not have a whore for a daughter. And if you refuse to comply with what I'm asking, I will tell you simply that you leave me no choice but to tell John Henry what you've done.'

'For God's sake, Papa . . . please . . .' She was sobbing almost hysterically now. 'This is my life . . . you'll kill him . . . Papa . . . please . . .'

'You're a disgrace to my name, Raphaella.' He stared at her without coming closer, and then went to his chair behind the desk again and sat down.

She looked at him, understanding the horror of what had happened, and for the first time in her life hating someone as she never had before. If Kay had stood in the same room with her at that moment, she would have killed her, gladly, and with her bare hands. Instead, she turned to her father with a look of despair.

'But Papa . . . why . . . why must you do this? I'm a grown woman . . . you have no right . . .'

'I have every right. You have obviously been too long in America, my dear. And perhaps, also, you have been too long on a loose leash, while your husband has been sick. Madame Willard tells me that she tried to reason with you but that you and this man persist. She tells me that if it were not for you, he would go back to his wife, that if it were not for you, he could settle down and have children.' He looked at her reproachfully, 'How can you do that to someone you pretend to love?' His words and the look on his face were like a knife cutting through her, as his gaze never wavered from her eyes. 'But my concern is not with this man, it is with your husband. It is to him that you should feel the strongest allegiance. And I'm quite serious, Raphaella, I will tell him.'

'It will kill him.' She spoke very quietly, her eyes still pouring tears down her face.

'Yes,' Her father said curtly. 'It will kill him. And his blood will be on your hands. I want you to think about that in Santa Eugenia. And I want you to know why I made arrangements for you to leave tonight.' He stood up and there was suddenly an air of dismissal on the granite like face of her father. 'I will not have a whore under my roof, Raphaella, not even for one night.' He walked to the door of his study then, pulled it open, bowed slightly, and waved her outside. He stared at her long and hard for an endless moment as she shivered, looked ravaged by what had passed between them, and he only shook his head, and spoke two words to her. 'Good afternoon.' And then he shut the door firmly behind her, and she had to walk to the nearest chair and sit down.

She felt so sick and shaky that she felt sure she would faint in a moment. But she just sat there, dazed, horrified, hurt, embarrassed, angry. How could he do this to her? And had Kay known what she was doing? Could she possibly have known the cataclysmic effect her letter would have? Raphaella sat stunned for more than half an hour, and then, glancing at her watch, she realised that since her father had changed her flight she would have to leave the house then and there.

She walked slowly to the staircase, with a backward glance, towards her father's study. She had no desire to say good-bye to him now. He had said everything he had to say, and she knew that he would turn up at Santa Eugenia. But she didn't give a damn what he did, or threatened or said, he had no right to interfere with her life with Alex. And she didn't give a damn what he threatened to do to her. She wouldn't give Alex up. She marched down the stairs to the front hallway, put on the little black straw hat with the veil, and picked up her bag. She realised now that her valises had never been taken out of the Citroën, and that the chauffeur was still standing just ourside the door. In effect, she had been banished from her father's house, but she was so angry that she didn't care. He had treated her like an object, a piece of furniture, some kind of chattel, and she would not let him do that. He hadn't sold her to John Henry. She had married him. And her father couldn't threaten to tell John Henry. She wouldn't let him. She slipped back into the Citroën with a sigh of fatigue, and a ravaged look in her eyes, caused by more than the long trip from the States, and she said not a single word on the trip back to the airport. She just sat there and thought about what her father had said.

Chapter 24

In San Francisco, at the same time as Raphaella was being
driven back to the airport outside Paris, Alex had just
received a most unusual call. He sat staring at his folded
hands at his desk, and wondered why he had received the
call. It most certainly had to do with Raphaella, but more
than that he did not know. And he felt an odd and terrible
weight as he waited for the appointed hour. At five minutes
after nine that morning, he had received a call from one of
John Henry's secretaries, and had been asked to come to the
house that morning, if he could. He had told him only that
Mr Phillips wanted to see him on a personal matter of
considerable importance. Further explanation was not
offered and he didn't dare ask. Immediately after he had
hung up, he had dialled his sister, but Congresswoman
Willard was not available that morning, and he knew that
there was nowhere else to seek an answer. He would have to
wait until he saw John Henry, in another two hours. He
feared above all that someone had told him, and now the old
man was going to tell him not to see Raphaella again.
Perhaps he had already spoken to her himself and she hadn't
told Alex. Perhaps he had already arranged with her family
to keep her in Spain. But he sensed something terrible about
to happen, and due to John Henry's advanced age and the
obvious gravity of the situation, he couldn't refuse to go and
see him, but he would have liked to as he parked his car
across the street from the house.

Slowly, he crossed to the enormous oak door he had seen
so often. He rang the bell, and waited, and a moment later, a
serious-faced butler appeared. Alex felt, for a moment, as
though each member of the household knew his crime and
was about to pass judgement on him. He was a small boy
about to be scolded for stealing apples, but no, this was
much, much worse. If he had allowed himself, he would

have been truly terrified. But he felt that this was the instance in which he had absolutely no choice. He owed it to John Henry Phillips to appear before him, no matter what the old man chose to do or say.

The butler led him to the main hall, where a maid escorted him upstairs, and outside John Henry's suite of rooms, an elderly man walked towards Alex, smiled benignly and thanked him for coming to see Mr Phillips on such short notice. He identified himself as Mr Phillips's secretary, and Alex recognised the voice he had heard on the phone.

'Very kind of you to come so quickly. This is most unusual for Mr Henry. He hasn't asked anyone to come here to see him in several years. But I gather that this is a somewhat urgent personal matter, and he thought that you might be able to help him.' Once again, Alex felt apprehensive.

'Certainly.' He found himself muttering inanities to the ancient secretary and wondered if he was going to faint as they waited for a nurse to usher them inside. 'Is he very ill?' It was a stupid question he knew, as the man nodded, since he knew from Raphaella just how sick John Henry was, but he found himself totally unnerved just from being here outside John Henry's bedroom doorway, in 'her' home. These were the halls she walked in every day. It was the house in which she had breakfast each morning, to which she came after she left him, after they had made love.

'Mr Hale . . .' The nurse had opened the door and the secretary beckoned. For a moment, Alex seemed to falter, and then in his dark suit and white shirt and navy blue polka dot tie he walked towards the doorway, feeling like a man going to his own execution, but at least he was going in style. He would not disgrace her, neither by proving himself a coward in refusing to come here, or by looking less than appropriate when he did. He had stopped at home to change his clothes for a dark pin striped suit he had bought in London, white shirt and Dior tie, but even that didn't help as he crossed the threshold and looked at the shrunken figure in the massive antique bed.

'Mr Phillips?' Alex's voice was barely more than a whisper as behind him both the secretary and the nurse instantly disappeared. They were alone now, the two men who loved Raphaella, one so beaten and so old and so broken, the other so young and tall as he stood looking at the man Raphaella had married fifteen years before.

'Please come in.' His speech was garbled, and difficult to understand, but it was as though Alex sensed his words with ease, so attuned was he to expect what was coming. He had felt more of a man because he had come so willingly to accept whatever anger or insults John Henry chose to hurl at him, but he felt less of a man now when he realised how small and pained his opponent was. He waved vaguely towards a chair near the bed, indicating to Alex to take it, but there was nothing vague about the sharp blue eyes which watched him, taking his measure, inch by inch, hair by hair. Alex sat down cautiously in the chair, wishing that he would wake up in his bed to find that this had only been an anxious dream. It was one of those moments in a lifetime which one would like to wish away.

'I want to . . .' He laboured with his speech, but his eyes never left Alex as he did so, and even now there was about him the aura of command. There was nothing overbearing about him, just a kind of quiet strength, even in his broken condition, one sensed that this had once been a great man. It was easier now to understand what he might once have been to Raphaella, and why she still loved him now. There was more than loyalty here, there was someone very special, and for an instant, Alex felt shame at what they had done. 'I want . . .' John Henry struggled on, fighting with the side of his mouth which no longer chose to move, 'to thank you . . . for coming.' It was then that Alex realised that the eyes were not only piercing, but also kind. Alex nodded at him, not quite sure what to say. 'Yes, sir' would have seemed appropriate. He felt in awe of this man.

'Yes. Your secretary said that it was important.' They both knew that this was the understatement of the year. Despite the crippled mouth, John Henry attempted to smile.

'Indeed, Mr Hale . . . in . . . deed.' And then after a brief pause, 'I hope . . . I did not . . . frighten you . . . in asking you . . .' he seemed barely able to finish but determined to do so. It was rough going for them both. '. . . to come here. It is very important,' he said more clearly, 'to all three . . . of us . . . I do not need to explain.'

'I . . .' should he deny it, Alex wondered. But there had been no accusation. There had only been the truth. 'I understand.'

'Good.' John Henry nodded, looking pleased. 'I love my wife very much, Mr Hale . . .' The eyes were strangely bright. 'So much so that it has pained me . . . terribly . . . to keep her trapped here, while I . . . I am a prisoner of this useless, finished body . . . and she goes on . . . chained to me . . .' He looked grief stricken as his eyes reached out towards Alex, '. . . like this. It is not a life for a . . . young . . . woman . . . yet . . . she is very good to me.'

Alex couldn't stop himself then. And his voice was hoarse as he spoke. 'She loves you a great deal too.' He felt ever more the intruder. They were the lovers. He was the interloper. It was the first time he had truly understood. She was this man's wife, not his. And by virtue of what they felt for each other, she belonged here. And yet, could he truly believe that? John Henry was a very old man, approaching death by infinitely small, measured steps. As he himself seemed to know, it was a cruel existence for her. He looked at Alex helplessly now.

'This has been a terrible thing to do . . . to her . . .'

'You didn't wish it.'

There was the ghost of a smile. 'No . . . I did not . . . But . . . it happened . . . And still . . . I live on . . . and I torment her . . .'

'That's not true.' They sat here like two old friends, each acknowledging the other's existence and importance, it was a very strange moment in both men's lives. 'She doesn't resent one moment of her time with you.' Again he had had to fight the urge to add 'sir'.

'But she should . . . resent it . . .' He closed his eyes for a moment. 'I do.' He opened his eyes again and they were as sharp as before. 'I resent it . . . for her . . . and for me . . . But I did not ask you here to tell you my regrets . . . and my sorrows . . . I called you here to ask you . . . about you.'

Alex's heart pounded, and he decided to take the bull by the horns. 'May I ask you how you know of me?' Had he known all along? Did he have her followed by servants as a routine?

'I received . . . a letter.'

Alex felt a strange flame within him begin to glow. 'May I ask from whom?'

'I do not . . . know.'

'It was anonymous?'

John Henry nodded. 'It told me only . . . that . . . you and . . .' He didn't seem to want to say her name in Alex's presence, it was enough that they sat here together, speaking the truth. 'That you and she had been involved for . . . almost a year . . .' He began to cough softly, and Alex worried, but John Henry waved his hand to indicate that all was well and a moment later he went on. 'It gave me your address and telephone number, explained that you . . . are . . . an attorney . . . and it said quite clearly . . . that I would be wise . . . to put a stop to this . . .' He looked at Alex with curiosity. 'Why is that so? Was the letter . . . from your wife?' He seemed intrigued, but Alex shook his head.

'I don't have a wife. I've been divorced for several years.'

'Is she . . . still . . . jealous?' He fought to go on.

'No. I believe the letter you received was from my sister. She's a politician. A congresswoman, in fact. And she is a dreadful, selfish, evil woman. She thinks that if any word of this, my, er, our involvement ever leaked out, it would damage her politically, because of the scandal.'

'She is probably . . . right . . .' John Henry nodded his head. 'But does anyone know?' He found that hard to believe of Raphaella.

'No.' Alex was adamant. 'No one. Only my niece, and she adores Raphaella and is very discreet.'

'Is she a small child?' John Henry seemed to smile.

'She is sixteen and she is the daughter of that same sister. In recent months, Amanda, my niece, has been staying with me. She was injured on Thanksgiving day and while her mother has been most unkind to her, your . . . er . . . Raphaella,' he decided to go ahead and say it, 'has been wonderful to her.' His eyes lit with warmth as he said the words, and John Henry smiled again.

'She would be wonderful . . . in a case like that. She is a

most . . . unusual . . . person.' On that they both agreed, and then his face grew sad. 'She should have had . . . children.' And then, 'Perhaps . . . one day . . . she will.' Alex said nothing. And at last John Henry went on. 'So, you think it is . . . your sister?'

'I do. Did she threaten you in any way in the letter?'

'No.' He looked shocked. 'She only relied . . . on . . . my . . . ability to put a stop . . . to it . . .' He looked suddenly amused, and waved at his useless limbs beneath the sheets. 'What confidence to have . . . in an old, old man.' But he didn't seem so old in spirit as his eyes met Alex's 'Tell me, how . . . may I ask . . . how did it begin?'

'We met on a plane, last year. No . . . that's not true . . .' Alex frowned and closed his eyes for a moment, remembering the first time he had seen her on the stairs. 'I saw her one night . . . sitting on the steps, looking out at the Bay . . .' He realised that he didn't want to tell John Henry she'd been crying. 'I thought she was incredibly beautiful, but that was all. I never expected to see her again.'

'But you did?' John Henry looked intrigued.

'Yes, on the plane I mentioned. I glimpsed her in the airport and she disappeared.'

John Henry smiled at him benignly. 'You must be a romantic.'

Alex blushed slightly, with a sheepish smile. 'I am.'

'So is she.' He spoke as her father, and he didn't offer the information that he had been a romantic too. 'And then?'

'We spoke. I mentioned my mother. She was reading one of her books.'

'Your mother writes?' His interest seemed to grow.

'Charlotte Brandon.'

'Most . . . impressive . . . I read some of her early . . . books . . . I would have liked to meet her.' Alex would have liked to tell him that he would, but they both knew that that would not happen. 'And your sister is . . . a Congresswoman . . . quite a group.' He smiled benevolently at Alex and waited for the rest.

'I invited . . . her . . . to lunch with my mother in New York, and . . .' he faltered for only the fraction of a second, 'I didn't know who she was then. My mother told me after lunch.'

'She knew?'

'She recognised her.'

'I'm . . . surprised . . . few people know her . . . I have kept her well hidden from . . . the press.' Alex nodded. 'She had not . . . told you . . . herself?'

'No. The next time I saw her she told me only that she was married and could not get involved.' John Henry nodded, seemingly pleased. 'She was very definite, and I'm afraid that . . . I . . . I pressed her.'

'Why?' John Henry's voice was suddenly harsh in the still room.

'I'm sorry. I couldn't help it . . . I . . . as you said, I'm a romantic. I was in love with her.'

'So soon?' He looked sceptical, but Alex held firm.

'Yes.' He took a deep breath. It was difficult to be telling it all to John Henry. And why? Why did the old man want to know it all? 'I saw her again, and I believe she was drawn to me too.' It was none of his business that they had gone to bed in New York. They had a right to their privacy too. She was not only his, but Alex's as well. 'We flew back to San Francisco on the same plane, but I only saw her once more here. She came to tell me that she couldn't see me again. She didn't want to be unfaithful to you.'

John Henry looked stunned. 'She is an . . . amazing . . . woman . . .' Alex clearly agreed. 'And then? You pressed her again?' It was not an accusation, only a question.

'No. I left her alone. She called me two months later. And I think we had both been equally unhappy.'

'It began then?' Alex nodded. 'I see. And how long has that been?'

'Almost eight months.'

John Henry nodded slowly. 'I used . . . to wish . . . that she would find someone. She was so lonely . . . and I can do nothing . . . about it. After a time, I stopped thinking . . . about it . . . she seemed to set in living her life . . . like this.' He looked at Alex once again without accusation.

'Is there any reason . . . why . . . I should stop it? Is she . . . unhappy?' Alex slowly shook his head. 'Are you?'

197

'No.' Alex sighed softly. 'I love her very deeply. I'm only sorry that this had to come to your attention. We never meant to hurt you. She above all couldn't have borne that.'

'I know.' John Henry looked at him gently. 'I know . . . and you . . . have not . . . hurt me. You have taken nothing from me. She is as much my wife as she ever has been . . . as much as she can be . . . now. She is as kind to me as ever . . . as gentle . . . as loving. And if you give her something more, some sunshine . . . some joy . . . some kindness . . . some love . . . how could I begrudge her that? It is not right . . . for a man of my age . . . to keep a beautiful young woman locked in a trap . . . No!' His voice echoed powerfully in the room. 'No . . . I will not stop her!' And then his voice softened again, 'She has a right to happiness with you . . . just as she once had a right to happiness with me. Life is a series of moving seasons . . . moving stages . . . moving dreams . . . we must move with them. To stay locked in the past will condemn her to the same fate as mine. It would be immoral to allow her to do that . . . that would be the scandal . . .' he smiled gently at Alex, 'Not what she shares with you.' And then almost in a whisper. 'I am grateful to you . . . if you . . . have made . . . her happy, and I believe that you have.' And then he waited for a long moment. 'And now? What do you plan with her, or do you?' He looked worried again, as though trying to settle the future for a beloved child.

Alex wasn't sure what to tell him. 'We seldom talk about it.'

'But do you think . . . about it?'

'I do.' Alex was honest with him. He had been too kind not to be.

'Will you . . .' His eyes filled with tears on the words, 'take care of her . . . for me . . .'

'If she will let me.'

John Henry shook his head. 'If they will . . . let you . . . if anything happens to me, they will come and get her . . . and take her away.' He sighed softly, 'She needs you . . . if you will be good to her, she needs you very much . . . just as once . . . she needed me.'

Alex's own eyes were damp now. 'I promise you. I will take care of her. And I will never, never pull her away from you.

Not now, not later, not in fifty years or ten years or two. I want you to know that.' He reached out and took John Henry's frail hand in his own. 'She is your wife, and I respect that. I always have. I always will.'

'And one day, you will make her . . . yours?' Their eyes met and held.

'If she lets me.'

'See that . . . she does.' He squeezed Alex's hand hard, and then his eyes closed, as though he were exhausted. He opened them a moment later with a small smile. 'You're a good man, Alexander.'

'Thank you, Sir.' He had finally said it. And he felt better. It was as though they were father and son.

'You were brave to come here.'

'I had to.'

'And your sister?' His eyes questioned Alex and Alex only shrugged.

'She can't really make trouble between us.' He looked at John Henry. 'What more can she do? She told you. She can't make it public, the voters would find out then.' He smiled. 'She has no power at all.'

But John Henry looked worried. 'She could hurt . . . Raphaella.' He said it so gently it was almost a whisper. But he had said her name at last.

'I won't let her.' And Alex sounded so strong as he said it, that John Henry looked completely at peace.

'Good.' And then after a moment. 'She will be safe with you.'

'Always.'

He looked at Alex for a long time then, and then stretched out his hand again. Alex took it in his, and he pressed it and whispered softly. 'You have my blessing, Alexander . . . tell her that . . . when the time comes . . .' There were tears in Alex's eyes as he kissed the frail hand he held, and a few minutes later he left the old man to rest.

He left the stately mansion with a feeling of peace he had never before known. Without meaning to, his sister had bestowed on him an infinitely precious gift. Rather than ending the affair with Raphaella, she had given them the key to their future. In a strange old-fashioned way, in the ritual of bestowing a blessing, John Henry Phillips had passed on Raphaella to Alexander Hale, not as a possession or a burden, but as a precious treasure which each, in his own time, had vowed to love and protect.

Chapter 25

'Raphaella, darling . . .' Her mother threw her arms around her as she came off the plane in Madrid. 'But what is this madness? Why didn't you stay in Paris for the night? When your father told me you were going to come straight through like this, I told him it was quite mad.' Alejandra de Mornay-Malle looked at the dark circles forming under her daughter's eyes and scolded her gently, but the way she did it told Raphaella that she had no idea why her plans had changed. Obviously her father had said nothing about the letter from 'Madame Willard', or the affair with Alex, and that she was in disgrace.

Raphaella smiled tiredly at her mother, wanting to feel happy to see her, wanting a feeling of homecoming, of a safe haven from her father's anger. Instead all she felt was exhaustion, and all she could hear was the echo of her father's words, 'I don't want a whore in my house, Raphaella, not even for one night.'

'Darling, you look exhausted, are you sure you're not ill?' The striking flaxen beauty that had made Alejandra de Santos y Quadral famous as a girl had dimmed only slightly with the onset of middle age. She was still a remarkably beautiful woman, her beauty impaired only by the fact that she was insipid and the brilliant green eyes held no very interesting light. But as a statue she would have been lovely, and as a portrait she had been very beautiful, quite a number of times. But she had none of Raphaella's smoky beauty, or the stark contrasts of her jet black hair and ivory skin. There was none of Raphaella's depth in her mother, none of her intelligence or her wit or her excitement. Alejandra was just a very elegant woman with a very lovely face, a kind heart, excellent breeding, good manners, and an easy gracious way.

'I'm fine, Mother. I'm just very tired. But I didn't want to waste time in Paris, since I can't stay for very long.'

'Can't you?' Her mother looked dismayed at the prospect of a short visit. 'But why not? Is John Henry ill again, darling?'

Raphaella shook her head as they wended their way from the airport towards Madrid. 'No. I just don't like to leave him for very long.' But there was a look of strain and anguish about her daughter, which Alejandra noticed about her again as they left for Santa Eugenia the next day.

The night before she had excused herself early, saying that all she needed was a night of rest and she would be fine. But her mother sensed a reserve, almost a recalcitrance, that made her worry, and on the trip to Santa Eugenia the next day, Raphaella said not a word. It was then that she became almost frightened and called her husband in Paris that night.

'But Antoine, what is it? The girl is positively mourning over something. I don't understand it, but everything is very wrong. Are you sure it's not John Henry?' After eight years of his illness it seemed odd that Raphaella should be feeling it so much now. It was then with a sigh of regret, Antoine told her, and that she listened with dismay. 'Poor child.'

'No. Alejandra, no. There is nothing here to pity. She is behaving abominably, and it will become known very shortly. How will you feel when you read about it in the gossip columns, or when you see a photograph of her in the papers somewhere, dancing at a party with a strange man?' He sounded very old and very stuffy, and at her end of the phone, Alejandra only smiled.

'That doesn't sound like Raphaella. Do you suppose she really loves him?'

'I doubt it. It doesn't really matter. I put things to her very clearly. She has absolutely no choice.' Alejandra nodded again, wondering, and then shrugged. Antoine was probably right. He almost always was, as were her brothers, at least most of the time.

But later that night, she broached the subject to Raphaella, who had been taking a long quiet walk on the elaborately sculptured ground. There were palm trees and tall dark cypress, flower gardens, and fountains, and hedges in the shapes of birds, but Raphaella saw none of it as she walked along thinking of Alex. All she could think of was the letter Kay had sent her father, and that she would not give in to his threats, no matter how adamant he was. She was, after all, a grown woman. She lived in San Francisco, was married, and led her own life. But the truth of how much her family still controlled her came back to her again and again as she pondered her father's words.

'Raphaella?' She jumped when she heard her name and then saw her mother, wearing a long white evening dress and an endless rope of perfectly matched pearls. 'Did I frighten you? I'm sorry.' She smiled and gently took her daughter's arm. She was good at consoling and advising other women, she had had a lifetime of that in her life in Spain. 'What were you thinking when you were walking?'

'Oh . . .' Raphaella exhaled slowly. 'About nothing special . . . some things in San Francisco . . .' She smiled at her mother, but her eyes stayed tired and sad.

'Your friend?' Suddenly Raphaella stopped walking, and her mother slipped an arm around her daughter's shoulders. 'Don't get angry. I talked to your father tonight. I was very worried . . . you look so upset.' But there was no reproach in her voice, only sorrow and gently she led Raphaella along down the winding path. 'I'm sorry that something like that has happened.'

Raphaella didn't say anything for a long time, and then she nodded. 'So am I.' She wasn't sorry for herself, but in a way she was sorry for Alex. She always had been, right from the start. 'He's a wonderful man. He deserves much more than I can give him.'

'You should think about that, Raphaella. Weigh it in your conscience. Your father is afraid of the disgrace, but I don't think that's what is really so important. I think you ought to think if you're ruining someone's life. Are you destroying this man? You know,' she smiled gently and squeezed Raphaella's shoulders again, 'everyone once or twice in a lifetime . . . commits an indiscretion. But it's important that it is not with someone who can be hurt by it. Someone you know well usually makes more sense, sometimes even a cousin, maybe someone else who is also a married man. But to play with people who are free, who want more from you, who have hopes for something you can't give is a cruelty, Raphaella. More than that, it's irresponsible. If that is what you are doing, then it is wrong for you to love this man.'

Her mother had just added yet another burden to the enormous weight she had felt pressing down on her since she'd arrived. After she had recovered from her anger at the words of her father, she had been overwhelmed with depression at the truth of at least some of his accusations. The fact that she might be taking something from John Henry, in the way of time or spirit or devotion or even just a fraction of a feeling, had worried her all along, and the fact that she was keeping Alex from something more productive had been for her another regret about the relationship from the first.

Now her mother was telling her to have an affair with a cousin or someone as married as she was but not with Alex. She was telling her that loving Alex was being cruel. And suddenly as the emotions poured over her, Raphaella couldn't bear it for a moment longer. She shook her head, squeezed her mother's arm, and ran back along the pathway all the way to the house. Her mother followed more slowly, with tears in her eyes for the anguish she had seen on Raphaella's face.

Chapter 26

The days Raphaella spent at Santa Eugenia that summer
were among the unhappiest she had ever spent there, and
each day weighed on her like a yoke of cast iron which she
wore around her neck. This year even the children didn't
enchant her. They were loud and unruly, constantly played
practical jokes on the grown-ups and annoyed Raphaella in
every possible way. The only bright spot was that they had
loved her stories, but even that didn't seem to matter to her
very much now. She put the manuscripts back in her
suitcase after her first few days there, and refused to tell them
any more stories during the rest of her stay. She wrote two or
three letters to Alex, but suddenly they all seemed stilted and
awkward. It was impossible not to tell him what had
happened, and she didn't want to do that until she had
resolved it all in her own mind. Each time she tried to write
to him, she felt more guilty, each day she felt more oppressed
by her father's and her mother's words.

It was almost a relief when after the first week her father
came for the weekend, and after a formal luncheon at which
everyone at Santa Eugenia was present, thirty-four people
that day, he told Raphaella he wanted to see her in the small
solarium which adjoined his room. When she joined him
there, he looked as ferocious as he had in Paris, and she
unconsciously sat down in a striped green and white chair as
she would have as a child.

'Well, have you come to your senses?' He came directly to
the point, and she fought with herself not to tremble at his
words. It was ridiculous that at her age he should impress
her, but she had spent too many years taking orders from
him not to be impressed by the power he wielded, because he
was her father and because he was a man. 'Have you?'

'I'm not sure I know what you mean, Father. I still don't
agree with your position. What I've been doing has not hurt
John Henry, however much you may disapprove.'

'Really? Then how is his health, Raphaella? It was my understanding that he was not doing very well.'

'He's not doing badly.' Her voice faltered and then she got out of the chair and walked around the room, finally coming to a stop to face her father with what was the truth. 'He is seventy-seven years old, Papa. He has been bedridden, more or less, for almost eight years. He has had a number of strokes, and he has very little desire to go on living the way he is. Can you really blame that on me?'

'If he has so little desire to go on living, can you dare to take a chance with the little desire he has left? Can you dare to take the chance that someone will tell him, and that for him, it will be the last straw? You must be a very brave woman, Raphaella. In your shoes, I would not take that chance. If only because I would not be entirely certain that I could live with myself if I killed him . . . which, I will add, your circumstances might. Or hadn't that thought occurred to you?'

'It has. Often.' She sighed softly. 'But Papa . . . I love . . . this man.'

'Not enough to do what's best for him though. That saddens me. I thought there was more to you than that.'

She eyed him sadly. 'Must I be so perfect, Papa? Must I be so very strong? I have been strong for eight years . . . for eight . . .' But she couldn't go on, she was crying again, and then she looked up at him tremulously, 'Now this is all I have.'

'No.' He spoke firmly. 'You have John Henry. You have no right to more than that. One day, after he is gone, then you can consider other possibilities. But those doors are not open to you now.' He looked at her sternly, 'And I hope, for John Henry's sake, that they are not open to you for a long time.' She bowed her head then for a moment, and then looked up and walked to the door of the little room.

'Thank you, Papa.' She said the words very softly and left the room.

Her father left for Paris the next day, but it was obvious to him as well as to her mother, that some of what they had said to Raphaella appeared to have taken hold. Much of the fight had gone out of her, and finally after four more days at Santa Eugenia, and five more sleepless nights, she got out of bed at five o'clock one morning, went to the desk in her room, and pulled out a piece of paper and a pen. It was not that she could no longer fight her parents, it was that she could no longer fight the inner voice which they had spawned. How could she know that what she was doing was not hurting John Henry? And what they said of Alex was true as well. He had a right to more than she could give him, and perhaps she would not be free to give him more for many years.

She sat at her desk, staring down at the blank paper, knowing what she had to say. Not because of her father or her mother or Kay Willard, she told herself, but because of John Henry, and Alex, and what she owed them. It took her two hours to compose the letter which she could hardly see when she finally signed it with a last stroke of her pen. The tears were pouring down her face so copiously that it was only a blur before her, but the meaning of her words to him was anything but a blur. She had told him that she did not wish to continue. That she had given it all a great deal of thought during her vacation in Spain, that there was no point in their dragging on a love affair that had no future. She had realised now that he was not suited to her, and to the life she would lead one day when she was free. She told him that she was happier in Spain with her family, that this was where she belonged, and that since he was divorced, and she was a Catholic, she could never marry him anyway. She drew on every lie and excuse and insult she could find, but she did not want to leave him with a single doubt about continuing. She wanted to free him completely so that he could find another woman, and not wait for her. She wanted to know that she had given him the final gift of freedom, and if she had to do that by sounding unkind in the letter, then she was willing to do that, for Alex. It was her last gift to him.

But the second letter she wrote was almost harder. It was a letter to Mandy which she sent to Charlotte Brandon's address in New York. It explained that things had changed between her and Alex, that they wouldn't be continuing to see each other when she got back to San Francisco, but that she would always love Mandy, and treasure the months which they had shared.

By the time she finished both letters, it was eight o'clock in the morning, and Raphaella felt as though she had been beaten from midnight until dawn. She put on a thick terry cloth robe and ran silently to the main hall where she left the two letters on a silver platter. Then she walked slowly outside and across the grounds to a remote spot on the beach which she had discovered as a child. She stripped away the robe and the nightgown beneath it, and kicked off the sandals she had worn, and threw her body into the water with a vengeance, swimming as hard and as far as she could. She had just renounced the one thing she lived for, and now she didn't give a damn if she lived or died. She had saved John Henry for another day or a year or a decade or even two, had freed Alex to marry and have babies, and she had nothing, except the emptiness which had consumed her for the last lonely eight years.

She swam as far out as she could manage, and then swam back until every inch of her body ached. Slowly she walked out of the water and back to the bathrobe, and she lay down on it on the sand, her long lean naked limbs gleaming in the morning sunlight as her shoulders shook and she sobbed. She lay there like that for almost an hour, and when she went back to the house, she saw that the servants had taken her two letters off the giant silver salver and taken them into town to mail. It was done.

When Alexander received the letter in San Francisco it mattered little that he had had John Henry's blessings two weeks before. Raphaella had made her own decision, and it was obvious when she wouldn't take his frantic phone calls that nothing would change her mind. Alex had lived with the possibility that John Henry might force her to end it, after Kay's letter but not that Raphaella would end the affair herself for no reason at all, except that it was what she wanted. As he sat, bereft, John Henry's blessing seemed suddenly cruel.

Chapter 27

When she left Spain and returned to San Francisco the days seemed endless to Raphaella. She sat by John Henry's side for hours every day, reading, thinking, sometimes talking. She read him parts of the newspaper, tried to unearth books which had once pleased him, sat in the garden with him, and read books of her own while he napped more and more. But each hour, each day, each moment dragged past her with lead weights attached to them. It seemed to her each morning that she would never get through one more day. And by nightfall, she was exhausted by the effort it had taken, just to sit there, barely moving, her own voice droning in her ears, and then his soft snore as he slept while she read.

It was a life of slow torture to which she felt condemned now. It was different than it had been before she'd met Alex, the previous year. Then she hadn't known anything else, she hadn't had the joy of fixing up a room for Mandy, hadn't baked bread, or pottered in the garden, or waited impatiently for him to come home, she hadn't raced laughing up the stairs beside Mandy, or stood looking at the view with Alex just before the dawn. Now there was nothing, only endlessly bleak days during the warm summer, sitting in the garden watching great puffs of white cloud roll by overhead, or sitting in her room late at night listening to the foghorns bleating on the bay.

Sometimes she was reminded of her earlier summers in Santa Eugenia, or even summers she had spent away with John Henry some ten years before. But now there was no swimming, no laughing, no running on a beach with the wind in her hair. There was nothing, no one, only John Henry, and he was different too than he had been a year before. He was so much more tired, worn out really, and introverted, so much less interested in the world beyond his bed. He didn't care any more about the political situation, about large oil deals with the Arabs, or potential disasters that intrigued the world. He didn't give a damn about his old firm or any of his partners. He really didn't care about anything, and he was querulous suddenly if the least little thing went wrong. It was as though he resented everything and everybody, hating them finally for the agonies of the past eight years. He was tired of dying slowly, he told Raphaella one morning. 'If I'm going to die sooner or later anyway, then I might as well do it right now.'

He talked constantly now of wishing it was over, of hating the nurses, of not wanting to be pushed around in his chair. He didn't want to be bothered by anyone, he insisted, and it was only with Raphaella that he made the supreme effort, as though he didn't want to punish her for the way he felt. But it was obvious to everyone who saw him that he was desperately unhappy, and it never failed to remind Raphaella of her father's words. Maybe he'd been right after all that John Henry needed her full attention. Certainly he did now, even if he hadn't before. Or maybe it was because she had nothing else to do now that he only seemed to need her so much more. But he seemed to swallow up every moment, just because she felt obliged to sit with him, to be near him, to sit and watch him while he slept. It was as though she had made one last commitment, to give up her whole life for this man. And at the same time, it was as though John Henry had finally given up his will to live. Raphaella felt that weigh on her more now too. If he was tired of living, what could she do to make him want to stay alive? To infuse him with her youth, with her own vitality, with her will to live? But her life was no happier than John Henry's. Since she had given up Alex, there was no longer any reason which Raphaella could see which justified her existence, except as a kind of life-giving serum for John Henry. There were days when she thought that she couldn't bear it any more.

She almost never went out any more, and when she did, she had the chauffeur drive her somewhere so that she could take a long walk. She hadn't been downtown since returning from Spain earlier that summer, and she was afraid to wander in the neighbourhood, even in the evening, for fear that somehow, somewhere Alex would be there. He had gotten her letter the day before she had left Santa Eugenia, and she had sat terribly still for a long moment when the butler told her there was a call from America, wanting it to be Alex, and yet fearing that at the same time. She didn't dare refuse the call for fear that it was something about John Henry.

So she went to the phone with her heart pounding and her hands trembling, and when she had heard his voice at the other end, she had closed her eyes tightly and tried to fight back the tears. She told him very quietly and calmly that she had come to her senses here, at Santa Eugenia, and that there was nothing more to say that she hadn't already said in the letter he had just received. He had accused her of being crazy, had said that someone must have pressured her into it, asked her if it had anything to do with something Kay might have said in New York. She assured him that it was none of those things, that it was her own decision, and when she had hung up the phone, she had cried for several hours. Giving up Alex was the most painful decision of a lifetime, but she could no longer take a chance that her divided allegiance would kill John Henry, nor would she continue to deprive Alex of all that he deserved with someone else. In the end her father and Kay had won. And now all that remained was for Raphaella to live up to it for the rest of her days. By the end of the summer she saw the years stretching ahead of her, like a lifetime of bleak empty rooms.

In September, as John Henry began to sleep for several hours in the morning, just to keep herself busy she picked up the manuscript of the children's books again. Feeling silly for even putting it together, she finally typed it, and sent the final version to a publisher of children's books in New York. It had been an idea Charlotte Brandon had given her, and it seemed vaguely silly to even do it, but she had nothing to lose, and even less to do.

With the book completed, Raphaella once again was haunted by her memories of last summer. Above all, there were times when she resented her father terribly, and she wondered if she would ever forgive him for the things he had said. He had only relented slightly when she told him on the phone from Santa Eugenia that she had 'taken care of everything in San Francisco'. He had told her that it was nothing she should be praised for, that it was only her duty, and that it had pained him to use such force to alter a course which she should have altered herself long before. He pointed out that she had disappointed him severely, and even her mother's gentler words left her, in the end, with a sense of having failed.

It was this feeling that she carried with her into the autumn in San Francisco, and which made her turn down her mother's offer to meet her in New York for a few days when she was there on her way to Brazil with the usual horde. Raphaella no longer felt that she should do things like go to New York to meet her mother. Her place was with John Henry, and she would not leave him again until the day he died. Who knew if her months of ricocheting between her own home and Alex's had not in some way speeded John Henry towards his death. It would have been useless of course to tell her that any speed in that direction would have been welcomed by no one as much as by John Henry himself. Now she almost never left him except for her occasional walks.

Her mother had been vaguely disturbed at Raphaella's refusal to join her at the Carlyle and wondered briefly if she were still angry at her father for what had passed between them in July. But Raphaella's letter of refusal didn't sound like she was pouting. It sounded more as though she were oddly withdrawn. Her mother promised herself that she would call her from New York and make sure that nothing was the matter, but with her sisters and her cousins and her nieces and their constant errands and shopping and the time difference, she left for Rio de Janeiro without ever having had a chance to call.

It wouldn't have mattered to Raphaella anyway. She had no desire to talk to her mother or her father, and had decided that summer that she would not return to Europe again either, until after John Henry had passed on. He seemed to be living in a state of suspended animation, sleeping most of the time, depressed when he wasn't, refusing to eat, and seeming to lose whatever abilities had remained. The doctor told her that all of it was normal, in a man of his age, with the shocks he had suffered from the strokes. It was only surprising that the determination of his spirit had not been more acute before. It seemed only ironic to Raphaella that as she devoted herself to him fully he seemed to be at his worst. But the doctor told her that he might also get a little better, that perhaps after a few months of lethargy, he might inexplicably perk up. It was certainly obvious that Raphaella was doing everything to entertain him, and now she even began to cook small gourmet dishes in order to tempt his palate and induce him to eat. It was a life about which most people would have had nightmares, and which Raphaella seemed not even to notice. Having given up the only thing which she had cared about, and relinquished the only two people she had loved in a long time, Alexander and Amanda, it no longer really mattered to her what she did with her time.

November disappeared like the months before it, and it was December when she got the letter from the publishing house in New York. They were enchanted with the book she had sent them, surprised that she didn't have an agent, and wanted to pay her five thousand dollars as an advance for the book, which they would have illustrated and hoped to release the following summer and fall. For a moment she stared at the letter in amazement, and then for the first time in a long time, she broke out in a broad smile. Almost like a schoolgirl she raced up the staircase with the letter to show John Henry. When she got there, she found him sleeping in his wheelchair, his mouth open, his chin on his chest, making a soft purr. She stood there for a time, watching him, and then suddenly felt desperately lonely. She had wanted so much to tell him, and there was no one else to tell. Once again, she felt a familiar pang for Alex, but she pushed the thought instantly away, telling herself that by now he had found someone else to replace her, that Mandy was happy, and Alex might even be married or engaged. In another year he might even have children. She felt for the hundredth time that she had done a good deed.

She folded the letter and went back downstairs. She

realised too that John Henry had known nothing about the stories she'd been concocting for the children, and he would find it very strange if she brought him the news of a book now. It was better to say nothing. And of course her mother wouldn't be interested, and she had no desire to write to tell her father. In the end there was no one to tell, so she sat down and answered the letter, thanked them for the advance, which she accepted, and then later wondered why she had. It was an ego trip which suddenly seemed very foolish, and after she gave the letter of acceptance to the chauffeur to mail she was sorry she had done it. She was so used to denying herself everything she wanted that even that little treat now seemed out of place.

Feeling annoyed with herself for doing something so silly, she later asked the chauffeur to drive her out to the beach, while John Henry slept away the afternoon. She just wanted to walk in the fresh air, and see the dogs and the children, feel the wind on her face and get away from the stale air of the house. She had to remind herself that it was almost Christmas. But it didn't really matter this year. John Henry was too tired to care if they celebrated it or not. Briefly she found herself dwelling on the Christmas she had shared with Alex and Mandy and then once again forced the memories out of her head. She seldom even allowed herself even those now.

It was almost four o'clock when the chauffeur pulled the car up alongside the vans and the pick-ups and the old jalopies, and smiling at the incongruous vision she knew she presented, she slid into a pair of black Spanish loafers she often wore at Santa Eugenia, and slipped out of the car into the stiff breeze. She was wearing a little curly lamb jacket with a red turtleneck sweater and a pair of grey slacks. She didn't dress as elaborately as she used to any more. To sit beside John Henry while he slept, or dine on a tray in his room as he gazed sightlessly at the news on the television, there didn't seem to be much point in getting dressed.

Tom, the chauffeur, watched Raphaella disappear down the stairs on to the long sandy beach, and then he glimpsed her again as she wandered near where the surf broke. Eventually he could no longer distinguish her from the others, and he climbed back into the car, turned on the radio, and lit a cigarette. By then, Raphaella was far down the beach, watching three labradors chase each other in and out of the water, and a group of young people wearing blankets and blue jeans were drinking wine and playing their guitars.

The sound of their singing followed her further down the beach as she wandered and at last, she sat down on a log and took a deep breath of the salt air. It felt so good to be there, to be out in the world for a few moments, to at least see others living even if she could not do much living herself. She just sat there and watched people passing, arm in arm, kissing, side by side, talking and laughing or jogging past each other. They all seemed to be bent on going somewhere and she wondered where they all went when the sun went down.

It was then that she found herself watching a man who was running. He came from far down the beach in a straight line, running almost like a machine without stopping, until finally, still moving with the smoothness of a dancer he slowed to a walk and kept coming down the beach. The fluidity of his movement in the distance had intrigued her, and as he came closer, she kept her eyes on him for a long time. She was distracted by a group of children, and when she looked for him again she saw that he was wearing a red jacket and was very tall, but his features were indistinct until he came still closer. Suddenly she gasped as she saw who he was. She just sat there staring, startled, unable to move to turn so that he wouldn't see her face. She just sat there watching, as Alex came closer and then stopped as his eyes fell on her. He didn't move for a long time, and then slowly, deliberately, walked towards where she sat. She wanted to run away, to vanish, but after seeing him run down the beach she knew she didn't have a chance and she had ventured miles from where she had left the car. Now relentlessly, with his face set, he came towards her, until he stood before her, looking down at her sitting on the log.

Neither of them spoke for a long moment and then, as though in spite of himself, he smiled. 'Hello. How are you?' It was difficult to believe that they hadn't seen each other in five months. As Raphaella looked up at the face she had seen in her mind so clearly and so often, it seemed as though they had been together only the day before.

'I'm fine. How are you?'

He sighed and didn't answer. 'Are you fine, Raphaella? I mean really . . .' She nodded this time, wondering why he hadn't answered when she asked him how he was. Wasn't he happier? Hadn't he found someone to replace her? Wasn't that why she had released him? Surely her sacrifice had instantly borne fruit. 'I still don't understand why you did it.' He looked at her bluntly, showing no inclination to leave. He had waited five months to confront her. He wouldn't have left now if they'd dragged him away.

'I told you. We're too different.'

'Are we? Two different worlds, is that it?' He sounded bitter. 'Who told you that? Your father? Or someone else? One of your cousins in Spain?' No, she wanted to tell him, your sister fixed it for us. Your sister, and my father with his goddamn surveillance, and threatening to tell John Henry, whether it killed him or not . . . that, and my conscience. I want you to have the babies that I'll never have . . .

'No. No one told me to do it. I just knew it was the right thing to do.'

'Oh really? Don't you think we might have discussed it? You know, like grown-ups. Where I come from, people discuss things before they make major decisions that affect other people's lives.'

She forced herself to look at him coldly. 'It was beginning to affect my husband, Alex.'

'Was it? Strange that you only noticed that when you were six thousand miles away from him in Spain.'

She looked at him pleadingly then, the agony of the past five months beginning to show in her eyes. He had already noticed how much thinner her face was, how dark the circles beneath the eyes, how frail were her hands. 'Why are you doing this now, Alex?'

'Because you never gave me the chance to in July.' He had called her once in San Francisco, and she had refused to take the call. 'Didn't you know what that letter would do to me? Did you think of that at all?' And suddenly as she saw his face, she understood better. First Rachel had left him, giving him no chance to win against an invisible opponent, a hundred thousand dollars a year job in New York. And then Raphaella had done almost the same thing, flaunting John Henry and their 'differences' as an excuse to walk out. Suddenly she saw it all differently and she ached at what she saw in his eyes. Beneath his piercing gaze she dropped her eyes now, and touched the sand with one long thin hand.

'I'm sorry . . . Oh God . . . I'm so sorry . . .' She looked up at him then and there were tears in her eyes. And the pain he saw there brought him to his knees beside her on the sand.

'Do you have any idea how much I love you?'

She turned her head away then, and put a hand up as though to stop him from speaking, whispering softly, 'Alex, don't . . .' But he took the hand in his own, and then with his other hand brought her face back until she looked at him again.

'Did you hear me? I love you. I did then, and I do now, and I always will. And maybe I don't understand you, maybe there are differences between us, but I can learn to understand those differences better, Raphaella. I can if you give me the chance.'

'But why? Why only a half life with me when you can have a whole one somewhere else?'

'Is that why you did it?' At times he had thought so, but he had never been able to understand why she had severed the tie so quickly, so bluntly. It had to be more than just that.

'Partly.' She answered him honestly now, her eyes looked in his. 'I wanted you to have more.'

'All I wanted was you . . .' And then he spoke more softly. 'That's all I want now.' But she shook her head slowly in answer.

'You can't have that.' And then after a long pause. 'It's not right.'

'Why not, dammit?' There was fire in his eyes when he asked the question. 'Why? Because of your husband? How can you give up all that you are for a man who is almost

217

dead, for a man who, from what you yourself have told me, has always wanted your happiness, and would probably love you enough to set you free if he could?'

Alex knew John Henry had in a sense set Raphaella free already. He couldn't tell Raphaella of that meeting however. Her face bore witness to the terrible strain she was suffering under. To add to that, to tell her that John Henry knew of their relationship, was unthinkable.

But Raphaella wouldn't listen. 'That wasn't the deal I made. For better or worse . . . in sickness and in health . . . until death do us part . . . Not boredom, not strokes, not Alex . . . I can't let any of that hinder my obligations.'

'Fuck your obligations.' He exploded and Raphaella looked shocked and shook her head.

'No, if I don't honour what I owe him, he'll die. I know that now. My father told me that this summer and he was right. He's barely hanging on now, for God's sake.'

'But that has nothing to do with you dammit, don't you see that? Are you going to let your father run your life too? Are you going to be pushed around by your "duties" and "obligations" and your sense of "*noblesse oblige*"? What about *you*, Raphaella? What about what *you* want? Do you ever allow yourself to think of that?' The truth was that she tried not to think of it. Not any more.

'You don't understand, Alex.' She spoke so softly that he could barely hear her in the wind. He sat next to her on the log, their bodies so close that it made Raphaella shiver. 'Do you want my jacket?' She shook her head. And then he went on. 'I do understand. I think you did something insane this summer, you made one giant sacrifice in order to atone for what you thought was one giant sin.'

But again she shook her head. 'I just can't do it to John Henry.' Alex could not, try as he might, tell her that the one constant in her life – her relationship with her husband – had already been altered.

'Do what for God's sake? Spend a few hours away from the house? Do you have to chain yourself to his bedpost?'

She nodded slowly. 'For the moment, yes.' And then, as though she owed it to him to tell him, she went on. 'My father was having me followed, Alex. He threatened to tell

John Henry. And that would have killed him. I had no choice.'

'Oh my God.' He stared at her in amazement. And what she hadn't even told him was that the surveillance was due to a letter from his sister Kay. 'Why would he do a thing like that?'

'Tell John Henry? I'm not sure he would. But I couldn't take the chance. He said he would, so I had to do what I did.'

'But why would he have you followed?' She shrugged and looked him in the eye.

'It doesn't really matter. He just did.'

'And you, you sit there, and wait.'

She closed her eyes. 'Don't say it like that. I'm not waiting. You make it sound as though I'm waiting for him to die, and I'm not. I'm simply doing what I set out to do fifteen years ago, be his wife.'

'Don't you think circumstances warrant a little bending of the rules on this one, Raphaella?' His eyes pleaded with her, but once again she shook her head. 'All right, I won't push you.' He realised again how much pressure she must have been under in Spain. It was hard to imagine her father having her followed and threatening to tell her husband that she was having an affair.

Alex pondered with well-hidden fury what he would have liked to do to Raphaella's father, and then he looked her in the eye. 'I'm going to just leave it open. I love you. I want you. On any terms you want, whenever you can. If that's tomorrow, or in ten years. Come knock on my door and I'll be there. Do you understand that, Raphaella? Do you know that I mean what I'm saying?'

'I do, but I think it's crazy for you to do that. You have to lead a life.'

'And you don't?'

'That's different, Alex. You're not married, I am.' They sat silent for a while on the log, looking out at the sea. It felt good just being there together again, after so long. Raphaella wanted to prolong the moment, but the light was already growing dim and the fog was beginning to roll in.

'Is he still having you followed?'

'I don't think so. There's no reason to now.' She smiled gently at Alex, and wished that she could just touch his cheek. But she knew that she couldn't let herself do that. Never again. And what he was saying was madness. He couldn't sit around waiting for her for the rest of his life.

'Come on.' He stood up and held a hand out to her. 'I'll walk you back to your car.' And then he smiled at her. 'Or is that not such a great idea?'

'It's not.' She smiled in answer. 'But you can walk me back part of the way.' It was getting dark quickly enough that she was not enchanted at the prospect of walking back to her car alone. She looked up at him with a gentle look of enquiry, her brows knit, her eyes seeming even larger now that her face was thinner than it had been. 'How is Amanda?'

Alex looked down at Raphaella with a gentle smile. 'She misses you . . . almost as much as I do . . .'

Raphaella didn't answer. 'How did the summer go?'

'She lasted exactly five days with Kay. My darling sister had planned the entire month so that she would be showing Mandy off to the voters every moment. Mandy tried it on for size and told her to shove it.'

'Did she come home?'

'No, my mother took her to Europe early.' He shrugged. 'I think they had a nice time.'

'Didn't she tell you?'

He looked long and hard at Raphaella. 'I don't think I heard anything anyone told me until about November.' She nodded, and they walked on. And then at last she stopped.

'I should walk on alone from here.'

'Raphaella . . .' He hesitated, but then decided he had to ask her. 'Can I see you some time? Just for lunch . . . or a drink . . .'

But she shook her head. 'I couldn't do that.'

'Why not?'

'Because we'd both want more than that, and you know it. It has to be the way it is now, Alex.'

'Why? With me so lonely for you I can't see straight, and you wasting away? Is that how it has to be? Was that why your father threatened to tell John Henry, so he could be assured that we'd both live like this? Don't you want more, Raphaella?' And then unable to stop himself, he reached out and took her so gently in his arms. 'Don't you remember how it was?'

Her eyes filled with tears and she buried her face in his shoulder, nodding, but not wanting to see his face. 'Yes . . . yes . . . I remember . . . but that's over . . .'

'No, it's not. I still love you. I will always love you.'

'You must not do that.' She looked up at him finally, with agony in her eyes. 'You must forget all that, Alex. You have to.'

Alex said nothing, and only shook his head. 'What are you doing at Christmas?' It was an odd question and Raphaella looked at him, puzzled, not understanding what he had in mind.

'Nothing. Why?'

'My mother is taking Amanda to Hawaii. They leave at five in the afternoon on Christmas Day. Why don't you come over in the evening for a cup of coffee? I promise, I won't push you or bug you, ask you for any promises. I just want to see you. It would mean a lot to me. Please, Raphaella . . .' His voice trailed off and she stood there, and then finally, painfully, agonisingly, she forced herself to shake her head.

'No.' It was barely more than a whisper. 'No.'

'I won't let you do this. I'll be there. Alone. At my place on Christmas night. Think about it. I'll be waiting.'

'No . . . Alex . . . please.'

'It doesn't matter. If you don't come, it's all right.'

'But I don't want you to sit there. And I won't come.'

He said nothing but there was a hopeful light in his eyes. 'I'll be there.' He smiled then. 'Goodbye now.' He kissed the top of her head then and patted her shoulders with his big hands. 'Take care, babe.' He stood there and she said nothing as slowly she turned away.

She turned back once to see him standing there, in his red parka with the wind in his dark hair. 'I won't come, Alex.'

'It doesn't matter. I want to be there. In case you do.' And as she walked away towards the stairway which would lead her back to the car, he shouted after her. 'See you on Christmas Day.'

As he watched her climb into the limousine he thought of her devotion to John Henry, to him, to all her obligations. He would let her make her own decision.

But he could not leave her.

Chapter 28

The small tree they had put on the card table across the room twinkled merrily as Raphaella and John Henry ate their turkey on the all too familiar trays. He seemed quieter than usual, and Raphaella wondered if the holiday depressed him, if it reminded him of ski vacations in his youth, or the trips he had taken with Raphaella, or the years when his son had been a boy and there had been a giant tree in the foyer downstairs.

'John Henry . . . darling . . . are you all right?' She leaned over and spoke to him gently, and he nodded, but he didn't answer. He was thinking of Alex and their talk. Something was wrong, but he'd been so depressed over the last months that Raphaella's condition had remained unnoticed. She usually fooled him with her extraordinary determination to keep his spirits up, camouflaging her own pain. He lay back against the pillows with a sigh.

'I'm so tired of all this, Raphaella.'

'What, Christmas?' She looked surprised. The only sign of it was the tiny tree in his bedroom, but maybe the light hurt his eyes.

'No, all of it. Living . . . eating dinner . . . watching the news when nothing is ever new. Breathing . . . talking or sleeping . . .' He looked at her bleakly, and there was no sign of anything even remotely happy in his eyes.

'You're not tired of me, are you?' She smiled gently at him and made a move to kiss his cheek, but he turned away.

'Don't . . . do that.' His voice was soft and sad, muffled by his pillows.

'John Henry . . . what's wrong?' She looked surprised and hurt as she watched him, and slowly he turned to face her again.

'How can you ask that? How can you . . . live like this . . . any more? How can you bear it? . . . sometimes I think . . . about the old men . . . who died in India . . . where they

223

burned . . . their young wives on the funeral pyre. I'm no better than that, Raphaella.'

'Don't say that . . . don't be silly . . . I love you . . .'

'Then you're crazy.' He didn't sound amused but angry. 'And if you are, then I'm not. Why don't you go somewhere? Take a vacation . . . do something, for God's sake . . . but don't just sit here, wasting your life. Mine is over, Raphaella . . .' His voice dropped to a whisper. 'Mine is gone. It has been for years.'

'That's not true.' Tears sprang to her eyes as she tried to convince him. The look on his face broke her heart.

'It is true . . . and you have . . . to face it. I've been dead . . . for years . . . But the worst part of it is . . . I'm killing you too. Why don't you go home to Paris for a while?' He had again wondered what was happening between her and Alex but he didn't want to ask. He didn't want her to know that he knew.

'Why?' She looked astonished. 'Why Paris?' To her father? After what had happened during the summer? The very idea made her ill. But John Henry looked adamant at her from his bed.

'I want you . . . to go away . . . for a while.'

She shook her head firmly. 'I won't go.'

'Yes, you will.' They were like children arguing, but neither of them was amused, and neither of them smiled.

'No, I will not.'

'Dammit, I want you to go somewhere.'

'Fine, then I'll go for a walk. But this is my home too, and you can't send me away.' She took the tray from him and set it down on the floor. 'I think you're just bored with me, John Henry.' She tried to tease him, but his eye would not catch the sparkle of mischief beginning to glow in hers. 'Maybe what you need is a new sexy nurse.' But he wasn't amused. He just lay there glowering, it was part of the querulousness that she noticed more and more.

'Stop talking rubbish.'

'I'm not talking rubbish.' She spoke to him gently, leaning forward earnestly in her chair. 'I love you and I don't want to go away.'

'Well, I want you to go away.'

She sat back in silence for a while as he watched her and then suddenly he spoke softly in the quiet room. 'I want to die, Raphaella.' He closed his eyes as he continued to speak. 'That's all I want to do. And why don't I ... God, why don't I?' He opened his eyes and looked at her again. 'Tell me that. Where the hell is justice?' He looked at her accusingly. 'Why am I still alive?'

'Because I need you.' She said it softly and he shook his head and turned his face away again. He said nothing for a very long time then, and when she approached the bed carefully she saw that he had fallen asleep. It made her sad to realise how unhappy he was. It was as though she weren't doing enough.

The nurse came in on tiptoe and Raphaella motioned to her that John Henry had fallen asleep. They stepped out for a whispered conference. The consensus was that he was probably asleep for the night. He had had a long, difficult day, and Christmas had made no difference. Nothing really did any more. He was sick of it all.

'I'll be in my room if you need me.' She whispered it to the nurse, and then walked pensively down the hall. Poor John Henry, what a rotten existence. And in Raphaella's mind the injustice was not that he was still living, but that he had had the strokes at all. Without them, at his age, he could still have been vital. Slower perhaps than he had been at fifty or sixty, a little more tired, but happy and busy and alive. But the way things were, he had nothing, and he was right in a way. He was barely alive.

She walked slowly into her little study, thinking of him, and then letting her mind drift to other things. Her family celebrating Christmas at Santa Eugenia, her father, and then inevitably the Christmas she had shared with Alexander and Amanda the year before. And then for the hundredth time since that morning, she remembered what he had said to her three weeks before on the beach. 'I'll be waiting ... I'll be there ...' She could still hear him say it. And as she sat there, alone in her study, she wondered again if he really was. It was only seven-thirty, a respectable hour, and she could easily have gone for a walk, but where would it lead her? What would happen if she went there? Was it smart, was it wise? Did it make sense at all? She knew that it didn't, that her place was there in John Henry's huge empty house. As the hours ticked slowly onwards, she suddenly felt she had to go there, just for a moment, for half an hour, just to see him. It was madness and she knew it, but at nine-thirty she flew out of her chair, unable to stay in the house a moment longer. She had to go.

She quickly slipped a red wool coat over the simple black dress she had been wearing, put on long thin black leather boots, slipped a black leather handbag on her shoulder and ran a comb through her hair. She felt her heart flutter at the prospect of seeing him, reproaching herself for going but suddenly smiling as she thought ahead to the moment when he would open the door. She left a note in her room that she had gone for a walk and to drop in on a friend, in case someone came to find her, and her feet fairly flew as she hurried the few blocks to the little house she hadn't seen in five and a half months.

When she saw the house she simply stood there, looking at it, and she sighed softly. She felt as though she had been lost for almost half a year and she had finally found her way home. Unable to suppress the smile on her face, she crossed the street and rang the doorbell, and then suddenly there was the rapid thump of his footstep on the stairs. There was a pause, and then the door opened and he stood there, unable to believe what he saw, until suddenly the smile in her eyes was matched by his.

'Merry Christmas.' They said in unison and then laughed together as he stood aside with a bow and then rose to face her with a warm smile. 'Welcome home, Raphaella.' Saying not a word, she walked inside.

There was furniture in the living-room now. He and Mandy had put it together, gone to auctions and garage sales and department stores and art galleries and thrift shops, and what they had put together was a comfortable combination of French Provincial, Early American, a handsome fur throw, soft French impressionist paintings, lots of silver and some pewter, some handsome old books, and there were huge jugs filled with flowers on the tables, and there were plants in every corner and crawling all over the little marble mantelpiece in the double parlour. The couch was off-white, the little throw cushions were made of fur and tapestry and there were several needlepoints that Amanda had made for Alex while they were doing the house. With Raphaella gone she was even closer to her uncle, and felt an obligation to 'take care of him' now that there was no one else who would. She nagged him about eating the right foods, taking his vitamins, getting his sleep, driving too fast, working too hard, and not weeding the garden. He teased her about her boyfriends, her cooking, her make-up, her wardrobe, and yet somehow managed to make her feel that she was the prettiest girl alive. Together they ran a nice little household, and as she stepped across the threshold, Raphaella could feel the love that they shared, it exuded from every corner of the room.

'Alex, this is lovely.'

'Isn't it? Mandy did most of it after school.' He looked proud of his absent niece as he led Raphaella into the living-room, and it was something of a relief to sit in a room that had not been one they had shared. She had been somewhat nervous that he would take her up to the bedroom to sit in front of the fireplace and she couldn't have borne the memories there, or in the study, or even in the kitchen downstairs. This was perfect, because it was warm and pretty, and it was new.

He offered her coffee and brandy. She accepted the former, declined the latter, and sat down on the pretty little couch, admiring the details of the room again. He was back in a minute with the coffee, and she saw that his hands were trembling as badly as hers when he set down the cup.

'I didn't really know if you'd be here,' she began nervously, 'but I decided to take a chance.'

He eyed her seriously from a chair next to the couch. 'I told you I would be. And I meant it, Raphaella. You should know that by now.' She nodded and sipped the hot espresso.

'How was Christmas?'

'All right.' He smiled and shrugged. 'It was a big event for Mandy, and my mother flew in last night to take her to Hawaii. She's been promising her that trip for years, and this seemed a good time. She just finished a book and she

227

could use the rest too. As the saying goes, she's not getting any younger.'

'Your mother?' Raphaella looked both shocked and amused. 'She'll never be old.' And then she remembered something she had forgotten to tell him when they met on the beach. 'I'm having a book published too,' and then she blushed and laughed softly, 'though nothing as important as a novel.'

'Your children's book?' His eyes lit up with pleasure and she nodded.

'They just told me a few weeks ago.'

'Did you use an agent?' She shook her head.

'No. Just beginner's luck, I guess.' They smiled at each other for a long moment and then Alex sat back in his chair.

'I'm glad you're here, Raphaella. I've wanted to show you this room for a long time.'

'And I've been wanting to tell you about the book.' She smiled gently. It was as though they had both retrieved a friend. But what would they do now? They couldn't resume what they once had. Raphaella knew that. It would rock the boat too badly, with Kay, with her father, her mother, John Henry. She wished that she could tell him what the previous summer had been like, what kind of a nightmare it had been for her.

'What were you thinking about just then?' She had looked devastated as she stared into the fire.

She looked up at him honestly. 'Last summer.' She sighed softly. 'It was such an awful time.'

He nodded, looking pensive too, and then he sighed with a small smile. 'I'm just happy you've come back at all, and that we can talk. That was the hardest part for me, not being able to talk to you any more . . . or see you . . . knowing you wouldn't be here when I got home. Mandy said that was the hardest part for her too.' What he said turned the knife in Raphaella's heart and she looked away from him so he wouldn't see the pain in her eyes. 'What do you do now Raphaella?' His voice was gentle, and she stared pensively into the fire.

'I'm with John Henry most of the time. He hasn't been well at all in the past few months.'

'It must be hard for both of you.'

'Mostly for him.'

'And you?' He eyed her pointedly and she didn't answer. But then, without saying more, he leaned towards her and gently kissed her lips. She didn't stop him, she didn't think about what they were doing. She just kissed him, gently at first, and then with the passion and the sorrow and the loneliness and the aching for him that had drowned her since the summer before. It was as though it all washed over her with that first kiss, and she could feel him battling with his own passions too.

'Alex . . . I can't . . .' Not again. She couldn't start this again but he nodded.

'I know, babe. It's all right.' They sat there for a while, talking, looking into the fire, talking about themselves, about each other, about what had happened to them, and what they had felt, and then suddenly they were talking about other things, about people, about things that had amused them, about funny moments, as though for six months they had stored it all. It was three in the morning when Raphaella left him, at the corner around the bend from her house. He had insisted on walking her home. And then, like a schoolboy he hesitated briefly and decided to plunge in. 'Can I see you again, Raphaella? Just like this . . .' He didn't want to frighten her away again, and he had just glimpsed the pressures she lived with, both real, and in her own mind. She seemed to think about it, but only briefly, and she nodded.

'Maybe we could go for a walk on the beach?'

'Tomorrow?'

She laughed at the question and nodded. 'Very well.'

'I'll pick you up right here and we can go in my car.' It would be Saturday, and he was free. 'Twelve o'clock?'

'Okay.' Feeling very young and girlish, she smiled at him and waved, and then she was gone, grinning to herself all the way home. She didn't think of John Henry, or her father, or Kay Willard, or anyone else. She thought only of Alexander . . . Alex Hale . . . and of seeing him at noon the next day and going to the beach.

Chapter 29

By the end of a week, Alex and Raphaella were meeting every afternoon, either for a walk on the beach, or to sit lazily in front of the fire, drinking espresso and talking about life. She showed him her contract for the book when it arrived from New York, and he told her about his latest cases, and they went back to Fort Point. They shared afternoon hours when he wasn't working, and a few hours in the evening after John Henry went to bed. They were always hours when she couldn't be with John Henry because he was sleeping, so she didn't feel that she was stealing a single precious life-giving moment from him. She gave to Alex the time which was her own, a half hour here, an hour there, a spare moment, to walk and breathe and think and be. They were some of the happiest hours they had spent together, hours in which they discovered each other once again. Only this time they discovered more than they had a year earlier, or perhaps it was that they had both grown so much in the time they were alone. In both cases, the sense of loss had been staggering, yet it had prodded each of them in different ways. But the relationship between them was still very tenuous, it was all very new and they were both afraid. Raphaella was terrified to create the same cataclysmic disaster she had once before, arousing his sister's ire, her own father's, and the problem of keeping Alex from a fuller relationship with somone else still remained. But Alex was only frightened of scaring her off again. He had, after all, John Henry's blessing, so he had no guilt at all. They advanced carefully, inching slowly towards each other, until the day after New Year's when she came over at two in the afternoon, after John Henry had declared that he wanted to sleep all day, and he seemed bent on doing just that.

Raphaella wandered over to see Alex, rang the doorbell, not even sure that he was home, and he opened it to her in jeans and a comfortable old turtleneck sweater, with a look of immense pleasure to see her standing at the door.

'What a nice surprise. What are you doing here?'

'I just thought I'd come to visit. Am I disturbing you?' With a blush, she suddenly realised that she had taken a great deal for granted, he could have had some woman upstairs in his room. But he instantly read the look on her face and chuckled.

'No, Madam. You are not "disturbing" me at all. Want a cup of coffee?' She nodded, and followed him downstairs to the kitchen.

'Who's been doing those?' She waved a hand at the shining copper pots as she slid into a kitchen chair.

'I have.'

'Have you really?'

'Of course.' And then he smiled at her. 'I have many talents you don't know about.'

'Really? Like what?' He handed her a cup of warm coffee and she took a sip as he watched her happily from his chair.

'I'm not sure I should give up all my secrets at once.'

They sat quietly together for a while, sipping their coffee and enjoying each other's company, and then they began, as always, to discuss a dozen different things. Their time together always seemed to pass so quickly. Then suddenly he remembered the manuscript to his mother's new book.

'Oh Alex, can I read it?' Raphaella's eyes shone.

'Sure. I have it upstairs. It's all over my desk.'

Her eyes danced with pleasure at the prospect, and abandoning their coffee, she hastily followed him upstairs. She glanced at a few pages, loved what she was reading, and smiled up at Alex. She suddenly realised that this was her first time back in his room. Cautiously then she glanced across the hall at his bedroom, and then silently their eyes met and held. He kissed her then, slowly, artfully, hungrily, and her back arched with pleasure as he held her in his arms. He was waiting for her to stop him, but she didn't as he let his hands begin to rove, and then as though by mutual agreement, they wandered slowly across the hall.

For the first time in his adult life, he was frightened, of what he was doing, of the consequences of what they had just

231

found again. He was so desperately afraid of losing her, but it was Raphaella who whispered softly to him. 'It's all right, Alex.' And then as he peeled off her sweater, 'I love you so much.' It seemed like a ballet as he slowly unclothed her, and then as she took off his clothes as well. They tasted and felt and held and caressed and lingered and it seemed to take them all afternoon to make love, but when at last they lay with each other and their bodies were sated and their minds and hearts were full, they both looked happier than they ever had with each other. Alex looked down at her from one elbow with a smile that she had never seen before.

'Do you know how happy it makes me to see you here?'

She smiled softly. 'I missed you so much, Alex . . . in every possible way.' He nodded and lay down beside her, his fingers roving, his mouth hungry, his loins beginning to tingle, and suddenly he knew that he wanted her again. It was as though he couldn't get enough now, as though she might leave him again and there would never be more. They made love again and again and again in the evening, and then they took a warm bath together, as Raphaella sat in it dreamily with her eyes closed.

'Darling, you are exquisite.'

'And very sleepy.' She opened one eye and smiled. 'I have to wake up and go home.' But it seemed odd to be going anywhere, odder still to call the other house 'home'. This was home again, where Alex was, where they shared their lives and their souls and their bodies and their loving. And she didn't give a damn what her father threatened this time. She would never let Alex go. Let Kay write him another damn letter. Let them all go to hell. She needed this man. And she had a right to him after all.

He kissed her again as they sat there soaking and she teased him that if he touched her again she would call the police. But he was as tired as she was, and as he drove her home, he yawned happily, kissed her once more, and then as always, let her walk the last block alone.

When she let herself into the house, there was a strange stillness, as though all the clocks had stopped somewhere, as though some sound which had existed subliminally in the huge mansion had somehow stopped. She decided that it was only her imagination and pure exhaustion, and with a grin and a yawn she began to climb the stairs. But as she reached the first landing, she suddenly saw two of the maids and two of the nurses clustered in a small group outside John Henry's door. For an instant, her heart skipped a beat and she wondered, and then she stopped at the head of the stairs as they saw her.

'Is something wrong?'

'It's . . .' The nurse looked red-eyed as she faced Raphaella. 'It's your husband, Mrs Phillips.'

'Oh my God.' She said it softly. She knew as she saw them, there was no mistaking the looks on their faces.

'Is he . . .?' She couldn't finish the sentence and the nurse nodded.

'He's gone.' But then overcome by her own emotions, she burst into tears again and was instantly taken into the other nurse's arms.

'How did it happen?' Raphaella approached them slowly, her back very straight and her voice verysoft. Her eyes looked enormous. John Henry had died while she lay in bed with Alex, playing and cavorting and making love. The indecency of it struck her like a slap across the face and in a single instant she remembered the impact of her father's words the previous summer. He had called her a whore. 'Did he have another stroke?'

For an instant, the foursome stood frozen, and then the nurse who had been crying cried louder, and the two maids seemed to instantly disappear. It was then that the second nurse looked at Raphaella, and she knew that something had gone very wrong while she was gone.

'The doctor wants to speak to you, Mrs Phillips. He's been waiting for two hours. We didn't know where you were, but we found the note in your room and assumed that you'd be home soon.' Raphaella felt sick as she stood there.

'Is the doctor still here?'

'He's in Mr Phillips's room, with the body. But they'll be coming to take him away soon. He wants an autopsy just to be certain.' Raphaella stared at her dumbly and then hurried into John Henry's room. She stood very still as she came to the bed and saw him lying there. He looked as though he were sleeping, and once she thought that she saw him move his hand. She didn't even see the doctor as she stood there. All she could see was John Henry, so tired, so shrivelled, so old, and looking only as though he were asleep.

'Mrs Phillips? . . . Raphaella?'

Raphaella spun quickly when she heard the voice beside her, and then sighed when she saw who it was, 'Hello, Ralph.' But then as though drawn by a magnet, her eyes went back to the face of the man she had been married to for fifteen years. She wasn't even sure what she felt yet. Sorrow, emptiness, regret, grief, something, but she was not yet sure what. She didn't really understand that he was gone. Only a few hours before he had said that he was tired, and now he looked like he had gone to sleep.

'Raphaella, let's go in the other room.'

She followed the doctor into the dressing-room which the nurses had so often used, and they stood there together like two conspirators, but he looked unhappy as he stared at Raphaella and it was clear that he had something to say.

'What is it? What is it that no one is telling me? It wasn't a stroke, was it?' Suddenly, she instinctively knew, And the doctor shook his head and confirmed her worst fears.

'No, it wasn't. It was a horrible accident. A terrible mistake, an almost unforgivable thing, except that it wasn't done maliciously, and no one could have known how he felt.'

'What are you trying to tell me?' Her voice was rising, and she felt as though something in her head were going to explode.

'That your husband . . . John Henry . . . the nurse gave him a sleeping pill, and she left the bottle on the night-table . . .' There was a long pause, as she stared at him in horror. 'He took the pills, Raphaella. The whole bottle. He committed suicide. I don't know how else to tell you. But that's what happened.' His voice faltered, and Raphaella felt herself wanting to scream. He had killed himself . . . John Henry had killed himself while she was out screwing Alex . . . she had killed him . . . killed him as though she had done it with her bare hands. Was it that he knew about Alex? Was it that he sensed something? Could she have stopped it if she'd been there? Could it . . . would it . . . what if . . . her mind raced as her eyes grew wide with what she was thinking, but she could not make a sound. She could say nothing. Her father had been right. She had killed him. John Henry had committed suicide. At last she brought herself to look at the doctor.

'Did he leave me a note?' He shook his head in answer. 'Nothing.'

'Oh my God,' she said almost to herself, and then sank to the floor at his feet, in a dead faint.

Chapter 30

Antoine de Mornay-Malle arrived from Paris at six o'clock
the following evening, and he found Raphaella sitting
staring out at the Bay when he arrived. As she heard his
voice behind her, she rose from her chair, turned to greet
him, and when she did so he saw that her eyes were almost
glazed. She had not gone to bed the previous evening, and
despite the doctor's offers of a sedative she had refused. Now
she stood looking very tired and very thin in a black wool
dress which seemed to shrink her further, her hair pulled
severely back, her eyes huge and almost gouged into the
ghostly pale face. When he glanced at her legs, he saw that
she wore the black stockings of mourning, and she was bereft
of jewellery except for the heavy gold knot she had worn for
fifteen years on her left hand.

'Papa . . .' She came towards him slowly, as he
approached her, and his eyes searched her face. He had
known from her voice when she called him that something
was desperately wrong, more than just the death of her
husband. There was something about it which she had not
yet revealed.

'Raphaella, I'm very sorry.' He unbent a little, and
settled himself in a chair next to hers. 'Was it . . . was it
quick?'

She said absolutely nothing, staring out at the bay and
holding tightly to his hand. 'I don't know . . . I think so . . .'

'You weren't with him?' He stared at her face and began
to frown. 'Where were you?' His voice was suddenly filled
with suspicion and she couldn't bear to look him in the eye.

'I was out for a little while.'

Her father nodded. 'It was another stroke? . . . or did his
heart just give out?' Like many people his age, he wanted to
know exactly how the end had come, possibly so that when it
came to him, he would know what he should be expecting.
But still, he found something odd about the look on his

236

daughter's face. As she sat there, she was seriously thinking of not telling him, but she also knew that it was pointless to lie to him. Knowing her father, he would engage in conversation with everyone, the servants, the nurses, the doctor. Accidentally or on purpose, he would discover the truth. Everyone in the household already knew it. The doctor had agreed with her to say absolutely nothing about the circumstances of John Henry's passing, but the nurses told the maid who mentioned it to the butler, who gave the news to the chauffeur with a look of astonishment and dismay. And it wouldn't be long before one of them told a friend in one of the other houses, and eventually word would be out all over town. John Henry Phillips had committed suicide. And somehow, Raphaella knew that her father would find it out too.

'Papa . . .' Slowly she turned to face him, and at last she met his eyes. 'It wasn't a stroke . . .' She closed her eyes tightly for a moment, gripped her chair, opened her eyes again and went on. 'It was . . . he took pills, Papa . . .' Her voice was barely audible as he looked at her, not understanding what she was trying to say. 'I . . . he . . . he's been so depressed lately . . . he hated being sick . . . he's been . . .' She faltered as tears filled her eyes and a sob clutched her throat.

'What are you trying to tell me?' He stared at her, not moving at all in his chair.

'I'm telling you that . . .' She took a big gulp of air. 'The nurse left the sleeping pills next to him on the table . . . and he took them . . . all of them.' She said it clearly now.

'He killed himself?' Her father looked horrified, but slowly she nodded. 'My God, where were you? Why didn't you see that the nurse put the medication away? Why weren't you here?'

'I don't know, Papa . . . but no one knew that he wanted to die. I mean, I knew it . . . he was so tired, and lately he was so sad from having been sick for so long. But no one thought . . . I didn't think . . . I never thought he would . . .'

'My God, are you crazy? How could you not be more careful? How could you not watch everything the nurses did? It was your responsibility, your duty . . .' He prepared to go on but Raphaella leapt from her chair, looking as though she were about to scream.

'Stop it, Papa! Stop it! I couldn't help it . . . nobody could! It was no one's fault . . . it was . . .'

'You'll bring charges against the nurse, won't you?' He looked businesslike, as he watched her from his chair. But Raphaella shook her head, once again looking broken and bereft.

'Of course not. She couldn't know . . . it was an accident, Papa.'

'An accident which killed your husband.' Their eyes met and held for a long time. And then, as though he sensed something more which she hadn't told him, he narrowed his eyes as he watched her. 'Is there more, Raphaella? . . . something you haven't told me?' And then, as though it had come to him more clearly, not as a guess, but as a certainty of her guilt, he sat very straight in his chair and stared at his daughter. 'Where were you when he did this, Raphaella?' She looked woefully at her father, feeling not like a woman, but more like a child. 'Where were you?' He put horrible emphasis on the words when he asked the questions, and there was nothing she could say.

'I was out.'

'With whom?'

'No one.' But it was useless. He had already sensed it and she knew that he knew. She looked at him now, her face an agony of self-recrimination which told its own tale.

'You were with *him*, weren't you, Raphaella? Weren't you?' His voice rose ominously, and unable to see her way clear of the obstacle before her, she simply nodded her head. 'My God then, you killed him. Do you understand that? Do you know why he took those pills?' Her father looked at her in open revulsion, but again Raphaella shook her head.

'He didn't know about it, Papa. I'm sure of that.'

'How can you be? The servants must have known it, they must have told him.'

'They wouldn't have done that to him, and I don't think they knew.' She walked listlessly towards the window. The worst was over now. He knew the truth. He couldn't say anything more. It was all out on the table, her perfidy, her betrayal, her failure of John Henry which had ended up in his death, by pills, instead of by the hand of God.

'Then you lied to me when you said you wouldn't see him any more?'

'No, I told you the truth.' She turned to face him again. 'I didn't see him again, until about two weeks ago. We met accidentally.'

'So of course you climbed right back into his bed.'

'Papa . . . please . . .'

'Didn't you? Isn't that what killed your husband? Think about it. Can you really live with that? Can you?'

Her eyes filled with tears again and she shook her head. 'No, I can't.'

'You're a murderess, Raphaella,' he slid the words out of his mouth like snakes, their venom poisoning all within reach, 'a murderess as well as a whore.' And then drawing himself to his full height he faced her. 'You have disgraced me, and in my heart I disown you, but for my own sake, and the sake of your mother, I will not let you disgrace me again. I have no idea what you plan to do about your lover. I'm sure you would like nothing better than to run off with him the minute they put John Henry in the ground. But that, my dear girl, is not going to happen. Not for a moment. What you do later is none of my business, and as you keep pointing out, you're a grown woman. A repulsive one, an immoral one, but grown you certainly are. So, in a year, after a decent period of mourning, you are welcome to go about your whoring again. But in the meantime, for one year, you will be decent, to me, to your mother, and to the memory of a man I loved a great deal, even if you did not. After the funeral, you will fly to Spain with your mother. And you will stay there for one year. I will attend to all the business matters that come up in relation to the estate, it will take almost that long to settle it anyway, and after a year you can come back here and do whatever you want. But one year, one year you owe the man whom you murdered. If you went to prison, it would be for the rest of your life. And the fact is, young woman, that what you have done you will have to live with for the rest of your days.' He walked solemnly to the door and turned around. 'Be prepared to leave on the day of the funeral. I won't discuss it with you further. A year of decent mourning for a man you drove to suicide is a small price to pay.' As she stood there and watched him leave the room, the tears slid slowly down her face.

It wasn't until the next morning that she heard from Alex. They had kept it out of the papers for a day, but on the following morning it was there, on the first page. John Henry Phillips was dead. It explained that he had been bed-ridden since his first illness, that he had had several strokes and had been incapacitated for eight years. The article barely mentioned Raphaella, except to mention that he was survived by no children, but by his second wife, the former Raphaella de Mornay-Malle y de Santos y Quadral, after that it mentioned the corporations he had founded, the fortune he had inherited, the important international deals he had consummated over the years. But that was not what had interested Alex. He had stared at the paper in amazement when he picked it up outside on his way to work.

He had stood there, motionless, reading, for several minutes, and then had run back inside to call Raphaella. He had wondered why she hadn't come to see him the night before, and he had been terrified that she might have had second thoughts about resuming their relationship, and that their lovemaking the night before had filled her with guilt and driven her away again. Now he wondered what it would mean to her that John Henry had died while she was with him. He could figure out that much from what he had read. It mentioned the night that he had died, and Alex knew that he had either died while Raphaella was out or shortly after she got home. He tried to imagine the scene that had met her when she returned from their hours together, and he shuddered to himself as he dialled the phone. It had taken her several minutes to come to the phone herself after the butler answered, and when she did her voice sounded lifeless and flat. But at her end, when she picked up the receiver, and heard his voice, she felt a tremor run through her. It was like a brutal reminder of what she had been doing when her husband had taken the lethal pills.

'Raphaella?' His voice was gentle and it was obvious that he was upset. 'I just read the paper. I am so sorry . . .' And then after a moment's pause. 'Are you all right?' She had said nothing so far except hello.

'Yes.' She spoke very slowly. 'I am.' And then, 'I'm sorry . . . I was busy just now when you called.' She had been selecting the suit they would put on John Henry, and her father had been standing by wearing an expression that mingled accusation of her with grief for his lost friend. 'The funeral is tomorrow.' What she told him sounded bleak and disjointed and he sat on the stairs with the phone in his hand and closed his eyes. It was obvious what had happened. She was consumed with guilt over the death of her husband. He had to see her. To talk to her. To find out how she really was.

'Can I see you after the funeral, Raphaella? Just for a minute. I just want to know that you're all right.'

'Thank you, Alex. I'm fine.' She sounded like a zombie and he was suddenly frightened. It sounded as though she were heavily sedated, or worse yet, as though she were in some kind of shock.

'Can I see you?'

'I'm leaving tomorrow for Spain.'

'Tomorrow? Why?'

'I'm going back with my parents. My father felt I should spend the period of mourning there.'

Oh Jesus. Alex shook his head. What had happened? What had they done to her? What had they told her? 'How long is the period of mourning?'

She answered him expressionlessly. 'One year.'

He stared at the floor in stupefaction. She was going away for a year? He had lost her again and he knew it, and he also knew that this time it was for good. If she associated John Henry's death with their reunion, then their affair would remain always an ugly moment she would want to forget. And all that he knew was that he had to see her. For a minute, ten seconds, anything, to bring her back to reality, to remind her that he really loved her, that they had done nothing wrong and that they had not caused John Henry's death. 'Raphaella, I have to see you.'

'I don't think I can.' She glanced over her shoulder and could see her father in the next room.

'Yes, you can.' Then Alex thought of something. 'On the

steps, where I first saw you, outside your garden. Just go down there, and I'll meet you. Five minutes, Raphaella . . . that's all . . . please?'

There was such a tone of pleading in his voice that she pitied him, but she felt nothing for anyone any more. Not for herself, not for Alex, maybe not even for John Henry. She was a murderess now. An evil woman. She was numb. But it wasn't Alex who had killed John Henry. She had. There was no reason to punish him.

'Why do you want to see me?'

'To talk to you.'

'What if someone sees us?' But what did it matter? She had already committed the ultimate sin. And her father knew about Alex, knew she had been with him when John Henry took the pills. What difference would it make now, if it made things easier for Alex? She was leaving the next day for Spain.

'They won't see us. And I won't stay more than a few minutes. Will you meet me?'

She nodded slowly. 'Yes.'

'Ten minutes. I'll be there.'

They hung up, and ten minutes later he was waiting nervously at the bottom step where he had first seen her, her face silhouetted in the lamplight, the lynx coat swathing her in softness. He was not prepared for the vision which came to him now, as she walked down the flight of stairs. Everything about her was rigid and dark and depressing. She wore a severe black dress, no make-up, the thick black stockings, black shoes, and a look in her eyes that frightened him to his very core. He didn't even dare to approach her. He simply stood there and waited as she came to him and then stood before him, with that haunting look of agony in her black eyes.

'Hello, Alex.' It was almost as though she were dead too. Or as if someone had killed her, which in effect her father had.

'Raphaella . . . oh baby . . .' He wanted to reach out to her but he didn't dare to, instead he just watched her with a look of anguish in his own eyes. And then, 'Let's sit down.' He let himself down on the steps and motioned to her to join him.

Like a little robot she did, hugging her knees close to her chest in the chill air on the cold steps. 'I want you to tell me what you're feeling. You look so bottled up that it scares me, and I think you're blaming yourself for something you had nothing to do with. John Henry was old, Raphaella, and sick, and very tired. You told me that yourself. He was sick of living, he wanted to die. The timing was only coincidental.'

Raphaella smiled bleakly at him and shook her head, as though she pitied him for being such a fool. 'No, not coincidental, Alex. I killed him. He didn't die in his sleep as it said in the papers. Or he did, but it was not a natural sleep. He took a bottle of sleeping pills.' She waited for it to sink in, as she watched him with her own lifeless eyes. 'He committed suicide.'

'Oh my God . . .' He looked startled, as though someone had slapped him, but now he understood what he had heard in her voice, and what he now saw in her face. 'But do you know that for certain, Raphaella? Did he leave a note?'

'No, he didn't have to. He just did it. But my father is sure that he knew about us, so in effect, I killed him. That's what my father says, and he's right.' For an instant, Alex wanted to kill her father, but he said nothing to her.

'How does he know that?'

'Why else would John Henry do it?'

'Because he was so damn tired of living like a dead man, Raphaella. How often had he told you that himself?' But she only shook her head now. She wouldn't listen. Alex was proclaiming their innocence, while she knew only too well the extent of their guilt. And if not his, then assuredly her own. 'You don't believe me, do you?'

She shook her head slowly. 'No, I don't. I think my father is right. I think someone must have seen us, and told him, maybe one of the servants, maybe a neighbour when we came home one night.'

'No Raphaella, you're wrong. The servants didn't tell him.' He looked at her gently. 'My sister did, when you were in Europe last summer.'

'Oh my God.' Raphaella looked as though she might faint, but he reached out and took her hand.

'It wasn't like that. Kay meant it to be, but it wasn't. One

243

of his secretaries called and asked me to come to the house.'

'And you did?' She looked shocked.

'I did. He was a wonderful man, Raphaella.' There were tears in his eyes now, as well as hers.

'What happened?'

'We talked for a long time. About you. About me, I guess. About us. He gave me his blessing, Raphaella.' The tears spilled from Alex's eyes. 'He told me to take care of you, afterwards . . .' He reached out to her then but she pulled back. The blessing didn't count now. Even Alex knew it. It was too late for that. 'Raphaella, darling, don't let them hurt you. Don't let them take something away that we both want, that even John Henry respected, something that is so right.'

'We're not right. We were very, very wrong.'

'Were we?' He faced her squarely as they sat there. 'Do you really believe that?'

'What choice do I have, Alex? How can I believe differently? What I did killed my husband, drove him to suicide . . . can you really tell me that I've done nothing wrong?'

'Yes, and so would anyone else who knew the story. You're innocent, Raphaella. No matter what your father says. If John Henry were alive, I'm sure he would tell you the same thing. Are you sure he didn't leave you a letter?' He searched her eyes as he asked her, it seemed odd that John Henry had left nothing. He seemed like the kind of man who would, but she only shook her head again.

'Nothing. The doctor checked when he got there, and so did the nurses. There was nothing.'

'You're sure?' She nodded again. 'So now what? You go to Spain with your mother to atone for your sin?' She nodded once more. 'And then what? You come back here?' He mentally resigned himself to a long, lonely year.

'I don't know. I'll have to come back to settle things. I'll put the house on the market after the estate has been cleared. And then,' she faltered and stared at her feet as she spoke in a monotone. 'I suppose I'll go back to Paris, or maybe Spain.'

'Raphaella, that's crazy.' He couldn't keep his hands

from hers any more. He clasped her long thin fingers in his own. 'I love you. I want to marry you. There's no reason for us not to. We haven't done anything wrong.'

'Yes, Alex.' She pulled away from him very slowly, retrieving her hand from his. 'We have. *I* have done something very wrong.'

'And for the rest of time you'll bear that burden, is that it?' But more to the point, he knew as he sat there that for the rest of time he would remind her of what she considered her great sin. He had lost her. To a quirk of fate, of timing, to the insanity of a tired old man, to the evil interpretations of her father. He had lost her. And then, as though she knew what he was thinking, she nodded and stood up. She stood looking at him for a long moment, and then softly she whispered 'Goodbye'. She didn't touch him, or kiss him, and she didn't wait for an answer. She simply turned, and walked slowly up the stairs, as Alex watched her, aghast at what he was losing, at what she was doing. In her unrelenting black garb she looked like a nun. This was the third time he had lost her. But this time he knew it was for good. When she reached the well-concealed garden door, she pushed it open, and closed it behind her. She did not look back at Alex, and there was no sound after the door had closed. Alex just stood there for what felt like hours, and then slowly, aching, and feeling as though he were dying, he walked painfully up the stairs, got into his car, and drove home.

Chapter 31

The funeral was as private as they could keep it, but there were still well over a hundred people in the pews of the little church. Raphaella sat in the front pew with her mother and father. There were tears on her father's cheeks, and her mother sobbed openly for a man she had barely known. In the pew immediately behind them were the half dozen relatives who had accompanied her mother from Spain, Alejandra's brother and two of her sisters, a cousin and her daughter and son. The group had allegedly come to lend support to Raphaella as well as Alejandra, but Raphaella felt more as though they were the prison guards, come to escort her back to Spain.

It was she who sat dry-eyed through the funeral, staring blindly at the coffin covered in a blanket of white roses. Her mother had taken care of the flowers, her father the rest of the arrangements. Raphaella had had to do nothing, except sit in her room and think of what she had done. Now and then she thought of Alex, of his face when she had last seen him, of what he had told her. But she knew that he was wrong in what he was thinking. It was all so obviously her fault, as her father had told her, and Alex was only trying to assuage her guilt. It was strange to realise that she had lost both of them at the same time. She had lost Alex as much as she had John Henry, and she knew as she sat there stiffly, listening to the music, that she would never see either of them again. It was then that the tears began to flow slowly, rolling mercilessly down her cheeks beneath the thick black veil until they fell silently on to her delicate hands folded in her lap. She never moved once during the entire ceremony. She only sat there, a criminal at a tribunal, with nothing to say in her own defence. For a single mad moment she wanted to jump up and tell them, that she hadn't killed him on purpose, that she was innocent, that it was all a mistake.

But she wasn't innocent, she reminded herself silently. She was guilty. And now she would have to pay.

When it was over, they drove to the cemetery in silence. He was to be buried beside his first wife and their son, and Raphaella knew as she looked at the grassy knoll where they were buried, that she would never rest there with him. It was unlikely that she would ever again live in California. She would return for a few weeks, in a year, to pick up her things, and sell the house, and then one day, she would die and be buried in Europe. It seemed more fitting somehow. She had no right to lie here with him. She was the woman who had killed him, his murderess. It would have been blasphemy to bury her in his plot. And at the end of the prayer said by the priest at the graveside, her father glanced at her as though saying the same thing.

They drove back to the house once again in silence, and Raphaella returned to her room. Her packing was almost done. She had nothing to do, and she didn't want to speak to or see anyone. No one seemed particularly anxious to speak to her. The whole family knew what had happened. Her aunts and uncles and cousins did not know about her affair, but they knew that John Henry had committed suicide, and their eyes seemed almost accusing to Raphaella as though they were saying again and again that it was her fault. It was easier for her not to see them, not to see their faces or their eyes, and now she sat in her room, again like a prisoner, waiting, and envying John Henry for his courage. If she had had the same bottle of pills, she would have taken them. She had nothing left to live for, and she would have been grateful to die. But she also knew that she had to be punished, and dying was too easy. She would have to live on, knowing what she had done in San Francisco, and enduring the looks and whispers of her family in Spain. She knew that forty or fifty years later they would still tell the story, and suspect that there was more that they didn't know. By then, perhaps word of Alex's existence would have accompanied the rest of the story. People would talk about 'Tia Raphaella' who had cheated on her husband . . . you remember, he committed suicide . . . I don't know how old she was . . . maybe thirty . . . you know, she was really the one who killed him.

As she heard the words in her head, she dropped her face in her hands and began to cry. She began to cry for the children who would never know her, or know the truth about what had happened to her here, she cried for Alex and what had almost been, for Mandy whom she would never see again, and at last for John Henry . . . for what he had done . . . for what he had once been . . . for the man who had loved her so long ago, and proposed to her as they walked along the Seine. She sat alone in her room and cried for hours, and then silently she walked to his bedroom, and looked around for a last time.

At nine o'clock her mother came upstairs to tell her that it was time to leave the house to catch their plane. They were taking the ten-thirty night flight to New York, which would get them in around six in the morning New York time, and at seven o'clock they would catch the flight to Spain. The plane would arrive at eight o'clock that evening local time in Madrid. She had a long journey ahead of her, and a very long year. As the man who did their heavy cleaning picked up her two bags and took them downstairs, she walked slowly down the main staircase, knowing that she would never live here again. Her days in San Francisco were over. Her life with John Henry was gone now. Her moments with Alex had ended in disaster. Her life was, in a sense, over.

'Ready?' Her mother looked at her gently, and Raphaella looked at her with the empty eyes Alex had seen that morning, nodded, and walked out the door.

Chapter 32

In the Spring, she received, via San Francisco, a copy of her children's book which was due out sometime late in July. She eyed it quietly, with a sense of distance. It seemed a thousand years since she had started that project, and it seemed so unimportant now. She felt nothing for it at all. As little in fact as she now felt for the children, for her parents, her cousins, or even for herself. She felt nothing for anyone. For five months, she had moved like a zombie, gotten up in the morning, dressed in her black clothes of mourning, gone to breakfast, returned to her bedroom, answered the scores of letters they were still forwarding to her from San Francisco, all of them letters of condolence to which she responded on the heavily black bordered stationery suited to the task. At lunchtime, she would emerge again from her bedroom, and immediately afterwards she would once again disappear. Now and then she would take a solitary walk before dinner, but she was careful to discourage companionship, and to beg off if someone insisted on coming along.

It was clear that Raphaella wanted to see no one, and that she was taking her year of mourning very much to heart. She had even decided immediately after her arrival, that she had no desire to stay on in Madrid. She wanted to sequester herself at Santa Eugenia, to be alone, even in the bosom of her family, and at first her parents agreed. In Spain, her mother and the rest of the family were accustomed to the business of mourning, they did it for a year, and the widows and children of the dead always wore solid black. And even in Paris it wasn't an entirely unusual thing. But the zeal with which Raphaella threw herself into her mourning, struck everyone strangely. It was as though she were punishing herself and atoning for countless unspoken sins. After the first three months, her mother suggested she go to Paris, but

249

the suggestion met with an instant refusal. She wanted to stay at Santa Eugenia, she had no desire to go anywhere else. She shunned everyone's company, even her mother's. She did nothing anyone knew of except stay in her room, write her endless letters in response to the cards and letters of condolence, and go for her solitary walks.

Among the letters, which came after her arrival was a long and heartfelt one from Charlotte Brandon, reaching out to the young woman. She told her bluntly but kindly that Alex had explained the circumstances of John Henry's passing and that she hoped that Raphaella would be wise enough not to blame herself. There was a long philosophical part of the letter, concerning Henry's infirmities. She wrote that she had known of him as a young man and how she had gathered over the years that his infirmities must have come as a spirit-crushing blow, that in the light of what he had been and then had become, in light of his affection for Raphaella, his life must have been a prison which he had longed to flee, and that what he had done, while certainly difficult for those who survived him to understand, may well have been the final blessing for him. 'Although a selfish act,' Charlotte wrote to Raphaella, 'it is one which I hope you will come to accept and understand, without the egocentricity of self-accusation and self-flagellation.' She urged Raphaella to simply accept it, be kind to his memory, and to herself, and move on. It was a plea to Raphaella to be good to herself, whatever that might mean.

It was the only letter to which Raphaella did not respond immediately, as she sat by herself for endless hours in her Ivory Tower. The letter from Charlotte languished for weeks on the desk unanswered. Raphaella simply did not know what to say. In the end, she answered simply, that she was grateful for the kind words and the woman's thoughts, and hoping that if she found herself in Europe, that she would stop at Santa Eugenia and say hello. However painful for Raphaella the mental association of Charlotte and Alex, she had been fond enough of Charlotte in her own right and in time, she would like to see her again. But when she made the suggestion, she did not anticipate a note from Charlotte in late June. She and Mandy had just flown to London, as usual to promote Charlotte's latest book. There was also going to be a movie tie-in and she was very busy. She was scheduled to fly on to Paris and then Berlin, but as long as she was in Europe, she was thinking of flying to Madrid to see some friends. She and Mandy were longing to see Raphaella and wondered if they could either lure her to Madrid or drive to Santa Eugenia to see her for an afternoon. They were willing to undertake the trip to see her, and Raphaella was deeply touched. Enough so that she didn't dare refuse to see them, but attempted to discourage them with kind words. She explained that it was awkward for her to leave Santa Eugenia, that her assistance was needed to keep an eye on the children, and see that things ran smoothly for her mother's innumerable guests, none of which was true of course. Since the rest of the family had begun to arrive for the summer, Raphaella had been more elusive than ever, and often took her meals on a tray in her room. To the emotional Spaniards around her it didn't seem an unusual posture during mourning, but nonetheless her mother was growing increasingly concerned.

The letter which Raphaella addressed to Charlotte in Paris was put on the same silver salver where the family left all of their outgoing mail. But on the particular day Raphaella left it, one of the children scooped it all up in his knapsack, to mail it in town when he went shopping for candies with his sisters and brothers, and the letter to Charlotte slipped out of his hand before he reached the box. Or at least that was the only explanation Raphaella could discover, when Charlotte called her three weeks later, in July, having heard not a word.

'May we come to see you?' Raphaella faltered for a long moment, feeling at the same time rude and trapped.

'I . . . it's so hot here, you'd hate it . . . and you know, it's so awkward to get here, I hate to put you to so much trouble.'

'Then come to Madrid.' Charlotte's voice had been filled with good cheer.

'I really can't leave here, but I'd love to.' It was a blatant lie.

'Well, then it looks as though we have no choice, do we?

How about tomorrow? We can rent a car and come down after breakfast. How does that sound?'

'A three hour drive, just to see me? Oh Charlotte . . . I feel awful . . .'

'Don't. We'd love to. Is that all right for you?' For a moment she wasn't sure if Raphaella really wanted them, and she suddenly wondered if she was pressing herself on her and she would rather not see them at all. Perhaps the link with Alex was still too painful for her to bear. But she sounded well to Charlotte, and when she answered again she sounded as though she'd be pleased to see them.

'It'll be wonderful to see you both!'

'I can hardly wait to see you, Raphaella. And you'll barely recognise Mandy. Did you know she's going to Stanford in the fall?'

At her end of the conversation, Raphaella smiled gently. Mandy . . . her Amanda . . . it pleased her to know that she would still be living with Alex. He needed her as much as she needed him. 'I'm glad.' And then she couldn't help asking. 'And Kay?'

'She lost the election, you know. But you must have known that before you left. That was last year.' As it so happened, she had known it, because she had seen it in the papers, but Alex had refused to discuss his sister with her during the brief revival of their relationship. For him, there had been an irreparable break between them over Amanda, and Raphaella had often wondered what he would have done if he had known about Kay's letter to her father. He would probably have killed her. But Raphaella had never told him. And now she was just as glad. What did it matter? Their life together was over, and Kay was his sister after all. 'Darling, we'll catch up on all this tomorrow. Can we bring you anything from Madrid?'

'Just yourselves.' Raphaella smiled and hung up, but for the rest of the day she paced her room nervously, why had she let them talk her into it? And what would she do when they came? She didn't want to see Charlotte or Amanda, didn't want any reminders of her past life. She was leading a new life now, at Santa Eugenia. This was all she would ever have now. What was the point of staying in touch with the past?

When she came down to dinner that evening, her mother noticed the nervous tremor of her hands, and she made a mental note to herself to speak to Antoine. She thought that Raphaella should see a doctor. She had been looking ghastly for months. Despite the brilliant summer sunshine, she stayed in her room and remained ghostly pale, she had lost fifteen or twenty pounds since she'd arrived from San Francisco, and she looked frankly unhealthy compared to the rest of her family, with her huge dark unhappy eyes in the painfully gaunt waif-like face.

She mentioned to her mother however in passing that she was having two guests from Madrid the next day. 'Well, actually, they're from the States.'

'Oh?' Her mother looked at her warmly. It was a relief that she was seeing someone. She hadn't even wanted to see her old acquaintances in Spain. It was the most earnest period of mourning Alejandra had ever seen. 'Who are they, darling?'

'Charlotte Brandon, and her granddaughter.'

'The writer?' Her mother looked surprised. She had read some of her books, translated into Spanish and she knew that one of her sisters had read them all. 'Your aunt Anna Christina will be thrilled.' Alejandra looked pleased, but Raphaella did not.

'Will my aunt be here?'

'She's arriving tomorrow also. She'll be staying for a week. And your friends? Would you like them to spend the night?' Raphaella shook her head absently and went back upstairs to her room.

She was still there late the next morning, when one of the servants came upstairs and knocked softly on her door. 'Donna Raphaella . . . you have guests.' She hardly even dared to disturb Raphaella. The door opened and the fifteen-year-old girl in the maid's uniform visibly quailed.

'Thank you.' Raphaella smiled, and walked to the stairs. She was so nervous that her legs felt like wooden posts beneath her. It was odd but she hadn't seen any friends in so long, that she didn't know what to say. Looking serious and

253

a little frightened, in one of the elegant black summer dresses her mother had bought her in Madrid, still wearing the black stockings, she walked down the stairs looking frighteningly pale.

At the foot of the stairs, Charlotte waited, and she gave an unconscious start when she saw Raphaella approach. She had never seen anyone looking so anguished and unhappy, and she looked like a portrait of sorrow in her black dress with her huge grief-stricken eyes. There was instantly a smile there for Charlotte, but it was more like a sad reaching out across an unbridgeable chasm. It was as though she had slipped into another world since she had last seen her, and as she watched her, Charlotte felt an almost irresistible urge to cry. She managed somehow to quell it, and took the girl in her arms with a warm tender hug. She realised as she watched the gaunt beauty hug Amanda that in some ways she was even more beautiful than before, but it was the kind of beauty one only looked at, one never touched, and one never really came to know. Throughout their visit she was hospitable and gracious, charming to them both, as she showed them the house and the gardens, the historical chapel built by her great-grandfather, and introduced them to all the children who were playing with their nannies in a special garden built just for them. It was an extraordinary place to spend a summer, Charlotte found herself thinking, and it was a relic of another life, another world, but it was no place for a young woman like Raphaella to be buried, and it frightened her when Raphaella told her that she planned to stay there.

'Won't you go back to San Francisco?' Charlotte looked upset.

But Raphaella shook her head quickly. 'No. Eventually I have to go back to close the house of course, but I may even be able to do that from here.'

'Then won't you want to move to Paris or Madrid?'

'No.' She said it firmly and then smiled at Amanda, but Amanda had said almost nothing. She had only stared at Raphaella for the most part since they had arrived. It was like seeing the ghost of someone they had once known. This wasn't Raphaella. It was a kind of broken dream. And like

Charlotte, Mandy spent the afternoon trying not to cry. All she could think of were the times with Alex, when he and Raphaella had been so happy, when she had been there when Mandy got home from school every day. But now as she looked at this woman, she was a stranger, something different and foreign. She reminded Mandy of Raphaella, but nothing more than that. It was a relief when at last Raphaella suggested she go swimming, and as Raphaella had so long ago she tried to work out her feelings with a long, exhausting swim, which gave Charlotte an opportunity to be alone with Raphaella, something she had longed for all day. Now as they sat side by side in comfortable chairs in a secluded corner of the garden, Charlotte looked at her with a tender smile.

'Raphaella . . . may I speak to you as an old friend?'

'Always.' But the look of the frightened doe came to her quickly. She didn't want to answer any questions, didn't want to have to explain about her decisions. This was her life now. And she didn't want it exposed to anyone but herself.

'I think you are tormenting yourself beyond anything that anyone can imagine. I see it in your face, in the haunted look in your eyes, in the way you speak . . . Raphaella . . . what can I tell you? What can anyone say to set you free?' She had gone right to the heart of the matter in a single minute, and Raphaella turned her face away so that the older woman would not see the shimmer of tears in her eyes. She appeared to be looking at the garden, but slowly, sadly, she shook her head.

'I will never be free again, Charlotte.'

'But you are imprisoning yourself in this life. You are wrapped in guilt over something I will never believe was your doing. Never. I will always believe that your husband was tired of living, and if you let yourself, I think you'd know that too.'

'I don't know that. I never will. It doesn't matter anyway. I had a full life. I was married for fifteen years. I want nothing more. I am here now. I have come home.'

'Except that it's not home to you any more, Raphaella. And you're talking like an old woman.'

Raphaella smiled. 'That's how I feel.'

'That's crazy.' And then, on the spur of the moment, she looked Raphaella in the eye. 'Why don't you come to Paris with us?'

'Now?' Raphaella looked shocked.

'We're going back to Madrid tonight, and we fly back to Paris tomorrow. How does that sound?'

'Slightly mad.' Raphaella smiled gently. It appealed to her not at all. She hadn't been to Paris in a year now, but she had absolutely no desire to go.

'Will you think about it?' Raphaella shook her head sadly.

'No, Charlotte. I want to stay here.'

'But why? Why must you do this? It's not right for you.'

'Yes,' she nodded slowly, 'it is.' And then, finally, she dared to ask the question that had been on her mind all day long. 'How is Alex? Is he all right now?' He had written to her twice and she had not answered, but she had seen in his letters that he was distraught over what had happened, and it was compounded by her removal, her silence, and her original insistence that they would not meet again.

Charlotte nodded slowly. 'He's coping.' But this had been much harder than his separation from Rachel, and she was no longer entirely certain that he would ever be quite the same. She wasn't sure whether or not she should say that to Raphaella. She wasn't sure that Raphaella could bear any more guilt than she was already carrying around. 'You never wrote to him, did you?'

'No.' She looked Charlotte squarely in the eye. 'I thought it would be better for him if I cut the cords all at once.'

'That was what you thought once before, wasn't it? And you were wrong that time too.'

'That was different.' Raphaella looked vague, remembering the scene in Paris with her father only a year before. How intense it had all been, how important, and now everything had changed and none of it mattered any more. Kay had lost her precious election, she had lost Alex, John Henry was dead . . . Raphaella glanced up at Charlotte now. 'Kay wrote a letter to my father, telling him about the affair with Alex, begging him to stop us, which he did.' Seeing how shocked she was by this revelation, she decided not to add the information about the letter to John Henry which had been an even crueller act. She smiled at Alex's mother. 'He threatened to tell my husband, he had me followed. He also insisted that I was being selfish and destroying Alex's life by keeping him from marrying and having children.' She sighed softly. 'That time I really had no choice.'

'And this time?'

'My father wanted me to come here for a year. He thought it was the least I could do,' her voice dropped to barely more than a whisper, 'after killing John Henry.'

'But you didn't kill him.' A moment passed between them, and then, 'What happens after the year? Will your family be unhappy if you leave here?'

'I don't know. It doesn't make any difference, Charlotte. I won't. This is where I belong. This is where I will stay.'

'Why do you belong here?'

'I don't want to discuss it.'

'Stop punishing yourself dammit!' She reached out and took Raphaella's hands in her own. 'You're a beautiful young woman with a fine mind and a good heart, you deserve a full happy life, children, a husband . . . with Alex, or with someone else, that's up to you, but you can't bury yourself here, Raphaella.'

Raphaella pulled her hands slowly out of Charlotte's. 'Yes, I can. I can't live anywhere else with what I've done. Whoever I touched, whoever I loved, whoever I married, I would think of John Henry and of Alex. One man I killed and the other I nearly destroyed. What right do I have to touch the life of anyone else?'

'Because you have neither killed nor destroyed anyone. God, I wish I could get that across to you.' But she knew that it was almost hopeless. Raphaella was locked in her private dungeon and could barely hear what was being said. 'Then you won't come to Paris?'

'No,' she smiled gently, 'but I thank you for the invitation. And Mandy looks wonderful.' It was the signal that Raphaella no longer wished to talk about herself. She was no longer willing to discuss her decisions. She suggested instead that they visit the rose gardens at the far end of the estate. After that they rejoined Amanda, and a little while later it was time for them to go. She watched them leave with a look of regret and then walked back into the big house and across the pink marble hallway and made her way slowly up the stairs.

As Charlotte pulled their rented car through the main gates of Santa Eugenia Amanda burst into tears. 'But why wouldn't she come to Paris?'

There were tears in Charlotte's eyes as well. 'Because she didn't want to, Mandy. She wants to bury herself alive here.'

'Couldn't you talk to her?' Mandy blew her nose and dabbed at her eyes. 'God, she looked awful. She looks like she died, not him.'

'In a way, I think she did.' Charlotte let the tears roll down her cheeks as she turned on to the highway to Madrid.

Chapter 33

It was in September that Alejandra began to push
Raphaella. The rest of the family had gone back to
Barcelona and Madrid, and Raphaella was determined to
sit out the winter at Santa Eugenia. She insisted that she
wanted to work on another children's book, but it was a
lame excuse. She had no interest in writing any more and she
knew it. But her mother insisted that Raphaella return with
her to Madrid.

'I don't want to, Mother.'

'Nonsense. It'll be good for you.'

'Why? I can't go to the theatre or the opera, or any dinner
parties.'

Her mother looked pensive as she gazed at the wan tired
face before her. 'It's been nine months, Raphaella. You
could go out with me once in a while.'

'Thank you . . .' She looked bleakly at her mother, 'But I
want to stay here.' The discussion had gone nowhere for
over an hour, and as usual, afterwards, Raphaella had
disappeared to her room. She would sit there for hours,
looking out at the gardens, thinking, dreaming. There were
fewer letters to answer now. And she never read books any
more. She just sat there, thinking, sometimes about John
Henry, sometimes about Alex, and about moments they had
shared. Then she would think about the trip to Paris, when
her father had thrown her out of his house and called her a
whore. After that she would think of the scene she had found
when she came home that night, after John Henry . . . and
then her father's arrival . . . his calling her a murderess. She
would simply sit there, living in her memories, and staring
outside, seeing nothing, going nowhere, doing nothing, as
she dwindled away. Her mother was even afraid to leave
Santa Eugenia, there was something frightening about the
way Raphaella behaved. She was so removed, so distracted,
so distant, so indifferent. She never seemed to eat any more,

259

never spoke to anyone unless she had to, never entered into jokes or discussions or moments of laughter. It was ghastly to see her that way. But at the end of September her mother finally insisted.

'I don't care what you say, Raphaella. I'm taking you back to Madrid. You can lock yourself up there.' Besides, she was tired of the dreary autumn in the country. She herself was hungry for amusement, she couldn't understand how a young woman of thirty-four could bear the life she led. So Raphaella packed her bags and went with her, saying nothing on the drive, and then going upstairs to the large suite of rooms she always occupied in her mother's house. No one even seemed to notice her any more as she drifted among them. The aunts or the cousins or the brothers or the uncles. They had simply come to accept her the way she now was.

Her mother began the season with a round of parties, there was music and dancing and laughter in the house. She endorsed several benefits, and took large groups to the opera, gave large and small dinners, and seemed to constantly entertain an army of friends. By the first of November, Raphaella could no longer stand it. It seemed as though every time she went downstairs there were forty people waiting there in evening dresses and black ties. And her mother had flatly refused to allow her to continue to eat in her rooms. She insisted that it was unhealthy and even if she was in mourning, she could at least eat with her mother's guests. Besides it did her good to see people, her mother insisted, but Raphaella didn't agree. At the end of the first week of December, she picked up the phone and decided to get away. She made a reservation on a plane to Paris, figuring that a few days in the solemnity of her father's quarters would be something of a relief. She always wondered how the two of them had stood each other, her mother so gregarious, so flighty, so social, her father so serious and so austere. But the answer of course was that her mother lived in Madrid, while her father stayed in Paris. Nowadays, he very seldom came to Spain. He felt he was too old for Alejandra's frivolous entertainments, and Raphaella had to admit that she had come to feel that way herself.

She called her father to let him know that she was coming,

but assumed that it would present no particular problem for him. She had a room in his house too. There was no one home when she called his number, and at first the phone was answered by a new maid. She decided then to surprise him, and reminded herself that she hadn't been in the house since the year before he had confronted her about the affair with Alex. But now, for nine months she had atoned for at least some of her sins, with her agonising monastic life in Spain. She knew that her father approved of what she was doing, and after the ferocity of his accusations, it was a relief to know that he might approve of her a little more now.

The plane to Paris was half empty. She took a taxi in from Orly Airport, and stood for a moment looking up at the splendour of her father's house when she arrived. In a way, it always felt odd to be back here. This was the house she had lived in as a child, and she could never quite return without feeling somehow as though she weren't a woman, but was once more that small child. The house also reminded her of John Henry, and his early trips to Paris, their long walks in the Luxembourg gardens, and their meandering along the Seine.

She rang the doorbell, and the door was opened, again by an unfamiliar face. It was a maid in a starched uniform with a sour face and thick black eyebrows who looked at her enquiringly as the taxi driver brought her bags inside.

'Yes?'

'I am Madame Phillips, Monsieur de Mornay-Malle's daughter.' The little maid nodded at her, looking neither impressed nor interested in the new arrival, and Raphaella smiled. 'Is my father at home?'

The young woman nodded with an odd look in her eyes. 'He's . . . upstairs.' It was eight o'clock in the evening, and Raphaella hadn't been entirely sure that she would find her father at home. But she knew that he would either be in, dining alone, or out for the evening. She ran no risk of encountering a party like those at her mother's, with dancing, laughing couples drifting through the halls. Her father was a good deal less social and he preferred to meet people in restaurants instead of at home.

Raphaella nodded pleasantly again at the woman. 'I'll go

up to see him. Would you be so kind as to have one of the men bring the bags up to my room in a while?' And then realising that the woman might not know which one it was. 'The big blue bedroom, on the second floor.'

'Oh,' said the maid, and then suddenly she clamped her mouth shut as though she couldn't bring herself to say more. 'Yes, Madame.' She nodded her head at Raphaella, and hurried back to the pantry, as Raphaella walked slowly up the stairs. There was no particular joy for her in coming back here, but it was peaceful at least, and it was a relief after the constant movement in the house in Spain. She realised as she reached the second landing that after she sold the house on San Francisco, she would have to set up an establishment of her own. She was thinking of buying a little piece of land near Santa Eugenia, and putting up a small house adjoining the main grounds. While it was under construction, she could live peacefully at Santa Eugenia. It would give her the perfect excuse not to be in town. All of that was part of what she wanted to discuss with her father. He had been handling the estate for her since she left San Francisco, and now she wanted to know where things stood. In a few more months, she wanted to go back to California and close up the house.

She hesitated for a moment in front of her father's study, looking at the elaborately carved double doors, and then she walked on quietly to her own room, to take off her coat, wash her hands, and comb her hair. There was no rush to see her father. She assumed that he would probably be reading in his library, or going over some papers, smoking a cigar.

Without stopping to think of what she was doing, she turned the large brass knob and stepped into the ante-room of her old room. There were two sets of double doors which sealed off the entrance, she passed through one set, and then casually opened the next ones and walked into the room. But there was the suddenly startling feeling of having walked into the wrong apartment. There was a tall heavy-set blonde woman seated at her dressing table, wearing a blue lace peignor ringed with a soft fluff of feathers around the neck, and when she stood up to face Raphaella with a look of audacious enquiry, Raphaella saw that her blue satin slippers matched her robe. For an endless moment,

Raphaella only stood there, not able to understand who the woman was.

'Yes?' With an air of authority she gazed at Raphaella, and for a moment, Raphaella thought that she was going to be told to leave her own room. And then suddenly she realised, that it was quite obvious that her father had guests, and here she had arrived totally unannounced. But it was no problem really. She could sleep in the large yellow and gold guest room on the third floor. It did not occur to her as she stood there that it was odd that her father's house guests did not have that room instead of hers.

'I'm terribly sorry . . . I thought . . .' She didn't know whether to advance and introduce herself, or back out saying nothing at all.

'Who let you in here?'

'I have no idea. There seems to be a new maid.'

The woman advanced on her angrily, and for a moment, Raphaella got the feeling that this was the heavy-set woman's house. 'Who are you?'

'Raphaella Phillips.' She blushed faintly and the woman stopped in her tracks. And as Raphaella watched her, she got the feeling that she had met this woman somewhere before. There was something vaguely familiar about the blonde helmet, the set of her eyes, something about her, but Raphaella couldn't place it, and with that, her father came in through the boudoir door. He was wearing a dark red silk bathrobe, and he looked pomaded and clean and perfectly groomed, but all he wore was the bathrobe, hanging slightly open, his legs and feet bare, and the grey tufts on his chest peeking through the open robe. 'Oh . . .' Raphaella backed towards the door as though she had walked into a room she should never have entered. As she did so, she realised that it was exactly what she had done. She had walked right into an assignation, and as the realisation of that hit her, the woman's identity struck her with full force. 'Oh my God.' And then Raphaella just stood there, staring at her father, and the blonde woman, who was the wife of the most important Cabinet minister in France.

'You may be excused, Georgette.' His tone was austere, but his face looked nervous, and the woman had flushed and

263

turned away. 'Georgette . . .' he spoke to her softly, nodding towards the boudoir, and she disappeared and he faced his daughter, pulling the robe tightly closed. 'May I ask what you're doing here like this, unannounced, and in this room?'

She looked at him for a long time before answering, and suddenly the rage that she should have felt a year earlier washed over her with a force she could neither stop nor resist. Step by step she advanced towards him with a light in her eyes he had never seen there before. Instinctively, his hand went out to the back of the chair near him, and something inside him trembled as he faced his child.

'What am *I* doing here, Papa? I came to visit you. I thought I'd come to see my father in Paris. Is that surprising? Perhaps I should have called, and spared Madame the embarrassment of being recognised, but I thought it might be more amusing to come as a surprise. And the reason I am standing in this room, Father, is because it used to be mine. But I think what is far more to the point is what are *you* doing in this room, Father? You, with the saintly morals and the endless speeches. You, who threw me out of this house over a year ago, and called me a whore. You who called me a murderess because I "killed" my seventy-nine-year-old husband who had been almost dead for almost nine years. And what if Monsieur le Ministre has a stroke tomorrow, Papa, then will you be a murderer too? What if he has a heart attack? What if he finds out he has cancer, and kills himself because he can't bear it, then will you bear the guilt and punish yourself as you've punished me? What if your affair with his wife ends his political career? And what about her, Papa? What about her? What are you keeping her from? What right do you have to this, while my mother sits in Madrid? What right do you have that I did not have a year ago with a man I loved? What right . . . how dare you! How dare you!' She stood before him, trembling, and shouting in his face.

'How dare you have done to me what you did last year? You threw me out of this house and sent me to Spain that night because you said you would not have a whore under your roof. Well, you have a whore under your roof, Papa.' She pointed hysterically at the boudoir, and before he could stop her, she strode to the door, where she found the Minister's wife sitting on the edge of a Louis XVI chair crying softly into a handkerchief as Raphaella looked down at her. 'Good day, Madame.'

Then she turned to her father, 'And goodbye. I will not spend a night under the roof as a whore either, and you, Papa, are the whore, not Madame here, and not I. You are ... you are ...' She began to sob hysterically, 'What you said to me last year almost killed me ... for almost a year I've tortured myself over what John Henry did while everyone else told me that I was innocent, that he did it because he was so old and so sick and so miserable. Only you accused me of killing him and called me a whore. You said that I disgraced you, that I had risked a scandal that would destroy your good name. And what about you, damn you? What about her?' She waved vaguely at the woman in the blue peignoir. 'Don't you think this would be a scandal to top all scandals? What about *your* servants? What about Monsieur le Ministre? What about the voters? What about your clients at the bank? Don't you care about them? Or is it that I am the only one who can be disgraceful? My God, what I did was so much less than this. And you have a right to this, if that's what you want, who am I to tell you what you can and can't do, what's wrong and what isn't, but how dare you call me names? How dare you do what you did to me?' She hung her head for a moment sobbing and then glared at him again. 'I will never forgive you, Papa ... never ...'

He looked like a broken man as he stared at her, his ageing body hanging loosely in the bathrobe, his face registering the pain of what she had just said. 'Raphaella ... I was wrong ... I was wrong ... This happened afterwards. I swear it. It started this summer ...'

'I don't give a damn when it started.' She fired the words at him as he stood looking at her and at his mistress, crying in her chair. 'When I did it, you called me a killer. Now that it's you, it's all right. I would have spent the rest of my life at Santa Eugenia, eating out my soul. And do you know why? Because of what you said. Because I believed you. Because I felt so desperately guilty that I accepted all the misery you heaped on my head.' She shook her head then, and walked out of the boudoir to the door of the main room. He followed her, looking lamely after her, and she stopped for only an instant at the door to look back at him with an expression of scorn.

'Raphaella . . . I'm sorry . . .'

'What are you sorry about, Father? That I found you out? Would you have come to tell me? Would you have told me that you had changed your mind, that I hadn't killed my husband? Would you have let me know that you'd thought things over, and perhaps you were wrong? Just when would you have told me? If I hadn't walked in on you, just when would you have come to me and said that? When?'

'I don't know . . .' His voice was a hoarse whisper. 'In time . . . I would have . . .'

'Would you?' She shook her head firmly. 'I don't believe you. You'd never have done it. And all the while you'd have been carrying on here with your mistress, and I would have buried myself in Spain. Can you live with yourself, knowing that? Can you? The only one who has destroyed anyone's life Father, is you. You almost destroyed mine.'

And with that she slammed the door. She was down the stairs in a moment and saw her bags still standing in the hall. With a trembling hand she picked up a bag in each hand, and slipped her handbag over her shoulder, opened the door, and marched out of the house to find the nearest taxi stand. She knew there was one around the corner, and she didn't give a damn if she had to walk to the airport, she was going back to Spain. She was still trembling and shaken when she finally found a taxi, and when she told the driver to take her to Orly, she put her head back on the seat, and closed her eyes.

She was suddenly filled with hatred and anger against her father. What a bastard he was, what a hypocrite . . . what about her mother? What about all the accusations he'd made? All the things he'd said? But as she raged silently to herself all the way to the airport, she found herself thinking that in truth he was only human, as human as her mother probably was, as human as she herself had been, maybe as human as John Henry himself had been once upon a time.

266

Maybe she really hadn't killed John Henry. Maybe in fact he simply hadn't wanted to go on.

As she flew home to Madrid she stared into the night sky and mulled it all over, and for the first time in close to a year, she felt free of the agonising weight of her own burdens of guilt and pain. She found herself feeling sorry for her father, and suddenly laughing softly to herself at the vision of him in his red robe, and the heavy-set middle-aged mistress in the peignoir with the feathers around her fat neck. As the plane landed in Madrid, she was laughing softly, and she was still grinning when she got off the plane.

Chapter 34

The next morning, Raphaella came down to breakfast, and although her face was as pale and gaunt as it had been for a year there was a different light in her eyes, and she answered her mother lightheartedly as she drank her coffee, that she had discussed all her business with her father, and had decided to come home.

'But in that case, why didn't you just call him?'

'Because I thought it would take longer than it did.'

'But that's silly. Why didn't you stay and visit with your father?'

Raphaella put down her coffee cup quietly. 'Because I wanted to get back here as soon as I could, Mother.'

'Oh?' Alejandra sensed something brewing and carefully watched her daughter's eyes. 'Why?'

'I'm going home.'

'To Santa Eugenia?' Alejandra looked annoyed. 'Oh not that again for heaven's sake. At least stay in Madrid until Christmas, and then we'll all be there together. But I don't want you there now. It's much too dreary at this time of year.'

'I know it is, and that's not where I'm going. I meant San Francisco.'

'What?' Her mother looked stunned. 'Is that what you discussed with your father? What did he say?'

'Nothing.' Raphaella almost smiled at the memory of the red bathrobe. 'It's my decision.' What she had learned of her father had finally freed her. 'I want to go home.'

'Don't be ridiculous. This is your home, Raphaella.' She waved around her at the elaborate house that had been in the family for fifty years.

'Yes, partly. But I have a home there too. I want to go back there.'

'And do what?' Her mother looked unhappy. First, she

had hidden at Santa Eugenia like a wounded animal, and now she wanted to flee. But she had to admit that there was something alive there. It was only a glimpse . . . a glimmer . . . but it was a reminder of the woman Raphaella had once been. She was still strangely quiet, oddly private, even now she would not say what she was going to do. Alejandra found herself wondering if she had heard from that man again, if that was why she was going, and if that was the case, she was not very pleased. It had only been ten months since the death of her husband after all. 'Why don't you wait until the Spring?'

Raphaella shook her head. 'No. I'm going now.'

'When?'

'Tomorrow.' She decided as she said it, put down her coffee cup, and looked her mother in the eye. 'And I don't know how long I'll stay, or when I'll be back. I may sell the house there, I may not. I just don't know. The only thing I do know is that when I walked out on everything I had there I was in shock. I have to go back.' Her mother knew that it was true. But she was afraid to lose her. She didn't want Raphaella to stay in the States. She belonged in Spain.

'Why don't you just let your father take care of everything for you?' It was what Alejandra would have done herself.

'No.' Raphaella looked at her firmly. 'I'm not a child any more.'

'Do you want to take one of your cousins?'

Raphaella smiled gently. 'No, Mother. I'll be fine.'

She attempted to discuss it several more times with Raphaella, but to no avail, and it was too late when her father received her message. The next day, with trembling hands, he picked up the phone and called Spain. He thought that perhaps Raphaella had told her, that his own marriage was going to explode now in a burst of flame. But what he learned was only that Raphaella had flown back to California that morning. It was too late to stop her, but Alejandra wanted him to call her and tell her to come home.

'I don't think she'll listen, Alejandra.'

'She'll listen to you, Antoine.' He heard the words with a sudden vision of the scene Raphaella had walked in on two

269

days before and he found himself suddenly very grateful that she hadn't told her mother. Now he only shook his head. 'No, she won't listen to me, Alejandra. Not any more.'

Chapter 35

The plane landed at San Francisco International Airport at three o'clock in the afternoon on a brilliantly clear December day. the sun was shining brightly, the air was warm, the wind brisk, and Raphaella took a deep breath, wondering how she had survived without that crisp air. It felt good in her soul just to be there, and when she checked her bags out of customs herself, she felt strong, and free and independent, as she walked outside with the porter and hailed a cab. There was no limousine this time waiting for her, there had been no special exit from the plane. She hadn't asked to be escorted through customs. She had come through just like everyone else, and it felt good. She was tired of being hidden and protected. She knew that it was time she take care of herself. She had called ahead to tell John Henry's staff that she was coming, there were only a few people at the house now anyway. The others had all been let go by her father, some with pensions, some with small sums left to them by John Henry, but all with regret at the era they saw close. They all believed that Raphaella would never come back again, and it was with amazement that the remaining few had heard that she was on her way.

When the cab pulled up in front of the mansion and she rang the doorbell, she was greeted with warmth and friendly smiles. They were all happy to see her, happy to have someone in the house again besides each other, although they all suspected that her return was an omen of change too. That evening they fixed her a handsome dinner, with turkey and stuffing, and sweet potatoes and asparagus, and a wonderful apple pie. In the pantry they all commented on how painfully thin she had gotten, and how unhappy she looked, how tired, and how they had never seen such sad eyes. But she looked better than she had looked at Santa Eugenia for the past year, not that any of them could have known that.

To please them, she had eaten in the dining-room, and afterwards she wandered slowly around the house. It looked sad somehow, empty, unloved, a relic of another era, and as she looked around her she knew that it was time to bring it to a close. If she stayed in San Francisco which she was not at all sure of, she would have no need of a house like this. She knew as she wandered slowly upstairs that it would always depress her. She would always remember John Henry here, diminished as he had been in his last years.

In a way, she was tempted to stay in San Francisco, but if she did she would need a much smaller house . . . like Alex's house . . . on Vallejo . . . despite all her efforts not to let it do that, her mind drifted once again back to him. It was impossible to walk into her bedroom and not think of all the nights when she'd waited impatiently to go to him. She thought of it now as she stood looking around her, wondering how he was, what had happened, what he'd done with his life in the last year. She had never heard again from Amanda or Charlotte, and she somehow suspected that she would not. Nor did she plan to contact them . . . or Alex . . . she had no intention of calling him to tell him she was back. She had come to face the memories of John Henry, to close the house, to pack up his belongings, to face herself. She no longer thought of herself entirely as a killer, but if she was going to live with what had happened, she knew that she had to deal with it, where it had happened and face it all squarely before she went on, and either stayed in San Francisco or went back to Spain. Where she stayed was no longer important. How she felt about what had happened would determine the whole course of her life. She knew that all too well as she roved restlessly from room to room now, trying not to think of Alex, not to let her mind wander, not even to allow herself to feel guilty again for the way that John Henry had died.

It was almost midnight when she finally had the courage to walk into his bedroom. She stood there for a long moment, looking around, remembered the hours she had spent with him, reading to him, talking, listening, eating dinners on trays, and then for some reason she remembered the poems he had been so fond of . . . and as though she had always meant to do that, she walked slowly to the bookcase and began to look over the books. She found the slim volume on the bottom shelf where someone had put it. Much of the time he had kept it on the night-table next to his bed. She remembered now that she had seen it there the next morning . . . the night after . . . she found herself wondering now if he had been reading it when he died. It was an odd romantic notion which was not very likely to have much to do with the truth, but she felt close to him again as she sat down near the bed, holding the slim volume, and remembering the first time they had read it together, on their honeymoon in the South of France. This was the same volume he had bought when he was a very young man. Now, smiling softly, she began to leaf through it, and stopped suddenly at a familiar passage, where the book had been marked with a single blue page. As the book opened to where the paper had been inserted, her heart suddenly leapt strangely as she realised that the single sheet was covered in the shaky scrawl John Henry had developed in his final years. It was as though he had left her something, some message, some last words . . . and then as she began to read, she realised that that was precisely what he had done, and as she glanced at the foot of the letter, her eyes filled with tears.

'My Darling Raphaella,' she read the words again through a blur of tears which began slowly to spill down her cheeks. 'It is an endless evening, at the conclusion of an endless lifetime. A rich lifetime. A richer one because of you. What a priceless gift you have been, my darling. One perfect flawless diamond. You have never ceased to fill me with awe, to bring me pleasure, to give me joy. Now, I can only beg you to forgive me. I have thought of this for so long. I have wanted for such a long time to be free. I go now, without your permission, but I hope with your blessing. Forgive me, my darling, I leave you with all the love I have ever had to give. And think of me not as gone, but as free. With all my heart, John Henry.'

She read the words again and again. 'Think of me not as gone but as free.' He had left her a letter after all. The relief was so overwhelming that she could barely move. He had asked her to forgive *him*. How absurd it all was. And how wrong she had been . . . not gone . . . but free. She thought of him that way now, and she blessed him, as he had begged her to a year before. And the blessing was returned. Because suddenly, for the first time in a year, Raphaella felt free as well. She walked slowly through the house, knowing they were both free. She and John Henry. He had moved on, as he had wanted to so badly. He had chosen the path that was right for him. And now she was free to do the same. She was free to leave . . . to move on . . . She was whole again. And suddenly she wanted to call Alex to tell him about the letter, but she knew that she could not. It would have been a cruelty beyond words to step back into his life after all that time. But she wanted so much to tell him. They hadn't killed John Henry after all.

As she walked slowly back to her bedroom at three o'clock that morning, she thought of both men, tenderly, lovingly, and she loved them both more than she had in a long time. They were all free now . . . all three of them. At last.

She called the real estate agent the next morning, listed the house, called several museums, the libraries at both UC and Stanford, and a moving company, asking for several men and some boxes and tape. It was time to go now. She had made up her mind. She wasn't sure where she was going, or what she would do, but it was time to get out of the house that had been John Henry's and never hers. Maybe it was even time to go back to Europe, but of that she was not yet sure. With John Henry's letter, she was absolved of her 'sin'. She folded it neatly and put it in her handbag. She wanted to put it in the bank with some of her important papers. It was the most important piece of paper she had ever owned.

By the end of the week, she had made her endorsements to the museums, and the two universities she had called had divided up the books. She kept only a handful of the ones she had shared with John Henry, and of course the book of poems in which he had left the last letter to her the night he died. She had already gotten a phone call from her father, and she told him about the letter. There had been a long silence at his end of the phone then, and when he spoke to her again his voice was husky as he apologised for all that he

274

had said. She assured him that she bore him no malice, but as they hung up, they each wondered how one got back a year, how one put balm on wounds that might never heal. But it was John Henry who had bandaged up Raphaella's anguish, he who had given her the finest gift of all with the letter, the truth.

It all seemed like a dream, as Raphaella and the servants packed the last of the boxes. It had taken them a little less than two weeks, and by the following week, on Christmas, Raphaella planned to be back in Spain. There was really no reason for her to be here. The house was all but sold to a woman who was madly in love with it, but whose husband needed just a little more time to make up his mind about their final bid. The furniture was all going to auction, except for a few small pieces she was sending to her mother in Spain. There was really nothing left for her to do there, and in a few days Raphaella would move to a hotel for her last nights before leaving San Francisco for good. Only the memories remained now, drifting through the house like old ghosts. Memories of dinners in the dining-room with John Henry silk dressed or wearing pearls, of evenings in front of the fire ... of the first time she had seen the house. She would have to pack up the memories and take them with her, she told herself as they finished packing, exactly one week before Christmas, at six o'clock. It was already dark out and the cook made her a dinner of eggs and bacon, which was precisely what she wanted, and with a stretch and a sigh, she looked around John Henry's mansion, as she sat on the floor in a pair of old khaki slacks. Everything was ready for the movers to take to the auctioneers, and to the shipping company, which would be sending the few things that she wanted on to Spain. But as she sat finishing the last of her eggs and bacon, her mind drifted again to Alex and the day they had met again on the beach, exactly a year before. She wondered if she would see him again if she went back there, but she smiled to herself at the improbability of it. That dream was over now too.

When she finished the eggs, she took her plates back to the kitchen. The last of the help would be leaving in a few days, and it was strangely pleasant, she had discovered, to take care of her own needs in the oddly dismantled house. But now there were no books to read, no letters to write, no television to watch. She thought, for the first time, of going to a movie, and decided instead to go for a brief walk and then go to bed. She still had some things to do the next morning and she had to go down to the airline to get her return ticket to Spain.

Glancing at the view now and then, she wandered slowly down Broadway, looking at the sedately handsome houses, and knowing that she wouldn't miss them when she left. The house that she had missed so acutely was much smaller, much simpler, painted beige with white trim and bright flowers in the front garden in the Spring. Almost as though her feet knew what her head was thinking, she found herself walking in that direction, until she turned the corner, and saw that it was only a block away. She didn't really want to see it. Yet somehow she knew that she wanted to be there, to sense once again the love she had known there. She had said goodbye at last to the house she had known with John Henry, now it was as though she had to let go of the place where she had known Alex. And maybe then she would be free to find another home, a place of her own this time, and maybe one day a man she could love, as she had loved Alex, and John Henry before that.

She felt almost invisible as she walked there, drawn by some powerful lure she couldn't really explain. It was as though she had waited all week to come here, to see it again, to acknowledge all it had meant to her, and to say goodbye, not to the people, but the place. The house was dark when she got there, and she knew that no one was inside. She wondered even if he were away, in New York maybe, and then she remembered Mandy was in college. Perhaps she had gone home already for Christmas vacation, to Kay or to Hawaii again, with Charlotte. All of those people seemed suddenly so far from Raphaella's life, and she stood there for a long time, looking up at the windows, remembering, feeling all that she had felt there, wishing Alex well, wherever he might be. What she did not see as she stood there was that the garage door had opened, and the black Porsche had stopped at the corner, as the tall dark-haired man at the wheel sat and stared. He was almost certain that it was Raphaella standing across the street from the house, looking up at the windows, but he knew that it wasn't possible, that it was an illusion, a dream. The woman who stood there, dreamily staring seemed taller and much thinner, and she wore old khaki pants and a thick white sweater, with her hair tied in a familiar knot. The silhouette was much like Raphaella and something about her expression, from what he could see at that distance, but he knew that Raphaella was in Spain, and according to his mother, she had just about given up life. He had lost all hope of being able to reach her. She had never answered his letters, and from what his mother had said she was beyond hope. She had cut herself off from everything she had once cared about, given up dreaming and being and feeling. It had almost killed him for a year, but now he had made his peace with what was. Just as he had learned that he couldn't go on tormenting himself over Rachel, he had also learned that he couldn't hang on to Raphaella any more. She didn't want him to. He had understood that much, and so, reluctantly, after a year of sorrow he had given up. But he would always remember . . . always . . . he had never loved any woman as he had loved her.

And then, deciding that the woman outside his house wasn't Raphaella, he put the car back into gear and drove into the garage. Across the street, the boy who so passionately loved the black Porsche came home, stood gazing at the car with his usual awe. He and Alex were friends now. One day, Alex had even given him a ride down the block. But now it wasn't the boy who caught Alex's attention. It was the woman's face that he saw in his rear view mirror. It was she . . . it was . . . he got out of the low-slung Porsche as quickly as his long legs would allow and darted rapidly under the automatic door just before it closed, and then suddenly he stood there, barely moving, only watching her, as across the street she stood trembling, watching him. Her face was much thinner, her eyes larger, her shoulders seemed to sag a little in the clothes she had worn to pack boxes, and she looked tired. But it was Raphaella, the woman he had dreamed of for so long and had finally understood he would never see again. And now suddenly, she was here, watching him, and he wasn't quite sure if she was laughing or crying. There was a small smile on her lips, but the street lights caught the shimmer of a tear drifting slowly from her eye.

Alex said nothing, he only stood there, and then slowly she began to come towards him, carefully, as though she were fording a stream that ran between them, as the tears began to run swiftly down her cheeks, but the smile widened, and now he smiled at her. He wasn't sure why she was there, if she had come to see him, or only to stand there and remember and dream. But now that he had seen her, he wouldn't let her leave him. Not again, not this time, and suddenly he took the last step towards her and pulled her into his arms. His lips were on hers and he could feel his heart pounding as he held her, and then hers as he pressed her still closer and kissed her again. They stood in the middle of the street, kissing, but there were no cars around them. There was only one small boy who had come to see the black Porsche, and had wound up seeing them kissing instead. But it was the Porsche that filled him with wonder, not the two grown-ups clinging to each other in the middle of Vallejo laughing softly, as the man wiped the tears from the woman's eyes. They kissed one last time as they stood there, and then slowly arm in arm, they walked into his garden and disappeared into the house, as the boy shrugged his shoulders, glanced for a last time at the garage which housed his dream car, and went home.

PALOMINO

Danielle Steel

To ride over the hills,
on a fine horse,
with a dream,
looking for love,
before sunset,
is what life is about ...
and to find it
is the culmination
of a lifetime.

1

Hurrying up the steps of the brownstone on East Sixty-third Street, Samantha squinted her eyes against the fierce wind and driving rain, which was turning rapidly into sleet. It whipped her face and tingled as it pricked at her eyes. She made a soft purring noise, as though to urge herself on, and then stopped, gasping, as she fought with the lock, her key refusing to turn. Finally, finally, the door gave, and she fell into the warmth of the front hall. For a long moment she just stood there, shaking the dampness off her long silvery blonde hair. It was a colour one rarely saw, like spun silver meshed with fine gold; a towhead they had called her as a child, and she had hated it, and then in her teens and twenties her hair had won her lavish praise. Now at thirty she was used to it, and when John told her that she looked like a fairy princess, she laughed at him, her blue eyes dancing, her beautiful, delicately angular face in sharp contrast to the full breasts and softly rounded hips. Her legs were long and thin and endless.

She was a woman of a thousand contrasts, huge dancing eyes with a sharp look that saw all, in sudden contrast to the sensual fullness of her mouth, the narrow shoulders, large breasts, the long graceful hands; the softness of her voice in contrast to the intelligent precision of her words. Somehow one expected Samantha Taylor to have a southern drawl, to languish on a velvet chaise longue, her form framed by a negligee trimmed in marabou. Instead she was given to jeans and bounded across rooms with a long stride. She was filled with energy and life, except tonight, except for the past hundred nights.

1

She stood now, as she had since late August, silent, still, waiting, the rain running off the tips of her hair, listening . . . but for what? There was no one here anymore. She was alone in the old brownstone. The couple who owned it had been in London for six months, their duplex apartment had been lent to a cousin who was almost never there. A reporter for *Paris-Match,* he spent more time in New Orleans, Los Angeles, and Chicago than he did in New York. And then there was the top floor. Samantha's domain . . . Samantha's . . . only hers now, although once upon a time it was Samantha and John's, an apartment they had put together with such devotion and such care. Every elegant inch of it, dammit. Samantha thought of it again with a small frown as she left her umbrella in the front hall and made her way slowly upstairs. She hated to come home now and managed to see to it that she came home later every night. It was almost nine o'clock this evening. But it had been later than that the night before. She wasn't even hungry. She hadn't been since she had first heard the news.

'You're what?' She had stared at him in horror on a broiling August evening. The air conditioner was broken, and the air was heavy and still. She had come to greet him at the front door, wearing only white lace underpants and a little lilac bra. 'Are you crazy?'

'No.' He had stared at her, looking wooden and strained. Only that morning they had made love. And now his Viking-like blond beauty seemed . . . beyond her reach. He looked like someone she didn't even know. 'I can't lie to you anymore, Sam. I had to tell you. I've got to get out.'

For what seemed like hours she had only stared at him. He couldn't mean it. He had to be kidding. But he wasn't. That was the insanity of it. He was deadly serious. She knew it from the look of agony on his face. She walked slowly towards him, but he shook his head and turned away. 'Don't . . . please don't.' His shoulders shook softly, and for the first time since he had spoken she felt pity slice through her like a shaft of pain. But why was she feeling sorry for him? Why? How could she feel sorry for *him* after what he had just said?

'Do you love her?' The shoulders she had loved so much only shook more, and he said nothing. But the pity began to fade now as Samantha moved toward him. Anger began to boil within her soul. 'Answer me, dammit.' She yanked hard on his shoulder, and he turned to look into her eyes.

'Yes. I think so. But, Sam, I don't know. I just know I have to get out of here for a while so I can figure it out.'

She stalked across the room, stopping only when she reached the far side of the delicate French rug that looked like a carpet of flowers beneath her bare feet. There were tiny violets and small dusky-coloured roses, and a myriad of still smaller flowers one had to stoop to see. The overall impression was one of pastel pinks and reds and mauves; it was a warm link to the soft pinks and mauves and deep dusty green on the couches and chairs that filled the large wood-panelled room. The house was an old brownstone, and the top floor was theirs. And Samantha had taken two years to decorate it, lovingly, with beautiful pieces of Louis XV furniture that she and John bought together at antique shops and auctions at Sotheby Parke Bernet. The fabrics were all French, the vases constantly filled with freshly cut flowers, the paintings all Impressionistic, and the overall feeling of the apartment was decidedly European and very elegant. Yet there was a cosy side to it too, as there was to Sam. It wasn't the beauty of the apartment she was seeing now as she stood with her back to her husband, wondering if they would ever be the same again. It was as though one of them had just died, as though everything had been instantly and irretrievably shattered and would never be repaired. And all with a few well-chosen words.

'Why didn't you tell me?' She turned and her face

was filled with accusation.

'I . . .' He began but couldn't finish. There was nothing he could say now to make it better, to take back the pain he had just inflicted on the woman he had once so greatly loved. But seven years was a long time. It should have been long enough to solder them to each other forever, and yet it hadn't, and somehow, somehow, during the election coverage the year before, he had slipped. He had meant to end it when they all got back from Washington. He had really meant to. But Liz hadn't let him, and it had gone on. And on, and on . . . until now she had forced his hand. And the bitch of it was that she was pregnant and refused to get rid of the kid. 'I didn't know what to tell you, Sam. I didn't . . . and I thought — '

'I don't give a damn what you thought!' Suddenly her eyes blazed at the man she had known and loved for eleven years. They had become lovers at nineteen. He had been the first man she had ever slept with, when they were both at Yale. He had been so big and blond and beautiful, a football hero, the big man on campus, the golden boy everybody loved, including Sam, who worshipped him from the first moment they met. 'You know what I thought, you son of a bitch? I thought you were faithful to me. That's what I thought. I thought you gave a damn. I thought' – her voice quavered for the first time since he'd said the awful words – 'I thought you loved me.'

'I do.' There were tears running slowly down his cheeks as he said the words.

'Oh, yeah?' She was crying openly now and she felt as though he had just torn out her heart and thrown it on the floor. 'Then how come you're moving out? How come you walked in here like a crazy person, dammit, and when I said, "Hi, babe, how was your day?" you said, "I'm having an affair with Liz Jones and I'm moving out." ' Her voice was growing hysterical as she advanced on him. 'Can you explain that to me? And just how long have you been involved with her anyway?

4

God damn you, John Taylor . . . God damn you . . .' As though she couldn't stop herself, she rushed at him, fists flailing, and then pulling at his hair, trying to maul his face; he resisted her with ease and pulled her arms behind her as he forced her down to the floor, where he cradled her in his arms.

'Oh, babe, I'm so sorry . . .'

'Sorry?' It was a shriek between laughter and tears as she struggled free. 'You come in here and tell me that you're leaving me for someone else and you're "sorry"? Jesus Christ . . .' She took a deep breath then and pushed away from him. 'Let me go, dammit.' She looked at him with raw pain, and when he saw that she was calmer, he let go of her arms. She was still breathless from her attack on him, but now she walked slowly to the dark green velvet couch and sat down. She looked smaller suddenly, and very young, the thick sheet of pale blonde hair hanging down as she buried her face in her hands, and then slowly she raised her face again, her eyes awash with tears. 'Do you really love her?' Somehow it was impossible to believe.

'I think so.' He nodded slowly. 'The worst part is that I love you both.'

'Why?' Samantha looked past him into an empty space, seeing nothing and understanding still less. 'What was missing between us?'

Slowly he sat down. It had to be told. She had to know. He had been wrong to keep it from her for so long. 'It happened during the election coverage last year.'

'And it's been going on since then?' Her eyes widened as she wiped away fresh tears with the back of one hand. 'Ten months, and I didn't know it?' He nodded and said nothing. 'My God.' And then she looked at him strangely. 'Then why now? Why did you walk in here today like this and tell me? Why don't you stop seeing her? Why aren't you trying to save a marriage we've had for more than seven years? What the hell do you mean "I'm having an affair and I'm moving out"?

5

Is that all this means to you?'

She was beginning to shriek again and John Taylor almost cringed. He hated this, hated what he was doing to her, but he knew he had to, he had to go. Liz had something he desperately wanted, she had a quality that he needed, a kind of low profile that pleased him. He and Samantha were too much alike in some ways, too visible, too spectacular, too quick, too beautiful. He liked Liz's sensible plainness, her less-dazzling intelligence, her quiet style, her willingness to take a backseat, to be obscure, while helping him to be more of what he was. She was the perfect foil for him, it was why they worked so well as a team. On camera, doing the news, John was undeniably the star, and Liz helped make him look that way. He liked that. She was so much quieter than Samantha, so much less flamboyant, so much less exciting, and he had finally discovered that that was what he wanted. He didn't feel anxious when he was with her, he didn't have to compete. He was automatically the star.

And there was more to it now. She was pregnant and it was his child, he knew it. It was the one thing he wanted more than all else. A son, to play with and love and teach to play football. It was what he had always wanted, and what Samantha couldn't give him. It had taken the doctors three years to discover what the problem was, and when they did, they were sure. Samantha was sterile. She would never have a child. 'Why now, John?' Samantha's voice dragged him back to the present, and he slowly shook his head.

'It doesn't matter. It's not important. It just had to be done. I had to tell you. There is no good day for something like this.'

'Are you willing to end it?' She was pushing and she knew it, but she had to ask, had to push him; she still couldn't understand what had happened, and why. Why on this blistering hot day had her husband come home from the television station where he reported the news every night and told her that he was leaving her for

6

someone else? 'Will you stop seeing her, John?'

Slowly he had shaken his head. 'No, Sam, I won't.'

'Why?' Her voice had dwindled, childlike, and there had been a fresh wave of tears. 'What does she have that I don't have? She's plain, and she's boring . . . and you —you always said you didn't like her . . . and you hated working with her, and—' She couldn't go on, and he watched her, almost feeling her pain as his own.

'I have to go, Sam.'

'Why?' She grew frantic as he moved into the bedroom to pack his clothes.

'Because I do, that's all. Look, it's not fair of me to stay here and let you go on like this.'

'Please stay . . .' Panic crept into her voice like a dangerous beast. 'It's okay, we'll work it out . . . honest . . . please . . . John . . .' The tears were streaming down her face, and he suddenly turned hard and distant as he packed. He became almost frantic, as though he had to leave in a hurry before he fell apart too.

And then suddenly he turned on her. 'Stop it, dammit! Stop it . . . Sam, please . . .'

'Please what? Please don't cry because my husband is leaving me after seven years, eleven if you count the time at Yale before we were married? Or please don't make you feel guilty while you leave me for some goddamn whore? Is that what you want, John? For me to wish you luck and help you pack? Christ, you walk in here and blow my whole life apart and what do you want from me? Understanding? Well, I can't give it to you. I can't do anything except cry, and if I have to, I'll beg . . . I'll beg, do you hear me . . . ?' And with that, she collapsed in a chair and began to sob again. With a firm hand he clasped the suitcase into which he had thrown half a dozen shirts, a pair of sneakers, two pairs of dress shoes, and a summer suit. Half of it was hanging out of the suitcase, and he was carrying a fistful of ties in one hand. It was impossible. He couldn't think straight, let alone pack.

'I'll come back Monday when you're at work.'

'I'm not going to work.'

'Why not?' He looked dishevelled and distracted, and Samantha looked up at him and laughed softly through her tears.

'Because my husband just left me, you jackass, and I don't think I'm going to feel like going to work on Monday. Do you mind?'

He hadn't smiled, hadn't softened in any way. He just looked at her awkwardly, nodded, and walked quickly out the door. He dropped two ties as he went, and after he was gone, Samantha picked them up and held them for a long time as she lay on the couch and cried.

She had done a lot of crying on the couch since August, but John hadn't come back. In October he had gone to the Dominican Republic for a long weekend, gotten a divorce, and five days later had married Liz. Samantha knew now that Liz was pregnant, and when she had first heard, the news had cut through her like a knife. Liz had announced it one night on the broadcast, and Sam had watched her, her mouth open, shocked. So that was why he had left her. For a kid . . . a baby . . . a son that she couldn't give him. But in time she came to understand that it wasn't only that.

There had been a lot about their marriage that she hadn't seen, hadn't wanted to see, because she loved John so much. His sense of competition with her, his sense of insecurity over Sam's success in her own field. No matter that he was one of the top newscasters in the nation, no matter that people flocked for his autograph everywhere they went, John always seemed to feel that his success was an ephemeral thing, that any day it could be over, that they might replace him, that the ratings could change his life. For Sam, it was different. As assistant creative director of the second largest advertising agency in the country, her position was tenuous, but less so than his. Hers was a fickle profession as well, but she had too many award-winning

8

campaigns behind her to make her feel vulnerable to the winds of change. As she sat alone in her apartment all through the autumn, she remembered bits and pieces, snatches of conversations, things he had said . . .

'For chrissake, Sam, you've made it to the top at thirty. Shit, with bonuses you make more money than I do.' And now she knew that that had bugged him too. But what should she have done? Quit? In her case why not work? They couldn't have a baby and John had never wanted to adopt one. 'It's not the same if it's not your own.' 'But it becomes your own. Look, we could adopt a newborn, we're young enough to qualify for the best. A baby would mean so much, sweetheart, think about it . . .' Her eyes had glowed when they had discussed it, his had always glazed, and then he would shake his head. The answer to the question of adoption was always no. And now he didn't have to worry about it anymore. In three more months he would have his first child. His own. The thought of it always hit Samantha like a physical blow.

Samantha tried not to think about it as she reached the top landing and opened her front door. The apartment had a musty smell these days. The windows were always closed, the heat was too high, her plants were all dying and she had neither thrown them out nor taken care of them. The entire apartment had an aura of unlove, of disuse, as though someone were only changing clothes there, but nothing more than that. And it was true. Samantha hadn't cooked anything more than coffee there since September. She skipped breakfast, ate lunch with clients as a rule, or with other executives of Crane, Harper, and Laub, and dinner she usually forgot. Or if she was absolutely starving, she grabbed a sandwich on the way home and ate it in the waxed paper, juggling it on one knee as she glanced at the news on TV. She hadn't seen her plates since the summer and she didn't really care. She hadn't really lived since the summer, and sometimes she wondered if she ever would again. All she could think of was what had happened, how he had told her, why he had left her, and that he was no longer hers. Pain had given way to fury, which led to sorrow, which grew to grief, which reverted once again to anger, until at last by Thanksgiving her emotions were so frayed at the edges that she was numb. She almost blew the biggest campaign of her career, and two weeks before that she had had to go into her office, lock the door, and lie down. For a moment she had felt as though she were going to have hysterics, faint maybe, or perhaps just put her arms around someone—anyone—and burst into tears. It was as though there were no one now, no one to whom she belonged, no one who cared. Her father had died when she was in college, her mother lived in Atlanta with a man she found charming but whom Sam did not. He was a doctor, and pompous and self-satisfied as hell. But at least her mother was happy. Anyway, Sam wasn't close to her mother, and it wasn't to her that she could turn. In fact she hadn't told her of the divorce until November, when her mother had called one night and found Sam in tears. She had been kind, but it did little to strengthen the bond between them. For Sam and her mother it was too late. And it wasn't a mother that she longed for, it was her husband, the man she had lain next to, and loved, and laughed with for eleven years, the man she knew better than her own skin, who made her happy in the morning and secure at night. And now he was gone. The realisation of it never failed to bring tears to her eyes and a sense of desolation to her soul.

But tonight, cold as well as weary, for once Samantha didn't even care. She took off her coat and hung it in the bathroom to dry, pulled off her boots, and ran a brush through her silvery gold hair. She looked in the mirror without really seeing her face. She saw nothing when she looked at herself now, nothing except a blob of skin, two dull eyes, a mass of long blonde hair. One by one she peeled off her clothes as she stood there, dropping the black cashmere skirt, the black and white

10

silk blouse she'd worn to work. The boots she'd pulled off and thrown on the floor beside her were from Celine in Paris, and the scarf she unknotted at her neck was a black and white geometrical pattern from Hermès. She had worn large pearl and onyx earrings and her hair had been severely knotted at her neck. The coat, which hung damply beside her, was bright red. Even in her dazed state of loss and sorrow, Samantha Taylor was a beautiful woman, or as the creative director of the agency called her, 'a hell of a striking girl.' She turned the tap and a rush of hot water ran into the deep green tub. Once the bathroom had been filled with plants and bright flowers. In summer she liked to keep pansies and violets and geraniums there. There were tiny violets on the wallpaper, and all of the fixtures were French porcelain, in a brilliant emerald green. But like the rest of the apartment, it lacked lustre now. The cleaning woman came to keep everything from getting dusty, but it was impossible to hire someone to come three times a week to make the place looked loved. It was that that had left it, as it had left Samantha herself, that polish, that lustre that comes only with a warm touch and a kind hand, the rich patina of good loving that shows on women in a myriad tiny ways.

When the tub was full of steaming water, Samantha slipped slowly into it, let herself just lie there, and closed her eyes. For a brief moment she felt as though she were floating, as though she had no past, no future, no fears, no worries, and then little by little the present forced itself into her mind. The account she was currently working on was a disaster. It was a line of cars the agency had coveted for a decade, and now she had to come up with the whole concept herself. She had come up with a series of suggestions relating to horses, with commercials to be shot in open country or on ranches, with an outdoorsy-looking man or woman who could make a big splash in the ads. But her heart wasn't really in it, and she knew it, and she wondered briefly for how long this would go on. For how long would she feel somehow impaired, damaged, as though the motor ran but the car would never again get out of first gear? It was a feeling of dragging, of pulling down, like having lead hair and hands and feet. When she stepped out of the tub, with her long silky hair piled in a loose knot atop her head, she wrapped herself carefully in a huge lilac towel and then padded barefoot into her room. Here again there was the feeling of a garden, a huge four-poster was covered with white eyelet embroideries and the bedspread was scattered with bright yellow flowers. Everything in the room was yellow and bright and frilly. It was a room she had loved when she did the apartment, and a place she hated now as she lay in it night after night alone.

It wasn't that there had not been offers. There had been, but she was immobilised by the interminable sensation of being numb. There was no one whom she wanted, no one about whom she cared. It was as though someone had turned off the faucet to her very soul. And now as she sat on the edge of the bed and yawned softly, remembering that she had eaten only an egg-salad sandwich for lunch and skipped both breakfast and dinner, she jumped as she heard the buzzer from downstairs. For a moment she thought about not answering, and then, dropping the towel and reaching hastily for a quilted pale blue satin robe, she ran toward the intercom as she heard the bell again.

'Yes?'

'Jack the Ripper here. May I come up?'

For a fraction of an instant the voice was unfamiliar in the garbled static of the intercom, and then suddenly she laughed, and as she did she looked like herself again. Her eyes lit up, and her cheeks still wore their healthy glow from the warm tub. She looked younger than she had in months. 'What are you doing here, Charlie?' she shouted into the speaker in the wall.

'Freezing my ass off, thanks. You gonna let me in?'

She laughed again and rapidly pressed the buzzer, and a moment later she could hear him bounding up the stairs. When he arrived in her doorway, Charles Peterson looked more like a lumberjack than the art director of Crane, Harper, and Laub, and he looked more like twenty-two than thirty-seven. He had a full, boyish face and laughing brown eyes, dark shaggy hair and a full beard, which was now dusted with sleet. 'Got a towel?' he said, catching his breath, more from the cold and the rain than from the stairs.

She rapidly got him a thick lilac towel from her bathroom and handed it to him; he took off his coat and dried his face and beard. He had been wearing a large leather cowboy hat that now funnelled a little river of ice water onto the French rug. 'Peeing on my carpet again, Charlie?'

'Now that you mention it . . . got any coffee?'

'Sure.' Sam looked at him strangely, wondering if anything was wrong. He had come to visit her once or twice before at the apartment, but usually only when something major was on his mind. 'Something happen with the new account that I should know?' She glanced out at him from the kitchen with a worried look, and he grinned and shook his head as he followed her to where she stood.

'Nope. And nothing's going to go wrong. You've been on the right track with that all week. It's going to be fabulous, Sam.'

She smiled softly as she started the coffee. 'I think so too.' The two exchanged a long, warm smile. They had been friends for almost five years, through countless campaigns, winning awards and teasing and joking and working till four A.M. to co-ordinate a presentation before showing it to the client and the account men the next day. They were both the wunderkinder of Harvey Maxwell, titular creative director of the firm. But Harvey had sat back for years now. He had found Charlie at one agency and hired Samantha from another. He knew good people when he found them. He had given them their heads and sat back with glee as he watched what they created. In another year he would retire, and it was everyone's bet, including Samantha's, that she would inherit his job. Creative director at thirty-one was not bad at all. 'So what's new, kiddo? I haven't seen you since this morning. How's the Wurtzheimer stuff going?'

'Well . . .' Charlie threw up his hands with an expression of acceptance. 'How much can you do for one of the largest department stores in St. Louis that has big bucks and no taste?'

'What about the swan theme we talked about last week?'

'They hated it. They want flash. Swans ain't flash.'

Sam rolled her eyes and sat down at the large butcher-block table as Charlie sprawled his lanky form into one of the chairs across from her. It was strange, she had never been drawn to Charlie Peterson, not in all the years they had worked together, travelled together, slept on planes together, talked into the wee hours together. He was her brother, her soul mate, her friend. And he had a wife she loved almost as much as he did. Melinda was perfect for him. She had decorated their big friendly apartment on East Eighty-first with brightly coloured tapestries and beautifully woven baskets. The furniture was all covered in a deep mahogany-coloured leather and everywhere one looked were wonderful little art objects, tiny treasures Melinda had discovered and brought home, everything from exotic seashells they had collected together in Tahiti to one perfect marble she had borrowed from their sons. They had three boys, all of whom looked like Charlie, a large unmannerly dog named Rags, and an enormous yellow Jeep Charlie had driven for the past ten years. Melinda was also an artist, but she had never been 'corrupted' by the workaday world. She worked in a studio and had had two successful shows of her work in the past few years. In many ways she was very different from Samantha, yet the two women had a gentleness in common, a softness beneath the bravado that Charlie treasured in both. And in his own way he loved

Samantha, and he had been rocked to the core by what John had done. He had never liked him anyway and had always pegged him for an egocentric ass. John's rapid desertion of Samantha and subsequent marriage to Liz Jones had proved to Charlie that he was right, as far as he was concerned at least. Melinda had tried to understand both sides, but Charlie hadn't wanted to hear it. He was too worried about Sam. She'd been in lousy shape for the past four months, and it showed. Her work had suffered. Her eyes were dead. Her face was gaunt.

'So what's doing, madame? I hope you don't mind my coming over so late.'

'No.' Samantha smiled as she poured him a cup of coffee. 'I just wonder how come you're here. Checking up on me?'

'Maybe.' His eyes were gentle above the dark beard. 'Do you mind that, Sam?'

She looked up at him sadly and he wanted to take her in his arms. 'How could I mind that? It's nice to know someone gives a damn.'

'You know I do. And so does Mellie.'

'How is she? Okay?' He nodded. They never had time to talk about things like that in the office.

'She's fine.' He was beginning to wonder how he was going to lead into what he wanted to tell her. It wasn't going to be easy, and he knew that she might not take it well.

'So? What's up?' Samantha was suddenly looking at him with amusement. He feigned an innocent expression and Samantha tweaked his beard. 'You've got something up your sleeve, Charlie. What is it?'

'What makes you say that?'

'It's pouring with rain outside, it's freezing cold, it's Friday night, and you could be at home with your warm, cosy wife and your three charming children. It's difficult to imagine that you came all the way over here just for a cup of coffee with me.'

'Why not? You're a lot more charming than my

15

children. But'—he hesitated briefly—'you're right. I didn't just happen to drop by. I came here to talk to you.' God, it was awful. How could he tell her? He suddenly knew that she'd never understand.

'And? Come on, out with it.' There was a spark of mischief in her eye that he hadn't seen for a long time.

'Well, Sam . . .' He took a deep breath and watched her closely. 'Harvey and I were talking—'

'About me?' She looked instantly uptight, but he nodded and went on. She hated people talking about her now. Because they always talked about how she was and what John had done.

'Yeah, about you.'

'Why? The Detroit account? I'm not sure he understands my concept, but—'

'No, not about the Detroit account, Sam. About *you*.'

'What about me?' She thought that was over, that they weren't talking about her anymore. There was nothing left to talk about. The separation was over, the divorce had come and gone, and John was married to someone else. She had survived it. So? 'I'm fine.'

'Are you? I think that's amazing.' He looked at her with feeling and a trace of anger he had felt all along for John. 'I'm not sure I'd be so fine in your shoes, Sam.'

'I don't have any choice. Besides, I'm tougher than you are.'

'You probably are.' He smiled gently. 'But maybe not as tough as you think. Why not give yourself a break, Sam?'

'What's that supposed to mean? Go to Miami and lie on the beach?'

'Why not?' He forced a smile and she looked at him, shocked.

'What are you telling me?' Panic crept rapidly into her face. 'Is Harvey firing me? Is that it? Did he send you here to play hatchet man, Charlie? They don't want me anymore because I'm not as cheerful as I used to be?' Just asking the questions, she felt her eyes fill with tears. 'Christ, what did you expect? I had a rough

16

time . . . it was . . .' The tears began to choke her and she hurriedly stood up. 'I'm okay, dammit. I'm fine. Why the hell—' But Charlie grabbed her arm and pulled her back down to her seat with a gentle look in his eyes.

'Take it easy, babe. Everything's okay.'

'Is he firing me, Charlie?' A lone, sad tear crept down her cheek. But Charlie Peterson shook his head.

'No, Sam, of course not.'

'But?' She knew. She already knew.

'He wants you to go away for a while, to take it easy. You've given us enough to run with for a while on the Detroit account. And it won't kill the old man to think about business for a change. We can get along without you, as long as we have to.'

'But you don't have to. This is silly, Charlie.'

'Is it?' He looked at her long and hard. 'Is it silly, Sam? Can you really take that kind of pressure and not buckle? Watching your husband leave you for someone else, seeing him on national television every night chatting with his new wife as you watch her pregnant belly growing? Can you really take that in stride without missing a step? Without missing a goddamn day at work, for chrissake, insisting on taking on every new account in the house. I expect you to crack yourself wide open sooner or later. Can you really put yourself on the line like that, Sam? I can't. I can't do that to you, just as your friend. What that son of a bitch did to you almost brought you to your knees, for God's sake. Give in to it, go cry somewhere, let go of it all and then come back. We need you. We need you desperately. Harvey knows that, I know it, the account guys know it, and you damn well better know it, but we don't need you sick or crazy or broken and that's how you're going to wind up if you don't take the pressure off now.'

'So you think I'm having a nervous breakdown, is that it?' She looked hurt as well as shocked, but Charlie shook his head.

'Of course not. But hell, a year from now, you could.

17

The time to take care of the pain is now, Sam, not later, when it's buried so deep that you can't find it anymore.'

'I've already lived with it for this long. It's been four months.'

'And it's killing you.' It was a flat statement on his part and she didn't deny it.

'So what did Harvey say?' She looked sad as her eyes met those of her friend. She felt somehow as though she had failed, as though she should have been able to handle it better.

'He wants you to go away.'

'Where?' She wiped a tear from her cheek with the back of her hand.

'Anywhere you want.'

'For how long?'

He hesitated for only an instant before answering. 'Three or four months.' What they had decided was that she would be better off away until John and Liz had had their much publicised child. Charlie knew what a blow it was to Samantha, and he and Harvey had talked it out over many a lunch, but neither could have been prepared for the look Charlie saw now on her face. It was a look of total disbelief, of shock, almost horror.

'*Four months?* Are you crazy? What the hell is going to happen to our clients? What the hell will happen to my job? Jesus, you really took care of it, didn't you? What is it? You want my job all of a sudden, is that it?' She jumped up from the table again and stalked away, but he followed her and stood facing her, looking down at her with sorrow in his eyes.

'Your job is a sure thing, Sam. But you've got to do this. You can't push yourself like this anymore. You have to get out of here. Out of this apartment, out of your office, maybe even out of New York. You know what I think? I think you should call that woman you like so much in California and go stay with her. Then come back when it's out of your system, when you're back among the living. It'll do you a hell of a lot of good.'

18

'What woman?' Samantha looked blank.

'The one you told me about years ago, the one with the horse ranch, Carol or Karen something, the old woman who was the aunt of your college roommate. You used to talk about her as though she were your dearest friend.' She had been. Barbie had been her closest confidante besides John, and they had been college roommates. She had died two weeks after graduation in a plane crash over Detroit.

There was suddenly a gentle smile in Samantha's eyes. 'Barbie's aunt . . . Caroline Lord. She's a wonderful woman. But why on earth would I go there?'

'You like to ride, don't you?' She nodded. 'Well, it's a beautiful place and it's about as different and as far from Madison Avenue as you can get. Maybe what you need is to park your fancy business wardrobe and pour that sexy body of yours into some jeans and chase cowboys for a while.'

'Very funny, that's all I need.' But the idea had struck some kind of chord. She hadn't seen Caroline in years. She and John had stopped to visit her once, it had been a three-hour drive north and east from L.A. and John had hated it. He didn't like the horses, thought the ranch was uncomfortable, and Caroline and her foreman had looked askance at him for his prissy city ways. A horseman he wasn't, but Samantha was an elegant horsewoman. She had been since she was a child. There had been a wild pinto pony on the ranch when they visited and she had ridden it, to Caroline's dismay. But she hadn't got hurt in spite of the horse throwing her half a dozen times as she tried to help break him to the saddle, and John had been instantly impressed by her skill. It had been a happy time in Sam's life and seemed a long time in the past as she looked up at Charlie now. 'I'm not even sure she'd have me. I don't know, Charlie. It's a crazy idea. Why don't you guys just leave me alone to finish my work?'

'Because we love you, and you're going to destroy yourself like this.'

'No, I'm not.' She smiled valiantly at him, and slowly he shook his head.

'It doesn't matter what you say to me now, Sam. It was Harvey's decision.'

'What was?'

'Your leave of absence.'

'It's definite, then?' Once again she looked shocked and again he nodded his head.

'As of today. Three and a half months leave, and you can extend it to six if you want.' They had called the station to ascertain Liz's due date, and tacked two more weeks from there.

'And I won't lose my job?'

'No.' He slowly pulled a letter out of his pocket and gave it to Samantha to read. It was from Harvey and guaranteed her job even if she stayed away for six months. It was unheard of in their business, but as Harvey had put it, Samantha Taylor was 'a fairly extraordinary girl.'

Sam looked up sadly at Charlie. 'Does this mean I'm off as of today?' Her lower lip trembled.

'That's what it means, lady. You're on vacation as of right now. Hell, I wish I were.'

'Oh, my God.' She sank into a chair and covered her face with one hand. 'Now what am I going to do, Charlie?'

He gently touched her shoulder. 'Do what I told you, baby. Call your old friend on that ranch.'

It was a mad suggestion, but after he left, she began to think about what she was going to do. She went to bed still in a state of shock. For the next three and a half months, she was out of a job. She had nowhere to go, nothing to do, nothing she wanted to see, and no one to see it with. For the first time in her adult life she was totally without plans. All she had to do was have one meeting with Harvey the next morning to explain everything on her desk and after that she was free. As she lay there in the dark, feeling frightened, suddenly she began to giggle. It was crazy really, what the hell was she going to do with herself until April 1? April fool . . . the joke's on you . . . Europe? Australia? A visit to her mother in Atlanta? For an instant she felt freer than she ever had before. When she had left Yale, she had had John to think of, and now she had no one at all. And then, on an impulse, she reached for her address book in the darkness and decided to follow Charlie's advice. She flicked on the light and found the number easily under *L*. It would be nine thirty in California, and she hoped that it wasn't too late to call.

The phone was answered on the second ring by the familiar smoky voice of Caroline Lord. There followed a lengthy explanation on Sam's part, friendly silence from Caroline as she spoke, and then a strange, anguished sob as Sam let herself go at last. Then it was like coming home to an old friend. The older woman listened, really listened. She gave Sam a kind of comfort she had forgotten over the years. And when Sam hung up the phone half an hour later, she lay staring at the canopy above her, wondering if maybe she really was going crazy after all. She had just promised to fly to California the following afternoon.

2

It was a frenzied morning for Samantha, she packed two suitcases, called the airlines, left a note and a cheque for the cleaning woman, and attempted to close up the apartment as best she could. Then, with her two suitcases, she took a cab to the office, where she gave Charlie the key to the apartment and promised to send Christmas presents for the boys from the coast. Then she met with Harvey for more than two hours, explaining everything he wanted to know.

'You know, you don't have to do this for me, Harvey. It isn't what I want.' Her eyes reached out toward him as they concluded the meeting that would send her on her way.

He eyed her quietly from across his vast marble and chrome desk. 'It isn't what you want, Sam, But it's what you need, whether you know it or not. Are you getting out of town?' He was a tall, spare man with iron-grey hair that he wore as closely cropped as any Marine. He wore white Brooks Brothers shirts, striped suits, looked like a banker, and smoked a pipe, but behind the steely grey eyes was a brilliant mind, a creative spirit, and a rare and beautiful soul. He had been, in a sense, like a father to Samantha, and now that she thought it over, it didn't really surprise her that he was sending her away. But they hadn't spoken of her plans all morning. All they talked about were the accounts.

'Yes, I'm going away.' She smiled at him from across the forbidding desk. It was easy to remember how frightened she had been of him at first, and how much she had come to respect him over the years. But the respect was mutual, as she knew. 'In fact'—she looked at her watch—'my plane leaves in two hours.'

'Then get the hell out of my office.' He put his pipe down and grinned, but Sam hesitated for a moment in her chair.

'You're sure I'll get my job back, Harvey?'

'I swear it. You have the letter?' She nodded. 'Good. Then if you don't get your job back, you can sue me.'

'That's not what I want. I want the job.'

'You'll get it, and probably mine eventually, too.'

'I could come back in a few weeks, you know.' She said it tentatively, but he shook his head and the smile faded quickly from his eyes.

'No, Sam, you can't. April first, and that's it.'

'For any special reason?' He didn't want to tell her, so again he shook his head.

'No, that was the date we picked. I'll send you plenty of memos to keep you abreast of what's happening here, and you can call me anytime you want. Does my secretary know where to find you?'

'Not yet, but she will.'

'Good.' He came around the desk then pulled her toward him without saying another word. He held her close for a long moment and then kissed the top of her head. 'Take it easy, Sam. We'll miss you.' His voice was gruff and there were tears in her eyes as she held him close for one moment and then strode rapidly toward the door. For just one tiny instant she felt as though she were being banished from her home, and she felt panic wash over her as she considered begging him not to make her leave.

But when she left his office, Charlie was waiting for her outside in the hallway, and he smiled gently at her, slung an arm over her shoulders, and gave her a squeeze. 'Ready to go, kiddo?'

'No.' She smiled damply at him and then sniffed, burrowing closely into his side.

'You will be.'

'Yeah? What makes you so sure?' They were walking slowly back to her office, and more than ever she wanted to stay. 'This is crazy. You know that, don't you, Charlie? I mean, I have work to do, campaigns to co-ordinate, I have no right to—'

'You can keep talking if you want to, Sam, but it won't make any difference.' He looked at his watch. 'Two hours from now I'm putting you on that plane.'

Samantha suddenly stopped walking and turned to look at him belligerently, and he couldn't resist smiling at her. She looked like a very beautiful and totally impossible child. 'What if I won't get on it? What if I just won't go?'

'Then I'll drug you and take you out there myself.'

'Mellie wouldn't like that.'

'She'd love it. She 's been begging me to get out of her hair all week.' He stopped, eyeing Samantha.

Slowly she smiled. 'I'm not going to talk you out of it, am I?'

'Nope. Nor Harvey. It really doesn't matter where you go, Sam, but you've got to get the hell out of here, for your own sake. Don't you want to? Don't you want to get away from all the questions, from the memories, from the chance of running into . . . them?' The word had a painful ring to it, and she shrugged.

'What difference does it make? When I turn on the news in California, they'll still be there. The two of them. Looking . . .' Her eyes filled with tears just thinking of those two faces that she was magnetically drawn to every night. She always watched them, and then hated herself for it, wanting to turn the knob to another channel but unable to move her hand. 'I don't know, dammit, they just look like they belong together, don't they?' Suddenly her face pulled into a mask of sadness and the tears began to roll down her face. 'We never looked like that, did we? I mean—'

But Charlie said nothing, he only pulled her into his arms. 'It's okay, Sam. It's okay.' And then as she cried softly into his shoulder, oblivious of the glances of secretaries hurrying past her, he swept a long strand of the blonde hair off her forehead and smiled down at her again. 'This is why you need a vacation. I think it's called emotional exhaustion, or hadn't you noticed?'

She grunted disapproval and then chuckled softly through her tears. 'Is that what they call it? Yeah . . .' She pulled away from him, sighed, and wiped the tears from her cheeks. 'Maybe I do need a vacation.' And then, valiantly swinging her hair back over her shoulders, she attempted to glare at her friend. 'But not for the reasons you think. You bastards have just worn me out.'

'You're damn right we have. And we have every intention of doing so again when you return. So enjoy yourself while you're out there. Horse freak.' A hand on both their shoulders suddenly made them both turn.

'Haven't you left yet, Samantha?' It was Harvey, pipe clenched in his teeth and a bright light in his eyes. 'I thought you had a plane to catch.'

24

'She does.' Charlie grinned at her.

'Then put her on it, for chrissake. Get her out of here. We have work to do.' He smiled gruffly, waved the pipe, and disappeared down another hallway as Charlie looked at her again and saw the sheepish smile.

'You don't really have to put me on the plane, you know.'

'Don't I?' She shook her head in answer, but she wasn't paying attention to the art director, she was looking at her office as though for the last time. Charlie caught her expression and grabbed her coat and bags. 'Come on, before you get maudlin on me. Let's catch that plane.'

'Yes, sir.'

He crossed the threshold and waited, and with two hesitant steps she followed him. With a deep breath and one last glance behind her she softly closed the door.

3

The plane ride across the country was uneventful. The country drifted below her like bits and pieces of a patchwork quilt. The rough brown nubby textures of winter fields drifted into snowy white velvets, and as they reached the West Coast, there were signs of deep satiny greens and rich shiny blues, as lakes and forests and fields ran beneath them. At last, with a fiery sunset to welcome them, the plane touched down in L.A.

Samantha stretched her long legs out in front of her, and then her arms as she looked out of the window once again. She had dozed most of the way across the country, and now she looked out and wondered why she had come. What point was there in running all the way to California? What would she possibly find there? She knew as she stood up, tossing her long blonde mane behind her, that she had been wrong to come all this way. She wasn't nineteen years old anymore. It didn't make any sense to come and hang out on a ranch and play cowgirl. She was a woman with responsibilities and a life to lead, all of which centred around New York. But what did she have there really? Nothing—nothing at all.

With a sigh she watched the rest of the passengers begin to deplane, and she buttoned her coat, picked up her tote bag, and fell in line. She had worn a dark brown suede coat with a sheepskin lining, jeans, and her chocolate leather boots from Celine. The tote bag she had brought was in the same colour and tied around the handle was a red silk scarf, which she took off and knotted loosely round her neck. Even with the worried frown between her eyebrows, and the casual clothes she had worn on the trip, she was still a strikingly beautiful woman, and heads turned as men noticed her making her way slowly out of the giant plane. None of them had seen her during the five-hour trip because she had only left her seat once and that to wash her face and hands before the late lunch that was served. But the rest of the time she had just sat there, numb, tired, dozing, trying to reason out once again why she had let them do this, why she had allowed herself to be talked into coming west.

'Enjoy your stay. Thank you for flying . . .' The phalanx of stewardesses spoke the familiar words like a chorus of Rockettes, and Samantha smiled at them in return.

A moment later Samantha was standing in the Los Angeles airport, looking around with a sense of disorientation, wondering where to go, who would find her, not sure suddenly if they would even meet her at all. Caroline had said that the foreman, Bill King, would probably meet her, and if he wasn't available, one of the other ranch hands would be there. 'Just look

26

for them, you can't miss 'em, not in that airport.' And then the old woman had laughed softly, and so had Sam. In an airport filled with Vuitton and Gucci and gold lamé sandals and mink and chinchilla and little bikini tops and shirts left open to the navel, it would be easy to spot a ranch hand, in Stetson and cowboy boots and jeans. More than the costume, it would be easy to spot the way they moved and walked, the deep tan of their skin, their wholesome aura as they moved uneasily in the showily decked-out, decadent crowd. Sam already knew from her other visits to the ranch that there would be nothing decadent about the ranch hands. They were tough, kind, hardworking people who loved what they did and had an almost mystical tie to the land that they worked on, the people they worked with, and the livestock they tended with such care. They were a breed Samantha had always respected, but certainly a very different breed than she was accustomed to in New York. For a moment, as she stood there, watching the typical airport chaos, she suddenly realised that once she got to the ranch she would be glad she had come. Maybe this was what she needed after all.

As she looked around for the sign that said BAGGAGE CLAIM, she felt a hand on her arm. She turned, looking startled, and then she saw him, the tall, broad-shouldered, leathery old cowboy that she remembered instantly from ten years before. He stood towering over her, his blue eyes like bits of summer sky, his face marked like a landscape, his smile as wide as she remembered it; a feeling of great warmth exuded from him as he touched his hat and then enfolded her into a great big bear hug. It was Bill King, the man who had been the foreman on the Lord Ranch since Caroline had bought it some thirty years before. He was a man in his early sixties, a man of slight education, but with vast knowledge, great wisdom, and even greater warmth. She had been drawn to him the first time she'd seen him, and she and Barbara had looked up to him like a wise uncle, and he had championed their every cause. He

27

had come with Caroline to Barbara's funeral and had stood discreetly behind the family with a floodtide of tears coursing down his face. But there were no tears now, there were only smiles for Samantha as the huge hand on her shoulder squeezed her still harder and he gave a small shout of glee.

'Damn, I'm happy to see you, Sam! How long has it been? Five, six years?'

'More like eight or nine.' She grinned up at him, equally happy to see him and suddenly delighted that she had come. Maybe Charlie hadn't been so wrong after all. The tall, weathered man looked down at her with a look that told her she had come home.

'Ready?' He crooked an arm and with a nod and a smile she took it, and they went in search of her baggage, which was already spinning lazily on the turntable when they got downstairs. 'This it?' He looked at her questioningly, holding the large black leather suitcase with the red and green Gucci stripe. He held the heavy case easily in one hand, her tote slung over his shoulder.

'That's it, Bill.'

He frowned at her briefly. 'Then you can't be meaning to stay long. I remember the last time you came out here with your husband. You must have had seven bags between the two of you.'

She chuckled at the memory. John had brought enough clothes with him for a month at Saint-Moritz. 'Most of that was my husband's. We had just been to Palm Springs.'

He nodded, saying nothing, and then led the way to the garage. He was a man of few words but rich emotions. She had seen that often during her early visits to the ranch. Five minutes later they had reached the large red pickup, stowed her suitcase in the back, and were driving slowly out of the parking lot of the Los Angeles International Airport, and Sam suddenly felt as though she were about to be set free. After the confinement of her life in New York, her job, her

28

marriage, and now the confusion of bodies pressing around her on the plane and then in the airport terminal after the trip, finally she was about to go out to open places, to be alone, to think, to see mountains and trees and cattle, and to rediscover a life she had almost forgotten. As she thought of it, a long, slow smile lit up her face.

'You look good, Sam.' He cast an eye at her as they left the airport, and he shifted into fourth gear as they reached the freeway beyond.

But she only smiled and shook her head at him. 'Not as good as all that. It's been a long time.' Her voice softened on the words, remembering the last time she had seen him and Caroline Lord. It had been a strange trip, an awkward mingling of past and present. The ranch hadn't been much fun for John. And as they drove along the highway, Sam's mind filled with memories of the last trip. It seemed a thousand years later when she felt the old foreman's hand on her arm, and when she looked around, she realised that the countryside around them had altered radically. There was no evidence of the plastic ugliness of the L.A. suburbs, in fact there were no houses in sight at all, only acres and acres of rolling farmland, the far reaches of large ranches, and uninhabited government preserves. It was beautiful country all around her, and Sam rolled down the window and sniffed the air. 'God, it even smells different, doesn't it?'

'Sure does.' He smiled the familiar warm smile and drove on for a while without speaking. 'Caroline sure is looking forward to seeing you, Sam. It's been kind of lonely for her ever since Barb died. You know, she talks about you a heck of a lot. I always wondered if you'd come back. I didn't really think so after the last time.' They had left the ranch early, and John had made no secret of the fact that he'd been bored stiff.

'I would have come back, sooner or later. I was always hoping to stop here when I went to L.A. on business, but I never had enough time.'

'And now? You quit your job, Sam?' He had only a vague idea that she had something to do with commercials, but he had no clear picture of what, and he didn't really care. Caroline had told him that it was a good job, it made her happy, and that was all that counted. He knew what her husband did, of course. Everyone in the country knew John Taylor, by face as well as by name. Bill King had never liked him, but he sure as hell knew who he was.

'No, Bill, I didn't quit. I'm on leave.'

'Sick leave?' He looked worried as they drove through the hills.

Sam hesitated for only a moment. 'Not really. Kind of a rest cure, I guess.' For a minute she was going to leave it at that and then she decided to tell him. 'John and I split up.' He raised a questioning eyebrow but said nothing, and she went on. 'Quite a while ago actually. At least it seems like it. It's been three or four months.' A hundred and two days, to be exact. She had counted every one of them. 'And I guess they just thought I needed the break at the office.' It sounded lousy to her as she said it, and suddenly she felt panic rise in her as it had that morning when she spoke to Harvey. Were they really firing her and just didn't want to tell her yet? Did they think she'd already cracked up? But when she looked at Bill King, she saw that he was nodding, as though it all made perfect sense to him.

'Sounds right to me, babe.' His voice was reassuring. 'It's damn hard to keep on going when you hurt.' He stopped for a moment and then went on. 'I found that out years ago when my wife died. I thought I could still handle my job on the ranch I was working on then. But after a week my boss said, "Bill, my boy, I'm givin' you a month's money, you go on home to your folks and come back when the money's gone." You know, Sam, I was mad as fire when he did it, thought he was telling me that I couldn't handle the job, but he was right. I went to my sister's outside Phoenix, stayed for about six weeks, and when I came back, I was myself again. You can't expect a man nor a woman to keep going all the time. Sometimes you have to give him room for his grief.'

He didn't tell her that he had taken three months off twenty-five years later, time off from the Lord ranch, when his son was killed during the early days of Vietnam. For three months he had been so stricken that he had barely been able to talk. It was Caroline who had nursed him out of it, who had listened, who had cared, who had finally come to find him in a bar in Tucson and dragged him home. He had a job to do on the ranch, she had told him, and enough was enough. She barked at him like a drill sergeant and heaped work on him until he thought he would die. She had shouted, yelled, argued, bullied, until finally one day they had almost come to blows out in the south pasture. They had got off their horses, and she had swung at him, and he had knocked her right on her ass, and then suddenly she had been laughing at him, and she laughed until the tears ran from her eyes in streams, and he laughed just as hard and knelt beside her to help her up, and it was then that he had kissed her for the first time.

It had been eighteen years ago that August, and he had never loved another woman as he loved her. She was the only woman he had actually ached for, longed for, lusted after, laughed with, worked with, dreamed with, and respected more than he respected any man. But she was a very special kind of woman. Caroline Lord was no ordinary woman. She was a superwoman. She was brilliant and amusing, attractive, kind, compassionate, intelligent. And he had never been able to understand what she wanted with a ranch hand. But she had known her mind from the beginning and never regretted the decision. For almost twenty years now she had secretly been his woman. And she would have made the affair public long before, had he let her. But he felt that her position as mistress of the Lord Ranch was sacred, and although here and there it was suspected, no one had ever known for certain that they

31

were lovers, the only thing anyone knew for certain was that they were friends. Even Samantha had never been sure that there was more between them, though she and Barbara had suspected and often giggled, but they had never really known.

'How's Caroline, Bill?' She looked over at him with a warm smile and saw a special glow come to his eyes.

'Tough as ever. She's tougher than anyone on that ranch.' And older. She was three years older than he. She had been one of the most glamorous and elegant women in Hollywood in her twenties, married to one of the most important directors of her day. The parties they had given were still among the early legends, and the home they had built in the hills above Hollywood was still on some of the tours. It had changed hands often but was still a remarkable edifice, a monument to a bygone era rarely equalled in later years. But at thirty-two Caroline Lord had been widowed, and after that, for her, life in Hollywood had never been the same again. She had stayed on for two more years, but they had been painful and lonely, and then suddenly without explanation she had disappeared. She had spent a year in Europe, and then another six months in New York. It took her another year after that to decide what she really wanted, but as she drove for hours, alone in her white Lincoln Continental, she suddenly knew where it was she longed to be. Out in the country, in nature, away from the champagne and the parties and the pretence. None of it had had any meaning for her after her husband was gone. All of that was over for her now. She was ready for something very different, a whole new life, a new adventure, and that spring, after looking at every available piece of property in a two-hundred mile radius of Los Angeles, she bought the ranch.

She paid a fortune for it, hired an advisor and the best ranch hands around. She paid everyone a handsome wage, built them pleasant, cosy quarters, and offered them a kind of warmth and comfort that few men could deny. And in return, she wanted sound advice and good teaching, she wanted to learn how to run the ranch herself one day, and she expected them all to work as hard as she did herself. It was in her first year at the ranch that Bill King found her, took the place in hand, and taught her all he knew himself. He was a foreman of the kind most ranchers would die for, and it was purely by accident that he landed on the Lord Ranch. And even more so that he and Caroline Lord wound up as lovers. All that Samantha knew of Bill's history on the ranch was that he had been there almost since the beginning and had helped make the place a financial success.

Theirs was one of the few California cattle ranches that showed a profit. They bred Angus cattle and sold a few Morgan horses as well. Most of the big ranches were in the Midwest or the Southwest; only a precious few in California had good luck, and many were kept in operation as tax losses by their owners—city dwellers, stockbrokers, lawyers, and movie stars who bought them as a kind of game. But the Lord Ranch was no game, not to Bill King or Caroline Lord, or to the men who worked there, and Samantha also knew that while she stayed there she would be expected to perform certain chores as well. No one came to the ranch just to be lazy. It seemed indecent, considering how hard everyone else worked.

When Sam had called Caroline this time, she had told Sam that at the moment they were short two men and Samantha was welcome to help out. It was going to be a busy vacation for Samantha, of that she was sure. She figured that most likely she would do small jobs in the stables, take care of some of the horses, and maybe help clean out some of the stalls. She knew just how unlikely it was that she would get a chance to do much more. Not that she wasn't able to. Samantha had long since proven her skill on a horse. A rider at five, in horse shows at seven, Madison Square Garden at twelve, and three blue ribbons and a red, jumping competitions thereafter, and a couple of years when she had dreamed of the Olympics and when she had spent every living moment she had with her own horse. But once she'd gone to college there hadn't been much time for horses, the dream of the Olympics faded, and in the years afterward she almost never had time to ride. It was only when she had visited the ranch with Barbara, or when she met someone with horses once in a great while, that she still got the chance to ride. But she knew that as a 'city gal,' she would not likely be trusted by hands to work with them, unless Caroline interfered on her behalf.

'Been riding much lately?' As though reading her thoughts, Bill leaned toward her with a smile.

She shook her head. 'You know, I don't think I've been on a horse in two years.'

'You'll be mighty sore by this time tomorrow.'

'Probably.' They exchanged a quiet smile as they drove on in the early evening. 'But it'll probably feel good. That's a nice kind of sore.' Tired knees and aching calves— it wasn't like the aching spirit she had borne these last months.

'We've got some new palominos, a new pinto, and a whole mess of Morgans, all of which Caroline bought this year. And then'—he almost grunted as he said it—'she's got this crazy damn horse. Don't ask me why she bought it, except some damn fool nonsense about he looks like a horse in some movie her husband made.' He looked at Sam disapprovingly. 'She bought herself a Thoroughbred. Hell of a fine horse. But we don't need a horse like that on a ranch. Looks like a damn racehorse . . . runs like one too. She's going to kill herself on it. No doubt about it. Told her so myself.'

He glared at Sam and she smiled. She could just imagine elegant Caroline on her Thoroughbred, racing across the fields as though she were still a young girl. It would be wonderful to see her again, wonderful to be back there, and suddenly Samantha felt a wave of gratitude wash over her. She was so glad she had come after all. She cast a sideways glance at Bill as he drove the last few miles toward the ranch that had been his home for more than two decades, and Samantha found herself wondering again just exactly how far his involvement with Caroline went. At sixty-three he was still virile and handsome, the broad frame, the long legs, the strong arms, the powerful hands, and the brilliant blue eyes all combined to give him an aura of power and style. On him the Stetson looked marvellous, on him the blue jeans seemed to be moulded to his legs. None of it looked trite or silly. He was the best of his breed, the proudest of his kind. The rugged lines of his face only helped to enhance the well-chiselled features, and the deep husky baritone voice was precisely what it had been. He was easily six feet four without the Stetson, and with it, he was literally a towering man.

As they drove through the front gates of the ranch, Samantha breathed a sigh of relief—of pain—of lots of feelings. The road stretched on for another mile after the sign that said LORD RANCH with a handsomely carved L, which they also used in their brand. Samantha felt like an anxious child as she caught her breath, expecting to see the house suddenly loom toward them, but it was another ten minutes before they rounded the last turn in the private road, and then suddenly there it was. It looked almost like an old plantation, a beautiful big white house with dark blue shutters, a brick chimney, a wide front porch, broad front steps, surrounding flower beds, which became a riot of colour in the summer, and, behind it all, a veritable wall of gigantic, handsome trees. Just down the slope from the house was a single willow tree and a little pond, which was covered with lilies and filled with frogs. Near at hand were the stables, beyond them the barns, and all around were cottages for the men. In Sam's mind it always stood out as the way a ranch should look, but whenever she had seen others, she had rapidly discovered that few did. Few other ranches were as impeccably kept, as handsome, as well run ... and none of them boasted either Caroline Lord or Bill King.

'Well, little lady, how does it look to you?' The pickup had stopped, and as he always did, Bill looked around with obvious pride. He had helped to make the Lord Ranch something special, and that was just what it was, most of all to him. 'Does it look different?'

'No.' She smiled as she looked around her in the darkness. But the moon was high, the house was well lit, there were lights on in the men's cottages and the main hall where they ate and played cards, there was a strong light near the stables, and it was easy to see that not much had changed.

'There are a few technical improvements, but you can't see them.'

'I'm glad. I was afraid it might all have changed.'

'Nope.' He sounded the horn twice and a tall slim white-haired woman stood in the doorway, smiling first at Bill, and then instantly at Sam. There was only a moment's hesitation as she stood gazing at the young woman, and then with a light step she ran down the stairs, held out her arms, and took Samantha in a tight hug.

'Welcome home, Samantha. Welcome home.' And then suddenly, as she smelled the dusty rose of Caroline Lord's perfume, felt her thick white hair brush her cheek, she felt tears in her eyes and a sense of having come home. After a moment the two women parted, and Caroline stood back and looked at her with a smile. 'My God, you're pretty, Sam. Prettier even than last time.'

'You're crazy. And good Lord, look at you!' The older woman was as tall and as thin and as ramrod straight as she ever had been, her eyes were bright, and her whole being suggested sparkle and life. She was as pretty as she had been the last time Sam saw her in her fifties, and now at sixty-six, she was still beautiful, and even in jeans and a man's cotton shirt she had her own undeniable style. There was a bright blue scarf knotted at her neck, she wore an old Indian belt, and her cowboy boots were a deep-jade green. Samantha

36

happened to look down as she followed Caroline up the steps to the ranch house and gasped with a little exclamation of delight. 'Oh, God, they're wonderful, Caroline!'

'Aren't they?' Caroline had understood instantly and looked down at them with a girlish smile. 'I had them made specially. It's a final extravagance at my age, but what the hell. It may be my last chance.' Sam was suddenly struck by that kind of reference, and it jolted her just to realise that Caroline thought like that now. Sam was silent as she walked into the familiar house, and Bill followed her with her bags. The entrance hall they stood in boasted a handsome Early American table, a brass chandelier, and a big bright-coloured hooked rug. In the living room beyond there was a huge fire blazing in the fireplace, surrounded by a cluster of comfortable well-upholstered chairs covered in a deep blue. It was a colour picked up again in an antique rug, this one littered with bright flowers woven into the hooked design. The room was entirely done in blues and reds and greens, there was a brightness to it that seemed to perfectly reflect Caroline herself, and all of it was set off by the many antique pieces in rich woods. There were leather-bound books, brass fixtures everywhere, andirons in front of the fireplace, candelabra, buckets and planters, and sconces on the walls with lights like delicate candles. It was a wonderful old-fashioned room with elegance and warmth, much like Caroline herself, and it was perfectly in keeping with the fact that it was on the ranch. It was a room that would have been perfect in *Town & Country* or *House and Garden,* but which, of course, Caroline had never shown. It was her home and not a showplace, and after the very visible years she had spent in Hollywood she felt very strongly about her privacy now. In effect, for all but a few, she had virtually disappeared some twenty-five years before.

'Do you need some more firewood, Caroline?' Bill was now looking down at her from his great height, his snow-white hair revealed now that he had his big-brimmed Stetson in his hand.

She smiled and shook her head, looking ever more youthful, the light in his eyes reflected in her own. 'No, thanks, Bill. I've got enough for the rest of the night.'

'Fine. Then I'll see you ladies in the morning.' He smiled warmly at Sam, nodded respectfully to Caroline, and with his long stride rapidly left the living room and went out. They heard the door close gently behind him, and as Samantha and Barbara had decided a hundred times during the visits while they were in college, Sam decided once again that the two couldn't be involved with each other after all. Not if they said good night to each other like that. And their greetings were never more personal than they had just been, friendly nods, casual smiles, warm greetings, serious conversations about the ranch. Nothing else was ever evident between them, and yet as one watched them one had a feeling, as though they had some secret understanding, or as Sam had one put it to Barbara, 'as though they were really husband and wife.'

But before Samantha could ponder the matter further, Caroline put a tray on a low table near the fire, poured a cup of hot chocolate, uncovered a plate of sandwiches, and waved Sam to sit down.

'Come on, Sam, sit down and make yourself comfortable.' And then, as she did, the older woman smiled at her again. 'Welcome home.'

For the second time that evening Sam's eyes filled with tears and she reached a long graceful hand toward Caroline. They held hands for a moment, as Sam held the bony fingers tight.

'Thank you for letting me come here,'

'Don't say that.' Caroline let go and handed her the hot chocolate. 'I'm glad that you called me. I've always loved you . . .' She hesitated for a moment, glancing into the fire and then back at Sam, 'Just as much as I loved Barb.' And then she sighed softly. 'Losing her was like losing a daughter. It's hard to believe it's been almost ten years.' Sam nodded silently, and then Caroline smiled at her. 'I'm glad to know that I didn't lose you too. I've loved your letters, but for the last few years I've been wondering if you'd ever come back.'

'I wanted to, but . . I've been busy.'

'Do you want to tell me about all that, or are you too tired?' It had been a five-hour flight, and then a three-hour drive. By California time it was only eight thirty, but by Sam's time, in New York, it was eleven thirty at night. But she wasn't even tired, she was just exhilarated to see her old friend.

'I'm not too tired . . . I just don't know where to start.'

'Then start with the hot chocolate. Then the sandwiches. Then talk.' The two women exchanged another smile, and then Sam couldn't resist reaching out to her again, and Caroline gave her a warm hug. 'Do you know how good it is to have you back here?'

'Only half as good as it is to be back.' She took a big bite out of a sandwich and then sat back against the couch with a broad grin. 'Bill says you have a new Thoroughbred. Is he a beauty?'

'Oh, God, Sam, he sure is!' And then she laughed again. 'Better even than my green boots.' She looked down with amusement and then back at Sam with a sparkle in her eye. 'He's a stallion and so full of fire that even I can hardly ride him. Bill is terrified I'll kill myself riding him, but when I saw him, I really couldn't resist. The son of one of the other ranchers near here bought him in Kentucky, and then needed some quick money so he sold him to me. It's almost a sin to ride him just for pleasure, but I can't help it. I just have to. I don't give a damn if I'm an arthritic old woman, or what kind of fool anyone thinks me, he is the one horse in my lifetime I want to ride till I die.' Sam flinched again at the mention of death and old age. In that sense both she and Bill had changed since the last time. But after all, they were both in their sixties now, maybe it was indeed a preoccupation that was normal for their age. Nonetheless it was impossible to think of either of them as 'old people,' they were too handsome, too active, too powerful, too busy. And yet, it was obviously an image of themselves that they both now had. 'What's his name?'

Caroline laughed out loud and then stood up and walked toward the fire, holding out her hands for warmth. 'Black Beauty, of course.' She turned toward Samantha, her exquisite features delicately lit by the fire until she looked almost like a carefully etched cameo, or a porcelain figure.

'Has anyone told you lately how beautiful you are, Aunt Caro?' It was the name Barbara had used for her, and this time there were tears in Caroline's eyes.

'Bless you, Sam. You're as blind as ever.'

'The hell I am.' She grinned and nibbled the rest of her sandwich before taking a sip of the hot chocolate that Caroline had poured from a Thermos jug. She was the same gracious hostess she always had been in the days when Samantha had first visited the ranch and all the way back to her legendary parties in Hollywood in 1935. 'So.' Sam's face sobered slowly. 'I guess you want to know about John. I don't suppose there's much more than what I told you the other night on the phone. He had an affair, he got her pregnant, he left me, they got married, and now they await the birth of their first child.'

'You say it so succinctly.' Then after a moment, 'Do you hate him?'

'Sometimes.' Sam's voice fell to a whisper. 'Most of the time I just miss him and wonder if he's all right. I wonder if she knows that he's allergic to wool socks. I wonder if anyone buys him the kind of coffee he loves, if he's sick or healthy or happy or freaked out, if he remembers to take his asthma medicine on a trip . . . if—if he's sorry—' She stopped and then looked back at Caroline still standing by the fire. 'That sounds crazy, doesn't it? I mean, the man walked out on me, cheated on me, dumped me, and now he doesn't even call to find out how I am, and I worry that his feet itch because his wife might make a mistake and buy him wool socks. Is that crazy?' She laughed but it was suddenly a half sob. 'Isn't it?' And then she squeezed her eyes shut again. Slowly she shook her head, keeping her eyes tightly closed, as though by closing them she wouldn't see the images that had danced in her head for so long. 'God, Caro, it was so awful and so public.' She opened her eyes. 'Didn't you read about it?'

'I did. Once. But it was just some vague gossip that you two were separated. I hoped that it was a lie, just some stupid publicity to make him seem more appealing. I know how those things are, how they get planted and don't mean a thing.'

'This one did. You haven't watched them together on the broadcast?'

'I never did.'

'Neither did I.' Samantha looked rueful. 'But I do now.'

'You ought to stop that.'

Samantha nodded silently. 'Yeah, I will. There's a lot I have to stop. I guess that's why I came out here.'

'And your job?'

'I don't know. I've somehow managed to keep it through all this. At least I think so if they meant what they said when I left. But to tell you the truth, I don't know how I did it. I was a zombie every waking minute I was in the office.' She dropped her face into her hands with a soft sigh. 'Maybe it's just as well that I left.' She felt Caroline's hand on her shoulder a moment later.

'I think so too, Sam. Maybe the ranch will give you time to heal, and time to collect your thoughts. You've been through a tremendous trauma. I know. I went through the same when Arthur died. I thought it would kill me too. That's not quite the same thing as what happened to you, but in its own way death is a rejection.' There was a vague frown in her eyes as she said the last words, but it rapidly flitted away as she smiled again at Sam. 'But your life isn't over, you know,

41

Samantha. In some ways perhaps it's just begun. How old are you now?'

Samantha groaned. 'Thirty.' She made it sound like eighty and Caroline laughed, a delicate, silvery sound in the pretty room.

'You expect me to be impressed?'

'Sympathetic.' Samantha spoke with a grin.

'At my age, darling, that's too much to ask. Envious, perhaps, that would be more like it. Thirty.' She looked dreamily into the fire. 'What I wouldn't give for that!'

'What I wouldn't give to look like you do now, age be damned!'

'Flattery, flattery . . .' But it was obvious that it pleased her, and then she turned to Sam again with a question in her eyes. 'Have you been out with anyone else since it happened?' Sam rapidly shook her head. 'Why not?'

'Two very good reasons. No one decent has asked me and I don't want to. In my heart I'm still married to John Taylor. If I went out with another man it would feel like cheating. I'm just not ready. And you know?' She looked sombrely at the older woman. 'I don't think I ever will be. I just don't want to. It's as though part of me died when he walked out that door. I don't care anymore. I don't give a damn if nobody ever loves me again. I don't feel lovable. I don't want to be loved . . . except by him.'

'Well, you'd better do something about that, Samantha.' Caroline eyed her with gentle disapproval. 'You've got to be realistic, and you can't wander around like a mobile dead body. You have to live. That's what they told me, you know. But it does take time. I know that. You've had how many months now?'

'Three and a half.'

'Give it another six.' She smiled softly. 'And if you're not madly in love by then, we'll do something radical.'

'Like what? A lobotomy?' Samantha looked serious as she took another sip of hot chocolate.

'We'll think of something, but I don't really think we'll have to.'

'Hopefully by then I'll be back on Madison Avenue, killing myself with a fifteen-hour workday.'

'Is that what you want?' Caroline looked at her sadly.

'I don't know. I used to think so. But now that I look back at it, maybe I was in competition with John. Still, I have a good shot at becoming creative director of the agency, and there's a lot of ego involved in that.'

'Do you enjoy it?'

Samantha nodded and smiled. 'I love it.' And then she cocked her head to one side with a shy smile. 'But there have been times when I've liked this kind of life more. Caro—' She hesitated, but only for an instant. 'Can I ride Black Beauty tomorrow?' She suddenly looked like a very young girl.

But Caroline slowly shook her head. 'Not yet, Sam. You ought to warm up on one of the others. How long has it been since you've been on a horse?'

'About two years.'

'Then you don't want to start with Black Beauty.'

'Why not?'

'Because you'll land on your backside halfway out the gate. He's not easy to ride, Sam.' And then more gently, 'Not even for you, I suspect.' Caroline had seen years before that Samantha was a splendid rider, but she knew only too well that Black Beauty was an unusual horse. He even gave her a hard time, and he terrified the foreman and most of the ranch hands. 'Give it time. I promise I'll let you ride him when you feel sure of yourself again.' They both knew that it wouldn't take Sam long. She had spent too much time with horses to feel rusty for long. 'You know, I was hoping you wanted to do some serious riding. Bill and I have spent the last three weeks tearing our hair out over the ranch papers. We have a lot of things to tie up at year end. As I told you, we're two men short on top of it. We could use an extra hand. If you want to, you could ride with the men.

'Are you serious?' Samantha looked stunned. 'You'd let me do that?' Her big blue eyes lit up by the light of the fire, her golden hair was alight with its glow.

'Of course I would let you. In fact I'd be grateful to you.' And then, with a gentle smile, 'You're as competent as they are. Or you will be again after a day or two. Think you'd survive starting out with a full day in the saddle?'

'Hell yes!' Samantha grinned, and Caroline walked toward her with a look of affection in her eyes.

'Then get to bed, young lady. You have to be up at four o'clock. In fact I was so sure you'd say yes, I told Tate Jordan to expect you. Bill and I have to go into town.' She looked at her watch then. It was a simple watch that Bill King had given her that Christmas. Once, thirty years earlier, the only watches that had graced her wrist had been Swiss and encrusted with diamonds that her husband had bought her in Paris, at Cartier's. But she had long since put it away. Sometimes she found it hard to believe that she had ever had another life. She stood looking at Samantha now with a warm smile and gave the younger woman another firm hug. 'Welcome home, darling.'

'Thank you, Aunt Caro.'

With that, the two women walked slowly down the hall. Caroline knew that the fire was safely contained in the fireplace, and she left the tray for the Mexican woman who arrived every morning to work on the ranch and clean her house.

She walked Samantha to her bedroom doorway and watched as Sam eyed the room with delight. It was a different room than she had shared with Barbara during the summers. Caroline had long since turned that room into a study. It had pained her too much to remember the young girl who had visited and lived there, growing into young womanhood in the pink frills of that room. This room was entirely different. It was equally feminine, but stark white. Everything was white eyelet and wonderfully frilly, from the canopied bed to the handmade cushions to the wicker chaise longue. Only the wonderful patchwork bedspread folded back on the bed introduced some colours, and here were a riot of bright colours, reds and blues and yellows, all carefully worked in a log-cabin design. There were matching cushions on two comfortable wicker chairs near the fireplace. And on the large wicker desk rested a huge vase of multicoloured flowers. And through her windows Samantha would have a perfect view of the hills. It was a room in which one would want to spend hours, if not years. The touches of Hollywood hadn't entirely left Caro. She still decorated every room with the special touches and infinite good taste that had characterised her Hollywood years.

'It sure doesn't look like the bedroom of a ranch hand.' Sam chuckled as she sat down on the edge of the bed and looked around.

'Not exactly. But if you'd prefer, I'm sure one of the men would be happy to share a bunk in one of the cottages.' They grinned at each other, kissed again, and then Caroline softly closed the door. Samantha could hear the heels of the cowboy boots echo on the hardwood floors all the way down the hallway to the other side of the house where Caro had her own apartment: a large bedroom, a small den, a dressing room, a bathroom, all done in bright colours not unlike the quilted bedspread, and here she still kept pieces of long-ago-collected art. There was one very fine Impressionistic painting. The others were all pieces she had bought in Europe, some with her husband, some after she lost him, but they were the only treasures she still kept from her old life.

In her own room Sam slowly unpacked her suitcase, feeling as though in the space of a few hours she had entered an entirely different world. Could she really have been in New York that morning, sleeping in her own apartment, talking to Harvey Maxwell in his office? Could one come this far in so short a time? It seemed more than unlikely as she listened to the horses neighing softly in the distance and felt the winter wind brush her face as she opened the window and looked out. Outside there was a landscape lit by the moon beneath a sky brilliant with every star in the heavens. It was a miraculous scene and she was more than glad to be there, glad to be visiting Caroline, and glad to be away from New York. Here she would find herself again. She knew as she stood there that she had done the right thing. And as she turned away from the window, somewhere in the distance she heard a door close near Caroline's bedroom, and for a moment she wondered, as she and Barbie had so long ago, if it was Bill King.

4

The alarm went off next to Sam's bedside at four the next morning. She groaned as she heard it and then reached out a hand to turn it off. But as she did she felt the breeze on her fingers and suddenly realised that something was different. She opened one eye, looked around, and realised that she wasn't at home. Not in her own at least. She looked around once more, in total confusion, and then up at the frilly white canopy above her, and suddenly she knew. She was at Caroline Lord's ranch, in California, and that morning she was going to ride with the other hands. The idea sounded a little less appealing than it had the previous evening. The prospect of leaping out of bed, taking a shower, and actually leaving the building before she had even had breakfast, and then, after being faced with a plate heaped high with sausages and eggs, getting on a horse, all probably before six A.M., sounded exceedingly grim. But this was what she had come west for, and as she considered sleeping in for the first morning, she knew she couldn't do it. Not if she was going to make friends with the men. Besides, letting her ride with the men was a privilege Caroline had given her. And if she was to be respected by the ranch hands, she would have to show herself as tough, as willing, as knowing, as good with a horse, as ready to ride, as any of them.

She wasn't greatly encouraged when she peered into the darkness after her shower and saw that the countryside was shrouded in a thin veil of rain. She climbed into an old pair of blue jeans, a white button-down shirt, a thick black turtleneck sweater, wool socks and her own riding boots that she had worn religiously when she rode in the East. They were beautiful custom-made boots from Miller's and not at all the kind of thing to wear on a ranch, but she figured that she could buy a pair of cowboy boots in town that weekend, and in the meantime she'd have to make do. She pulled her long blonde hair into a tight knot at the nape of her neck, splashed some more cold water on her face, grabbed an old blue down parka that she had worn skiing and a pair of brown leather gloves. Gone were the days of Halston, Bill Blass and Norell. But what she was going to be doing was no longer that kind of work. Elegance didn't matter, only warmth and comfort. And she knew that when she returned to her room that evening she would do so with every muscle shrieking, every joint aching, her seat numb, her knees raw, her eyes blurred from the wind, her face tingling, her hands clenched in the position she would use all day with the reins. Knowing that was certainly no incentive to get up. She slipped out of her room into the hall and noticed the narrow sliver of light under Caroline's door. She thought of saying good morning but it seemed an ungodly hour to disturb anyone, and on tiptoe Sam continued toward the front door. She closed it softly behind her, pulling the hood of her parka over her head and pulling the string tight in the soft rain, her boots making little squishing noises in the puddles that had already formed on the ground.

It seemed to take forever to reach the main hall where the men ate and where some of them gathered at night to play pool or cards. It was a large, freshly painted, rambling building, with beamed ceilings, a brick fireplace tall enough to stand in, a record player, a TV, several game tables, and a handsome antique pool table. As Sam had always known her to, Caroline Lord treated her men well.

For just an instant as Sam reached the doorway, her hand froze on the knob and she suddenly wondered what she had done. She was about to invade the all-male sanctum, share their meals with them in the morning and lunchtime, work beside them, and pretend to be one of them. What would they think of the intrusion? Suddenly Samantha's knees trembled as she wondered if Caroline or Bill had warned them, and she stood there almost too terrified to go inside. As she stood there in the rain, hesitating, with her hand on the doorknob, a voice just behind her muttered, 'Come on, dammit, man, it's cold.' She wheeled around, startled at the voice she hadn't expected, and found herself face to face with a stocky man with dark brown hair and dark eyes, of approximately her own height and age. He looked as surprised as she did, and then with a rapid hand to his mouth at the error, his face broke into a broad grin. 'You're Miss Caroline's friend, aren't you?' She nodded speechlessly, attempting to smile. 'Sorry . . . but could you open the door anyway? It is cold!'

'Oh . . .' She heaved the door wide. 'I'm sorry. I just . . . did she . . . did she say anything about me?' Her porcelain cheeks were flushed from embarrassment and the chill rain.

'Sure did. Welcome to the ranch, miss.' He smiled and moved past her, welcoming but not particularly anxious to say more. He instantly greeted two or three of the other ranch hands and then moved toward the huge open kitchen, greeted the cook, and grabbed a cup of coffee and a bowl of Cream of Wheat.

Samantha saw then that room was filled with men like the one who had just entered, all wearing blue jeans, sturdy jackets, heavy sweaters, their hats left on pegs on the wall, their cowboy boots clattering loudly as they made their way across the wood floor. There were more than twenty of them in the large hall that morning, talking in small groups or drinking coffee alone. Half a dozen were already seated at the long table, eating eggs and bacon or hot cereal, or finishing a second or third cup of coffee. But wherever one looked, there was a man engaged in his own morning ritual, in a man's world, about to engage in man's work, and for the first time in her life Samantha felt totally out of place. She felt her face flush hotly again as she walked hesitantly toward the kitchen, smiled nervously at two of the men as she helped herself to a cup of black coffee, and then attempted to disappear into the woodwork at the far end of the room.

At first glance there was not a single face she remembered. Most of them were young and probably relatively new there, and only two or three of them looked as though they could have worked anywhere for a long time. One was a broad, heavyset man in his early or mid-fifties who looked a lot like Bill King. He had the same kind of build, but his eyes weren't as warm and his face wasn't as kind. He glanced only once at Samantha and then turned his back on her to say something to a young freckled redhead. They both laughed and then walked across the room to a table where they joined two other men. For an instant of paranoia Samantha wondered if she would be the source of amusement, if it had been totally crazy for her to come here, and even crazier for her to want to ride with the men. This was a far cry from her days here with Barbara, when they had come to play around on the ranch. For one thing they had both been very young and very pretty and it had delighted all the men just to watch them hang around and ride. But this was different. Samantha was trying to masquerade as their equal, something they would surely not tolerate, if they even noticed her presence at all.

'Aren't you going to have some breakfast?' The voice next to her was husky but gentle, and Sam found herself looking into the face of another man of the old foreman's vintage, but this one did not look as unpleasant as the first one. In fact, after another glance at him, she gave a soft gasp.

'Josh! Josh! It's me, Sam!' He had been there every summer when she had come with Barbara, and he had always taken care of them. Barbara had told Sam how gently he had taught her to ride when she was a little girl. He had a wife and six kids somewhere, Sam remembered. But Sam had never seen them anywhere on the ranch. Like most of the men he worked with, he was used to living his life in an exclusively male world. It was a strange, solitary life, a lonely existence carried out among others who were equally apart. A society of loners who banded together, as though for warmth. And now he looked at Samantha, blankly for a moment and then with rapid recognition and a warm smile. Without hesitation he reached out and hugged her, and she could feel the rough stubble of his beard against her cheek.

'I'll be damned! It's Sam!' He gave a soft whoop and she laughed with him. 'Now why the hell didn't I figure it out when Miss Caroline told us about her "friend"?' He slapped his leg and grinned at her some more. 'How've you been, dammit? Boy, you look good!' She found it hard to believe with her face still half asleep and her body encased in her worst and oldest clothes.

'So do you! How are your wife and kids?'

'Grown and gone, thank God. Except for one and the wife.' And then he lowered his voice, as though telling some terrible secret. 'They live here on the ranch now, you know. Miss Caroline made me. Said it wasn't right for them to live in town with me living here.'

'I'm glad.'

He rolled his eyes in answer and they both laughed.

'Aren't you going to eat some breakfast? Miss Caroline told us that a friend of hers was coming from New York to help us out.' He grinned evilly for a moment. 'You should have seen their faces when she told them her friend was a woman.'

'They must have been thrilled.' Samantha said sarcastically as they made their way toward the kitchen. She was dying for some coffee and the food was beginning to smell good now that she had found Josh.

And then as she helped herself to a large bowl of oatmeal, Josh leaned toward her conspiratorially. 'What are you doing here, Sam? Aren't you married?'

'Not anymore.' He nodded sagely and she volunteered no other information as they went and sat down at one of the tables. For a long time as Sam ate her oatmeal and nibbled some toast, no one joined them, and then eventually curiosity got the better of two or three of the men. One by one Josh introduced them, and for the most part they were younger than Sam and had the rugged look of hardworking men who all but lived in the outdoors. It was by no means an easy profession, particularly at this time of year. And it was obvious how Bill King had come by the rugged lines in his face that made him look like a heavily carved statue, they had been worn by time and the elements as he rode for some fifty years on the different ranches where he worked. Josh's face was no different as Sam watched him, and she could easily see that some of the others would look very much like them in a short time.

'Lotta new faces, huh, Sam?' She nodded, and he left her for a second for more coffee. She noticed on the big clock over the fireplace that it was five forty-five. In fifteen minutes they would all head for the barn to claim their horses and officially their workday would begin. She wondered who was going to assign her a horse for the day. Caroline hadn't mentioned it the previous evening, and she was suddenly anxious as she looked around for Josh. But he had disappeared somewhere with one of his cronies, and Sam found herself looking around her like a lost child. Despite the few curious glances cast her way, on the whole there was no visible interest and she suspected that what was happening was that they didn't want to pay attention to her, so most of them pretended to look away. It made her want to shout or stand on a table, just to catch their attention once and for all, tell them that she was sorry she was invading their world and that if they wanted her to she'd go home now, but the precise way in which they were ignoring her was beginning to drive her nuts. It was as though they were determined that she shouldn't be

51

there, so they pretended to themselves and each other that she was not.

'Miss Taylor?' She spun around at the sound of her name and found herself staring into a broad chest wearing a thick wool plaid shirt in blue and red.

'Yes?' Her eyes travelled upward until she found herself looking into a pair of eyes of a colour she had seldom seen. They were almost emerald with gold flecks. The hair was black and the temples were touched with grey. The face was leathered, the features sharp, and he was taller than any other man on the ranch, including Bill King.

'I'm the assistant foreman here.' He offered only his title, no name. And there was something cold and forbidding in his voice as he said it. Had she met him in a dark alley, a chill would have rippled up her spine.

'How do you do?' She wasn't quite sure what to say to him, and he was looking down at her with a tight frown.

'Are you ready to come out to the barn?' She nodded in answer, awed by his commanding style, as well as his great height. She noticed, too, now that the others were watching, wondering what he was saying to her and obviously noticing that there was no trace of warmth in the way he spoke, no welcoming words, and no smile.

Actually she had wanted another cup of coffee but she wasn't about to tell him that as he led the way to the door. She grabbed her jacket off the peg where she had finally left it, struggled into it, pulled up the hood, and closed the door behind her, feeling somehow like a child who has done something wrong. The idea of Samantha riding with them clearly irked him as he walked rapidly into the barn. Samantha shook the rain off her hood as she slipped it off her hair and watched him. He picked up a clipboard with a list of men's names and those of horses and then with a pensive frown he walked to a nearby stall. The name outside the stall was LADY, and for some reason she wasn't sure she could have explained, she found herself instantly irritated by his choice. Just because she was a woman she had to ride Lady? She instinctively felt that she was going to be stuck with that horse during the entire duration of her stay and found herself fervently hoping that Lady would at least prove a decent mount.

'You ride fairly well?' Again she only nodded, afraid to toot her own horn, afraid to offend him, when the truth would have been that she probably rode better than most of the men on the ranch, but he would have to see that for himself, if he even bothered to look. Samantha watched him again as he went back to his list, and found herself watching the sweep of his neck as his dark hair brushed his collar. He was a powerful, sensuous-looking man, somewhere in his early forties. There was something frightening about him, something fierce and stubborn and determined. She could sense it without knowing him, and she felt almost a ripple of fear go through her as he turned to her again and shook his head. 'No good. She might just be too much for you. I want you to ride Rusty. He's on the far side of the barn. Grab one of the free saddles in the tack room and mount up. We ride out in ten minutes.' And then with a look of annoyance, 'Can you be ready by then?' What did he think, she wondered, that it took her two hours to saddle a horse?

Suddenly as she watched him her temper flared. 'I can be ready in five. Or less.' He said nothing in answer and merely walked away, put the clipboard back on the wall from which he'd taken it, and strode quickly across the barn to the stalls, where he saddled his own horse and led it slowly outside. Within five minutes all the men had returned from breakfast and the barn was a madhouse of catcalls and laughter and noises mixed with the sounds of horses shifting their feet, greeting their habitual riders, and whinnying at each other as the men who rode them took them from their stalls, creating a veritable traffic jam at the entrance as the entire group emerged into the damp yard beyond and congregated happily in the light rain.

Most of the men had donned slickers over their jackets, and Josh had handed Sam one as she walked her horse slowly outside. He was a large unexciting-looking chestnut, with no particular verve and no spark to his step. Samantha already suspected that what she could anticipate was a horse that would want to stop by the stream, walk when he could, nibble at bushes, graze on whatever grass he could find, and beg to go home whenever Sam happened to turn even slightly in the direction of the barn. It promised to be a day filled with aggravation, and she found herself suddenly remorseful over her anger about Lady only moments before. But more than that, what she felt as she waited was that she wanted to prove to the assistant foreman that she was worthy of a much better mount. Like Black Beauty, she smiled to herself as she thought of Caroline's Thoroughbred stallion. She was looking forward to riding him, and wouldn't that just show this rigid chauvinist ranchman what kind of a rider she was. She wondered if Bill King had ever been like him, and had to admit to herself that he had probably been worse. Bill King had been, and was still, a tough foreman, and this one hadn't really done much to Sam except offer her a pretty tame horse, which, she had to admit in spite of herself, was a reasonable thing to do with an unknown rider out from a place like New York. How did he know she could ride, after all? And if Caroline hadn't tried to prejudice them in her favour, it was just as well.

The men sat on horseback in the rain in their slickers, chatting in little clusters, waiting for the assistant foreman to give them their instructions for the day. The twenty-eight ranch hands never rode together, but usually broke into four or five goups to perform whatever needed doing at various ends of the ranch. Every morning Bill King, or his assistant, moved among them, verbally giving out assignments, telling which men to work with which others and where. Now, as he did every morning when Bill King wasn't around, the tall dark-haired assistant foreman quietly moved among them, giving them their assignments for the day. He assigned Josh four men to work the south end of the ranch, looking for strays and cattle in trouble. Two other groups went to check some fences he thought were down. Another foursome had two sick cows to bring in down by the river. And he and another four men and Samantha were checking the north boundaries for three cows he knew were loose and about to calve. Samantha followed the group quietly out of the main compound, riding sedately on Rusty and wishing that the rain would stop. It seemed forever before they got into a good canter, and she had had to remind herself again that in a Western saddle you didn't post to trot. It was odd to sit in the big comfortable saddle, she was far more accustomed to the smaller, flatter English saddles she had always used for jumping and competition in Madison Square Garden, but this was a whole other life.

Only once did she smile to herself and wonder what was happening that morning in her office. It was insane to think that only two days before she had been wearing a blue Dior suit and conducting a creative meeting with a new client, and now she was out looking for stray cows on a ranch. The very thought of it almost made her laugh aloud as they crested a small hill, and she had to concentrate to keep from openly smiling, the whole contrast of what she had done and what she was doing was so totally absurd. Several times she noticed the assistant foreman's eyes on her, as though checking to see if she could manage her mount. Once she almost said something unpleasant to him as he reminded her to rein in as he rode past her, while Rusty was desperately trying to nibble at some grass. For just a moment Samantha had let the animal have his way, hoping to pacify the dull-spirited beast before they moved on. The dark-haired tyrant seemed to think that Samantha couldn't control him, and the very thought of that made her almost scream. 'I did it on purpose,' she wanted to shout after him, but he seemed totally uninterested in her doings as he moved on to talk quietly to two of his men. She noticed also that all of them seemed to regard him as something of an authority. The men had the same way of dealing with him as they did with Bill King, with quiet awe, curt respectful answers, and quick nods. No one questioned what he suggested, no one argued with what he said. There was very little humour exchanged between him and the others, and he smiled very rarely as the men talked or he talked to them.

55

Somehow Sam found that he annoyed her. The very sureness with which he spoke was an open challenge to her.

'Enjoying your ride?' he asked her a little while later as he rode along beside her for a moment.

'Very much,' she said through clenched teeth as the pouring rain grew worse. 'Lovely weather.' She smiled at him, but he didn't answer. He only nodded and moved on, and she mentally accused him of being a humourless pain in the ass. As the day wore on, her legs grew tired, her seat ached, the insides of her knees screamed from the no-longer-unfamiliar friction of saddle against jeans. Her feet were cold, her hands were stiff, and just as she wondered if it would ever end they broke for lunch. They stopped at a small cabin on the far reaches of Caroline's ranch, set aside for just such occasions. It boasted a table, some chairs, and the equipment they needed to assist them with making lunch: hot plates and running water. Sam discovered that the assistant foreman himself had brought the necessary provisions in his saddlebag, and everyone was handed a fat sandwich filled with turkey and ham, and two huge Thermoses were brought out and rapidly emptied. One had been filled with soup, the other with coffee, and it wasn't until she was cherishing the last of her coffee that he spoke to her again.

'Holding up all right, Miss Taylor?' There was the faintest trace of mockery in his voice, but this time there was a kinder light in his eyes.

'Fine, thanks. What about you, Mr ... er ... you know, I don't know your name.' She smiled sweetly at him and this time he grinned. There was definitely some pepper to the girl. He had sensed that right at the first, when he had suggested Lady. He had seen the look of annoyance flare up in her eyes, but he hadn't given a damn what kind of horse she wanted. He was going to give her the quietest mount on the place. He didn't need some dizzy broad from New York breaking her ass on the north boundary that morning. That was all he needed, but so far she seemed to have managed all right. And he had to

56

admit that it was hard to figure out what kind of rider she was on that lazy horse.

'My name's Tate Jordan.' He held out a hand, and once again she wasn't sure if he was mocking her or being sincere. 'How are you enjoying your stay?'

'Terrific.' She smiled angelically at him. 'Great weather. Superb horse. Wonderful people . . .' She faltered a moment and he raised an eyebrow.

'What? Nothing to say about the food?'

'I'll think of something.'

'I'm sure you will. I must say, I'm surprised you decided to ride today. You could have waited for a better day to start out.'

'Why should I? You didn't, did you?'

'No.' He looked at her almost derisively. 'But that's hardly the same thing.'

'Volunteers always try harder, or didn't you know that, Mr. Jordan?'

'I guess I didn't. We haven't had too many around here. Have you been out here before?' He looked her over with interest for the first time, but it was curiosity, rather than any friendship he was intending to form.

'Yes, I have, but not in a long time.'

'Did Caroline let you ride with the men before too?'

'Not really . . . oh, once in a while . . . but it was more for fun.'

'And this time?' The questioning eyebrow raised again.

'I guess this is for fun too.' She smiled at him more genuinely this time. She could have told him it was therapy, but she wasn't about to disclose her secrets to him. On the spur of the moment she decided to thank him instead. 'I do appreciate your letting me ride with you. I know it must be difficult having someone new around.' She wasn't going to apologise for being a woman. That would have been too much to bear. 'I hope that eventually I might be of some use.'

'Maybe so.' He nodded at her then and moved on. He didn't speak to her again for the rest of the afternoon. They never found the strays they had been concerned

57

about, and by two o'clock in the afternoon they met up with one of the parties mending fences and joined them. Samantha was of only minimal use in what they were doing, and the truth of it was that by three o'clock she was so tired, she was ready to fall asleep, in the pouring rain, on the horse, and despite whatever conditions prevailed. By four she was looking truly miserable, and by five thirty when they got back, she was sure that once she got off the horse she would never move again. She had been on horseback and in the rain for eleven out of eleven and a half hours, and she thought that there was a distinct possibility that she might die that night. She could barely crawl off the horse when they got back to the barn, and only Josh's firm hands assisting her kept her from falling bowlegged and exhausted onto the ground. She met his concerned look with an exhausted chuckle and gratefully took a firm hold of his supporting arm.

'I think maybe you overdid it today, Sam. Why didn't you go home early?'

'Are you kidding? I'd have died first. If Aunt Caro can do it, so can I . . .' And then she looked ruefully at her old buddy. 'Or can I?'

'I hate to tell you this, babe, but she's been doing it for a lot longer than you have, and every day. You're going to hurt like the devil tomorrow.'

'Never mind tomorrow! You should know what it feels like right now.' All of this was being conducted in whispers from just inside Rusty's stall. Rusty was already impervious to them, gorging himself on hay.

'Can you walk?'

'I'd better. I'm sure as hell not going to crawl out of here.'

'Want me to carry you?'

'I'd love it.' She grinned at him. 'But what would they all say?' They both laughed at the thought of it, and then as Sam glanced up, suddenly her eyes took on a new sparkle. She had just noticed the name on a pretty little bronze plaque outside another stall. 'Josh.' Suddenly her eyes didn't look as though she were in any kind of agony.

'Is that Black Beauty?'

'Yes, ma'am.' He said it with an admiring grin, for her as much as for the Thoroughbred. 'Want to see him?'

'I would take my last dying steps across a bed of nails to see him, Joshua. Take me to him.' He put an arm under hers to support her and helped her hobble across the barn to the other stall. All of the others had gone by then, and there were suddenly no other voices in the barn except theirs.

From the distance the stall appeared to be empty, but as Samantha approached it she saw him in the far corner and whistled softly as he walked slowly toward them and nuzzled her hand. He was the most beautiful horse she had ever seen in her entire lifetime, a masterpiece of black velvet with a white star on his forehead and two perfectly matched white socks on his front legs. His mane and his tail were the same perfect shiny raven-black as the rest of his body, and his eyes were large and gentle. His legs were incredibly graceful, and he was also the biggest horse Sam thought she had ever seen. 'My God, Josh, he's incredible.'

'He's a beauty, ain't he?'

'Better than that, he's the best-looking horse I've ever seen.' Sam sounded awed. 'How big is he?'

'Seventeen and a half hands, almost eighteen.' Josh said it with pride and pleasure and Samantha whistled softly in the big barn.

'What I'd give to ride that.'

'Think she'll let you? Mr. King doesn't even like her to ride him, you know. He's got a hell of a lot of spirit. Almost threw her a couple of times, and that ain't easy to do. I ain't seen a horse yet could throw Miss Caro.'

Samantha never took her eyes off the horse. 'She said I could ride him, and I'll bet he doesn't try to throw me.'

'I wouldn't chance it, Miss Taylor.' The voice from directly behind her wasn't Josh's voice, it was another voice, a deep, smoky one that spoke softly, but without warmth. She turned slowly to see Tate Jordan and suddenly her eyes blazed.

'And why don't you think I should chance it? Do you think Rusty is more my style?' She was suddenly very angry as exhaustion, pain, and annoyance mingled almost beyond control.

'I don't know about that. But there's a world of difference between these two horses, and Miss Caroline is probably the best woman rider I've ever seen. If she has trouble with Black Beauty, you can bet that you'd fare a lot worse.' He looked too sure of himself, and Josh looked suddenly uncomfortable at the exchange.

'Oh, really? How interesting, Mr. Jordan. I notice that you qualify Caroline as the "best *woman* rider" you've ever seen. I take it you don't feel she compares with men?'

'It's a different kind of riding.'

'Not always. I'll bet you that I could handle this beast a lot better than you could.'

'What makes you think so?' His eyes flashed, but only for an instant.

'I've been riding Thoroughbreds for years.' She said it with the venom of sheer exhaustion, but Tate Jordan looked neither pleased nor amused.

'Some of us haven't had those advantages. We just do the best we can, with whatever we've got.' As he said it she felt her face flush; he touched his hat, nodded at her without looking at the ranch hand beside her, and then strode out of the barn.

For a moment there was silence, and then Josh watched her to see what was happening in her face. She tried to look nonchalant as she patted Black Beauty's muzzle, and then glanced over again at Josh. 'Irritating son of a bitch, isn't he? Is he always like that?'

'Probably. Around women. His wife ran off and left him years ago. She ran off with the ranch owner's son, married him too. And he even adopted Tate's boy. Till they was killed. His wife and the ranch owner's boy got themselves killed in a car wreck. Tate got his boy back, though the boy still don't use his name. I don't think Tate cares much what name the boy uses. He's crazy as hell about his son. But he don't never mention his wife. I think she left him with a kind of sour taste in his mouth about women. Except for—' Josh blushed furiously for a moment. 'Except for . . . you know, easy women. I don't think he's never been involved with no one else. And hell, he says his boy's twenty-one, so you know how long that's been.'

Sam nodded slowly. 'Do you know the boy?'

'Nope. I know Tate got him a job around here last year, but he don't usually say much about himself, or the boy. He keeps pretty private. Most of the men do. But he goes to see him about once a week. He's over at the Bar Three.'

Another loner, Sam found herself thinking, wondering if cowboys were anything but. She was intrigued about something else about him. He showed a quick intelligence, and she found herself wondering briefly just who and what Tate Jordan was, as Josh shook his head with his familiar grin. 'Don't let it worry you none, Sam. He don't mean no harm. It's just his way. Underneath all them porcupine quills he's gentle. You should see him with the kids on the ranch. He must have been a good father to his boy. And Tate's got an education too. Not that that makes much difference here. His dad was rancher and sent him to some fine schools. Even went to college and got some kind of degree in something, but his old man died and they lost the ranch. I think that's when he went to work on the other ranch and his wife ran off then with his boss's son. I think it must have all done something to him. I don't think he wants much more than he got. For himself or his boy. He's just a ranch hand like the rest of us. But he's smart and he'll be a foreman someday. If not here, then he'll do it somewhere else. You can't deny what a man is. And ornery or not, he's a hell of a good man on a ranch.' Sam thought of what she'd just heard. She knew more than she really wanted to, thanks to Josh's loose tongue. 'Ready to head back for the big house?' He looked warmly at the pretty young woman with the tired face and the damp clothing. 'Can you make it?'

'If you ask me that again, Josh, I'll kick you.' She glared at him ferociously and he laughed.

'Hell no, you won't.' He laughed more. 'You couldn't

lift your leg high enough to kick a short dog, Samantha.'
And then he laughed over his joke all the way to the big
house. It was a few minutes after six when Caroline
opened the door to them, and Josh left her at the front
door in Caroline's care. She couldn't help smiling at her
young friend as Sam struggled into the cosy living room
and collapsed, groaning, onto the couch. She had shed the
damp jacket on the way, and as her pants had stayed dry
beneath the slicker, she knew that she wasn't damaging
the furniture and she needed to sit down.

'Good God, did you ride all day?' Sam nodded, barely
able to speak, she was so tired and stiff. 'Why in heaven's
name didn't you come home when you'd had enough?'

'I didn't want to look like a sissy . . .' She groaned
horribly but managed to grin at Caroline, who collapsed
on the couch with a chuckle and a smile.

'Oh, Samantha, you foolish girl! You'll be in agony
tomorrow!'

'No, I won't. I'll be back on that damn horse.' And then
she groaned again, but more at the memory of the horse
than at the pain.

'Which one did they give you?'

'A miserable old beast called Rusty.' Sam looked at
Caroline with open disgust and Caroline laughed harder.

'Oh, God, they didn't. Did they really?' Samantha
nodded. 'Who on earth did that? I told them you could
ride as well as any of the men.'

'Well, they didn't believe you. At least Tate Jordan
didn't. He almost gave me Lady, and then decided Rusty
was more my speed.'

'Tomorrow tell him you want Navajo. He's a beautiful
Appaloosa, no one rides him except Bill and myself.'

'Will that make the other men resent me?'

'Did they today?'

'I'm not sure. They didn't say much.'

'They don't say much to each other either. And if you
rode with them since this morning, how could they
possibly resent you? My God, and all those hours on the
first day!' She looked truly horrified at what Samantha
had done.

'Wouldn't you have done the same thing?'

She thought about it for a minute, and then, with a sheepish grin, nodded yes.

'By the way, I saw Black Beauty.'

'What do you think of him?' Caroline's eyes glowed.

'I think I'd like to steal him, or at least ride him. But'—her eyes suddenly flashed again—'Mr. Jordan doesn't think I ought to. According to him, Black Beauty isn't a horse for a woman.'

'What about me?' Caroline looked vastly amused.

'He thinks you're the "best *woman* rider" he's ever seen. I challenged him about that, why not the "best rider" without qualifying it?' But Caroline only laughed at her. 'What's so funny, Aunt Caro? You *are* the best damn rider I've ever seen.'

'For a woman,' she countered.

'You think that's funny?'

'I'm used to it. Bill King thinks the same thing.'

'Liberated in these parts, aren't they?' Samantha groaned as she got off the couch and pointed herself in the direction of her room. 'In any case if I can squeeze a better horse out of Tate Jordan tomorrow, I'll feel as though I've won a major battle for womankind. What was the name of that Appaloosa?'

'Navajo. Just tell him I said so.'

Samantha rolled her eyes as she disappeared down the hall. 'Good luck,' Caroline called after her. But as she washed her face and brushed her hair in the pretty bedroom, she realised that it was the first time in three months that she hadn't moved heaven and earth to watch John and Liz's evening broadcast, and she hadn't even missed it. She was in another world now. A world of horses named Rusty, and Appaloosas, and assistant foremen who thought they ruled the world; but it was all very simple and very wholesome, and the most pressing problem she had was what horse she was going to ride the next day.

She thought once more to herself as she lay in bed shortly after dinner that it was the most blissfully simple existence she had known since she was a child. And then, as the thoughts faded from her mind, just before she drifted into sleep, she heard the familiar door close again and she was sure this time that she heard muffled footsteps and soft laughter in the hall.

5

The next morning Samantha climbed out of bed with a horrific groan, she staggered to the shower and stood there for a full fifteen minutes with the hot water raining down on her sore limbs. The insides of her knees were almost scarlet from her eleven-hour day in the saddle, and she padded her long johns with pads of cotton as she gingerly stepped back into her jeans. The only encouraging sign for the day ahead was that it was no longer raining, and she glanced around her in the early morning darkness, noticing that there were still stars in the sky, as she made her way to the main dining hall for breakfast. This morning she felt less timid as she walked in, hung her jacket on a hook, and went straight to the coffee machine, where she filled a tall steaming mug. She saw her old friend Josh at a far table and went over to him with a smile as he beckoned to her to sit down.

'How you feelin' today, Samantha?'

She grinned ruefully at him and lowered her voice conspiratorially as she took over the empty chair. 'It's a good thing we're riding today. Josh, that's all I can tell you.'

'How's that?'

''Cause I sure as hell couldn't walk. I just about crawled here from the big house.' Josh and the other two men chuckled and one of them praised her for her hard ride the day before.

'You sure are a damn fine rider, Samantha.' Not that

64

she had had the opportunity to show them her stuff in the driving rain.

'I used to be. It's been a long time.'

'Don't make no difference,' Josh told her firmly. 'You got a good seat, good hands, you got 'em for the rest of your life. You gonna ride Rusty again today, Sam?' He raised one eyebrow and she shrugged as she sipped her coffee.

'We'll see. I don't think so.' Josh only smiled. He knew that Sam wouldn't put up with an old nag like that for long. Sure as hell after she saw Black Beauty. It would be a miracle if she wasn't riding him before long. 'What did you think of the big boy?' He grinned with pleasure.

'Black Beauty?' Her eyes filled with a special light as she said his name. There was something about horse people and a Thoroughbred stallion. It was a kind of passion other people would never understand. Josh nodded and grinned. 'He's the best piece of horseflesh I've ever seen.'

'Miss Caro going to let you ride him?' He couldn't resist asking.

'If I can talk her into it—and don't think I won't try!' Sam smiled back over her shoulder as she headed for the line waiting for breakfast. She returned five minutes later with a plate of sausages and fried eggs. Two of the men had moved to another table, and Josh was already squaring the hat on his head. 'Going out early, Josh?'

'I told Tate I'd give him a hand in the barn before we ride out this morning.' He smiled at her, turned to call out to one of his friends, and then disappeared.

Twenty minutes later when Samantha went out to the barn to saddle up, she looked around hesitantly for Tate, not entirely sure how to broach the change of mounts with him. But on a day like this there was no way she was going to ride a nag like the one he'd assigned her. She was sure that if Navajo was Caroline's suggestion, he would be much more her style.

A couple of men nodded to her as they walked past her. They seemed less annoyed by her presence than they had been the previous morning. She suspected that even though they had been expecting her they hadn't imagined her quite as she was. But she also knew that if nothing else would win them over, riding as hard and as long as they did in the driving rain would eventually win their hearts. And if she was going to spend the next three months on Caroline's ranch, acting like any other ranch hand, then it was important to her that the men come to accept her as one of them. Still she knew that one or two of the younger ones had been stunned by her looks and her youth, and she had caught one of them staring at her in fascination the evening before when she had pulled the rubber band out of her hair at the end of the long day and shook out her wet mane of silvery blonde hair. She had smiled at him briefly and he had blushed furiously and turned away.

'Morning, Miss Taylor.' The firm voice broke into Sam's reverie, and when she looked up at Tate Jordan, she suddenly knew that however uncomfortable he may have made her, or wanted to, she was not willing to ride a bad horse all day in order to prove that he was in charge. There was something stubborn and determined just in the way he looked at her, and it set her back up just watching the way he moved his head. 'Tired after yesterday?'

'Not really.' Not to him would she admit the aches and the pains. Tired? Of course not. Just to look at him one knew how powerful and important he thought he was. Assistant foreman on the Lord Ranch. Not bad, Mr. Assistant Foreman. And Sam knew it was possible that at sixty-three, Bill King might retire at any moment and leave Tate Jordan his oversize shoes to fill. Not that Jordan would fill them as intelligently or as kindly or as wisely . . . She didn't know why, but Tate Jordan annoyed the hell out of her, and there was an unspoken friction between them one could sense instantly as he brushed past. 'Ahh . . . Mr. Jordan.' She suddenly felt an odd pleasure in putting a spoke in his wheels.

'Yes?' He turned to face her, holding a saddle perched on one shoulder.

'I thought I'd try a different ride.' Her eyes were cool as glass as his slowly began to blaze.

'What did you have in mind?' There was an undertone of challenge.

She was dying to say Black Beauty, but decided not to waste the irony of the suggestion on him. 'Caroline thought that Navajo might do.'

He looked momentarily annoyed, but then nodded and turned away, muttering distractedly over his shoulder, 'Go ahead.' The very words irritated Samantha. Why did she need his permission for what horse she rode? Reason provided a simple answer, but she still bristled at his style as she found Navajo's stall and his saddle and bridle in a little tack room just beyond it and went back to saddle up. He was a beautiful Appaloosa, mottled whipped-cream-and-chocolate face, rich brown flanks, and the characteristic white hindquarters with big brown spots. He was gentle as Samantha put the saddle on him and then strapped the girth beneath him, but it was also evident as she led him out of his stall that he had a great deal more spirit than Rusty. In fact she had to work to control him once she was astride, and he pranced for a full five minutes as she attempted to join the others beginning to move out. She had been assigned the same group as the previous day, and she saw Tate Jordan watching her with open disapproval as they rode toward the hills.

'Think you can manage him, Miss Taylor?' His voice was clear as a bell and Samantha suddenly felt a strong urge to hit him as he rode alongside her and observed the frisky manoeuvres of her horse.

'I'll certainly try, Mr. Jordan.'

'I think we should probably have given you Lady.' Samantha said nothing at all in answer and moved on. Half an hour later they were all engrossed in what they were doing: looking for strays and once again checking fences. They found a sick heifer, which two of the men roped in order to lead back to one of the main cattle barns. And by the time they stopped for lunch, they had already put in six hours of work. They stopped in a clearing and tied the horses to the surrounding trees. The usual sandwiches and soup and coffee were handed around, and conversation was sparse but relaxed. No one said much to Samantha, but she was comfortable with them nonetheless and let her thoughts drift as she sat for a few moments with her eyes closed in the winter sun.

'You must be tired, Miss Taylor.' It was that voice again. She opened one eye.

'Not really. I was enjoying the sunshine. Does that bother you very much?'

'Not at all.' He smiled pleasantly. 'How are you enjoying Navajo?'

'Very much.' She opened both eyes and smiled at him. And then she suddenly couldn't resist teasing him a little. 'Not as much as I'd enjoy Black Beauty of course.' She smiled mischievously at him and it was hard to tell if she meant it or not.

'That, Miss Taylor'—he returned the smile to her like a rapid volley in tennis—'is a mistake I hope you never make.' He nodded wisely. 'You'd get hurt. And that'— he smiled gently at her again—'would be a great shame. A stallion like that, there are damn few people who should ride him. Even Miss Lord herself has to be careful when she takes him out. He's a dangerous beast, and not . . .' He looked for the right words. ' . . . not the kind of horse a "sometime rider" ought to play with.' The green eyes looked infinitely patronising as he gazed down at her with his steaming cup of coffee in his hand.

'Have you ridden him?' The question was blunt and her eyes didn't smile.

'Once.'

'How did you find him?'

'He's a beautiful animal. No doubt about that.' The green eyes smiled again. 'He's quite a different ride than Navajo.' But there was an implication in his words that suggested that Navajo was all she could handle. 'Looks like he gave you a little bit of a hard time when we started out.'

'And you thought I couldn't handle it?' She was almost amused.

'I was concerned. After all, if you get hurt, it's my responsibility, Miss Taylor.'

'Spoken like a true foreman, Mr. Jordan. But I don't really think Miss Lord would hold you responsible for what happens to me with a horse. She knows me too well.'

'What does that mean?'

'That I'm not used to riding horses like Rusty.'

'But you think you're up to a stallion like Black Beauty?' He knew that neither Caroline Lord nor Bill King would let her ride him. Hell, they'd only let him ride the exquisite Thoroughbred once.

Samantha nodded quietly. 'Yes, I think I could ride him.'

He looked amused. 'Do you? You're that sure of yourself are you?'

'I just know how I ride. I ride hard. I take chances. I know what I'm doing, and I've been riding since I was five. That's been a while.'

'Every day?' There was a challenge again. 'Ride much in New York, do you?'

'No, Mr. Jordan.' She smiled sweetly. 'I don't.' But as she said it she vowed to ride Black Beauty as soon as Caroline would let her, because she wanted to, and because she wanted to show this arrogant cowboy that she could.

A moment later he strode back toward his men and gave them the signal. They mounted up and he spent the rest of the afternoon checking the boundaries of the ranch. They found some more loose heifers at the outermost reaches and drove them home at sunset, when once again Samantha wondered if she would even be able to get off her horse. But Josh was waiting for her outside the barn when they got there, and he gave her a hand as she swung her leg over Navajo with a groan.

'You gonna make it, Sam?'

'I doubt it.' He grinned at her in answer as she untacked her horse and almost staggered to the tack room to put her saddle and bridle away.

'How'd it go today?' He followed her and stood in the doorway.

'All right, I guess.' She realised with a tired smile that she was beginning to speak like the rest of the cowboys, in the same sparse fashion. Only Jordan spoke differently than they did, and only when he was speaking to her. Then the education he'd had was obvious; the rest of the time he sounded just like them. Not unlike Bill King, who was subtly different when he was with Caroline, but not as much. Bill King and Tate Jordan were very different men. Jordan was much less of a rough diamond than most.

'Long way from New York, ain't it, Samantha?' The wizened little old cowboy grinned, and she rolled her eyes.

'It sure is. But that's why I came out here.'

He nodded. He didn't really know why she had come. But he understood. A ranch was a good place to be when one had problems. Lots of hard work, fresh air, good food, and good horses would cure almost anything. Your belly got full, your rump got tired, the sun came up and went down, and another day went by with nothing more complicated to worry about than your horse needed new shoes or the fence on the south forty needed fixing. It was the only life Josh had ever known but he had seen plenty of other people try other things and come back to it. It was a good life. And he knew it would do Sam good too. Whatever she was running away from, it would help her. He had noticed the dark circles under her eyes the previous morning. They already looked clearer today.

Together, they wandered past Black Beauty, and almost instinctively Sam reached out and patted his neck. 'Hello, boy.' She spoke softly to him and he whinnied as though he knew her. She gazed at him thoughtfully, as though once again seeing him for the first time. And then an odd light came into her eyes as she left the big barn with Josh at her side, bid him good night, and walked slowly back to the big house, where Bill King was talking to Caroline. They stopped when she came in.

'Hello, Bill . . . Caro.' She smiled at them both. 'Am I

70

interrupting something?' She looked embarrassed for a moment, but they were both quick to shake their heads.

'Of course not, dear.' Caroline kissed her and Bill King picked up his hat and got up.

'I'll be seein' you tomorrow, ladies.' He was quick to leave them and Samantha sprawled out on the couch with a sigh.

'Hard day?' Caroline looked at her gently as she lay there. She herself hadn't ridden all week. She and Bill still had a lot of paperwork to do before year's end, and there were only two weeks left in which to do it. She'd at least have to get out and ride Black Beauty one of these days before he became totally wild, but she didn't really even have time for that. 'Are you very tired, Sam?' Caroline looked sympathetic.

'Tired? Are you kidding? After sitting at a desk for all these years? I'm not tired. I'm broken. If Josh didn't drag me off that horse every night, I'd probably have to sleep out there.'

'That bad, huh?'

'Worse.' The two women laughed and the Mexican woman who helped Caroline with the cleaning and cooking signalled from the kitchen. Dinner was ready. 'Mmm, what is it?' Samantha wrinkled her nose happily on the way into the big handsomely done country kitchen.

'Enchiladas, chiles rellenos, tamales . . . All my favourites, I hope some of them are yours.'

Samantha smiled at her happily. 'After a day like that you could feed me cardboard, as long as there was lots of it, with a bath and bed at the end of the meal.'

'I'll remember that, Samantha. Otherwise how's it going? Everyone being civil to you, I hope?' She furrowed her brows as she asked the question, and Samantha nodded and smiled.

'Everyone's perfectly pleasant.' But there was a tiny catch in her voice and Caroline was quick to hear it.

'Except?'

'No *except*'s. I don't think Tate Jordan and I will ever be best friends, but he's perfectly civilised. I just don't think

71

he approves of what he calls "sometime riders." '

Caroline looked amused. 'Probably not. He is an odd sort. In some ways he thinks like a rancher, but he's perfectly happy to break his back working on the ranch. He is the last of the real thing. Real cowboys, the hard-riding, hardworking, down-to-the-core ranchman who would die for the ranchers he works for and do anything he could to save the ranch. He's a good man to have here, and one day,' she sighed softly, 'he'll be the right man to step into Bill's shoes. If he stays.'

'Why wouldn't he? He has a hell of a nice life here. You've always provided your men with more comforts than anyone else.'

'Yes.' She nodded slowly. 'And I've never been convinced that that mattered to them as much as I thought it should. They're a funny breed. Almost everything they do is a matter of pride and honour. They'll work for one man for nothing because they feel they owe him or because he's done right by them, and then leave someone else because they feel they should. It's impossible to predict what any of them will do. Even Bill. I never even fully know with him what he's going to do.'

'It must be quite something to try and run a ranch like that.'

'It's interesting.' Caroline smiled. 'Very interesting.' And then suddenly she noticed Samantha glancing at her watch. 'Something wrong, Sam?'

'No.' Sam looked suddenly strangely quiet. 'It's six o'clock.'

'Yes?' For a moment Caroline didn't understand and then she did. 'The news broadcast?' Samantha nodded. 'Do you watch it every night?'

'I try not to.' The look of pain was back in Sam's eyes as she said it. 'But in the end I always do.'

'Do you think you ought to?'

'No.' Slowly Samantha shook her head.

'Do you want me to have Lucia-Maria bring the television in? She can, you know.' But Sam shook her head again.

'I have to stop watching sometime.' A tiny sigh escaped her. 'I might as well stop watching right now.' It was like fighting an addiction. The addiction of staring into John Taylor's face every night.

'Can I offer anything to help distract you? A drink? A rival newscast? Hard candy? Some tissues to shred?' She was teasing and Samantha laughed then. What a wonderful woman she was and she seemed to understand it all.

'I'll be all right, but come to think of it . . .' She looked across the table at Caroline, looking like a very young girl with an enormous request, like Mom's mink stole for the senior prom. And the long blonde hair loose on her shoulders only helped to make her look younger in the soft light. 'I do have a favour to ask.'

'What's that? I can't imagine anything here you can't have.'

'I can.' Samantha grinned like a little kid.

'And what might that be?'

Samantha whispered the two magic words. 'Black Beauty.'

For a moment Caroline looked pensive, and then suddenly she looked amused. 'So that's it, is it! I see . . .'

'Aunt Caro . . . may I?'

'May you what?' Caroline Lord sat back in her chair with a regal air and a twinkle in her eye.

But Samantha would not be easily put off. 'May I ride him?'

There was no answer for a long moment as Caroline grew anxious. 'Do you think you're up to it yet?'

Samantha nodded slowly, knowing the truth of what Josh had said: If you had it, you never lost it. 'I do.'

Caroline nodded slowly. She had watched Sam riding into the main compound as she and Bill had stood at her large picture windows. Sam just had horses in her bones. It was part of her, instinctively, even after not riding for over a year. 'Why do you want to ride him?' She cocked her head to one side, her dinner forgotten.

When Samantha answered, her voice was gentle and her eyes had a faraway look, her ex-husband's broadcast forgotten, along with the woman to whom he had fled. All she could think of now was the ravishingly beautiful black stallion in the stables and how badly she wanted to feel him beneath her as together they raced into the wind.

'I don't know why.' She looked up at Caroline honestly. And then she smiled. 'I just feel as though, as though—' she faltered for a moment, her eyes distant again—'as though I have to. I can't explain it, Caro. There's something about that horse.' She smiled a distant smile, which was instantly reflected in Caroline's eyes.

'I know. I felt it too. That was why I had to have him. Even if it makes no sense for a woman my age to have a horse like him. I had to, just this one last time.' Samantha nodded her complete understanding and as the two women looked into each other's eyes they felt the same bond that had always held them together, across the years, across the miles. In some ways they were as one, as though in their souls they were mother and daughter.

'Well?' Samantha looked at her hopefully.

'Go ahead.' Caroline smiled slowly. 'Ride him.'

'When?' Sam almost held her breath.

'Tomorrow. Why not?'

6

In the morning as Samantha poured her aching body out of bed, she only felt its pain for the first few instants. After that she remembered her conversation with Caroline, and nothing hurt anymore as she ran to the shower and stood there, with the hot water pounding down on her shoulders and her head. This morning she wasn't even going to take the time for breakfast. She didn't care about breakfast. Not today. All she needed was a cup of coffee from Caroline's kitchen, and after that she would sail out to the barn. Just thinking about it made her smile. It was all she could think of this morning. And the smile was still dancing in her eyes as she ran the last steps to the barn. Two of the men were talking quietly in one corner, but other than that there was no one there. It was still much too early for most of them to be there. They were eating breakfast and trying to wake up as they gossiped about the local news and the usual ranch talk in the main dining hall.

Quietly, almost stealthily, Samantha picked up Black Beauty's saddle and walked toward his stall. But as soon as she had done so she saw the two men eyeing her, one with raised eyebrows. They had both stopped talking and were watching her with a silent question. Just as silently she nodded and slipped into the stall. She made soft murmuring noises to soothe him, running a hand down the long graceful neck and patting the powerful flanks as he eyed her nervously at first, backing and sidling, and then stopping as though to sniff the air near where she stood. She rested the saddle on the stall door, and then slipping the bridle over his head, she led him from the stall.

'Ma'am?' The voice surprised her as she looped the reins around the convenient post so she could saddle Black Beauty. She turned around to see who it was. It was one of the two men who had been watching her, and she realised then that he was a good friend of Josh. 'Miss Taylor?'

'Yes?'

'Uh . . . do you . . . I don't mean . . .' He was mortified, but clearly worried, and Sam smiled her golden smile. This morning her hair was loose down her back, her eyes brilliant, her face pink from the chill December air. She looked incredibly beautiful as she stood beside the coal-black Thoroughbred stallion, like a tiny palomino at his side.

'It's all right.' She was quick to reassure him. 'I have Miss Lord's permission.'

'Uh . . . ma'am . . . does Tate Jordan know?'

'No.' She shook her head firmly. 'He doesn't. And I

75

don't see why he should. Black Beauty belongs to Miss Caroline, doesn't he?' The man nodded, and Sam smiled the dazzling smile again. 'Then there shouldn't be any problem.'

He hesitated and then backed off. 'I guess not.' And then with a worried frown, 'You ain't scared to ride him? He's got one hell of a lot of power in those long limbs.'

'I'll bet he does.' She looked at his legs with pleasure and anticipation and then swung the saddle onto his back. For Black Beauty, Caroline had also acquired an English saddle, and it was this that Samantha was strapping to him now. It was as though he knew the feel of the smooth brown leather, unlike the cumbersome Western saddle Samantha had been riding for two days. This was a saddle she knew better, and a breed of horse she had often ridden, but a horse as fine as this one was a rare gift in any horseman's life.

A few minutes after she had saddled him, she tightened the girth again, and then hesitantly one of the two ranch hands moved closer and gave her a leg up onto the gigantic black horse. At the feel of a rider on his back, Black Beauty pranced nervously for a moment, and then with the reins well in hand, Samantha nodded at the two ranch hands and walked Black Beauty quickly away. He pranced and sidestepped quite a lot on the way to the first gate, and then as she let him through it, she allowed him to break into a trot, which rapidly became a swift canter as they made their way across the fields. The sky was by then streaked with the first signs of daybreak, and the light around her was pale grey becoming almost gold. It was a magnificent winter morning and she had beneath her the most magnificent horse she had ever ridden. Unconsciously a broad smile broke out on her face and she let Black Beauty gallop as she moved with him across the fields. It was the most extravagant feeling of freedom she had ever known and it was almost like flying, as together, like one body, they sailed along. It seemed hours later when she forced herself to make him change direction, and slowing him only a little, she began to head home. She still had to

76

ride with the men that morning, and what she had done was forfeit breakfast to ride this magnificent horse across the fields. It was only a quarter of a mile from the main complex that she finally succumbed to temptation and jumped the huge horse across a narrow stream, which he cleared with ease, and only after they had passed it did she notice that not far from them Tate Jordan was riding his own handsome black and white pinto and glaring at her as she raced along. She reined in a little, veered and rode toward him, wanting, just for one moment, to rush him and show him how well she rode. But instead she resisted the temptation and just allowed herself to gallop gaily in his direction on the back of the handsome beast. She slowed him down to a canter, and Black Beauty was prancing happily as they reached Tate.

'Good morning! Want to run with us?' In her eyes was victory beyond measure, and the answering look in Tate Jordan's eyes was fierce.

'What the hell are you doing on that horse?'

'Caroline said I could ride him.' She sounded like a petulant child as she slowed him further, and Tate fell into step beside her as they rode back. She was remembering everything he had said to her the day before and she was enjoying her moment of triumph as he fumed. 'Remarkable, isn't he?'

'Yeah. And if he'd stumbled at the stream back there, he'd have a remarkably broken leg, or didn't you think of that when you raced him toward it to jump it? Didn't you see the rocks back there, dammit? Don't you know how easily he could slip?' His voice carried across the early morning silence, and Samantha looked at him with annoyance as they rode on.

'I know what I'm doing, Jordan.'

'Do you?' He eyed her with unbridled fury. 'I doubt that. Your idea of knowing what you're doing is showing off and going as fast as you can. You could ruin a lot of horses that way. Not to mention what you could do to yourself.'

As she rode along beside him she wanted to scream. 'Do

77

you really think you could do better?'

'Maybe I know enough not to try. A horse like that should be a racehorse or a show horse. He doesn't belong on a ranch. He shouldn't be ridden by people like you, or me, or Miss Caro. He should be ridden by highly trained people, Thoroughbred people, or he shouldn't be ridden at all.'

'I told you, I know what I'm doing.' Her voice rose in the stillness, and without warning, he reached out and grabbed her reins. Almost instantly both horses and their riders came to a full stop.

'I told you yesterday, you don't belong on that horse. You'll hurt him or kill yourself.'

'Well.' She looked at him angrily. 'Did I?'

'Maybe next time you will.'

'You can't admit it, can you? That a woman can ride as well as you. That's what galls you, isn't it?'

'The hell it is. Damn city playgirl, you come out here to have a good time and play at "ranch girl" for a few weeks, ride a horse like that, jump him on terrain you don't know—dammit, why don't people like you stay where they belong? You don't belong here! Don't you understand that?'

'I understand it perfectly, now let go of my horse.'

'Damn right I will.'

He threw the reins at her and drove off. And feeling somehow as though she had lost rather than won, she rode back to the barn, but more sedately. She didn't know why, but his words had hurt her. And there was one grain of truth in his tirade. She had been wrong to jump Black Beauty headlong over the stream. She didn't know the country she was riding, at least not well enough to take chances like that. But on the other hand, it had felt wonderful, flying over the countryside on a horse with the speed of the wind.

She could see the men gathering in the yard of the complex and hurried back into the barn to put Black Beauty in his stall. She was going to rub him down just for a moment, cover him with a blanket, and then leave. She could give him a good rubdown that night, but when she reached his stall, Tate Jordan was already waiting, his green eyes smouldering emerald fire, his face harder than she had ever seen it before, but he was looking taller and more handsome than any cowboy on a poster and for an insane moment she thought of her agency's new car ads. He would have been perfect as the male model, but this was not a commercial and this wasn't New York.

'Just what exactly are you planning to do with that horse?' His voice was low and taut.

'Rub him down for a minute and then cover him up.'

'And that's it?'

'Look.' She knew what he was saying and now her delicate skin flushed to the roots of her golden hair. 'I'll come back later and take care of him properly.'

'When? In twelve hours? Like hell you will, *Miss* Taylor. If you want to ride a horse like Black Beauty, you'd damn well better live up to the responsibility. Walk him, cool him off, rub him down. I don't want to see you out with the others for another hour, if then. Is that clear? I know you're not much on taking advice or suggestions, but how are you on orders, do you understand them? Or is that a sometime thing with you too?' As she looked at him she almost wanted to slap him. What a hateful man he could be, but he was also a man who loved horses, and he was right about what he had just said.

'Fine. I understand.' Her eyes dropped, and she took Black Beauty's bridle in her hands and prepared to walk away.

'Are you sure?'

'Yes, dammit! Yes!' She turned back to shout at him, and there was an odd light in his eyes. He nodded and walked back toward his own horse, the reins looped easily over one of the hitching posts outside. 'By the way, where will you all be working today?'

'I don't know.' He strode past her, 'Find us.'

'How?'

'Just gallop the hell all over the ranch. You'll love it.' He grinned sarcastically at her as he got back on his horse and rode off, and Samantha wished for only a moment that she were a man. At that precise moment she would have loved to hit him, but he was already gone.

As it turned out, it took her two hours to find them. Two hours of riding through brush, of following a few familiar trails and getting lost on others. At one point she almost wondered if Tate hadn't purposely chosen some activity that would keep them out in the more remote areas so she wouldn't find them. But at last she did. And despite the chill December air, she was warm in the bright winter sunshine after riding everywhere she could think of looking for them. She had found two other small work groups, and one larger one, but of Tate's there had been no sign.

'Have a nice ride?' He looked at her with amusement as she stopped and Navajo pawed the ground.

'Charming, thank you.' But there was a feeling of victory nonetheless to have found them at all, and she watched the emerald eyes glinting in the sun. And then, without saying anything further, she wheeled her horse and joined the men, dismounting a few moments later to help carry a newborn calf in a sling made of a blanket. The mother had died only hours before, and the calf looked as if she might not make it either. One of the men hoisted the small, scarcely breathing animal in front of his saddle and rode steadily toward the livestock barn, where he would bring her to another cow in the hopes of giving her a foster mother. It was only half an hour later when Sam spotted the next one on her own, this one even smaller than the first, and the mother had obviously been gone for several more hours. This time with no assistance she fashioned the sling on her own, hoisted the calf onto her saddle with the help of a young ranch hand who was far too intrigued by Samantha to be of much use with the calf. Then, without waiting for instructions, she began to canter at a steady pace after the other ranch hand, toward the main barn.

'Can you manage it on your own?' She looked up, startled, to see Tate Jordan riding along smoothly beside her, his sleek black and white pinto making an interesting pair with her brown and white Appaloosa.

'Yeah, I think I can manage.' And then with a look of concern at the animal in front of her saddle, 'Do you think this one will live?'

'I doubt it.' He spoke matter-of-factly as he watched her. 'But it's always worth a try.' She nodded in answer and rode harder, and this time he veered away and turned back. A few minutes later she was at the main barn, and the orphaned calf was taken into expert hands that worked on him for over an hour, but the little calf didn't live. As she walked back to Navajo waiting patiently outside the livestock buildings, she felt tears sting her eyes, and then as she swung her leg over the saddle she suddenly felt anger. Anger that they hadn't been able to save him, that the poor little beast hadn't survived. And she knew there were others like him out there, whose mothers had, for one reason or another, died as they delivered in the cold night. The men always had an eye out for livestock in trouble on the hills, but it was inevitable that there were some who escaped their notice and died on the hills every year. It was common for those who delivered in winter. The others had come to accept it, but Samantha had not. Somehow the orphaned calves seemed almost symbolic of the children she could not bear, and now she rode back out to the others with a vengeance and a determination that the next one she brought back would live.

She brought in three more that afternoon, riding hell for leather as she had that morning on Black Beauty, the calves wrapped in the blankets, the men watching her with combined intrigue and awe. She was a strange and beautiful young woman, bent low over her horse's neck, riding as no woman had on the Lord Ranch before, not even Caroline Lord. The extraordinary thing was that as they watched her fly across the hills, Navajo moving like a brown streak until they saw him no more, they knew just how good Samantha was. She was a horsewoman like few others, and as they rode back to the barn that night the men joked with her as they hadn't before.

'Do you always ride like that?' It was Tate Jordan

again, his dark hair ruffled beneath the big black Stetson, his eyes bright, his beard beginning to cast a shadow across his face by the end of the day. There was a kind of rugged masculinity about him that had always made women pause when they saw him, as though for just a moment they couldn't catch their breath. But Samantha did not suffer from that affliction. There was something about the self-assured way he moved that annoyed her. He was a man who was sure of his world and his job, his men and his horses, and probably his women as well. For a moment she didn't answer his question, and then she nodded with a vague smile.

'For a good cause.'

'And this morning?' Why did he want to push her? she wondered. Why did her care?

'That was a good cause too.'

'Was it?' The green eyes pursued her as they rode home after the long day.

But this time Samantha faced him frankly, her blue eyes locking into his green. 'Yes, it was. It made me feel alive again, Mr. Jordan. It made me feel free. I haven't felt like that in a long time.' He nodded slowly and said nothing. She wasn't sure if he understood, or if he even cared, but with a last look at her he moved on.

7

'Aren't you going to ride Black Beauty this morning?'

For a moment she almost snapped at him as she swung a leg over Navajo and settled herself in the saddle, and then for no particular reason, she grinned at him. 'No, I thought I'd give him a rest, Mr. Jordan. How about you?'

'I don't ride Thoroughbreds, Miss Taylor.' The green eyes laughed at her as his lively pinto danced.

'Maybe you should.' But he said nothing and rode off to lead his men into a distant part of the ranch. Their group was larger than usual, and today Bill King and Caroline were riding with them too. But Samantha scarcely saw them. She was too busy doing the job she had been assigned to do, and by now she knew that the men were beginning to accept her. They hadn't planned to, they hadn't really wanted to. But she had worked so hard and ridden so well, and hung in for such endless hours, and worked so diligently to save the orphaned calves, that suddenly this morning it was 'Heyyyyyo! Over here . . . Sam! . . . Hey, Sam, dammit . . . right now!' No more Miss Taylor, not a single ma'am. She totally lost track of time and everything except her work and her surroundings, and it wasn't until dinner that night that she stopped to talk to Caroline again.

'You know, Sam, you're a marvel.' She poured a second cup of coffee for Samantha and sat back in the comfortable kitchen chair. 'You could be in New York, sitting behind a desk, creating exotic commercials, and living in an apartment that's the envy of everyone you know, and instead you're out here, chasing cows, carrying sick calves, knee deep in manure, mending fences with my men, taking orders from men who have a fifth-grade education, getting up before dawn, and riding all day long. You know, there aren't many people who would understand that.' Not to mention the fact that she had once been the wife of one of the most desirable young men on TV, Caroline thought. 'What do you think about what you're doing?' Caroline's blue eyes danced at her and Samantha smiled.

'I think I'm doing the first sensible thing I've done in a very long time, and I love it. Besides'—she grinned girlishly—'I figure if I stick around here long enough, I'll get to ride Black Beauty again.'

'I hear Tate Jordan didn't take too kindly to it.'

'I don't think he takes too kindly to me on the whole.'

'You been scaring him half to death, Samantha?'

'Hardly. As arrogant as he is, it would take a lot more than me to scare him.'

'I don't think that's the case. But I hear he thinks you can ride. From him that's high praise.'

'I suspected that this morning, but he'd rather die than say so.'

'He's no different than the rest. This is their world, Samantha, not ours. On a ranch a woman is still a second-class citizen, most of the time anyway. They're all kings here.'

'Does that bother you?' Samantha watched her, intrigued, but the older woman visibly softened as she grew pensive, and something very gently veiled her eyes.

'No, I like it like that.' Her voice was strangely gentle, and then she smiled up at Samantha and looked almost like a girl. In that flash of a moment it explained everything about Bill King. In his own way he ruled her, and she loved it. She had for many years. She respected his power and his strength and his masculinity, his judgement about the ranch and his way of handling the men. Caroline owned and ran the ranch, but it was Bill King behind her who had always helped run it, who silently held the reins along with her. The ranch hands respected her, but as a woman, a figurehead. It was Bill King who had always made them jump. And Tate Jordan who was making them jump now. There was something terrible macho and animal and appealing about all of it. It was a pull one wanted to resist as a modern woman, yet one couldn't. The lure of that kind of masculinity was almost too strong.

'Do you like Tate Jordan?' It was an odd, direct question, yet Caroline said it in such a naive way that Samantha laughed.

'Like him? I don't think I could.' But that wasn't what Caroline had meant, and she knew it, and now she laughed a little silvery laugh as she sat back in her chair.

'He's good at what he does. I suppose I respect him, though he's certainly not an easy man to get along with, and I don't think he much likes me. He's attractive, if that's what you mean, but unapproachable too. He's an odd man, Aunt Caro.' Caroline nodded silently. She had once said almost the same things about Bill King. 'What made you ask?' There was certainly nothing between them, nothing Caroline could have sensed or seen as she had watched them all work all day long.

'I don't know. Just a feeling. I get the impression he likes you.' She said it simply, as young girls do.

'I doubt that.' Samantha looked both amused and sceptical. And then she spoke more firmly. 'But in any case that's not why I'm here. I'm here to get over being involved with one man. I don't need to cure it by getting involved with another. And certainly no one here.'

'What makes you say that?' Caroline looked at her strangely.

'Because we're all foreigners to each other. I'm a stranger to them, and I suppose in their own way, they're strangers to me. I don't understand their ways any more than they understand mine. No,' she sighed softly, 'I'm here to work, Aunt Caro, not play with the cowboys.' Caroline laughed at the words she used and shook her head.

'That's how those things start though. No one ever intends . . .' For a moment Sam wondered if Caroline was trying to tell her something, if after all this time she was going to admit to an affair with Bill King, but the moment passed quickly, and now Caroline stood up, put the dishes in the sink, and a few minutes later began to turn off the kitchen lights. Lucia-Maria had long since gone home. Samantha was suddenly sorry that she hadn't encouraged Caroline to say more, but she had the impression that Caroline was anxious not to say anything further. Silently a door had already closed.

'You know, the truth of it is, Aunt Caro, that I'm already in love with someone else.'

'Are you?' The older woman instantly stopped what she was doing and looked stunned. She had had no inkling before that Samantha was already involved.

'Yes.'

'Would it be rude to ask who?'

'Not at all.' Samantha smiled at her gently. 'I'm very

much in love with your Thoroughbred horse.' They both laughed and bid each other good night a few minutes later. And tonight Sam found herself listening for the now familiar opening and closing of the front door. She was certain now that it was Bill King coming to spend the night with Caroline, and she wondered why they hadn't married if this had gone on for as long as she now suspected it had. Maybe they had their reasons. Maybe he already had a wife. She found herself pondering, too, the questions Caroline had asked about Tate Jordan and wondered why Caroline should suspect Samantha of being attracted to him. She wasn't really. If anything, he annoyed her. Or did he? She suddenly found that she was questioning herself. He was brutally handsome, like someone out of a commercial . . . like someone out of a dream. But he wasn't her kind of dream; tall, dark and handsome. She smiled to herself, her mind instantly darting back to John Taylor . . . John with his glorious golden beauty, his long legs, his huge, almost sapphire coloured eyes. They had been so perfect together, so alive, so happy, they had done everything together . . . everything . . . except fall in love with Liz Jones. That John had done alone.

At least, she consoled herself as she pulled her mind wilfully away from him again, she hadn't been watching the newscast. At least she didn't know how the pregnancy was going or have to listen to Liz thank another thousand viewers for the little hand-knitted booties and crocheted blankets or 'darling little pink hats.' It had been almost unbearable, but she hadn't been able to stop watching the broadcasts while she was still in New York. Even when she worked late, she watched them. It was as though there were an alarm clock buried somewhere in her body that let her know when it was six o'clock and then forced her inexorably toward a television set so she could watch the programme. At least here she hadn't thought of it in almost a week. And in another week it would be Christmas, and after she survived that—her first Christmas without John, the first time in eleven years that she wouldn't be with him—then she knew that she'd live. And in the meantime all she had to do was work from morning till night, follow the cowboys, spend twelve hours a day riding Navajo, find those little orphaned babies, and bring them back alive. And day by day, month by month, she'd make it. She was finally beginning to know that she would live. She congratulated herself again on the wise decision to come west as her eyes closed and she drifted off to sleep, and this time along with Liz and John and Harvey Maxwell there were suddenly other people in her dreams too: Caroline trying desperately to tell her something that she could never quite hear; and Josh, laughing, always laughing; and a tall dark-haired man on a beautiful black horse with a white star on its forehead and two white socks. She was riding behind him, bareback, holding tightly to him as they raced along through the night. She was never quite sure where they were going or from where they had come, but she knew that she felt perfectly safe there as they rode along in perfect unison. And as she woke up with her alarm at four thirty, she felt oddly rested, but she couldn't quite remember her dream.

8

Just before they would normally have had their lunch-break, Tate Jordan gave the signal and the large group of men working together gave a whoop and headed home. Sam was among them, joking with Josh about his wife and children, and being teased by two of the other men. One of them was accusing her of probably having run away from a boyfriend who beat her 'and rightly so after listening to you run that big mouth of yours,' but the other one claimed that she was probably the mother of eleven children and too lousy a cook so they threw her out.

'You're all right.' Samantha laughed with the men she

was riding with. It had been an easy morning's work and they were all anxious to knock off work early for lunch. It was the twenty-fourth of December, and that night there would be a huge Christmas feast in the main hall, wives and children and even girlfriends were invited. It was an annual event, beloved by all. It made them all feel more than ever like a family, linked together and bonded by their love for the ranch. 'The truth is that I had fifteen illegitimate children and they all beat me, so I ran away. How's that?'

'What, no boyfriend?' One of the old timers guffawed. 'A pretty little palomino like you and no boyfriend, awww come on!' They were all beginning to liken her to a palomino, but she was fond enough of horses and she took it as a compliment. The truth was that she was daily beginning to look more like one. Her long shining hair was whitening in the sun, and her face was getting tanned a rich honey-brown. It was a beautiful combination, and one which all of the men had noticed, whether they mentioned it or not. 'Don't tell me you ain't got no man, Sam!' The old timer persisted in the question a number of them had pondered when she wasn't around.

'Nope. Of course there were fifteen fathers for the fifteen illegitimate children, but now'—she laughed along with them and then shrugged, calling over her shoulder as she rode ahead back to the barn—'I'm too mean for any man.'

Josh watched her go with a gentle look in his eyes, and the man riding closest to him leaned closer to ask him, 'What's really her story, Josh? Got any kids?'

'Not that I know of.'

'Married?'

'Not anymore.' But he said nothing further. Partly because he figured if Sam wanted them to know something she'd tell them, and besides that, he didn't know any more about her life himself.

'I think she's out here running away from something,' a very young cowboy volunteered, blushing.

'Mebbe so,' Josh agreed and moved on. No one really wanted to discuss it. It was Christmas, they had their own women and children to think of and it was her business after all. Despite the superficial gossipy tendencies that exist in any situation of communal living, the ranch on the whole bred considerable respect. These were, for the most part, men who believed in keeping their own counsel, and they thought too highly of each other and their own privacy to pry. Most of them were not overt talkers, and most of their conversation usually centred around the livestock and the ranch. Sam was safe in their midst and she knew it. No one was going to ask about John or Liz or about why she had never had babies, and how did she feel now that she was divorced . . . 'Tell me, Mrs. Taylor, now that your husband has ditched you for another woman, how do you feel about . . .' She had been all through that in New York. And now she was free.

'See you later!' She called the words gaily to Josh as she made her way hurriedly to the big house. She was going to shower and change into fresh jeans, and then she had promised to come back over to the main hall to help decorate the tree. There were groups and committees devoted to everything from singing Christmas carols to baking. Christmas was an event second to none on the Lord Ranch.

When she walked into the house, Caroline was pouring over an enormous ledger with her deep frown, and Samantha sneaked behind her and gave her a big hug.

'Oh! You startled me!'

'Why don't you relax for a change? It's Christmas!'

'Do I look like Scrooge yet?' Caroline's face relaxed into a warm smile. 'Should I say "Bah humbug"?'

'Not yet. Wait till tomorrow. And then we can all haunt you with the ghost of Christmas Past!'

'Oh, there have been a few of those.' For a moment Caroline became pensive as she put the big ranch ledger away. Suddenly she had thought back to Hollywood and her extravagant Christmases there. And as she watched her Samantha knew exactly what was on her mind.

'Do you miss all that still?' What she meant was 'Do you still miss your husband?' and Samantha's eyes were suddenly sad as she asked. It was as though she needed to know for herself how long it would go on.

'No.' Caroline answered the question gently. 'I'm not sure I ever really did, not after the beginning. Oddly enough this was always more my style. For a long time I didn't know that, but I discovered that once I came here. I've always been happy here, Samantha. It's the right place for me to be.'

'I know. I've always sensed that about you.' She envied her. Sam had not yet found her own place. All she had was the apartment she had shared with John Taylor. There was nothing that was exclusively Sam's.

'Do you miss New York terribly, Sam?'

Sam shook her head slowly. 'No, not New York. Some of my friends. My friend Charlie and his wife, Melinda, and their three little boys. One of them is my godson.' She felt suddenly lonely and bereft as she said it, homesick for the people she had left behind. 'And my boss maybe, Harvey Maxwell. He's the creative director at CHL. He's been like a father to me. I suppose I miss him too.' And then, as she said the words, she felt a wave of loneliness overtake her as she thought of John again—and this first Christmas without him. Involuntarily her eyes suddenly filled with tears and she looked away, but Caroline saw them and gently reached out and took her hand.

'It's all right. I understand . . .' She reached out and pulled Samantha to her. 'I remember what it was like when I first lost my husband. That was a very difficult year for me too.' And then after a moment, 'But it gets better. Just give it time.' Sam only nodded, and her shoulders shook gently as she bowed her head on Aunt Caro's delicate shoulder, and then a moment later she sniffed and pulled away.

'I'm sorry.' She smiled in embarrassment through her tears. 'How maudlin. I don't know why that happened.'

'Because it's Christmas and you were married to him for all those years. It's perfectly normal, you know, Sam. For God's sake, what do you expect?' But again, as she sat there, as she had been a thousand times since she'd heard that John had left Sam, Caroline was outraged at what he had done. How could he leave this perfectly exquisite young woman for that cold little bitch that she had stealthily watched on TV the other night, trying to understand what had happened, trying to see some reason why he had chosen her instead of Sam. The only reason she could see was the baby, but that hardly seemed a reason to go totally crazy and leave a woman like Sam. Nonetheless he had done it, however little she understood what he had done. 'Are you going over to help decorate the tree?'

Sam nodded and smiled valiantly again. 'I also promised to bake cookies, but you may be sorry about that. The men I've been working with all tease me that any woman who can ride the way I do probably can't cook. And the worst of it is that they're right.' They both laughed and Sam gently kissed Aunt Caro and then held her close one more time. 'Thank you.' It was a fierce whisper.

'For what? Don't be silly.'

'For being my friend.' She let go of the older woman then, and when she did, there were tears in Caroline's eyes as well.

'Foolish woman. Don't ever thank me for being your friend! Or I won't be!' She tried to look angry but couldn't, and then shooed Sam out the door to go decorate the tree. A half an hour later Sam was in the main dining hall, perched on a tall ladder, hanging silver and green and red and blue and yellow baubles on the tree. There were small children working on the lower branches, and tiny ones hanging up little paper ornaments they'd made. There was an older group stringing popcorn and cranberries together, and a circle of men and women choosing ornaments and making as much noise, or more, as their kids. It was a large and happy congregation, with women circulating large bowls of popcorn, platters of brownies, boxes of cookies, all made on the ranch or sent from 'back home.' There were people working everywhere in the best of the Christmas spirit, even Tate Jordan had come in, and as the official ranch giant, he had just agreed to put

91

the star on the top of the tree. He was carrying a child on each shoulder and the black Stetson hung on a hook near the door. It was only when he reached the tree that he saw Samantha, and then, setting the children down, he smiled. From her perch on the ladder for once she was actually taller than he.

'Put you to work, did they, Sam?'

'Of course.' She smiled, but ever since her earlier moment of nostalgia there had been something sparkling missing from her smile. For a moment he commandeered the ladder and clambered up it quickly to hang the huge gold star. He added a few angels and some bright Christmas balls near the top, adjusted the lights, and then stepped down and handed Samantha up again. 'Very nice.'

'There have to be some advantages to being as tall as I am. Do you want a cup of coffee?' He said it casually, as though they had always been friends, and this time when she answered there was more life in her smile.

'Sure.'

He came back with two cups and some cookies and proceeded to hand her an assortment of ornaments, which she hung from her perch as occasionally she sipped her coffee and munched a cookie and he commented on where she should hang the next ball. At last she grinned at him after he had just told her where to hang a little silver angel.

'Tell me, Mr. Jordan, do you always give orders?'

He stopped to think for a moment and then nodded. 'Yeah, I guess I do.'

She sipped her coffee and watched him. 'Don't you find it tiresome?'

'No.' And then he looked at her pointedly. 'Do you . . . find it tiresome to give orders, I mean?' He sensed that she was used to running things too. There was something about her that suggested an aura of command.

She answered without hesitation. 'Yes. Very.'

'And that's why you're here?' It was a very direct question and she looked at him for a minute before answering.

'Partially.' As she answered he found himself wondering if she had had a nervous breakdown. He was sure that there was a serious reason why she had come to the ranch, and he was also sure that this was not just an ordinary housewife running away from home. But there was nothing to indicate that she was even slightly crazy. He really had no clue.

'Samantha, what do you do when you're not in California working on ranches?'

She didn't really want to answer but she liked his openness as he stood there talking to her. She didn't want to spoil their working relationship by being cute with glib answers and scaring him away. This was a man she liked and respected, sometimes detested, but thought was good at his job. What was the point of playing games with him now?

'I write commercials.' It was an oversimplification of her job, but it was a start. In an odd way she was not unlike the assistant foreman at Crane, Harper and Laub. Realising that suddenly made her smile.

'What's so funny?' He looked puzzled as he watched her.

'Nothing. I just realised that in some ways our jobs are alike. At the advertising agency where I work there's a man named Harvey Maxwell. He's kind of like Bill King. And he's also old and one of these days he's going to retire, and—' Suddenly she was sorry she had said it. All he would do is resent her if he thought she was going to step into a man's job, but Tate Jordan was smiling as she abruptly ended her recital.

'Go ahead, say it.'

'Say what?' She tried hard to look blank.

'That you'll probably get his job.'

'What makes you think that?' Despite the fresh suntan she was blushing. 'I didn't say that.'

'You didn't have to. You said our jobs were alike. So you're an assistant foreman, are you?' For some reason she couldn't fathom, he looked pleased, as though that amused him. 'Very nice. Do you like what you do?'

'Sometimes. Sometimes it's hectic and crazy and I hate it.'

'At least you don't have to ride twelve hours in the rain.'

'There is that.' She returned the smile, suddenly intrigued by this big gentle man who had been so harsh and so demanding during her first days on the ranch, and so livid with her for riding Black Beauty, and now he seemed like a totally different person as they drank coffee and ate cookies next to the Christmas tree. She looked at him closely for a moment and then decided to ask him something. She suddenly felt that she had nothing to lose. As he stood there he looked impossible to anger, impossible to annoy. 'Tell me something. Why did you get so furious with me for riding Black Beauty?'

He stood very still for a moment and then set down his coffee cup and looked deep into her eyes. 'Because I thought it was dangerous for you.'

'Because you didn't think I was good enough to ride him?' This time it wasn't a challenge, it was a straight question, and he gave her a straight answer.

'No, I knew you were good enough that first day. The way you sat on Rusty in the pouring rain and even got a little work out of the old nag, I knew damn well you were good. But it takes more than that to ride Black Beauty. It takes caution and strength, and I'm not sure you're long on either. In fact I'm sure you're not. One day that horse is going to kill somebody. I didn't want it to be you.' He paused for a moment, his voice husky. 'Miss Caroline should never have bought him. He's a bad horse, Sam.' He looked at her strangely. 'I feel it in my gut. He frightens me.' And then he startled her again by speaking ever so softly. 'I don't want you to ride him again.' She said nothing in answer, and after a long moment she looked away. 'But that's not like you, is it? To turn down a challenge, to pass up a risk? Maybe especially now.'

'What do you mean by that?' She was puzzled by what he had just said.

He looked her straight in the eye again as he answered.

'I have the feeling you've lost something very precious to you . . . someone, most likely—that's the only thing most of us give a damn about. Maybe right now you don't care about yourself as much as you should. That's a bad time to ride a demon horse like that stallion. I'd rather see you on any horse on the ranch except that one. But I don't suppose you'd give up riding a Thoroughbred stallion just for me.' She wasn't sure what to say to him when he stopped talking, and her voice was husky when she answered at last.

'You're right about a lot of things, Tate.' His name was new and strange on her lips, and when she lifted her eyes to his, her voice grew softer. 'I was wrong to ride him—the way I did. I took a lot of chances that morning.' And then after a brief pause, 'I won't promise you that I won't ride him again, but when I do, I'll be careful. I will promise you that. Broad daylight, terrain I know, no jumping over a rock bed and a stream I can barely see . . .'

'My God, how reasonable!' He looked down at her and grinned. 'I'm impressed!' He was teasing her and she grinned.

'You should be! You can't imagine the crazy things I've done on horses over the years.'

'You ought to quit doing stuff like that, Sam. It's not worth the price you may have to pay.' They both fell silent for a moment. They both knew of the accidents that befell others, the paraplegics who spent the rest of their lives in wheelchairs because they risked a mad jump and fell. 'I never did see the point of that crazy Eastern jumping. Christ, you can kill yourself like that, Sam. Is it worth it?'

She let her eyes drift into his. 'Does it matter?'

He looked at her long and hard. 'It may not matter to you right now, Sam. But one of these days it will again. Don't do something foolish. You can't change that back.' She nodded slowly and smiled. He was a strange and perceptive man, and she could see that he had qualities she hadn't originally noticed. At first she had seen him only as a tyrannical but effective assistant foreman. Now she saw that he was a man of much greater depth. The years he had spent around people and ranchers and ranch hands, living and losing and working till he almost dropped, hadn't been wasted. He had learned what he did well, and along with it he had learned to read people—no simple art. 'More coffee?' He looked down at her again with a small smile and she shook her head.

'No, thanks, Tate.' This time his name seemed easier on her lips. 'I should be moving on. I'm on cookie-making detail. What about you?' He grinned at her and stretched to whisper in her ear.

'I'm Santa.' He said it with mixed embarrassment and glee.

'What?' She looked at him with confused amusement, not sure if he was kidding.

'I'm Santa.' He said it again, barely doing more than mouth the words, and then, leaning closer to her, he explained. 'Every year I get all dressed up in a costume and Miss Caroline's got this huge bag of toys for the kids. I play Santa.'

'Oh, Tate, you?'

'Hell, I'm the tallest guy here. It makes sense.' He tried to pass it off as ordinary but it was obvious that he enjoyed it. 'The kids really make it worthwhile.' And then he looked down at her questioningly again. 'You got kids?'

She shook her head slowly, her eyes giving away nothing of the emptiness she felt. 'You?' She had momentarily forgotten the ranch gossip she'd heard from Josh.

'I've got one. Works on a ranch near here now. He's a good kid.'

'Does he look like you?'

'Nope. Not at all. He's kind of slight and redheaded like his mother.' He smiled slowly as he said it, thinking of the boy with obvious pride.

Her voice was husky again when she sopke to him. 'You're a very lucky man.'

'I think so too.' He smiled at her. And then his voice lowered again as it almost caressed her. 'But don't worry, little palomino, one of these days you're gonna be lucky too.' He touched her gently on the shoulder and then moved on.

96

9

'Santa . . . Santa! . . . Over here . . .'

'Now just a minute, Sally. You've got to wait for me to come over that side of the room.' Tate Jordan in the heavy white beard and red velvet costume was slowly making his way around the room, endowing each child with a much awaited present, bestowing candy canes and other candies, pats on the cheek, hugs, and even kisses. It was a side of Tate Jordan that no one knew except the people who saw him do this every year on the ranch. It made one actually believe in Santa, just to watch him chuckle and cavort and pull yet another surprise from his enormous sack. Had he not told her earlier that evening that he was playing Santa, Samantha would never have suspected that it was he. Even his voice sounded different as he chatted and chuckled gently, exhorting children to be good to their mummies and daddies this year, to stop teasing their little sisters, to do their homework, and to stop being mean to the cat or the dog. He seemed to know everything about everyone, which of course wasn't difficult on a ranch. But as they touched him and were touched by him, the children were ecstatic, and even Samantha was caught up in the magic of his 'ho ho ho'. The entire performance seemed to take him hours, and when he was through, after eating a whole plate of cookies and six glasses of milk, he vanished with a last 'Ho ho ho' toward the barn, not to be seen again for another year.

Forty-five minutes later, bereft of makeup, padded belly, white wig, and red suit, he reappeared in the main hall, unnoticed as he wandered through the crowd admiring the toys and the dolls and tickling and teasing the children. Soon he made his way to where Samantha stood, with Bill and Caroline, in a simple black velvet skirt and a very pretty white lace blouse. Her hair was knotted loosely at her neck and tied with a black velvet ribbon, and she was wearing makeup for the first time since she had come to the ranch.

'Is that you, Sam?' he teased her after accepting a glass of punch and a fervent thank you to his employer.

'I could say the same to you, you know.' And then in a soft voice. 'That was just terrific. Are you that good every year?'

'I get better and better.' He grinned happily. The Santa Claus role always made Christmas for him.

'Is your son here?'

'No.' He shook his head quickly. 'Jeff's boss isn't as generous as mine.' He smiled at Samantha. 'He's working tonight.'

'That's too bad.' She looked genuinely sorry.

'I'll see him tomorrow. And it's all right. He's a big guy now. He doesn't have time for his old man.' But there was no resentment as he said it. He had enjoyed watching his son become a man. For a moment he wanted to ask Samantha why she had had no children, he had been watching her all evening as she hungrily eyed all the little boys and girls, but he finally decided that it was far too personal a question and he settled instead for a question about New York.

'It's a lot colder there, but I don't think I've ever been anywhere where there's as much Christmas spirit as this.'

'That has nothing to do with California. That's Caroline Lord, and nothing else.' Samantha nodded, and this time when they exchanged a smile their eyes met and held.

Shortly thereafter Samantha met Josh's wife and two of his married children, and a number of the men she'd been riding with for the last two weeks sheepishly brought her their wives or their girl friends, their sons and their daughters and their nieces, and for the first time since she'd come there, she knew that she belonged.

'Well, Sam? Very different from your usual Christmas?'

Caroline was looking at her with a warm smile and Bill was standing nearby.

'Very different. And I love it.'

'I'm glad.' It was only a few minutes after Caroline had warmly hugged her and wished her a merry Christmas that Samantha noticed that she seemed to have disappeared. And shortly thereafter she realised that the old foreman had too. She wondered how many others had noticed. But Samantha was equally aware of the fact that she never heard any gossip about them on the ranch. She wondered if perhaps she was jumping to inappropriate conclusions. It didn't seem likely that she was, but one never knew.

'Tired?' It was Tate Jordan's voice just above her again, and she turned toward him with a little nod.

'I was just about to go back to the house. I was looking for Aunt Caro, but I guess she's already gone.'

'She always leaves quietly so as not to spoil anyone's fun.' He spoke with nothing but the greatest admiration. It was a bond that he shared with Sam. 'Are you ready to go too?' Sam nodded and tried unsuccessfully to squelch a yawn. 'Come on, sleepyhead, I'll walk you home.'

'Can I help it if the guy I work for is a slave driver? It's a wonder I don't fall out of my saddle half dead by the end of the day.'

'Once or twice'—he grinned at her—'I thought you might.' And then he laughed out loud. 'That first day, Sam, I thought you'd stick it out if you died in the saddle.'

'I almost did. Josh almost had to carry me home.'

'And you still got up on Black Beauty after that! You're crazy!'

'About that horse . . . yes!' He looked unhappy after she said it, and she changed the subject as they stepped into the frosty night. 'Feels like snow.'

'It does, but it's not very likely. At least I hope not.' He looked up at the sky but didn't seem overly concerned. And by then they had already reached the door of the big house, where Sam lived.

Samantha hesitated for a moment and then as she

opened the door she stepped aside and looked up at the dark-haired giant with the deep green eyes. 'Would you like to come in, Tate, for a glass of wine or a cup of coffee?' But he was quick to shake his head, almost as though she had suggested something outrageous that he could never accept.

'I promise,' she added, grinning at him, 'I won't attack you. I'll sit on another couch.' He let out a roar of laughter as she said it, and it was difficult to recognise the man she had been at odds with for more than two weeks.

'It's not that, but ranch etiquette, I guess. This is Miss Caroline's house. It wouldn't be appropriate for me to . . . it's difficult to explain . . .'

Samantha smiled at him pleasantly from the doorway. 'Would you like me to wake her so she can ask you in herself?'

He rolled his eyes. 'Hardly, but thanks for the thought. Another time.'

'Chicken.' She looked like a kid as she stood there, and he laughed.

10

Because she had done so for the past ten days, Samantha woke up at four thirty the next morning. She forced herself to lie in bed, pretending even to herself to be asleep, and finally, after an hour of lying with her eyes closed and her mind racing, she got out of bed. It was still dark outside and the stars were shining brightly, but she knew that in little over an hour, life on the ranch would begin. Christmas morning or no, the animals would be stirring, there would be men in the corral tending to the horses, even though no one would be riding the hills.

On bare feet Samantha silently padded to the kitchen,

plugged in the electric coffee maker Caroline used, and then sat waiting in the dark kitchen, letting her mind drift back to the night before. It had been a lovely Christmas party she had shared with the others. Like one gigantic family, all of them linked to each other, each one caring about the other, the children familiar with everyone who lived there, happy and shouting and running around the big beautifully decorated Christmas tree. Thinking about the children at the Christmas party the night before suddenly made her think of Charlie and Melinda's children. This was the first Christmas that she hadn't sent them gifts. She remembered her promise to Charlie with a pang, but she had been nowhere near a store. As Samantha sat in the empty kitchen she felt suddenly very lonely, and without warning her thoughts shifted instantly and very painfully to John. What was his Christmas like this year? How did it feel to be married to a woman who was pregnant? Had they already done the nursery? The pain Samantha felt knife through her was almost beyond bearing, and as though by reflex action she felt herself reach for the phone. Without thinking, yet desperately wanting to reach out and hear a friendly voice, she dialled a familiar number and only a moment later she heard Charlie Peterson answer the phone. His mellifluous voice boomed into the receiver with a resounding rendition of 'Jingle Bells'. He was halfway into the second verse before Sam could squeeze in her name.

'Who? . . . "O'er the fields we go . . ." '

'Shut up, Charlie! It's me, Sam!'

'Oh . . . hi, Sam . . . "Dashing all the wayyyy . . ." '

'Charlie!' She was laughing as she listened, between rounds of trying to outshout him, but despite the amusement of listening to him, there was another pang of loneliness and she felt terribly far away. She suddenly wished she were with them, and not three thousand miles away on a ranch. There was no choice but to wait for him to finish singing.

'Merry Christmas!'

'You mean you're through? You're not going to sing

101

"Silent Night"?'

'I wasn't planning to, but if you're making a special request, Sam, I'm sure I could . . .'

'Charlie, please! I want to talk to Mellie and the boys. But first'—she almost gulped as she said it—'tell me how things are at the office.' She had forced herself not to call. Harvey had practically ordered her not to and she had obeyed. They had her number if they needed her, and her boss had thought it would do her good to forget about them as completely as she could. And actually she had done better than she expected to. Until now. 'How are my accounts doing? Have you lost them all yet?'

'Every one of them.' Charlie beamed into the phone with pride and lit a cigar, and then suddenly he frowned and looked at his watch. 'What in hell are you doing up at this hour? It must be . . . what? Not even six o'clock in the morning out there! Where are you?' He suddenly wondered if she had abandoned the ranch and returned.

'I'm still here. I just couldn't sleep. I've been getting up at four thirty every morning, now I don't know what to do with myself. This feels like the middle of the afternoon.' Not quite, but she was certainly wide awake. 'How are the kids?'

'Wonderful.' There was a moment's hesitation in his voice, and he hurried on to ask her how she was. 'They riding you ragged out there, I hope?'

'Absolutely. Come on, Charlie, tell me what's happening back there.' Suddenly she wanted to know everything, from the office gossip to who was threatening to steal which account from another house.

'Nothing much, kiddo. New York hasn't changed much in the last two weeks. What about you?' He sounded serious for a moment and Sam smiled. 'You happy out there, Sam? You all right?'

'I'm fine.' And then with a small sigh, 'It was the right thing to do, much as I hate to admit it. I guess I needed something as radical as this. I haven't watched the six o'clock news all week.'

'That's something at least. If you're up at four thirty,

you're probably asleep by six o'clock at night.'

'Not quite, but close.'

'And your friend . . . Caroline, and all the horses? They're okay?' He sounded so much like a New Yorker that it made her laugh as she pictured him puffing on his cigar and staring into space wearing his pyjamas and his bathrobe and maybe something the children had given him for Christmas, like a baseball cap or a mitt or a pair of red-and-yellow-striped socks.

'Everyone here is fine. Let me talk to Mellie.' She did, and Melinda didn't catch Charlie's signal. She almost instantly told Sam the news. She was pregnant. The baby was due in July, and she had just found out that week. For just a fraction of a second there was a strange silence and then suddenly Sam was full of effusive congratulations as in the distance Charlie closed his eyes and groaned.

'Why did you tell her?' He was whispering hoarsely at his wife as she attempted to continue to talk to Sam.

'Why not? She'll find out when she comes back anyway.' Melinda had put her hand over the phone, whispered back to him, then took her hand away and went on. 'The kids? They all say they want another brother, but if it isn't a girl this time, I quit.' Charlie made impatient gestures, let her say a rapid good-bye, and recovered the phone.

'How come you didn't tell me, kiddo?' Sam tried to sound nonchalant, but as always when she heard that kind of news, especially lately, it touched something very old and sad and still sensitive near her very core. 'Afraid I couldn't take it? I'm not mentally ill, you know, Charlie, I'm just divorced. That is *not* the same thing.'

'Who cares about that stuff anyway.' There was something sad and worried in his voice.

'You do.' Sam's voice was very soft. 'And Mellie does. And I do. And you're my friends. She was right to tell me. Don't yell at her when you get off the phone.'

'Why not?' He grinned guiltily. 'She needs to be kept in line.'

'Some way you have of keeping her in line, Peterson.

It's a good thing you're the most overpaid art director in the business. You're going to need it for all those kids.'

'Yeah,' he growled contentedly, 'ain't I just.' And then after a long moment, 'Well, kid, be good to your horses, and call if you need us. And Sam'—there was a heavy pause—'we all think about you a lot, and we miss you. You know that, don't you, babe?' She nodded, unable to speak, her voice and her eyes instantly filled with tears.

'Yeah, I know.' It was all she could finally choke out. 'And I miss you too. Merry Christmas!' And then, as she smiled through her tears and blew him a kiss, she hung up. She sat in the kitchen afterward for almost half an hour, her coffee cold in the cup, her eyes riveted to the table, her heart and her mind three thousand miles away in New York. And when she looked up again, she saw that outside the day was slowly breaking, the night had faded from deep blue to pale grey, and she stood up and slowly walked with her cup over to the sink. She stood very still and knew exactly what she wanted to do. With a determined step she walked down the hall, slipped quietly into her clothes, and bundled herself up in two warm sweaters and a jacket, put on the cowboy hat Caroline had lent her a few days before, and with a last look over her shoulder to make sure that no one was stirring, she walked quietly out of her room, down the hall, and out the front door, closing it softly behind her.

It took her only a few minutes to reach the stables, and when she did, she stopped a few feet away from his stall. There was no sound stirring within, and she wondered if he was still sleeping, the giant shining ebony animal she suddenly knew that she wanted to ride. She gently opened the half door and stepped inside, running a hand smoothly down his neck and his flanks and speaking so gently that she almost cooed. He was awake, but he wasn't restless. Black Beauty looked as though he had been waiting for her to come; he gazed meaningfully at her from behind the bristling black lashes, and Samantha smiled at him as she quietly let herself out of the stall, went to get his saddle and bridle, and returned to prepare him for their ride.

There had been no one in the stable to see her when she got there, and there was still no one there now.

When she led him slowly out of the main door a few minutes later into the early morning, there was no one in the vast yard outside. She walked Black Beauty to a nearby block and quickly climbed it. After hoisting herself into the saddle with ease and pulling the reins taut, she moved away toward the now familiar hills. She knew exactly where she wanted to ride him, she had seen a trail through some woods a few days before and now she knew that this was where she wanted to go. At first she cantered gently toward her destination, and then after a while, sensing the huge beast straining to go faster, she let him lope from a canter into a gallop as he made his way toward the rising sun. It was one of the most exquisite feelings she could remember, and she held her knees to his flanks and pressed harder as effortlessly they cleared a series of low bushes and then a narrow stream. She remembered the first time she had jumped him but knew that this was different. She was taking no chances with Black Beauty this morning, but she wasn't angry either. She only wanted to become part of Black Beauty's very body and soul. She felt like an ancient myth, or Indian legend, as she let him slow on the crest of a hill, and she watched the sun begin in earnest its climb into the sky. It was only then that she heard the hooves behind her, then that she knew she'd been followed, and then that she turned in surprise. But when she saw him riding the ivory and onyx pinto toward her, she wasn't really surprised to see Tate Jordan. It was as though he were also a part of the legend, as though he also belonged there, as though he too had fallen from the fiery golden morning sky.

He rode toward her in a straight line, with the pinto at a full gallop, making his way toward her with almost fierce determination, and then at the last moment he swerved to fall in right at her side. She eyed him carefully for an instant, not sure of what she'd see there, afraid that once again he'd be angry, that he'd spoil the moment, and that the friendship that had been conceived only the night before would already die. But what she saw instead in those deep green eyes that looked at her so fiercely was not anger this time, but something much gentler. He said nothing to her, he only watched her, and then nodded and led the pinto on. It was clear that he wanted her to follow him, and she did, with Black Beauty moving effortlessly down the trails that he sought out, over the hills, and into the valleys, until at last they were on a part of the property she had never seen. There was a small lake there, and a little cabin, and as they came over the last hill and saw it Tate and the steaming pinto slowed. He turned to smile at her in the early morning, and Samantha returned the smile as she watched him rein in his horse and dismount.

'Are we still on the ranch?'

'Yes.' He looked up at her. 'Over past that clearing is where it ends.' The clearing was just behind the cabin.

Samantha nodded. 'Whose is that?' She indicated the cabin, wondering if there was anyone there.

Tate didn't give her a direct answer. 'I found it a long time ago. I come here now and then, not often, but when I want to be alone. It's locked up, and no one knows I come out here.' It was a bid for secrecy and Samantha understood.

'Do you have the keys?'

'More or less.' The handsome leathered face broke into a grin. 'There's a key on Bill King's ring that fits it. I helped myself to it once.'

'And made a copy?' Samantha looked shocked, but he nodded his head. Above all else Tate Jordan was an honest man. If Bill King had asked him, he would have told him. But Bill never had, and Tate figured he wouldn't care. Above all he didn't want to draw attention to the forgotten cabin. It meant a lot to him.

'I keep some coffee in there, if it hasn't gone stale. Want to get down for a bit and step inside?' He didn't tell her that he kept a bottle of whisky there too. Nothing with which to commit excesses, but something to keep him warm and soothe his mind. He came here sometimes when he was worried, or if something was bothering him and he needed to be alone for a day. Many was the Sunday he had spent at this cabin, and he had his own ideas as to what kind of purpose it had once served. 'Well, Miss Taylor?' Tate Jordan watched her for a long moment and she nodded.

'I'd like that.' The lure of coffee appealed to her, this morning it was unusually cold. He gave her a hand down and helped her tie up the handsome horse, and then he led the way toward the door of the cabin, extracted his copy of the key, opened the door, and stepped aside to let her in. Like the rest of the cowboys on the ranch, he was always gallant. It was like a last touch of the Old West, and she looked up and smiled at him as she walked slowly in.

There was a dry, musty smell in the cabin, but as she looked around her her eyes widened instantly in surprise. The large airy single room was decorated in pretty flowered chintzes, they were somewhat old-fashioned, but still very handsome and appealing. There was a little couch, two thickly cushioned wicker chairs, and in a corner by the fire was a huge handsome leather chair that Samantha knew instantly was an antique. There was a small writing desk in a corner, there was a radio, a small record player, there were several shelves of books, a large friendly fireplace, and a number of funny objects that must have meant something to the person who owned the cabin: two large handsome trophies, a boar's head, a collection of old bottles, some funny old photographs in ornate old-fashioned frames. There was a thick bear rug spread out in front of the hearth and a delicate antique rocking chair with a needlepoint footstool standing nearby. It was like a haven in a fairy tale, hidden deep in the forest, the kind of place one would want to come to hide from the rest of the world. And then through an open doorway Sam saw a small pretty little blue room with a large handsome brass bed and a beautiful quilt, soft-blue walls, another impressive bear rug, and a little brass lamp with a small shade. The curtains were blue and white and very frilly, and there was a large handsome landscape of another part of the ranch hanging over the bed. It was a room where one would want to spend the rest of one's life.

'Tate, whose is this?' Samantha looked vaguely puzzled, and Tate only pointed to one of the trophies perched on a little shelf on the near wall.

'Take a look.'

She moved closer and her eyes widened as she looked at the trophy and then Tate and then back again. It bore the legend WILLIAM B. KING 1934. The second one was Bill King's too, but dated 1939. And then Sam looked over her shoulder again at Tate, this time with fresh concern.

'Is this his cabin, Tate? Should we be here?'

'I don't know the answer to the first question, Sam. And to the second, probably not. But once I found this place, I could never stay away.' His voice was deep and smoky as his eyes reached out for Sam's.

She looked around silently and nodded again. 'I can see why.'

As Tate moved quietly toward the kitchen she began to look at the old photographs, and although she thought there was something familiar about them, she was never really sure. And then, feeling almost embarrassed, she drifted into the bedroom, her eye caught by the large landscape over the bed. As she reached it and could easily read the signature, suddenly she stopped. The artist had signed her name in red in the lower right-hand corner. C. Lord. Sam turned around then and was about to flee the tiny bedroom, but the room was blocked by Tate's vast frame in the doorway. He was holding out a cup of steaming instant coffee and watching her face.

'It's theirs, isn't it?' Here was the answer to her question, the question she and Barbara had mused over so often, and laughed about, and giggled over. Finally, in this tiny cosy blue room with the patchwork quilt and the huge brass bed that almost filled the room, she knew. 'Isn't it, Tate?' Suddenly Sam wanted confirmation from him if no one else. He nodded slowly and handed her the bright yellow cup.

'I think so. It's a nice place, isn't it? Somehow, all put together it's just like them.'

'Does anyone else know?' She felt as though she had uncovered a holy secret and had a responsibility to both of them to know if it was secure.

'About them?' He shook his head. 'At least no one's ever been sure. But they've been awfully careful. Neither of them ever gives it away. When he's with the men he talks about "Miss Caroline" just like the rest of us, even calls her that most of the time to her face. He treats her with respect, but no particularly marked interest, and she does the same with him.'

'Why?' Samantha looked puzzled as she sipped her coffee and then set down the cup and sat on the edge of the bed. 'Why didn't they just let people know years ago and get married if that was what they wanted?'

'Maybe they didn't want that.' Tate looked as though he understood it, and as she looked up at his weathered face, it was clear that Sam did not. 'Bill King's a proud man. He wouldn't want it said that he married Miss Caro for her money, or for her ranch or her cattle.'

'So they have this?' Sam looked around her in fresh amazement. 'A little cottage in the woods, and he tiptoes in and out of her house for the next twenty-five years.'

'Maybe it kept the romance fresh for them.' Tate Jordan was smiling as he sat down next to Samantha on the bed. 'You know, there's something very special about what you see here.' He looked around himself with warmth and respect that were almost akin to awe. 'You know what you see, Samantha?' He didn't wait for the answer but went on. 'You see two people who love each other, whose lives blend perfectly, her paintings and his trophies, their old photographs and records and books, his comfortable old leather chair and her little rocking chair and her footstool by the fire. Just look at it, Sam.' Together they glanced out of the bedroom doorway. 'Just look. You know what you see out there? You see love. That's what love is, those copper pots, and that old needlepoint cushion, and that funny old pig's head. That's two people you see out there, two people who've loved each other for a long time, and still do.'

109

'You think they still come here?' Sam was almost whispering and Tate laughed.

'I doubt it. Or if they do, not much anyway. I probably come here more than they do. Bill's arthritis has been bothering him a lot in the last few years. I suspect'— he lowered his voice—'that they stay pretty close to the big house.' As he said it Samantha remembered the nightly opening and closing of doors. Yet even after all these years they met in hidden ways at midnight hours.

'I still don't understand why they keep it a secret.'

Tate looked at her for a long time and then shrugged. 'Sometimes that's just the way it is.' And then he smiled at her. 'This isn't New York, Samantha. A lot of old-fashioned values still apply.' It didn't make sense to her anyway. In that case they should have got married. Good Lord, it had gone on for twenty years after all.

'How did you find this place, Tate?' She stood up again and wandered back out to the living room and a few minutes later sat down in Caroline's comfortable old rocking chair.

'I just happened on it one day. They must have spent a lot of time here years back. It's got the same kind of feeling as a real home.'

'It is a real home.' Sam stared into the empty fireplace dreamily as she said it, thinking back to the elegant apartment she had left behind her in New York. It had none of the qualities she felt here, not anymore, none of the love, none of the warmth, none of the tender comfort, the solace that she felt just sitting in the old rocking chair.

'Feel like you could stay forever, don't you?' He smiled at her and let his huge frame down into the leather chair. 'Want me to light a fire?'

She quickly shook her head. 'I'd worry too much about it after we left.'

'I wouldn't leave it burning, silly.'

'I know that.' They exchanged another smile. 'But I'd worry anyway. You know, maybe a stray spark or something . . . this is too special to mess with. I wouldn't want to do anything to jeopardise what they have here.' And

110

then, looking at him more seriously, 'I don't even feel like we should be here.'

'Why not?' The sharp chin jutted out just a little.

'It's not ours. It's theirs, and it's private and secret. They wouldn't want us to be here, or to know about them . . .'

'But we knew about them anyway, didn't we?' He asked the question gently and she nodded slowly.

'I always suspected. Barb—Aunt Caro's niece and I – we used to talk about it for hours, trying to guess, assuming and then not assuming. We were never really sure.'

'And once you grew up?'

She smiled in answer. 'Then I sensed it. But still I always wondered.'

He nodded slowly. 'So did I. I always thought I knew for certain. But I didn't really. Until I came here. This tells its own story.' He looked around again. 'And what a nice story it tells.'

'Yeah.' Sam nodded agreement and began to rock slowly in the old chair. 'It would be nice to love someone like that, wouldn't it? Enough to build something together, and to keep for twenty years.'

'How long did your marriage last, Sam?' It was the first personal question he had asked her, and she looked at him squarely and answered him quickly, seemingly without emotion. But she couldn't help wondering how he knew she'd ever been married.

'Seven years. Yours?'

'Five. My boy was just a little guy when his mum took off.'

'I'll bet you were glad when you got him back.' And then suddenly she blushed furiously, remembering the story and what an insensitive thing she had inadvertently said. 'I'm sorry, I didn't mean—'

'Hush.' He waved a hand gently. 'I know what you meant. And hell, I was glad. But I was damn sorry his mum died.'

'Did you love her even after she left you?' It was an

111

outrageous question but suddenly it didn't matter. It was as though here, in this shrine of Bill and Caro's, they could say anything and ask anything they wanted, as long as it mattered, as long as it wasn't designed to hurt.

Tate Jordan nodded his head slowly. 'Yes, I loved her. In some ways I still do, and she's been dead near fifteen years. It's a funny thing. You don't always remember the way things got in the end. What about you, Sam, you too? You remember your husband when you first loved him, or remember what a son of a bitch he was at the end?'

Sam laughed softly at his honesty and nodded her head as she rocked. 'God, isn't that the truth. Why? I keep asking myself. Why do I remember him when we went to college, when we got engaged, on our honeymoon, on our first Christmas? How come my first thought of him isn't with his socks and my guts hanging out of his suitcase when he walked out the door?' They both smiled at the image she'd created, and Tate shook his head and then turned to her again, his eyes filled with questions.

'Was that how it was, then? He walked out on you, Sam?'

'Yes,' she answered bluntly.

'For someone else?' She nodded, but she didn't look pained this time. She was just admitting to a simple truth. 'That's how it was with my old lady too.' Sam noticed as she listened that now Tate sounded more like the other cowboys. Maybe here he could relax. He no longer had to impress her, and there was no one else around. 'Tears your heart out, doesn't it? I was twenty-five years old, and I thought I'd die.'

'So did I.' Sam looked at him intently. 'So did I. In fact,' she sighed softly, 'I guess everyone in my office did too. That's why I'm here. To get over it. To get away.'

'How long has it been?'

'Since last August.'

'That's long enough.' He looked matter-of-fact and she bridled.

'Is it? For what? To forget him? To not give a damn

anymore? Well, you're wrong on that one, buddy, try again.'

'Do you think about him all the time?'

'No.' She answered him honestly. 'But too much.'

'You divorced yet?'

She nodded. 'Yes, and he's already remarried, and they're having a baby in March.' Might as well tell him everything at one sitting. And in an odd way it felt good to get it all out of the way, all the painful truths, the true confessions. It was wonderful to get it over with. But she found now that he was watching her intently.

'I'll bet that hurt a lot.'

'What?' For a moment she didn't follow what he was saying.

'About the baby. Did you want children?'

She hesitated for only an instant, and then nodded as she suddenly left the rocking chair. 'As a matter of fact, yes, Mr. Jordan. But I'm sterile. So my husband got what he wanted—somewhere else . . .' As she stood at the window, looking out at the lake, she didn't hear him coming, and then suddenly he was standing behind her, with his arms around her waist.

'It doesn't matter, Sam . . . and you're not sterile. Sterile is someone who can't love, who can't give anything, who is locked up and closed up and sold out. That's all that matters and that's not you, Sam. That's just not you.' He turned her around slowly to face him and there were tears in her eyes. She didn't want him to see them, but she couldn't resist the magnetic pull of his hands as he had turned her slowly by the waist. He gently kissed both her eyes, and then pressed his mouth down on hers so hard and for so long that at last she had to fight for breath.

'Tate . . . don't . . . no . . .' She was fighting, but weakly, and he only pulled her closer to him again. She could smell the scent of saddle soap and tobacco on him and feel the rough wool of his shirt beneath her cheek as she turned away and rested her face against his chest.

'Why not?' He put a finger under her chin and made her

look up at him again. 'Sam?' She said nothing, and he kissed her again. His voice was gentle in her ear when he spoke to her, and she could feel her heart pounding against her chest. 'Sam, I want you, more than I've ever wanted any woman before.'

She spoke softly, but with feeling, as her eyes gazed into his. 'That isn't enough.'

He nodded slowly. 'I understand.' And then after a long moment, 'But I don't offer anything more than that anymore.'

Now it was her turn. She smiled gently and asked the same question. 'Why not?'

'Because—' He hesitated and then chuckled softly in the pretty little cabin. 'Because I really am sterile. I don't have all of that left to give.'

'How do you know? Have you tried lately?'

'Not in eighteen years.' His answer was quick and honest.

'And you think it's too late to love anyone again?' He didn't answer and Sam looked around, her eyes pausing at the trophies and then coming back to him. 'Don't you think he loves her, Tate?' He nodded. 'So do I. He can't be any braver than you are, and he's one hell of a man.' And then as she looked at Tate, 'So are you.'

'Does that mean . . .' He spoke softly, his lips playing with hers and her heart wreaking havoc between her ribs, wondering what she was doing kissing this stranger, this cowboy, and trying to justify to him why he should fall in love. She wanted to ask herself what in hell she thought she was doing, but there wasn't time. 'Does that mean,' he went on, 'that if I told you I loved you, that we'd be making love right now?' He looked amused, and with a small smile she shook her head. 'I didn't think it did. So what are you trying to convince me of, and why?'

'I'm trying to convince you that it's not too late to fall in love again. Look at them, when they started out, they were older that we are now. They had to be.'

'Yeah . . .' But he didn't sound convinced. And then he turned his eyes back to her with a pensive expression.

114

'What difference does it make to you if I ever fall in love again?'

'I'd like to know that it's possible.'

'Why? Are you doing research for science?'

'No,' she whispered. 'For myself.'

'So that's it.' He ran a hand gently down her pale blonde mane, fighting with the pins that held it firmly in the knot at the nape of her neck, and then suddenly he unleashed it and it all came tumbling down her back. 'My God, your hair is lovely, Sam . . . palomino . . .' He said it ever so softly. 'Little palomino . . . how beautiful you are . . .' The sun glinted in the window and danced among the gold threads in her hair.

'We should go back now.' She said it gently but firmly.

'Should we?'

'We should.'

'Why?' His lips were kissing her chin and her jawbone and her neck. She wasn't objecting, but she was also not going to let him go any farther than that. 'Why should we go back now, Sam? Oh, God, you're so lovely . . .' She could feel a shiver run through him, and she pulled away slowly with a small shake of her head.

'No, Tate.'

'Why not?' For a moment there was fire in his eyes, and she was almost afraid.

'Because it's not right.'

'For chrissake, I'm a man, you're a woman . . . we're not children here. What do you want?' He raised his voice in lustful irritation. 'The perfect romance, a wedding ring on your finger before you go to bed?'

'What do you want, cowboy? Just a quick roll in the hay?' The force of her words hit him like a bullet, and he looked stunned as slowly he shook his head.

'I'm sorry.' He spoke coldly and then moved to the sink to wash their cups. But when he had finished, she was still standing there, watching him, and she spoke up.

'I'm not sorry. I like you. In fact'—she reached out and put a hand on his arm—'I like you a hell of a lot. But I don't want to get hurt next time.'

'You can't have the kind of guarantees you want, Sam. Not from anyone. And not from me. The only guarantees you'll ever get are lies.' There was some truth in that and she knew it, but it wasn't just the promise she wanted but something real.

'You know what I want?' She looked around at the cabin as she asked the question. 'I want this. I want this kind of meshing and blending and loving after more than twenty years.'

'You think they were so sure of that in the beginning? You think they knew then what they do now? Hell no. She owned the ranch and he was a ranch hand. That was all they knew.'

'You think so?' Samantha's eyes exploded sparks at him. 'You know what else I'll bet they knew then?'

'What?'

'I'll bet they knew they were in love. And until I find that, until a man loves me and I love him, then I'm not coming out to play again.'

He opened the door and locked it behind them. 'Come on.' But she had seen as she walked past him that he wasn't angry. He had understood all that she had told him, and she found herself wondering what he would do now, what she would do herself. For a moment, just a moment, she had wanted to abandon all restraint and caution, but she had decided not to. Not because she didn't want him, but because she wanted him so much. Tate Jordan was one hell of a man.

'Can we come back here?' She eyed him squarely as he cupped his hands and offered her a leg up to the huge Thoroughbred horse.

'Do you really want to?'

She nodded slowly, and he smiled at her and said nothing. She took the leg up and flew into her saddle. A moment later she had the reins in her hands, her heels in the horse's flanks, and she was flying beside Tate Jordan into the wind.

11

'Have a nice ride, dear?' Caroline looked at her benevolently as Samantha strode into the living room, her hair loose, her face flushed, her eyes bright. She looked like a vision of youth and health and beauty, and Caroline couldn't help envying her a little as she watched the young limbs coil into a comfortable chair.

'Very, thanks, Aunt Caro.' She was dying to tell her that she had seen their cabin, but she knew she couldn't. But still the excitement lingered. From that and the kiss she and Tate had shared in Black Beauty's stall. It had been a kiss that seared her very edges and reached into the nether regions of her soul. He was a man different from any other, more powerful and more independent and more alluring than any she had ever known or would.

'See anyone this morning?' It was a casual question, born of thirty years of almost communal living on a large ranch. Not a single hour went by that one didn't hang out with someone, talk about something, and hear something about someone else.

Sam had been about to say 'No one,' and then decided to tell Caroline the truth. 'I saw Tate Jordan.'

'Oh.' It was a very small word without any great emphasis or interest. 'How is Santa Claus after last night? The kids sure enjoy him every year.'

Sam was tempted to say 'So do I,' but didn't dare say it. 'They should. He's a very nice man.'

'You mean you've relented? You don't hate him anymore?'

'I never did.' She tried to look casual as she poured herself a cup of coffee. 'We just didn't see eye to eye over my ability to ride your horse.'

'And he's changed his mind?' Samantha nodded with a

117

grin of satisfaction. 'No wonder you like him. How heartily we approve of those who approve of us. He's a good man though, no matter what he may have said about your riding Black Beauty. He knows this ranch every bit as well as Bill and I.' Every bit ... even the cabin, Samantha found herself thinking and had to take a sip of coffee so as not to smile.

'What are you doing today, Aunt Caro?'

'The books, as usual.'

'On Christmas?' Samantha looked shocked.

Caroline nodded dutifully. 'On Christmas.'

'Why don't we have Christmas dinner instead?'

'As I recall,' Caroline said, looking at her with amusement, 'we already did that last night.'

'That was different. That was everyone. Why don't you and I cook dinner today for Bill King and Tate?' Caroline eyed her very hard for a moment and then shook her head.

'I don't really think that would work.'

'Why not?'

Caroline sighed softly. 'Because they're ranch hands, Samantha, and we're not. There really is a very definite hierarchy on a ranch.'

'Don't you ever have dinner with Bill?' Sam looked shocked.

'Very rarely. Only on state occasions, when someone gets married or dies. Only on nights like last night, at Christmas, do all the fences come down. The rest of the time, you are who you are, and they —they're careful to keep the fences up, Sam.'

'But why?'

'Out of respect. That's just the way it is.' She seemed to accept it, but it continued to annoy Sam.

'But it's all so stupid. What difference does the hierarchy make, for heaven's sake! Who cares?'

'They do.' Caroline's voice was like a splash of cold water. 'They care very much, about form, about position, about who you are and the respect they feel they owe you. As a ranch owner, you're put on a pedestal by them, and they never let you come down. It's tiring sometimes, but that's the way it is. You have to accept it. If we invited Bill and Tate here today, they would be genuinely shocked.' But Sam found it hard to believe as she remembered Tate's earlier entreaties to sleep with him at the cabin. It hadn't occurred to her yet that that was different; it was private. It wasn't like having dinner together at the big house.

'Well, it still doesn't make sense to me.'

Caroline smiled warmly at her. 'It never did to me either, but I accept it now, Sam. It's simpler that way. That's just the way they are.' Was that the reason for the cabin, then? Because he was a ranch hand and she was something very different, the ranch owner? Could all the secrecy have been for something as simple as that? She was suddenly dying to ask her but knew that she could not. 'There will be cold turkey dinners all day at the main hall, Samantha. You could go over there and chat with whoever's around. But I really have to work with Bill for a few hours in my office. I feel terrible about neglecting you on Christmas, Sam, but we have to get this done.' Caroline and Bill's single-minded purpose together, over all the years, had always been the ranch. But now Sam found herself wondering if they ever missed the cabin. They would have to. It was such a perfect place to hide out. She wondered, too, how long it had been since they had last been there, how often they had gone in the beginning, if they'd had it then . . . and she wondered too, how soon she would go there again with Tate.

'I'll be fine, Aunt Caro. I have some letters to write. I'll go and get something to eat at the main hall when I get hungry.' And suddenly she realised that she wanted to catch a glimpse of Tate again. It was as though he had got under her skin that morning and now she couldn't get him out. All she could think of was him, and his hands and his lips and his eyes . . .

But when she went to the main hall for lunch half an hour later, she found that there was no sight of him, and Josh mentioned to her casually when she saw him near the barn a few hours later that Tate had gone to the Bar Three Ranch, twenty-five miles away, to visit his son.

119

12

In the silvery early morning darkness Tate Jordan gave the signal, and the two dozen ranch hands who followed his orders, kicked their horses and followed him toward the main gate. Today most of them were rounding up young bulls for castration, and Tate himself and another small group were riding to a narrow canyon to see if the bridge there was down. When they reached it an hour later, they saw that all was pretty much in order, but on the way back they found that two trees had been hit by lightning and had gone through the roof of a shed, damaging a tractor and some small tools. For two hours the men worked pulling branches away from the building, checking over the tools, trying to start the tractor, and finally activating a huge saw so that they could remove the broken trees. It was gruelling work for all of them, and most of all Samantha, and when they stopped at long last for lunch, Samantha's long blonde hair was damp from her efforts and her thick flannel shirt clung to her chest.

'Coffee, Sam?' Tate handed it to her as he did to the others, and only for a fraction of an instant did she think that she saw something special lingering in his eyes. But a moment later when he gave her some more instructions on what he wanted done with the broken tools, she felt certain that she'd imagined the earlier attention. It was obvious that their relationship was once again strictly business. And by the end of the day she was sure. He treated her well now, as he did the others, joked with her once or twice, and told her to rest when he saw that she could do no more. But he offered her no special words, no particular encouragement, as she sweated and laboured.

At the end of the day, when she left Navajo in his stall, Tate said nothing to her as he left the barn and headed back to his own cabin not far from the main hall.

'Hard work today, eh, Sam?' Josh called to her over his shoulder as he put up his saddle, and she nodded, glancing briefly at Tate's back and suddenly wondering if the moments at the hidden cabin had been a kind of aberration, a brief flash when they both had lost control and then regained it. And she was suddenly glad that she hadn't succumbed to the powerful attraction she had felt. By now he would have been laughing at her, she thought briefly, trying to remember what Josh had said. 'You look beat.'

'Don't we all! It's always hard work out here.' But she didn't look unhappy about it as she said it, and she was glad, as she had been that morning, that she had been spared the all-day session of castrating the young bulls. From what she had seen of it years before it was a bloody and unpleasant experience, and she would rather have spent the day as she had with Tate and the others, fighting with the branches of the stricken trees and wrestling with the awkward farm tools in the crushed shed. 'See you tomorrow!' She waved at him with a tired smile and headed toward the big house, suddenly eager for a hot bath and some dinner, and shortly thereafter her warm bed. Her life on the ranch seemed to grow simpler daily. She slept, she got up, she ate, and she worked her tail off. But it was just what she wanted. She barely had any time to think. Though lately there were thoughts that seemed to crowd her: visions of Tate's face as they had stood side by side in the cabin, talking about Bill and Caro . . . and themselves.

When she walked into the friendly ranch house, she called out to Caroline but was met with only silence. And a few minutes later, in the kitchen, she found a note that explained that Caroline had driven a hundred miles with Bill King. There were problems with some of the tax material that couldn't be explained on the phone, so they had gone to see the accountant. They would either be back late that night or in the morning, but in either case obviously, Sam was not to wait up. There was a chicken already roasted in the oven, a big baked potato alongside it, and a salad in the fridge. But despite the hard day's work Sam found that she wasn't as hungry as she'd thought a few moments earlier. The prospect of eating alone didn't have much appeal. Instead she wandered slowly into the living room, thinking that later she'd make herself a sandwich, but almost without thinking, she stooped, flicked a switch, and turned on the TV. And then she could almost feel something akin to an electric shock run through her as she heard John's voice boom into the cosy living room, and then moments later saw Liz's swelling belly and her smiling face. It brought home again just what had happened, and as Sam watched them her eyes held the same sadness that she had brought with her from New York. She was staring at them and listening to them go through their usual patter, when she suddenly realised that for the past few minutes someone had been knocking on the door. For what had seemed like hours she had been mesmerised by the two smiling people on the evening newscast, and she had been almost unable to tear herself away. With a quick flick of the switch they disappeared from the screen, and with a small unhappy frown around her eyes, Sam walked to the door and pulled it open. Gone was the New York caution of 'Who is it?' Here it could only be ranch hands or friends, there were simply no foes. As she pulled open the door she found herself staring at a navy-blue plaid shirt and a familiar denim jacket, and she let her eyes move rapidly upward until they reached Tate Jordan's face.

'Hi, Tate.' She looked tired and distracted as she stood there, her mind still crammed with the images of her ex-husband and his new wife.

'Something wrong?' He looked instantly worried as he watched her, but she shook her head. 'You look like you've had bad news.'

'No.' She looked vague as she said it. Even if she felt lousy, she could hardly call it 'news' anymore. 'Not really,

I guess I'm just tired.' She smiled at him but it wasn't the easy, relaxed smile he was growing used to, and he wondered what had made her unhappy enough to look like that. He thought maybe she'd had a phone call from back home, or a nasty letter from her ex-husband. He knew that kind of look himself from his own hassles with his ex-wife years before.

'You worked your ass off out there today, little Palomino.' His smile was like a reward at the end of a hard day, and this time when Sam grinned it was real.

'I'm glad you noticed.' But she knew now that Tate Jordan saw everything. It was part of why he was such a valuable man to have on the ranch. He knew all of his men, the quality of their work, their loyalty, their devotion, what they took from and gave to the Lord Ranch in every possible way. And then, eyeing him with a question, she stood aside. 'Would you like to come in?'

'I didn't mean to bother you, Sam.' He looked momentarily embarrassed as he stepped inside. 'I just heard that Bill and Caroline drove in to see the accountant. I thought I'd make sure you were okay. Want to come over to the hall for dinner?' She was touched by his thoughtfulness and suddenly wondered if she saw something more in his smile. But it was difficult to tell with Tate Jordan. There were times when one could read nothing at all in the deep green eyes and even less on the heavily lined face. 'Have you already eaten?' He could smell the chicken still in the oven, and she shook her head.

'No, Caroline left me a chicken, but I wasn't . . . I didn't have time to . . .' She flushed suddenly, remembering the evening broadcast she had sat and stared at instead of eating. And then, as she looked at him, she waved at the kitchen and cocked her head to one side, brushing her thick blonde mane off her shoulders and down her back.

'Do you want to have dinner with me here, Tate? There's plenty to eat out there.' They could divide the potato, there was the whole chicken, and the salad was big enough to feed half the men on the ranch. Caroline always cooked as though she were expecting an army. It came from years of being surrounded by ranch hands and friends.

'Wouldn't that be a lot of trouble for you?' He looked hesitant, his big bulk suddenly seeming too large for the low ceilings, but Samantha quickly shook her head.

'Don't be silly. Caroline left enough food here for ten.' He laughed and followed her into the kitchen, and as they chatted about the ranch and the day's work, she set the table, and a few minutes later they were devouring the chicken and the salad as though they ate dinner together every day.

'What's New York like?' He looked at her, grinning, after he had finished his meal.

'Oh . . . crazy, I guess, is the best way to describe it. Too crowded, too noisy, too dirty, but exciting too. Everyone in New York seems to be doing something: going to the theatre, starting a business, rehearsing for a ballet, going broke, getting rich, getting famous. It really isn't a place for mere mortals.'

'And you?' He eyed her carefully as she got up to pour them both coffee.

'I used to think I loved it.' She shrugged as she set down the cups of steaming coffee and sat down again. 'Now sometimes I'm not so sure. It all seems terribly far away right now, and not very important. It's funny, three weeks ago I couldn't have left my office to get a haircut without calling three times in an hour just to make sure everything was okay. And now I've been gone for almost three weeks and who knows the difference? They don't. I don't. It's as if I never lived back there.' But she also knew that if she had flown back that night, by the next morning it would seem as though she had never left, and she would feel once again that she never could. 'I think the thing about New York is that it's addictive. Once you break the habit, you're all right, but while you're hooked'—she smiled warmly at him—'watch out!'

'I've known women like that in my lifetime!' His eyes danced mischievously as he sipped steaming coffee in the delicate white cup.

124

'Have you now, Mr. Jordan? Would you care to tell me about that?'

'Nope.' He smiled again. 'What about you? Did you leave anyone waiting for you in New York, or did you run away from all of that too?'

Her eyes grew serious for a moment after he asked her and then she shook her head. 'I didn't run away, Tate. I left. For a vacation . . .' She hesitated again. 'A sabbatical, I think they called it at the office. And no, I didn't leave anyone waiting back there. I thought you understood all of that the other day.'

'It never hurts to ask.'

'I haven't been out with anyone since my husband.'

'Since August?' She was surprised that he had remembered but she nodded. 'Don't you think it's about time?'

She didn't want to tell him that she was beginning to think so right now. 'Maybe. It'll all happen at the right time.'

'Will it?' He spoke softly as he leaned toward her and kissed her as he had before. Once again she felt her heart pounding against the table as her body moved toward him, and with one hand he gently cupped her face as the other smoothed her silken hair. 'My God, you're beautiful, Sam. You take my breath away, do you know that?' He kissed her again, and then pushed the plates across the table and pulled her toward him, until suddenly they were both breathless as they kissed in the silent house. It was then that Sam gently pulled away from him, with a small embarrassed smile on her lips.

'Aunt Caro would be shocked, Tate.'

'Would she?' He looked unconvinced. 'Somehow I doubt that.' And at the same moment they both found themselves thinking of Caroline and Bill King on their little trip. They would probably spend the night together somewhere on the road. It made Sam think again of the little hidden cabin, and Tate smiled as his mind drifted back to it too. 'If it weren't so dark we could ride out there. I liked being there with you, Sam.'

'At the cabin?' She had understood immediately what

125

he had been thinking, and he nodded.

'I felt the other day'—his voice caressed her and he stood up—'as though it had been made just for us.' She smiled at him and slowly he pulled her to her feet until she stood before him, dwarfed by his size, her own tall frame tiny beside his, her breasts suddenly pressed against him as he pulled her to him, and her mouth hungry for his once again as gently he stroked her back and her hair. He pulled away then and his voice was only a whisper. 'I know this sounds crazy, Sam, but I love you. I knew it the first time I saw you. I wanted to touch you and to hold you and to run my hands through that palomino hair.' He smiled gently down at her but Samantha looked pensive. 'Do you believe me, Sam?'

Her big blue eyes found his green ones and she looked troubled. 'I don't know what I believe, Tate. I was thinking of what I said to you the other day, that just making love with someone wouldn't be enough. Is that why you said all this?'

'No.' His voice was still a whisper, his mouth near her ear as he kissed her neck. 'I said it because I mean it. I've been thinking about you a lot since the other day. What you want isn't different from what I feel, Sam.' His voice grew stronger as he reached out and took her hands. 'You just want me to put words to my feelings. I'm not used to doing that. It's easier to say "I want to make love to you" than it is to say "I love you." But I've never met a woman I've wanted as much as I want you.'

'Why?' She spoke in a hoarse whisper with all the hurt John had left her sharply etched in her eyes. 'Why do you want me?'

'Because you're so lovely . . .' He reached out gently and touched her breasts with his powerful yet careful hands. 'Because I like the way you laugh and the way you talk . . . and the way you ride that damn horse of Caro's . . . the way you work like an ox with the men even though you don't have to . . . because I like'— he grinned and let his hands slip around her—'the way your ass sits on top of your legs.' She laughed in answer and gently

126

pushed his hands away. 'Isn't that good enough reason?'

'Good enough reason for what, Mr. Jordan?' She was teasing him now as she turned away from him and began to clear the table, but before she could get their plates to the sink, he had taken them from her, set them down, and picked her up easily in his arms and carried her out of the room, making his way across the living room until he reached the long hall that led to her room. 'Is this the way, Samantha?' His voice was ever so gentle and his eyes burned into hers. She wanted to tell him to stop, to turn back, but she found that she couldn't. She only nodded and pointed vaguely down the hall, and then, giggling suddenly, she pushed away from him.

'Come on . . . stop, Tate. Put me down!' His laughter joined hers but he didn't do as she told him. Instead he stopped at a half-open door at the end of the hall.

'Is this yours?'

'Yes.' She crossed her arms as he held her in his as though she were a very small child. 'But I didn't invite you in, did I?'

'Didn't you?' One eyebrow rose and he crossed the threshold and looked around with interest. And then with no further words he set her down on the bed, took her in his arms, and kissed her hard on the mouth. The games between them were suddenly over, and the passion he unleashed in her took her very much by surprise. She was stunned at the force with which he held her to him, at the hunger of his mouth and his hands and his whole body as it reached out for hers. It seemed only moments later that he lay beside her and that her clothes seemed to melt away from her body, as did his. All she was aware of was the soft doeskin of his flesh against hers, the gentleness of his hands—ever searching, ever thrilling— the endless legs wound around hers, and his mouth drinking her own. He held her closer to him until she could bear it no longer and she pressed against him, moaning softly, longing to be his. It was then that he pulled away from her, that he looked hard into her eyes, asking her a question without words. Tate Jordan had never taken a woman, and would not

127

take this one, not ever, and not now, unless this was what she wanted, unless he was certain, and as he searched her eyes she nodded slowly, and then seconds later he took her, pressing deep and hard into her flesh with his own. She gave a sharp gasp of pleasure as he thrust deeper, and then with another moan she let herself go to the ecstasy he brought her to again and again and again.

It seemed hours later when he lay still beside her, the room was dark, the house quiet, and she felt his long powerful body stretched out next to her, content, sated, and she felt with pleasure his lips gentle on her neck. 'I love you, Palomino. I love you.' The words sounded so real, but suddenly she wanted to ask him 'Do you?' Was it real? Would anyone ever really love her again? Love her and mean it, love her and not hurt her, love her and not go away? A small trickle of tears suddenly fell from the corner of her eye to the pillow, and he looked at her sadly and nodded his head. He pulled her into his arms then and cradled her gently, crooning to her softly meaningless words as one would have to a wounded animal or a very small child. 'It's all right, babe. It's all right now, I'm here with you . . .'

'I'm sorry . . .' Her words were muffled as suddenly the sobs of a lifetime broke from her, and the grief that had lived pent up inside her broke from her like a flock of wild birds. They lay like that, locked together, for almost an hour, and when her tears were spent, she felt a familiar stirring beside her and she smiled slowly and reached down to touch him, and then guide him to the same spot again.

'You all right now?' His voice was husky in the darkness, and she nodded. 'Answer me.'

'I'm all right'. He would go no further and his eyes were riveted to hers.

'You sure?'

'Yes, I'm sure.' With her body she showed him the gratitude that she didn't know the words for, arching toward him and giving him as much pleasure as he had given her. It was a meshing of two people beyond any she

128

had ever known in the years before him, and as she lay beside Tate Jordan and slept, Samantha wore a small happy smile.

When the alarm went off at her bedside the next morning, she awoke slowly, with a smile, expecting to see him, and what she saw instead was a note beneath the small clock. He had set it for her when he had left her bed quietly at two o'clock that morning. He had turned on the alarm and written her a note on a little scrap of paper. It said only I LOVE YOU, PALOMINO. And as she read it she lay back on her pillows again, closed her eyes, and smiled. This time there were no tears.

13

At the end of the day's work Samantha looked as fresh and alive as she had at the beginning, and Josh commented on it with disgust as she hung up her saddle with a grin.

'Christ, woman! Look at you, Sam, tough as nails. Three weeks ago you could hardly walk after a day's ride, you were so out of shape. Now you fly off that damn horse and look as bright-eyed at six o'clock at night as you do in the morning when you get up. Makes me sick. You ought to be carrying *me* back to *my* cabin. My ass is sore as hell, and my arms are killing me from roping those damn steers. Maybe what you need is to shake your butt and work a little harder.'

'Bullshit. I worked harder than you did today!'

'Oh, yeah?' He snarled playfully at her and swatted her behind with his hat as she walked past.

'Yeah!' She ran past him with a grin on her face and a long blonde ponytail tied with a bright red ribbon. She had almost flown in her saddle all day long. All she had been able to think of was Tate Jordan, but neither of them had given anything away as they worked. If anything, he had been indifferent and almost surly, and she had done her best to ignore him the few times they might have had occasion to speak. He spoke to her casually only once over coffee at lunchtime and then strolled away to chat with some of the other men while Sam hung back with the ranch hands she knew best. It was only now that the day was over that she allowed her thoughts to soar toward Tate again. All day she had remembered moments of their night together, an instant, a glimmer, the shape of his leg as he had lain naked and uncovered amidst the tousled sheets, a look in his eye as he leaned toward her to kiss her again, the way the back of his neck looked as he lay down for a moment with a happy sigh and let her run long, tantalising fingers slowly down his tingling spine. She loved the way he looked and the way he felt and what he did to her, and now it was all she could think of as she ran back to Aunt Caro's house. She had no idea when she might see him alone again. His cabin was highly visible, so near to the main hall where the men ate, and Aunt Caro was back from her brief trip with Bill. It was obvious that a meeting between them would take some arranging, but she felt certain that he would find a way. The thought that now he and Bill King would both tiptoe into the house and then creep out again at midnight brought a gurgle of laughter to her lips as she opened the front door.

'My, aren't you happy this evening, Miss Samantha.' Caroline eyed her with pleasure from where she sat. And for the first time in four months she saw John's familiar face and felt not a twinge. She checked for a moment, narrowed her eyes pensively as she watched him, and then shrugged with a small quiet smile as she went to her room to wash up.

'I'll be back in a minute, Aunt Caro.'

When she returned, they shared dinner, only tonight Samantha found herself wondering where Tate was. Was he in the main dining hall with the others? Had he opted to stay in his cabin and cook for himself, as a few of the men did? But most of them preferred to eat dinner with the others. Even the men with wives on the ranch often came to the main hall after dinner for coffee and a smoke and the companionship of the men they rode with all day long. Suddenly Samantha ached to be with them, but she also sensed that if she joined them all of a sudden in the evening they would begin to wonder why she was there. They accepted her in their midst in the daytime, but in the evening they expected her to stay at the big house with Caroline, where she belonged. It would have shocked them to see her there in the evening, and it would have been impossible to seek out Tate without causing comment. Someone would have easily figured it out. Gossip on any ranch was rampant, and there was a kind of sensitive radar that all of them seemed to have. Romances and marriages and divorces were almost instantly discovered, along with illicit affairs and illegitimate babies, which made it all the more remarkable that Bill King and Caroline had kept their secret for so long. Even if some of the old timers, or those who knew them well, suspected, no one on the ranch had ever been sure. Samantha found now that she respected that and understood all the more how difficult the clandestine life-style must have been. Now she felt herself fairly throbbing with excitement, aching to be with the man, to talk to him, to laugh, to tease him, to touch him, to go for a walk in the night air, to look up at him with interest and pride and hold his hand, and after that to come back to her bedroom and discover each other's bodies once again, as they had the night before.

'Do you want more salad, Samantha?' They were halfway through dinner before Samantha seemed to remember where she was. For half an hour she had been silent and dreamy and drifting as Caroline watched her and wondered what was the cause. Sam didn't look unhappy, so she didn't think she was upset that Caroline had been watching the newscast. She didn't look homesick. In fact she looked fine, so it had to be something else. 'Something wrong, Sam?'

'Hmm?'

131

'Something right?'

'What? . . . Oh . . . I'm sorry.' Samantha blushed like a schoolgirl and then shook her head with a brief girlish laugh. 'No, I was just distracted. It was a long day today, but I enjoyed it.' It was the only way she could explain the outrageous glow she knew she wore and the look on her face.

'What on earth did you do?'

'Nothing special. Roped some horses, checked the fences, the men roped some steers this afternoon . . .' She tried to remember. Mostly she had dreamed about Tate. 'It was just a nice day really.'

The wise old woman watched her closely. 'I'm glad that you're happy here on the ranch.'

Samantha's face grew oddly serious as she remembered. 'I am, Aunt Caro. I'm happier here than I've been anywhere else in a long time.'

Caroline nodded and addressed herself to her salad as Samantha went back to dreaming of Tate. But it wasn't until the next morning that she saw him. The night before she had heard Bill King come and go, with envy this time. But there had been no way that Tate could come to her, and as she lay in her bed, longing for him, she smiled to herself, it was like being eighteen and having an illicit affair. She felt suddenly young and girlish, terribly clandestine, and impatient to be with him again.

It was seven o'clock the next morning, Sunday, when she gulped her coffee, zipped up her jeans, donned her jacket, brushed her hair one last time, and then ran out to the barn, hoping that she might find him there. As it turned out, when she got there, there as no one. The men who had come to feed the horses had already gone back to the main hall to eat, and she was alone in the huge barn with the familiar horses, each one in its stall, quietly eating or resting or softly greeting each other, as Samantha slowly made her way to Black Beauty's stall. She ran a hand slowly down his muzzle and then felt the soft whiskered lips brush her hand, looking for something to eat.

132

'I didn't bring you anything this morning, Beauty. I'm sorry, boy.'

'Never mind him.' The low voice came from behind her. 'What did you bring me?'

'Oh!' She wheeled around to face him, startled, and before she could catch her breath, he had taken her swiftly in his arms, almost crushing the air out of her lungs as he held her and kissed her quickly, and then let her go.

'Good morning, Palomino.' He spoke in a whisper and she blushed.

'Hello . . . I missed you.'

'I missed you too. Do you want to go to the cabin this morning?' Anyone even a few feet from them couldn't have heard him speaking, and Samantha nodded quickly with a bright light of anticipation in her eyes.

'I'd like that.'

'I'll meet you at the south fence, in the clearing. Do you know where that is?' He looked suddenly worried as he watched her as though he were afraid she might get lost, but she only laughed.

'Are you kidding? Where do you think I've been all week long while you've been working?'

'I don't know, babe.' He grinned at her. 'Same place I've been, I suspect. Halfway out of your head.'

'You're not far wrong.' And then, as he made to go, she grabbed at his sleeve and whispered, 'I love you.'

He nodded, brushed her lips with his own, and whispered in answer, 'I love you too. See you at ten.' And then he was gone, his heels clicking loudly on the barn floor, and a moment later as he turned a bend there was a shouted greeting to two of the men coming to tend to their horses. A moment earlier and they would have seen him kissing Samantha. Instead all they saw now was Sam diligently feeding Caroline's best horse.

14

They met at five minutes before ten in the south clearing, their horses fresh, the sky blue, their eyes bright with desire. It was a little crazy, this brand-new passion, she couldn't explain it but deep in her gut, she knew that she had to be with him, and she was ready to make a commitment to him for the rest of her life. She tried to explain it to him later that morning, as they lay in the big comfortable brass bed in the pale blue bedroom, their bodies tired, their hearts light, and his arm encircling her as she nestled at his side.

'I don't know, Tate, it's as if . . . as if I've always been waiting for you. As if suddenly I know what I was born for . . .'

'You mean screwing?' He grinned at her and rumpled the exquisite hair.

'Don't call it that.' She looked hurt.

'I'm sorry.' He kissed her softly and touched her face. 'Making love. That's what it is, you know, no matter what I call it.'

'I know it is.' She moved closer to him with a happy smile and closed her eyes. 'It must be wrong to be this happy. It's certainly indecent.' Her eyelids fluttered and he kissed the tip of her nose.

'Is it? Why?' He looked just as happy as she as he lay there. 'Why don't we have a right to feel like this?'

'I'm not sure. But I hope we do and for a very long time.' Their thoughts went in unison to Bill and Caroline, who had lain in the same bed before them and were still together after such a long time.

'It's crazy, Tate, it's all so new between us and it just doesn't feel like it, does it?'

'No, but if you don't stop talking about it, I'm going to

134

start treating you like you've been around for the last twenty years.'

'And then what?'

'I'll ignore you.'

'Just try it.' She ran a slender finger up the inside of his thigh and stopped interestingly where his legs joined.

'And just what is that all about, Miss Samantha?'

'Hang around and I'll show you.' She teased in a sultry voice and he put a hand between her thighs. They were the oddest combination of teasing and serious, and through the entire morning there was always the feeling that they had been there before and been part of each other's lives for a very long time. It was almost impossible to realise that the relationship was a brand-new one, and Tate seemed to feel as comfortable as she did as they wandered naked through the tiny house.

'Did you see the photo albums, babe?' he called out to her as she made sandwiches in the cheerful little kitchen from the provisions he'd brought. He sat on the couch, with a blanket over his naked shoulders, his feet extended toward the bright fire. The fireplace hadn't been cleaned since the last person had used it, so they felt certain that no one would discover that they'd been there from whatever ashes they eventually left in the grate.

'Yeah, they're great, aren't they?' There were photographs of Bill and Caroline, and other people on the ranch, dating all the way back to the early fifties, and the two new lovers chuckled fondly as they glanced through the pages, watching people cavort years ago in front of outdated cars, in funny bathing suits and odd hats. There were a few pictures of rodeos, and there were even some photographs of the ranch before some of the newer buildings had been built. 'Gee, it used to be a lot smaller.'

He smiled in answer. 'One day it should be a lot bigger than this. This could be the finest ranch in the state, maybe one of the best in the country, but Bill King is getting old, he isn't anxious to see it grow. Leastways not anymore.'

'What about you? Is that what you want, Tate? To run

135

this ranch someday?' He nodded slowly, being honest with her. He had a great deal of ambition, all of it centred around this ranch.

'Yeah. I'd like to make it something very special one day, if Miss Caro will let me. I'm not sure she will, while old Bill is around.'

Samantha spoke softly, almost reverently. 'I hope he always will be, Tate, for her sake.'

He nodded slowly. 'So do I. But one day, one day . . . there are some things I'd like to change on this ranch.' Closing the album carefully, he began to tell her. An hour later he glanced at the electric clock in the kitchen and stopped. 'Listen to me, Sam. I could go on like this for hours.' He smiled sheepishly but it was obvious that she had enjoyed it.

'I like hearing about it.' And then after a minute, 'Why don't you start your own ranch?'

But he laughed and shook his head. 'With what, little Palomino? Good wishes and old beer cans? Do you have any idea what it would cost to start a decent ranch? A fortune. Not on my pay, babe. No, all I want is to be one hell of a foreman, not an assistant foreman, but the real thing. The man in power. Hell, most of the ranchers don't know their ass from a hole in the ground. The foreman is the one who keeps the place running.'

'You do that here.' She eyed him proudly and he gently touched her hair and then cupped a hand under her chin.

'I try, little Palomino. I try when I'm not playing hookie with you. You could make me almost sorry I'm working. All I wanted to do yesterday was come here with you, and make love to you and sit by the fire and feel good.'

Samantha stared into the fire with dreams in her eyes. 'So did I.' And then after a moment she turned her eyes back to him. 'What are we going to do, Tate?'

'About what?' He was teasing her. He knew what she meant.

'Don't be cute. You know what I mean.' And then she giggled. 'The other night I had this vision of you and Bill King tiptoeing into the house and bumping into each other in the dark.' They both laughed at the image and he pulled her close, with a pensive look in his eyes. He had already mulled over the possibilities, and all of them were complicated, none of them was ideal.

'I don't know, Sam, it would be a lot easier if it were summer. We could come here every night after work and ride back in the moonlight under the stars. But it's dark as hell now when we finish, and I'd be afraid one of the horses might stumble and get hurt.'

'We could carry lanterns.'

'Sure.' He grinned at her. 'Or hire a helicopter, why not?'

'Oh, shut up. Well . . . what are we going to do? Do you want to try sneaking into Aunt Caro's?'

He shook his head slowly. 'No. They'd hear us, just like you told me you hear him coming in every night. And my place is so damn wide open. All it would take would be for one of the men to see you, just once, and it would be all over for us.'

'Would it?' Samantha looked strained as she said it. 'Would it really be so awful if they knew?' He nodded slowly. 'Why?'.

'It's not right, Sam. You are who you are and I am who I am. You don't want them talking and neither do I.' But the truth was that she didn't give a damn. She thought she loved him, and she didn't give two pins what anyone said. What could they do to hurt them? But she saw in his face that it was a sacred rule. Ranchers didn't fall in love with ranch hands.

Samantha looked at Tate squarely. 'I'm not going to play the same game they've played, Tate, not forever. If we stay together, I want people to know it. I want to be able to be proud of what we have, not afraid of who might find out.'

'We'll cross that bridge later.' But she had the feeling that he wasn't prepared to move an inch in her direction, and suddenly she bridled and the light in her eyes was as stubborn as his.

'Why? Why not start dealing with it right now? Okay, I

understand we don't have to advertise to everybody right this minute that we're having an affair. But hell, Tate, I'm not going to sneak around forever.'

'No.' He said it very quietly. 'Eventually you're going back to New York.' The words hit her like a wave of cold water, and when she spoke again, there was ice and pain in her voice.

'What makes you so sure?'

'Because that's where you belong, just like I belong here.'

'Is that right? How do you know that? How do you know that I'm not like Caroline, that I haven't decided I don't want that kind of life anymore, not that my life is like hers was?'

'You know how I know?' He looked at her with the full wisdom of his forty-plus years. 'Because when Caroline came here, she was a widow, she wanted to give up the life she had shared with her husband, because he was gone. And she was forty years old, Sam, that's not the same as thirty or thirty-one. You're young, you still have a lot of living to do, a lot of your crazy commercials to put together, a lot of deals to make, a lot of buses to catch, phone calls to make, planes to miss, parties to go to . . .'

'And I couldn't do some of that here?' She looked hurt and he eyed her gently, with wisdom and tenderness and love.

'No, little one, you couldn't. This isn't the place for that. You came here to heal, Sam, and that's what you're doing, and maybe I'm just part of that. I love you. I never laid eyes on you before three weeks ago, and I haven't really given a damn about a woman in years, but I know I love you. I knew it the first day we met. And I hope you love me. But what happened to Bill and Caro is a miracle, Sam, they don't belong together, and they never will. She's educated, he isn't. She's led one hell of a fancy life, and his idea of class is a solid-gold toothpick and a fifty-cent cigar. She owns the ranch and he ain't got a hill of beans. But she loves him, and he loves her, and this was all she wanted. For my own reasons I think she was a little

138

crazy, but she'd had another life, and maybe after that this was enough for her. You're different, Sam, you're so much younger, and you've got a right to so much more than I could give you here.' It was totally crazy, they had known each other for less than a month, and only been lovers for two days, and yet they were talking about the future as though it really mattered, as though there were even a question of their staying together for the rest of time. Samantha eyed him with amazement and then looked at him with a small smile.

'You're crazy, Tate Jordan. But I love you.' And then she took his face in her hands and kissed him, hard, on the lips, and then sat back and crossed her arms. 'And if I want to stay here, if this is the life I want, whether I'm thirty or ninety or eighteen, then that's my decision. I am not Caroline Lord, and you are not Bill King, and you can save your damn self-sacrificing speeches, mister, because when the time comes, I'm going to do exactly what I want to do. If I don't want to go back to New York, you can't make me, and if it's you I want for the rest of my life, then I'll follow you to the ends of the earth and bug you to death until you announce it to every last goddamn ranch hand, and Caroline and Bill. You're not going to get rid of me as easily as you'd like to. You got that?' She was grinning at him, but she saw that there was still a broad streak of resistance in his eyes. It didn't matter though, he didn't know her, and the truth of it was that with only one recent exception, what Sam Taylor wanted, she got. 'Got that, mister?'

'Yeah, I got it.' But without saying more, this time it was Tate who kissed her and silenced her almost completely as he threw off the warm blanket and cast it over both of them. Only moments later they were once more blended together, their legs and their arms and their bodies one shimmering tangle as their lips held and the fire crackled nearby. And when it was over, he pulled his lips from hers breathlessly and carried her back to the little blue bedroom where they began again. It was after six o'clock when they noticed that it was nighttime. They had slept and made love and slept and made love all afternoon, and now regretfully Tate swatted her bottom, and then went into the bathroom to run a hot tub. They took a bath together, his endless limbs wrapped around her, as she giggled and told him stories of her early summers on the ranch.

'You know, we still haven't solved our problem.'

'I didn't know we had one.' He lay his head back on the edge of the tub and closed his eyes in the hot bath.

'I mean about where and how to meet.'

He fell silent for a long moment as he thought it over and then shook his head. 'Damn, I wish I knew. What do you think, Sam?'

'I don't know. My room at Aunt Caro's? I could let you in the window.' She laughed nervously. It really had overtones of being fifteen years old and very "fast". 'Your place?'

He nodded slowly. 'I guess so. But I don't like it.' And then suddenly he brightened. 'I've got it. Hennessey's been bitching for two months about his house. Says the cabin's too small for him, it sits in the wind, it's too far from the chow hall. He's been driving us all nuts.'

'So?'

'I'll trade him. His place is on the edge of the camp, almost behind Caro's. At least if you go there, no one should see you. It's a hell of a lot better than where I am right now.'

'You don't think they'll suspect?'

'Why should they?' He grinned at her in the steam from the bathtub. 'I don't plan to pinch your ass every day at breakfast or kiss you on the mouth before we ride.'

'Why not, don't you love me?'

He said nothing, but only leaned forward, kissed her tenderly, and then fondled her breasts. 'Matter of fact, little Palomino, I do.'

She raised herself on her knees in the old bathtub and then knelt facing him with everything she felt in her eyes. 'So do I, Tate Jordan. So do I.'

They rode back that night after seven, and Sam was

intensely grateful that she knew Caroline had gone to dinner at another ranch. Otherwise Caroline would have been frantic. But the day had slipped past them, with their chatter and their laughter and their loving, and now as Sam came back to the main ranch house she felt a sudden loss at not being with him. It was as though someone had severed her right arm. It was an odd feeling to have about a man she had known for so little time, but isolated as they were from the rest of the world, there was something special and intense about their feelings, and she found herself longing for him again as she sat alone in the empty house. Caroline had left her a note that expressed concern at her long absence but not panic, and she had also left a warm dinner on the stove, which Sam only picked at before going to bed at eight thirty and lying there in the dark, thinking of Tate.

When Caroline came home that night with Bill King beside her, they tiptoed stealthily into the darkened house, and Bill went immediately to her room. Sam's presence in the house had made things a little awkward, and Caroline had to remind him every night not to close the front door so hard, but he didn't hear. Now Caroline walked softly down the hall to Sam's room, opened the door, peered into the moonlit darkness, and saw the beautiful young woman asleep in her bed. She stood watching her for a moment, feeling that her own youth had come back to haunt her, and then silently she walked into the room. She thought that she knew what was happening, yet as she had known it for herself, it was something that couldn't be changed or stopped. One had to live one's life. She stood there for a long time, gazing down at Samantha, her hair fanned out on her pillow, her face so unlined and so happy, and with tears in her eyes, Caroline reached out and touched the sleeping girl's hand. It did nothing to wake Sam as she lay there, and on still-silent feet Caroline left the room again.

When she returned to her own room, Bill was waiting in his pyjamas and taking a last puff on his cigar. 'Where were you? Still hungry after all that dinner?'

'No.' Caroline shook her head, oddly quiet. 'I wanted to

make sure that Sam was all right.'

'Is she?'

'Yes. She's sleeping.' They had thought so when they saw the darkened house.

'She's a nice girl. That guy she was married to must've been a damn fool to run off with that other woman.' He hadn't been impressed with what he'd seen of Liz on TV.

Caroline nodded silent agreement and then wondered how many of them were damn fools. She to have let Bill force silence on her for two decades, keeping their love for each other secret; Bill for living like a criminal, as he tiptoed in and out of her house for more than twenty years; Samantha for falling for a man and a way of life that were both as foreign to her and possibly as dangerous as jumping off the top of the Empire State Building; and Tate Jordan for falling in love with a girl he couldn't have. Because Caroline knew exactly what was happening. She sensed it in her bones, in her gut, in her soul. She had seen it in Sam's eyes before Sam even knew it, sensed it on Christmas when she saw Tate look at Sam while she was busy doing something else. Caroline saw it all, and yet she had to pretend that she saw nothing, knew nothing and no one, and suddenly she didn't want that anymore.

'Bill.' She looked at him strangely, took his cigar away, and set it down in the ashtray. 'I want to get married.'

'Sure, Caro.' He grinned and fondled her left breast.

'Don't.' She brushed him away. 'I mean it.' And something suddenly told him that she did.

'You're senile! Why would we get married now?'

'Because at our age you shouldn't be sneaking in and out of our house in the middle of the night, it's bad for my nerves and your arthritis.'

'You're crazy.' He lay back against the headboard with a look of shock.

'Maybe. But I'll tell you something. By now I don't think we'll surprise anyone. And what's more, I don't think anyone would care. No one would remember what or where I come from, so all your old arguments are nonsense. All they know after all this time is that I'm

142

Caroline Lord and you're Bill King of the Lord Ranch. Period.'

'Not period.' He looked suddenly ferocious. 'They know you're the rancher and I'm the foreman.'

'Who gives a damn?'

'I do. And you should. And the men do. There's a difference, Caro. You know that after all these years. And I'll be damned'—he almost roared it at her—'if I'll make you a laughingstock. Running off and marrying the foreman—the hell I will.'

'Fine.' She glared at him. 'Then I'll fire you, and you can come back as my husband.'

'Woman, you're crazy.' He wouldn't even discuss it. 'Now turn the light out. I'm tired.'

'So am I . . .' She looked at him unhappily. 'Of hiding, that's what I'm tired of after all these years. I want to be married, dammit, Bill.'

'Then marry another rancher.'

'Go to hell.' She glared at him and he turned off the light, and the conversation was ended. It was the same conversation they had had a hundred times over the last twenty years, and there was no winning. As far as he knew, she was the rancher, and he was the foreman. And as she lay on her side of the bed, her eyes filled with tears, her back to him, she fervently prayed that Samantha would not fall hopelessly in love with Tate Jordan, because she knew that it would end no differently than this. There was a code that these men followed, a code that made sense to no one but them, but they lived by it, and Caroline knew that they always would.

15

The exchange of cabins between Tate Jordan and Harry Hennessey was completed within four days. Hennessey was enchanted with Tate's offer, and with the appropriate amount of grumbling, Tate eventually moved his things. He claimed that he didn't particularly like his cabin, was sick and tired of hearing Hennessey bitch, and had no vested interest in any of the cabins. No one took any particular notice of the transaction, and by Thursday night Tate had unpacked all his things. In her room at Aunt Caro's, Samantha waited patiently in the dark until nine thirty, when Caroline was safely in her room. Samantha left via her window and padded through the garden at the rear of the house, until only a few moments later she reached Tate's front door. His new cabin was almost directly behind the house and could be seen by no other. It was even protected from the view of the big house by the fruit trees at the back end of the garden, so there was no one who could see Samantha slip quietly through the door. Tate was waiting for her, barefoot, bare-chested, and in blue jeans, his hair almost blue-black, with salt at the temples and liquid green fire in his eyes. His skin was as smooth as satin, and he folded her rapidly into his arms. Moments later they were between clean sheets on his narrow bed. It was only after they had made love that they indulged in conversation, that she giggled about sneaking out of her window and told him that she was sure that at that very moment Bill King was tiptoeing through the front door.

'Doesn't this all seem ridiculous at our age?' She was amused but he wasn't.

'Just think of it as romantic.' Like Bill King with his concern for Caro, Tate Jordan had no intention of turning

Sam into a laughingstock on the ranch. She was no quick piece of ass, no easy lay from New York. She was one hell of a special lady, and now she was his woman, and he would protect her if he had to, even from herself. And she understood nothing of the code of behaviour between ranchers and ranch hands. What they did was their business and no one else's, and always would be, no matter what Samantha said. It was a point that she no longer chose to argue, there were always too many other things to say. She knew his position now, and he was well aware of hers, there was nothing left to be said for the moment about their clandestine arrangements. And it was comfortable enough for a while. For some reason, in her own mind, she had decided to make it an 'open secret' by summer. She figured by then they would have been lovers for six or seven months, and he would be less uptight about the others knowing the score. And she realised as she thought of the summer that suddenly she was thinking of staying on at the ranch. It was the first time that she had admitted to herself that she might stay there, and it brought up the question of what she would do with her job in New York. But she figured that there was time to work that out too. It was still only December, although it already felt as though she had been on the Lord Ranch, and was Tate Jordan's woman, for a number of years.

'Happy?' he asked her just before they drifted off to sleep, linked together, her legs entwined in his, and his arm around her shoulders.

'Mmmm . . .' She smiled at him with her eyes closed, and he kissed her eyelids once just before she drifted off to sleep. She awoke when he did at four o'clock the next morning and made her way back through the orchards behind the garden, slipped in through her half-open window, and turned on the lights. She showered as she always did, dressed, went to the main hall for breakfast, and thus, for Samantha Taylor, began a new life.

16

On Valentine's Day she got a card from Charlie Peterson from her office that made reference to her empty office. For the first time she thought of the job waiting for her in New York. She told Tate about it that night as she lay in his arms. It was a nightly ritual now. She was there each night no later than nine o'clock, after eating dinner with Aunt Caro and then taking a bath.

'What's he like?' Tate watched her with interest as she flung herself on the couch with a happy grin.

'Charlie?' She narrowed her eyes at the man who now felt like her husband. 'Are you jealous?'

'Should I be?' His voice was even.

'Hell no!' The words were blended with a shout of laughter. 'He and I have never been involved, besides he has a wife and three sons and she's pregnant again. I just love him like a brother, you know, kind of like my best buddy. We've worked together for years.'

He nodded. And then, 'Sam, don't you miss your job?'

She was silent and pensive for a moment before answering and then shook her head. 'You know, the amazing thing is that I don't. Caroline says it was that way for her too. When she left her old life, she just left it. And she never had any desire to go back. I feel that way too, I miss it less and less every day.'

'But you miss it some?' He had trapped her, and she rolled over on her stomach now and looked into his eyes as she lay on the couch and he sat near her with his back to the fire.

'Sure, I miss some of it. Like sometimes I miss my apartment, or some of my books, or my things. But I don't miss my life there. Or my job. Most of the things that I do miss are all the things that I could bring here if I wanted

146

to. But the job . . . it's so strange, I spent all that time working so hard, and trying so damn hard to become important, and now . . .' She shrugged at him and looked like a very young, very blonde sprite. 'I just don't give a damn about that anymore. All I care about is if the steers are rounded up, if there's work to be done, if Navajo needs new shoes, if the fence in the north pasture is down. I don't know, Tate, it's as though something happened. As though I became a different person when I left New York.'

'But somewhere in you, Sam, is still that old person. That person who wanted to write prize-winning commercials and be important in your line of work. You're going to miss that one day.'

'How do you know that?' She looked suddenly angry. 'Why do you keep pushing me to be what I don't want to be anymore? Why? Do you want me to go back? Are you scared of the commitment, Tate, of what it might mean?'

'Maybe. I have a right to be scared, Sam, you're a hell of a woman.' He knew that she wasn't willing to keep their life together a secret forever, that she wanted their love out in the open. That was something that worried him a great deal.

'Well, don't push me. Right now I don't want to go back. And if I do, I'll tell you.'

'I hope so.' But they both knew that her leave of absence had only six more weeks to run. She had promised herself that she would make a decision by mid-March. She still had a month. But only two weeks later, as they rode slowly back from the secret cabin where they still spent idyllic Sundays, he looked mischievous and told her that he had a surprise.

'What kind of surprise?'

'You'll see when we get home.' He leaned over toward her from where he sat on his pinto and kissed her full on the lips.

'Let's see . . . what could it be . . . ?' She managed to look both naughty and pensive, and also very young, at the same time. She had her long blonde hair in two pigtails tied with red ribbons, and she was wearing a brand-new pair of red snakeskin cowboy boots. Tate had teased her horribly about them, telling her that they were even worse than Caro's green ones, but with the Blass and Ralph Lauren and Halston wardrobe cast off since she'd arrived at the ranch, they had been her only whimsical purchase in three months. 'You bought me another pair of boots? Violet ones this time?'

'Oh, no . . .' he groaned as they rode slowly home.

'Pink?'

'I think I'm going to throw up.'

'All right, something else. Let's see . . . a waffle iron?' He shook his head. 'A new toaster?' She grinned, she had set fire to theirs only last week. 'A puppy?' She looked hopeful and he smiled but once again shook his head. 'A turtle? A snake? A giraffe? A hippopotamus?' She laughed and so did he. 'Hell, I don't know. What is it?'

'You'll see.'

As it turned out, it was a brand-new colour television, which he had just bought through Josh's brother-in-law in the nearest town. Josh had promised to drop it off at Tate's place on Sunday. And Tate had told him to leave it inside while he was out. And when he and Samantha came through the door, he pointed with an expression of pride mixed with glee.

'Tate! Babe, this is great!' But she was a lot less excited than she knew he was. She had been perfectly happy without one. And then she pouted coyly. 'Does this mean the honeymoon is over?'

'Hell no!' He was quick to prove it, but afterward he turned on the TV. The Sunday news report was on. It was a special weekly wrap-up usually done by someone else, but tonight for some reason John Taylor was handling it, and as Sam saw him she suddenly stopped and stared at him, as though she was seeing him for the first time. It had been almost three months since she'd seen his face on TV, five since she'd seen him in person, and she realised now that she didn't care anymore. All that terrible hurt and pain had faded and all that was left now was a vague feeling of disbelief. Was this truly the man she had once

148

lived with? Had she really loved that man for eleven years? Now as she watched him she thought he looked plastic and pompous, and suddenly the clear realisation of how totally self-centred he was came to her for the first time and she wondered why she had never seen it before. 'You like him, Sam?' Tate was watching her with interest, his angular rugged countenance in complete contrast to the baby-smooth golden boy looks of the younger man on the TV screen. And with an odd little smile Sam slowly shook her head, and then turned to face Tate.

'No, I don't.'

'You're sure watching him pretty close.' And then Tate grinned. 'Go on, you can tell the truth. Does he turn you on?'

This time it was Samantha who grinned. She smiled with a look of freedom and relief and suddenly, finally, she knew it was over. She no longer had any tie whatsoever to John Taylor. She was her own woman now, and it was Tate Jordon whom she loved. In fact she didn't give a damn if they'd had their baby, and she didn't care if she never saw either John or Liz again. But Tate was persistent as he watched her, sprawled out in the bed he had bought to accommodate their loving, with the soft blue blanket held to her chest.

'Come on, Sam, does he?'

'Nope,' she finally answered with a note of triumph. She kissed Tate playfully on the neck then. 'But you do.'

'I don't believe you.'

'Are you kidding?' She whooped with laughter. 'After what we just did all day you can doubt that you turn me on? Tate Jordon, you are craaaaaazzyyyy!'

'I don't mean that, silly. I mean about him. Look . . . Look . . . look at that pretty blond newsman.' He was teasing her and Sam was laughing. 'Look how pretty he is. Don't you want him?'

'Why? Can you get me a special deal? He probably sleeps in a hair net, and he's sixty years old and has had two face-lifts.' For the first time in her life she was enjoying making fun of John. He had always taken himself so damn seriously, and she had let him. The face and body and image and life and happiness of John Robert Taylor had been of prime importance to both of them. But what about her? When had Sam really mattered, if ever? Certainly not at the end when he ran off with Liz. Her face grew serious again as she remembered.

'I think you like him and you're too chicken to admit it.'

'Nope. You're wrong, Tate. I don't like him at all.' But she said it with such an air of conviction that he turned his head to look at her again, this time with a look of serious enquiry that hadn't been there before.

'Do you know him?' She nodded, but she looked neither moved nor amused. Mostly she looked indifferent, as though they were talking about a plant or a used car. 'Do you know him well?'

'I used to.' She could see Tate bridle, and she wanted to tease him just a little. She placed a hand on his powerful naked chest and then smiled. 'Don't get yourself excited, sweetheart. It was nothing. We were married for seven years.' For a moment everything seemed to stop in the little room. She could feel Tate's whole body tense beside her, and he sat up in the bed next to her and stared down at her with a look of dismay.

'Are you putting me on, Sam?'

'No.' She looked at him matter-of-factly, unnerved by his reaction, but not sure what it meant. It was probably just shock.

'He was your husband?'

She nodded again. 'Yes.' And then she decided that the occasion needed further explanation. It wasn't every day that one saw the ex-husband of one's current lover on the television screen as one went to bed at night. She told him everything.

'But the funny thing is that I was just thinking as I watched him that I really don't give a damn anymore. When I was in New York, every night I used to watch that damn broadcast. I'd watch both of them, John and Liz, doing their cutesy little routine and talking about their precious baby as though the whole world cared that she was pregnant, and it used to turn me inside out. Once when I came in, Caro was watching it, and I almost felt sick. And you know what happened tonight when that plastic face came on the screen?' She looked at Tate expectantly but got no answer. 'Absolutely nothing happened. Nothing. I didn't feel a damn thing. Not sick, not nervous, not pissed off, not left out. Nothing.' She smiled broadly. 'I just don't care.'

With that, Tate got up, stalked across the room, and turned off the set. 'I think that's wonderful. You used to be married to one of America's best-looking young heroes, clean-cut preppie John Taylor of television fame, and he leaves you and you find yourself a tired old cowboy, some ten or twelve years older than our hero, without a goddamn dime to his name, shovelling shit on a ranch, and you're trying to tell me that this is bliss? Not only is this bliss, but it's permanent bliss. Is that it, Samantha?' He was steaming, and Samantha felt helpless as she watched. 'Why didn't you tell me?'

'Why? What difference does it make? Besides, he is not nearly as well known or successful as you seem to think he is.' But that wasn't quite true.

'Bullshit. You want to see my bank account, baby, and compare it to his? What does he make every year? A hundred grand? Two? Three? You know what I make, Samantha? You want to know? Eighteen thousand before taxes, and that was a big raise for me because I'm the assistant foreman. I'm forty-three years old, for chrissake, and compared to him, I don't make shit.'

'So what? Who gives a damn?' She was suddenly shouting as loud as he was, but she realised that it was because she was scared. Something had just happened to Tate when he learned that she and John had been married, and it frightened her. She didn't expect him to take it this hard. 'The point is . . .' She made a conscious effort to lower her voice as she smoothed the blanket over her legs. By now Tate was pacing the room. 'The point is what happened between us, what kind of people we were, what we were like to each other, what happened at the end, why he left me, how I felt about him and Liz and their baby. That's what matters, not how much money he makes or the fact that they're on TV. Besides, *they're* on television, Tate, I'm not. What difference does is make? Even if you're jealous of him, just look at him, dammit, he's a fool. He's a plastic little preppie that made good. He got lucky, that's all, he's got blond hair and a pretty face and the ladies around America like that. So what? What does that have to do with you and me? If you want to know what I think, I think it has absolutely nothing to do with us. And I don't give a shit about John Taylor. I love *you*.'

'So how come you didn't tell me who you were married to?' He sounded suspicious of her now, and she lay back in the bed and tugged at her hair, trying not to scream before she sat up to face him again, which she did with a look in her eye almost as ferocious as the look in his.

'Because I didn't think it was important.'

'Bullshit. You thought I'd feel like two cents, and you know something, sister?' He walked across the room and started to pull on his pants. 'You were right. I do.'

'Then you're crazy.' She was shouting at him openly now, trying to fight his illusions with the truth. 'Because you're worth fifty, a hundred, John Taylors. He's a selfish little son of a bitch who hurt me, for chrissake. You're a grown man, and a smart one, and a good one, and you've done nothing but be good to me since we met.' She looked around the room where they had spent all their evening hours for three months, and saw the paintings he had bought her to cheer the place up, the comfortable bed he had bought, even the colour TV now to amuse her, the pretty sheets they made love on, the books he thought she'd like. She saw the flowers that he picked her whenever he thought no one was looking, the fruit he had brought just for her from the orchards, the sketch of her he done one Sunday at the lake. She thought of the moments and the hours and the gestures, the rolls of film they had taken and the secrets they had shared and she knew once again, for the hundredth time, that John Taylor wasn't fit

152

to lick Tate Jordan's boots. There were tears in her eyes when she spoke again and her voice was suddenly husky and deep. 'I don't compare you to him, Tate. I love you. I don't love him anymore. That's all that means anything. Please try to understand that. That's all that matters to me.' She reached out to him but he kept his distance, and after a few minutes she let her hand drop to her side as she knelt naked on the bed with tears rolling slowly down her face.

'And you think all of that will mean something to you in five years? Oh, lady, don't be so naive. Five years from now I'll be just another cowboy, and he'll still be one of the most important people on television in this country. You think you won't stare at the set every night while you wash dishes and ask yourself how you wound up with me? This isn't playacting, you know. This is real life. Ranch life. Hard work. No money. This isn't a commercial you're making, lady, this is real.' She began to cry harder now at the fierceness of his words.

'Don't you think it's real to me?'

'How could it be, for chrissake? How could it be, Sam? Look at what you came from and how I live. What's your apartment in New York like? A penthouse on Fifth Avenue? Some fancy-schmancy number with a doorman and a French poodle and marble floors?'

'No, it's a top floor in a town house, a walk-up, if that makes you feel any better.'

'And it's filled with antiques.'

'I have some.'

'They ought to look real cute here.' He said it with feeling and turned away from her to put on his shoes.

'Why the hell are you so angry?' She was shouting again and crying at the same time. 'I'm sorry if I didn't tell you I was married to John Taylor. As it so happens, you're much more impressed with him than I am. I just didn't think it mattered as much as you seem to think.'

Anything else you didn't tell me? Your father is president of General Motors, you grew up in the White House, you're an heiress?' He looked at her with hostility, and stark naked, she sprang from his bed like a long, lithe cat.

'No, I'm an epileptic and you're about to give me a fit.' But he didn't even smile at her attempt to tease him out of his mood. He simply went into the bathroom and closed the door, while Sam waited, and when he came out, he glanced at her impatiently.

'Come on, put on your clothes.'

'Why? I don't want to.' She felt terror creep into her heart. 'I'm not leaving.'

'Yes, you are.'

'No, I'm not.' She sat down on the edge of the bed. 'Not until we hash this thing out. I want you to know once and for all that that man doesn't mean anything to me and that I love you. Do you think you can get that through your fat head?'

'What difference does it make?'

'It makes a big difference to me. Because I love you, you big dummy.' She lowered her voice and smiled gently at him, but he didn't return the smile. Instead he looked at her pointedly and picked up a cigar, but he only played with it, he didn't light it.

'You should go back to New York.'

'Why? To chase after a husband I don't want? We're divorced. Remember that? I like it that way now. I'm in love with you.'

'What about your job? You're going to give that up for ranch life too?'

'As a matter of fact . . .' She took a deep breath and almost trembled. What she was about to say now was the biggest step of all, and she knew that she hadn't yet completely thought it through, but it was the time to say it, tonight. She didn't have more time to think it out. ' . . . that's exactly what I've been thinking of doing. Quitting my job and staying here for good.'

'That's ridiculous.'

'Why?'

'You don't belong here.' He sounded exhausted as he said the words. 'You belong there, in your apartment, working at your high-powered job, getting involved with some man in that world. You don't belong with a cowboy, living in a one-room cabin, shovelling horse shit, and roping steer. Besides, for chrissake, you're a lady.'

'You make it sound very romantic.' She tried to sound sarcastic again but tears stung her eyes.

'It isn't romantic, Sam. Not a bit. That's the whole point. You think it's a fantasy and it's not. Neither am I. I happen to be real.'

'So am I. That's the issue. You refuse to believe that I'm real too, that I have real needs and am a real person and can exist away from New York and my apartment and my job. You refuse to believe that I might want to change my life-style, that maybe New York doesn't suit me anymore, that this is better and it's what I want.'

'So buy yourself a ranch, like Caroline.'

'And then what? You'll believe I'm for real?'

'Maybe you can give me a job.'

'Go to hell.'

'Why not? And then I could sneak in and out of your bedroom for the next twenty years. Is that what you want, Sam? To end up like them, with a secret cabin you're too old and tired to go to, and all you've got left are secret dreams? You deserve a lot better, and if you're not smart enough to know that, then I am.'

'What's that supposed to mean?' She eyed him with terror, but he would not meet her eyes.

'Nothing. It means put your clothes on. I'm taking you home.'

'To New York?' She tried to sound flip and failed.

'Never mind the smart shit, just put on your clothes.'

'Why? What if I don't want to?' She looked like a frightened belligerent child, and he walked over to where she had dropped her clothes in a pile when they made love earlier that evening; he scooped them all up and dumped them in her lap.

'I don't care what you want. This is what I want. Get dressed. I seem to be the only grown-up here.'

'Like hell you are!' She jumped to her feet and dropped

the pile of clothes to the floor. 'You're just locked into your old-fashioned ideas about ranchers and ranch hands, and I won't listen to that bullshit anymore! It's a cop-out and you're wrong and it's stupid.' She was sobbing as she stooped to the floor, picked up her clothes piece by piece, and began to dress. If he was going to be like this, she would go back to the big house. Let him stew in his own juice overnight.

Five minutes later she was dressed and he stood looking at her, with despair and disbelief, as though tonight he had discovered a side of her he had never known, as though she were suddenly a different person. She stood staring at him unhappily and then walked slowly toward the door.

'Do you want me to walk you home?'

For a moment she almost relented, but then she decided not to. 'No, thanks, I can manage.' She tried to calm herself as she stood in the doorway. 'You're wrong, you know, Tate.' And then she couldn't help whispering softly, 'I love you.' As tears filled her eyes she closed the door and ran home, grateful that once again Caroline was away at a nearby ranch. She did that often on Sundays, and tonight Samantha didn't want to see her as she came through the front door, her face streaked with tears.

17

The next morning Sam lingered in Caroline's kitchen over coffee, staring bleakly into the cup and thinking her own thoughts. She wasn't sure if she should try to talk to him again that evening, or let it sit for a few days and let him come to his senses on his own. She replayed in her mind the previous night's conversation, and her eyes filled with tears again as she stared into her cup. She was grateful that this morning there was no one around her. She had decided not to go to breakfast in the main hall. She wasn't hungry anyway, and she didn't want to see Tate until they went to work. She was careful not to go to the barn until five minutes before six, and when she saw him, he was in a far corner, with his familiar clipboard, quietly issuing orders, waving toward the far boundaries, pointing toward some of the animals they could see on the hills, and then turning to point to something else. Quietly Sam saddled Navajo as she did every morning, and a few minutes later she was mounted and waiting out in the yard. But for some reason he had put Josh in charge of Sam's group today, and it was obvious that he wouldn't be riding, or at least not with them. All of which annoyed Sam further, it was as though he was going out of his way to avoid her. And with a nasty edge to her voice she leaned toward him and said loudly as her horse walked past him, 'Playing hookie today, Mr. Jordan?'

'No.' He turned to look at her squarely. 'I've got some business to discuss with Bill King.' She nodded, not sure what to answer, but as she turned Navajo at the gate to lock it behind the others, she saw him standing in the yard, watching her with a look of sorrow, and then quietly he turned and walked away. Maybe he was sorry about the fuss he had made about her ex-husband. Maybe he had understood that the differences that existed between them were differences that may have mattered to him, but not to Sam. For an instant she wanted to call out to him, but she didn't dare, the others might hear her, so she spurred Navajo on and joined them for the usual hard day's work.

Twelve hours later, riding more slowly and slumping with fatigue in the heavy Western saddles, they all rode back into the main yard and dismounted, led their horses into the barn, and removed the bridles and the saddles and put them away. Samantha was particularly exhausted that evening, she had spent the whole day thinking about Tate and everything he had said the night before. She was vague and distracted when she said good night to the others, and she looked strained when she walked in Caroline's front door.

'You look beat, Sam. Are you feeling all right, dear?' Caroline looked at her worriedly and hoped that it was only hard work that had made her look so worn. But she had a sudden uneasy suspicion that it was more serious than that. But she was not going to add still further to Samantha's worries. She said nothing, only urged Sam to take a hot bath before dinner, while she put on some steaks and made some soup and a salad. But when Sam came back, it was in clean jeans and a plaid flannel shirt, and she looked more than ever like a tidy cowgirl, as Caroline commented with a smile.

Nonetheless dinner that evening was less than joyful and it seemed hours before Sam could flee through her window and make her way through the garden and past the orchard to the little cabin where she went to see Tate. But when she got there, she knew with a terrible certainty that he was even more upset than she had imagined. The lights were off and it was too early for him to be asleep. Either he was pretending or he was hanging out at the main hall with the others, which was unlike him, but certainly effective if he was trying to avoid her. Tentatively she knocked on the door and there was no answer. She turned the knob as she always did and walked in. But what greeted her was not the usual disarray of Tate's belongings. What met her eyes instead was a dusty, barren emptiness that engulfed her, and the sound of astonishment that she made reverberated against the empty walls. What had he done? Had he actually switched cabins again to avoid her? She felt a wave of panic engulf her as she realised that she had no idea where he was. With her heart pounding, as she steadied herself in the doorway, she reassured herself that wherever he was he couldn't have gone very far. She knew that somewhere in the complex there were still two or three empty cabins, and he had obviously spent the day moving lock, stock, and baggage to avoid her. If it hadn't been so unnerving, and such a sign of how ferociously he felt about what they had discussed the previous evening, she would have been amused. But as she walked back to Caroline's house in the darkness, she was anything but amused.

She scarcely slept that night as she tossed and turned, wondering why he had done something as radical as switch cabins, and at three thirty she got up, unable to bear it anymore. She pottered around her room for another half an hour, showered, and was still ready too early. She had another half hour to kill, with a cup of coffee in Caroline's kitchen, before she could go to the main hall to eat. And this morning she definitely wanted to be there. If she could catch him even for a moment, she wanted to ask him why he had changed cabins and tell him that he was acting like an impetuous child.

But as she stood in line, waiting for bacon and eggs and her third cup of coffee, she heard two of the men talking and turned to Josh with an expression of horror and a blank stare.

'What did they just say?'

'They were talking about Tate.'

'I know. What did they say?' Her face looked ghostly pale. She couldn't have heard right.

'They said it's too bad.'

'What's too bad?' She was trying desperately not to scream.

'That he left yesterday.' Josh smiled pleasantly and moved forward in the line.

'For where?' Her heart began to pound in her ears so loudly, she could barely hear his answers, but he only shrugged before answering this time.

'No one seems to know. His boy over at the Bar Three ought to know though.'

'What the hell do you mean?' She was almost shouting.

'Christ, Sam, take it easy. Tate Jordan. He quit.'

'When?' She thought for a moment that she might faint.

'Yesterday. That was why he stuck around to talk to Bill King. To tell you the truth, yesterday morning he told me he was going to when he asked me to ride for him. He told me he'd been wanting to do it for a long time. He said it was time to move on.' Josh shrugged. 'Damn shame. He would have been good in Bill King's shoes.'

'So he just left? No two-week notice, no breaking in someone new to do his job for him? That's it?' There were already tears stinging her eyes.

'Yeah, Sam, this ain't Wall Street. When a man wants to move on, he does. He bought himself a truck yesterday morning, put all his stuff in it, and took off.'

'For good?' She could barely choke out the words.

'Sure. Ain't no sense coming back. Never the same if you do. I did it once. It was a mistake. If he was unhappy here, then he done the right thing.' Oh? Did he? How lovely to hear it. And then Josh looked at her more closely. 'You okay, Sam?'

'Yeah. Sure.' But she was terrifying-looking, she was so grey. 'I haven't been sleeping too well lately.' She had to fight back the tears . . . had to . . . had to . . . besides, there was no reason to panic. Bill King would know where he was, and if he didn't, the boy would. She'd go and see him herself. But she wasn't going to let this man slip through her fingers. Never. And after she found him, he'd never do something like this to her again.

'You know'—Josh was still staring at her—'you looked lousy yesterday too. Think maybe you're getting the flu?'

'Yeah.' She tried to look unaffected by what he had just told her about Tate Jordan. 'Maybe.'

'Then why the hell don't you go back to the big house and climb back into bed?'

She started to resist him and then knew that there was no way she could ride for the next twelve hours, driving herself mad, wondering where Tate had gone. So she nodded vaguely, thanked Josh for the suggestion, and left the main hall. She hurried back to the big house, let herself in through the front door, and then just stood there, as uncontrollable sobs racked her and she dropped to her knees beside a couch and bowed her head in despair. She felt as though she wouldn't survive this second loss in her life, not now, not Tate. As she agonised over what had happened, sobbing uncontrollably into the

160

couch, she suddenly realised that Caroline was next to her, gently touching her shoulder and then smoothing the tangled blonde hair. Samantha looked up after a few moments, her face red and swollen, her eyes wild, and looked into her friend's eyes to learn what she could there, but Caroline only nodded and cooed gently and took her into her arms and slowly brought her to sit on the couch.

It was fully half an hour before she could speak. Caroline said nothing. She only sat there and rubbed her back gently and waited. There was nothing one could say. It cut her to the core to realise that Sam had come to her to recover from one major loss and had now sustained another. She knew in her gut about Sam and Tate. She had agonised over it the day before when Bill had told her that Tate Jordan had left. But it was too late to stop him, or to discuss it. He had already left when Bill told Caroline in the late afternoon, and all she could think of was how Samantha would take the news. But Caroline hadn't dared to tell her the night before. She had hoped it would wait.

Samantha looked at her then, her face blotched, her eyes hideously bloodshot and swollen, and there was no dissimulation in the look she gave her friend. 'He's gone. Oh, God, Caro, he's gone. And I love him . . .' She couldn't go on then, and Caroline nodded slowly. She understood only too well. She had tried to tell her that here things were different, that there were things that would matter to him that didn't seem important to her.

'What happened, Sam?'

'Oh, God, I don't know. We fell in love at Christmas . . .' She looked around nervously suddenly, wondering if any of the Mexican women were cleaning, but there was no one in sight. 'We went to—' She looked at Caroline in embarrassment. 'We found your cabin and we met there at first, but not often. We weren't snooping—'

'It's all right, Sam.' Caroline's voice was very quiet.

'We just wanted someplace to go and be alone.'

'So did we.' Caroline said it almost sadly.

161

'And then he switched cabins with someone else and I used to go to him every night . . . through the orchard . . .' Her speech was disjointed and her face awash with tears. 'And then the other night, he . . . we were watching television and John came on doing a special broadcast, and we were just kidding around at first, and he wanted to know . . . if I thought John was handsome or something . . .and I happened to mention that we'd been married . . . and Tate went nuts. I don't understand it.' She gulped horribly and went on. 'He just went crazy, telling me that I couldn't be married to a movie star one minute and a cowboy the next, that I'd never be happy, that I deserved better, that—' She couldn't go on then, she was overwhelmed by tears. 'Oh, God, and now he's left. What will I do? How will I find him?' Panic ran through her again as it had all morning. 'Do you know where he's gone?' Caroline shook her head sadly. 'Does Bill?'

'I don't know. I'll call him up right now at his office and ask him.' She walked away from Sam then and stepped to the phone on her desk. Sam listened in agony to the entire conversation, and it was clear at the end of it that Bill knew nothing at all, and he was sorry that Tate had gone too. He had been counting on him to take over for him one day when he was too old to run the ranch. But now that would never happen. He knew that Tate was gone for good.

'What did he say?' Samantha looked at her dismally as she came back and sat down.

'Not much. He said that Tate said he'd be in touch one of these days, but Bill says he wouldn't count on it. He knows the way these men are. He left no forwarding address.'

'Then I'll have to find his son at the Bar Three.' She said it almost with desperation, but Caroline shook her head.

'No, Sam. The boy quit and went with him. That much Bill knew. They packed the truck up together and then left.'

'Oh, my God.' Samantha dropped her head into her

hands and began to sob again, softly this time, as though her heart were already shattered and there were nothing left.

'What can I do for you, Sam?' There were tears now in Caroline's eyes too. She realised how easily it could have happened to her years earlier, and the conversation Sam had related sounded exactly like an argument that she and Bill had had for years. Eventually they had resolved it differently, but Bill was a good deal less stubborn than Tate. He was also just a shade less noble, a fact for which Caroline was deeply grateful as she sat helplessly and watched the agony of her young friend.

Sam looked at her now, in answer to her question. 'Help me find him. Please, oh, if you could do that . . .'

'How?'

Sam sat back against the couch and sniffed as she thought. 'He'll go to a ranch somewhere. He won't want any other kind of work. How would I get a list of ranches?'

'I can tell you all the ones I know in this area, the men can tell you others. No, let me ask them, we'll cook up some excuse, some reason. Sam'—Caroline's eyes lit up —'you'll find him.'

'I hope so.' She smiled for the first time in hours. 'I won't stop until I do.'

18

By mid-April Sam had contacted sixty-three ranches. At first she had called the ones in the area, looking for Tate, then those farther north, some farther south, then she had begun to call other states. Arizona, New Mexico, Nevada, Texas, Arkansas, she had even called one in Nebraska that one of the men had suggested. He had talked to Tate about the place and said the food and the pay were real good. But no one had seen Tate Jordan. Sam left her name and address and Caroline's number and asked them to call her if Tate should appear. She used Caroline Lord's name everywhere and it helped her, and the two pored hourly over directories, wanted ads, listings, advertisements, and the names they got from the men. She had long since asked her office for an extension and had promised them some kind of definitive answer by May 1. If she wasn't coming back to New York, they wanted to know by then. Until then the job would be hers. But she didn't give a damn about her job, all she wanted was Tate Jordan, and he was nowhere to be found. It was as though a month before he had dropped off the face of the earth never to be seen again. He had to be somewhere, Sam knew, but the question was where? It was becoming an obsession with her. She no longer rode with the men, no matter that that began rumours or confirmed their suspicions. From the day that he left she rode with them no more.

She went to the cabin once alone, but couldn't bear it, and had ridden home on Black Beauty, her face covered with tears. Now she seldom even rode the big black Thoroughbred, even when Caroline encouraged her to do so. All she wanted to do was stay at the house, make phone calls, go over lists, look at maps, write letters, and try to figure out where he was. So far it had all been fruitless, and secretly Caroline was beginning to think that it might stay that way. The truth was that it was a big country, and there were countless ranches. There was always the possibility that he had gone to a different line of work entirely, or that he wasn't using his real name. She was much too familiar with the scores of drifters who had worked on the ranch in the years she had owned it to be able to hold out great hope to Sam. It was entirely possible that he would turn up somewhere, someday, but it was equally possible that he would never be seen or heard from again. It was even possible that he had left the country, gone to Canada or Mexico, or even one of the big ranches in Argentina. Often the ranch owners let men like Tate work without papers, or with falsified ones, just so they could have them on their ranches. As ranch foremen went, Tate had a long list of good credentials, he was a reliable, hardworking man, and he had a great deal of expertise to offer any ranch. Any ranch owner with half a brain would recognise that, the question was— which ranch owner and which ranch.

By the end of April there was still nothing, and Sam had three days to call her office and tell them where things stood. She had told them a month before that Caroline was ill and it was suddenly difficult for her to leave when she had said she would. They had been understanding at first, but now Charlie was calling. The fun was over. Harvey wanted her back. They were suddenly having big trouble with her automobile client, and if she was coming back at all, then Harvey wanted it to be right now. She couldn't really blame him, but she couldn't tell them either that she was in worse shape now than she had been when she left New York. More than ever, now that he was gone, she knew how much she loved Tate, how much she respected him and his way of life. It was particularly painful to her now when she saw Bill and Caro, and it was agonising for Caroline to share in Samantha's loss.

'Sam.' As she looked at her young friend over coffee on the last day of April, she sighed deeply and decided to tell her what she thought. 'I think you should go back.'

'Where?' She was glancing again at one of her lists of ranches and wondered if Caroline had thought of one they should try again. But Caroline was quick to shake her head.

'I meant New York.'

'Now?' Sam looked shocked. 'But I haven't found him.'

Caroline gritted her teeth for what she wanted to say next, much as she hated to hurt Sam. 'You don't know that you ever will.'

'That's a rotten thing to say.' Sam looked at her angrily and pushed away her coffee. She had been testy and nervous since the whole nightmare had begun. She never slept, she never ate, she never got fresh air anymore. She only did one thing. She looked for Tate. She had even driven to some of the ranches, and flown briefly to one.

'But it's true, Sam. You have to face the truth now. You may never find him again. I hope like hell that you do, but you can't spend the rest of your life looking for a man who wants to be left alone. Because if you find him, you don't know that you'll be able to convince him that what you think is right and that he's wrong. He thinks that the two of you are too different. It could just be that he's right. And even if he isn't, if this is what he wants, you can't force him to change his mind.'

'What brought this on? Have you been talking about it to Bill?'

'No more than I have to.' Sam knew that he disapproved of her relentless search for Tate. He called it a 'fool manhunt' and thought Sam was wrong to push. 'The man said what he wanted to tell her when he left here, Caro. There's nothing more to say.' But then once he had admitted that if he had done the same thing he hoped she would have tried as hard to find him. 'I just think you ought to face the possibilities, Sam. It's been a month and a half.'

'So maybe it'll just take a little longer.'

'And a little longer . . . and a little longer . . . and a little longer than that. And then what? You spend twenty years looking for a man you barely knew.'

'Don't say that.' Sam looked exhausted as she closed her eyes. She had never worked as hard on any job as she had on the search for Tate. 'I knew him. I know him. Maybe in some ways I knew him too damn well, and that scared him off.'

'It could have.' Caroline agreed. 'But the point is that you can't go on living like this. It'll destroy you.'

'Why should it?' The bitterness in her voice was easy to read. 'Nothing else has.' John and Liz had had their baby, a little girl, and they had even shown her and victorious Liz in the delivery room on the evening news. But Sam didn't care about that anymore either. All she wanted was to find Tate.

'You have to go back, Sam.' Caroline sounded as stubborn as Sam herself.

'Why? Because I don't belong here?' She looked at Caroline angrily, but this time Caroline nodded at what she said.

'That's right. You don't. You belong back in your own world, at your desk, in your office, in your own apartment, with your own things, meeting new people and seeing old friends, being who you really are and not who you pretended to be for a while. Sam'—she reached out and touched her hand—'I'm not tired of having you here. If it were up to me, you could stay forever. But it's not good for you, don't you see that?'

'I don't care. I just want to find him.'

'But he doesn't want you to find him. If he did, he would let you know where he is. He must be taking care that you don't find him, Sam, and if that's true, then you've lost the battle. He could hide from you for years.'

'So you think I should quit. Is that it?'

There was a long silence between them, and then Caroline nodded almost imperceptibly. 'Yes.'

'But it's only been six weeks.' Tears flooded her eyes as she tried to combat the logic of what Caroline had said. 'Maybe if I wait another month—'

'If you do, you won't have a job, and that won't do you any good either. Sam, you need to go back to a normal life.'

'What's normal anymore?' She had almost forgotten. It had been a year since she had been 'happily' married to John Taylor, since she had led a perfectly ordinary life as an advertising executive in Manhattan, married to a man she loved and whom she thought loved her.

'Normal?' She looked at Caroline in horror. 'You must be kidding. I wouldn't know normal anymore if it introduced itself and bit me on the ass!' Caroline laughed at her bleak humour but the look in her eyes didn't waver, and at last Sam sat back in her chair with a long pensive sigh. 'But what the hell am I going to do in New York?'

'Forget all this for a while. It'll do you good. You can always come back.'

'I'd just be running away again if I left here.'

'No, you'd be doing something healthy. This isn't a life for you here, not like this.' It hadn't been since he left.

Sam nodded silently, left the table, and walked slowly back to her room. She placed the call to Harvey Maxwell two hours later and then she went out to the barn and saddled Black Beauty. She rode him for the first time in three weeks that afternoon, riding him headlong into the wind, at full gallop, taking every chance, every jump, every hedge, every stream. Had Caroline seen her, she would have feared for the horse's life, as well as that of her young friend. Had Tate seen her, he would have killed her.

But she was alone now, riding as fast and as hard as she could until she knew that the horse could go no more. She cantered him back to the main compound then and walked him slowly around the corral for half an hour. She knew that she owed that much to the animal, no matter how unhappy she was. And then, when she felt that she had sufficiently walked him and he was cooler, she led him back to his stall and took off the English saddle, stood looking at him for a long time, and then patted his flanks one last time with a whispered, 'Good-bye, old friend.'

19

The plane landed at Kennedy Airport on a glowing spring evening, and Samantha looked down at the city with a blank stare. All she could think of as she unfastened her seat belt was the last she had seen of Caroline at the airport, standing tall and proud next to the old foreman, with tears running down her cheeks as she waved good-bye. Bill had said almost nothing to her as she stood on tiptoe to kiss his cheek in the crowded terminal, and then suddenly he had squeezed her arm and growled fondly, 'Go on back to New York, Sam, and take care now.' It was his way of saying that he thought she was doing the right thing. But was she? she wondered as she picked up her tote bag and moved into the aisle. Had she been right to come home so soon? Should she have stayed longer? Would Tate have turned up if she'd just waited another month or two? Of course he still might appear, or call from somewhere. Caroline had promised to continue to ask around, and of course if anyone heard from him, she had promised to call Sam. Other than that there was nothing anyone could do. Sam knew that much herself as she sighed deeply and stepped into the airport.

The crowd around her was almost overwhelming, the noise level, the bodies, the confusion. After five months on the ranch she had forgotton what it was like to deal with that many people, to move as quickly as they were moving. She felt totally devoured by the press of people around her as she made her way to the baggage-claim area, feeling like a tourist in her own town and looking appropriately bewildered. There was of course not a single available porter, there were hundreds of people waiting for taxis, and when she finally got one, she had to share it with two Japanese tourists and a plastics salesman from Detroit. When he asked her where she had come from, she was almost too tired to answer, but finally murmured something about California.

'You an actress?' He seemed intrigued as he looked her over, taking in the shining blonde hair and the deep tan. But Sam was quick to shake her head as she looked absentmindedly out of the window.

'No, a ranch hand.'

'A ranch hand?' He stared at her in open disbelief and she turned to look at him with a tired smile. 'This your first time in the big city?' He looked hopeful but she shook her head and did whatever she could to discourage the conversation after that. The two Japanese tourists were chatting animatedly in their own language, and the driver spoke only in curses, darting between lanes of traffic. It was an appropriate re-entry into her city, and as they crossed the bridge from Queens into Manhattan, she looked at the skyline and suddenly wanted to cry. She didn't want to see the Empire State Building and the U.N. and all the other buildings. She wanted to see the big house, the barn, the beautiful redwood trees, and that vast expanse of blue sky. 'Pretty, isn't it?' The perspiring plastics salesman from Detroit moved closer, and Sam only shook her head and edged closer to the door next to where she sat.

'No, not really. Not after what I've seen lately.' She eyed him angrily, as though her return to New York were all his fault. He eyed one of the Japanese girls after that, but she only giggled and went on chattering in Japanese with her friend.

Mercifully the driver dropped Sam off first, and she stood for a long moment on the sidewalk, staring at her house, suddenly afraid to go in, sorry she'd come home, and longing more painfully for Tate than she ever had. What in hell was she doing here in this strange town, all alone, surrounded by all these people, going back to the apartment she had lived in with John? All she wanted was to go back to California, to find Tate, to live and work on the ranch. Why couldn't she have that? Was it so much to ask? she wondered as she unlocked the front door and struggled up the stairs with her bags. No twelve-hour day in the saddle had exhausted her as this one had, with a five-hour plane trip, two meals, a movie, and the emotional shock of coming back to New York. Groaning under the weight of her bags, she dropped them next to her front door on the landing, hunted for her key, fitted it in the lock, and shoved open the front door. The place smelled like the inside of a vacuum cleaner as she stepped inside. It was all there, where she had left it, looking vacant and unloved, and different somehow, as though while she'd been gone all the furniture had subtly altered, shrunken or grown or only slightly changed colour. Nothing looked exactly the same as it had. Yet it was, every bit of it, just as it had been when she and John had lived there. She felt like an intruder now, or a ghost returning to a scene from her past.

'Hello?' She wasn't even sure why she said it, but when no one answered, she closed the front door and sat down on a chair with a sigh, and then as she looked around, the sobs overtook her, her shoulders shook, and she dropped her face into her hands.

The phone rang insistently twenty minutes later, and she sniffed and blew her nose in a handkerchief and answered the phone, not even sure why she did. After all this time it was obviously going to be a wrong number, unless it was Harvey or Charlie. They were the only two people in New York who knew that she was coming back.

'Yes?'

'Sam?'

'No.' She gave a half-smile through her tears. 'It's a burglar.'

'Burglars don't cry, silly.' It was Charlie.

'Sure they do. There's no colour TV here to rip off.'

'Come over to our place, I'll give you mine.'

'I don't want it.' And then slowly the tears began flowing again, she sniffed loudly and closed her eyes as she tried to catch her breath. 'Sorry, Charlie. I guess I'm not exactly thrilled to be home.'

'Sounds like it. So? Why'd you come back?' He sounded matter-of-fact as he said it.

'Are you crazy? You and Harvey have been threatening murder and mayhem for the last six weeks, and you want to know why I'm here?'

'Okay, so come help us out with your crazy client and then go back. For good, if that's what you want.' Charlie's approach to life was always so damn practical.

'It's not that simple.'

'Why not? Look, Sam, life is very short and can be very sweet if you let it. You're a big girl, you're free now, you should be able to live wherever you want to. If what you want is to run around with a bunch of horses for the rest of your life, then go do it.'

171

'That simple, huh?'

'Sure. Why not? Tell you what, why don't you just try it out here for a while, kind of like a tourist, see how it feels to you after a couple of months, and if you're not happy . . . hell, Sam, you can always split.'

'You make it all sound so easy.'

'That's how it should be. In any case, pretty lady, welcome back. Even if you don't want to be here, we're happy as hell to have you around.'

'Thanks, love. How's Mellie?'

'Fat, but pretty. The baby's due in another two months, and this one's a girl, I just know it.'

'Sure, Charlie, sure. Haven't I heard that at least two other times?' She smiled at the phone and wiped the tears off her face. It was at least nice to be back in the same town with him again. 'The truth of it is, Mr. Peterson, you only know how to make boy babies. It's all the basketball games you go to, something in the air there gets into your genes.'

'All right, so maybe what I need to do more of in future is go to strip joints. That makes sense . . .' They chuckled together as Sam looked around her at the depressing apartment.

'I thought you were going to water my plants, Charlie.' There was more laughter than reproach in her voice as she gazed at the long-gone wisps of brownish green.

'For five months? You must be kidding. I'll buy you new ones.'

'Don't bother. I love you anyway. Tell me, by the way, how bad things really are in the office, now that you've got me home.'

'Bad.'

'Terrible-bad or just medium-bad?'

'Excruciatingly bad. Another two days and I'd have had an ulcer or killed Harvey. That son of a bitch has been driving me nuts for weeks. The client hasn't liked a single storyboard we've shown them, they think it all looks too prissy, too clean.'

'Didn't you use my horse theme?'

172

'Hell yes, we've seen every horsey model there is this side of the Mississippi, auditioned every female jockey, every trainer, every—'

'No, no, for chrissake, Charlie. They're right if that's what you're doing. I meant *horses*. Cowboys. You know, macho, sunsets, as in riding into the sunset on a big beautiful stallion...' As she said it her mind went instantly to Black Beauty and, of course, Tate. 'That's what you need for those cars. You're not selling a little woman's car, you're selling a low-cost sports car, and they want to give an impression of power and speed.'

'And you don't think a racehorse can do that?'

'Hell no.' She sounded adamant, and at his end he grinned.

'I guess that's why this one's your baby.'

'I'll take a look at what you've got tomorrow.'

'See you then, kid.'

'Give my love to Mellie, Charlie, and thanks for calling.' She hung up and looked around again and sighed, whispering to herself, 'Oh, Tate—why?'

Bit by bit she unpacked her suitcase, dusted things off, tidied up, looked around, and tried to convince herself that this was her home. At ten o'clock she was grateful to climb into bed with a notepad and some memos from Harvey. She wanted to get a head start on what she had to do the next day. It was after twelve o'clock when she set down the notepad, turned off the light, and tried to go to sleep. In the end it took her another two hours, as she lay thinking of the ranch and waiting to hear the familiar sounds that never came.

20

Samantha's return to the office the next morning felt, to her, like a strange trip backward in time toward a point that seemed totally foreign, her desk and her office and her colleagues suddenly seemed like part of another life. She could barely imagine a time when she had spent ten hours a day there, when the working of Crane, Harper, and Laub had preoccupied her every waking hour. Now the problems they dealt with seemed so childish, the clients they talked about so foolish and tyrannical, the concepts and the presentations and the ideas all seemed like child's play to her. She couldn't somehow bring herself to be truly frightened that they might lose a client, to care if someone were going to be angry, or the meeting might go awry. She listened with a serious expression all morning and when it was over, she felt as though she had wasted her time. Only Harvey Maxwell, the creative director, seemed vaguely to sense her feelings and he looked at her sharply after everyone else had left the conference room on the twenty-fourth floor.

'Well, Sam, how does it feel?' He eyed her closely, his brows knit, his pipe in his hand.

'Strange.' She had always tried to be honest with him.

'That's to be expected. You've been gone for a long time.'

She nodded slowly. 'Longer than I should have been maybe.' She looked up at him, her eyes hooked into his. 'It's hard to come back after such a long time. I feel—' She hesitated and then decided to say it, 'as though I've left a big part of me there.'

He sighed, nodded, and attempted to relight his pipe. 'I feel that too. Any special reason?' His eyes sought hers. 'Anything I ought to know about? You fall in love with a

174

cowboy, Sam, and plan to go back?' But he was asking her more than she wanted to tell him, so she only shook her head.

'Not really.'

'I'm not sure I like your answer, Sam.' He put down his pipe. 'It's a little vague.'

But Sam spoke to him quietly. 'I came back. You asked me to and I did, maybe that's all we both need to know for now. You let me go away at a time when I needed to do that desperately, much more than I realised at the time. And now you need me, so here I am. I'm here for as long as you need me. I won't run out on you, Harvey. I promise.' She smiled but Harvey Maxwell did not.

'But you think you might go back, Sam?'

'Maybe. I don't know what will happen.' And then with a small sigh she gathered up her things. 'Why don't we just worry about our client right now? What do you think about my ranch themes for the commercials, a cowboy riding along in the twilight or at sunrise, with a herd of cattle behind him . . . a man mounted on a splendid horse, emerging from the landscape, yet at one with his surroundings—'

'Stop!' He held up a hand and grinned. 'You'll make me buy the car. I like it. Work up some storyboards with Charlie and let's see if we can get this show on the road.'

The storyboards that she worked up over the next three weeks with Charlie were the best that any of them had ever seen. What they had on their hands was not only a series of powerful commercials, they had another award-winning campaign. As Sam sat back in her chair after the first client meeting, she looked happy and proud.

'Well, kiddo, you did it.' Charlie threw his arms around her as they waited for Harvey to join them. He had walked the client out to the elevator while Sam and Charlie talked. 'They loved it!'

'They should. Your artwork was stupendous, Charlie.'

'My pleasure.' He grinned and stroked his beard, and a moment later Harvey joined them, beaming for once and waving toward the boards set up around the room. There

175

were four commercials they had presented, in the hopes of talking the client into one or two. The client had accepted all four.

'Well, children, did we make a successful presentation or did we make a successful presentation?' Harvey couldn't get the grin off his face and Samantha smiled back happily at him. It was one of the first times she had looked happy since she'd come back, but it felt good to be doing something constructive, and to have done it so well.

'When do we start?'

'They want to go into production on it immediately. How soon can you start, Sam? Do we have any locations lined up? Christ, you must know enough ranches to get things rolling. What about the one you've been living on for the last six months?'

'I'll call. But we're going to need three more. And I think'—she mused about it while gnawing her pencil—'I think we're going to want some entirely different locations. Each ranch should be different, special, set apart from the others. We don't just want repeats of the one we shot before.'

'What are you suggesting?'

'The Northwest, the Southwest, the Midwest, California . . . maybe even Hawaii . . . Argentina?'

'Oh, Jesus. I knew it. Well, figure it all out and work it into the budget. We still have to get that past them, but I don't really think we'll have a problem with it. Just do me a favour, start finding locations. It sounds like this may take a little time. And call your friend out at your ranch. At least that will give us one. If we have to, we can start there.' Sam nodded. She knew that this shoot, like countless others, was going to be entirely hers. Now that she was back, Harvey was already talking about retiring again, and she knew that he would leave all the location work to her.

'I may have to fly out and look at some places next week, Harvey. Sound okay to you?'

'That sounds fine.' He left them then, still with a broad smile on his face, and Samantha and Charlie went back to

176

their offices, Samantha to her white-on-white office with chrome and glass desk, beige leather couch and chairs, and lithographs all coordinated in the same white and beige. Charlie's office looked more like an artsy-craftsy attic, cluttered and colourful and amusing, with odd-shaped boxes, huge plants, and funny signs. It looked exactly like an art director's office, one wall was white, one yellow, two were a deep heather blue, and the rug on the floor was dark brown. He had, of course, chosen his own decor. Sam's was part of the general scheme of the whole CHL office, all of it done in soft sand colours and cool textures with modern lines, and not a great deal of soul. But it was restful to work there. She never even saw the decor when she was working, and when she saw clients, she usually met them in one of the conference rooms, or at The Four Seasons for lunch.

She knew when she looked at her watch that it was the wrong time to call Caroline and ask if they could film there. At noon in California Caroline would be out in the hills with Bill and the other men. But she got out the list she had already glanced at that morning in anticipation and began to make phone calls to see what she could do. She knew damn well that she couldn't just pick up the phone and call ranches where she knew no one. She would have to fly out to the areas, then drive around and make her pitch to them in person, asking them if they would allow a commercial to be filmed on the ranch. It usually took weeks to find locations, but she was going to do it right, because she was going to produce the best damn commercials that anyone had ever seen. She was doing it as much for the client now as for herself. It meant a great deal to her to make everything perfect, to make it special and important and striking and effective—and maybe even find Tate. That was a possibility that hadn't escaped her. It wasn't why she had pushed for the concept. The cowboy-on-horseback theme was perfect for the product, but it also could be that while she was travelling and looking for locations, and maybe even while she was out there again for the shooting, maybe someone on one of the

177

ranches might have heard of Tate. The prospect of finding him was a goal she never lost sight of, and now it loomed larger then ever as she called the travel department and asked them to book her on flights to Phoenix, Albuquerque, Omaha, and Denver, and all during the following week.

'Looking for a location?' the voice asked.

'Yeah.' Sam was already deeply engrossed in the notes on her desk. She had a list of places she wanted to see, most of them concentrated in those four areas, and then of course there was Aunt Caro's ranch.

'Sounds like fun.'

'It should be.' And Sam's eyes began to dance.

21

The phone rang at the Lord ranch at six o'clock that evening as Sam sat in her apartment in a bathrobe, once again looking around at the lifeless decor. She decided as she waited for the phone to be answered that she was going to have to do something about the way the place looked, if she stayed there.

'Hello?' It was Caroline, and Sam immediately broke into a smile.

'Boy, it's good to hear your voice.'

'Sam?' Caroline smiled in answer. 'Are you all right?'

'I'm fine. I'm just working on a crazy project. And aside from wanting to know how you all are, I wanted to ask you a favour, but you have to say no if that's what you want.'

'First tell me how you are, and how it feels to be back.' Samantha noticed that Caroline sounded tired, but she put it down to a long day's work and reported in full on her return, how grim the apartment looked, what it felt like to go back to the office, and then her voice became alive with excitement as she explained about the commercials and her search the following week for other ranches.

'And you know what that means, don't you?' Her voice fairly flew. 'It means that maybe, just maybe, if I get lucky'—she barely dared to do more than whisper—'I could just find Tate. Hell, I'm going to be all over this country.' For a moment, Caroline said nothing.

'Is that why you're doing it, Sam?' Caroline sounded sad for her. She wanted Sam just to forget him. It would be better for her in the end.

'No, it isn't.' She withdrew a little. She had heard the dismay in the older woman's voice. 'But it's why I'm so excited about it. This is a great opportunity for me.'

'I'd say so professionally, in any case. This could be very important for you, if the commercials come out as well as you seem to think they will.'

'I'm hoping they do, which is part of why I called. Aunt Caro, how would you feel about our shooting at the ranch?' It was a candid, open question but there was a moment of silence at the other end.

'Normally, Sam, I'd have loved it. If nothing else, it would give us an excuse to see you. But I'm afraid that right now it's out of the question.' There was a catch in her voice as she said it, and Sam frowned. 'Is something wrong, Aunt Caro?'

'Yes.' A little sob shook her, but she pulled herself together quickly. 'No, really, I'm all right. Bill had a little heart attack last week. Nothing major. He's already back from the hospital, and the doctor says that it's nothing to be unduly alarmed about, but . . .' Suddenly fresh sobs shook her. 'Oh, Sam, I thought if something happened . . . I don't know what I'd do. I couldn't live without him.' It was the first time that they had faced that, and she was terrified now that she'd lose him. 'I just couldn't go on if something happened to Bill.' She sobbed softly into the phone.

'My God, why didn't you call me?' Samantha looked stunned.

'I don't know, it all happened so quickly. And I stayed

at the hospital with him, and I've been awfully busy since he got home. He was only there for a week, and the doctor says it's nothing . . .' She was repeating herself in her anxiety and Sam could feel tears sting her eyes too.

'Do you want me to come out there?'

'Don't be silly.'

'I'm serious. I don't have to be here. They lived without me all winter, they can manage fine. Especially now that I've done the groundwork for them, all they have to do is find the locations and then have a production house do the film. I could be out there tomorrow, Aunt Caro. Do you want me?'

'I always want you, darling.' The older woman smiled through her tears. 'And I love you very much. But we're fine really. You take care of your commercials and I'll take care of Bill and he'll be fine. I just didn't think that right now the disruption—'

'Of course not. I'm sorry I asked you, but I'm not really. If I hadn't asked, I would never have known about Bill. You're a rat not to have called me! You're sure you can manage?'

'Positive. And if I need you, I'll call you.'

'Promise?'

'Solemnly.' Caroline smiled again.

And then Sam asked the next question gently. 'Is he staying at the house?' She hoped so, it would be a lot easier for Aunt Caro, and a lot more agreeable for him.

But Caroline sighed and shook her head. 'No, of course not. He's so stubborn, Sam. He's staying at his old cabin. Now I'm the one sneaking in and out all night long.'

'That's ridiculous. Can't you pretend to put him up in the guest room? Hell, he's been the foreman there for almost thirty years, would that be so shocking?'

'He thinks so, and I'm not supposed to upset him so I let him have his way.'

'Men!' Sam snorted as she said it and Caroline laughed. 'I completely agree.'

'Well, give him my love and tell him to take it easy, and I'll call you in a few days to see how he is.' And then just before she hung up, she called out to her old friend, 'I love you, Aunt Caro.'

'I love you too, Sam dear.' And now they were bound in a common secret, the lives of women who loved ranch hands, who had to live shackled by the insane rules of courtship peculiar to ranch hands and ranchers. And now that Caroline had almost lost her beloved foreman, she suddenly knew how great was Sam's pain.

22

For ten days Sam flew from the Midwest to the Southwest, and then up north again, and only Caroline's insistence that Bill was so much better kept her away from California as well. In each place she stopped she rented cars, stayed at small motels, drove hundreds of miles, and spoke to every conceivable rancher she could lay her hands on, and for her own purposes she spoke to the ranch hands as well. For the purposes of Crane, Harper, and Laub, at the end of ten days she had just what she needed, four splendid ranches, each one totally different, surrounded by varied but always majestic countryside. They were all settings that would make extravagantly beautiful commercials. But for her own purposes, again and again Sam struck out. And as she flew back to New York her sense of victory at having found what she had wanted was vastly outweighed by her depression over not finding Tate. She had called Caroline from her hotel room every evening, inquired about Bill, and then told her who she had talked to, what they had said, and pondered for another hundred times what might have happened to Tate, where he might have gone, which direction he might have taken. By now she had spoken to so many ranchers since he had vanished three months before that she felt certain that if someone found him, met him, or hired him they would surely drop her a note. She had left her card at all the ranches she had visited, and surely some of that effort would pay off. Maybe he was just taking time to visit relatives along the way and was headed for a specific destination. But again Caroline reminded her that he could be anywhere, on any ranch, and there was always the possibility that he would never surface in Sam's life again. She felt that, for Sam's sake, it had to be faced.

'I'll never give up completely,' Sam had said stubbornly only the night before.

'No, but you can't spend the rest of your life waiting either.' She didn't say it, but Sam had thought quickly. 'Why not?' Instead they had turned the conversation back to Bill and his health. Caroline thought he was much improved, but still weak.

And now, as the plane landed in New York, Sam thought of him again, and inevitably of Tate. She knew also that for the next month she would think of him every day, every moment, as she interviewed actor after actor after actor to play the role in the commercials. They had already agreed with the client that what they wanted was not four cowboys, but one man. One man who would embody all that was powerful and masculine and good and true and sexy in this country. And all Sam could think of was someone who looked like Tate.

In the ensuing weeks, as she spent hours meeting the actors sent over by the city's biggest modelling agencies, she compared them all to him. She wanted someone tall, broad shouldered, in his early forties, with a deep mellifluous voice, kind, with interesting eyes and strong hands, a good seat in the saddle . . . what she really wanted was Tate. It was as though each time her secretary announced another group of actors to audition, Sam went to meet them expecting to see him. What she saw instead were dazzling blondes with broad shoulders; tall, dark, handsome men; ex-football-players, and even an ex-hockey goalie; men with rugged faces, deep-set eyes, and strong chins; but most of them seemed too plastic, some had bad voices, faces that were too pretty, one looked more like a ballet dancer than a cowboy. In the end, after four weeks of looking, she found her man, and it was a good thing. The shoot was only two weeks away, scheduled for July fifteenth.

The man they chose was actually English, but his Western accent was so perfect that no one would have known. For years he had been a Shakespearean actor at Stratford-on-Avon, and two years before he had decided to come to New York and start doing commercials, because he was tired of demanding roles with too little pay. Now he was advertising soft drinks, men's underwear, and a line of tools in national commercials that were paying him a handsome wage. He had shoulders from one side of the room to the other, a handsome angular face that was good-looking but not too pretty, deep blue eyes, and dark reddish-brown hair. He looked totally the part, and every man in America would want to identify with him and their wives would dream of the car being advertised, in the hopes that the cowboy in the commercial might somehow appear at the wheel. He was exactly what they needed for the commercial, and the only thing that amused Samantha, as she told Charlie, was that their new Western hero was decidedly gay.

'Does he look it?' Charlie looked worried.

'Hell no, he's an actor. And he is gorgeous!'

'Well, do yourself a favour, don't fall in love with him.'

'I'll try not to.' But the best part was that she liked him. His name was Henry Johns-Adams, and if nothing else he would be good company on the trip. He was extremely well-read, terribly polite, very cultured, and he seemed to have a good sense of humour as well. It would be a real relief from some of the self-centred, undisciplined egomaniacs she had had along on other shoots. 'You coming west with us, Charlie?'

'I don't know, Sam. I hate to leave Mellie. If she has the baby by then, it'll be okay. If not, I may have to send two of my assistants. Can you manage?'

'If I have to.' And then with a gentle smile, 'How's she feeling?'

'Fat, exhausted, fed up, bitchy. But I love her anyway. And it's almost over. The baby's due at the end of next week.'

'What are you going to name him?' She hadn't got off his back about it being a boy again.

'Her. And you'll see. We're not telling what we're going to name her. It's a surprise this time.'

'Come on, tell me, Charlie. Charlotte, if it's a girl?' She loved to tease him and he pinched her behind as he shook his head and disappeared.

As it turned out, Mellie had the baby that weekend, a week early for a change and a girl this time, finally. The surprise was that they named her Samantha. When Charlie told her in the office on Tuesday after the Fourth of July weekend, there were tears in Sam's eyes.

'Do you mean it?'

'Sure I do. Want to come see her?'

'Are you kidding? I'd love to. Mellie's not too tired?'

'Hell no. The fourth one's easy. It sounds disgusting but she walked out of the delivery room. Freaked me out, but the doctor said it was okay.'

'It makes me feel nervous just hearing about it.' Like all women who have never had children, Samantha was amazed by the entire process and the whole mystique.

They went to the hospital together at lunchtime, and Mellie looked happy and healthy and glowing in a lace-trimmed pink bathrobe, with pink satin slippers, a huge grin on her face, and the tiny pink and white baby nestled in her arms. For a long moment Sam said absolutely nothing. She just stood and stared at the delicate bundle, her eyes riveted to the baby's face.

'She's so beautiful, Mellie.' Sam said it in a whisper, in tones of awe, and Charlie chuckled from where he stood just behind her.

'Yeah. But we would have named her Samantha even if she'd been ugly.' Sam turned around and made a face at him. It dispelled the enormity of the moment, and Sam's sudden longing for what she could never have, the miracle of childbirth, and her own child. Lately she had seldom let her thoughts wander in that direction, but for the first time in a long time, as she stood there gazing down at the new baby, she felt her heart ache for the lost dream.

'Want to hold her?' Melinda looked lovelier than Sam had ever seen her. There was a kind of quiet glow that seemed to emanate from the very depths of her soul and at the same time envelop the baby as it lay precious and protected in its mother's arms.

'I don't think so.' Sam shook her head and sat down on a corner of the bed, her eyes still riveted to the small child. 'I'd be afraid to break her.'

'They're tougher than they look.' It was the claim of every mother. 'Here . . . try it.' Without warning Melinda dropped the baby into Sam's arms and settled her there as they all watched the baby stretch, curl herself up again, and then smile. She was sound asleep as she lay there, and Sam could feel the baby's warmth in her arms.

'She's so tiny!'

'No, she's not!' Mellie laughed. 'She weighs eight and a half pounds!'

But a moment later the brand-new Samantha discovered that she was hungry and awoke, looking for her mother, with a yowl. The elder Samantha returned her to the safety of Melinda, and a few minutes later she and Charlie went back to the office, as Samantha felt again how much was missing in her life. It was one of those times when the fact that she was sterile weighed on her like a boulder on her guts.

And then, as she stopped in the doorway of her office, she remembered and called out to Charlie. 'Does this mean you're coming west with me?'

He nodded, smiling. 'I would have had to anyway.'

'How come?' She looked surprised.

'Just to be sure you don't rape our cowboy!'

'Not likely.' She grinned at him and disappeared into her office. The agony of seeing the baby subsided slightly, though it didn't leave her completely for the rest of the day.

23

'Everybody ready?' Charlie looked at them with a broad grin, and then bowed at the entourage and waved them onto the airplane. They were travelling on a commercial airline to Arizona, but there were so many of them, it seemed as though they had bought out most of first class. There were seven people from the production company, and in addition Sam, Charlie, their two assistants, Henry Johns-Adams—the English actor—and his friend. To add to the mountain of luggage and equipment and miscellaneous crates and boxes, Henry and his roommate had brought along their dog, a tiny white poodle named Georgie, which Samantha prayed would not manage to dart underneath the feet of any horses. If it did, it was so little that it would probably be all over, and most likely so would the shoot.

In addition they were being met in Arizona by a makeup person and a hairdresser, both of whom had been working in L.A. and would continue on with the group from Crane, Harper, and Laub for the rest of the trip.

'Think they got all our luggage?' Henry's friend whispered to Samantha nervously, and she convinced him that it was assuredly all on the plane. 'But there's so much.'

'They're used to it. Besides'—she smiled reassuringly—'this is first class.' As though that made a difference, as though they wouldn't just as easily lose one of his matched Vuitton suitcases as they would one of the crew's pieces of Samsonite luggage or one of the zillion-dollar pieces of equipment. And once again she realised what a great deal of work she'd have on this journey. Having thought up the concept, almost completely written the ads herself, found the locations, cast the leading man, organised the troupes, selected the production house and approved their bid, what she was going to do now, for the next two weeks, in four different locations, was reassure everyone that they would be fed soon, it would only take a few more takes, the weather would be cooler tomorrow, the air conditioning in the hotel would be repaired by noon, and the food couldn't possibly be this bad in the next town. And having a nervous gay boyfriend and a French poodle along wouldn't help anything. On the other hand Henry Johns-Adams had already proved to be even tempered, amusing, and a good sport, and Sam was hopeful that he would keep both his lover and his pet in line. She didn't mind his being gay, but she was a little uptight about having him bring his little entourage. Nonetheless, he had insisted, and they wanted him badly enough to have brought his mother and fourteen of his dearest friends.

The drinks on the plane helped everyone's nerves and their spirits. Charlie was in grand form and entertained them all, and finally, half an hour out of Tucson, they all relaxed. They had no work to do that day. They were going to drive a hundred and fifty miles to their location, in three rented station wagons, with all the equipment, and then they'd all have a good dinner and a good night's sleep and get to work bright and early the next day. Sam's ranch hours were about to stand her in good stead, because she figured that she'd be up every morning by four thirty. And every night, for an hour or two after work, she had a plan. She had already made up the list of additional people she wanted to talk to, and after working on whichever ranch all day, she'd hang out with the ranch hands for a while and just chat. Maybe one of them had worked with Tate somewhere, maybe one of them would know a link—a relative, an old employer, someone who might know where he was by now. It was worth a try. Anything was. As the plane lowered its landing gear Samantha smiled to herself, feeling hopeful. You never knew, maybe one of these days she would walk onto a ranch, look up at a tall handsome cowboy leaning against a fence post, and it wouldn't be a stranger this time. It would be Tate, with those green eyes, and the gentle

187

smile, and the mouth that she so loved . . . Tate . . .

'You okay, Sam?' Charlie had tapped her arm, and when she turned in surprise, he was looking at her strangely.

'Huh?' She still looked startled.

'I've been talking to you for about ten minutes.'

'That's nice.'

'I wanted to know who you want to drive the other two cars.' She quickly brought her mind back to business and gave instructions, but it wasn't what she was thinking about as they landed and her eyes lingered on the horizon, wondering if by the next day, or the day after, she would have found him . . . Tate, are you there? She wanted to whisper the words, but she knew that there would be no answer. There was no way of knowing. She just had to keep looking. But that was why she was here.

They were among the first off the plane, and she organised the group quickly, picking up the station wagons, assigning drivers, handing out maps, buying boxes of sandwiches for the trip, giving out vouchers for their motel in case they arrived separately from each other in the three cars. She had thought of everything, as she always did.

In the car she drove she had Charlie, the hairdresser, the makeup artist, the star, his boyfriend, the poodle, and all the Vuitton luggage. The equipment, the crew, and the assistants went in the two other cars.

'All set?' Charlie looked around behind him and then handed out cans of cold fruit juice. It was hotter than hell in Arizona, and they were all relieved to be in an air-conditioned car. Henry was in the process of telling funny stories about being on tour in England, the boyfriend had kept them all in stitches with tales of what it had been like to discover that he was gay in Dubuque, the hairdresser and makeup girl had plenty of stories to tell about their recent trip to L.A. to coif and paint a noted rock star, and the trip went along pleasantly until they reached the hotel. Here, predictably, unfolded the first drama. The hotel owner didn't allow dogs, didn't think much of Henry's friend, looked with horror at the hair-dresser's flaming-red hair with the little blue punk fringe across the front, and scowled horribly at 'them ugly brown bags.' Henry's friend almost caressed his beloved Vuitton and threatened to sleep in the car if he had to, but he was not leaving the dog. A hundred dollar bill, which would appear on the expense account as tips and miscellaneous, helped grease the way for Georgie to stay in the hideous turquoise vinyl splendour of the hotel too.

'You look beat, Sam.' Charlie sprawled on a couch in her room and watched her pore over a sheet of notes on a clipboard. She looked up with a grin and threw a crumpled ball of paper that hit his left ear.

'You must be kidding. Me? Why would I look tired? I'm just dragging around the country with a bunch of eccentrics and a French poodle. Why should I be tired, Charlie?'

'I'm not tired.' He looked virtuous and she made a face.

'No wonder. You never work.'

'That's not my fault. I'm only the art director, here to make sure that the film is artistically beautiful. It's not my fault you're an ambitious bitch and you want to be C.D.' He had only been kidding, but suddenly Sam looked serious as she sat down on the bed.

'Is that what you think, that I want to be C.D.?'

'No, my love.' He smiled gently at her. 'I don't really think that's what you want. But I think it's what you'll get. You're damn good at what you do. In fact, much as I hate to admit it, sometimes you're brilliant. And Harvey knows it, and the clients know it, and I know it, and everyone in the business knows it, and sooner or later you're going to get yours. Either someone will hire you away at a salary even you can't resist, or Harvey will retire, as he keeps threatening to do, and you'll wind up the C.D.' Creative Director . . . it was an awesome thought.

'I don't think that's what I want. Not anymore.'

'Then you better do something about it while you still can, before it just comes at you and happens and it's too late to stop it.' And then, after he thought about it for a moment, 'What do you want, Sam?'

She looked at him for a long time and then signed softly, 'Oh, Charlie, that's a long story.'

'I had a feeling it would be.' His eyes didn't waver from hers. 'There was someone in California, wasn't there? On the ranch?' She nodded. 'So what happened?'

'He left me.'

'Oh, shit.' And right after John too. No wonder she had looked so rigid and unhappy when she had come back. 'For good?'

'I don't know. I'm still looking for him.'

'Don't you know where he is?' She shook her head, and he looked sad for her. 'What are you going to do?'

'Keep looking.' She said it with quiet determination and he nodded.

'Good girl. You're a strong lady, you know that, Sam?'

'I don't know, love.' She smiled and sighed again. 'Sometimes I have my doubts.'

'Don't.' He looked at her almost proudly. 'I don't think there's anything you couldn't pull through. Remember that, kiddo, if the going ever gets too rough.'

'Remind me.'

'I will.' They exchanged a warm smile and Sam was glad that he had come with her, he was the best friend she had, and it made the trip more fun to have him to joke with and laugh at and talk to, and behind all the clowning, there was a warm and intelligent man. It pleased her, too, to know that she had his respect and Harvey's. At first when she had come back from her months on the ranch, she had been aware that she was having to prove herself again, not only as assistant creative director, but as a person, as their friend. And now, in such a short time, she knew that she was back in the circle of their respect and affection. That meant a lot to her, and she stood up and went over to kiss Charlie on the cheek.

'You haven't told me anything about my namesake lately.'

'She's great. Brushing her teeth, tap dancing, doing the laundry.'

190

'Oh, shut up, you jerk. I'm serious. How is she?'

'Cute as a button. Girls sure are different from boys.'

'You're very observant, dear. By the way, are you hungry yet? I'm starving, and we have to shepherd all our little darlings to dinner at the taco joint down the street or they're going to bitch and moan.'

'That's what you're giving them for dinner? Tacos?' He looked shocked. 'I'm not sure little Mr. Vuitton will like that, not to mention the poodle.'

'Don't be nasty. Beside, in this town I doubt if there's anything else to eat.'

'Wonderful.'

But as it turned out, they all had a marvellous time, eating tacos, drinking beer, and telling jokes that got increasingly raunchy as they got more and more relaxed and more tired, and eventually the whole group went back to the hotel and went to bed. Charlie waved a last good night to Sam as he disappeared into his room, and she spent another half hour going over her notes to herself for the next day, and then, yawning, she turned off the light.

24

It was six o'clock the next morning when they got together for breakfast. And seven thirty when they finally made it to the ranch. They had decided not to shoot at sunrise on the first day, but to settle for full day shots, and eventually try for a sunset. But it was almost noon by the time everything was set up to the film crew's satisfaction and they were fully rolling with Henry Johns-Adams riding a good-looking black mare, which made Samantha long for Caroline's Thoroughbred stallion. This was no Black Beauty Henry was riding, but she was a pretty horse and would look good on film. She had a pleasing gait as they cantered again and again over the same hills, filming take after take, but the horse was as even tempered as her rider, and by the end of the day everyone was tired, but there were no frayed tempers. They were a good group to work with, and Samantha was pleased with the way it was going. She went over to talk to the ranch foreman and thanked him for letting them film on the ranch. She had already sent flowers to the ranch owner's wife and a case of bourbon to her husband, in addition to what they were paying per day in order to film there. But now she handed the foreman several bottles too, and he looked pleased with the gift and chatted with her. He was even more impressed when he learned that she had spent most of the year working on a ranch in California, and for a little while they discussed ranch business and horseflesh and cattle, and Sam felt almost as though she had come home. After a while she happened to mention Tate Jordan, and wondered if he'd met him, and said that there was a commercial she wanted to use him in, if he ever crossed the foreman's path. She described him as a fine man and someone she respected a great deal. Out of respect for Tate's sentiments about ranch people knowing about his relationship with her, she didn't let on about that. The foreman took her card and assured her that he'd be happy to let her know if he came across Tate, and after that she went back to the others and drove one of the bulging station wagons back to the hotel.

She struck out equally in her search for Tate at each stop of their trip in the next three weeks, although the filming of the commercials was going brilliantly. The production crew knew that they had got the most beautiful footage they'd ever had, and so far the entire shoot had gone off without a hitch. As a result spirits were soaring, friendships were cemented, humours were good, and everyone was willing to work endless hours in the hot sun and seldom complained. They had even managed to get two perfect sunrises on film and several sunsets. Only Sam seemed to be dragging by the time they got to their last stop. They were filming at a ranch in Steamboat Springs, Colorado, and Sam had just interviewed the last of the foremen and hung out for almost an hour with some of the ranch hands who had come by to watch them film. She knew now that if she found Tate it wouldn't be this time, and they were going home the next day, so once again her hopes had been dashed. She would go back to New York, and wait, and try again someday when she was near a ranch. And maybe, maybe, one day she would find him. Maybe. If.

As she stood looking at the mountains for a moment, she heard one of the men tell another that she had worked on the Lord Ranch in California. They knew of it, and the second cowboy looked her over with an appraising glance.

'Yeah?' She nodded. 'I figured you knew horses, but I didn't know how. I saw you riding this morning. You got a good seat, good hands.'

'Thank you.' She smiled at him, but her sorrow had somehow crept into her eyes now. She looked tired and deflated and the man looked her over, wondering why she looked so down at the mouth.

'You see our new stallion?' he asked her, chewing on a wad of tobacco. 'Got him last week. He's out in the far barn.'

'Could I see him?' Sam asked him the question more to be pleasant than because she had any real desire to see the stallion. She wanted to get back to the tiny motel where they were staying, wrap it all up, and get ready to go home the next day. For her, there was nothing left to stick around for. They had done the shoot, and she hadn't found Tate. But trying to look interested, she trudged after the old cowboy, and when she reached the barn beside him, she wasn't sorry she had come. What she saw in front of her was one of the biggest stallions she had ever seen, grey with a black mane and a black tail and a long white star on his forehead that seemed to make his eyes look even wilder as he pawed the ground. 'My God, he's a beauty.'

'Ain't he?' The ranch hand looked pleased. 'He's a little

193

devil to ride though. Gave everyone a toss or two yesterday.' He grinned. 'Even me.'

Sam smiled. 'I've spent plenty of time down on the ground too. But this boy is worth it.' She ran a hand down his neck and he whinnied, as though he liked the feel of her hand on his flesh and he wanted more. He was so big and splendid an animal that just seeing him was almost a sensual experience. She told the ranch hand then about Black Beauty, about how she had ridden him and what a great ride he had been.

'Thoroughbred, eh?' She nodded. 'Grey Devil here looks as fine to me. He runs like a racehorse, but he's a little too frisky for ranch work. I don't know but Mr Atkins may sell him after all. Damn shame too. He's a fine horse.' And then, as though bestowing the ultimate gift on Samantha, he turned to her. 'You want to ride him, miss? I warn you, you may land on your butt in the dirt, but I think you can handle him from what I've seen you do today.' She had ridden just off camera from Henry, urging him on at sunrise, almost angering him to make him seem less complacent and ride as hard as she wanted him to. In the process she had driven the horse she was riding as hard as he could be pushed, and Sam herself had accomplished the whole performance with obvious ease. She was a spectacular rider, and her precision and ability hadn't been wasted on the men who had watched her. They had talked about her over lunch, one of them had said that she looked like a little palomino filly, and it was a pleasure now to offer her Grey Devil, as he stood in his stall, waiting, as though he had been meant for her.

'Do you mean it?' She was awed by the offer, knowing that it was both a compliment and a gift. 'May I ride him?' It was going to be her last ride for a long time. She was flying back to New York the next day, and there were no ranches in her immediate future. Only hard work at her desk in New York. 'I'd love to.'

'Go on. I'll get his saddle.' He did so, and a moment later he had him saddled for Samantha, although he had to do it carefully so as not to get kicked. He had twice the devil in him that she had seen in Black Beauty, and he seemed to be almost bursting from his skin, aching to be allowed to run free. 'He's a little fresh. Go easy with him in the beginning . . . Miss . . .' He hunted for her name.

'Sam.' She smiled easily, suddenly anxious to get on the huge grey horse. He was even bigger than Black Beauty, and suddenly it was as though she could sense Tate beside her, shouting at her as he had about Caro's black stallion, trying to force her to ride horses like Lady and Rusty. She grinned to herself. Hell, he had left her. She could ride anything she wanted to now. And as she thought of it the full pain of having lost him ripped through her once again; she took the leg up the old ranch hand gave her, pulled the reins taut, and let the huge grey stallion dance her around. She didn't let him get out of hand, and his two efforts to toss her were fruitless, much to the old man's delight.

Slowly she walked past the big barn, toward the old corral. By then several of the men had seen her, at first they watched with interest, and then they began to cheer as they saw how she controlled the prancing grey beast. As though everyone nearby suddenly sensed an intriguing performance, they turned to watch Samantha as she rode Grey Devil through the ranch's main compound, past her crew, and Charlie, and Henry and his friend and the poodle; and then sensing her own passion for horses and the countryside surge within her, she forgot them all and began cantering out into the fields beyond. She cantered for only a few moments and then she gave him what he wanted, letting him free to gallop at his own speed, racing until it felt as if he were flying, his hooves beating hard on the ground. As Sam rode Grey Devil she was smiling, with the wind on her face and her heart pounding as they rode along. Riding this horse was like waging a special kind of battle, against the horse's strength and his mind, with only her capabilities and her skill on her side. But she was an even match for Grey Devil, and although several times he tried to throw her, he didn't succeed, and she felt all the tension and anguish and disappointment of not finding Tate well up within her, and she began to press Grey

Devil forward, urging him to go even faster than he had before. She would beat him at his own game, if she could.

It was then that the crowd watching grew silent. Until then she had been a beautiful sight to see, her golden hair stretched out behind her, in sharp contrast to the black mane and tail of Grey Devil, as they flew across the fields. She moved as one with the giant stallion, her every muscle in tune with his. But now one of the ranch hands jumped off the fence to stop her, several others caught their breath, and the foreman shouted, as though she could hear him. But it was already too late. There was a hidden narrow stream out in the field she had just sailed into. It was narrow enough to jump with ease if she saw it, but it was also very deep, and if the horse stumbled, she would be thrown into a rocky ravine. The foreman was running now, waving wildly, and Charlie saw him and began running too. It was as though both men knew what was coming, but at precisely that moment they saw her. The stallion stopped dead as he reached the stream he had seen before Sam did, and Samantha, unprepared, flew through the air with a wild, fearful grace, hair fanned out, arms extended, until she silently disappeared.

As Charlie saw it happen he ran for the station wagon, turned the key in the ignition, shoved it into gear, and surged forward—he didn't give a damn who he ran down. It was too far to run. He signalled wildly to the foreman, who hopped in, and drove off with the tyres screeching on the gravel and then bumping terribly as they crossed the fields. Charlie made horrible guttural sounds as he muttered to himself, praying all the way. 'What's over there?' he asked the foreman, without taking his eyes off the field. He was going almost sixty, and Grey Devil had flashed past him only moments earlier, hell-bent on the barn.

'A ravine.' The foreman looked tense as he answered, straining to see what was ahead. They could still see nothing and a moment later he shouted 'Stop!' which Charlie did, and the foreman led the way through the grass, down a little incline to where Grey Devil had balked at the stream. At first they saw absolutely nothing, and then Charlie saw her, her white shirt almost torn from her body, her chest and her face and her hands lacerated almost beyond recognition, her hair fanned out around her, as she lay there broken, bleeding, and terribly, terribly still.

'Oh, my God . . . oh, my God . . .' Charlie began crying as he rushed toward her, but the foreman was already kneeling beside her, with two fingers pressed gently to the side of her neck.

'She's still alive. Get in the car, go back to the house, call for the sheriff, tell him to bring the helicopter out here right away. And if he can get one, bring a paramedic, or a doctor, or a nurse.' The town of Steamboat Springs was not heavily endowed with medical personnel suited to the occasion. It was obvious from the position in which she lay, Sam had probably broken several bones, and possibly even her neck or her back. 'Go on, man, get going!' he shouted at Charlie, who wiped his face on his sleeve and ran back to the car, shot back a little distance, turned around, and pounded on the accelerator, wondering frantically if Samantha would live. 'Fucking horse,' he was shouting to himself as he drove back to where the others waited tensely. And then he jumped out of the car and gave orders.

He went back to Sam then and knelt beside her, trying to hold her and staunch the flow of blood from the cuts on her face with a towel he'd found in the car. And when he got into the helicopter beside her twenty minutes later, his face was grim. The two assistants were left to wrap up with the others. They were all to meet him in the hospital in Denver later that night.

It seemed to take forever for the helicopter to reach Denver, and by the time it did, it was obvious that Samantha's life was in grave danger. A paramedic had travelled with them, and for the last ten minutes of the trip he had given her artificial respiration as Charlie had sat anxiously by. He was aching to ask the paramedic if he thought she would make it, but he was afraid, so he said nothing and just watched them and continued to pray.

They set her down as gently as they could on the lawn of St. Mary's Hospital, having alerted all air traffic that they were coming through and coming down with a code blue. Charlie desperately searched his mind for what that meant, and thought he remembered that it meant someone was literally almost dead.

A doctor and three nurses were waiting on the lawn with a gurney, and she was rushed inside as soon as they landed, with Charlie left to follow as quickly as he could. He never thought to thank the young paramedic or the pilot, all he could think of was Samantha, so broken and so still. The only thing still recognisable about the long narrow form he saw draped in sheets a few minutes later was the tangled mass of golden palomino hair. It was then that he finally made himself say it, as two nurses stood by monitoring her vital signs while they prepared to take her to X ray and possibly surgery. They had already decided that the lacerations on her face were only superficial and could wait.

'Will she make it?' His voice was barely a croak in the brilliantly lit white hall.

'Excuse me?' His voice had been barely audible, and the nurse spoke to him without taking her eyes off Sam.

'Will she make it?'

'I don't know.' She spoke softly. 'Are you the next of kin? Her husband?'

Charlie shook his head dumbly. 'No, I'm—' And then he realised that maybe he should be. That if they thought he was family they'd tell him something more. 'I'm her brother. She's my sister.' He barely made sense as he stood there, feeling suddenly dizzy and sick as he realised that Sam might not live. She already looked as though she might be dead. But she was still breathing faintly, the nurse told him, and before she could say more, two residents, the doctor, and a whole flock of nurses in what looked like blue pyjamas came to whisk Sam away. 'Where is she going? Where is she . . . ?' No one listened and he just stood there, once again with tears coursing silently down his face. There was nothing they could tell him, they just didn't know.

It was an hour and a half later when they came back to find Charlie sitting frozen like a lost child in a waiting-room chair. He hadn't moved, he hadn't smoked, he hadn't even had a cup of coffee. He had just sat there, waiting, barely daring to breathe himself.

'Mr. Peterson?' Someone had taken his name when they had asked him to sign the admission forms. He had continued to claim that he was her brother, and he didn't give a damn if he lied, if it helped her, not that he was sure what difference it made.

'Yes?' He sprang to his feet. 'How is she? Is she all right?' Suddenly he couldn't stop talking, but the doctor nodded very slowly and looked Charlie full in the face.

'She's alive. Barely.'

'What is it? What happened?'

'To put it simply, Mr. Peterson, her back is broken. Her spine is fractured in two places. Bones are shattered. There's a hairline fracture in her neck, but we can work around that. The problem right now is her spine. There are so many small broken bones, we have to operate in order to take off some of the pressure. If we don't, there could be permanent damage to her brain.'

'And if you do?' Charlie had instantly sensed that the sword had two edges.

'If we do, she may not live.' The doctor sat down and indicated to Charlie to do the same. 'The problem is that if we don't, I can almost guarantee you that she'll be a vegetable for the rest of her life, and probably a quadri-plegic.'

'What's that?'

'Entirely paralysed. That means she'd have no control of her arms and legs, but could possibly move her head.'

'And if you do operate, that won't be the case?' Charlie suddenly felt a desperate urge to throw up, but he fought it. What in God's name were they discussing here, like buying carrots and onions and apples, move her head or her legs or . . . Jesus Christ!

The doctor was careful with his explanation. 'She'll certainly never walk again, Mr. Peterson, but if we do operate, we might salvage the rest of her. At best she'll wind up a paraplegic, with no use of the lower half of her body. But if we're lucky, we can save her mind. She might not be a vegetable if we go in now.' He hesitated for an interminable moment. 'The risk is much greater though. She's in bad shape, and we could lose her. I can't make you any promises.'

'All or nothing, isn't it?'

'More or less. In all fairness I should tell you even if we do nothing for her, or if we do everything we can, she might not live through the night. She's in a very critical condition.' Charlie nodded slowly, suddenly understanding that it was his decision and feeling desperately sorry that it was. He knew Sam had family still alive, but he had gone this far, and besides, she was closer to him than anybody . . . Oh, poor sweet Sam.

'You want an answer from me, Doctor?'

The man in the white coat nodded. 'I do.'

'When?'

'Right now.'

But how do I know you're any good, Charlie wanted to ask him. What choice do you have? another voice asked. Not to operate meant that Sam would die in effect, there would be nothing left but a lot of blonde hair and a broken body, no mind, no heart, no soul—he choked at the thought. To operate meant they might kill her . . . but . . . if she lived, she'd still be Sam. In a wheelchair, but still Sam.

'Go ahead.'

'Mr. Peterson?'

'Operate. Operate, dammit . . .operate!' Charlie was shouting and as the doctor hurried away, Charlie turned and began to pound the wall. It was when he stopped that he went to buy himself cigarettes and coffee and that he huddled in a corner, like a frightened animal, watching the clock. One hour . . . two hours . . . three . . . four . . . five . . . six . . . seven . . . At two o'clock in the morning

200

the doctor returned to find him wide-eyed and terrified and almost green with anguish as he waited, convinced that by now Sam must have died. She had died and no one had told him. And he had never been so frightened in his life. He had killed her with his lousy goddamn decision. He should have told the man not to operate, should have called her ex-husband, God, her mother . . . He didn't even begin to think of the consequences of his decision. The doctor had wanted an answer . . .

'Mr. Peterson?'

'Hmm?' He looked at the man as though he were in a trance.

'Mr. Peterson, your sister is all right.' He gently touched his arm, and Charlie nodded. He nodded again, and then the tears came, and then suddenly he was clasping the doctor tightly in his arms.

'My God . . . my God . . .' was all he could whimper. 'I thought she was dead . . .'

'She's all right, Mr. Peterson. Now you should go home and get some rest.' And then he remembered that they were all New Yorkers. 'Do you have a place to stay?' Charlie shook his head and the doctor jotted the name of a hotel on a piece of paper. 'Try that.'

'What about Sam?'

'I can't tell you much. You know the stakes we were playing for. We reconnected as much as we could. Her neck will be fine. Her spine . . . well, you knew . . . she will be a paraplegic. I'm almost sure there was no brain damage, neither from the fall, nor from the pressure before we operated. But we just have to wait now. It was a very long operation.' One could see that much on his face. 'We'll just have to wait.'

'How long?'

'We'll know a little more every day. If she makes it until tomorrow, we'll have much better odds.'

Charlie looked at him then, realising something. 'If she . . . if she lives, how long will she be here? Before we can take her back to New York?'

'Ohh . . .' The doctor exhaled slowly, staring at the

ground as he thought, and then looked back into Charlie's face. 'That really is hard to say. I would say though that if she does exceptionally well we could move her in an air ambulance sometime in the next three or four months.'

Three or four months? 'And then?' He dared to say the words.

'It really is too soon to even think about all this,' the doctor chided, 'but you're looking at at least a year in the hospital, Mr. Peterson. If not more. She's going to have to make a lot of readjustments.' Charlie shook his head slowly, only beginning to comprehend what lay in store for Sam. 'But first, let's just get her through tonight.' He left Charlie then, sitting alone in a corner of the waiting room, waiting for the others to arrive from Steamboat Springs.

They got there at three thirty in the morning, found Charlie asleep, hunched over with his head on his chest and snoring softly, and they woke him to hear the news. He told them what he knew, and there was sober silence among the others, and then quietly they left together to find a hotel. When they got there, Charlie sat staring in agony out of the window at Denver, and it was only when Henry and his friend came to sit with him, that at last he let it all go, all the pain and the terror and the worry and the guilt and the confusion and the sorrow, and he sobbed for over an hour as Henry held him in his arms. And from that moment on, as they sat with him through the night and brought him solace, they were his friends. It was the darkest night that Charlie could ever remember, but when they called the hospital in the morning, it was Henry who dropped his face in his hands and cried. Samantha was still alive.

202

25

The day after Sam's accident the entire crew disbanded, but after several long phone conversations with Harvey, Charlie opted to stay. He didn't know how long he'd have to be there, and he couldn't leave Mellie alone with four kids forever, but right now he knew he wasn't leaving. She was alone in a strange city, and she was almost half dead. Harvey had been stunned when he had heard the news. It had been easy for Charlie to convince him to let him stay. But Harvey had also suggested that Charlie at least try to contact Sam's mother in Atlanta. She was, after all, Sam's only living relative, and she had a right to know that her only child was in intensive care in Denver with a broken back. But when Charlie called her, he discovered that she and her husband were on vacation for a month in Europe, so there was nothing more he could do. He knew anyway that Sam wasn't overly fond of her mother, thought her stepfather was a horse's ass, and her father had been dead for years. There was no one else to call. By then of course, though, he had called Mellie, and she had cried like a baby at the news. 'Oh, poor Sam . . . oh, Charlie . . . how will she do it . . . in a wheelchair . . . and all alone . . . ?' They had cried for a few moments together, and then Charlie had got off the phone. He wanted to put another call in to Harvey, because he had wanted him to check on the doctor who did the operation, even though by now it was more than a little late. But he was relieved when he got back to Harvey. Harvey had called every bone man he knew in Boston, New York, and Chicago, he had even called a friend who was the chief orthopaedic surgeon for the Mets.

'Thank God for your social connections, Harvey. Anyway, what did he say?'

'He says the guy's tops.' Charlie let out a long sigh and a few minutes later he put down the phone. Now all he could do was go back to his waiting game. They let him see her for five minutes every hour. But there wasn't much he could do really. She hadn't regained consciousness yet, and she didn't all that day.

It was the next day around six o'clock in the evening, when he looked in on her for the eighth time that day. He expected only to stand there for a few minutes, as he had every hour on the hour since that morning, to watch her still, now bandaged face, and then, at the signal from the nurse, to close the door and walk away. But this time as he watched her he thought that something was different. The position of her arms had shifted slightly and her colour looked better. As he stood there he began gently to run a hand down the long sun-streaked blonde hair and softly say her name. He talked to her as though she could hear him, telling her that he was right there with her, that they all loved her, and that she'd be okay. And this time, before the nurse came to beckon him from her, Sam opened her eyes, saw Charlie, and whispered 'Hi.'

'What?' He looked astonished as he stood there, and his own word sounded like an explosion in the highly monitored room. 'What did you say?'

'I said hi.' It was barely more than a whisper, and as she said it he wanted to give a war whoop of glee. Instead he bent low so that she could hear him and he whispered too.

'Hey, kiddo, you're doing great.'

'Am I? . . . What . . . happened . . . ?' Her voice was fading and he didn't want to answer, but her eyes wouldn't let go of his.

'You kicked hell out of some horse.'

'Black Beauty?' She looked vague and groggy and he wondered if she was fading out again, but then the eyelids fluttered open. 'No . . . now I remember . . . the grey stallion . . . there was a ditch . . . a river . . . something . . .' Something, all right. A something that had changed her whole life.

'Yeah. Anyway, it doesn't matter. That's all over.'

'Why am I here?'

'So you can recover.' They were still whispering, and he smiled at her and ever so gently took her hand. He had never been so happy to see her as he was right now.

'Can I go home?' She sounded sleepy and childlike as she closed her eyes again.

'Not just yet.'

'When? Tomorrow?'

'We'll see.' Tomorrow . . . it would be several hundred tomorrows, but Charlie couldn't bring himself to feel sorry. He was just so damn glad that she had made it. She was alive, and she was conscious—that had to be a good sign.

'You didn't call my mother, did you?' She eyed him suspiciously and he quickly shook his head.

'Of course not.' He lied.

'Good. Her husband is an ass.'

Charlie grinned at her, thrilled with the soft patter of conversation, and then the nurse appeared at the window and gave him the sign.

'I have to go now, Sam. But I'll come back tomorrow. Okay, babe?'

'Okay.' She smiled sweetly at him, closed her eyes, and went back to sleep. And when Charlie went back to the hotel, he called Mellie and told her that Sam had regained consciousness at last.

'What does that mean?' She still sounded desperately worried, but he was buoyant with the news.

'I don't know, love. But right now it sure feels good. I thought . . . I thought maybe we had lost her.'

Mellie nodded at her end. 'So did I.'

* * *

He stayed in Denver with her for another two weeks, and then both Mellie and Harvey started making noises about his coming home. He knew he had to, and he missed Mellie and the kids terribly, but he just hated to leave

Sam. Still he knew he couldn't stay in Denver for another three months. But that night, as he tried to force himself to make a plane reservation for that weekend, he had an idea. And the next morning he waited for the doctor outside his office and nervously put forward his plan.

'What do you think, Doctor?'

'That it's very risky. Is it worth it? Why is it so important to take her back to New York?'

'Because she has her friends there. She has absolutely no one here.'

'What about your parents? Couldn't they come out?' Charlie looked at the doctor blankly for a moment and then remembered that he was still masquerading as Sam's brother, and then shook his head.

'No. They're travelling in Europe, and I don't think that I'll be able to reach them for another month.' By now he knew that if he had to reach her family Sam's stepfather's office could find him, but she had been adamant about it. She didn't want her mother called. 'I just don't want to leave her alone out here, and I really should get back.'

'I can understand that.' The doctor looked pensive. 'You know she would be in good hands.'

'I know that.' Charlie looked at him warmly. 'But . . . right now . . . once she figures out what she's up against, Doctor, she's going to need everyone she's got.'

He nodded slowly. 'I can't argue with that. Right now she's really not in any danger, as long as we keep everything pretty constant for her and make sure she doesn't get pneumonia.' That was still the greatest danger, and suspended on a great machine as she was in the giant plaster body cast—her 'barbecue spit,' as she called it—they turned her over, like a roast chicken, several times a day. But she still hadn't figured out the implications of what had happened, and the doctor didn't want to tell her until she was stronger. He felt that for the moment there was no need. 'You do have a point, Peterson. Once she knows, and that day will come fairly soon, she's going to need all of you. I can't keep it from her forever. It's only been two weeks. But she's less groggy now, she's more alert, eventually she'll put two and two together, and when she figures out that she'll never walk again, it's going to be very traumatic for her. I'd like to have you here.'

'Or her there. What do you think?'

'Can your firm charter a plane? Would they do it?'

'Yes.' He had called Harvey that morning and Harvey had told him to spare no expense. 'A nurse, a doctor, any kind of machinery you want. You run the show, we'll pay the bills.'

'All right,' the doctor said thoughtfully, 'all right, if her condition stays stable for the next few days, I'll make the arrangements for you and we'll fly her to New York this weekend.'

'You'll come too?' Charlie crossed his fingers and the doctor nodded. 'Hallelujah! Thank you, Doctor!' The doctor grinned, and Charlie hurried to tell Sam.

'You're going home, kid.'

'I am? I can leave?' She looked both startled and thrilled. 'But what about my barbecue? Won't they charge us a lot for excess baggage?' Although she was joking, he saw that she looked nervous at the prospect of leaving. She was beginning to understand just how much danger she had been in and that she wasn't totally out of the woods yet. The only thing she really didn't understand was about her legs. But she would. Charlie still cringed at the thought. As long as she was still in the cast, she wouldn't figure it out.

'No sweat—you should pardon the pun,' he said, grinning. 'We're taking the barbecue with us. Harvey says we can charter our own plane.'

'But, Charlie, that's crazy. Can't they just set me up with crutches or something, or if worse comes to worst, stick me in a wheelchair with my stupid body cast and let me fly home on the plane?'

'Only if you want to give me heart failure. Look, Sam, the truth is you kicked the shit out of yourself, so now why take chances? Why not go home in style? I mean, if you're going to do it, baby, *do it!*'

'A chartered plane?' She looked hesitant but he nodded with a grin.

'Of course we'll have to see how you do in the next couple of days.'

'I'll do fine. I want to get out of here.' She smiled wanly at him. 'I just want to go home to my own bed.' He realised then with a jolt that by 'home,' she had understood her apartment, when all he had meant was New York. He mentioned it later to the doctor, who reassured him.

'I'm afraid you're going to see a lot of that, Mr. Peterson. The human mind is a wonderful thing. It only accepts what it can handle. The rest it just kind of puts away somewhere, until it can deal with it. Somewhere, deep in her psyche, she knows that she is still too sick to go home, but she's not ready yet to accept that. When she is, she will, you don't have to say anything. Not yet at least. We can discuss that little matter at the New York airport if we have to. But she'll deal with it when she's ready to, just like she'll deal with the fact that she can't walk anymore. One day all the information she already has will fall into place and she'll know.'

Charlie exhaled softly. 'How can you be so sure she'll understand?'

There was a moment's pause before the doctor answered. 'She doesn't have any choice.'

Charlie nodded slowly. 'Do you think we'll be able to take her back there?'

'Sooner or later.' The doctor answered calmly.

'I mean this weekend.'

'We'll just have to see, won't we?' He smiled then and disappeared to make his rounds.

The next few days seemed to take forever, and Sam was suddenly impatient and nervous and jumpy too. She wanted to go home, but she was having problems. The body cast was chafing, she was coughing slightly, she had a rash on her arms from some of the medication, and her face itched terribly now that all the scabs were healing and dropping off.

'Christ, Charlie, I look like a goddamn monster!' She sounded irritated for the first time since she'd been there, and when he came into the room, he thought her eyes looked red.

'I don't think so. I think you look gorgeous. So what else is new?'

'Nothing.' But she sounded sullen, and he watched her carefully as he toured casually around the room. She was no longer in intensive care, but had a small room, almost entirely swallowed up by the bed, and in the corner was a table covered with flowers, from Henry and his lover, Jack, the rest of the crew, another bunch from Harvey, and still more from Mellie and him.

'Want to hear some of the office dirt?'

'No.' She lay in her cast and closed her eyes, and he watched her, praying that she wasn't getting sick. It seemed a long time before she opened them again. And when she did, she looked angry, and he saw that there were tears in her eyes again.

'What's up, babe? Come on, tell Papa.' He sat down in a chair next to the bed and took her hand.

'The night nurse . . . the one with the funny red wig . . .' The tears slowly spilled over. 'She said that when I go home . . .' Sam gulped down a sob and squeezed his hand, and as she did it Charlie was grateful that she could. 'She said I'm not going home . . . that I'm just going to another hospital . . . in New York . . . oh, Charlie,' she wailed like a small child, 'is that true?' He looked at her, wanting to hug her, like one of his children, but there was no way to put one's arms around the huge plaster cast or her surrounding machine, all he could do was hold her hand and gently touch her face. He knew he had to tell her the truth.

'Yeah, babe, that's true.'

'Oh, Charlie, I want to go home.' She sobbed in anguish and then winced at the pain.

'Don't do that, silly, you'll hurt yourself, but it's all

right to cry. Just keep it down.' He tried to tease her, but inside he was sad at what was happening. For Sam, it was the beginning of a long, difficult road she had only just begun to travel. Her old life had ended in the flash of an instant, at the feet of a grey horse. 'Come on, Sam, just getting back to New York would be a step in the right direction, wouldn't it?'

'I guess so.'

'Sure it would.'

'Yeah, but I want to go home. I don't want to go to a hospital.'

'Well'—he grinned at her lopsidedly—'at least we know you're not crazy. But okay, so you have to go to a hospital for a while, so what? I'll be able to visit you, and Mellie and Harvey and whomever else you want . . .'

'Not my mother!' Sam rolled her eyes and laughed through her tears. 'Oh, shit, Charlie, why did this have to happen to me?' The smile faded, and the tears began in earnest again. For a long time he just sat there and held her hand, and then he said the only thing he knew to tell her.

'I love you, Sam. We all do. And we're right here with you.'

'You're such a good friend, and I love you too.' It made her cry more, but the nurse arrived then with her lunch.

'I hear you're leaving us, Miss Taylor. Is that true?'

'I'm trying to.' She smiled at Charlie. 'But I'll be back. Under my own steam next time, just to visit!'

'I sure hope so.' The nurse smiled and left the room, as inwardly Charlie breathed a sigh of relief. For a moment he had been terrified that the nurse would give something away when Sam said 'under my own steam.'

'So,' she looked at Charlie, sipping some soup, 'when are we going home?'

'Does Saturday suit you, or do you have other plans?' He grinned at her, immensely pleased. She was trying. Oh, God, she was trying.

'No, Saturday sounds okay to me.' She was smiling as she looked at him, and he couldn't help thinking that the doctor had been right. When she was ready to know something, she would. He just wondered when she would be ready to face the rest. 'Yeah, Saturday sounds just fine. What hospital am I going to, Charlie?'

'I don't know. Do you care?'

'Do I have a choice?'

'I'll find out.'

'Try for Lenox Hill. It's in a nice neighbourhood, and it's near the subway. That way everyone I want to see will be able to come visit.' She smiled softly. 'Maybe even Mellie.' And then, 'Do you think she could bring the baby?'

There were tears in Charlie's eyes when he nodded. 'I'll sneak her in under my coat and tell them she's yours.'

'She kind of is, you know . . .' She looked embarrassed. 'Kind of . . . after all, she's got my name.' He bent over and kissed her forehead then, there was nothing more he could have said in answer without bursting into tears.

26

Charlie held his breath when the plane left the Denver airport on Saturday morning. They had Sam's orthopaedic surgeon with them, as well as a young resident, two nurses, a life-support unit, and enough oxygen to blow them all the way to South America, but Samantha was slightly sedated, seemed very relaxed, and was excited to be going home. The doctor seemed pleased with her condition and had made all the necessary arrangements both at Lenox Hill Hospital and with an ambulance unit that would be waiting for them at the airport when they arrived. In addition they were getting special clearance all along their route and were making themselves known to air-traffic control from sector to sector. If Sam had suddenly needed help they couldn't provide in the air, they could have come down almost anywhere along the way at a moment's notice. Everything that could have been thought of had been, and all that remained now was to fly safely back to New York.

It was a brilliantly sunny day in August, and Sam did nothing but talk about going home. She was also slightly punchy from the sedative she'd been given, and she giggled a lot and made a number of jokes in poor taste, which everyone laughed at, except Charlie, who was a nervous wreck. Once again he felt the responsibility upon his shoulders, and he felt that if something went wrong now it would be his fault. He shouldn't have pushed, he had rushed them, he should have left her in Denver. The doctor found him halfway through the flight, staring out a rear window, and he gently touched his shoulder and spoke softly so Sam wouldn't hear in case she woke up. She had just gone to sleep.

'It's all right, Peterson. It's almost over. And she's doing fine. Just fine.'

He turned to smile at the doctor. 'She may make it, but what about me? I think I've aged twenty years in the last two weeks.'

'It's a very trying experience, for the family as well.' The craziest part was that he wasn't even family, but he was her friend. He would have done it for anyone, for his brother-in-law, for Harvey, for . . . Sam . . . he would have sat at Sam's bedside for another month if he had to. He felt so damn sorry for her. What in hell was her life going to be like now? And she had no one, no husband, no boyfriend, that damn cowboy she'd mentioned had run out on her and she didn't even know where he was. Who did she have to take care of her? No one. For the first time in a long time he found himself hating John Taylor again. If the bastard had stuck around, like a decent husband, she wouldn't be alone now. But she was. The bitch of it was that she was all alone. The doctor was watching him as he thought it out, and his hand pressed gently on Charlie's shoulder. 'Don't overprotect her, Peterson. It

212

would be a terrible mistake. When the time comes, she'll have to stand on her own, so to speak. She's not married, is she?'

Charlie shook his head. 'No, not anymore. And that's what I was just thinking. It's going to be very rough.'

'It will be for a while. But she'll get used to it. Others do. She can lead a full life. She can help herself, help others, she can go back to her job in time. Unless she's a tap dancer by profession, it shouldn't make that much difference, except psychologically. That's where the problems arise. But they won't let her leave Lenox Hill until she's ready, psychologically as well as physically. They'll teach her how to take care of herself, be independent. You'll see. She's a beautiful young woman, a strong one with a fine mind, there's no reason why she shouldn't adjust perfectly.' And then after a moment he gave Charlie's shoulder one last squeeze and smiled. 'You've made the right decision . . . both times. It would have been a crime not to operate, to lose that spirit and that mind, and she should be in New York, surrounded by friendly faces.' Charlie turned to look at him then, with gratitude in his eyes.

'Thank you for saying that.' The doctor said nothing. He only patted Charlie's shoulder and went back to take a look at Sam.

Two hours later they landed at Kennedy Airport. The transfer to the large ambulance unit went perfectly smoothly, and a life-support unit with three paramedics travelled alongside. Their lights were flashing but there were no sirens as they made their way along the highway at full speed. And half an hour later they reached Lenox Hill without a problem.

Sam was smiling up at Charlie as they made the last leg of the trip. 'It's quicker this way, you know that, no baggage claim to hassle with and no cabs.'

'Look, next time,' Charlie said, grinning at her, 'do me a favour. Hassle me a little with the baggage and let's take a cab.'

She grinned up at him, but once they arrived at Lenox

213

Hill, she was busy. It took them more than two hours to process her into the hospital and settle her comfortably in her own room. The doctor assisted with all the arrangements, then she met the new doctor who had been awaiting her arrival, thanks to Harvey once again. When it was all over she and Charlie and the doctor from Denver were all exhausted. The rest of the group had been dispensed with. They had all been paid before the trip and they would all be returning to Denver on the ambulance plane later that evening. The doctor was going to spend a few days in New York observing at Lenox Hill and would return to Denver by commercial jet.

'Think you'll be okay now, Sam?' Charlie looked at her with a tired smile as she accepted a shot and began almost instantly to drift off to sleep.

'Yeah, babe . . . sure . . . I'll be fine . . . give Mellie my love . . . and thank you . . .' Five minutes later he was in the elevator with the doctor, and then he was in a cab, and ten minutes later he was on East Eighty-first Street with his arms tightly around his wife.

'Oh, baby . . . oh, baby . . .' He felt as though he had come back from a war zone, and suddenly he realised how desperately he had missed her and how exhausted he was. Sam's tragedy and Charlie's total responsibility for her had been an awesome weight to carry, and he hadn't let himself feel it until now, when suddenly all he wanted to do was make love to his wife. She had had the foresight to have hired a baby-sitter to be with the children, and after they all duly attacked their father, teased and played and ran him ragged, she shooed them off with the baby-sitter, closed the bedroom door, ran a bath for him, gave him a massage, and made love to him, before he smiled at her sleepily and fell asleep in their bed. She woke him up again two hours later, with dinner, champagne, and a little cake she had made for him that said "I love you. Welcome home".

'Oh, Mellie, I love you so much.'

'I love you too.' And then, as they ate the cake, 'Do you think we should call Sam?' But Charlie shook his head, he had given her all he had to give for a while. Just this once, just tonight, he wanted to be with Mellie. He didn't want to think of the horrible accident, of the grey horse that had haunted him in his sleep for three weeks, of Sam in her plaster cast or her 'barbecue' or the fact that she would never walk again. He just wanted to be with his wife, and to make love to her, until he fell into her arms and passed out, which he did shortly after midnight, with a last sleepy yawn and a broad smile.

'Welcome home,' she whispered to him softly as she kissed his neck and turned off the light.

27

'Mother, I'm fine really . . . don't be silly . . . there's no reason for you to come up . . . oh, for chrissake . . . yes, of course I'm still in a cast, but I'm fine here. No, I don't want to be moved to Atlanta. I just was moved here from Denver three weeks ago, that's enough . . . because this is my home, Mother. I don't know anyone in Atlanta. Yes, of course, I have you and George . . . Mother . . . now, Mother . . . please! I don't resent him . . .' She rolled her eyes at Melinda as she walked into Sam's hospital room, and made a horrible face at the receiver, mouthing 'My mother' to Melinda, who grinned. 'Honestly, Mother, the doctor is wonderful, I like him . . . I know he's competent because he told me so and his mother loves him. Come on, Ma. Give me a break. I'm fine, I'll call you. You can call me. When I feel up to it, I'll come to Atlanta . . . I don't know when I can go home . . . but I'll tell you. I promise . . . no, Mother, I have to go now . . . the nurse is waiting . . . no, you can't talk to her . . . good-bye, Mother.' She hung up and groaned. 'Hi, Mellie. Christ, what did I ever do to get saddled with my mother?'

215

'She's just worried about you, Sam.'

'I know. But she drives me nuts. She wants to come up here to visit. With George, who wants to consult with my doctor, and turn the whole hospital upside down. Tell me what an ear, nose, and throat man from Georgia can possibly have to contribute to my broken back?' Mellie grinned at the thought. 'How's life by you?'

'Okay. How are you?'

'Bored. I want to go home.'

'What do they say?'

'Something inane about patience. How's my namesake?' She beamed at the mention of little Sam.

'Wonderful.' Mellie smiled too. 'She does more at two months than any of the boys did at four.'

'It's the name,' Sam assured her with a grin. 'Just make sure she doesn't get into trouble with horses.' Mellie didn't answer and Sam sighed. 'I wish I knew how long I'll be stuck here.' But Mellie suspected that she didn't really want to know. Charlie had told her that Sam would probably be in the hospital for a year.

She got visits from everyone including Harvey, who sat nervously on the edge of his chair, fingering his hat, toying with his pipe, and staring nervously at Sam in her body cast lying helplessly on the bed.

'Don't look so uptight, for chrissake, Harvey. I won't bite you.'

'Will you sign a document to that effect?'

'I'd be glad to.' He smiled his rueful smile and she asked him when he was going to get smart and fire her.

'I can't, Sam. I'm saving you for my old age. Besides, I just saw the answer print of the first commercial from your great adventure out west. Sam'—he sounded almost breathless with admiration—'if you never do anything in your whole lifetime except lie there and eat chocolates, you can be proud of this.'

'That good?' She sounded stunned. He was generally not lavish with praise. But she had heard from Charlie that morning that the stuff was damn good.

'It's better than that. It's superb. And they say the

others will be better still. My dear, I'm in awe.'

She looked at him for a long moment and then grinned at him. 'I think I must be dying, for you to be talking like this.'

'Hardly. We'll get it all put on tape for you eventually and bring it up here with a video machine for you to see it before we ever put it on the air. But I'm afraid after all this, Miss Samantha, I really am going to retire and make you C.D.'

'Don't threaten me, Harvey.' She glared at him. 'I don't want your damn job, so you stay where you are, or I'll stay here.'

'God forbid.'

He came to see her once or twice a week. Charlie came to visit often at lunchtime, Henry Johns-Adams had already come to see her twice, bringing her a box of divine Godiva chocolates, and his friend had sent her a beautiful bed jacket from Bergdorf's, which she could hardly wait to wear when she got rid of her cumbersome cast. And Georgie, the French poodle, had sent her a get-well card and a book.

But a week later Sam got the visit to end all visits. Despite her protestations that she didn't want a visit from her mother, she arrived from Atlanta with her husband and did her best to turn the whole hospital upside down. She spent several hours trying to convince Samantha to sue her office, that if it weren't for them and their ridiculous commercials, she wouldn't have been on that trip, that it was obviously a dangerous assignment, that they didn't give a damn about her, and that her boss was undoubtedly some kind of a lunatic who didn't care two pins that she was now flat on her back. Her whole tack so enraged Samantha that she asked her to leave and then had to relent when her mother cried and insisted that Sam was a sadistic ingrate determined to break her mother's heart. On the whole it was an exhausting meeting, which left Samantha shaking and pale, but not nearly as upset as she was when her mother and George returned to see her the next day. They entered Sam's room with identical funereal expressions and it was clear that her mother had been crying, and once she sat down, she started again.

'Good God, Mother, what's the matter?' It made Sam nervous just to see them, and she was already upset. She had called Caroline Lord that morning to see how Bill was, and learned that he had had another heart attack, this one more serious than the first one. And chained to her bed in her body cast at Lenox Hill Hospital, she could do nothing to help Caro, and she suddenly felt useless and hemmed in. But Caro had been much more upset about the accident. She bit back the information about her own misfortune, thinking Caro had enough in her heart to carry around, but Charlie had obviously already told her. Caro was frantic with worry. Like all horsepeople, she knew the danger involved but she nevertheless was in a state of shock over Sam. She made Sam promise that she would call again. And if not, she would call Sam herself when she had a free moment from Bill.

But now all thought of Aunt Caro was pushed from her mind as she faced her mother, who was, as always, elegantly dressed, in a blue linen suit and a white silk blouse. She wore neat little spectator pumps and three strands of pearls and pearl earrings, and although she was a little plump woman of sixty, she still had the same extravagantly beautiful hair as Sam. Hers was snow white now, but once it had been as gold as Sam's. Her husband was tall and handsome and looked more like a naval captain than a doctor. He was barrel chested and florid, with a great shock of snowy white hair.

'Oh, Samantha . . .' her mother lamented as George held her hand and she sat back, almost inert, in the chair.

'For chrissake, what's wrong?' Samantha suddenly had an odd, creeping feeling, as though something terrible were about to happen to her, or maybe it already had.

'Oh, Samantha . . .'

'Jesus.' If she could have, she'd have screamed, or maybe just tapped her feet. But her feet had only tingled and hung like dead meat since her body had been surrounded by what felt like cement. The nurses all told her that it was normal to feel that way in a body cast, and Sam had found that comforting. For a while there she had been worried that her legs were shot. 'So what's up, guys?' She eyed them with irritation and hostility. She couldn't wait for them to go home. 'Don't keep me in suspense.' But her mother only cried more. It was her stepfather who eventually took the first step.

'Samantha, we have spoken at some length to your doctor this morning.'

'Which one? I have four.'

She felt like an irritable, sassy teenager as she watched them with suspicion. But she just wanted them to go away and leave her alone.

But her stepfather was a man of precision. 'In fact we spoke to two of them. Dr. Wong and Dr. Josephs. They were both very informative and very kind.' He looked at her with obvious pity, and his wife cast woeful eyes in his direction before she sobbed again and he went on.

'Did they say anything to bring all this hysteria on? Anything I should know?' She glanced at her mother in annoyance and then back at George.

'Yes, there is. And much as it pains us, we think it's time you knew. The doctors have simply been waiting until— until the right time. But now that we're here . . .' It sounded like the perfect beginning for an eulogy as he said it, and Samantha wanted to look around to see who was in the casket. He looked like an undertaker, not a sea captain, she decided and tried to fix her face politely as he went on. 'Now that we're here, we feel it's time you knew.'

'Knew what?'

'The truth.' Suddenly, as he said it, a little alarm went off somewhere near Sam's heart. It was as if she knew. As if she had known all along, without knowing, as though she sensed exactly what they were going to say.

'Oh?' was all she said.

'Yes.'

'The accident . . . well, Sam, it was a very grave injury you sustained when you fell. Your spinal column was severely fractured in two places. It was quite a miracle that you didn't die from the shock and those ruptures, and also that there was no brain damage, which of course they're sure now there wasn't.'

'Gee, thanks. That's nice. But the rest?' Her heart pounded but her face gave nothing away.

'As you know, as for the rest, you weren't so lucky, or you wouldn't be here in that unfortunate cast.' He sighed briefly but continued. 'What you don't know, however, and we feel you should, as do your doctors, I might add—it really is time. What you don't know, Samantha, is that'—he hesitated for only a fraction of a second before lowering the boom—'you are now a paraplegic.'

There was a moment's silence and she stared at him. 'What exactly does that mean, George?'

'That you'll never walk again. You will retain the full use of your upper torso, your arms, shoulders, et cetera, but the real damage was done just at your waistline. One can see it perfectly on the X rays,' he explained informatively with a professional air. 'From that point on there's nothing. You may have some sensation, as I suppose you already do now, but that's all. You'll have no muscle control certainly, no ability to use your legs. You will of course have to use a wheelchair.' And then he delivered the final shock. 'But of course your mother and I decided this morning that you will come to live with us.'

'No, I won't!' It was a shriek of panic, and both her mother and stepfather looked stunned.

'Of course you will, darling.' Her mother stretched out a hand and Sam shrank from it like a wounded animal, wanting desperately to run away. Her eyes were wild as she looked at them. They had no right to tell her this. It wasn't true . . . it couldn't be . . . no one else had told her . . . but she knew almost before she heard it that it was in fact the truth—and what she had been hiding from almost since the moment she'd gained consciousness in Denver. It was the one thing no one ever said. Except these two people. They had come here to tell her this, as though it were their mission, and she didn't want to hear anything that they had just said.

'I don't want to, Mother.' She spoke through clenched teeth, but they refused to understand.

'But you can't take care of yourself anymore. You'll be as helpless as a baby.' Her mother painted a picture that made Sam want to die.

'I won't! I won't, dammit . . . I'll kill myself first!' She was shrieking.

'Samantha! How dare you say such a thing!'

'I will if I want to, dammit. I will not be confined to this life, to the life of a cripple. And I don't want to be as helpless as a baby, living in Atlanta with my parents at the age of thirty-one. How could this have happened to me, dammit . . . it can't have happened, I won't let it happen.'

Her mother stood helplessly by as George put on his most professional bedside manner and attempted to soothe her but she just screamed louder, and her mother's eyes looked at her husband and implored him that they should go.

'Maybe we should come back and talk about this later . . .' They edged slowly toward the door. 'You need some time to yourself, Samantha, to adjust . . . we have plenty of time to discuss it, we're not leaving until tomorrow, and the doctors don't think you'll be leaving here anyway until May or June.'

'What?' It was a final wail of pain.

'Samantha . . .' For an instant her mother looked as though she would approach her, and Sam could only snarl from the bed.

'Get out of here, for God's sake . . . please . . .' She began to sob uncontrollably. 'Just go . . .' They did as she bid them, and suddenly she was alone in the empty room with the echo of their words. A nurse found her there half an hour later, sawing hopelessly at her wrists with the barely sharp edges of a plastic cup.

The damage she did was repaired with a few stitches, but the damage her mother and stepfather did took several months to heal.

'How's it going, kid?' Charlie shook the snow from his collar, took off his coat, and threw it on a chair. There was even snow in his beard and in his hair. 'So?' He looked at her expectantly, and she shrugged.

'What do you expect? For me to sit in my chair wearing a pink tutu and do an arabesque for you when you walk in?'

'Ooohhhhh-eeee, charming today, aren't we?'

'Get fucked.'

He looked at his watch with a pensive expression. 'I'd like to, but Mellie has a PTA meeting, and actually I don't have time. I have a client meeting at two.'

'Very funny.'

'That's more than I can say for you.'

'Well, I'm not funny anymore. That's life. I'm thirty-one years old and I'm a cripple in a wheelchair. That is neither funny, nor amusing, nor cute.'

'No, but it's not necessarily as pitiful as you'd like to make it either.' He had seen her this way for three and a half months. Ever since her idiot stepfather had broken the news. She was out of the body cast now and wearing a brace and moving around in a wheelchair. But now came the hard part, the gruelling months of physical therapy when she learned to live with her handicap, or not. 'It doesn't have to be as lousy as this, Sam. You don't have to be a "helpless cripple," as your mother puts it.'

'No? Why not? You going to make a miracle again and give me back the power over my legs?' She pounded on them as if they were old rubber.

'No, I can't do that, Sam.' He spoke gently but firmly. 'But you've got the power of your mind and your arms and your hands and'—he grinned for an instant—'the power of your mouth. You could do a lot with all of that, if you wanted to.'

'Really? Like what?' Today he had come prepared.

'As it so happens, Miss Smartass, I brought you a present from Harvey today.'

'One more box of chocolates from anyone and I'll scream.' She sounded like a petulant child and not the Sam he knew. But there was still hope that she would adjust. The doctors said that in time she would very probably come around. It was a hell of a tough adjustment, for anyone, especially a beautiful, active young woman like Sam.

'He didn't send you chocolates, kiddo. He sent you work.' For an instant he saw surprise in Sam's eyes.

'What do you mean, he sent me work?'

'Just that. We talked to your doctors yesterday and they said there's no reason why you can't do some of your work here. I brought you a dictating machine, some pens and paper, three files Harvey wants you to look over . . .' He was about to go on when Sam spun her chair away and almost snarled.

'Why the hell should I?'

But he decided that she had played the game for long enough. 'Because you've been sitting here on your ass for long enough. Because you have a fine mind, and you could have died and you didn't, Sam, so don't waste what you got.' He sounded angry and Sam was quieter when she spoke again.

'Why should I do anything for Harvey?'

'Why should he do anything for you? Why should he give you a five-month vacation because your husband left you, and then spare no expense to bring you home when you have an accident—I might remind you that you could still be sitting alone in Denver, if it weren't for Harvey—and then why should he give you unlimited sick leave and wait for you to come back?'

'Because I'm good at what I do, that's why?'

'Bitch!' It was the first time in months he had got angry at her and it felt good. 'He needs your help, dammit. He's snowed under and so am I. Are you willing to pick yourself up again and stop feeling sorry for yourself, or aren't you?'

She was very quiet for a long moment, her back turned in her chair, her head bowed. 'I haven't decided yet.' She said it very softly and he smiled.

'I love you, Sam.' And then she turned slowly to face him, and when she did, he saw that there were tears running slowly down her face.

'What the hell am I going to do, Charlie? Where am I going to live? And how? . . . Oh, Christ, I'm so afraid I'll end up with my mother in Atlanta. They call me every day to tell me what a helpless cripple I am now, and that's what I keep thinking . . . that I am . . .'

'You're not. There's nothing helpless about you. You may have to make some changes in your life, but nothing as radical as Atlanta. Christ, you'd go nuts there.' She nodded sadly, and he took her chin in his hand. 'Mellie and I won't let that happen, even if you have to come and live with us.'

'But I don't want to be helpless, Charlie. I want to take care of myself.'

'So do it. Isn't that what they're teaching you here?'

She nodded slowly. 'Yeah. But it takes forever.'

'How long is forever? Six months? A year?'

'Something like that.'

'Isn't it worth it, not to have to live in Atlanta?'

'Yes.' She wiped her tears away with her fancy bed jacket. 'For that, it would be worth five years.'

'Then do it, learn what you've got to, and then come on back out in the world and do your thing, Sam. And meanwhile'—he smiled at her and glanced at his watch— 'do me a favour and read those files and memos. For Harvey.'

'Never mind "for Harvey." You're both full of shit. I know what you're doing, but I'll try it. Send him my love.'

'He sent you his. He said he'd be up here tomorrow.'

'Tell him not to forget my Mickey Spillanes.'

She and Harvey were addicted to the detective books

and Harvey kept shipping her copies of them to amuse herself with.

'Oh, Christ . . . you two.' Charlie struggled back into his heavy overcoat, put on his galoshes, pulled up his collar, and waved at her from the door.

'So long, Santa Claus, Give my love to Mellie.'

'Yes, ma'am.' He saluted and disappeared, and for a long time she sat in her chair, staring at the files. It was almost Christmas again and she had been thinking of Tate all morning. Only a year before she had been on the Lord Ranch, and Tate had played Santa to the kids. It had been then that she had started to get to know him, then that it had all begun. It had been Christmas Day when he had taken her to the hidden cabin. Thinking about him made it all come alive again and she felt the familiar ache as she wondered again where he had gone.

She had talked to Caroline only that morning. Bill had had a small stroke after Thanksgiving, and in the past few months he had done nothing but go downhill. In the midst of the gloomy reports she hated to bother Caro with inquiries about Tate Jordan, but eventually she had anyway, and as always she had no news. Caroline herself was terribly despressed about the state of Bill's health. She had just hired a new foreman, a young man with a wife and three kids, and he seemed to be doing a good job. And as always, she had encouraged Sam to push on. The physical therapy that Sam was enduring was the hardest work of her life and she wondered if it was worth it; strengthening her arms so that she could almost swing like a monkey, get herself in and out of her chair, in and out of bed, on and off the pot, anything she would need to do to live alone. If she would cooperate, the staff would train her to manage totally independently. She had resisted, balking at the help offered her—in her heart she felt it didn't really matter anyway—but now, now suddenly it seemed important to push on. Charlie was right. She had lived— that was reason enough to push on.

Christmas Day itself was a difficult holiday for her.

Harvey Maxwell came by, and Charlie and Mellie and the kids. The nurse let them all in and she got to hold the baby, who was almost five months old now and prettier than ever. When they all left, she felt desperately alone. By the end of the afternoon she thought that she simply couldn't bear it, and out of sheer desperation she left her room and wheeled herself slowly down the hall. And then at the very end of the floor she found a little boy in a wheelchair like hers, sitting sadly by the window, staring out at the snow.

'Hi, my name's Sam.' Her heart ached for him, and then he turned toward her. He couldn't have been more than six, and his eyes were filled with tears.

'I can't play in the snow anymore.'

'Neither can I. What's your name?'

'Alex.'

'What did you get for Christmas?'

'A cowboy hat and a holster. But I can't ride horses either.'

She nodded slowly, and then suddenly she wondered. 'Why not?'

He looked at her as though she were very stupid. 'Because I'm in this wheelchair, dummy. I got hit by a car, riding my bike, and now I have to be in this thing forever.' And then he looked at her curiously. 'What about you?'

'I fell off a horse in Colorado.'

'Yeah?' He looked at her with interest and she grinned.

'Yeah. And you know something, I bet I could still ride, and I'll bet you could too. I saw this article once in a magazine that showed people like us riding horses. I think they had special saddles, but they did it.'

'Did they have special horses?' He looked enchanted at the idea and Sam smiled and shook her head.

'I don't think so. Just nice ones.'

'Did a nice horse make you fall off?' He stared at her legs and then her face.

'No. He wasn't a nice horse. But I was pretty silly to ride him. He was a real mean horse, and I did a lot of stupid things when I was riding him.'

'Like what?'

'Gallop all over the place and take a lot of chances.' It was the first time she had been that honest with herself. It was also the first time she had talked about the accident, and she was surprised by how little it hurt. 'Do you like horses, Alex?'

'I sure do. I went to the rodeo once.'

'Did you? I used to work on a ranch.'

'No, you didn't.' He looked disgusted. 'Girls don't work on ranches.'

'Yes they do. I did.'

'Did you like it?' He still looked doubtful.

'I loved it.'

'Then why did you stop?'

'Because I came back to New York.'

'How come?'

'I missed my friends.'

'Oh. You got kids?'

'Nope.' She felt a small twinge as she said it, thinking longingly of little baby Sam. 'Do you have any kids, Alex?' She grinned at him and he guffawed.

'Of course not. You're silly. Is your name really Sam?'

'Yup. It's really Samantha. My friends call me Sam.'

'Mine is Alexander. But only my mum calls me that.'

'Want to go for a ride?' She was feeling restless and he was as good a companion as any.

'Now?'

'Sure. Why not? You expecting a visitor?'

'No.' He looked momentarily sad again. 'They just went home. I was watching them leave from the window.'

'Okay, then why don't you and I take a little tour?' She grinned mischievously at him, gave him a push to start him, and told the nurse at the desk that she was taking Alex for a ride, and the entire nurses' station waved good-bye as they headed for the elevators and from there to the gift shop on the main floor. Sam bought him a lollipop and two candy bars, and some magazines for herself. Then they decided to buy some bubble gum too and they came back to their floor, blowing bubbles and playing guessing games.

'Wanna come see my room?'

'Sure.' He had a tiny Christmas tree covered with little Snoopy decorations, and the walls were pasted with pictures and cards from his friends at school.

'I'm gonna go back too. My doctor says I don't have to go to a special school. If I do my therapy, I can be just like everyone else, almost.'

'That's what my doctor says too.'

'Do you go to school?' He looked intrigued, and she laughed.

'No. I work.'

'What do you do?'

'I work at an advertising agency, we make commercials.'

'You mean like to sell kids junk on TV? My mum says that the people who write them are ireessperonss . . . susperonsible, or something like that.'

'Irresponsible. Actually I write commercials to sell junk to grown-ups mostly, like cars, or pianos, or lipstick, or stuff to make you smell good.'

'Yuck.'

'Yeah, well . . . maybe one day I'll go back to working on a ranch.' He nodded wisely. It sounded sensible to him.

'You married, Sam?'

'Nope.'

'How come?'

'No one wants me, I guess.' She was teasing but he nodded seriously. 'You married, Alex?'

'No.' He grinned. 'But I've got two girl friends.'

'Two . . . ?' And the conversation went on for hours. They shared dinner that night and Sam came back to kiss him good night and tell him a story, and when she went back to her room, she smiled peacefully to herself and attacked a stack of work.

29

Alex left the hospital in April. He went home with his mum and dad, and then back to school. He sent Sam a letter every week, telling her that he was just like the other kids again, he even went to a special baseball game every Sunday with his dad, and a bunch of other kids in wheelchairs. He dictated the letters to his mother and Sam saved them all in a special file. She sent him letters too, and bubble gum, and pictures of horses, and anything she found in the gift shop that looked like something he'd like. Their connection somehow made Sam feel stronger. More like pushing on. But the testing time for Sam came at the end of the month, when her doctor brought up the question of going home.

'Well, what do you think? Think you're ready?' She panicked at the thought and shook her head.

'Not yet.'

'Why not?'

'I don't know . . . I'm not sure I can manage . . . I'm not . . . my arms aren't strong enough . . .' Suddenly she had a thousand excuses, but that the doctor knew was normal. She felt safe in her cocoon, and she no longer wanted to leave. Doctor Nolan knew that when the time came they would have to push her gently, and she would resist them every inch of the way.

Indeed she had a comfortable routine all worked out for herself. Three hours of P.T. every morning, three hours of paperwork from her office every afternoon. The ads, which had won her seven new awards, and among them the much coveted Clio, had long since aired, and she was adding to the campaign with new concepts. Henry Johns-Adams and his friend and Charlie were about to head west to shoot two more ads.

One night Sam called Caroline to try one more time to use the ranch—thinking it would take Caroline's mind off Bill— but she was in for a terrible shock. Caroline picked up the phone, and when she heard Sam's voice, she broke down and sobbed deep racking sobs from the depths of her soul. 'Oh, Sam . . . my God . . . he's gone . . . he's gone.' Sam didn't know what to say—indeed what could she say—she simply kept in touch and tried to cheer her up. Now, a few months later, Caroline was still absolutely lost without him, and it killed Sam to hear her so bereft and so broken, her spirit bent, her soul torn, without the man she had loved for so long. It was Sam now who gave her the strength to continue, who encouraged her.

'But I have no one left, Sam. I have no reason to go on. All of my family is gone . . . and now Bill . . .'

'You still have the ranch, and me, and there are so many people who care about you.'

'I don't know, Sam.' She sounded so tired. 'I feel like my life is over. I don't even want to ride with the men anymore. I just let the new foreman handle everything for me. It doesn't mean anything without Bill, and'—Sam could hear the tears in her voice—'it all makes me so sad.' She had had him buried on the ranch, and there had been a memorial service. He had had his way to the end. He had died as the foreman of the Lord Ranch, and not her husband, though it didn't really matter anymore. Whether people had guessed or not, they had respected both of them, and his loss was felt by many who sympathised with Caro for losing a good friend, even if they didn't know he'd been her man.

There was of course still no news of Tate Jordan. Sam didn't even ask anymore. She knew that Caro would have told her. All of those people she had contacted, all of those ranches she had driven to, and all of the ranch hands and ranchers she had talked to on her trips, and none of them had seen him, no one knew him. She wondered where he had gone, and if he was happy, if he remembered as she did. Now there was really no point in finding him. She had nothing left to give him. Now she wouldn't have let him stay with her. It would have been Sam who would have run away. But she didn't have to. He had already been gone for a year.

It was spring when they finally pushed her gently from the nest, despite her mother's protests. Her doctor released her from the hospital on the first of May, on a splendid warm sunny day, and she went to see her apartment for the first time. She had had to rely once more on Charlie and Mellie, she had had to call movers and have everything packed up in her old place. With the stairs in her old apartment, she knew that there was no way she could manage entirely alone, and miraculously an apartment had turned up in Melinda and Charlie's building. It was a ground-floor apartment with a small sunny garden, and it was going to be perfect for Samantha because it had no stairs, an easy access, and a doorman. It was just exactly what the doctor ordered, and Samantha had instructed the movers to put the furniture as per the diagram she had drawn up for them and just to leave the crates of her belongings for her to unpack herself. It was going to be her first challenge after she left the hospital, and it was a big one.

She huffed and she puffed and she attacked the boxes and she sweated, and once she even fell out of her chair trying to hang a small painting on the wall. But she got up, she hung it up, she unpacked the crates, she made her bed, she washed her hair, she did all the things they had taught her. She felt so victorious by Monday morning that when she showed up at the office in a black skirt and a black turtleneck sweater, with fashionable black suede boots and a red bow in her hair, she looked younger and healthier than she had all that terrible year. When her mother called at noon to lament her daughter's fate, Sam was busy at a meeting. After that she went to lunch at Lutèce with Charlie and Harvey to celebrate her return, and by the end of the week she had seen her first client, and she had handled it with grace as well as ease. It intrigued her to see that men still looked at her like she was attractive, and even her terror that it was pity that motivated the looks couldn't dim the pleasure of knowing that even if she wasn't a functioning woman her femininity still existed. The question of dating was one she had refused to discuss with the psychiatrist at the hospital. She considered that a closed door, and for the time being they had left it alone and worked on the rest. She had made such progress in every other area that they figured sooner or later she would come around. She was after all only thirty-one, and incredibly pretty. It was unlikely that a woman like Sam Taylor would spend the rest of her life alone, no matter what she said now.

'Well.' Harvey, wearing one of his rare smiles, lifted a glass of champagne. 'I propose a toast to Samantha. May you live another hundred years, without taking a single day off from CHL. Thank you.' He bowed and the three of them chuckled, and then Sam toasted them. By the end of the lunch they were half drunk and Sam was making bad jokes about not being able to drive her chair. She ran into two pedestrians on the way back to the office, and Charlie took over and pushed her, ploughing her cheerfully into a policeman, who was almost brought to his knees.

'Charlie, for chrissake! Watch where you're going!'

'I was . . . I think he's drunk. Disgusting too, an officer on duty!'

The three of them laughed like kids, and had trouble sobering up when they got back to the office. Eventually they all gave up and left early. It had been a very big day.

That Saturday Sam took her little friend Alex to lunch, the two of them sunning in their chairs. They had hot dogs and French fries and she took him to a movie. They sat side by side in the aisle at Radio City, and his eyes were huge as he watched the show. When she took him home at the end of the day, she felt a little tug at her heart to give him back to his mother, and she took refuge at Mellie's apartment on the way home, where she played with the baby. Suddenly, as Sam rolled her wheelchair carefully and slowly across the room, little Sam stood up, and on tiptoe, with arms flailing, little Sam followed her, as 'Big

Sam,' as they called her in the baby's presence, sat in her wheelchair and gaped. And then, as the child fell cooing to the rug, Sam shouted for Mellie, who arrived just in time to see the baby do the same stunt again, and she was only ten months old.

'She's walking!' Mellie shouted to no one in particular, 'She's walking . . . Charlie! Sam's walking . . .' He arrived in the doorway with an expression of shock, not having understood that it was the baby, and then Sam looked at him in astonishment with tears rolling down her face, and then she smiled and held out her arms to the laughing baby.

'Oh, yes, she is!'

30

Crane, Harper, and Laub won a Clio again that year for another of Sam's commercials, and by year's end, she had brought in two more major accounts. Her mother's premonitions of doom had not come to pass. Instead she was working harder than ever, managing her apartment with ease, seeing a few friends, and having occasional Saturday-afternoon movie dates with now seven-year-old Alex. On the whole Sam was happy with her life. She was glad she had lived—glad she had survived. Still, she wasn't entirely sure where it was all going. Harvey was still the creative director and still threatening to retire but Sam never believed him until the first of November, when he called her into his office and pointed absentmindedly to a chair.

'Sit down, Sam.'

'Thank you, Harvey, I am.' She grinned at him with amusement and he looked momentarily flustered and then laughed.

'Don't make me nervous, dammit, Sam, I have something to tell you . . . no, ask you . . .'

'You want to propose after all these years?' It was a standing joke between them. He had been happily married for the last thirty-two years.

'No, dammit, I'm not kidding around today. Sam'—he stared at her almost fiercely—'I'm going to do it. I'm going to retire on the first of the year.'

'When did that hit you, Harvey? This morning?' She was still smiling. She never took his retirement threats seriously anymore, and she was perfectly happy with her job the way it was. Her salary had escalated satisfactorily over the years, and CHL had given her so much in terms of kindness and understanding during her various problems and illness that she felt an unseverable loyalty to them anyway. She didn't need Harvey's job. 'Why don't you just relax and take a nice vacation with Maggie this Christmas, someplace warm, like the Caribbean. And then come back like a big kid, roll up your sleeves, and get back to work.'

'I don't want to.' He suddenly sounded like a belligerent child. 'You know what, Sam? I'm fifty-nine years old, and all of a sudden I wonder what I'm doing. Who gives a damn about commercials? Who remembers anything we do by next year? And I'm missing the last of my best years with Maggie, sitting at this desk, working my ass off. I don't want to do that anymore. I want to go home, Sam, before it's too late. Before I miss my chance, before she gets sick, or I do, or one of us dies. I never thought that way before, but I'll be sixty years old next Tuesday and I just figured, screw it. I'm going to retire now, and you can't talk me out of it, because I won't let you. So what I called you in here to ask you was, do you want my job, Sam, because if you do, you can have it. In fact my asking you is only a formality, because whether you want it or not, it's yours.'

She sat there, awed, for a moment, not sure what she should say. 'Harvey, that was quite a speech.'

'I meant every bit of it.'

'Well, in a funny way I think you're right.' She had

234

spent months thinking about Bill King and Aunt Caro, and she wondered if they had enjoyed every moment they could, right until the end. They had been so busy hiding what they were doing for so many years that they had missed a lot of times together that they might otherwise have shared. To Sam, it seemed like a hell of a waste of energy they could have better spent together, but it was all in the past now. What concerned her more was Caro, who had been in such awful shape in the eight months since he had died. She had been in what Sam considered a deep depression for several months, and she wanted to go out and see her, but the one thing she hadn't tackled yet was travelling. She was comfortable on home turf now and knew she could manage, but leaving home to go any great distance still scared her. She hadn't been to Atlanta either, and knew she probably never would. But a visit to Aunt Caro would have been different. She just hadn't taken matters in hand and got organised to go. She was thinking vaguely about Christmas, but that wasn't sure. She had funny feelings about going back there at Christmastime and facing all her memories of Tate.

'Well, Sam, do you want to be C.D.?' It was a direct question that required a direct answer, and Sam looked at him with a small hesitant smile.

'You know, the funny thing is that I don't know. I like working for you, Harvey, and I used to think that being creative director was the end of the rainbow. But the truth is, in the last year or two my life has changed so much, so have my values, and I'm not sure I want everything that goes with it: the sleepless nights, the headaches, the ulcers, especially now. The other thing I'm concerned with is that the C.D. should really travel, and I'm just not comfortable doing that yet. I don't feel safe about it, that's why I haven't flown out to see my friend in California. I don't know, Harvey, maybe I'm not the right person anymore for the job. What about Charlie?'

'He's the art director, Sam. You know yourself how unusual it is for an art director to become C.D. It's a separate issue.'

'Maybe. But he could do it and he'd be good.'

'So would you. Will you think about it?'

'Of course I will. You're really serious though this time, aren't you?' She was as surprised by his decision as by her own hesitation to accept. But she wasn't sure anymore if that was what she wanted, and however well she was managing life from her wheelchair, she just wasn't sure if she had enough mobility for the job. 'How soon do you want to know?'

'In a couple of weeks.' She nodded and they chatted for a few moments before she left his office, and when she did, she had every intention of giving Harvey an answer at the end of two weeks time. But ten days later, life threw her a curveball, and she felt as though the sky had fallen in on her. She had felt like that fairly often in the last two years.

She sat in her office with the letter she had just got from Caroline's lawyer, and with tears running slowly down her face, she wheeled across the hall to Charlie's office and stopped in the doorway with a look of shock on her face.

'Something wrong?' He stopped what he was doing and came instantly toward her. It was a stupid question. She was white-faced and she nodded and continued into the room, holding out the letter, which he took and read, and then he stared at her with the same look of amazement on his face. 'Did you know?'

She was crying softly now as she shook her head and then answered. 'I never even thought of it . . . but I guess there's no one else.' And then suddenly she flung out her arms to him, and he held her. 'Oh, Charlie, she's gone. What am I going to do?'

'It's all right, Sam. It's all right.' But he was as stunned as Samantha. Caroline Lord had died the previous weekend. For an instant Sam was hurt that no one had called her—where was Josh, why hadn't he let her know? But the moment passed. They were drifters, it wouldn't have occurred to them to call her in New York.

In accordance with Caroline's will, the ranch had been left to Sam. She had died in her sleep, without pain or problem. And Charlie suspected, as Sam did, that she just willed it to happen. She hadn't wanted to live without Bill King.

Samantha wheeled slowly away from Charlie then and went to stare out of the window. 'Why would she leave me the ranch, Charlie? What the hell am I going to do with it? I can't do anything with it now.' Her voice trailed off as she thought of the happy times she had spent there, with her friend Barbara, with Caroline and Bill, and with Tate. She thought of the secret cabin, of Black Beauty, of Josh, and the tears only flowed more swiftly down her face.

'What do you mean you can't do anything with it?' Charlie's voice questioned her, as did his eyes when she turned to face him again.

'Because however much I may not like to admit it, however much I may try to pretend I'm normal with my job and my friends and my living alone and my taking cabs, the fact is, Charlie, as my dear mother says, I'm a cripple. What the hell would I do with a ranch? Watch them ride the horses? A ranch is for healthy people, Charlie.'

'You're as healthy as you allow yourself to be. The horse has four legs, Sam. You don't need any. Let him do the walking. It has a lot more style than your chair.'

'You're not funny.' She sounded angry as she said it, and she spun around and left the room.

But five minutes later he had followed her to her office, and he wanted to discuss it, no matter how angry she got, how loud she screamed.

'Leave me alone, dammit! A woman I loved a great deal just died and you want to bug me about how I should go out there and ride horses. Leave me alone!' She screamed the words at him but it didn't convince him.

'No, as a matter of fact I won't. Because I think the truth is that although it's damn sad that she died, she just gave you the gift of a lifetime, not because of what the place must be worth, but because that is a dream you could live with for the rest of your life, Sam. I've watched you here since you came back, and you're as good at it as you always were, but the truth of it is, I don't think you care anymore. I don't think you want to be here. I think that ever since you fell in love with that cowboy and worked on the ranch, all you want is that, Sam. You don't want to be back here. And now your friend has given it to you, all of it, lock, stock, and barrel, and suddenly you want to play cripple. Well, guess what, I think you're a coward, and I don't think you should be allowed to play that game.'

'And how do you plan to stop me from "playing cripple," as you put it?'

'Kick some sense into you, if I have to. Take you out there, rub your nose in it, remind you how much you love it all. Personally I think you're crazy and anything west of Poughkeepsie might as well be East Africa to me, but you, you're nuts about all that stuff. Christ, on that shoot last year, your eyes sparkled like light bulbs every time you saw a horse or a cow or talked to a foreman. It drove me nuts and you loved it, and now you're going to give all that away? What about doing something with it? What about bringing to life one of your dreams? You've talked so often to little Alex about that special riding class you'd read about once. The last time he came up here to pick you up for lunch, he told me you had said he could go riding one day, and maybe you'd take him—what about turning her ranch into a place for people like you and Alex, what about doing something like that?' Sam stared at her friend in amazement as the tears stopped rolling down her cheeks.

'But I couldn't do that, Charlie . . . how would I start it, how could I? I don't know anything about all that.'

'You could learn. You know about horses. You know something about being in a wheelchair. You'll have plenty of people to help you run the ranch, all you have to do is coordinate it, like a giant commercial, and hell, you're good at that.'

'Charlie, you're crazy.'

'Maybe.' He looked at her with a grin. 'But tell the truth, Sam, wouldn't you enjoy being a little crazy too?'

'Maybe,' she answered honestly. She was still staring at

him with a look of amazement. 'What do I do now?'

'Why don't you go out there and look around again, Sam. Hell, you own it.'

'Now?'

'Whenever you have time.'

'By myself?'

'If you want.'

'I don't know.' She turned away again and sat staring into space, thinking of the ranch and Aunt Caro. It would be so painful to see it again without her this time. It would be filled with memories of people she had cared about who were no longer there. 'I don't want to go out there alone, Charlie. I don't think I could handle it.'

'Then take someone with you.' He sounded matter-of-fact.

'Who do you suggest?' She looked at him sceptically. 'My mother?'

'God forbid. Hell, I don't know, Sam, take Mellie.'

'What about the kids?'

'Take all of us, then. Or never mind "taking us," we'll take ourselves. The kids would love it, so would we, and I'll tell you what I think once we get there.'

'Are you serious, Charlie?'

'Totally. I think this will be the most important decision you've ever made, and I'd hate to see you screw it up.'

'So would I.' She looked at him sombrely and suddenly thought about something. 'What about Thanksgiving?'

'What about it?'

'It's in three weeks, what if we all go out then?'

He thought for a minute and then grinned at her. 'You've got a deal. I'll call Mellie.'

'Think she'll want to go?'

'Hell yes. And if she doesn't'—he grinned— 'I'll go alone.' But Mellie offered no objection when he called her, and neither did the boys when they told them, and they didn't tell anyone else. They just quietly made reservations for a four-day trip over Thanksgiving. Samantha didn't even tell Harvey. She was afraid to upset him, and she still hadn't given him an answer about the job.

239

31

Samantha grew strangely quiet as they drove the last miles through the rolling hills on the familiar strip of highway. But the others didn't notice. The boys were so excited, that they were jumping up and down in the rented car. Mellie had left the baby with her mother, and the trip had gone smoothly so far. It was obviously an unorthodox Thanksgiving, the grown-ups at least thought it would be worth it. They had eaten a dry little slice of turkey and some dressing on the airline, and Mellie had promised to put together a real turkey dinner the next day on the ranch.

Samantha had spoken to Josh again only that morning. The boys were going to sleep in sleeping bags in one of the two guestrooms, and Charlie and Melinda were going to sleep in Aunt Caro's room. Sam would sleep in the room she had last had. The house was large enough to accommodate all of them, and Josh had assured her that there were groceries and that if she liked he would pick them all up at the plane in L.A. But Sam had insisted that she didn't want to spoil his Thanksgiving, she would see him when they got to the ranch. He had told her then, in his pained, halting way, how glad he was that she owned the ranch now and that he would do whatever he could to help her. He just hoped she wouldn't do something foolish like sell it, because he thought she could turn out to be one of the best damn ranchers around. She had smiled wistfully as he said it, wished him a happy Thanksgiving, and hurried to meet Mellie and Charlie and the boys in the lobby. They had had to take two cabs to the airport, and now they were crowded into a huge station wagon and the boys were singing songs.

But all Samantha could think of as they approached the

ranch was how it had been the last time she had seen it, with Caroline and Bill King strong and healthy. Then she thought back once again to her days there with Tate. It all seemed like a dream now, it was so distant, the moments of joy she had shared with him, the hours at the cabin, the rides that they took on his pinto and Caro's handsome Thoroughbred stallion. She had been able to walk then. She felt a black cloud descend on her slowly as they turned the last bend in the road and she realised once again how much everything had changed.

'There it is.' She said it softly from the backseat, pointing a shaking finger. They passed through the main gate, drove up the winding road, and then she saw it; Aunt Caro's house. But there were no lights on, and although it was only five o'clock in the afternoon, it looked bleak and lonely and sad in the failing light. 'Josh said he'd leave the door open. If you want to go inside, Charlie, the living room lights are all on a panel on the right just behind the door.' Sam just sat there with her eyes riveted to the house. She kept expecting to see the lights come on, to see the familiar white hair, to see Aunt Caro's smiling face and a wave of the hand. But as Charlie went in to turn the lights on and then walked quickly back to the car, there was no one beside him, and even the boys grew quiet as they looked around the ranch.

'Where are the horses, Sam?'

'In the barn, love. I'll show you tomorrow.'

'Can't we see them now?'

She smiled at Charlie over their heads and then nodded. 'Okay, let's get our stuff inside, and then I'll take you all over.' But now that she was here, she didn't want to go into the house, or the barn, she didn't want to see Black Beauty standing in his stall, or Navajo, or the other familiar horses. All she wanted was to see Caroline and Bill King and Tate Jordan, and live a life that she never would see again. There was a lump in her throat the size of an apple as she got herself into her wheelchair and let Charlie back her up the stairs. She rolled herself slowly into the house then and looked around. Then, ever so slowly, she began to roll toward her own room down the hall. A minute later the boys scampered past her, and she forced a smile as she showed them their room, and then she returned to the living room to find Charlie and Melinda. She pointed in the opposite direction, to their room, but she didn't want to see it. She didn't want to see the empty bedroom that had been Caro and Bill's.

'You all right?' Melinda looked at her gently and she nodded.

'I'm okay. Honest.'

'You look tired.'

She wasn't though, she was just desperately unhappy. 'I'm fine.' She was remembering once again with all too painful precision just how she had felt when she had left the ranch, not knowing where Tate was, or if she would ever find him, but still hopeful. And now she knew for certain that she would never see him again. Not only that but she had lost Caro . . . The thought of it weighed on her like wet cement. And then as she sat gazing out of the window at the dim hills in the twilight, she saw a bandy-legged little figure coming toward her, like an elf or a little wood sprite, and suddenly with damp eyes she was beaming. It was Josh. He had seen the lights in the house and he had hurried to see her. With a broad smile she pushed her way out the door and waited for him in her wheelchair on the porch. But as she did she saw him stop dead where he was standing, and she could see the look of shock on his face and hear the words. 'Oh, my God . . .' And then suddenly, without knowing when she had started, she was crying, and so was he, and he was halfway up the stairs and she was reaching down, and he bent over her and held her, as together they cried, for Bill and for Caro and for Tate, and for Sam as well. For what seemed like hours there was only the muffled sound of their crying, and then after a time the wizened old cowboy sniffed loudly and stood up.

'Why didn't nobody never tell me, Sam?'

'I thought Miss Caro . . .' He shook his head with a look of despair.

'How did it happen?'

She closed her eyes for a moment and then opened them. It was as though she too had shared in his shock. As though suddenly she saw herself as he saw her, crippled, in a wheelchair, no more the proud young palomino who had run all over the ranch. It was as though her life were over, as though she had suddenly grown old. And at that moment she knew she couldn't keep the ranch now. There was no way she could run it. All the men would react the same way to her as Josh had. She was a cripple now—no matter what they had told her at the hospital in New York.

'Sam . . .'

'It's okay, Josh.' She smiled gently at him and took a deep breath. 'It happened in Colorado, about fifteen months ago. It was something stupid I did with a horse.' The memory was blurred now, but she would always remember the grey stallion . . . Grey Devil . . . and the endless moment when she had flown through the air. 'I took a chance with a wild stallion. He was a real bitch to ride and he threw me into a ravine.'

'Why—why did you do it?' His eyes filled again as he watched her. He knew instinctively that she had pushed the horse too hard, and she didn't deny it.

'I don't know.' She sighed again. 'I was crazy, I guess. I think Black Beauty made me think I could handle any stallion I ever came up against and I was upset about something.' She had been depressed about Tate, but she didn't tell him that. 'So, that's what happened.'

'Will you . . . can they . . . ?' He didn't know how to finish, but she easily understood him and shook her head.

'No. This is it. I thought you knew though. I figured Caroline would have told you.'

'She never did.'

'Maybe she was too wrapped up with Bill. He had just had his first heart attack around that time. I wanted to come out but I was too busy with work, and then—' She faltered but went on. 'I was stuck in the hospital for ten months.' She looked around her at the familiar buildings.

243

'I should have come back though afterwards, but I don't know . . . I think I was afraid to. Afraid to face what I couldn't do anymore, so I never saw her again, Josh'—her lip tembled—'and she was so damn sad after Bill died, and I never helped her.' She closed her eyes and held out her arms and she clung to the old cowboy again.

'She was all right, Sam. And she went like she wanted to. She didn't want to hang around without him.' Did he know, then? Had they all known? Had the pretence been a farce for all those years? Sam looked into his face and saw that it was no secret. 'They were as good as married, Sam.'

She nodded. 'I know. They should have got married.'

He only shrugged. 'You can't change old ways.' And then he looked down at her again, his eyes filled with questions. 'What about you?' He understood suddenly how unlikely it was that she'd keep the ranch now. 'You going to sell this place now?'

'I don't know.' She looked troubled as they lingered on the porch. 'I don't see how I could run it. I think maybe I belong in New York.'

'You live with your folks now?' He seemed interested in how she managed but she shook her head with a small smile.

'Hell no. I live alone. I live in the same building as the friends who brought me out here. I had to get a new apartment, one without steps. But I can take care of myself.'

'That's terrific, Sam.' There was only a faint hint that he was talking to a cripple, but she knew he'd still have to make the adjustment. In some ways she still did too, so she didn't hold it against him. And then what he had said next shocked her. 'Why couldn't you do that out here? Hell, we'd all help you. And shit, there's no reason why you can't ride. As long as you ride careful now.' He almost glared at her as he said it, and then he smiled.

'I don't know, Josh. I've been thinking about it, but it's all pretty scary. That was why I came out here. I didn't want to make the decision to sell till I came out here again to see for myself.'

'I'm glad you did. And you know'—he narrowed his eyes and stroked his chin, staring at the darkening horizon—'I think we got an old saddle in there I can fix up for you just fine. And I'll tell you one thing.' He turned back to glare at her. 'You ain't riding Black Beauty, if I have to kick your ass to keep you off him!'

'Try and stop me!' She was laughing now, it was almost like the old days, but he wasn't kidding around.

'It'll be my pleasure. I'd like to know who was the fool who let you ride that other stallion.'

'Someone who saw me ride.'

'Damn show-off.' It was the kind of thing Tate would have said and her eyes grew serious again as she looked at Josh.

'Josh?'

'Yeah?'

'Did you ever hear any more about Tate Jordan?' It had been more than a year and a half since he left, but Josh just shook his head.

'Nope. Just another cowboy. Drifted off God knows where. He would have made you a good foreman though, Sam.' Not to mention a good husband, but Sam didn't say what was in her heart.

'How's the new man?'

'All right. But he's leaving. He's already had an offer. He told the lawyer that yesterday morning. He don't want to take no chances that you might sell the ranch and he might lose his job, so he's movin' on while he can. He's got a bunch of kids,' Josh said by way of explanation and Sam watched him thoughtfully.

'What about you, Josh? You staying?'

'Hell yes. This has been my home for too many years for me to go anywhere. You're going to have to sell me with the ranch.'

'Tell you what, if I don't, how would you like to be foreman?'

'You kidding, Sam?' His eyes lit up with interest. 'I'd sure as hell like that, and my wife would be so full of herself she'd make us all sick. But I could live with that.'

They grinned at each other and he stuck out a rough hand, which she shook.

'Sam?' Charlie peeked out the screen door then, he had heard her talking and wondered who it was. She wheeled quickly in her wheelchair, made the introductions, and they talked for a few minutes about the ranch.

And then finally Josh looked down at her again. He had forgotten her for a minute in the conversation that went on above her head. 'How long you staying, Sam?'

'Just till Sunday. We have to get back. Charlie and I work together in New York. He's an artist.'

'I am not, I'm a genius.' They all grinned.

'Can you ride?' He shook his head and Josh smiled broadly. 'We'll teach you. And Sam says you've brought your kids.'

'Three of them. My sons.'

'How many you got in all?' Josh raised an eyebrow.

'Four. We left a baby girl at home.'

'Shit,' he guffawed, 'that ain't nothin'. I got six.'

'God save me!' Charlie looked faint and they all laughed.

Josh came in then to meet Mellie and the boys, and then they all trooped out to the barn to look at the horses, and the boys were so excited that they were jumping up and down in the straw and squealing while the others laughed. Plans were made for the next day to give them lessons, and then Sam stopped for a few moments to look at Black Beauty, sedate and splendid as ever in his stall.

'He's a fine looking horse, Sam, ain't he?' Even Josh looked him over with pride, and then he glanced at Sam as though he had just remembered something. 'He's yours now, Sam.'

'No.' Sam shook her head slowly, looking at Josh. 'He'll always be Caro's. But I'll ride him.' This time she smiled, but he didn't.

'No, you won't.'

'We can fight about that in the morning.' He looked doubtful but they wandered back to the big house, and he left them on the porch, with a last tender look at Sam. It was then that she realised that it had been a homecoming. That even if the others were gone now, she still had Josh. And she had the beautiful ranch that Caroline had left her, and the memories of what her old friend had shared with Bill, and her own memories of Tate in their cabin— none of that would ever leave her, especially if she stayed right here.

32

'Okay now, Sam . . . we got you . . .' Two cowboys made a seat for her and held her while two more held the horse firmly. It wasn't Black Beauty they held between them, and not even Navajo, but a new horse named Pretty Girl. But this time the name didn't annoy her. She was surprised herself at how squeamish she felt and the horse was supposed to be very docile. Suddenly she was glad. They hoisted her into the saddle quickly, and Josh tied a bunch of straps around her, and then she sat there, perched in her saddle, staring down at them in amazement.

'By God, we did it. Look at that, I'm riding!' She looked like an ecstatic kid.

'No, you ain't.' Josh grinned at her with obvious pleasure. 'You're just sittin'. Get her movin' a little, Sam, and see how it feels.'

She looked down at him and whispered. 'Would you believe it, I'm scared.' She just sat there with a frightened expression alternating with a nervous smile, and after a moment Josh gently took the bridle and began to walk her on the quiet horse.

'You're okay, Sam. Come on, I'll walk you around the corral.'

'Josh, I feel like a baby.'

He looked over his shoulder with a tender smile. 'You are. Got to learn to walk, you know, before you can trot.' But a moment later he let go of the bridle and she began to trot slowly, and suddenly Sam's face broke out in a huge grin.

'Hey, guys, I'm running,' she was shouting, 'I'm running . . . look!' She was so excited, she could hardly stand it. For the first time in over a year, she wasn't moving along in a wheelchair, she was actually running again, and even if it wasn't under her own steam, the exhilaration of trotting along with the wind in her hair was the best feeling she'd known in years. It took Josh an hour to convince her that she'd had enough. And when they helped her down, she was so high, she was almost flying, her eyes were dancing, and her delicate face was framed by wisps of her golden hair.

'You sure looked good on that horse, Sam.' He smiled gently at her as they set her down in her chair.

She grinned a grin of confession. 'You know, at first I was scared to death.'

'Stands to reason. You'd have to be crazy not to be after what happened.' And then he looked at her thoughtfully. 'How did it feel?'

'So good, Josh.' She just closed her eyes and grinned. 'Like I was a normal person again.' The grin faded as she looked into his wise old eyes. 'It's been a long time.'

'Yeah.' He scratched his chin. 'But I keep thinkin', it don't have to be a long time anymore. Sam, you could come back here, and you could get back into ranchin' . . .' He had thought about it all night, but now she looked at him pensively, her head cocked to one side.

'You want to know what I've been thinking?' He nodded. 'Charlie and I talked about it in New York, and maybe it's totally crazy. But I wonder if, maybe, I could turn this into a special ranch, for'—she hesitated, not sure how to say it—'people like me. Kids mostly, but some grown-ups. Teach them to ride, help them get back to a normal life. Josh, I can't even begin to tell you what it just felt like. Here, in the chair, I'm different and I always will be. But up on that horse, I'm no different than I used to be. Oh, maybe a little, but I won't be once I get used to riding again. Imagine showing people that, giving them horses to ride, teaching them . . .' She didn't notice but there were tears in his eyes and her own as she spoke. He was nodding slowly, glancing around at the buildings.

'We'd have to make some changes, but we could do it . . .'

'Would you help me?'

He nodded slowly. 'I don't know much about . . . about . . .' He tried to be tactful, he had been about to say cripples. 'About people like that, but hell, I know horses, and I could teach a blind man to ride if I had to. Had my kids ridin' by the time they was three.' She knew it was true too, and he had just been as patient and as loving as any therapist she had worked with. 'You know, Sam, we could do it. Hell, I'd sure like to try it.'

'So would I. But I have to think it over. It would take some money, and I'd have to have therapists and nurses and doctors, people would have to be willing to trust me with their children, and why should they?' But she was talking more to herself than to Josh, and a moment later Charlie and Mellie interrupted them to ask Josh more questions about the ranch.

Sunday morning came too quickly, and they all looked regretful as they said good-bye. Josh was almost heart-broken as he took Sam's hand before they left for the airport and squeezed it with a thousand questions written on his face. 'Well? You goin' to keep it?' If not, he knew that he might never see her again. And he couldn't let that happen. He wanted to help her to find herself, and to build the ranch for special kids. He had sensed in the past few days how lonely and hurt she was.

'I don't know yet, Josh.' She answered him honestly. 'I have to do some research, and to think it over. I promise I'll let you know as soon as I make up my mind.'

'How soon do you think that will be?'

'Has another job come up for you?' She looked worried.

'If I said yes,' he said, grinning softly, 'would that make you jealous enough to keep it?'

She laughed in answer. 'You're a sly one.'

His face sobered. 'I just don't want to see you give up this ranch.'

'I don't want to either, Josh. But I just don't know enough about ranching to make it worth it. The only thing that makes sense is if we do what we said.'

'Well, why don't we?'

'Give me a chance to think it over.'

'You do that.' And then he leaned down and gave her a bear hug and turned to say good-bye to Charlie and Melinda and the three boys.

They waved good-bye to him for as long as they could see him, and in comparison to the trip out, it was a very quiet trip back. The boys were exhausted and disappointed that they were going back to New York. Charlie and Mellie alternated sleeping on part of the trip, and Sam was pensive all the way to New York. She had a lot to think about, about whether she herself could make it, about whether selling the livestock on the ranch would give her enough money to make the improvements, about whether or not it was what she wanted. Was she really ready to leave the safety of her life in New York? She had been so engrossed in the makings of her decision that all the way home she had barely thought of Tate.

She left Charlie and Mellie in the lobby of their building and disappeared into her apartment to make some notes, and she still looked preoccupied the next morning at the office when Charlie knocked on her door.

'Well, cowgirl, make up your mind yet?'

'Shhh!' She put a finger to her lips and beckoned him in. No one else knew in the office and she particularly didn't want Harvey to know yet. Not until she was sure.

'What are you going to do, Sam?' He threw himself down on the couch and grinned at her. 'Want to know what I would do if I were you?'

'No.' She tried to look forbidding, but he always made

her laugh. 'I want to make up my own mind.'

'That's smart. Just don't make any mistakes and tell your mother what you're considering. She'd probably have you locked up in the nut house.'

'Maybe she'd be right.'

'Hardly. Or at least not for those reasons.' He smiled at Sam and sat up just as Harvey's secretary appeared in the doorway.

'Miss Taylor?'

'Yes?' Sam turned to face her.

'Mr. Maxwell would like to see you.'

'God himself?' Charlie looked impressed and went back to his office as Sam followed Harvey's secretary down the hall.

And when she reached his office, she found him looking tired and pensive. There was a mountain of papers on his desk and he only glanced at Samantha as he finished some notes. 'Hi, Sam.'

'Hi, Harvey, what's up?' It was another minute before he turned his attention to her, and he went over the amenities before getting down to the reason she had been called.

'How was Thanksgiving?'

'Very nice. Yours?'

'Fine. How did you spend it?' It was a loaded question and Sam felt suddenly nervous.

'With the Petersons.'

'That's nice. At their place or yours?'

'Mine.' But it was truthful, she reassured herself. The ranch was hers now after all.

'That's terrific, Sam.' He smiled at her. 'You're really doing amazingly well.'

'Thank you.' It was a compliment that meant a lot to her, and for a moment they exchanged smiles.

'Which brings me to why I called you into the office this morning. You haven't given me your answer.' He looked expectant and Samantha sighed and slumped back in her chair.

'I know I haven't, Harvey . . . I feel awful about that,

but I just needed time to think.'

'Is it really a choice?' He looked surprised. What choice did she have after all? 'If you're still worried about the travel, all you have to do is hire a competent assistant'—he grinned at her—'like I did, and you'll be all set. The rest you can certainly handle. Hell, Sam, you've been doing my job and your own for years now!' He was teasing but she wagged a finger at him.

'Now you admit it! I should ask you to sign a statement to that effect.'

'Not on your life. Come on, Sam, get me off the hook. Give me an answer.' He sat back and smiled at her. 'I want to go home.'

'The bitch of it is, Harvey,' she said, looking at him sadly, 'so do I.'

But it was obvious that he didn't understand her. 'But this is your home, Sam.'

She shook her head slowly. 'No, Harvey, I just realised something this weekend. It's not.'

'You're unhappy at CHL?' He looked shocked. That possibility hadn't even occurred to him. Did she mean that she wanted to quit?

But she quickly shook her head. 'No, I'm not unhappy. Not here . . . but . . . well . . . I don't know if I can explain it, but it has to do with New York.'

'Sam.' He held up a hand to stop her. 'I'm warning you, if you've come in here to tell me that you're moving to Atlanta with your mother, I will go into shock. Call my doctor now if that's what you're going to tell me.' She could only laugh in answer and shake her head again.

'No, it is most certainly not that.'

'Then what is it?'

'I've been holding out on you, Harvey.' She looked guiltily at her boss of ten years. 'My friend Caroline left me her ranch.'

'Left it to you?' He looked startled. 'Are you going to sell it?'

Samantha shook her head slowly. 'I don't think so. That's just it.'

252

'You're not going to keep it, Sam, are you? What could you possibly do with it?'

'A lot of things.' And then, as she looked at him, she knew her answer. 'It's just something I have to do. Maybe I won't be able to do it, maybe it'll be too much for me, maybe it'll be a terrible fiasco, but I just want to give it a try. I want to set it up as a place to teach handicapped kids to ride, teach them how to be independent, to cover ground in something other than a wheelchair—on a horse.' Harvey was looking thoughtfully at her. 'You think I'm crazy, don't you?'

He smiled sadly. 'No, I was wishing that you were my daughter. Because I would wish you luck, and give you all the money I have and tell you to do it. I wish I could tell you that I think you're crazy, Sam, but I don't. It's a long way from being a creative director on Madison Avenue though. Are you sure that's what you want?'

'The funny thing is that I wasn't sure. Until right now when I told you, but now I know. I am sure.' And then with a small sigh. 'What are you going to do about the job? Give it to Charlie?' He thought for a minute and nodded.

'I guess so. He'll do a good job.'

'Are you sure you want to retire, Harvey?' But she had to admit that he looked ready and that she would do the same thing in his place.

He nodded, looking at her. 'Yes, Sam, I'm sure. As sure as you are about your ranch, which is to say that I want to retire and it's always a little scary to deal with the unknown. You never know for sure that you're doing the right thing.'

'I guess not.'

'Think Charlie will want the job?'

'He'll be thrilled.'

'Then it's his. Because it has to be like that. You have to want to work fifteen hours a day, take it home on the weekends, louse up your vacations, eat, sleep, and drink commercials. I just don't want that anymore.'

'Neither do I. But Charlie does.'

'Then go tell him he has a new job, or should I?'

'Would you let me do it?' It was the last thing she would do at CHL that would mean something to her.

'Why not? You're his closest friend.' And then he looked at Sam sadly. 'How soon are you leaving us?'

'What would be reasonable?'

'Why don't I leave that up to you.'

'First of the year?' It was in five weeks. That was a reasonable notice, and Harvey seemed to think so too.

'We'll retire together then. Maggie and I may even come to visit you on the ranch. My advanced age should be sufficient handicap for us to qualify as guests.'

'Bull.' She moved her wheelchair around his desk and came over to kiss his cheek. 'You'll never be that old, Harvey, not until you're a hundred and three.'

'That happens to be next week.' He put an arm around her shoulders and kissed her. 'I'm proud of you, Sam. You're quite a girl.' And then he coughed in embarrassment, fumbled on his desk, and waved her out. 'Now go tell Charlie he has a new job.'

Without saying anything further, she left his office and rolled her way down the hall, wearing a broad smile. She stopped in the doorway of Charlie's office, which was in its usual state of chaos, and she barged in on him as he attempted to find his tennis racket under the couch. He had a date to play lunchtime, and all he could find were the balls.

'What are you looking for, slobbo? I don't know how you find anything in this mess.'

'Huh?' He emerged, but only briefly. 'Oh, it's you. I don't. You don't happen to have a spare tennis racket, do you?' Only from Charlie could she take jokes like that.

'Sure. I play twice a week. Ice skating too. And cha-cha lessons.'

'Oh, shut up. You're disgusting. What's the matter? Don't you have any decency, any taste?' He eyed her with mock outrage and she started laughing.

'Speaking of which, you'd better buy some of both, you're going to need them.'

'What?' He looked blank.

'Taste.'

'Why? I've never needed taste before.'

'You were never creative director of a large ad agency before.' He stared at her, not comprehending.

'What are you saying?' His heart pounded for a moment. But it couldn't be. Harvey was offering the job to Samantha . . . unless . . . 'Sam?'

'You heard me, Mr. Creative Director.' She beamed at him.

'Sam . . . ? Sam!' He jumped to his feet. 'Did he — am I?'

'He did. And you are.'

'But what about you?' He looked shocked. Had they passed her over for the job? If that was the case, he wouldn't take it. They would both quit, they could open up shop together, they could . . .

She could see his mind racing and held up a hand. 'Relax. The job is yours. Me, I'm going to California, Charlie, to run a ranch for handicapped children. And if you're real nice to me, maybe I'll let you and the kids come and visit me in the summers and—' He didn't let her finish. Instead he ran to her and hugged her tight. 'Oh, Sam, you did it! You did it! When did you decide?' He was as thrilled for her as he was for himself. He was almost jumping up and down like a kid.

'I don't know.' She was laughing as he held her. 'I think just now in Harvey's office . . . or last night on the plane . . . or yesterday morning when I talked to Josh . . . I don't know when it happened, Charlie. But I did it.'

'When are you going out?'

'When you get your new job. On January first.'

'My God, Sam, does he really mean it? Creative director? Me? But I'm only thirty-seven.'

'It's all right,' she reassured him. 'You look fifty.'

'Gee, thanks.' He was still beaming as he reached for the phone to call his wife.

255

33

'So? How is it going? When do you open?' Charlie called her every week, to cry on her shoulder about all the work on his desk and find out about the progress at the ranch.

'We open in two weeks, Charlie.'

'What is that? Like a bank? You give out toasters and balloons and party hats?'

She smiled into the phone. For the past five months he had done nothing but encourage, and it had been a long haul. In the course of a lifetime five months was nothing, but her working sixteen and eighteen hours a day made it seem like ten years. They had torn down small buildings, put up new sheds, altered cottages, put in ramps, built a swimming pool, sold the livestock for the most part, except for a handful of cows to give them milk and to amuse the kids. There had been therapists to hire, nurses to see, doctors to contact, and then inevitably there had been the travelling. Sam had flown to Denver to see the doctor who had first operated on her back, to Phoenix, to Los Angeles, and to San Francisco, and then finally to Dallas and Houston, and in each city she had seen the top orthopaedic men. She had hired a secretary to travel with her, which made it easier for her and made it look more businesslike. She wanted to explain her programme to the doctors, so that they would refer patients to her, children who would spend four to six weeks on the ranch, learning to enjoy life again, to ride horses, to be with other children with similar disabilities, and to be independent of their parents and able to take care of themselves.

In her presentation she showed photographs of the ranch as it had been and architectural renderings of what it was going to be. She detailed the facilities and the plans for physical therapy, and gave résumés of the staff and detailed references for herself. And everywhere she went, she got a warm reception, and the doctors were impressed. All of them referred her to other doctors, most of them invited her to their homes to meet their wives and families. And in Houston she could even have had a date, but she declined graciously, and still won the doctor over. By the time she had finished her travels, she was certain that at least forty-seven doctors in six cities were going to refer patients to her ranch.

She still called it the Lord Ranch and she had kept on a handful of the old cowboys. Josh was, as promised, made the foreman, and she had even given him a bronze plaque to put on his front door, and he had been thrilled. But what she needed was a new breed of ranch hands, and she and Josh had picked them all carefully, for their attitudes about children, about handicaps, about horses. She didn't want anyone too old, or impatient, or ornery, or willing to take risks with the children or the horses. Just hiring the men had taken them almost two months. But she had a dozen ranch hands now, two of them from the old days, and the other ten all new. Her favourite among them was a broad-shouldered, handsome, redheaded, green-eyed 'young'un,' as Josh called him, named Jeff. He was shy and closed up about his own life, but he was always willing to talk for hours about what they were going to do with the ranch. His references told her that at twenty-four he had been working on ranches since he was sixteen, and in eight years he had been on five ranches in three states. When she asked him why, he said only that he used to travel a lot with his father, but now he was on his own, and when she called the last two ranches he had worked at, they told her to do anything she had to to hang on to him, and if he didn't stay with her, send him back to them. So Jeff Pickett became assistant foreman, and Josh was pleased with his new team.

The only problem Sam had had for a while had been the money she needed, but it was amazing what could happen if you really wanted something badly enough, and she did. Caroline had left her a small sum of money which had been absorbed by the alterations on the ranch within the first few weeks. After that the sale of the cattle had been a big help, and then Josh had come up with an idea to help her. They weren't going to need a lot of the fancier pieces of ranch equipment anymore, tools and tractors and trucks to transport the cattle, so she sold those and that paid for six new cottages and the swimming pool. After that she began to look into grants and discovered a wealth of untapped resources she hadn't considered, and once she'd got three of those, she applied for a loan at the bank.

Only a month before, Harvey called her from Palm Springs, where he and Maggie were on vacation while he played golf in a tournament with some old friends, and he had asked if they could come and see her, and when they had, he had insisted that he wanted to invest fifty thousand dollars in her ranch. It was just over the final amount she needed, and it was a godsend for her, as she told him when he wrote the cheque. And now she was going to be all right until they opened, and hopefully after that, within a year or two they'd be in the black and totally self-supporting. She didn't want to get rich on what she was doing. She just wanted to make enough money to be comfortable and support the ranch.

The opening date, as she now told Charlie, was June 7, and in a few days the rest of the physical therapists would be arriving, along with some new horses. The Jacuzzis were all installed, the pool looked terrific, the cabins were cosy, and she already had reservations for thirty-six kids over the next two months.

'When can I come?'

'I don't know, love, anytime you want. Or maybe, just give me a chance to catch my breath after we get started. I think I'm going to have my hands full for a while.'

As it turned out, that was the understatement of the century. She hadn't counted on being nearly as busy as she was. She was snowed under every morning, after they opened, with mountains of paperwork, letters from doctors, requests from parents, and she spent the entire afternoon teaching children, with Josh. One of the grants had gone toward having special saddles made for the children. They had fifty now, and had already applied for another grant for another fifty saddles, which Sam suspected they would soon need. Her patience with the children proved to be endless, as she taught them in groups of two or three. And invariably each time, after the initial terror as they sat there clutching the pommel, the horse would begin to walk as Josh led them, and the feeling of freedom and movement and actually walking would so completely overwhelm the children that they would squeal with glee. Sam never got over her own feeling of excitement and jubilation as she watched them, and time and again she watched Josh and the other cowboys stealthily brush away a tear.

All the children seemed to love her and, as the old ranch hands had more than two years before, they began calling her Palomino because of her sun-bleached fair hair. Suddenly everywhere on the ranch were shouts of 'Palomino! . . . Palomino!' as she wheeled herself about, checking on children in therapy, at the pool, making their beds, or sweeping their rooms in the pretty little cottages. Sam kept an eye on them everywhere, and at night, in the main hall where everyone ate now, including Samantha, there were endless discussions about who would sit at her table, who would sit at her right or her left, and at the campfire, who would get to hold her hand. The oldest child there was a boy of sixteen, who had arrived surly and hostile from twelve operations over nineteen months, after injuring his spinal cord in a motorcycle accident in which his older brother had been killed. But after four weeks on the ranch he was like a new person. Redheaded Jeff had become his mentor, and the boy and he had become fast friends. The youngest was a little girl of seven, with enormous blue eyes, easy tears, and a lisp. Her name was Betty and she had been born with stumps instead of legs and she was still a little afraid of horses, but she was having a great time with the other kids.

Sometimes when she looked around herself in amazement, as the summer wore on and the numbers of children grew, Sam marvelled at the fact that the handicaps didn't upset her. There had been a time in her life when only perfection seemed normal and when she wouldn't have known how to handle any of the problems that were now part of the ordinary day: children who wouldn't cooperate, artificial limbs that didn't fit, diapers for boys of fourteen, wheelchairs that got stuck, braces that broke. The mechanics of it all sometimes struck her as extraordinary, but most extraordinary of all was that it had become a way of life. And for a woman who had once longed for children, her prayers had been answered: by the end of August she had fifty-three. And now a new aspect had been added. They had bought a specially equipped van, with yet another grant, and made arrangements with the local school, so that after Labour Day the children who came to her, or stayed on, would go to school. For many of them it would be a reintroduction to schooling with normal children, and it was a good place for them to make the adjustments before they went back to their hometowns. There was almost nothing that Sam hadn't thought of, and when Charlie and Mellie came out in late August, they were absolutely stunned by what they saw.

'Has anyone done an article about you yet, Sam?' Charlie was enthralled as he watched a group of advanced senior riders cantering back from an afternoon on the hills. The children, for the most part, loved the horses, and even the horses had been specially picked by Sam and Josh for their docility and the steadiness that they showed.

But now, in answer to Charlie's question, she shook her head. 'I don't want any publicity, Charlie.'

'Why not?' Living in the vortex of visibility in New York, he was surprised.

'I don't know. I like it this way, I guess. Nice and quiet. I don't want to show off. I just want to help the kids.'

'I'd say you're doing that.' He beamed at her as Mellie chased baby Sam down the road. 'I've never seen kids look so happy. They love it, don't they?'

'I hope so.'

They did, as did the parents, the doctors, and the people who worked there. What Sam had done had been a dream come true. It gave the children all the independence Sam had hoped to give them, gave the parents new hope for their children, gave the doctors a kind of gift to brokenhearted parents and children, and it gave the people who worked there a new meaning to their lives that they'd never had before. And most of the time they got children who made it all worth it. Now and then they got one whom even the most devoted therapists and counsellors, and even Sam's loving efforts, couldn't help. There were those who just weren't ready or who didn't want help yet, or maybe never would. It was difficult to accept that they couldn't help a child, but they did their best nonetheless as long as the child stayed.

Amazingly enough, despite the magnitude of the handicaps with which they were dealing, it was always a happy place filled with laughter and smiling faces and squeals of delight. Sam herself had never been as happy and relaxed in her entire lifetime, and now when she met ranchers, or ran into ranch hands, or interviewed new personnel, she asked no questions except about the business at hand. Her endless, hopeless, fruitless search for Tate had finally been put to rest. And she accepted with an equanimity that still upset Charlie, the fact that she would be alone for the rest of her life, running the ranch, and being with 'her kids.' It seemed to be all she wanted, and now and then Josh thought it was a damn shame. At thirty-two she was an extravagantly beautiful woman, and it pained him to think that she was alone. But none of the men who crossed her path seemed to intrigue her and she was always careful not to offer encouragement or innuendos when she met single fathers of new campers, or therapists or doctors. One sensed with Sam that her love life no longer existed, that for her it was a closed door. Yet it was difficult to feel sorry for her, surrounded as she was by children who adored her and whom she seemed genuinely to love.

It was in October that she was called to her office on an

261

unusually warm day to see a new child coming in who was something of an exception. He had just been referred to the Lord Ranch by a judge in L.A. who had heard of what Sam was doing, and the child's 'tuition' was to be paid by the courts. Sam knew that he was expected that morning, and she also knew that there were special circumstances regarding him, but the social worker had told her on the phone that he would explain it all to her when they arrived. She was intrigued by the nature of the new referral, but she had had some work to do with Josh that morning and she didn't want to wait in her office. She had a lot to do before the kids came back from school. There were currently sixty-one staying at the ranch. In her own mind she had already decided that eventually a hundred and ten would be their limit, but in the meantime they still had room to grow.

But when Jeff came to find her out near the Jacuzzis, talking to Josh, he wore an odd expression, and when she got back to her office, she saw why. In a small broken wheelchair sat a shrunken blond child with huge blue eyes, his arms were covered with bruises, and he was clutching a ragged teddy bear. As Sam saw him she almost stopped, because he looked so different from the others. For the past five months she had seen nothing but handicapped children, they had cried, they had wailed, they had argued, they had sulked, they had pouted on arrival. They didn't want to go to school, they were afraid of horses, they didn't see why they had to make their own beds now, but no matter how much they grouched and eventually adjusted, what they all had in common was that they were all children who had been lavishly taken care of, almost pampered, by parents who loved them and were heartbroken at what had been dealt to them by the Fates. Never before had there been a child on the ranch who was so clearly unloved, so obviously bruised in spirit as well as in body, as this one, and as Sam wheeled her chair up closer to talk to him and held out her hands, he cowered from her and began to wail. She glanced quickly at the social worker, and then back at the child clutching his teddy bear, and spoke softly.

'It's okay, Timmie. No one's going to hurt you. My name's Sam. And this is Jeff.' She waved at the young redhead, but Timmie squeezed his eyes shut and cried more. 'Are you scared?' It was the merest whisper in her softest voice, and after a minute he nodded and opened one eye. 'I was scared when I first came here too. Before I got hurt, I used to ride all the time, but I was afraid of the horses at first when I got here. Is that what you're scared of?' He shook his head vigorously. 'You're not?' He shook his head again. 'Then what are you scared of?' He opened the other eye and regarded her with terror. 'Come on, you can tell me.'

It was a tiny broken whisper as he stared at her. 'You.'

Sam was shocked, and with her eyes she signalled Jeff and the social worker and her secretary to back off. They wandered slowly across the room. 'Why are you afraid of me, Timmie? I won't hurt you. I'm in a wheelchair just like you.'

He looked at her for a while and then nodded. 'How come?'

'I got hurt in an accident.' She no longer told them that she was thrown by a horse. It didn't serve her purposes, trying to introduce them to riding. 'But I'm okay now. I can do lots of things.'

'Me too. I can cook my own dinner.' Did he have to? she suddenly wondered. Who was this child and why was he so battered and bruised?

'What do you like to cook for dinner?'

'Spaghetti. It comes in a can.'

'We have spaghetti here too.'

He nodded sadly. 'I know. They always have spaghetti in jail.'

Sam's heart reached out to him and she gently reached out and took his hand. This time he let her, though the other one still clung tightly to his bedraggled bear. 'Did you think this was like jail?' He nodded. 'It's not. It's kind of like camp. Did you ever go to camp?' He shook his head, and she noticed that he looked more like four than six, which she knew he was. She also knew that he'd had polio when he was a year old. It had totally crippled both legs and hips.

'My mum is in jail.' He volunteered the information.

'I'm sorry to hear that.'

He nodded again. 'She got ninety days.'

'Is that why you're here?' Where was his father . . . his grandma . . . anyone, someone who loved this child? It was the first admission she'd ever had that upset her. She wanted to shake someone for what they'd done to the boy. 'Will you stay with us the whole time she's gone?'

'Maybe.'

'Would you like to learn to ride a horse?'

'Maybe.'

'I could teach you. I love horses, and we've got some real pretty ones. You could pick out one that you like.' Right now there were still a dozen left unassigned. Each child always rode the same horse for his entire stay at the ranch. 'How about that, Timmie?'

'Uh-huh . . .yeah . . .' But he was glancing nervously at Jeff. 'Who's that?'

'That's Jeff.'

'Is he a cop?'

'No.' She decided to speak his language. 'We don't have any cops here. He just helps with the horses and the kids.'

'Does he beat kids?'

'No.' She looked shocked, and then she reached out and touched his face. 'No one here will ever hurt you, Timmie. Never. I promise.' He nodded, but it was obvious that he thought it was a lie. 'As a matter of fact, how about if you and I stick together for a while, huh? You could watch me teach riding, and we could swim in the pool.'

'You got a pool?' The eyes began to light up.

'We sure do.' But the first pool she wanted to get him in was the bathtub. He was filthy from head to foot. He looked like he hadn't had a bath in weeks. 'Would you like to see your room?'

He shrugged, but she could see that interest was dawning, and with a small smile she handed him a colouring book and some crayons and told him to wait there. 'Where are you going?' He looked at her with suspicion and fresh fear.

'I think the man who brought you here wants me to sign some papers. I'll do that and then I'll take you to your room and show you the pool. Okay?'

'Okay.' He began to pull out the crayons and she crossed the room in her wheelchair and signalled to the social worker to join her in her secretary's office. In a whisper she asked Jeff to stay.

The social worker was a tired man in his late forties. He had seen it all by now, and this kid was no worse then the rest. But a child in Timmie's condition was new to Sam.

'Good Lord, who's been taking care of him?'

'No one. His mother went to jail two weeks ago, and the neighbours thought he had been sent somewhere else. The mother never even told the cops about him when they picked her up. He's just been sitting around in the apartment, watching TV and eating out of cans. We talked to his mother though.' He sighed and lit a cigarette. 'She's a heroin addict. She's been in and out of jail for years, in and out of treatment centres and hospitals and God knows what. The kid was a trick baby, and she never got him any of his shots. Hence the polio.' The social worker looked annoyed and Sam looked confused.

'I'm sorry. What is a "trick baby"?' He didn't look like any trick to her, that child was real. But the social worker smiled.

'I forget that there are any decent people left who don't know expressions like that. A trick baby is a child conceived by a prostitute. She doesn't know the father. He was a "trick," a "john," whatever. Charming, isn't it?'

'Why is she allowed to retain custody? Why don't the courts take him away from her?'

'They might. I think the judge is considering it this time. In fact she's thinking of giving him up. She considers herself one of the early Christian martyrs, being stuck with a crippled kid, having taken care of him for six years, she's had it.' He hesitated for a moment and then looked Sam in

265

the eye. 'I might as well tell you, there's also a question of child abuse here. The bruises on his arms—she beat him with an umbrella. Almost broke the kid's back.'

'Oh, my God, and they'd even consider giving him back to her?'

'She's been rehabilitated now.' He said it with all the cynicism that went with his job. Sam had never been exposed to anything like it before.

'Has he had any psychiatric help?'

The social worker shook his head. 'Our assessment of him is that he's normal, except for his legs of course. But mentally, he's all right. As all right as any of them are.' Sam wanted to scream at him, how all right could he be if his mother had been beating him with an umbrella? The child was terrified. She had already seen that much. 'Anyway, she's been in for two weeks, and with time off for good behaviour and credit for time served, she'll be out in two months. You got him for sixty days.' Like an animal, like a car, like a rental. Rent-a-Kid. Rent-a-Cripple. It made Sam feel sick.

'And after that?'

'She gets him back unless the court decides otherwise or she doesn't want him. I don't know, maybe you could keep him as a foster child, if you want to.'

'Can't he be adopted by decent people?'

'Not unless she gives up custody, and you can't force her to do that. Besides'—the social worker shrugged—'who's going to adopt a kid in a wheelchair? Any way you look at it, he's going to wind up in an institution.' 'Jail,' as Timmie had already said himself. What a grim life for a six-year-old child.

Sam looked sorrowful as the social worker walked to the door. 'We're happy to have him. And I'll keep him longer if necessary. Whether the court pays or not.' The social worker nodded.

'Let us know if you have any problems. We can always keep him in juvenile hall till she gets out.'

'Isn't that like jail?' Sam looked horrified and he shrugged again.

'More or less. What else do you think we can do with them while their parents are in jail? Send them to camp?' But the beauty of it was that they just had.

Sam turned the chair around and went back into her own office, where Timmie had torn a page out of the colouring book and scribbled across it relentlessly in brown.

'Okay, Timmie, all set?'

'Where's the cop?' He sounded like a little gangster and Sam laughed.

'He's gone. And he's not a cop, he's a social worker.'

'Same thing.'

'Well, anyway, let's get you to your room.' She attempted to get his chair going for him but it locked every few feet and one of the sides had fallen down. 'How do you get anywhere in this thing, Timmie?'

He looked at her strangely. 'I never go out.'

'Never?' She looked shocked again. 'Not even with your mother?'

'She never takes me out. She sleeps a lot. She's very tired.' I'll bet, Sam thought. If she was a heroin addict, she must have slept a hell of a lot.

'I see. Well, it seems to me that the first thing you're going to need is a new chair.' That was one commodity they didn't have. They didn't have any spare chairs, but she kept a narrow extra one in the back of her station wagon, in case anything ever happened to her own. 'I've got one you can use for now. It'll be a little big, but we'll get you a new one by tomorrow. Jeff—she smiled at the young redhead— 'can you get me my spare chair? It's in the back of my car.'

'Sure.' He was back five minutes later and Timmie was ensconced in the big grey chair, as Sam wheeled along beside him, helping him with the wheels.

As they wheeled past the other buildings, she explained to him what everything was, and they stopped at the corral for a few minutes so that he could look at the horses, and as he did he stared at one of the horses and then at Sam's hair. 'That one looks like you.'

'I know. Some of the other kids call me Palomino. That kind of horse is a palomino.'

'Is that what you are?' For a minute he looked amused.

'Sometimes I like to pretend that I am. Do you ever pretend stuff like that?' Sadly he shook his head and they drove on to his room. Now she was especially grateful that she had reserved him this particular room. It was big and sunny and all done in blue and yellow. There was a big cheerful bedspread and there were drawings of horses in frames on the walls.

'Whose is this?' He looked frightened again as she wheeled him into the room.

'Yours. While you're here.'

'Mine?' The eyes were as big as saucers. 'You mean it?'

'I mean it.' There was a desk, without a chair, a chest of drawers, and a little table where he could play games. He had his own bathroom, and there was a special speaker in case he got in trouble and needed help from one of the counsellors nearby. 'Do you like it?'

All he could say was 'Wow!'

She showed him the chest of drawers and then told him that that was where he could put his things.

'What things?' He looked blank. 'I don't have any things.'

'Didn't you bring a suitcase with some clothes?' She suddenly realised that she hadn't seen one.

'Nope.' He looked down at the spotted T-shirt that had once been blue. 'This is all I've got. And Teddy.' He squeezed the bear tight.

'Tell you what.' Sam glanced at Jeff and then back at Timmie. 'Right now we'll borrow you some stuff, and then I'll go into town later and get you some jeans and stuff. Okay?'

'Sure.' He didn't seem to care one way or the other, he was happy with his room.

'Now, about a bath.' She wheeled herself into the sunny bathroom and turned on the tap after flicking a special switch at a comfortable level that would close the drain. Everything had been specially installed. And the john had hand bars on each side. 'And if you want to use the toilet, all you have to do is push this button and someone will come and help.'

He stared at her, not comprehending. 'Why do I have to take a bath?'

'Because it's a nice thing to do.'

'You gonna do it?'

'I could have Jeff do it if you like.' She wasn't sure if at six he'd be modest, but he wasn't and now he vehemently shook his head.

'Uh-huh. You.'

'Okay.' For her this was a new adventure. It had only taken her ten months to learn how to bathe herself, but to bathe a child from a wheelchair, that was going to be something new.

She sent Jeff off to find clothes that would fit Timmie, rolled up her sleeves, and told him how to get himself in, but when he slipped and she tried to grab him, they both almost wound up on the floor. In the end she managed to get him into the bathtub, wound up soaked herself, and as she helped haul him out, she got him into the chair she had lent him just in time to lose her balance and fall out of her own. And for some reason she found herself on the floor, looking up at him and laughing as he laughed down at her too.

'Pretty silly, huh?'

'I thought you were supposed to teach me how to do it.'

'Well, there are other people here who do that.' She hoisted herself carefully off the wet floor and back into her chair.

'What do you do?'

'Teach riding.'

He nodded and she found herself wondering what he was thinking, but mostly she was grateful that he no longer seemed to be afraid of her, and when Jeff brought them the clothes he had borrowed from various cabins, Timmie almost looked like a new child. But she was soaking wet from his bath and she had to go back to her room to change. 'Want to come see my house?' Hesitantly he nodded, and after she helped him dress, she led the way. There was an easily accessible ramp into the big house now, and he followed her into the living room and down the hall to her bedroom, while she pulled some fresh jeans and a shirt out of the closet, which had been entirely rebuilt for her. She kept Caroline's old room as her best guest room, but she almost never used it, and visited it as seldom as she had to. It still pained her to feel its emptiness without her old friend.

'You got a nice house.' Timmie was looking around with interest. The teddy bear had come with him too. 'Who sleeps in the other rooms?'

'No one.'

'Don't you have kids?' He looked amazed.

'No. Except all the kids who live here on the ranch with me.'

'You got a husband?' It was a question a lot of the children asked her and she always smiled and said no, and it ended there.

'Nope.'

'Why not? You're pretty.'

'Thank you. I just don't.'

'Do you wanna get married?'

She sighed softly as she looked at the beautiful blond child. He was actually very pretty now that he was clean. 'I don't think I do want to get married, Timmie. I lead kind of a special life.'

'So does my mum.' He nodded his understanding, and Sam was at first shocked and then laughed but she couldn't say 'Not like that.'

She tried to explain her views to him. 'I just think I wouldn't have enough time for a husband with the ranch and you kids here and stuff.'

But he was looking at her intently, and then waved at her chair. 'Is it because of that?' What he had just asked her hit her like a punch in the stomach, because it was the truth, but she couldn't admit it, not to anyone, and barely to herself.

'No, it's not because of that.' But she wondered if he

270

knew she was lying, and then, without giving him time to ask her more questions, she ushered him back outside. They visited the stables and the main hall, looked at two cows in a pen, and went to the swimming pool, where she took him for a quick swim before lunch. There were only a few younger children on the ranch at that hour of the day in October. The others were all in school, having been dropped off by the huge adjusted school bus that Sam had bought to get the kids there. But the children who were around greeted Timmie with warmth and interest, and when the others got back at three thirty, he was hardly even shy. He watched them have their riding lessons, swoop down on the pool in their wheelchairs, and chase each other down the wide well-paved walks. He met Josh and solemnly shook his hand, and watched Samantha during all her lessons, and when she was finished, he was still standing by.

'You still here, Timmie? I thought you'd have gone back to your room.' He only shook his head, holding on to his teddy bear with big eyes. 'Want to come back to my house before dinner?' He nodded and reached out for her hand, and hand in hand, they wheeled back to the big house where she read him stories until the big old school bell sounded, and it was time to go eat.

'Can I sit with you, Sam?' Once again he looked worried, and she reassured him. But she suspected that by now he was tired after his long first day at the ranch. He sat beside her at dinner, yawning loudly, and before dessert had arrived, she turned to see that his little chin had dropped onto his chest and he was slumped in a corner of the big grey wheelchair. The teddy bear was still clutched in his arms, and she smiled gently and took off her heavy sweater, settled it around him like a blanket, and left the table to take him home. In his room she gently lifted him from the chair to the bed with one powerful smooth gesture, her own arms had gained much strength from the constant use they got. She took off his clothes as he stirred gently, undid his braces, changed his diapers, turned off the light, and ran a gentle hand over the soft

271

blond hair. For a brief moment she was suddenly reminded of Charlie's children, of the sweet faces and the
big blue eyes, and she suddenly remembered that fierce
longing she had felt when she had first held their last
baby, little Samantha, and how she had known then that
it was a void that, in her life, would never be filled. And
now, as she looked at Timmie, she felt her heart reach out
and embrace him as though he had been her child. He
stirred gently as she kissed his forehead, and whispered,
'Good night, Mummy . . . I love you . . .' Sam felt tears
spring to her eyes. They were words she would suddenly
have given her life for, and then, with head bowed, she
wheeled out of the cabin and closed the door.

34

By the end of the first month Timmie was riding the pretty
little palomino. Her name was Daisy and he loved her the
way any little boy would have loved his first horse. But far
more than the palomino, he loved Samantha, with a
passion that startled everyone with its vehemence and
strength. He appeared at the big house every morning,
knocked on the door, and waited for her to come and
answer it. Sometimes it took her longer than others,
because sometimes she was already making coffee and
sometimes she was still in bed. But the moment he saw
her, his face lit up like a sunburst, and as he wheeled in the
chair that she had bought him, he always looked around
him, like a puppy who's been kept outdoors all night.
They had a comfortable early morning patter. Sometimes
he told her what he'd dreamed about, or what one of the
kids had done at breakfast, or what the palomino had been
doing when Timmie sped past the corral in his chair to bid
the gentle horse good morning. And Samantha told him

what she would be doing that morning, they'd talk about his riding lesson, and once or twice she inquired if he had changed his mind about school, but he remained adamant on that subject. He wanted to stay on the ranch, not go to school with the others, and Samantha figured that for the first month at least she would let him settle in.

The bruises that his mother had inflicted upon him had long since faded, and the social worker called once a week to see how Timmie was, and when at the end of the month he came out to see them, he looked from Timmie to Samantha and then back again, and he was clearly stunned.

'What in God's name did you do to him?' he asked her when they were finally alone. Prying Timmie from Sam's side wasn't easy, but she had sent him to check on Daisy and tell Josh that they would be riding in a few minutes to show the social worker how well he had done. 'He looks like a different child.'

'He is a different child,' Sam said proudly. 'He's a child who's been loved and it shows.'

But the social worker only looked at her sadly. 'You know how hard you've made it for him?' She thought he was joking and she started to smile but she saw then that he meant it and knit her brows.

'What do you mean?'

'Do you know what it'll be like for him to go back to an apartment in a tenement with a drug-addict mother who feeds him stale crackers and beer?'

Sam took a deep breath and stared out of the window. She wanted to say something to him. But she didn't know if it was the right time. 'I wanted to talk to you about that, Mr. Pfizer.' She turned to face him again. 'What about the possibilities of not sending him back?'

'And keep him here?' She nodded, but he started to shake his head. 'I don't think the judge would buy that. The courts are paying for it right now, but it was just kind of a trial thing, you know . . .'

'I don't mean like that.' She took another deep breath and decided to ask him. What could she lose? Nothing.

And she might win everything . . . everything . . . For the third time in her life, Sam had fallen in love. And this time not with a man, but with a six-year-old boy. She loved him as she had never loved another human being, with a kind of depth and feeling she had never suspected that she had, as though some sort of well had reached right past her heart into her spirit and now she was able to give him all she had to give. And there was a lot of loving left over from the men who had left her, a lot that she had left to give. And now it was Timmie's, with all of her heart. 'What if I adopt him?'

'I see.' The social worker sat down heavily in a chair and looked at Samantha. He didn't like what he was seeing. He could see that she loved the child. 'I don't know, Miss Taylor. I would hate to get your hopes up. His mother may still want him.'

A strange light came into Sam's eyes. 'By what right, I might ask, Mr. Pfizer? As I recall, she beat him, not to mention her drug habits—'

'All right, all right . . . I know.' Oh, Jesus. This he didn't need, not today—not any day, in fact. People only got hurt thinking the way she did. The truth was that his mother could most likely keep him, whether Sam liked that idea or not. 'The fact is she's the boy's natural mother. The courts lean over backward to respect that.'

'How far do they lean?' Her voice was both frightened and cold. It was frightening to have let herself love the child as much as she did now, and to have to face the possibility that he might leave.

The social worker looked at her sadly. 'To tell you the truth, they lean pretty far.'

'Couldn't I do something?'

'You could.' He sighed. 'You could hire a lawyer and fight her, if she still wants him. But you might lose . . . you probably will.' And then he thought to ask her about the child. 'What about the boy? Have you asked him? That could weigh with the court, even though he's still very young. A natural mother would have a strong case here, no matter how rotten she is. You know, the worst of it is

274

that with the state rehabilitating her, we really can't afford to say now that she's not okay. If we do, then we're admitting that our whole rehabilitation system doesn't work, which it does not. But it's kind of a Catch-22 situation. See what I mean?' Sam nodded vaguely. 'What about the boy, have you asked him?' She shook her head. 'Why don't you?'

'I will.'

'All right. Then give me a call after that. If he wants to go back to his mother, you should let it go. But if he wants to say here'—he paused, thinking it over— 'I'll go talk to the mother myself. Maybe she won't give you any problem.' And then he bestowed a wintry smile. 'I hope for your sake that she makes it easy, the boy would sure be better off here with you.'

It was an understatement but Sam let it pass. The fact was that Timmie would be better off anywhere than with her, and Sam was determined to protect the child with all her will.

They went out to see Timmie ride then, and as happened with parents who saw their children ride for the first time, Martin Pfizer, the hardened, tired, old social worker, had to wipe away a stray tear. It was incredible to see what had happened to Timmie. He was beautiful and blond and clean and happy, he laughed all the time now, looked at Sam with an air of pure adoration, and he was even funny, and the oddest thing of all was that he even looked a lot like her.

When Martin Pfizer left at the end of the day, he said something again to Sam in a whisper as he squeezed her arm. 'Ask him and call me.' And then, tousling Timmie's hair, he shook Sam's hand and waved a last good-bye as he drove off.

It wasn't until after dinner that night when she took Timmie back to his room that she asked him, while he buttoned his pyjamas and she put his braces away.

'Timmie?'

'Yeah?'

She turned to look at him, feeling something tremble

inside her. What if he didn't want her? If he wanted to go back to his mother? She wasn't sure if she could stand the rejection, but she had to ask him. And that would only be the beginning. 'You know, I was thinking about something today.' With a look of interest he waited. 'I was wondering what you would think about sticking around here . . .' It was ghastly, she hadn't realised that it would be so hard to ask him. 'You know, kind of forever . . . I mean—'

'You mean stay here with you?' His eyes grew huge in the little tanned face.

'Yeah, that's what I mean.'

'Oh, wow!' But she knew as he said it that he hadn't understood her. He thought she just meant an extended visit, and she knew that she had to tell him it would mean giving up his mum.

'Timmie . . .' He had his arms around her now and she pulled him away so she could see his face. 'I don't mean just like the other kids here.' He seemed puzzled. 'I mean . . . I mean . . .' It was like a proposal of marriage. 'I want to adopt you, if they'd let me. But you have to want that too. I would never do anything you didn't want.' She was having to fight back the tears and he stared at her in amazement.

'You mean you want me?' He seemed astounded.

'Of course I want you, silly.' She hugged him tight again, the tears spilling from her eyes. 'You're the best little kid in the whole world.'

'What about my mum?'

'I don't know, Timmie. That would be the hard part.'

'Would she come to see me?'

'I don't know. Maybe we could arrange that, but I think it would be harder for everyone that way.' She was being honest with him, she knew she had to. It was a big step for him to take.

But he looked frightened when she looked down into his face again and she could feel him tremble. 'Would she come and beat me?'

'Oh, no.' It was a cry of anguish. 'I wouldn't let her do that.'

276

And then suddenly he started to cry and he told her things that he had never told her, about his mother and what she had done to him. When it was over, he lay in Sam's arms, spent, but he was no longer frightened, and after she pulled the sheets up to his chin, she sat next to him in the dark for over an hour, just watching him sleep and letting her tears flow. The last thing he had said to her as his eyes closed was 'I want to be yours, Sam.' And that was all she had wanted to hear.

35

The next morning Sam called Martin Pfizer and told him what Timmie had said. She also told him some of the other things he had told her, about the beatings and the neglect, things he had kept inside for a long, sad time. Pfizer shook his head.

'I hate to say it, but it doesn't surprise me. All right, I'll see what I can do.'

But by the next day he knew that he could do nothing. He had spent two hours with the woman, tried to reason with her, had talked to her counsellor at the facility where she had been incarcerated, but he knew that it was useless to say more. With a heavy heart he called Sam that evening and found her alone in the big house.

'She won't do it, Miss Taylor. I tried everything, reason, threats, everything. She wants him.'

'Why? She doesn't love him.'

'She thinks she does. She spent hours telling me about her father and mother, how her father beat her, her mother whipped her. It's the only thing she knows.'

'But she'll kill him.'

'Maybe. Maybe not. But there isn't a damn thing we can do now until she tries.'

'But can I sue for custody?' Sam's hand trembled as she waited.

'Yes. That doesn't mean that you have a chance. She's the natural mother, Miss Taylor. You're a single woman, and a— a handicapped person.' He caught himself quickly. 'That won't look well in court.'

'But look what I've done for him already. Look at the life he could have here.'

'I know. That makes sense to you and me, but there's an element of precedent involved, and you'll have to convince the judge. Get youself a lawyer, Miss Taylor, and give it a try. But you have to be realistic. Treat it as a test case, an experiment. If you lose, you lose, if you win, you get the boy.' Was he crazy? Didn't he understand that she loved Timmie and he loved her?

'Thank you.' Her voice was chilly when she hung up, and she spun around the room half a dozen times, mumbling to herself and thinking, and it drove her nuts that she had to wait until morning before she could call.

But when Timmie turned up the next morning, she gave him several errands to do for her, so that she could call Caroline's old lawyer and see if he could refer her to someone who might take the case.

'A child-custody suit, Samantha?' He sounded surprised. 'I didn't know you had children.'

'I don't.' She smiled grimly into the phone. 'Yet.'

'I see.' But of course he didn't. But he gave her two names of lawyers he had heard of in L.A. He knew neither of them personally, but assured her that their reputations were first-rate.

'Thanks.' When she called them, the first lawyer was on vacation in Hawaii, and the other was due back from the East he next day. She left a message for him to call her and spent the next twenty-four hours on pins and needles, waiting for him to call. But he did, as his secretary promised, at exactly five o'clock in the afternoon.

'Miss Taylor?' The voice was deep and mellifluous, and she couldn't tell if he was young or old. In as little time as she could, she explained the problem, told him what she wanted to do, what Timmie wanted, what the social worker had said, and where Timmie's mother was. 'My, my, you do have a problem, don't you?' But he sounded intrigued by what she had told him. 'If you don't mind, I'd really like to come out and see the boy.' She had told him that both she and Timmie were bound to wheelchairs, but she had explained to him about the ranch and how well Timmie had done. 'I think an important part of your case would hinge on the surroundings, and I should see them if I'm to make any sense. That is, of course, if you decide that you'd like me to represent you.' But so far she had liked what he had said.

'How do you feel about the case, Mr. Warren?'

'Well, why don't we talk about it at greater length tomorrow? On the surface I'm not overly optimistic, but this could be one of those highly emotional situations that get resolved in a most unorthodox way.'

'In other words, I don't have a chance. Is that what you're saying?' Her heart sank.

'Not exactly. But it won't be easy. I think you know that already.'

She nodded. 'I suspected that much from what the social worker said. It doesn't make any sense to me though, dammit. If that woman is a junkie and a child abuser, why is she even considered a possibility as Timmie's custodial parent?'

'Because she's his natural mother.'

'Is that really enough?'

'No. But if he were you're son, wouldn't you want every chance to keep him, no matter how screwed up you were?'

Samantha sighed into the phone. 'What about the good of the child?'

'That's going to be our best argument, Miss Taylor. Now tell me where you are and I'll come and see you tomorrow. Route Twelve, you said? Let's see, how far is that from . . .'

She gave him the appropriate directions and he appeared the next day at noon. He was driving a dark green Mercedes, wore a pair of dark brown slacks and a beige cashmere jacket, an expensive silk tie, and a very good-looking cream-coloured shirt. He was a man clearly in his mid-forties. His watch was Piaget, his hair was iron-grey, and his eyes were steel blue. His full name was Norman Warren. And Samantha couldn't resist a smile when she saw him. She had worked for too many years among people who looked so much like him. She held out a hand from her wheelchair with a grin.

'Forgive me, but are you from New York?' She had to know. But he laughed right out loud.

'Hell yes. How did you know?'

'So am I. Not that you can tell anymore.' Nonetheless she had worn a soft lilac sweater with her jeans today instead of her usual flannel shirt, and her dark blue cowboy boots were brand-new.

They shook hands and exchanged pleasantries, and she led him to the big house, where she had prepared sandwiches and hot coffee, and there was a hot apple pie she had 'stolen' from the main hall when she took Timmie to lunch there a few minutes before. He had been very annoyed when she had left him but she had explained that she was expecting a grown-up for lunch at the house.

'Why can't I meet him too?' He had pouted ferociously as she left him with Josh and the handful of kids who weren't in school. They all accepted Timmie as their mascot, he was the youngest in the place and he looked so much like Samantha that somehow they regarded him almost as though he were her son, and of course she did too.

'You'll meet him but I want to talk to him first.'

'What about?'

'Business.' She grinned at him in answer to the question he didn't quite dare ask. 'And no, he is not a cop.' Timmie laughed his bright little laugh.

'How did you know that was what I thought?'

'Because I know you, silly, now go eat.' He had gone off with the others, complaining because they were eating leftover stew. She promised to come and get him when they were finished talking business.

And as she sat over her own lunch with Norman Warren, she told him everything she could about the child. 'May I see him?' he finally asked. When they went to find him at the main hall, Warren looked around himself with interest and eyed the dazzlingly beautiful woman in the lilac sweater, perfectly at ease in her chair. Just being there was an experience for Norman Warren, he could see from the way the place was kept, and from the happy people he saw around them, that what Samantha had done was a success. But nothing had prepared him for what he saw when he' met Timmie, or when the boy mounted a palomino with Josh's help, or when he saw Sam ride beside him on Pretty Girl, or when the others came home from school and took their lessons. Norman Warren didn't leave until after dinner, and when he did, he did so with regret.

'I want to stay forever.'

'I'm sorry, I can't adopt you too.' Samantha laughed with him. 'And fortunately you don't qualify to come here as a student. But anytime you'd like to just come and visit and ride with us, we'd love it.'

He looked sheepish and almost whispered, 'I'm scared shitless of horses.'

She whispered back, 'We could cure you.'

Another sotto voce, 'No, you couldn't. I won't let you.' And then they both laughed and he drove off. They had come to terms on the agreement—she would pay him a fee of ten thousand dollars to represent her in her suit. She liked him very much, and he seemed to like Timmie, and there was every reason to hope that she at least had a chance to win him, and if she didn't, she could appeal it. He stressed once again that it wouldn't be easy, but it wasn't impossible either, and there were a lot of sympathetic factors in her favour, not least among them the way she and Timmie loved each other, and he hoped the fact that they were both in wheelchairs would add drama and sympathy to her side rather than work against them. But that remained to be seen. She had signed papers that afternoon. He would file the complaint in Los Angeles the next morning, and they would get a hearing date as soon as they could.

'Think he can help us, Sam?' Timmie looked up at her sadly as she accompanied him back to his room. She had explained to him who Norman Warren was and what he was going to do.

'I hope so, love. We'll see.'

'What if he can't do it?'

'Then I'll kidnap you and we'll hide in the hills.' She was teasing but his eyes sparkled as she pushed open the door to his room and turned on the light for him.

'Okay.'

Only when she left the room did she begin to wonder the same thing ... what if he couldn't ... but he had to ... he had to win the case for her. She couldn't bear losing Timmie. And by the time she got back to her own room, she convinced herself that she never would.

36

They shared Christmas in peace, and for the first time in Timmie's life he had the kind of Christmas of which children dream. There were presents stacked high in boxes, things to wear, and games, and puzzles, a bright fire engine with a hat for him to wear, and a sweater for his teddy bear, and even some things Sam had made for him. And in the main hall was a huge tree surrounded by presents. There were toys for all the children currently staying at the ranch. And one of the counsellors, at her request, had dressed up as Santa, and it reminded Sam and Josh of the year when Tate Jordan had been Santa. The memory of the man she still so loved placing the angel on the Christmas tree came back to her like a knife stab to her heart. Suddenly she was reminded of so many things about Tate and about John, whom she so seldom thought of now. They had had another baby, she knew, and Liz had finally been fired by the network, because she was so tiresome on the air. John Taylor's career was still booming but once in a great while when Sam watched him she found him plastic and empty and too pretty and terribly boring, and she wondered why she had ever cared. It seemed amazing now to watch eleven years of one's life fly out the window and not even care, but she just didn't. It was different when she thought of Tate.

'Sam . . . can I ask you a crazy question?' Josh asked her as they stood apart in a corner, watching the kids open their gifts.

'Sure. What?' But she already knew.

'Were you in love with Tate Jordan?' She looked into Josh's eyes and nodded her head slowly.

'Yes, I was.'

'Was that why he left?'

'I suppose. He decided not to work things out, I guess. And I had told him I didn't want to play the same game as Caro and Bill. But he didn't think a lady should love a ranch hand. At least not openly.' She looked sad as she spoke. 'So he left.'

'I figured it was something like that.'

'And he had some kind of fit when he found out who my ex-husband was . . . thought he wasn't good enough for me, or something equally dumb . . .'

'Shit.' Josh looked instantly angry. 'He was worth ten of that jerk. Oh—' His face flushed bright red. 'I'm sorry, Sam . . .'

She chuckled. 'Don't be. I was just thinking the same thing.'

'And he never wrote you or nothing?'

'No. I think I must have looked for him on every ranch in this country, but I never found him.'

Josh looked sorry again as he glanced at Sam. 'It's a damn shame, Sam. He was a good man, and I always thought he loved you. Maybe he'll turn up someday, just to say hi to Bill or me or Caro, and find you here instead.'

Sam shook her head with a taut expression on her face. 'I hope not. He'd be in for one hell of a shock.' She meant her legs, but this time Josh shook his head.

'You think he'd care?'

'It doesn't matter, Josh. I would. That's all over now. I've got the kids instead.'

'At your age, Sam? Don't be crazy. What are you, twenty-eight, twenty-nine?'

She grinned at the old man. 'Josh, I love you. I'm thirty-three.'

'All sounds the same to me. Try fifty-nine and see how you like the feel of that.'

'On you it looks good.'

'Sweet-talker, but I love it.' He grinned at her, and then his face grew serious. 'You're talking bullshit though, you know, about Tate. And it don't matter if it's Tate or someone else, you're too damn young to treat yourself like an old maid.' And then he narrowed his eyes and lowered his voice. 'The truth is, Sam, you're a damn liar. You spend all your time teaching these kids that they don't have to live or think or act like cripples, and then in your heart you think of yourself as one.' He had hit a nerve but she said nothing and kept her eyes on the kids. 'It's true, Sam . . . dammit, it's true. I saw that lawyer from Los Angeles talking to you the other day. He likes you, like a woman, dammit, and do you pay him any mind? No, hell no, you just act like a happy little old lady and give him iced tea.'

'There's nothing wrong with iced tea.' She grinned at him this time.

'No, but there's a lot wrong with pretending you're not a woman anymore at thirty-three.'

'Watch out, Josh,' she said, trying to glare at him. 'I might attack you next time we're alone.' And with that, she blew a kiss in his direction and wheeled herself into the midst of the kids. It was her way of telling him that she didn't want to hear any more. He had come a little too close to home.

It took them all two days to recover from the excitement

of Christmas. There weren't even any riding lessons, just some casual groups that rode out over the hills, but neither Timmie nor Sam were among them. They were both spending a lot of time alone, as though they each had a deep need to be together. The hearing was set for December 28.

'You scared?' The night before the hearing, she had put Timmie in her smallest guest room, next door to her own room, and she was just tucking him into bed.

'About tomorrow?' Her face was close to his, and she touched it with one long graceful hand. 'A little. Are you?'

'Yeah.' She saw now that the big blue eyes were filled with terror. 'A lot. What if she hits me?'

'I won't let her.'

'What if she takes me?'

'She won't.' But what if they let her take him? That was the ghost that haunted Samantha, and she couldn't promise him that that wouldn't happen. She didn't want to lie. She had already told him that if they lost it she would appeal it, if that was what he wanted, and she had also told him that if what he wanted was to be with his mummy then that was okay too. It tore at her heart to give him that option, but she knew she had to. She didn't want to steal him from his own mother. She wanted him to come to her with an open heart. 'It'll be all right, sweetheart. You'll see.'

But she didn't look nearly as certain the next day as Josh pushed both their wheelchairs up the ramp at the Los Angeles County Courthouse. She and Timmie were ferociously holding hands, and when they pressed into the elevator in their wheelchairs, they both felt awkward and conspicuous until Josh helped pull them out. Norman Warren was waiting for them just outside the courtroom, in a dark blue suit. He looked eminently respectable, as did Sam. She had worn a pretty pale blue wool dress, which was a remnant of her New York wardrobe, a matching light blue mohair coat, and plain black leather Gucci shoes. She had bought Timmie new clothes especially for the occasion, little navy blue slacks with a matching jacket and a pale blue turtleneck sweater, which accidentally matched Sam's dress. They looked very much like mother and son as they sat there waiting, and Norman once again noticed the striking resemblance of his towhead, her blonde hair, and the same enormous blue eyes.

The hearing took place in a small courtroom, and the judge entered, wearing glasses and a quiet smile. He did his best not to intimidate Timmie when he looked at him, and he sat at a desk on a slightly raised platform, which was less impressive than some of the desks he had sat at in other courts. He was a man in his early sixties, and he had been doing child-custody hearings for a great many years. He was admired in Los Angeles for his fairness and his kindness to children— a number of times had saved children from unfortunate adoptions. He had a profound respect for children and natural mothers, and often encouraged the mothers to think over their decisions before they gave away their babies, their faces drenched in tears. Many women had come back to thank him, and it was something he would always carry with him when he retired. And now he looked at Timmie with interest, and at Samantha and her attorney, and a few minutes later at the tiny, fragile-looking young woman who slipped into the courtroom with her attorney. She was wearing a grey skirt and a white blouse and she looked more like a schoolgirl than an addict or a hooker. And Sam learned then for the first time that she was only twenty-two. She had a kind of fragile beauty and looked like the sort of girl who couldn't possibly take care of herself. One wanted instantly to love, cherish, and protect her. It was part of why Timmie had always felt sorry for her after she beat him. Because she looked so hurt and so distraught herself. It always made him forgive her and made him want to help her, instead of expecting her to help him.

The court was called to order, the files were handed to the judge, but unnecessarily, as he had already read all the existing documents the day before. He said at the outset that it was an interesting case because of the aspects introduced by Samantha, a handicapped child, a hand-

286

icapped adopting mother, but they had to keep in mind, all of them there, that what was being looked for by the court, and should remain everyone's goal, was the ultimate good of the child. The judge offered the option to have the child removed, but Sam and Timmie had already discussed it. He said he wanted to be there, he didn't want to be 'taken away by the cops.' She assured him that he could wait outside with Josh, but he insisted that he wanted to be with her. She noticed then that he never let his eyes roam toward his mother, as though he were frightened to acknowledge her presence, or even see her, and he kept his hand in Sam's and his eyes toward the judge.

The opposing attorney called Timmie's mother as his first witness, and as Sam sat staring her full in the face, she realised full well what she was up against. A sweet face, a soft voice, a sob story from beginning to end, and the assurance that this time she had learned a lesson and had done nothing but read psychology books to learn more about herself and how she might help her precious son. Timmie's eyes fell into his lap the whole time her testimony was being heard and he didn't raise them again until she'd left the stand. Sam's attorney put on record that he would cross-examine her later, and the next witnesses were called, a psychiatrist who had examined Timmie's mother for the county, declaring her to be a warm, feeling young woman who had had an unfortunate youth. They felt that she had no intention of hurting her child, but had been under enormous pressure financially, but that now she was about to go to work in a big hotel downtown everything was looking up. Norman Warren made the psychiatrist look foolish, and the implication was made that she would have ample opportunity in the hotel to start picking up johns. The comment was stricken from the record, Norman was admonished, and the witness was excused from the stand. There were additionally two counsellors called, and then a doctor attesting to the mother's health and to the fact that she was in no way addicted to drugs anymore. And last of all, there was a priest who had known her since she was eleven, in fact he had baptised Timmie. He said that he felt absolutely certain that the child belonged with the mother who loved him, and as he said it Sam felt her stomach flip over in her gut. She held tightly to Timmie's hand through the entire proceeding, and when the priest left the stand, they adjourned for lunch. Norman had cross-examined them all except the mother herself and the priest. He was going to call Timmie's mother to the stand after the lunch break, but he explained to Sam that he had no intention of tackling the Catholic Church on the stand.

'Why not?'

'The judge is Catholic, my dear. Besides, what am I going to do to impeach what the man is saying? We're better off not touching that one.' Nonetheless he had made all the others look slightly shady, and he interrogated them almost with an air of amusement and derision, as though their testimony itself was tainted due to association with the woman herself. But none of what he had done to them even came close to what he did to Timmie's mother, and at a sign from Sam, Josh had firmly wheeled Timmie out of the room, protesting in a hoarse whisper, but he wasn't given any choice by Samantha, who blew him a kiss and turned back to watch what was happening on the stand. The girl was shaking in her seat, and almost before she started talking, she started crying. And it was admittedly difficult to envision this frail child as the villian in the piece. But despite what she looked like it was nevertheless made clear that she had discovered drugs at twelve, heroin at thirteen, had been arrested for prostitution at fifteen, gotten pregnant with Timmie at sixteen, had had five abortions to date, had been in seven drug programmes, had been arrested nine times as a juvenile, and three as an adult.

'But,' her attorney insisted as he objected, 'the court must keep in mind that this woman is no longer addicted, that she has just been through a very arduous state-run drug programme, and if we are to say that this woman is not rehabilitated, then we are in fact saying that our entire system of rehabilitation does not work.' The objection was duly noted and sustained. Her arrest record was stricken from the record as per Californian law, the rest stayed.

Her testimony took well over an hour, she sobbed throughout and talked remorsefully about 'my baby' whenever she had the chance, but every time Sam looked at her, she thought of the shots she hadn't got for him, which was why he had contracted polio, she thought of the beatings he had had at her hands, the torment, the loneliness, the terror, and all Sam wanted was to rise out of her wheelchair and scream.

For their side, Norman Warren called the social worker, Martin Pfizer, who was unemotional, matter-of-fact, and not particularly exciting as a witness; there was Sam's own physician; Josh; and there had been a packet of letters from important people, like judges and doctors, about the marvellous work she was doing on the ranch. And then at last there was Sam herself. The fact that she was divorced was brought out, that she was not remarried and had no 'prospects,' as the opposing attorney put it, at the present time, the fact that she was indeed irreversibly handicapped. The whole sad, long list was emphasised over and over until Sam almost started to feel sorry for herself. Norman objected and got that line of questioning stopped. In the end she wound up sounding like a kindly, interested do-gooder who wanted to help Timmie, but unlike his half-hysterical mother she did not shout 'my baby' and have to be led from the room.

The final witness was the hardest. It was Timmie himself, and his mother was asked if she could possibly quell her tears, or if she would like a recess during which she might compose herself once again. She chose to subdue herself there and then, still sniffing loudly as she listened while Sam watched the look of terror in the child's face. Everything that had previously been brought out was now tested. What his life was like with his mother, what his life was like with Sam, how his mother provided for him, what Sam bought him and gave him, how he felt about the two women, and then suddenly, 'Are you afraid of your mother, Timmie?' But the question itself obviously frightened him so much that he shrank back in his wheelchair, holding his teddy, shaking his head violently.

'No . . .no!'

'Does she ever beat you or hit you?'

There was no answer and then he shook his head and was finally asked to speak up. All they got was a hoarse 'No.' Sam closed her eyes in despair. She understood what he was doing. There was no way he could tell the truth with his mother there. It went on for another half hour and then they were all sent home. The judge kindly asked them to return the following morning. He said that he had all of their phone numbers, and that if, for some reason, he felt that he would not be able to reach a verdict quickly, he would let them know. But if they did not hear from him that evening, they were to return to the same court the next morning, bringing Timmie— this was a glance at Sam—and the verdict would be returned. He felt that in the interest of the child, and to avoid any additional pain to all parties, it was best to have the verdict returned right away. With that, the judge rose and the bailiff announced that court was adjourned.

On the drive back to the ranch Sam felt her whole body ache with exhaustion and Timmie fell asleep in her arms almost as soon as they left the kerb. He had trembled with terror as his mother had begun to approach him, clutched at Sam's hand, and Norman had whisked him from the courtroom as Josh helped Samantha, and they got away as quickly as they could. She realised later as she held him what a brave thing Timmie had done by being willing to try to go through the custody hearings. If his mother won him back, she might do anything to get even, and he had known better than anyone. But Sam understood now too as she held him close. How on earth was she going to give him to that woman if she had to? How could she bear it? As she lay in bed that night she knew she couldn't, that it would kill her. For hours she lay there and thought of taking him and running away somewhere. But where and how, and what was the point really? Two people in wheelchairs wouldn't get very far, and then she thought of the secret cabin, which she hadn't visited since she got back to the ranch. But she knew that even there they would find her. It was hopeless. All they could do was believe in justice and hope for the best.

37

Sam was awake long before sunrise the next morning. In fact, she realised as she looked at the clock, she had only slept for an hour and a half. But when she wheeled her way into Timmie's room, beside hers, she found that he was awake too.

'Hi, sweetheart . . .' She kissed him on the tip of the nose and reached for his braces. 'Good morning.'

'I won't go with her.'

'Why don't we worry about that after breakfast?' Sam tried to sound lighthearted, but he burst into tears and clung to her. Thus had begun the day. They had eaten breakfast alone again that morning. The rest of the children had no idea what was going on, and only a few of the therapists and counsellors had been told by Samantha. They were all trying to keep it as low-key as they could. But it was obvious when she left again with Josh and Timmie that something major was going on. As though they sensed something wrong around them, the children were unusually quiet as they boarded the bus to go to school.

In Los Angeles Samantha and Josh and Timmie met Norman outside the courtroom, and they all looked grim.

'Take it easy, Sam.' Norm gently touched her arm. She was wearing grey slacks and a grey cashmere sweater, and Timmie was wearing the same suit as the day before, this time with a red and white plaid shirt.

The judge began the proceedings by asking to have Timmie in the room, and then addressed himself to the boy, explaining that he had listened to all the evidence and had tried to make a good decision that would make Timmie happy for a very long time. He smiled at him like a benevolent grandfather and then asked him if he could wheel himself to the front of the room, explaining that it was only a formality, because he was the most important person there, after all, and all of this was about him. Timmie looked questioningly at Sam and then she smiled and nodded, and he rolled himself front and centre as the judge had asked.

With that, the judge turned his attention to Sam, explaining that he understood that what she was doing was not only admirable, but saintly, that he had talked to several people about the ranch, and that he was impressed beyond anything he could describe to her. Once again he favoured her with a warm smile. But then he went on to say that although there was no doubt that her intentions were excellent, and that she could certainly materially provide better for Timmie than could his mother, and although Timmie certainly had a difficult life with this young woman who had tried so hard to find the right road for herself and her handicapped child, he did however feel certain now, particularly after talking to Father Renney, that Timmie's mother had found her feet at last. Therefore, he beamed down at Timmie, he had found that Timmie belonged with his rightful mother. 'And now'—he gestured to the startled young girl in the pink blouse and with the tousled hair—'you may reclaim your son.' And then with an official bang of his gavel that felt like Sam's heart hitting bottom as she stared, he announced in a booming voice, 'The court finds in favour of the natural mother.' He got up then and left the room as Sam tried desperately not to scream. Timmie's mother, however, did not restrain herself in a similar fashion, and ran to him, almost knocking him out of his chair. All Sam could see was Timmie flailing wildly, trying to move away from her, and his chair being firmly held by the lawyer as he was embraced by his mother shrieking loudly all the while, 'My baby . . . my baby . . .'

'Sam . . . Sam!' It was a plaintive wail that almost tore her asunder and instinctively she turned toward him and tried to push her wheelchair past Josh and Norman to reach the child. But Josh grabbed the handles on the back of the wheelchair and Norm blocked her, the two men had instantly understood each other without a word. It would do no good now. The mother was all over her child.

'Stop . . .' Sam pushed at Norm. 'I have to see him.'

'You can't, Sam!' He spoke quietly but firmly, and Josh wouldn't let go of the chair as she pushed.

'I have to, dammit . . . Josh, let go!' She was beginning to sob now, but already Timmie's mother's lawyer was pushing his little wheelchair from the room as in anguish Timmie turned back toward Samantha, waving his little arms with a grief-stricken face.

'Sam . . . Sam!'

'I love you!' she called out. 'I love you, Timmie! It's okay!' And then he was gone. And as though the last ounce of strength had left her, she dropped her face in her hands and began to sob. For a long moment neither man knew what to do, and then Norman knelt beside her.

'I'm so sorry, Sam . . . we can appeal it.'

'No.' She could barely speak as she reached for her handkerchief and shook her head at Norm. 'No. I can't do that to him.' He nodded and stood up and then signalled Josh. There was no reason to stay there. It was all over for Samantha and Timmie. The boy was gone.

38

For the rest of the week Sam stayed at the big house, never leaving the building, and for the first day not leaving her room. Norman had come to pick up Timmie's things to return them to the social worker for Timmie, but Sam had refused to see him. Josh was taking care of everything for her. Twice that morning Norman had knocked on the door. He had even tried to call her. But she didn't want to see anyone, except Timmie. She had just lost the last love of her life.

'Will she be all right?' Norman asked Josh with a look of sorrow, and the old man shook his head with tears in his eyes.

'I don't know. She's tough, but she's lost a lot. And this . . . you don't know how she loved him.'

Norman nodded sadly. 'Yes I do.' For the first time in his career, as he left the courthouse the previous evening, he had stepped on the gas as hard as he could in his Mercedes, and as he drove home at eighty miles an hour he had cried too. 'I'd like to see her when she's ready. And I want to talk to her about an appeal. I think it would be worth it. This is an unusual case, because what she had against her is the fact that she is both single and crippled. But it's absolutely incredible that the court should find for a prostitute and a drug addict because she's a natural mother against a woman like Sam. I want to take this one all the way to the Supreme Court.'

'I'll tell her.' Josh looked as though he approved. 'When I see her.'

And then suddenly Norman looked worried. 'She wouldn't do anything crazy, would she?'

Josh thought for a while. 'I don't think so.' He didn't know she had tried that once before in the hospital in New York. But this time she wasn't suicidal. She just wished she were dead, but some faint, irrational hope that one day she might get Timmie back kept her from doing anything truly crazy. Instead, she just lay in bed, without moving, without eating, only dragging herself to the bathroom, for two whole days. She just cried and slept and then cried some more when she awoke, and at the end of the second day she awoke to hear someone pounding on her door. She lay silently in bed, fully intending not to answer, and then she heard glass breaking and knew that someone had just come through her front door.

'Who is it?' She sounded frightened. Maybe it was a burglar, she wondered. But as she sat up in bed with a look of confusion and terror, the lights in the hall suddenly went on, and she saw Jeff with his shock of red hair. His arm was bleeding as he stood there and then he looked suddenly embarrassed, and as always he flushed beet-red. 'What are you doing here?'

'I came to see you. I couldn't take it anymore, Sam. I haven't seen a light on in here for two days, and you didn't answer the other times when I came to the door . . . I thought maybe . . . I was afraid . . . I wanted to know if you were all right.' She nodded, smiling at him for caring, and then the tears came again and suddenly he was holding her tightly in his arms. The odd thing was that as he held her it was a familiar feeling, as though he had held her before, as though she knew his arms and his chest and his body, but she knew that this was a crazy thought and she pulled away from him and blew her nose.

'Thanks, Jeff.'

He sat down on the edge of the bed and looked at her. Even after two days of just lying there, she looked lovely. And for just an instant he had a wild urge to kiss her, and as he thought of it he flushed bright red again. But as he did she was suddenly laughing through her tears and he looked at her in confusion. 'What are you laughing at?'

'When you get embarrassed, you look just like a radish.'

'Thanks at lot.' He grinned. 'I've been called carrot-top, but never radish-face.' And then with a gentle smile, 'You okay, Sam?'

'No. But I will be, I guess.' And then another trickle of tears coursed down her face. 'I just hope Timmie'll be okay.'

'Josh says your lawyer wants to appeal it, all the way to the Supreme Court.'

'Yeah?' She looked cynical and angry. 'He's full of shit. He doesn't have a chance of winning. The fact is that I'm a cripple and I'm single. They probably don't even care if I'm single, but I'm a cripple. That's enough. Prostitutes and drug addicts make better mothers than cripples, or didn't you know?'

'The hell they do.' He almost snarled it.

'Well, that's what the judge decided.'

'The judge sucks.' She suddenly laughed at the outrageous comment and then realised that she smelled beer on his breath. She frowned as she looked at the young redhead.

'You drunk, Jeff?'

He looked embarrassed and blushed again but he shook his head. 'I just drank two beers. It takes more than that.'

'How come?'

'It just does. I usually don't get tight till five or six.'

'No.' She laughed at him. 'I mean how come you drank the two?' She didn't like the men to drink around the kids and Jeff knew it, but she knew from the darkness outside that it was after hours.

'It's New Year's Eve, Sam.'

'Is it?' She looked surprised and then counted backward . . . the hearing had been on the twenty-eighth, the verdict on the twenty-ninth, that had been two days ago. 'Oh, shit. So it is. And you're going out partying?'

'Yeah. I'm going over to the Bar Three. Did I ever tell you I used to work there?'

'No, but you seem to have worked on every damn ranch in the West.'

'I forgot to tell you about that one.'

'Are you taking a date?'

'Mary Jo.' This time he turned fire-engine red.

'Josh's girl?' She looked amused and he grinned at her. 'Yeah.'

'What did Josh have to say to that?'

'That he'd kick my ass if I got her drunk. But hell, she's almost nineteen. She's legal.'

'I'd watch out though, if I were you. If Josh said he'd kick your ass, he means it.' And then her face grew sober again. 'How is he?'

'Worried about you.' Jeff's voice was gentle in the quiet room. 'We all are, the ones who know. Your lawyer was here yesterday.'

'I figured he would be. To pick up Timmie's things?' Jeff hesitated and then nodded. 'Did he get all his Christmas stuff?' She began to cry again. 'I want him to have all of it.'

'He has it, Sam.' And then, not knowing what else to do for her, he took her in his arms and held her, and she lay her head against him and cried. He wanted to tell her then that he loved her, but he was afraid to. He had loved her the first time he saw her, with that incredible pale gold hair. But she was nine years older than he was and she never acted like she was interested in any man. He wondered sometimes if she could still do it, but he didn't even care, he just wanted to hold her and tell her he loved her one day. They lay like that for a long time, and then the tears stopped.

'Thank you.' She looked at him for a long, quiet time, stirred by his strength and his youthful beauty. 'You'd better get out of here now or you'll end up spending New Year's Eve with me instead of May Jo.'

'You know something?' His voice was deep and sexy. 'I'd like that.'

'You would, would you?' Her eyes were teasing but she could see that his were not. But she didn't think what she was suddenly feeling was what Jeff needed. He didn't need an older woman, and a cripple yet, on his hands. He was young. He had is whole life in front of him, filled with girls like Mary Jo. But she was suddenly so desperately lonely that she wanted to reach out to him, and before she did something foolish, she wanted him to go. 'Okay, kiddo, go celebrate New Year's Eve in style.' She sat up in her bed and tried to smile.

297

'And you, Sam?'

'I'm going to take a hot bath, make myself something to eat, and come back to bed. I guess maybe tomorrow I'm going to have to come out of my hole and face the world.'

'I'm glad to hear it. For a while there you had me scared.'

'I'm tough, I guess, Jeff. Time does that to you.' Time, and heartbreaks, and loss.

'Does it? It sure makes you beautiful too.'

'Go on, Jeff.' She looked worried. 'It's time for you to go.'

'I don't want to leave you, Sam. I want to stay here.'

But she shook her head as she looked at him, took his hand, held it to her cheek, and then kissed the fingertips gently as she let it go. 'You can't stay, Jeff.'

'Why not?'

'I won't let you.'

'You don't believe in ranchers and ranch hands mixing?' He bridled like a young stallion and she smiled.

'No, nothing like that, love. It's just that my life is behind me now and yours isn't. You don't need something like this.'

'You're crazy. Do you know how long I've wanted you?'

She put a finger to his lips. 'I don't want you to tell me. It's New Year's Eve, people say things they shouldn't on nights like this. I want us to be friends for a long time, Jeff. Please don't spoil it.' And then, with tears in her eyes again, 'I need you right now. You and Josh, and the children, but especially you and Josh. Don't do anything to change that. I just . . . I couldn't take it . . . I need you too much.' He held her once again then, kissed the top of her head, and then stood up and looked down at her.

'I'll stay if you want me to, Sam.'

She looked up into the brilliant green eyes and shook her head. 'No, babe, it's okay. You go.' He nodded slowly then and stood looking at her for one last moment in the doorway, and then she heard his cowboy boots echo in the hallway and then the front door close.

39

'Sam? . . . Sam?' It was six o'clock in the morning on New Year's Day and she was dressed and in her kitchen, making coffee for the first time in three days, when she heard Josh pounding on the door. She smiled to herself. One by one they would all break her door down if she didn't come out now. She still felt the terrible emptiness of Timmie's loss, but she knew that she couldn't let herself go. She owed more than that to the other kids. Slowly she wheeled her chair to the front door and opened it, looking out into the grey light before dawn as Josh stood in his heavy jacket on the front porch.

'Hi, Josh. Happy New Year.'

He stood there, saying nothing, and she wondered what was wrong. He looked as though he had been crying. 'You okay?' He shook his head and walked slowly into the room. 'Come and sit down.' She had thought that he had come to offer her solace and now she knew that he was in trouble. 'What is it?' She eyed him, her own brow furrowed with worry, and he gazed at her as he fell heavily into a chair and then dropped his head into his hands.

'The kids, Jeff and Mary Jo. They went out to some party last night'—he stopped and swallowed hard—'and they got drunk as skunks, and then drove home.' Sam felt her heart begin to race. She was afraid to ask the next question but he answered it for her. He looked up with an air of great pain and she saw two great big tears creep down his face. 'They ran into a tree and bounced off into a ravine . . . Mary Jo broke both her arms and legs, and tore up her face pretty bad . . . Jeff's dead.' Sam closed her eyes and reached for his hand, thinking of the boy who had held her only the night before and wondering if she had asked him to stay with her after all, that none of it would ever have happened. But it would have been wrong for her to seduce a boy of twenty-four, she told herself as she thought back over the night before. Wrong? she questioned herself. Wrong? Was it better for him to be dead?

'Oh, God . . .' She opened her eyes and looked at Josh, and then she reached out and held him. 'Will Mary Jo be okay, Josh?' He nodded and then sobbed into Sam's arms.

'But I loved that boy too.' He had only been with them for a year but it felt like half a lifetime, and now she understood the references he'd had from other ranchers, still wanting him to come back.

'Does he have folks we should call?'

'I don't know.' He blew his nose on a red handkerchief from his pocket and then replaced it with a sigh. 'I guess we should go through his things. I know his mum was dead, because he said something about it once or twice, but I don't know if he has sisters or brothers or a dad. He never talked about his life much, just about the kids here, and you, and how happy he was around the kids and the horses.'

Sam closed her eyes again and took a deep breath. 'We'd better to through his stuff. Where is he now?'

Josh sighed and stood up. 'I told them to keep him at the hospital, and we'd call and tell them what to do. If his folks are somewhere else, they may want him sent back.'

'I just hope we find something in his things that tells us who they are. What do we do if he doesn't have anything like that, Josh?' This was a new problem for her.

'Bury him with Bill and Miss Caro, I guess, or in town.'

'We can bury him here.' He was one of her people now, and he had loved the ranch. It was mad to be talking of burying that boy though, only a few hours before he had been sitting on a corner of her bed, holding her in his arms. She forced the memories from her mind, reached for her own jacket on a low peg near the front door, and turned her wheelchair slowly out the door.

Josh looked at the broken window in surprise then and turned to Sam. 'What happened?'

'Jeff. He wanted to be sure I was okay last night. He came to see me before they went out.'

'I had a feeling he'd do that, Sam. He looked at this house for two days and I knew all he could think about was you.' Sam nodded and said nothing more until they reached his cabin. For her it was bumpy going, because the paths to the men's cabins didn't need the smoothly paved walks that were everywhere else to allow for the wheelchairs. But Josh pushed her over the bumps and ruts and eased her wheelchair into the comfortable little cabin. She looked around at the unmade bed and moderate chaos that the boy had left, and felt that if they looked hard enough, they would find him. Maybe he would come staggering out of the bathroom with a grin, or poke his head out of the covers, or come wandering in singing a song . . . He couldn't be dead . . . not Jeff . . . not that young boy. Josh looked at her with his own look of pain and sat down at the small maple desk and began to pull out papers. There were photographs and letters from friends, souvenirs from old jobs, pictures of girls, programmes from rodeos, and everything except what they needed to find now.

Finally Josh came up with something that looked like a little leather billfold and in it he found a card with Jeff's social security number on it, some insurance papers, a couple of lottery tickets, and a slip of paper. On the paper it said, 'In case I get hurt, please contact my father: Tate Jordan, Grady Ranch,' and there was a post-office number in Montana.

As Josh looked at it his mouth dropped open and he stared, and then suddenly he remembered . . . the Bar Three . . . why hadn't he thought to ask? Sure, Tate had had a boy over there. He looked up at Sam in disbelief and she frowned at him.

'What is it?'

There was nothing he could say to her now. He only handed her the slip of paper and walked slowly outside for a breath of air.

40

Sam stared at the piece of paper for almost half an hour, trying to decide what to do and feeling her heart pound in her chest while she thought of it. She had almost made love to Tate's son the night before—what an insane quirk of fate. And now because she hadn't, he was dead, and she had to call his father. But she knew that even if they had made love, he might have gone out drinking and could have died then too. Whatever had happened, there was no changing fate. And now she had to face the problem of what to tell Tate Jordan and how. It was ironic that after all the searching she had done, and all the looking and asking and calling, there it was finally, his address, lying in the palm of her hand. She slipped the piece of paper into her jacket pocket and wheeled outside.

Josh was waiting for her there, leaning against a tree, as the sun rose slowly in the morning sky. 'What are you going to do, Sam? You going to call him?' He knew the truth now, and he hoped to hell she would.

She nodded sombrely. 'We have to. It's only right.'

'You gonna do it?'

'No, you are. You're the foreman.'

'You scared?'

'No, if it were anyone else, I'd do it, Josh. But I don't want to talk to him. Not now.' It had been almost exactly three years since he'd run off.

'Maybe you should.'

'Maybe so.' She looked at him sadly. 'But I'm not going to.'

'Okay.' But when Josh called, they told him that Tate was in Wyoming for the week, at a cattle auction with some of the other hands. No one seemed to know where they were staying or how to reach them, and it meant that

Jeff was going to have to be buried, either at the ranch or in town. They couldn't wait a week.

The funeral was simple and painful for all. But it was part of nature, part of life, Sam told the children, and Jeff had been their friend, so it was right that they should bury him together. The local minister said a little piece over the casket, and that day the men buried him next to Caro and Bill, and the children rode out over the hills, each of them carrying a bunch of flowers, which they left on the fresh grave. And afterward they all stood around and sang their favourite songs. It seemed a fitting way to bury someone who had been one of them and had been a friend to many. And as they turned their horses back toward the ranch and cantered over the hills, Samantha watched them, with the sun setting to their right, and their horses' hooves beating softly on the ground, and the air cool around them, and she thought that she had never seen anything as lovely in her life. For a moment she felt as though Jeff were riding alongside them, and in silent tribute to their lost friend, the ranch hands had led out Jeff's horse riderless, with his colourful Western saddle. For some reason it brought back her own memories of Timmie, and once more she felt tears sting her eyes.

And as she wrote to Tate that night from her desk at the big house, it helped her to hold out a hand to him, whatever had passed between them and whatever was no more. She too, had lost a child now, though he had been hers differently than Jeff had been Tate's, but still she knew the agony of that loss and she felt it again now even more deeply as she wrote to the man she had sought in vain for so long. She found herself wishing, too, that she knew what Jeff had told him. The one thing she didn't want him to know was what had happened to her. But she decided to twist the truth a little and pray that Jeff had not told at all.

'Three years doesn't seem like a very long time,' she wrote from her kitchen table after the initial paragraph in which she told him the news as simply as she could. 'But what a great deal has changed here. Caroline and Bill are

303

both gone now, resting next to where we laid Jeff today, in the hills, near their cabin. And the children who share the ranch with me rode out with flowers to leave on Jeff's grave as the men led his horse in the sunset. It was a difficult moment, a beautiful day, a sad loss for us all. The children sang the songs he loved best, and somehow, as we rode back, I had the feeling that he was near us. I hope, Tate, that you always feel him near you. He was a wonderful young man and a dear friend to us all, and the waste of such a young life is a source of disbelief and sorrow and immeasurable pain. I can't help but feel though that he accomplished more in his short lifetime than most of us with so many more years, which we spend so much less well.

'I don't know if you were aware, but Caroline had left the ranch, after her death, for a special purpose. She wished it to be made into a special facility for handicapped children, and Josh and I worked for months afterward to get it ready. It was just before we opened our doors to these special children that Jeff joined us, and he had a gift for this kind of work that truly touched the heart. He did things that would take hours to relate but that should make you proud of him, and I will see now if in the slew of photographs we took in the beginning there are any of Jeff, which I will send you. It will undoubtedly give you a clearer idea of what he did here. The ranch is very different from what you once knew.

'Certainly none of us had realised that this was Caroline's intention for the ranch, but it has served a worthy purpose, as has your son. I grieve for you in your loss, I wish you well, and we will be sending you all of his things to avoid the need of your making this painful journey. If there is anything that we can do here in this regard, please don't hesitate to contact us. Josh is always here and I'm sure would be happy to help you.' She signed it, 'Cordially, Samantha Taylor.'

There was no trace in her letter of what had passed between them, and the day after the funeral, Sam had Josh and some of his boys pack up Jeff's things and ship them air express to Tate. And that night she herself went through the ranch albums as promised and carefully took out each of the photographs of Jeff, searched for the corresponding negatives and the next day went into town with the whole stack. When the pictures came back a week later, she carefully went over them again to make sure that there were none of her, and there weren't, and then she put them in an envelope, without anything else, and mailed them to Tate. For Sam, that ended the chapter of Tate Jordan. She had found him at last. She had had the choice of reaching out to him, of telling him she still loved him, of even asking him to come. But just as she had sent Jeff away that fateful night, because she knew it would be selfish of her to reach out and wrong for the boy, now she turned away again, for her own reasons, and she congratulated herself afterward for what she had done. She didn't belong in Tate's life anymore, not the way she was. And she wondered as she lay in bed that night if she hadn't been crippled if she would have reached out to Tate now. There was no way to know, of course, because if she hadn't been crippled, she wouldn't have had the ranch, wouldn't have known Jeff, wouldn't have . . . She drifted off to sleep and was only awakened the next morning by the phone.

'Sam?' It was Norman Warren and he sounded excited at the other end.

'Hi.' She was still half asleep. 'What's up?' And then she realised that he probably still wanted to discuss the appeal. With Jeff's funeral and the difficult letter to write to Tate, she hadn't got back to him after their last conversation, but she had definitely decided that she didn't want to put Timmie through the ordeal. She had spoken to the social worker twice, he had told her that Timmie was having a rough time readjusting and he wanted to come back to her, but that there was nothing anyone could do, and he had told Timmie as much the last time he'd stopped by at their home. She had asked him if his mother was being decent to him this time, but the social worker was vague and said that he assumed she was.

'Sam, I want you to come to L.A.'

'I don't want to discuss it, Norman.' She sat up in bed with an unhappy frown. 'There's no point. I won't do it.'

'I understand that. But there are some other matters we have to work out.'

'Like what?' She sounded suspicious.

'There are some papers you didn't sign.'

'Send them to me.'

'I can't.'

'Then bring them to me.' She sounded annoyed. She was tired and it was early. And then she realised, as she blinked again, that it was Sunday. 'What are you doing, calling me on a Sunday, Norm?'

'I just didn't have time to get to it last week. Look, I know this is an imposition, Sam, and you're busy too, but couldn't you please do me a favour? Could you come in today?'

'On Sunday? Why?'

'Please. Just do it for me. I'd be very grateful.'

And then suddenly she panicked. 'Is something wrong with Timmie? Is he hurt? Did she beat him again?' Sam felt her heart race but he was quick to reassure her.

'No, no, nothing like that. I'm sure he's fine. I'd just appreciate winding it all up today once and for all.'

'Norman,' she sighed and looked at the clock. It was seven in the morning. 'Personally I think you're demented. But you were a big help, and you tried, so I'll do you a favour, just this once. Do you realise what a long drive that is for us?'

'Will you bring Josh?'

'Probably. Where shall we meet you? At your office? And what exactly am I going to sign?'

'Just some papers that say you don't want to appeal.'

What could he be up to? 'Why the hell can't you mail them?'

'I'm too cheap to buy a stamp.'

She laughed at him. 'You're crazy.'

'I know. What time will you be here?'

'I don't know.' She yawned. 'How about after lunch?'

306

'Why not get it over with early?'

'You want me to come in my nightgown, Norman?'

'That would be nice. Shall we say eleven o'clock?'

'Oh, shit,' she sighed. 'All right. But it better not take too long. I have a lot of things to do here.'

'Fine.'

She called up Josh then and told him and he sounded as annoyed as she had. 'Why the hell can't he mail you the stuff?'

'I don't know. But if we have to do it, we might as well go in on a Sunday. I don't have time all week. I'm going to be too busy with the kids.' She was expecting eleven of them from different states.

'All right. Want to leave in half an hour?'

'Make it an hour.'

He did, and she swung herself into the car, wearing jeans and a red sweater, there was a red ribbon in her hair and she was wearing her favourite red cowboy boots.

'You look like a valentine, Sam.'

'I feel more like Halloween. I don't know why the hell we have to go to L.A. on a Sunday morning.' And when they reached Norman's house, he seemed terribly hyper and revved up and insisted they had to go to the court-house, because he didn't have all the papers he needed there after all.

'On Sunday? Norman, have you been drinking?' She really was not amused.

'Just trust me, for God's sake.'

'If I didn't, I wouldn't be here.' Josh looked at him suspiciously and drove the car to the courthouse on the other side of town from where Norman lived. But when they got there, Norman suddenly looked as though he knew what he was doing. He flashed a pass at the guard downstairs, the guard nodded and let them in. 'Seventh floor,' he told the lone elevator man on duty, and when they got out of the elevator on the seventh floor, they turned left and then right and then left again and then suddenly they were in a brightly lit room with a uniformed matron at a desk and a policeman chatting to her, and suddenly Sam gave a gasp and a shriek and she raced toward him. It was Timmie, sitting in his wheelchair, with his teddy, looking filthy dirty again, but wearing his good suit and a grin.

He held her tight for a long time and she felt him tremble in her arms, and he said nothing and all she said was 'I love you, Timmie . . . I love you, darling . . . it's all right . . .' She didn't know how long she would be able to see him, if it would be a minute or an hour or a day, but she didn't care, she would give him everything she had for as long as she could, for as long as they would let her. 'It's all right . . .'

'My mum's dead.' He stared at Sam and said the words as though he didn't understand what they meant. And then Sam saw that there were deep circles under his eyes and another bruise on his neck.

'What happened?' She looked horrified, as much by what she saw as by what he had just said. 'What do you mean?' But Norman came toward them then and took Sam's arm gently.

'She OD'ed, Sam, two days ago. The police found Timmie alone at the house last night.'

'Was she there?' Her eyes were wide as she held Timmie's hand.

'No, she was somewhere else. Timmie was alone at the apartment.' And then he took a deep breath and smiled at the woman who had become his friend. 'They called the judge last night about Timmie, because they weren't sure if they should put him in juvie—juvenile hall,' he translated for her, '—and he called me. He said he'd meet us here this morning with Timmie's file. Sam, it's going to be all over.' There were tears in Norman's eyes.

'Right now?' Norman nodded. 'Can he do that?'

'Yes, he can reverse his decision based on what has just occurred. Timmie won't have to go through all the business of becoming a ward of the court on an interim basis. He's yours, Sam!' He turned and looked at the small child in the wheelchair, holding Samantha's hand. 'You've got your son.' It had been two weeks since

Samantha had seen him wheeled, screaming, from the courtroom, and now he was hers. She reached out and pulled him onto her knees and held him, sobbing openly now and laughing and kissing him and stroking his hair, and slowly he began to understand and he held her and kissed her and then in a quiet moment he touched her face with his small grimy hand and said, 'I love you, Mum.' They were words Samantha had ached to hear all her life.

The judge arrived half an hour later with the file he had collected from his office on the way, signed several papers, had Sam sign them, the matron witness them; Josh cried, Norm cried, she cried, the judge grinned, and Timmie waved his teddy bear at the judge with a broad grin as they wheeled into the elevator. 'So long!' he shouted, and when the doors closed, the judge was laughing and crying too.

41

'And then I'm going to ride Daisy . . . and play with my train and my fire engine and—'

'Take a bath,' Sam filled in for him with a grin on the drive back. My God, what a gift they had just given her. She was laughing and giggling almost hysterically, she was so happy, and for the first time since the accident that had killed Jeff and broken Mary Jo's arms and legs, Sam saw Josh laugh. They had already told Timmie about Jeff when he had asked for him, and he had cried for a minute and then nodded.

'Just like Mum . . .' But he said nothing else about her, and Sam didn't want to press him. She knew from the little that Norm had told her that it had been rough. But now that part of Timmie's life was over, and whatever he remembered in years to come would be counterbalanced by the love she would lavish on him in the time ahead.

She told him about the new children coming in and the garden they were going to plant in the spring, and then she looked at him with a big grin. 'And guess what you're going to do in a few weeks.'

'What?' He looked excited, despite the dark circles under his eyes.

'You're going to school.'

'Why?' He looked less than pleased at the thought.

'I just decided.'

'But I didn't before.' It was a whine just like that of any child and she and Josh exchanged a smile.

'That's because before you were special, now you're regular.'

'Can't I be special again?' He looked at her hopefully and she laughed and tucked him under her arm. They were sitting three abreast in the front seat of the big station wagon, with Timmie in the middle.

'You'll always be special, sweetheart. But now we can just live a regular old life. We don't have to worry about you going away, or being taken away, or anything. You can just go to school like the rest of the kids.'

'But I want to stay home with you.'

'You can for a while, but then you've got to go to school. Don't you want to get smart like me and Josh?' She was giggling again, and suddenly Timmie was laughing too, and he groaned at what she had just said.

'You're not smart . . . you're just my mum now!'

'Thanks a lot!' But it was obvious that the love affair between them was far from over. That afternoon they baked cookies and visited the rest of the kids, and she read him a story before he went to sleep in the room next to hers, and before she had finished it, he was snoring softly. She stayed like that for a long time, just watching him sleep, and touching his hair, and thanking God for bringing him back to her.

It was two weeks later, when he had finally started school and the new arrivals had been admitted and had started to settle down, before Sam got to spend almost a full day in her office. She had worked her way through three stacks of mail, much of it from doctors, and some it from the East, which was new for her. So far they had only had referrals from western cities.

It was then, as she was putting down the last letter, that she saw him. She happened to glance out her window, and there he was, as he always had been, as tall and as lovely, with his raven-black hair and his broad shoulders and his sharply etched face, and his cowboy hat and his boots . . . only now she saw that there was a little more salt mixed in with the pepper at his temples, but if anything, it improved his looks, and she caught her breath as she watched him stop and talk to some of the kids. As she watched him she remembered how well he had played Santa. But suddenly she shrank from her office window, pulled down the shade, and called her secretary to her. Her face was flushed and she looked terribly nervous, and she glanced around the room as though she might hide. 'Find Josh!' was all she told her. And five minutes later he was in the room. By then, outwardly, she had regained her composure. 'Josh, I just saw Tate Jordan.'

'Where?' He looked startled. 'Are you sure?' Hell, it had been three years, he must have changed, maybe she had dreamed it.

'I'm sure. He was out in the big yard, talking to some of the kids. I want you to go find him, find out what he wants, and get rid of him. If he wants to see me, tell him I'm not here.'

'Do you think that's fair?' Josh looked at her reproachfully. 'His boy just died on the ranch, Sam. It ain't been five weeks, and he's buried out there.' He waved toward the hills. 'Don't we at least owe him some time here?'

Sam closed her eyes for an instant and then opened them to look at her old friend. 'All right, you're right. Show him Jeff's grave and then please, Josh, get him out of here. There's nothing to see. We sent him all of Jeff's things. There's no reason for him to be here.'

'Maybe he wants to see you, Sam.'

'I don't want to see him.' And then as she saw the look in his eyes she grew fierce and turned her wheelchair to face him. 'And don't tell me about fair, dammit. It wasn't fair to walk out on me three years ago. That wasn't fair. Now I don't owe him a damn thing.'

Josh stopped in the doorway for a moment with a look of regret on his face. 'The one you owe, Sam, is yourself.'

She wanted to tell him to go to hell, but she didn't. She sat in her office and waited, she didn't even know for what, but she just sat there, thinking. She wanted him to leave the ranch, to go away again, to leave her alone. It was her life now, he had no right to come back and haunt her. Except that she knew that there was some truth in what Josh had just said. He had a right to see where his son was buried.

Josh came back half an hour later. 'I let him ride Sundance to go out and see the boy.'

'Good. Has he left the barn?' Josh nodded. 'Then I'll go home. When you see Timmie, tell him I'm there.' But when he got back, he had a riding lesson with some of his friends, and she sat in her house alone, wondering if Tate had left yet. It was so strange knowing that he was so nearby, that if she had wanted to she could have gone out and touched him, or seen him, or talked to him, and she wasn't even sure of what she was afraid of. Her own feelings? What he might say? Maybe she wouldn't feel anything at all if she had a chance to spend some time with him, maybe what had left the wound open for so long was the fact that he had left her without any real explanation and no chance to fight back. It had been like sudden death, with no reprisal, and now, three years later, he was back and there was nothing left to say. Or at least nothing that seemed worth saying, nothing that she would let herself say.

It was almost dark when Josh knocked on her front door and she cautiously opened it. 'He's gone, Sam.'

'Thanks.' They looked at each other for a long moment and he nodded.

'He's a nice man, Sam. We talked for a long time. He's

312

real torn up about the boy. He said he'd stop by and see Mary Jo tonight at the hospital and tell her he's sorry. Sam . . .' His eyes questioned her and she shook her head. She knew what he was going to say, but instinctively she held up a hand.

'No.' And then, softly, 'Does he know . . . about me? Did he say anything?' Josh shook his head.

'I don't think so. He didn't say anything. He asked where you were, and I said you were gone for the day. I think he understood, Sam. You don't walk out on a woman and then come back three years later. He just said to thank you. He was real touched by where we buried Jeff. He said he wanted to leave it just like that. You know,' he sighed softly and looked out at the hills, 'we talked about a lot of things . . . about life, about people . . . Caroline and Bill King . . . Life sure does change in a few years, don't it?' Josh looked sad tonight, it had done something to him to see his old friend. Sam didn't ask but he volunteered the rest of what he knew. 'When he left here, he went up to Montana. Worked on a ranch. Saved his money, and then took out a loan and bought a small spread and turned rancher. I teased him about it. He said he was doing it to have something to leave the boy. He did real good, and now Jeff is gone. He says he just sold his place last week.'

'What's he going to do now?' Sam looked suddenly nervous. What if he stayed around there, or got a job at the Bar Three?

'He's going back up there tomorrow.' Josh had seen the fear in her eyes. And then, 'I'll see him tonight, Sam, if you should change your mind.'

'I won't.'

Timmie came home then and she thanked Josh again and went in to make dinner. For some reason she didn't want to eat in the main hall, and Timmie had been with the other kids all day. But she was nervous and jumpy all evening, and that night as she lay in the dark all she could think of was Tate. Was she wrong? Should she see him? What did it matter? It was too late now and she knew it, but suddenly, for the first time since she'd been back to the ranch, she wanted to go back to their old places, just to see them . . . the cabin he had lived in behind the orchards, the hills they had ridden, and the secret cabin. In all the time she'd been back on the ranch, over a year now, she had never gone back to the cabin or the little lake, until they buried Jeff nearby. But you couldn't see the cabin from the graves. She had promised herself for months that one day she would go out there, just to retrieve Caroline's things. She really ought to take the place apart, but she didn't have the heart to, or even to see it. All she would think of there would be Tate . . . Tate . . . Tate . . . his name rang in her ears all night long.

In the morning she was exhausted and shaken, and Timmie asked her if she felt sick when they went to breakfast in the main hall. She was relieved when he went off to school with the others and she had time to herself. She wheeled slowly over to see Black Beauty. Occasionally she took the stallion out for a ride, but she hadn't ridden him in a long time, and she kept him now more out of sentiment than anything else. He was too highly-strung for most of the others to ride, the ranch hands didn't really like him, he wasn't Josh's kind of horse, and when she taught or led the children, she really needed a quieter horse like Pretty Girl. But now and then, when she was alone, she still rode him. He was a sensitive animal and he seemed to gear himself down to accommodate her. Even after Grey Devil in Colorado, she wasn't afraid of him.

And now, as she looked at him, she knew what she had to do. She asked one of the men to saddle him up, and a few minutes later he lifted her up into the saddle. Sam walked the huge horse slowly out into the yard and turned toward the hills with a pensive expression. Maybe now was the time when she finally had to face it, when she had to go back and see it and know that it could no longer touch her, because none of it belonged to her anymore. Tate Jordan had loved a woman she hadn't been for years now, and never would be again. And as she began to canter slowly over the hills she knew that, and she looked

314

at the sky and wondered if she would ever love a man again. Maybe if she faced it once and for all and let his memory go, she could let herself care for someone, maybe someone on the ranch, or a doctor she met through the children, or a lawyer like Norman, or . . . But how pale they all looked next to Tate. As she thought of him in the yard only the day before, she smiled softly, and then piece by piece she remembered the time they had shared, the times they had run over these hills, the days they had worked side by side, the respect they'd had for each other, the nights she had spent in his arms . . . And then, as the full impact of what she had felt for him began to hit her, she came over the last hill, rounded the trees, and there she saw it, the little lake and the cabin where she had come with him. She didn't want to go any closer. It was as though, for her, it were haunted. It belonged to another lifetime, to different people, but she saw it and saluted it, and then slowly she wheeled the powerful black stallion and cantered over the little knoll where they had laid Jeff to rest. She stood there for a long moment and smiled at the people they had left there, a man and a woman and a boy, all of them people she had cared about a great deal. But suddenly, as she stood there, with tears running slowly down her face, she felt Black Beauty sidestep and buck gently, he whinnied and she looked around and saw him, sitting tall and proud in the saddle as always, Tate Jordan, astride a new Appaloosa she had just bought. He had come to say good-bye to his son. For a long moment he said nothing to her, and there were tears on his cheeks too, but his eyes bored into hers and she felt her breath catch as she watched him, not sure whether to say something or simply ride away. Black Beauty was dancing gracefully around, and as she reined him in she nodded at Tate.

'Hello, Tate.'

'I wanted to see you yesterday, to thank you.' There was something infinitely gentle in his face. Gentle and yet so powerful. He would have been frightening, had he not looked so kind. But his frame was so large, his shoulders so

315

broad, his eyes so deep set. He looked as though he could have picked up Samantha and her stallion and set them down gently somewhere else.

'You don't have to thank me. We loved him.' Her eyes were like blue velvet as she looked into his.

'He was a good boy.' He shook his head slowly then. 'He did a real foolish thing. I saw Mary Jo last night.' And then he smiled. 'My, she's got big.'

Sam laughed softly. 'It's been three years.'

He nodded, and then he looked at her, with a question in her eyes, and slowly he let the Appaloosa approach. 'Sam?' It was the first time he had said her name and she tried to feel nothing as he did. 'Will you ride with me for a few minutes?' She knew that he wanted to see the cabin, but she couldn't bear the thought of returning there with him. She had to fight with everything she had to keep her distance, not to reach out to this gentle giant who suddenly stood facing her across a chasm of three years. But each time she wanted to say something to him, to say his name, to reach out while she had the chance, she looked down at her legs, tightly strapped to the saddle, and knew what she had to do. Besides, he had left her three years ago, for his own reasons. It was better left as it had been.

'I should get back, Tate. I have a lot to do.' She also didn't want to give him time to figure out why there was a strap around her legs. But he hadn't seemed to notice. He was much too intent on her face.

'It's quite a place you put together. What made you do it?'

'I told you in my letter, it was in Caroline's will.'

'But why you?' Then he didn't know. She felt a sweep of relief.

'Why not?'

'You never went back to New York?' That seemed to shock him. 'I thought you would.' *Did you? Was that why you left, Tate? So I would go back to where you thought I belonged?*

'I did. For a while.' She sighed softly in the early morning. 'I came back after she died.' She looked out at the hills as she spoke. 'I still miss her.'

His voice was soft beside her. 'So do I.' And then, 'Can we ride? Just a few minutes. I won't be back here for a long time.' He looked at her, almost pleading, and then feeling her heart pull inside her, she nodded and let him lead the way. When they rounded the knoll, they stopped as they came to the little lake. 'Do you want to get down for a minute, Sam?'

'No.' She shook her head firmly.

'I don't mean go into the cabin. I wouldn't do that.' And then he looked at her with a question. 'Are their things still there?'

'I haven't touched them.'

He nodded. 'I'd like to talk to you for a minute, Sam.' But this time she shook her head. 'There's a lot I never said.' His eyes pleaded but hers were gentle.

'You don't have to say it, Tate. It's a long time ago. It doesn't matter anymore.'

'Maybe not to you, Sam. But it does to me. I won't bore you with a long speech about it. I just want you to know one thing. I was wrong.' She looked at him, suddenly startled.

'What do you mean?'

'To leave you.' He sighed softly. 'The funny thing is that I even had a falling-out with Jeff about it. Well, not about you, about running from the ranch. He said that all my life I ran away from the important things, from the things that mattered. He said I could have been a foreman, or owned a ranch if I wanted to. He and I drifted for about six months, and then we gave each other hell. I went up to Montana then and bought that little ranch.' He smiled then. 'I made a damn good investment, too, and all with a loan. I did it to show Jeff he was wrong, and now'—he shrugged—'it really doesn't matter anymore. Except for what I learned from it. I learned that it doesn't mean a damn if you're a rancher or a ranch hand or a man or a woman, if you live right and you love well and you do good, that's all that matters. Those two'—he nodded toward the cabin—'look at them, in the end they're buried

317

together side by side, because they loved each other, and no one cares whether or not they were married or whether Bill King kept it a secret all his life that he loved her. What a damn waste of time!' He looked annoyed with himself, and she smiled at him and held out her hand.

'It's all right, Tate.' Her eyes were damp but she was still smiling, and he took her hand and raised it to his lips. 'Thank you for what you just said.'

'It must have been hard as hell on you when I left, Sam, and I'm sorry. Did you stay long after?'

'I looked for you everywhere for about two months and then Caro pretty much threw me out.'

'She was right. I wasn't worth the effort.' And then he grinned. 'Then.'

She laughed at the correction. 'And I suppose you are now?'

'Maybe not. But I'm a rancher now too.' This time they both laughed, and how comfortable it felt to be talking to him. It was almost, but not quite, like old times, when she first knew him, after they had begun to become friends. 'Remember the first time we came here?' She nodded, knowing that they were getting onto delicate ground and they had already come far enough.

'Yes, but that's a long time ago, Tate.'

'And now you're an old woman.'

She looked at him oddly. 'Yes, I am.'

He returned her gaze. 'I thought you'd remarry.'

Her eyes turned hard for a moment. 'You were wrong.'

'Why? Did I hurt you that much?' He looked sad for her, but she only shook her head and didn't answer, and he held his hand out to her again. 'Let's go for a walk, Sam.'

'I'm sorry, Tate, I can't now.' She grew sad and insistent. 'I have to get back.'

'Why?'

'Because I have to.'

'Why won't you let me tell you what I'm feeling?' His eyes looked very green and very deep.

'Because it's too late.' She spoke softly, and as she said

318

it he happened to glance down at her saddle with a look of despair. As he did he frowned and was about to ask her a question, but she seized the opportunity to begin to ride away.

'Sam . . . wait . . .' And then, as he watched her ride along, suddenly he knew the answer, the piece that had been missing from the puzzle for the past two days, why she had done it, why she had come back and not remarried, why it was too late . . . 'Sam.' But she wouldn't listen. It was as though she sensed something different in his tone now, and smacking the reins against Black Beauty's neck, she urged him to go faster, and as he watched her again for a long moment he was sure. The heels that had been so tight in the stirrups, that had pressed the stallion's flanks three years before, hung lifeless, toes pointed down. Never would she have allowed that to happen if she'd had any control. Now he understood the strange aspect of her saddle. He'd been so busy watching her that he hadn't even seen the most important thing of all. But now he had to spur on the Appaloosa to catch her, and finally, just before the last hill before they got back to the main complex, he urged on the Appaloosa like a racehorse and reached out to the stallion's bridle and reined it in. 'Stop, dammit! I have something to ask you!' His green eyes bored into hers, but when she turned, her blue eyes blazed.

'Let go, dammit!'

'No, now I want to know something and I want the truth or I'll knock you off that damn horse I've always hated and we'll see what happens.'

'Try it, you bastard!' Her eyes dared him and she fought him for the reins.

'And then what would happen?'

'I'd get up and walk home.' She prayed that he would believe her.

'Would you? Would you, Sam? Well then maybe we ought to try it . . .' He made to push her gently from her seat and she forced the stallion sideways.

'Stop, damn you.'

'Why won't you tell me? Why?' His eyes were the greenest she had ever seen and on his face there was almost immeasurable pain. 'I love you, dammit, woman, don't you know that? I've loved you every minute since I left here three years ago. But I left for your sake, not for mine, so you could go back to where you belonged with the people you belonged with and forget about me. But I never, ever, forgot you, Sam, I've dreamed of you every lousy night for the last three years, and now suddenly here you are again, ten times more beautiful, and I want you just as much and you won't let me near you. Why? Is there someone else? Tell me, I'll go away and you'll never hear from me again. But it's something else, isn't it? You're like the others, aren't you? Like the children? And you're as big a fool as I was then. I thought being a ranch hand made a difference, now you think not being able to walk does, don't you, because you can't walk, can you, Sam? Can you? Dammit, answer me.' It was an anguished roar as the tears poured slowly down his cheeks and she looked at him, torn between despair and anger, and nodded slowly, and then, with her own tears pouring freely, she pulled the stallion's reins from him and began to walk the horse away.

But first she looked back over her shoulder. 'That's right. You're right, Tate. But the funny thing is that you were right. Oh, not then, but now. Some things do make a difference. And believe me, this does.' She wheeled the horse slowly. 'Now do me a favour. You've said good-bye to your son and you told me what you had to tell me, now go. For both our sakes, go.'

'I won't.' He was adamant, more powerful than the stallion that she rode. 'I'm not going, Sam. Not this time. If you don't want me, you tell me, and we'll see, but not because of your damn legs. I don't care if you can't walk or crawl or move. I love you. I love your head and your heart and your mind and your soul. I love what you gave me and what you gave my son, and what you've given to those children. He told me, you know, Jeff did. He wrote

320

to me about the extraordinary woman who ran the ranch. The stupid thing is that I never understood what he was doing. I never knew that it was you. He had a lady boss here, that's all I knew. I figured some saintly crazy had started something new on Caro's ranch. But I didn't know it was you, Sam . . . and now I'm not leaving.'

'Yes, you are.' Her face was hard. 'I don't want pity. I don't want help. I don't want anything anymore, except what I have—the children and my son.' It was the first he had heard of Timmie, and he still remembered what she had said in the past about not being able to have kids.

'You can explain that one later. Now what do you want to do? Race me for the hills? The barn? The highway? I'm not leaving you, Sam.' She glared at him for a moment, and then in utter fury she urged the stallion on again, back over the hills at an insane pace the Appaloosa was barely able to keep up with, but everywhere she went, Tate was right behind. At last, with even Black Beauty winded, Sam knew she had to stop. They were at the far boundaries of the ranch now, and Sam looked at him almost in despair as she slowed to a walk.

'Why are you doing this, Tate?'

'Because I love you. Sam, what happened?' She stopped at last and told him, and he shielded his eyes from the sun for a moment. She had told him about looking for him everywhere, about her trips and the commercials, about Grey Devil and the fateful ride. 'Sam, why?'

'Because I was desperate to find you . . .' And then she whispered softly, 'Because I loved you so damn much . . . I didn't think I could live without you.'

'Neither did I.' He said it with the sorrow of three years of lonely days and nights. 'I worked so hard day and night, and all I did was think of you, Sam. Every night I'd lie there and all I could think about was you.'

'So did I.'

'How long were you in the hospital?'

'About ten months.' And then she shrugged. 'The funny thing is, I don't mind that anymore. It happened. I can live with it. I just can't force it on someone else.'

'Is there anyone?' He hesitated and she smiled and shook her head.

'No, there isn't, and there won't be.'

'Yes.' He brought the Appaloosa right up next to her. 'There will.' And then, without further warning, he kissed her, pulling her body close to him and tangling his fingers in the precious golden hair. 'Palomino . . . oh, my Palomino . . .' And when she heard the words that she had longed for for so long, she smiled. 'I won't ever leave you again, Sam. Never.' His eyes held her tight, and then she threw all caution to the winds and told him.

'I love you. I always loved you.' Her voice was filled with awe as her eyes drank him in. Tate Jordan had finally come back. And when he kissed her this time, she murmured, 'Welcome home.' He took her hand then, and slowly, riding their horses as close together as they could, they walked them over the hills and went home.

Josh was waiting in the big yard when they rode slowly toward it, but he turned and walked into the barn, pretending not to have seen them. And when they reached the barn door, Sam reined in the handsome stallion and looked at Tate. Slowly, solemnly, he dismounted and stood looking into her face. His eyes asked her a thousand questions, and his heart poured into hers. She hesitated only for a moment, and then she smiled as he said the familiar words.

'I love you, Palomino.' And then in a voice that only she could hear, 'I want you to remember that every day, every hour, every morning, every night, for the rest of your life. From now on I'm going to be here with you, Sam.'

Her eyes never left his, and then slowly, ever so slowly, she began to unstrap her legs from the saddle. She sat there for a minute, watching him, wondering if she could trust him after the endless three years. Was he really back now? Or was it all an illusion, a dream? And would he run away again? Tate could sense the terror that she was feeling, and as he stood beside her he held out his arms. 'Trust me, babe . . .' And then after a long moment,

'Please.' His arms never wavered as she sat there, still and tall and proud in her saddle. There was nothing defeated about Sam. Nothing crippled. Nothing broken. This was no half-woman. This was a woman and a half. But Tate Jordan was more than just a man. 'Sam?' As their eyes held and they watched each other, it was as though the years between them melted, and as Sam put her hands carefully on his shoulders, one could almost feel the bond between them begin to form again.

'Help me down.' The words were quiet and simple, and he swept her from the saddle into his arms with ease, and then, having watched what was happening, Josh appeared suddenly with her chair. Tate hesitated for only a moment and then put her in it, fearing that when his eyes met hers again he would see sorrow and pain. But when he looked into her face now, she was smiling, and deftly she began to roll away. 'Come on, Tate.' She said it matter-of-factly, and suddenly he knew that things had changed. This was no frail broken woman for him to rescue, this was a woman of strength and beauty for him to love. There was a deep smile in the green eyes as he hurried to walk along beside her.

'Where are we going, Sam?' He strode along, and she looked up into his face with a look of peace mingled with unbridled joy.

She smiled at him and rolled on, whispering the word as she looked at him once more. 'Home.'

When they reached the big house, she sped up the ramp with Tate only a few steps behind her. She pulled open the door and watched him carefully for a long moment, his eyes tender with memory as they stood there remembering another time, another life. He wanted to carry her over the threshold, but he wasn't sure she would want that, so with a last look at Sam he quietly stepped inside, then she rolled in behind him and closed the door.

ONCE IN A LIFETIME

Danielle Steel

To John,
Forever,
Olive.

Once in a Lifetime

It only happens once,
   not twice,
      the moments
        vanishing
          like mice,
scurrying past,
    life much
       too fast,
and only for
      the very brave,
       the strong,
        the true,

and when the moment
  comes
    for you,
don't let it
    pass you by,
for in the twinkling
  of an eye,
the love is gone,
  the moment dead,
an empty ringing
  in your head,
your heart will know
  when fate
    has whispered
      in your ear...
oh never fear,
  beloved friend,
  for in the end
    it's worth
      the price,
        the fee,
          the cost,
    when all is lost,
      but love is won,
when true love
    comes,
      there is
        but one.

    d.s.

1

When it snows on Christmas Eve in New York, there is a kind of raucous silence, like bright colours mixed with snow. Looking at Central Park from a window, you can see the snow fall steadily, shrouding all in white. Everything looks so still, so quiet ... but down below, in the streets, there are the inevitable sounds of New York. Horns bleating, people shouting, the clatter of feet and traffic and excitement, only muffled, somewhat dimmed. And in the last-minute furore of Christmas Eve, there is something more, a kind of wonderful tension waiting to explode in laughter and gifts ... people hurrying home, with packages stacked high in their arms, carolers singing, the innumerable Santa Clauses, tipsy and red-faced, celebrating their last night in the deadly cold, women holding tight to children's hands, admonishing them to be careful not to fall, and then smiling, laughing. Everyone in a rush, in high spirits, in unison for this one night of the year ... Merry Christmas! ... doormen waving, happy with their Christmas tips. In a day, a week, the excitement will be forgotten, the gifts unwrapped, the liquor drunk, the money spent, but on Christmas Eve nothing is yet over, it has only just begun. For the children it is a culmination of months of waiting, for the adults the end of frenzied weeks, of parties, shopping, people, gifts ... bright hopes as fresh as falling snow, and nostalgic smiles, remembering distant childhoods and long-forgotten loves. A time of memories, and hope, and love.

As the snow fell steadily the traffic began to thin at last. It was bitter cold, and only a few hardy souls were walking in the snow as it crunched beneath their feet. What had turned to slush earlier that day had now turned to ice, which slid wickedly beneath the six inches of fresh snow. It was treacherous walking, and by eleven o'clock traffic had all but ground to a halt. For New York it was unusually silent. Only an occasional horn sounded in the distance, a random voice calling out for a cab.

The sound of a dozen people leaving the party at 12 East Sixty-ninth Street rang out like bells in the night. They were laughing, singing, they had had a wonderful time. The champagne had been abundant, and there had been hot buttered rum and mulled wine, a huge Christmas tree and bowls of popcorn. Everyone had been given small gifts as they left, bottles of perfume, boxes of chocolates, a pretty scarf, a book. The host was a former book reviewer of *The New York Times*, his wife a celebrated author, their friends an interesting crew, from budding writers to concert pianists of repute, great beauties and great minds, all crushed into the huge living room in their town house, with a butler and two maids passing hors d'oeuvres and serving drinks. It had been planned as their annual Christmas cocktail party, and as always it would go on until three or four. The group that left just before midnight was small, and among them was a tiny blonde woman wearing a large mink hat and a long dark mink coat. Her whole body was enveloped in the rich chocolate fur, her face barely peeking above her collar in the wind as she waved for a last time at her friends and began to walk home. She didn't want to share a taxi with them. She had seen enough people for one evening, she wanted to be alone. For her, Christmas Eve was always a difficult evening. For years she had stayed at home. But not tonight. Not this year. This time she had wanted to see friends, at least for a while. Everyone had been surprised and pleased to see her there.

'Nice to see you, Daphne. You're back. Working on a book?'

'Just starting one.' The big blue eyes were gentle and the delicate sweetness of her face belied her age.

'What does that mean? You'll finish it next week?' She was notoriously prolific, but had been working on a movie for the past year.

She smiled again, this time with more mirth. She was used to their teasing. A touch of envy ... curiosity ... respect. She was a woman who inspired all three. Daphne Fields was intensely private, hardworking, ambitious, determined, visible in literary circles, and yet even when she was present, she wasn't always really there. She always seemed as though she was just one step back, just out of reach, and yet when she looked at you, you could feel her touch your very soul. She seemed to see everything, and yet at the same time, she didn't seem to wish to be seen. She was different than she had been ten years before. At twenty-three she had been gregarious, funny, outrageous ... protected, safe, happy. She was quieter now, the laughter of the past only showed now in glimpses in her eyes, its echo buried somewhere in her soul.

'Daphne?' She turned around quickly at the corner of Madison Avenue as she heard footsteps behind her, muffled by the snow.

'Yes, Jack?' It was Jack Hawkins, the editorial director of her current publishing house, Harbor and Jones, his face red from the cold, his eyes a brilliant blue and watering in the wind.

'Don't you want a ride?'

She shook her head and smiled, and it struck him again how tiny she was, buried in the huge mink coat, her black suede gloved hands holding the collar close. 'No, but thanks. I really want to walk. I live just down the street.'

'It's late.' As always, when he saw her, he found himself wanting to take her in his arms. Not that he ever did. But he would have liked to. So would a lot of other men. At thirty-three she still looked twenty-five, and sometimes twelve ... vulnerable, fresh, delicate ... but

3

there was something more. There was a loneliness in the woman's eyes, which tore at your very soul, no matter how spectacular her smile, how warm her eyes. She was a woman alone. And she shouldn't have been. If life were fair, she wouldn't have been. But she was. 'It's midnight, Daff...' He hesitated before rejoining the others walking slowly west.

'It's Christmas Eve, Jack. And it's cold as hell.' She grinned, her sense of humour leaping to her eyes. 'I don't think I'll get raped tonight.'

He smiled. 'No, but you could slip and fall on the ice.'

'Aha! And break my arm and not be able to write for months, is that it? Don't worry. I don't have another deadline till April.'

'For chrissake, come on. You can come home with us for a drink.'

She stood on tiptoe and kissed his cheek as she patted his shoulder with one hand. 'Go on. I'm fine. But thanks.' She waved him off then, and turned and walked quickly along the street, burying her chin in her coat, looking neither right nor left, not glancing at the shop windows, or the faces of the few people who walked past her. The wind felt wonderful on her face, and as she made her way home she felt better than she had all night. It had been an exhausting evening, it always was at parties like that, no matter how pleasant they were, how many people she knew, they were always the same. But she had wanted to be there tonight. She didn't want to be alone in her apartment, she didn't want to hold on to the memories this year ... didn't want to ... couldn't stand it anymore ... Even now, as her face tingled in the snow, the same memories came back to her, and she walked faster as though to outrun them, as though she ever could.

Almost instinctively she ran to the corner, glanced to see if there was any traffic, saw none, and assumed that the light was green ... as though if she ran fast enough, if she crossed the street, she could leave the memories

4

behind. But she always took them everywhere with her ... especially on Christmas Eve.

Running faster across Madison Avenue, she almost lost her footing as she slipped and then regained her balance as her arms flailed wide. The corner met, she turned rapidly left, to cross the street, and this time she didn't look up in time to see the car, a long red station wagon filled with people, hurtling through the last of their green light, her red. There was a shriek from the woman sitting beside the driver, a thump, another scream from within the car, and a strange sliding noise as the car ground across the ice and stopped at last. For an interminable instant, everything was silence. And then all the car doors opened at once, and half a dozen people rushed outside. There were no voices, no words, no more screams as the driver hurried towards her and then stopped, staring down at the woman lying like a small broken rag doll, cast facedown into the snow.

'Oh, my God ... oh, my God ...' He stood there helplessly for a moment, and then turned frantically towards the woman standing beside him, a look of terror mixed with fury, as though someone had to be blamed for this, anyone but him. 'For chrissake, call the cops.' He knelt beside her then, afraid to touch her, to move her, yet even more afraid that she was dead.

'Is she ... alive?' Another man knelt in the snow beside the driver, bourbon still heavy on his breath.

'I don't know.' There were no plumes of icy vapour from her breathing, no movement, no sound, no life. And then suddenly the man who touched her began to cry softly. 'I killed her, Harry ... I killed her ...' He reached out towards his friend and the two men hugged in silent agony as they knelt there, as two cabs and an empty bus stopped and the drivers ran out.

'What happened?' Suddenly all was action, talking, explanations ... she ran out in front of the car ... never looked up ... didn't see her ... icy ... couldn't stop ...

'Where the hell are the police when you need them?' The driver cursed as the snow fell around him ...

5

thinking, for no reason he could understand, of the carol they had sung only an hour earlier . . . 'Silent night, holy night' . . . and now this woman lay in the snow in front of him, dead or dying, and there were no damn cops.

'Lady? . . . Lady, can you hear me?' The bus driver was kneeling beside her, his face next to hers, trying to feel her breath on his face. 'She's alive.' He looked up at the others. 'You got a blanket?' No one moved. And then, almost angrily, 'Give me your coat.' For a moment the driver of the station wagon looked shocked. 'For chrissake, man, the woman may be dying. Take your coat off.' He hurriedly complied then, as did two others, and they buried Daphne beneath a multitude of coats. 'Don't try to move her.' The old black bus driver looked as though he knew what he was doing as he tucked the heavy coats around her and gently cradled her face, to keep it from freezing in the snow. A moment later the flashing red light appeared. It was a city ambulance and they'd had a busy night so far. They always did on Christmas Eve. A police car was just behind them, its eerie whooping siren screeching hideously as it arrived.

The ambulance attendants hurried at once to Daphne, the police moved more slowly as they took in the scene, and the driver of the station wagon hurried towards them, calmer now, but trembling horribly from the cold, as his coat lay on the street. The bus driver watched as the ambulance attendants gently rolled Daphne on to the gurney. There was no sound from her, no consciousness of pain. He saw now that her face was skinned and cut in several places, but there had been no bleeding as she lay facedown in the icy snow.

The police took a report from the driver, and explained that he would have to take a sobriety test before he could be released. All the others clamoured that he was sober, that he had drunk less than anyone that evening, and that Daphne had run out in front of the car without even looking, and against the light.

'Sorry, it's routine.' The policeman showed no

particular sympathy for the driver, nor did he show any emotion as he glanced at Daphne's face. Another woman, another victim, another case. He saw worse than that almost every evening. Muggings, beatings, murders, rapes. 'She alive?'

'Yeah.' The ambulance driver nodded tersely. 'Just.' They had just slid an oxygen mask into place, and pulled open the mink coat to check her heartbeat 'But we're going to lose her if we don't hurry.'

'Where's she going?' The policeman was scribbling on his report, 'white female of undetermined age ... probably mid-thirties.'

The ambulance driver called over his shoulder as they closed the door on Daphne. 'We're going to take her to Lenox Hill, it's the closest. I don't think she'd make it farther than that.'

'Is she a Jane Doe?' That would be another headache. They'd already sent off two unidentified murder victims to the morgue that night.

'No. She had a purse.'

'Okay, we'll follow you. I can copy it down there.'

There was a tense nod as the driver disappeared to get his charge to Lenox Hill, and the police officer turned back to the shivering driver as he struggled back into his coat. 'Are you going to arrest me?' He looked terrified now. His Christmas had turned instantly into a nightmare as he remembered the vision of Daphne lying facedown in the street.

'Not unless you're drunk. We can give you the sobriety test at the hospital. Have one of your friends drive and follow us there.' The man nodded and slipped back into his car, nodding at one of his friends, who slipped rapidly behind the wheel. There was no talking now, no gaiety: only silence as they followed the double wail of sirens towards Lenox Hill.

2

In the emergency room there was an aura of frantic activity everywhere, with armies of people dressed in white seeming to move with the precision of a fine ballet. A team of three nurses and a resident had instantly taken over as the ambulance attendants wheeled Daphne in, and another resident and an intern had been called meanwhile. The mink coat was thrown over a chair and they rapidly cut off her dress. It was a sapphire-blue velvet cocktail dress she had bought at Giorgio's in Beverly Hills earlier that winter, but it meant nothing now as it lay in pieces around her on the emergency room floor.

'Fractured pelvis ... broken arm ... lacerations on both legs...' There was a deep gash on her thigh gushing blood now. 'Just missed the femoral artery on this one...' The resident worked quickly, taking stock, checking her pulse, watching her breathing. She was in shock by now, and her face looked as pale as the ice where she had lain. There was almost a strange otherworldliness about her now, a lack of individuality, as though she no longer had a face, a name. She was just another body. Just another case. But a serious one. And if they were going to save her, they all knew they were going to have to work fast and well. One shoulder had been dislocated, and the X rays would tell them if she also had a broken leg.

'Head injury?' The other resident was quick to ask as he started an IV.

He nodded. 'A bad one.' The senior resident frowned as he flashed the beam of a narrow flashlight into her eyes. 'Christ, she looks like someone dropped her off the top of the Empire State Building.' Now that she was no longer lying on the ice, her whole face was awash with blood, and she would need stitches in at least half a dozen places on her face. 'Call Garrison. We're going to need him.' The house plastic surgeon had his work cut out for him too.

'What happened?'

'Hit by a car.'

'Hit and run?'

'No. The guy stopped. The cops said he looks like he's about to have a stroke.'

The nurses watched in silence as the residents worked over Daphne, and then wheeled her slowly into the next room for X rays. She still hadn't stirred.

The X rays showed the broken arm and pelvis, the femur had a hairline crack, and the X rays of her skull showed that there was less damage than they had feared, but there was a severe concussion, and they were watching her for convulsions. Half an hour later they had her on an operating table, to set the bones, stitch up her face, and do whatever could be done to save her life. There was evidence of some internal bleeding, but considering her size and the force with which the station wagon had hit her, she was lucky to be alive. Very lucky. And her chart showed that she wasn't out of danger yet. At four thirty in the morning she was taken from surgery to intensive care, and it was there that the night nurse in charge went over her chart in detail and then stood staring down at her quietly, with a look of amazement on her face.

'What's up, Watkins? You've seen cases like that before.' The resident on the floor looked at her cynically, and she turned and whispered with annoyance in her eyes.

'Do you know who she is?'

'Yeah. A woman who was hit by a car on Madison Avenue just before midnight ... broken pelvis, hairline crack in her femur...'

'You know something, Doctor? You aren't going to be

worth a damn in this business unless you learn to see more than just that.' For seven months she had watched him exercise his craft with precision, and very little humanity. He had the techniques, but no heart.

'All right.' He looked tired as he said it. Getting along with the nurses wasn't always his strong suit, but he had come to understand that it was essential. 'So who is she?'

'Daphne Fields.' She said it almost with awe.

'Terrific. But she still has all the same problems she had before I knew her name.'

'Don't you ever read?'

'Yeah. Textbooks and medical journals.' But with the rapid-fire smart-aleck answer, suddenly a light dawned. His mother read all of her books. For a moment the brash young doctor fell silent. 'She's well known, isn't she?'

'She's probably the most famous female author in this country.'

'It didn't change her luck tonight.' He suddenly looked sorry as he glanced down at the small still form beneath white sheets and the oxygen mask. 'Hell of a way to spend Christmas.' They looked at her together for a long moment and then walked slowly back to the nurse's station, where monitors reported the vital signs of each patient in the brilliantly lit intensive care unit. There was no evidence of day or night there. Everything moved at the same steady pace twenty-four hours a day. At times there were patients who came near hysteria from the constant lights, and the hum of monitors and lifesaving equipment. It was not a peaceful place to be, but most of the patients in intensive care were too sick to notice, or care.

'Has anyone looked at her papers, to see if there's someone we should call?' The nurse liked to think that for a woman of Daphne's stature there would be a host of people anxious to be at her side, a husband, children, agent, publisher, important friends. Yet she also knew, from articles she had read in the past, how zealously

10

Daphne guarded her privacy. Hardly anyone knew anything about her. 'She didn't have anything on her except a driver's licence, some cash, some charge cards, and a lipstick.'

'I'll take another look.' She took out the large brown manila envelope that was going to go into their safe, and she felt both important and somewhat outrageous as she went through Daphne Fields's things. She had read all of this woman's books, she had fallen in love with the men and women born in Daphne's mind, and for years she had felt as though Daphne herself were her friend. And now she was going through her handbag as though she did so every day. People waited in bookstores on autographing lines for two and three hours just to get a smile and a signature in a book, and here she was rifling through her purse like a common thief.

'You're impressed by her, aren't you?' The young resident looked intrigued.

'She's an amazing woman with an extraordinary mind.' And then there was something more in her eyes. 'She has given a lot of people a great deal of joy. There were times...' She felt like a fool saying it, especially to him, but she had to. She owed it to this woman who was now so desperately in need of their care. 'There were times when she changed my life ... when she gave me hope ... when she made me give a damn again.'

As when Elizabeth Watkins had lost her husband in a plane crash and she had wanted to die herself. She had taken a leave from the hospital for a year, and she had sat home and mourned, drinking Bob's pension. But something in Daphne's books had turned things around for her again, as though she understood, as though Daphne herself had known that kind of pain. And she made Elizabeth want to hang in, to keep going, to fight back. She had come back to the hospital again, and in her heart she knew it was because of Daphne. But how could she explain that to him? 'She's a wise and wonderful lady. And if I can do anything for her now, I will.'

'She can use it.' And then he sighed and picked up another chart, but as he did so he made a mental note to himself to tell his mother the next time he saw her that he had treated Daphne Fields. He knew that, just like Elizabeth Watkins, his mother would be impressed.

'Dr Jacobson?' The nurse's voice was soft as he prepared to leave.

'Yeah?'

'Will she make it?'

He hesitated for a moment and then shrugged. 'I don't know. It's too soon to tell. The internal injuries and the concussion are still giving us a run for our money. She got quite a blow on the head.' And then he moved on. There were other patients who needed his attention. Not just Daphne Fields. He wondered, as he stood waiting for the elevator, just what made up the mystique of someone like her. Was it that she wove a good tale or was it something more? What made people like Nurse Watkins feel as though they really knew her? Was it all illusion, hype? Whatever it was, he hoped they didn't lose her. He didn't like losing any patient, but if an important, newsworthy one died, it was worse. He had enough headaches without that.

As the elevator door closed behind him Elizabeth Watkins looked down at Daphne's papers again. It was strange, there was no indication of anyone to call in case of emergency. There was nothing in her handbag of any significance at all ... Just then, tucked into a pocket, she found a photograph of a little boy. It was dog-eared and frayed but it looked fairly recent. He was a beautiful little blond child with big blue eyes and a healthy golden tan. He was sitting under a tree, grinning broadly and making a funny sign with his hands. But that was it, other than the driver's licence and charge cards, there was nothing else except for a twenty-dollar bill. Her address was on Sixty-ninth Street, between Park and Lexington, a building that the nurse knew would be handsome and well guarded by a doorman, but who was waiting for her at home? It was strange to realise that despite her fascination with this woman's books, she knew nothing about her at all. There wasn't even a phone number for them to call. As Elizabeth mulled it over an irregularity turned up on one of the monitors, and she and one of the other nurses had to check on the man in 514. He had had cardiac arrest the previous morning, and when they reached him, they didn't like the way he looked. They ended up having to spend over an hour with him. And it wasn't until her shift ended at seven in the morning that she stopped to look in on Daphne again. The other nurses had been checking her every fifteen minutes, but there had been no change in the past two hours since she'd come up to the fifth floor.

'How is she?'

'No change.'

'Are her vitals steady?'

'No change since last night.' Nurse Watkins glanced at the chart again and then found herself staring at Daphne's face. In spite of the bandages and the pallor there was something haunting about that face. Something that made you want her to open her eyes and look at you so that you could understand more. Elizabeth Watkins stood over her quietly, barely touching her hand, and then slowly Daphne's eyelids began to flutter, and the nurse could feel her heart begin to pound.

Daphne's eyes opened slowly as in a distant haze she seemed to look around. But she still looked very sleepy and it was obvious that she didn't understand where she was.

'Jeff?' It was the merest whisper.

'Everything's all right, Mrs Fields.' Nurse Watkins assumed Daphne Fields was a Mrs. Her voice was gentle and soothing, barely audible, as she spoke near Daphne's ear. It was a practised voice of comfort. She could have said almost anything in that tone of voice, and it would have brought a sigh of relief, and the knowledge that one was safe with her.

But Daphne looked frightened and troubled as her

13

eyes struggled to focus on the nurse's face. 'My husband...' She remembered the familiar wail of the sirens from the night before.

'He's fine, Mrs Fields. Everything's fine.'

'He went to find ... the baby ... I couldn't ... I don't...' She didn't have the strength to go on then, as Elizabeth slowly stroked her hand.

'You're all right ... you're all right, Mrs Fields...' But as she said it she was thinking of Daphne's husband. He must have been frantic by then, wondering what had happened to Daphne. But why had she been alone at midnight on Madison Avenue, on Christmas Eve? She was desperately curious about this woman, about the people who populated her life. Were they like the people she wrote about in her books?

Daphne fell back into her troubled, drugged sleep then, and Nurse Watkins went to sign out. But she couldn't resist telling the nurse who took over the station. 'Do you know who's here?'

'Let me guess. Santa Claus. Merry Christmas, by the way, Liz.'

'Same to you.' Elizabeth Watkins smiled tiredly. It had been a long night. 'Daphne Fields.' She knew that the other nurse had also read several of her books.

'For real?' Her colleague looked surprised. 'How come?'

'She was hit by a car last night.'

'Oh, Christ.' The morning nurse winced. 'How bad?'

'Take a look at the chart.' There was a large red sticker on it, to indicate that she was still critical. 'She came up from surgery around four-thirty. She didn't come to until a few minutes ago. I told Jane to put it on the chart.' The other nurse nodded and then looked at Liz.

'What's she like?' And then she felt foolish as she asked it. In the condition Daphne was in, who could possibly tell? 'Never mind.' She smiled in embarrassment. 'I've just always been intrigued by her.'

14

Liz Watkins admitted her fascination openly. 'So have I.'

'Does she have a husband?'

'Apparently. She asked for him as soon as she woke up.'

'Is he here?' Margaret McGowan, the nurse who had just taken over the station, looked intrigued.

'Not yet. I don't think anyone knew who to call. There was nothing in her papers. I'll let them know downstairs. He must be worried sick.'

'That'll be a rotten shock for him on Christmas morning.' Both women nodded soberly, and Liz Watkins signed out and left. But before leaving the hospital, she stopped at central registration and told them that Daphne Fields had a husband named Jeff.

'That's not going to help us much.'

'Why not?'

'Their number's not listed. At least there's nothing under Daphne Fields. We checked last night.'

'Try Jeff Fields.' And out of simple curiosity, Liz Watkins decided to hang around for a few minutes to see what they came up with. The girl at the desk dialled information, but there was no listing for a Jeff Fields either. 'Maybe Fields is a pen name.'

'That doesn't do much for us.'

'Now what?'

'We wait. By now her family will be panicked most likely. Eventually they'll call the police and the hospitals. They'll find her. It's not as though she's just any Jane Doe. And we can call her publisher on Monday.' The girl at central registration had recognised the name too. She looked at Liz curiously then. 'What's she look like?'

'A patient who's been hit by a car.' For an instant Liz looked sad.

'Is she going to make it?'

Liz sighed. 'I hope so.'

'Me too. Christ, she's the only writer I can ever read. I'll stop reading if she doesn't make it.' The remark was meant to be amusing, but Liz was annoyed as she left central registration. It was as though the woman upstairs wasn't really human, just a name on the front of a book.

As she walked out into the snow in the winter sunshine, she found herself thinking about the woman behind the name. It was rare that she took patients home with her. But this was Daphne Fields. The woman whom, for more than four years, she liked to think that she knew. And as she reached the Lexington Avenue subway at Seventy-seventh Street, she suddenly stopped and found herself looking downtown. The address on the charge cards was only eight blocks from where she stood. What was to stop her from going to Jeff Fields? He must have been half crazy by now, frantic about the whereabouts of his wife. It certainly wasn't normal procedure, but after all, they were all human. And he had a right to know. If she could tell him now, and save him some of the frantic searching, what was so wrong with that?

Almost as though her feet were moving without her telling them to, she walked along the salt spread out on the fresh snow, and turned right towards Park when she reached Sixty-ninth Street. A minute later she stood outside the building. It looked exactly as she had suspected it would. It was a large, handsome stone building, with a dark green canopy, and a uniformed doorman standing just inside the door. He opened the door for her with a look of determined inquisition and his only word was 'Yes?'

'Mrs Fields's apartment?' It was extraordinary, she said to herself as she faced him. For four years she had read her books, and now she was standing in the lobby of her house, as though she knew her.

'Miss Fields is not in.' She noticed then that he had an English accent. It was like something out of a movie, or a dream.

'I know. I'd like to speak to her husband.' The doorman knitted his brows.

'Miss Fields doesn't have a husband.' He spoke with

the voice of authority and she wanted to ask him if he was sure. Maybe he was new, maybe he didn't know Jeff. Or maybe Jeff was just her lover, but she had said 'my husband.' For an instant Liz felt confused.

'Is there someone else at home then?'

'No.' He looked at her cautiously, and she decided to explain.

'Miss Fields had an accident last night.' With a burst of inspiration she flashed open her coat then, revealing the white uniform and stockings, and she indicated the starched cap she always carried in a plastic bag. 'I'm a nurse at Lenox Hill Hospital and we couldn't find a notation of next of kin. I thought that maybe...'.

'Is she all right?' The doorman looked genuinely concerned.

'We don't know. She's still on the critical list, and I thought that... Does she live with anyone at all?' But he only shook his head.

'No one. There's a maid who comes in every day, but not on weekends. And her secretary, Barbara Jarvis, but she won't be back till next week.' Barbara had told him that with a smile when she gave him Daphne's Christmas tip.

'Do you know how I might reach her?' He shook his head again with confusion, and then Liz remembered the photograph of the little boy. 'What about her son?'

The doorman looked at her strangely then, almost as though he thought she was slightly mad. 'She has no children, miss.' Something defiant and protective came into his eyes, and for a split second Liz wondered if he was lying. And then he looked into Liz's eyes with an air of dignity and distance and said, 'She's a widow, you know.' The words hit Liz Watkins almost like a physical blow, and a moment later, with nothing left to be said, she walked back out into the frigid Christmas morning and felt tears sting her eyes, not from the cold, but from her own sense of loss. It was as though she could feel her own husband's death in her bones again, as she had with such intense pain for that whole first year after he had died in the crash. So she *had* known ... they weren't just stories she dreamed up in her head. She knew. She had been through it too. It made Liz Watkins feel closer to her again as she walked slowly back to the subway, at Sixty-eighth and Lexington Avenue. Daphne was a widow, and she lived alone. And she had no one, except a secretary and a maid. And Liz Watkins found herself thinking that it was a lonely existence for a woman who wrote books so filled with wisdom and compassion and love. Maybe Daphne Fields was as lonely as Liz was herself. It seemed yet another bond between them, as she walked down the stairs into the bowels of the subway beneath the streets of New York.

3

Daphne lay drifting in her own private haze as a bright light seemed to pierce through the fog from very far away. If she tried very hard to concentrate on it, it would come closer for a time, and then the fog would envelop her again, almost as though she were sailing away from shore towards a distant place, losing sight of the last, barely visible landmarks, the lighthouse blinking faintly at her in the distance. And yet there was something familiar about the light, the sounds, there was a smell she could almost remember as she lay there. She didn't know where she was, and yet she sensed that she had been there before. There was something strangely familiar about it, and even in its distant, intangible familiarity, she knew that there was something terrifying about the sounds and smells. Something terribly, terribly wrong. And once, as she lay there, dreaming, she let out a small agonised sound as, in her mind, she saw a wall of impenetrable flames. But the nurse on duty came to her side quickly, and administered another shot. A moment later there were no memories, no flames, and there was no pain. She floated out again on a blanket of soft, fluffy clouds, the kind one sees looking out of the windows of aeroplanes, unreal, immaculate, enormous ... the kind of clouds one wants to dance on and bounce on ... she could hear herself laughing in the distance, and she turned in her dream to see Jeff standing beside her, as he had been so long ago...

'I'll race you to that dune in the distance, Daffodil.'
... Daffodil ... Daffy Duck ... Daffy Queen ... Funny Face ... he had had a thousand nicknames for her, and there was always laughter in his eyes, laughter and

something gentler still. Something that was there just for her. The race was as much a lark as all their other youthful endeavours. His endless, well-muscled legs racing her thin, graceful ones, and beside him she looked like a child, dancing in the wind, a summer flower on a hillside somewhere in France ... her big blue eyes in her tanned face, and golden hair flying in the wind.

'Come on, Jeffrey ...' She was laughing at him as she raced beside him in the sand. She was quick, but she was no match for him. And at twenty-two, she looked more like twelve.

'Yes, you can ... yes, you can!' But before they reached the dune in the distance, he swept her off her feet and spun her into his arms, his mouth crushing hers with the familiar passion that left her breathless each time he touched her, just as though it were the first time, which had happened when she was nineteen. They had met at a Bar Association meeting, which she was covering for the *Daily Spectator* at Columbia. She was a journalism major, and with overwhelming seriousness and intense devotion, she was doing a series of articles on successful young attorneys. Jeff had spotted her instantly, and somehow managed to get away from his cronies and invite her out to lunch.

'I don't know ... I ought to ...' Her hair had been wound into a tight figure-eight knot at the base of her neck, a pencil stuck into it, a notebook tightly clasped in her hand, and those huge blue eyes looking up into his with just a hint of laughter. She seemed to be teasing him without saying a word. 'Shouldn't you be working too?'

'We'll both work. You can interview me over lunch.' Afterwards, months later, she had accused him of being conceited, but he wasn't. He just desperately wanted to spend some time with her. And they had. They had bought a bottle of white wine and a handful of apples and oranges, a loaf of French bread and some cheese. They had gone deep into Central Park and rented a boat, and they had drifted on the lake, talking about his work and

20

her studies, about trips to Europe, and childhood summers spent in southern California and Tennessee and Maine. Her mother had been from Tennessee, and there was something about her that suggested the delicate southern belle, until one listened to her, and realised how powerful and direct she was. It wasn't the kind of style Jeff associated with a southern belle. Her father had been from Boston and had died when she was twelve. They had moved back to the South then, and Daphne had hated it, enduring it until she left and came to college in New York. 'What does your mother think of that?' He had been interested in everything about her. Whatever she told him, he wanted to know more.

'She's given up on me, I think.' Daphne said it with a small smile of amusement, her eyes lighting up again in just the way that tore at something deep in Jeffrey's soul. There was something so damn alluring about her, at the same time so sexy and so sweet, and then at the very same time so outrageous and gutsy. 'She's decided that in spite of her best efforts, I'm a damn Yankee after all. And not only that, I've done something unforgivable, I've got a brain.'

'Your mother doesn't approve of brains?' Jeffrey was amused. He liked her. He liked her one hell of a lot in fact, he decided as he attempted not to stare at the slit in her pale blue linen skirt, and the shapely legs beneath.

'My mother doesn't approve of the overt use of brains. Southern women are very canny. Maybe wily is a better word. A lot of them are smart as hell, but they don't like to show it. "They play."' She said it with a southern drawl worthy of Scarlett O'Hara, and they both laughed in the summer sun. It had been a beautiful July morning, and the sun was hot on their bare heads at noon. 'My mother has a master's in medieval history, but she'd never admit it. "She's just a lazy southern belle, y'know..."' The drawl was back again as she smiled at him with those cornflower-blue eyes. 'I used to think I wanted to be a lawyer. What's it like?' She looked suddenly very young again as she asked, and with a sigh he leaned back comfortably in the little boat.

'A lot of work. But I like it.' His speciality was publishing and that intrigued her most of all. 'You thinking about law school?'

'Maybe.' And then she shook her head. 'No, not really. I did think about it. But I think maybe writing is more for me.'

'What kind of writing?'

'I don't know. Short stories, articles.' She blushed faintly in the summer sun, and lowered her eyes. She was embarrassed to admit to him what she really wanted to do. It might never happen. It was only now and then that she thought it would. 'I'd like to write a book one day. A novel.'

'Then why don't you?'

She laughed out loud as he passed her another glass of wine. 'Simple as that, eh?'

'Why not? You can do anything you want to.'

'I wish I were that sure. And what would I live on while I wrote my book?' She had used the last of the money her father had left her to go to school, and with one more year to go, she was already worrying that the meagre funds might not hold out. Her mother couldn't help her. She was working in a dress shop in Atlanta, an elegant one, but nonetheless there was barely enough for Camilla Beaumont to feed herself.

'You could marry a rich man.' Jeffrey was smiling at her, but Daphne didn't look amused.

'You sound like my mother.'

'Is that what she'd like?'

'Of course.'

'And what do you have in mind when you finish school?'

'A decent job, on a magazine, maybe a newspaper.'

'In New York?' She nodded, and he wasn't sure why, but he felt suddenly relieved. And then he looked at her with interest, his head tilted to one side. 'Aren't you going home this summer, Daphne?'

'No, I go to school in the summer too. That way I'll finish early.' There wasn't enough money for her to take her time.

'How old are you?' It was more like he was interviewing her than she him. She hadn't asked him a single question about the Bar Association meeting or his work as an attorney, they had only talked of themselves since they had shoved off from the dock in the little rented boat.

'I'm nineteen.' She said it with a sudden spark of defiance, as though she were used to being told that she was too young. 'And in September I'll be twenty and a senior.'

'I'm impressed.' His eyes were gentle as he smiled, and she blushed. 'I mean it. Columbia's a tough school, you must have worked damn hard.' She could tell by his tone of voice that he meant it and suddenly she was pleased. She liked him. Almost too much. Or maybe it was just the sunshine and the wine, but she knew as she looked at him that it was more than that. It was the curve of his mouth, the gentleness in his eyes, the graceful strength of his hands as he pulled lazily at the oars from time to time ... and the way he watched her, with intelligence and interest ... the sensitivity of the things he said.

'Thank you...' Her voice drifted off and sounded very soft.

'What's the rest of your life like?'

She looked confused at the question. 'What do you mean?'

'What do you do with your spare time? I mean other than pretend to interview slightly drunk attorneys in Central Park.'

She laughed at him then and the sound echoed as they passed beneath a little bridge. 'Are you drunk? It must be the sun as much as the wine.'

'No.' He shook his head slowly as they came out into the light again. 'I think it's you.' He leaned over then and kissed her, and they had both played hooky for the

23

rest of the afternoon. 'They'll never know the difference,' he assured her as they wandered south towards the zoo. They laughed at the hippopotamus, threw peanuts to the elephant, and ran all the way through the monkey house holding their noses and laughing. He wanted to put her on the pony ride as though she were a little girl, and laughing at him again, she refused. Instead they took a hansom cab ride through the park, and at last they strolled up Fifth Avenue beneath the trees, until they reached Ninety-fourth Street where she lived.

'Do you want to come up for a minute?' She smiled innocently at him, holding the red balloon he had bought her at the zoo.

'I'd love to. But would your mother approve?' He was twenty-seven years old, and in the three years since he had graduated from Harvard Law he hadn't once thought of anyone's mother or whether or not they would approve. It was a good thing too, since no one's mother would. He had been on an orgy of dating and free sex since he had left school.

Daphne laughed at him as she stood on tiptoe and put her hands on his shoulders. 'No, Mr Jeffrey Fields, my mother would not approve.'

'Why not?' He pretended to look hurt as a couple returning from work looked at them and smiled. They looked young and beautiful and perfectly matched, his hair a deeper gold than hers, his eyes a dazzling grey-green, his features as handsomely sculpted as her own, and his youthful strength in sharp contrast to her delicate size as he circled her with his arms. 'Because I'm a Yankee?'

'No...' She tilted her head to one side and he felt his insides melt as his hands touched the tiny waist. 'Because you're too old, and too good-looking...' She grinned and gently pulled free from his grasp. 'And because you've probably kissed half the girls in town' – she laughed again – 'including me.'

'You're right. My mother would be shocked too.'

'Well, then come on upstairs for a cup of tea, and I

won't tell your mother, if you don't tell mine.' Her roommate was gone for the summer, and the apartment was tiny and respectable, shabby but not ugly. She made him iced tea, which she served with mint and wonderful delicate lemon cookies. He sat beside her on the couch, and it was suddenly eight o'clock at night and he wasn't tired or bored. He couldn't take his eyes off her, and he knew that he had finally met the woman of his dreams.

'How about dinner?'

'Aren't you tired of me yet?' Her feet were curled up under her and the hours had flown like minutes. The sun had just set over Central Park, and they had been together since before noon.

'I don't think I'll ever get tired of you, Daff. Will you marry me?'

She laughed at the question, watching his face, and she noticed something strangely serious in his eyes. 'In addition to dinner or instead of?'

'I'm serious, you know.'

'You're crazy.'

'No' – he looked at her matter-of-factly – 'actually, I'm smart as hell. I graduated in the top five of my class, I have a damn good job, and one day I'm going to be a powerful and successful lawyer. You're going to write best-selling books, and' – he narrowed his eyes as though considering the matter further – 'we'll probably have three children. We should have two, but you're so damn young we'll probably sneak in a third before you're thirty. What do you say?'

She couldn't stop laughing now. 'I still say you're crazy.'

'All right, I concede. We'll make it two children. And a dog. A golden lab.' She laughed and shook her head. 'All right. A French poodle . . . a Chihuahua?'

'Will you stop?'

'Why?' He looked suddenly like a little boy, and she felt the same leap in her heart she had felt all afternoon at his side. 'Don't you like me?'

25

'I think you're terrific. And definitely crazy. Is this the line you use on everyone, or only innocent students like me?'

He looked totally serious and perfectly calm. 'I haven't proposed to anyone before, Daphne. Ever.' He leaned back against the couch. 'When are we going to get married?'

'When I'm thirty.' She crossed her arms and looked at him with amusement as they sat looking at each other from opposite ends of the couch, but he solemnly shook his head.

'When you're thirty, I'll be thirty-eight. I'll be too old.'

'And I'm too young. Call me in ten years.' She looked suddenly womanly and sure of herself and very, very strong and he loved it, as he moved slowly towards her on the couch.

'If I walked out of here right now, I would call you in ten minutes. If I could bring myself to wait that long. Now, will you marry me?'

'No.' But her insides turned to mush as he approached.

'I love you, Daff. Even if you do think I'm crazy. But I'm not. And whether you believe me right now, or not, we're going to get married.'

'I don't have a penny to my name.' She felt a need to tell him that, almost as if what he was saying was serious, as though he really meant it. But the craziest thing of all was that she knew he did.

'I don't have a dime either, Daff. But we will one day. Both of us. And in the meantime we can live on those fabulous cookies and iced tea.'

'Are you serious, Jeff?' She suddenly looked at him with something very fragile in her eyes. Suddenly she had to know. Maybe he was only playing with her. And she hoped not.

But his voice was hoarse and powerful and kind as he touched her cheek with one hand and reached out for her hand with the other. 'Yes, I am. I know right at this moment that whatever happens between us, it'll be all right, Daff. I feel that. I could marry you tonight, and I know it would be right for us for the rest of our lives. Something like this only happens once in a lifetime. And I'm not going to let it go. If you fight me, I'll pursue you until you listen to me. Because I'm right and I know it.' And after a silent moment between them, 'And I think you know it too.'

Her gaze bored into his then, and he could see that there were tears hovering on her lashes. 'I have to think about this ... I'm not sure I understand what happened.'

'I do. We fell in love. Simple as that. We could have waited another five years to find each other, or ten, but we didn't. I found you today, at that goddamn boring meeting, and sooner or later you're going to be my wife.' He kissed her gently then, and stood up, still holding tightly to her hand. 'And now I'm going to say good night, before I do something truly crazy, like attack you.' She laughed at him then, and felt perfectly safe. There were others she would never have let into her apartment, but instinctively with Jeff she had known that she was safe. It was one of the things she instantly loved about him. She felt safe and happy and protected. She felt it just wandering at his side as they walked from the boat pond to the zoo. It was an essence of power he exuded, and quiet strength, at the same time mixed with something gentle. 'I'll call you tomorrow.'

'I'll be at school.'

'What time do you leave in the morning?'

'Eight o'clock.'

'Then I'll call you before that. Can you meet me for lunch?' She nodded, feeling suddenly awed and a little dazed.

'Is this for real?'

'Very much so.' He kissed her in the doorway and she felt stirrings she had never felt before, and that night as she lay in bed thinking of him, trying to sort out her thoughts, she felt a longing she had never known.

But he had meant everything he said to her on that first evening. He called her the next morning at seven o'clock, and he appeared outside the school of journalism on schedule at noon. His jacket was slung over his shoulder, his tie was in his pocket, and his golden hair shone in the sun as she came hesitantly down the steps, feeling shy for the first time. This was different from the day before. There wasn't the hubbub of the Bar Association meeting around them, there was no wine, no boat, no sunset peeking through her windows. There was only this extraordinary golden man standing in the noonday sun, smiling proudly down at her as though he owned her. And in her heart she knew he did, and always would.

They hailed a cab and went to the Metropolitan Museum for lunch, and sat by the pool as they toyed with their food, and by the time he took her back to school, she felt entirely comfortable with him again. He had a remarkable way about him, and once again she felt the same strength and safety she had felt at his side the day before.

She made dinner for him at her apartment that night, and once again he left early. And that weekend he had taken her to Connecticut to visit friends, play tennis, and sail, and they had come home golden brown from the sun, and this time he took her to his place in the East Fifties and he made dinner. It was there that he finally took her in his arms and slid his hands carefully over her silky golden flesh and made her absolutely ache for him. She spent the night wrapped in his arms, and it was only the next morning that he made love to her, with all the tenderness and caution and solemnly bridled passion of a man very much in love with a virgin. He made it beautiful for her, and that night they made love in her apartment, and this time it was she who took the lead and surprised not him, but herself, with the force of her desire and passion.

They had spent the rest of the summer in and out of bed, working their schedules around those of their roommates, hers having returned in late August, until finally Jeff could stand it no longer and during the Easter vacation of her senior year, he flew to Tennessee with her, and they got married. It was a quiet ceremony attended by her mother and a dozen friends. She wore a long white organdy dress and a big hat, and carried a big bunch of wild flowers and daisies, and her mother cried, as much from relief as from the delight of seeing her daughter married.

Camilla was dying from leukaemia, but she had not told Daphne yet. Before they flew north again, she told Jeffrey. He promised her that he would take good care of Daphne forever and always. Three months later she was dead and Daphne was pregnant with their first child. Jeff flew to Atlanta with her for the funeral, and he handled everything and held her as she cried. She had no one left now except Jeffrey and the baby that was due in March.

Through the summer he watched her grieve for her mother as they furnished their new apartment with the few treasures they had shipped up from Atlanta. She had graduated from Columbia in June, and in September she got her first job, working at *Collins Magazine*, a highly respectable women's magazine. Jeffrey didn't think it made much sense to go to work since she was pregnant, but at last he agreed, and he had to admit that it did her a great deal of good. She took a leave of absence from the magazine after Christmas, and settled in for the remaining two months to wait for the baby. She was more excited every day, and finally he saw the grief of the previous summer leave her eyes. She insisted that if it was a boy she wanted to call him Jeffrey, but he wanted a little girl that looked like her. And late at night in their bed, he would touch her belly and feel the baby kick, with love and wonder in his eyes.

'Doesn't it hurt?' He worried about her a great deal, but at twenty-one she was the picture of health, and she laughed at his concern.

'No. It feels funny sometimes, but it doesn't hurt.' She

looked at him happily as she lay on her side, and he felt almost guilty as he reached out to touch her breasts. He always wanted her, even now, and they made love almost every night. 'Don't you mind, Jeff?'

'No. Of course not. You're beautiful, Daff. Even more beautiful than you were before.' There was something so soft and luminous about her face as her golden hair fell around her shoulders like a shaft of wheat, and her eyes lit up with a kind of inner light he'd read about and never seen. She seemed filled with promise and a kind of magical joy.

She called him at the office after the first few pains, and she sounded exuberant and almost high, and he rushed home to be with her, forgetting the client in his office, his coat behind the door, and carrying with him a law book he had had in his hand when she called, feeling more than a little frantic and more afraid than he would admit. But when he saw her waiting for him, sitting quietly in a chair, he knew that everything would be all right, as he had always known, and he caught her excitement and poured them each a glass of champagne.

'To our daughter.'

'To your son!' Her eyes teased and laughed and then became suddenly glazed with the pain. He flinched for her for a moment, reaching quickly for her hand, forgetting the champagne, and then remembering all that they'd learned in the class they'd taken for two months, helping her through each pain, timing them with the stopwatch he'd bought, until four o'clock when he sensed before she did that it was time to go. The doctor met them at the hospital, and Daphne smiled, looking almost regal, her head held high, so excited and so proud, and then just as quickly vulnerable as she leaned against him, panting softly as he coached, but her eyes still dancing at what they shared, almost impervious to the increasing pain.

'You're incredible, darling. And oh, God, how I love you.' He had helped her to the labour room, stood by and held her hand and breathed, donned a mask and gown and sped into the delivery room with her at nine o'clock that night, and at ten nineteen, with Daphne pushing with all her might, and tears streaming from Jeffrey's eyes as he looked on with astonishment and awe, their baby girl was born. Aimee Camilla Fields poked her head into the world with a giant howl as her mother gave a shout of victory and glee. The doctor held her aloft and she was quickly put into Daphne's arms as Jeffrey looked down at both of them, laughing and crying, stroking Daphne's damp hair with one hand and holding the baby's tiny fingers with another.

'Isn't she beautiful, Jeff?' Daphne was crying now, and smiling at the same time, looking up at him with all she felt as he bent to kiss her gently on the lips.

'You've never looked more beautiful to me, Daff.'

'I love you.' The nurses had stepped back, feeling, as they always did, never quite hardened to the miracles they saw each day, and the threesome stayed alone for as long as they could. And at last Daphne was brought back to her room, and when she slept, Jeffrey went home at midnight, to lie awake in their bed, thinking of their little girl, and his wife, and all that he had shared with her in two years.

The next three years had flown past. Daphne had gone back to work at *Collins* when Aimee was a year old. She had stretched her leave as long as she could, and she hated to go, but as much as she loved Aimee, she wanted to work, too. She knew that she needed that for herself, to remain who she was, and Jeff knew that it was important to her to be not only mother and wife, but someone unto herself. He always understood. They had a sitter every day, a grandmotherly woman Daphne had found after the baby was born, and Jeff helped her take care of the baby at night, and on weekends they went to the park, or drove out into the country to see friends. There was a magical quality to their life, which touched everyone they knew.

'Don't you two ever fight?' one of Jeff's friends from

31

work teased them when they came to Connecticut one weekend. He liked them both, and envied Jeff more than he would admit.

'Sure we fight. At least twice a week. We make appointments to fight. I kick her around a little bit, she calls me names, the neighbours call the cops, and after they leave, we watch TV.' Daphne grinned at him over Aimee's head and blew him a kiss. He was as he always had been, funny and loving and solid and everything she wanted in a man. He had remained, for her, a dream come true.

'You two make me sick.' Their friend's wife had groaned as she watched them. 'How can married people be so happy? Don't you two have any sense?'

'Not a bit,' Jeff had answered with an arm around Daphne's shoulders as Aimee leaped off her lap and ran off to chase the cat she had just seen. 'I guess we're just too dumb to know any better.' But that was the nice thing about them, they were so damn bright, so good to be with, and so much fun. 'The Perfect Couple,' their friends dubbed them, and sometimes it made Daphne nervous, for fear that it was too good to last just the way it was, but after five years things between them had only got better. They had grown into a single mould, and other than his passion for watching gory rugby matches in Central Park on Sunday afternoons, there was absolutely nothing that Daphne would have changed. It was simply a question of two people who had found precisely what suited them best, and had had the wisdom to treat it well. And the only problem that they faced was an occasional lack of funds, which never seemed to trouble either Daphne or Jeff. At thirty-two Jeffrey was making a decent salary as a lawyer. It was enough, and her money from *Collins* paid for the extras. They were thinking of a second child, and when Aimee was three and a half, they decided to try again, but so far nothing had happened.

'It's fun trying though, isn't it, kid?' He teased her on

a Sunday morning that was Christmas Day. 'Want to try again?'

'After last night? I'm not sure I've got the strength.' After getting the tree and the presents ready for Aimee, they had made love until 3 a.m. She had grinned at him and he swatted her behind. Their sex life was even better than it had been five years before. She grew prettier as she grew older, and at twenty-four she had a more womanly air as she strode across the room and stroked a single finger across his naked belly, circling slowly around the places that pleased him the most.

'If you do that, you're gonna get raped!' But Aimee had burst into the room, her arms filled with new toys, and he had quickly wrapped himself in a towel while Daphne went to help her dress the new doll Santa Claus had brought.

'Sorry, sweetheart.'

'Kids!' He rolled his eyes and went off to take a shower. It was a lazy, easy day, the three of them ate turkey and cranberry jelly and dressing till they could barely move, and when at last Aimee went to bed that night, they sat in front of the fireplace in their living room, reading the last of the *Sunday Times*, drinking mugs of hot chocolate, and looking at the tree. It had been a perfect Christmas on a relaxed Sunday afternoon and evening as Daphne stretched out on the couch and put her head in Jeffrey's lap.

'What's a mountain range in Peru?'

'I give up. What is it?' He had no knack whatsoever for the crossword puzzle she tackled every Sunday, even during the festivities of Christmas. 'How the hell do you do that damn thing, Daff? Christ, I went to Harvard Law School, did okay, and I still can't get three words right.' She finished the whole thing every week by Tuesday, and wouldn't give up until she did. He was no help at all and yet she always asked him. 'And don't ask me who Beethoven's sister was or I'll throw my hot chocolate at you.'

'That's it!' She grinned evilly and sat up. 'Violence! That's the one I couldn't get on twenty-six across.'

'You drive me nuts. Come on' – he stood up and held out a hand – 'let's go to bed.'

'Let's wait until the fire goes out.' Their bedroom and Aimee's was upstairs in the little duplex they had acquired the summer before with his last raise, and Daphne loved the fireplace but she always worried, especially now, so near to the Christmas tree.

'Turn your worry button off, it's almost out now.'

'Then let's wait.'

'Let's not.' He pinched her behind. 'I'm so horny I can hardly see straight. I think you put an aphrodisiac in my hot chocolate.'

'Bullshit.' She grinned at him and stood up. 'You've been a sex maniac ever since I met you. You don't need an aphrodisiac, Jeffrey Fields. You need saltpetre in your food just to keep you normal.' He laughed and chased her up the stairs to their bedroom, where he threw her gently into bed and began to caress her beneath her sweater and she wondered, as she had for the past two months, if she would get pregnant this time. 'Why do you think it's taking so long this time?' She looked only faintly worried. With Aimee she had got pregnant almost on the first try, but this time it hadn't taken yet. Jeffrey only shrugged and smiled.

'Maybe I'm over the hill . . . hell, maybe you ought to get a new model.'

Her eyes were serious as she looked at him across the bed as they undressed. 'I'd never find anyone like you, Jeff. I don't give a damn if we never have another baby. Do you know how much I love you?'

'How much?' His voice was deep and husky as he reached for her across their bed and pulled her slowly towards him.

'More than you'll ever know, my love.' Her words were swallowed by his lips as they kissed and held, and began to make love beneath the comforter she had bought for their big brass bed. The bed was a kind of joke

34

between them. The springs squeaked, and the bed creaked outrageously when they made love, but it was an antique they had bought at an auction and they loved it. They had bought a smaller one for Aimee, and Daphne had discovered a beautiful child's quilt her grandmother had made among her mother's things.

'Think I should check on Aimee?' She always did before they went to bed, but tonight she felt sensual and lazy as she lay sated in her husband's arms, and he felt the same, and for a prescient instant she wondered if there would be life in her womb again. Their lovemaking had had an ardour and a depth and seriousness to it that somehow seemed as though it ought to result in their longed-for second child. She was thinking of the baby they wanted, and not the one they had, as she lay sleepily in Jeffrey's arms.

'She's all right, Daph.' He always teased her because she stood so solemnly beside Aimee's bed every evening, staring down at the golden-haired little girl who looked so much like her. And if she slept too soundly, Daphne would put a finger just beneath her nose to make sure that she was breathing. 'Just stay put tonight. She's fine.' Daphne smiled drowsily then, and a moment later was sound asleep curled up within Jeffrey's comfortable clasp. She lay there like that asleep for hours, until she stirred slowly in a distant dream. They were standing beside a waterfall, all three of them, she, Jeffrey, and Aimee, and the sound of the cascading water was so loud that it disturbed her sleep, but there was something more, too, a smell in the woods that somehow she couldn't escape from, and at last she stirred beside Jeffrey, coughing, opened her eyes to flee the dream, and looked through their bedroom doorway to discover that the sound of water that had roused her was the roar of fire, and that beyond their bedroom was a wall of flame.

'Jeff! ... My God, Jeff!' She jumped from the bed feeling dazed and dizzy and he stirred slowly as she shook him and began to scream. 'Jeff! Aimee!' He was awake then and saw instantly what was happening as he struggled from their bed, heading naked towards their bedroom doorway. Daphne was right behind him, her eyes wide with terror as he was forced back by the flames. 'Oh, God, Jeff, the baby!' There were tears streaming from her eyes from the pungent smoke and raw fear, but he turned to her swiftly and grabbed her shoulders tightly in his hands, shouting above the roar of the fire.

'Stop it, Daff! The fire's in the hall. We're safe, so is she. I'm going to get her now and she's going to be fine. I want you to put the blanket around you and crawl as fast as you can down the stairs to the doorway. I'm going to grab Aimee out of bed and I'll be right behind you. There's nothing to be afraid of! Do you understand me?' He was wrapping her in the blanket as he spoke, his movements quick and agile as he shoved her down towards the floor in the doorway of their bedroom and spoke clearly into her ear. 'I love you, Daff. It'll be fine.' He spoke with absolute conviction and then dashed the few feet towards Aimee's bedroom as Daphne headed down the stairs, trying not to panic, knowing that Jeff would keep Aimee safe, he always took care of them . . . always . . . always . . . she said it over and over to herself as she crawled down the stairs, trying to glance behind her, but the smoke seemed to have grown more dense and she could barely breathe, she felt as though she were swimming in the acrid smoke, and she couldn't see, and suddenly there was the sound of an explosion behind her, but as she heard it, it seemed to come from a great distance, and she was back in the dream she had had, standing beside the waterfall with Aimee and Jeff, and suddenly she wondered if the fire had only been a dream too. She felt comforted as she realised that it was . . . just a dream . . . just a dream . . . as she drifted off to sleep and felt Jeff at her side . . . she heard voices then in the dream as she slept on and after she heard a strange and eerie wail . . . that familiar sound again . . . that sound . . . and the lights coming at her through the fog . . . Mrs

Fields, the voices said, Mrs Fields . . . and then the lights had been too bright, and she was in an unfamiliar, frightening place, and she had felt terror course through her like hot blood, unable to remember how she had gotten there or why, and she had looked everywhere for Jeff . . . trapped between reality and dreams . . . there had been bandages on her hands and legs, and a thick coating of ointment on her face, and a doctor had looked down at her with despair as she cried . . . 'no, NO! Not my baby! . . . not Jeff!!! NOOO . . .'

Daphne Fields called out in the night in an anguished broken voice, remembering when she had seen those bright lights before . . . after the fire . . . It was Christmas morning when she woke, and the day nurse in intensive care came running to see her, lying there, shaking, her eyes wild, her face frozen with remembered pain. She had waked then as she did now, feeling the same shaft of agony slice through her like a guillotine, just as it had then, nine years before, the night Jeff and Aimee died in the fire.

4

Barbara Jarvis arrived at Lenox Hill two hours after Liz Watkins had called. She had looked up Barbara's number when she got home, and Barbara came at once, shaking from head to foot at the news. It was nine o'clock in the morning, and unlike the starched nurse who led her down the hall, Barbara Jarvis looked as though she hadn't slept all night. She had been up late, and the news of Daphne's accident rocked her to the core. She had been told that her employer was in intensive care at Lenox Hill and that she could visit for fifteen minutes on the hour and should notify whatever relatives there were. Liz Watkins had wondered, after she called, if the secretary would come and what she would be like. She hadn't sounded very friendly on the phone, hadn't thanked Liz for her call, and had sounded almost suspicious in answer to the nurse's words. Liz suspected that she was a strange one, and the nurse who saw her appear at the desk would have agreed. Not strange, but far from friendly either, she had a fierce, protective way about her as she asked for Daphne's room. Her questions suggested a kind of paranoia that left the nurse feeling both angry and annoyed. She wanted to know if the press had been called, if anyone had been to see Miss Fields yet, if her name appeared on any central register, and if the general nursing staff was aware of who she was.

'Yes, some of us are.' The nurse stared down at her. 'We read her books.'

'Maybe so. But she isn't writing here. I don't want Miss Fields disturbed.' Barbara Jarvis looked ferocious as she stood to her full, rather impressive height, her dark hair pulled into a knot, her eyes deeply troubled.

38

'Is that clear? If any of the newspapers call, there are to be no comments, no stories, no reports. Miss Fields hates publicity, and at a time like this she is entitled to be left alone.'

The nurse on duty was quick to snap, 'We had the governor of New York here last year, Miss...' She was so damn tired she couldn't even remember the woman's name, and a sudden urge to call her Miss Bitch almost overtook her. 'And he enjoyed total privacy while he was here. Miss Fields will do the same.' But it was obvious that the dark-haired amazon standing before her didn't believe a word she said. She was in total contrast to her employer, so tiny, so frail, so delicate and blonde as she lay in her hospital bed.

'How is she?'

'There's been no change since you were called. She had a difficult night.'

Little lightning bolts of worry darted into Barbara Jarvis's eyes. 'Is she in a great deal of pain?'

'She shouldn't be. She's being well medicated, but it's hard to tell.' And then she wondered if Barbara could shed some light on the obvious terrors Daphne had suffered the night before. Her voice softened as she looked at Barbara Jarvis. 'She had a rough night.' She explained the nightmares Liz Watkins had described in the chart and something in Barbara Jarvis's eyes said that she knew, but she wasn't going to give anything up. 'She had nightmares ... dreams ... it could be from the concussion. I'm not really sure.' The secretary said not a single word. 'If you'd like to see her, you can see her briefly. She floats in and out of consciousness and she may not know who you are.' Barbara nodded and looked rapidly at the rooms all along the well-lit hall. There was an eerie quality to intensive care, even to a healthy person. Nowhere in the hall was there a trace of daylight, everything was brilliant and fluorescent and technical and bright. It was more than a little frightening and Barbara Jarvis had never seen an intensive care unit before. But she knew that Daphne had. She had come to her long after the tragic fire, but Daphne had told her about it one night. She knew all about it, and about Aimee and Jeffrey, and after the past three years with Daphne she knew a great deal more than that.

'May I see her now?'

The nurse nodded and led the way to Daphne's room. She walked into the room on swift, silent feet and stood looking down at Daphne, glancing at the monitors again and satisfied that all was well. She'd had another shot of Demerol an hour before and she would sleep now for several hours. The nurse glanced at Barbara and saw tears sliding slowly down her cheeks as she reached towards Daphne and took her tiny white hand in her larger one and held it as though Daphne might have been her child. Her pulse was still weak, and it was still too soon to tell if she would live. Barbara held her breath as she watched, trying not to cry but she couldn't help it. The nurse left them alone at last, and Barbara stood staring at Daphne miserably until the nurse came back and signalled to Barbara from the doorway. The tall, sturdy woman stood exactly where she had when the head nurse left her, and she gently replaced Daphne's hand on the bed, and then left the room. As she walked slowly back down the hall, she looked grief-stricken for a long unguarded moment and then put back her mask as they stood beside the desk.

'Will she be all right?' Barbara's eyes sought something they couldn't have, some encouragement, some hope, a promise. But it was difficult to believe that Daphne would make it, lying there, so still, so small, so immobile. She almost looked as though she were already gone. Liz took small comfort in knowing that Daphne inspired the same kind of passionate devotion from those who knew her as from those who read her books. But Barbara Jarvis was looking at her now, wanting an answer, an answer that no one had, save God.

'It's too soon to say. She could very well make it.' And her voice gentled with long years of practice. 'Or she might not. She has suffered a very extensive trauma.'

40

Barbara Jarvis nodded in silence and walked slowly away and into a phone booth. When she came out she asked when she could see Daphne again and they told her in half an hour. 'Would you like a cup of coffee? You can see her again for fifteen minutes, on the hour. Or . . .' Maybe she would leave, she was only her secretary after all.

Barbara read their minds. 'I'll stay.' She tried to smile faintly, but the effort seemed enormous. 'I'd like coffee.' And then, almost with pain, 'Thank you.' A student nurse led her to a coffee machine placed conveniently near a blue vinyl couch that had seen several lifetimes of sorrow. The couch itself seemed depressing to her as she thought of people waiting here for loved ones to live or die, more often the latter. The nurse in blue stripes poured a cup of steaming black coffee and handed it to Barbara as the taller woman stood for a moment looking into the young girl's eyes. 'Do you read her books?' Blushing, the young nurse nodded. And then she went away. And at three o'clock Liz Watkins came back, to do a double shift. Barbara was still there, looking frantic and exhausted. Liz checked the chart, and saw that there was no improvement.

Liz came to chat with Barbara after a while, and poured her a fresh cup of coffee. She wondered about Barbara then, guessed her to be about Daphne's age, and for an insane moment she wanted to ask Barbara what Daphne was really like, but she knew that to do so was to invite the secretary's hostility to rise again like an angry cloud around her.

'Is there any family who should be called?' It was all that she dared to ask.

Barbara hesitated for only a fraction of an instant and then shook her head. 'No. No one.' She wanted to say that Daphne was alone in the world, but that wasn't exactly true, and either way it was none of this woman's business.

'I understand that she's a widow.'

Barbara looked surprised that she knew, but she

41

nodded and took a sip of the hot coffee. It had come out on *The Conroy Show* once, but she had never discussed it again. She didn't want anyone to know it. Now she was known only as 'Miss' Fields, and the implication was that she never had been married. At first it had felt to Daphne like a treason to Jeff, but in the long run she knew it was better. She couldn't bear to speak of him and Aimee. She only spoke of them to . . . But Barbara forced the thought from her mind, panicking at what might happen to him now.

'There've been no calls from the press?' She looked up from her coffee, suddenly worried.

'None.' Liz smiled reassuringly. 'And I'll handle those. Don't worry. We won't let them near her.'

For the first time Barbara smiled a small, genuine smile, and it was strange, for a fraction of an instant she looked almost pretty. 'She hates publicity with a passion.'

'That must be pretty rough. They must chase after her a lot.'

'They do.' Barbara smiled again. 'But she's a genius at avoiding them when she wants to. On tour it can't be helped, but even then she's very adept at dodging inappropriate questions.'

'Is she very shy?' Liz was so hungry for some piece of the real Daphne. She was the only celebrity she had actually longed to meet, and now here she was, so near, and yet Daphne was still a total enigma.

Barbara Jarvis was once again cautious, but not hostile. 'In some ways, she is. In other ways, not at all. I think "retiring" suits her better. She is very, very private. She's not afraid of people. She just keeps her distance. Except' – Barbara Jarvis looked distant and thoughtful for a moment – 'except with the people she cares about and is close to. She's like an excited happy child with them.' The image seemed to please both women, and Liz smiled as she stood up.

'I've always admired her through her books. I'm sorry to come to know her this way.' Barbara nodded, her own smile faded, her eyes sad. She couldn't believe that the woman she had worshipped might be dying. And her sorrow showed in her eyes as she looked up at Liz Watkins. 'I'll let you know as soon as you can go back in to see her.'

'I'll wait here.'

Liz nodded and hurried off. She had lost almost half an hour and she had ten thousand things to do. The day shift was the busiest of all, it was like working two shifts instead of one, and she still had to do her own shift that night. It was going to be a long, brutal day, for her, and Barbara Jarvis.

5

When the two women walked into Daphne's room again, Barbara saw her eyes open for a minute, and then flutter closed, as Barbara looked rapidly towards the head nurse who had brought her in. Barbara's face was filled with panic. But Liz was quiet and calm as she checked Daphne's pulse, and smiled as she nodded to Barbara.

'She's coming out of the sedation a little.' And almost as she said it Daphne's eyes opened again and tried to focus on Barbara.

'Daphne?' She spoke softly to her employer and friend as Liz watched, and Daphne's eyes opened again with a blank look. 'It's me ... Barbara ...' The eyes stayed opened this time and there was the faintest hint of a smile and then she seemed to drift back to sleep for a minute or two, and then she looked at Barbara again and seemed about to say something as Barbara bent near to hear her better.

'It must have ... been ... some ... party ... I have ... a hell of a headache ...' Her voice drifted off as she smiled at her own joke. Tears filled Barbara's eyes, even as she laughed. She was suddenly filled with relief that Daphne was even talking, and she turned towards Liz with a victorious look as though her firstborn had spoken her first words, and Liz's own eyes felt damp, with fatigue and emotion. She reproached herself silently for growing soft, but there was a tenderness to the scene that touched her. These two women were a strange pair, the one so small and fair and the other so tall and dark, the one so strong through her words although so tiny, the other so powerfully built, and yet so obviously in awe of Daphne. Liz watched as Daphne made the effort to

44

speak again. 'What's new?' It was the merest whisper and Liz could barely hear her.

'Not much. Last I heard you ran over a car. They tell me it was totalled.' It was the kind of banter they exchanged every morning, but Daphne's eyes looked sad as she looked at Barbara.

'Me ... too ...'

'That's a lot of crap and you know it.'

'... tell ... me ... the truth ... how am I?'

'Tough as nails.'

Daphne's eyes looked to the nurse she could see now as well, as though she wanted reassurance. 'You're much better, Miss Fields. And you'll feel a great deal better tomorrow.' Daphne nodded, like a small, obedient child, as though she believed it, and then suddenly her eyes seemed filled with worry. She sought Barbara again with her eyes and there was something very adamant in her face as she spoke again.

'Don't ... tell ... Andrew ...' Barbara nodded. 'I mean it. Or ... Matthew ...' Barbara's heart sank at the words. She had been afraid she would say that. But what if something happened? If she didn't 'feel better tomorrow,' as the nurse promised. 'Swear ... to ... me ...!'

'I swear, I swear. But for chrissake, Daff ...'

'... no ...' She was obviously growing weaker, the eyes closed and then opened again, with curiosity this time. 'Who ... hit ... me?' As though knowing would make a difference.

'Some jackass from Long Island. The police said he wasn't drunk. The guy claimed you didn't look where you were going.'

She tried to nod but instantly winced, and it took her a moment to catch her breath as Liz watched and checked the time on her wrist. It was almost time to end the visit. But Daphne seemed determined to speak again. '... telling ... the truth ...' They waited but nothing more came, and then Barbara bent to ask, 'Who is, love?'

The voice was soft and the eyes smiled again. 'The ... jackass ... I ... didn't look ... I was thinking ...' And then her eyes went to Barbara's. Only she knew how unbearable Christmas was for her, how painful it had been every year since Jeff and Aimee died in the fire on Christmas night. And this year she was alone, which was worse.

'I know.' And now the memory of them had almost killed her, or was it that she didn't care anymore? A horrifying thought struck Barbara. Had she stepped in front of the car on purpose? But she wouldn't. Not Daphne ... not ... or had she? 'It's all right, Daff.'

'... don't let them ... make ... trouble ... for him ... Not his fault ... Tell ... them ... I said so ...' She looked at Liz then as though to confirm it. She had been a witness. 'I ... don't ... remember ... anything ...'

'That's just as well.'

And then she looked sad and tears filled her big blue eyes. '... except ... the sirens ... it sounded like ...' She closed her eyes and the tears slid slowly out of the corners of her eyes and on to her pillow as Barbara reached down and took her hand, tears in her own eyes.

'Don't. Daphne, don't. You have to get well now.' And then, as though to pull Daphne back, 'Think of Andrew.'

Her eyes opened then, and she looked long and hard at Barbara as Liz pointed to her watch and nodded at Daphne.

'We're going to let you rest now, Miss Fields. Your friend can come back in to see you in a little while. Would you like anything more for the pain?' But she shook her head and seemed grateful to close her eyes again. She was asleep before they left the room, and after walking halfway down the hall side by side, Liz turned and looked at Barbara. 'Is there anything we should know, Miss Jarvis?' Her eyes dug deep into Barbara's. 'Sometimes information that may seem too personal makes a big difference in helping a patient.' She wanted to add 'helping a patient choose between living or

46

dying,' but she didn't. 'She had some awful nightmares last night.' There were a thousand questions in her voice and Barbara Jarvis nodded, but the walls went up instantly to protect Daphne.

'You already know that she's a widow.' It was all that she would say and Liz nodded.

'I see.' She left Barbara then and went back to her desk, and Barbara went back to the blue vinyl couch after pouring herself another cup of black coffee. She sat down with a sigh and she felt totally exhausted. And why the hell had she made her promise not to tell Andrew? He had a right to know that his mother was perhaps dying. And if she did, then what? Daphne had more than amply provided for him from the books in the past years, but he needed so much more than that. He needed Daphne and no one else ... and if she died ... Barbara shuddered, and looked out at the snow beginning to fall again outside. And she felt as bleak as the winter landscape.

Daphne had told her nothing about him for the first year that she worked for her. Nothing at all. She was a successful author, apparently single, working harder than anyone Barbara had ever known, with almost no personal life, but even that hadn't seemed surprising. How could she have had time for that, putting out two major books a year? She couldn't and she didn't. But it was on Christmas Eve when Barbara had worked late that she suddenly found her in her office, sobbing. It was then that she had told her about Jeff ... and Aimee ... and Andrew ... Andrew, the child she had conceived the night of the fatal fire ... the baby who had come nine months later, when she was so alone, with no family, no husband, no friends she would see because they all reminded her of Jeff, and his birth had been so different from Aimee's. Aimee who had been born with Jeff holding her hand, with a great gust of a cry, and her parents looking on with tears of joy intermingled with victorious laughter. Andrew had taken thirty-eight hours to come, a breech birth, with the umbilical cord threatening his every breath, until both he and his mother were finally, mercifully, released by an emergency Caesarean.

The doctor had reported that he made a strange, muted little sound when he first emerged, and he had been almost blue as they worked fiercely to save both him and Daphne. And when the anaesthetic had worn off, she had been too sick to see him, or hold him. But Barbara still remembered the look in Daphne's eyes when she spoke of the first moment she had held him. He had lain in her arms, put there by a nurse, and suddenly nothing hurt, nothing mattered in the world, except that baby, who lay staring up at her with a determined little stare, looking exactly like Jeffrey. She had named him Andrew Jeffrey Fields. She had wanted to name him after his father, but she couldn't bring herself to do it. It would have brought too many painful memories back each time she called him 'Jeff,' so instead she named him Andrew. It was a name they had chosen for a boy when she had been pregnant with Aimee. And she had told Barbara too of her shock and joy when she had discovered six weeks after the fire that she was pregnant. It was the only thing that had kept her going during those lonely nightmarish months, the only thing that had kept her from wanting to die too. And she hadn't, she had lived, as had Andrew, despite his traumatic arrival. He had been a beautiful, rosy-cheeked, happy baby. And he had Daphne's cornflower-blue eyes, but he continued to look exactly like his father.

She had rented a tiny apartment for the two of them, and she had filled the nursery with pictures of Jeffrey, so that one day he would know what his father had looked like, and in a small silver frame was a photograph of his sister. It wasn't until he was three months old that Daphne suspected that there was something different about Andrew. He was the most good-natured child she had ever seen. He was fat and healthy, but one day she dropped a whole stack of dishes as he lay peacefully in

48

a basket on the kitchen table, and he hadn't even started. She had clapped her hands at his ear after that, and he had just smiled at her. She had felt a whisper of terror run through her. She couldn't face calling the doctor, but on their next visit she had casually asked some questions, and he had instantly known what she suspected. Her worst fears had proven true. Andrew was deaf from birth. He made odd little sounds from time to time, but they couldn't know until later if he was mute as well. It was impossible to know if it had been as a result of the shocks she had sustained right after his conception, or from the medication she'd been given in the hospital for her own burns and injuries from the fire. She had been in the hospital for over a month, heavily medicated, no one had even suspected that she was pregnant. But whatever the reason for his hearing loss, it was permanent and it was total.

Daphne came to love him with a fierce, protective zeal and determination. By day she spent every waking moment with him, setting her alarm for five thirty every morning, so she could be sure to be awake before he was, ready for what the day would bring him and to assist him with each difficult moment. And they were many. At first she was obsessed with the potential hazards that constantly lay in wait for him. In time she grew accustomed to anticipating the constant dangers of warnings he couldn't hear, car horns he was never aware of, growling dogs and pans of sizzling bacon. But the stress she was under was constant. And yet there were endless precious moments, times when tears of tenderness and relief flowed down her cheeks as she shared her life with her baby. He was the happiest, sunniest child imaginable, but again and again she had to face the fact that his life would never be normal. Eventually, everything in her life stopped except her activities with Andrew. There were no friends she saw, no movies she went to. She devoted every single moment of the day to Andrew, afraid to leave him with anyone else, terrified that they wouldn't understand as well as she the dangers

49

and frustrations that confronted him. She took every burden of his life on to her own shoulders, and each night she fell into bed exhausted, drained by what the effort had cost her. There were times too when her own frustrations in dealing with a deaf child almost overwhelmed her, when the urge to shout at him for what he could not do or hear made her clench her teeth and her fists so that she wouldn't slap him. It was not Andrew she wanted to hit, but the cruelty of fate that had deafened her beloved child. She laboured under a silent but leaden mantle of guilt, secretly feeling that it was her fault, that she should have been able to prevent it. She hadn't been able to keep Jeff and Aimee from dying in the fire, and now she couldn't keep this final brutal reality from Andrew. She was helpless to change it for him. She read every book she could find about children who were deaf from birth, and she took him to every specialist in New York, but there was nothing they could do for Andrew, or Daphne. She faced the reality of it almost with fury, like an enemy to be fought. She had lost so much, and now Andrew had too. The unfairness of it burned within her like a silent rage, and at night she would have nightmares about the fire and awake screaming.

The specialists she had seen had suggested to her that eventually she would have to put Andrew in a special school, that it would be best for him, that it would be impossible for him to deal with normal children. And they also pointed out again and again that, despite Daphne's Herculean efforts with the child, there were stumbling blocks that she was unable to get over. Although she knew him better than anyone else did, even she had difficulties communicating with him, and the specialists warned her that in time she would come to resent him for her failures. She was not a professional, after all, they insisted, and he needed more sophisticated skills than she was able to give him. In addition, his constant isolation from other children made him suspicious and hostile on the rare occasions when he did see

50

them. Hearing children didn't want to play with him because he was different, and their cruelty caused Daphne so much pain that she hadn't taken him to a playground since he was an infant. But still she resisted the idea of his being with other children like him, so she kept him to herself, the two of them prisoners in her tiny apartment, as the specialists continued to badger her about sending him away to a special school.

'An institution?' she had screamed at the specialist she knew best. 'I won't do that to him. Ever!'

'What you're doing is a lot worse.' The doctor's voice had been gentle. 'It doesn't have to be forever, Daphne. But you have to face facts. You can't teach him at home what he needs to know. He needs totally different skills than you can give him.'

'Then I'll learn them!' She had shouted at him because she couldn't shout at Andrew's deafness, or at life, or fate, or the gods who had been so unkind to her. 'Dammit, I'll learn them and I'll stay with him night and day to help him!' But she had already done that, and it wasn't working. Andrew was living in total isolation.

'And when you die?' the pediatrician asked bluntly. 'You don't have a right to do that to him. You'll make him totally dependent on you. Give him the right to his own life, for God's sake. A school will teach him independence, it will teach him how to function in the normal world when he's ready.'

'And when will that be? When he's twenty-five? Thirty? When he's so totally used to being out of the world that he's institutionalised? I saw those people up there, I talked to them, through an interpreter. They don't even trust what they call "hearing people." They're all freaks, for chrissake. Some of them are forty years old and have never lived anywhere but an institution. I won't do that to him.' He had sat, watching them talk, fascinated by the gestures and the expressions on their faces, but Andrew had heard none of the angry words between his mother and his doctor.

For three years she had fought her private war, to the

slow but steady detriment of Andrew. It had become obvious long since that Andrew could not speak, and when he was three, her renewed efforts to introduce him to hearing children at the playground were a disaster. Everyone shunned him. It was as though they somehow knew that he was terribly, terribly different, and one day she watched him sitting in the sandbox alone, watching the other children with tears running down his face, and then looking at his mother as though to say 'What's wrong with me?' She had run to him and held him, rocking him gently as they both cried, feeling isolated and afraid. Daphne felt that she had failed him. A month later, for Daphne, the war was over. With lead in her heart she began to visit the schools she so desperately hated, feeling as though at any moment Andrew would be torn from her. She couldn't face another loss in her life, and yet she knew that not to do it would destroy him. Freeing him was the ultimate gift she had to give him. And at last she found the only school where she could bear to leave him. It was in a small, comfortable town in New Hampshire, with birch trees surrounding it, and a pretty little pond, and a small river that ran along the grounds, where she watched the children fish. And what she liked best about it was that there were no 'students' there older than twenty. They weren't called patients, or residents or inmates, as she had heard in other institutions. They were called children and students, like 'real' people. And most were sent back to their families in their late teens, to attend colleges when they could, or take jobs, and return to the families who had stood behind them for so long and waited. As Daphne walked slowly around the grounds with the director, a stately woman with white hair, she felt the weight of her loss again, knowing that Andrew might live there for as long as fifteen years, or at least eight or ten. It was a commitment that tore her heart from her. This was her last child, her last love, the only human being alive who was related to her, and she was going to leave him. Her eyes filled with tears again at the thought, and she felt the same shaft of unbearable pain she had felt for months as she had come to terms with the decision, and as the tears poured down her face she felt the director's hand on her arm, and suddenly she was in the older woman's arms, being held close in a strong comforting grasp, sobbing out the pain of the past four years, since even before the birth of Andrew.

'You're doing a wonderful thing for your son, Mrs Fields, and I know how hard it is.' And then, after the sobs had finally subsided, 'Are you currently employed?' The question had come as a shock. Did they doubt her ability to pay his tuition? She had hoarded whatever money she and Jeff had had, and she had been desperately frugal. She hadn't bought so much as a new dress for herself since the few she had bought after the fire, and she was planning to use all of Jeff's insurance money for the school, for as long as it would last. But now of course, with Andrew gone, she could go back to work. She had not worked again since Jeff's death. She had had to recover herself, and then she had found out she was pregnant. She couldn't have worked anyway then, she was too distraught after their deaths. And *Collins* had given her a generous severance when they accepted her resignation.

'No, I'm not employed, Mrs Curtis, but my husband left me enough to . . .'

'That's not what I meant.' The director's smile was filled with compassion. 'I was wondering if you would be free to stay up here for a while. Some of our parents do that. For the first months, until the children adjust. And Andrew being so young . . .' There were five other children his age, which was part of what had convinced Daphne. 'There's a charming little inn in town, run by an Austrian couple, and there are always a few houses to rent. You might give it some thought.' She felt as though she'd had a reprieve. And her face lit up like a sunbeam.

'Could I see him every day?' Tears filled her eyes again.

'At first.' Mrs Curtis's voice was gentle. 'Eventually it will be better for both of you if you begin to cut the visits down. And you know' – the smile was warm – 'he's going to be awfully busy with his friends.'

Daphne's voice was forlorn. 'Do you think he'll forget me?'

They stopped where they stood and the older woman looked at her. 'You're not losing Andrew, Mrs Fields. You're giving him all that he needs for a successful life in the world again.'

A month later she and Andrew made the trip, and she drove as slowly as she could through New England. These were the last hours of their old life and she wanted to drag them out as long as she could. She knew she wasn't ready to leave him. And somehow, the beauty of the countryside made it even harder. The leaves were turning, and the hills were a riot of deep reds and bright yellows, there were cottages and barns, horses in fields, and tiny churches. And suddenly she was reminded of the big beautiful world beyond their apartment that she wanted to share with him. There were cows and lots of sights lining the road he had never seen, and he pointed and made his odd little familiar sounds to ask her questions. But how could she explain to him a world filled with people, and aeroplanes, and exotic cities like London or San Francisco or Paris? She realised suddenly how deprived he had been and how little she had actually taught him, and the familiar feeling of failure washed over her again as they drove on through the scarlet hills of New England.

All of Andrew's favourite treasures and toys were in the car, his teddy bear and a stuffed elephant he loved, and the picture books they had leafed through together, but which no one could read to him. Daphne found herself thinking of it all as they drove, and suddenly what stood out to her now was all that she hadn't accomplished rather than all that she had, and she found herself wondering what Jeff would have done in her place with his son, if he'd had the chance. Perhaps he would have had more ingenuity, or greater patience, but he could have had no greater love than she had for this child. She loved him with every ounce of her soul, and if she could have given him her own ears with which to hear, she would have.

An hour before they reached the school they stopped for a hamburger at a roadside stand, and her bleak mood brightened a little. Andrew seemed excited by the trip, and he was watching everything around him with delight. She wished, as she watched him, that she could tell him about the school, but there was no way to do that. She couldn't tell him what it was like or what she felt, or why she was leaving him there or how much she loved him. For all of his life she had only been able to meet his physical needs, or show him fire trucks racing silently by in the street. She had never been able to share her thoughts or feelings with him. She knew that he had to know that she loved him, she was with him every moment after all. But what would he think now when she left him at the school? How could she explain it to him? It only added to her private anguish to know that she couldn't. Mrs Curtis, the director at the school, had rented a little cottage for her in the town, and Daphne planned to stay until Christmas, so that she could visit Andrew every day. But that would be very different from what they had shared in the past, their every waking moment spent side by side. Their lives would never be the same again, and Daphne knew it. The hardest thing she had ever done in her life was letting go of this child, whom she wanted to hold on to more than life itself, but knew she couldn't.

They arrived at the school shortly after dusk, and Andrew looked around in surprise, as though he didn't understand why they were there. He looked at Daphne with confusion and she nodded and smiled as he glanced worriedly at the other children. But these children were different from the ones he had met in Central Park in New York, and it was as though he instinctively sensed that they were like him. He watched them play, and the

55

signs they made, and again and again they came over to him. It was the first warm welcome he had ever had from children his own age, and as one little girl came over and took his hand and then kissed his cheek, Daphne had to turn away so he wouldn't see the tears pouring down her face. Andrew just stared at the little girl in amazement. It was Mrs Curtis who helped him join in at last, took his hand and led him around as Daphne watched, feeling as though she had done the right thing and a new world was opening to Andrew. Something extraordinary happened as she watched, he began to reach out to these children so much like him. He smiled and he laughed and for a moment he forgot Daphne. He began to watch the signs that they made with their hands, and laughing once he imitated one of them, and then making a funny little noise, he walked over to the little girl who had approached him before and kissed her. Daphne went over to him later and waved to show that she was going away, but he didn't cry, he didn't even look frightened or unhappy. He was having too good a time with his friends, and she held him for a last moment, with a brave smile on her face, and then she ran away before the tears came again. And he never saw the ravaged look on his mother's face as she drove out of the driveway.

'Take care of my baby . . .' she whispered to a God she had long since come to fear, and this time she prayed that He would hear her.

6

Within two weeks Andrew had totally adjusted to his new life at the school, and Daphne felt as though she had lived in the cosy New England town forever. The cabin Mrs Curtis had helped her find was warm in the autumn wind, it had a perfect little country kitchen with a brick fireplace for baking bread, a tiny living room filled with a well-worn couch and deep easy chairs, there was a fireplace here too, and shining copper pots filled with plants, and in the bedroom a four-poster bed with a bright quilt. It was here that Daphne spent most of her time, reading books and writing in a journal. She had started keeping a journal when she was pregnant with Andrew, it was filled with notes about what her life was like, what she thought and felt, little essays about what life meant to her. She always thought that one day, when he was older, she would share her writings with Andrew. And in the meantime, it gave her a place to empty her soul, on long, lonely nights, like the ones in New Hampshire. The days there were bright and sunny, and she took long walks down wooded paths and beside streams, thinking of Andrew, and looking at the snowcapped mountains. This was a whole different world from New York. There were barns with horses, cows in the pastures, hills and meadows where she could walk without seeing a soul, and often did. She only wished she could share it with Andrew. For years now, he had been her only companion. And every few days she went to the school to see him. For her it was still an enormous adjustment. For four years her life had centred around him, and now suddenly he was gone, and there were times when the emptiness almost overwhelmed her. She found herself thinking more and more of Jeff, and of Aimee. She would have been eight years old by then, and at times when Daphne saw a little girl the same age, she turned away, her eyes filled with tears, her arms aching to hold her. But it wasn't as though she had lost Andrew the same way, she kept reminding herself. He was alive and happy and busy, and she was doing the right thing for him and she knew it. But time after time she would go to the school, and sit on a bench outside with Mrs Curtis, watching him play and learning to sign now. She was also learning the hand signs in order to communicate with him better.

'I know how difficult this is for you, Mrs Fields. It's easier for the children to adjust, than for their parents. For the little ones it's a kind of release. Here they are finally free of a world that didn't accept them.'

'But will it ever accept him?'

'Yes.' There was absolute certainty in the director's voice. 'It will. He'll always be different. But with the right tools there will be almost nothing he can't tackle in time.' She smiled gently at Daphne in the breeze. 'One day he'll thank you.' But what about me? she suddenly wanted to ask ... what happens to me now? What do I do without him? It was as though the older woman had read her thoughts. 'Have you thought about what you'll do when you go back to New York?' For a woman alone, like Daphne, Andrew's absence would create an enormous void, and she already knew that Daphne hadn't worked since she was pregnant almost five years before. At least most of the parents had each other, other children, jobs, activities to fill their lives in the absence of these special children. But it was obvious that Daphne didn't. 'Will you go back to work now?'

'I don't know...' Daphne's voice trailed off as she stared out at the hills. How empty it would all be without him. She almost hurt more now than she had when she first left him. The reality of it was finally sinking in. Her life would never be the same again ... never ... 'I don't know.' She pulled her eyes back from the hills and looked at Mrs Curtis. 'It's been so long. I doubt if they'd even want me.' She smiled and the passage of time showed in her eyes. The years had taught her lessons filled with pain.

'Have you thought of sharing with others what you've learned with Andrew?'

'How?' Daphne looked surprised. The thought had never occurred to her.

'There aren't enough good books on this subject. You mentioned that you were a journalism major in college, and you worked at *Collins*. Why not write a book or a series of articles? Think of how something like that would have helped you when you first found out about Andrew.' Daphne remembered the terrible feelings of being alone, of no one in the world seeming to share her problem.

'It's a thought.' She nodded slowly, and watched Andrew hug a little girl, and then chase a big red ball across the playground.

'Maybe you're just the one to do it.'

But the only thing she seemed to write now was her journal, night after night. She had nothing but time on her hands now, and she was no longer exhausted at night, as she had been for years since she had Andrew. He was just like any other small child, constantly busy, but he needed even more attention than most, to be sure that he didn't run into danger from something he couldn't hear, and there was always his frustration to deal with, at not being able to communicate with others.

When she closed her journal that night, she lay in the dark and thought again of Mrs Curtis's suggestion. It was a good idea, and yet, she didn't want to write about Andrew. Somehow it seemed a violation of him as a person, and she didn't feel ready to share her own fears and pain. It was all too fresh, just as Jeff's and Aimee's deaths had been for so long. She had never written about that either. And yet she knew that it was all bottled up inside, waiting to come out, along with feelings that she hadn't faced in years. Those of being still young, and a woman. For four years now, her only close contact had been with her son. There had been no men in her life, and few friends. She didn't have time for them. She didn't want pity. And going out with another man would have seemed a betrayal of Jeffrey, and all that they had shared. Instead, she had submerged all of her feelings, locked all of those doors, and gone on year after year taking care of Andrew. And now there was no excuse left. He would live at the school, and she would be alone in their apartment. It made her never want to go back to New York. She wanted to hide in the cabin in New Hampshire forever.

In the mornings she went for long walks, and once in a while she stopped at the little Austrian Inn for breakfast. The couple who ran it were well matched – both rotund and kind, and the wife always asked about her son. She knew why Daphne was there from Mrs Curtis. As in every small country town, people knew who belonged and who did not, why they were there, when they had arrived, and when they were leaving. People like Daphne weren't so rare here, there were other parents who came to town to visit their children. Most stayed at the inn, and a few did what Daphne was doing, usually in the summer. They rented cottages and small houses, brought their other children with them, and generally made it a festive occasion. But Mrs Obermeier sensed that Daphne was different. There was something much quieter, much more withdrawn, about this tiny, delicate, almost childlike woman. It was only when you looked into her eyes that you realised she was wise well beyond her twenty-eight years, and that life had not always been kind to her.

'Why do you think she's alone like that?' Mrs Obermeier asked her husband one day as she put sweet rolls in a basket and slid a tray of cookies into the oven. The cakes and pies she prepared made everyone's mouth water.

'She's probably divorced. You know, children like

that can destroy a marriage. Maybe she paid too much attention to the boy and her husband couldn't take it.'

'She seems so alone.'

Her husband smiled. His wife always worried about everybody. 'She probably just misses the boy. I think Mrs Curtis said he was very young, and he's her only child. You looked like that too when Gretchen went to college.'

'That wasn't the same.' Hilda Obermeier looked at him, knowing that there was something he wasn't seeing. 'Have you looked into her eyes?'

'Yes,' he admitted with a grin and a flush of his full jowls, 'they're very pretty.' He patted his wife's behind then and went outside to bring in some more firewood. They had a house full of guests at the inn that weekend. In the dead of winter there were always those who went cross-country skiing. And in the fall, people came from Boston and New York to see the changing of the leaves. But the brilliant orange and magenta leaves were almost gone now. It was November.

On Thanksgiving Day, Daphne went to the school and shared turkey dinner with Andrew and the other children. They played games afterwards, and she was stunned when he grew angry at her and signed to her, 'You don't know anything, Mom.' The rage in his eyes cut her to the quick, and she felt a separation from him she had never felt before. She suddenly resented the school for taking him from her. He wasn't *hers* anymore, he was *theirs*, and she hated them for it. But instead she found herself taking it out on Andrew, and signing angrily at him. Mrs Curtis saw the exchange and spoke to her about it later, explaining that what they were both feeling was normal. Things were changing very quickly now for Andrew, and consequently for Daphne. She couldn't sign as quickly as he, she made mistakes and felt clumsy and stupid. But Mrs Curtis assured her that in time they would have a better relationship than the one they'd had before and it would all be worth it.

And at dinnertime she and Andrew had made friends

again, and they had gone to the table hand in hand, and when he signed the prayer at the start of the meal, she was so proud she thought she would burst, and afterwards he grinned at her. After dinner he played with his friends again, but as he wore down he came to sit on her lap and cuddle, as he had in years past, and she smiled happily as he fell asleep in her arms. He purred softly in his sleep, and she held him, wishing she could turn the clock back. She carried him to his room, changed his clothes, and slipped him gently into bed as one of the counsellors watched. And then, with a last look at the sleeping blond child, she walked softly out of the room and went back downstairs to the other parents. But she didn't want to be with them tonight. Once Andrew was in bed, she was anxious to get back to her cabin. She had grown used to her solitude and her own thoughts, and the comfort of spilling her soul into her journal.

She drove home by a familiar back road and gave a startled gasp as she heard something snap and the car suddenly sank forward and stopped. She had broken an axle. She was shaken but not hurt, and instantly realised how lucky she had been that it hadn't happened sometime when she was on the highway. But this was a mixed blessing too. She was alone on a deserted road and about seven miles from her cabin. The only light was that of the moon and she could see her way clearly, but it was bitter cold and it would be a long walk home in the sharp wind. She pulled her collar tightly around her, wishing that she had worn a hat and gloves and more sensible shoes, but she had worn high heels and a skirt for Thanksgiving dinner. Her eyes watered in the cold, and her cheeks tingled and her hands grew rapidly numb, even in her pockets, but she buried her chin in her coat, and with no other choice she kept walking.

It was almost an hour later when she saw headlights coming towards her on the road, and she was suddenly engulfed in panic. Even in this sleepy town something unpleasant could happen. She was a woman alone on a dark country road and if something happened to her, there would be no one to hear her screams, or come to help her. Like a frightened rabbit, she suddenly stopped in the road as she watched the headlights come towards her. And then, instinctively, she ran behind a tree, her heart pounding so loudly she could hear it as she hid there. She wondered if the driver had seen her flight. He had still been a good distance away when she ran from the road. And as the vehicle approached she saw that it was a truck. For a moment it looked as though it would drive past her, and then it ground to a sudden halt as she held her breath, terrified, waiting.

The door to the truck opened and a man stepped out. 'Hello? Anyone there?' He stood looking around for a few minutes and all she could see was that he was very tall, and she felt suddenly very foolish hiding there. As her feet and legs ached with the cold, she wanted to come out from behind the tree and ask for a ride, but how would she explain that she was hiding? It had been a stupid reaction, and now she had to stay there. He walked slowly around the truck, shrugged, hopped back into his truck, and kept going. And then he was gone, and Daphne walked slowly out from behind the tree with a foolish grin, talking to herself.

'You dummy. Now you'll freeze your ass off all the way home. Serves you right.' She began to hum then, amused by her own stupidity, and knowing that she had lived in cities for too long. There was no reason that she should have felt threatened, except that she had noticed that feeling more and more in the past few years. It was as though she had grown fearful, from her lack of contact with people. And she always felt so totally responsible for Andrew that she was suddenly desperately afraid something might happen to her.

She walked on down the road for another mile, and suddenly she was startled to hear a car behind her in the distance. Once again she thought of running off the road, and this time she shook her head, saying softly to herself, 'There's nothing to be afraid of.' She felt even more foolish for the spoken words, but she stood her ground as she moved to the side of the road and watched the same truck she had seen before come towards her. The truck stopped again and this time she could see the man as the light went on when he opened the door. He had a rugged face, grey hair, and broad shoulders and he was wearing a heavy sheepskin coat that he pulled close around him.

'Is that your car back there?'

She nodded and nervously smiled, noticing that his hands were large and rough as he took them out of his pockets. The same shiver of fear ran through her that she had felt before, but she forced herself not to run from him. If he was a decent man, he would think she was crazy. And if he wasn't, it was too late to hide from him now. She would have to deal with whatever happened in whatever way she could. She smiled, but her eyes were wary. 'Yes, it is.'

'Did I pass you awhile back?' He looked confused about it as he looked down at her. 'I thought I saw someone on the road, but when I stopped I didn't see a soul. When I saw your car back there, I figured I'd missed you.' His eyes seemed to understand something she didn't want him to know, and his voice was deep and husky and gentle. 'Broke your axle, I see. Can I give you a ride? It's an awful cold night to be walking.' They stood there like that for a long moment as she searched his eyes, and then nodded.

'I'd like that very much. Thank you.' She hoped he thought the tremor in her voice was from the cold, and by now even she wasn't sure. She was frozen to the bone, and she could barely manage the door handle with her numb fingers. He opened it for her and she slipped inside, and then a moment later he came around to his side and slipped behind the wheel, with scarcely a glance at her.

'You were lucky you weren't on the main road going fifty. Did it give you any warning at all?'

'No, it just snapped and the front end collapsed and

that was it.' She felt better now and the inside of the little truck was wonderfully warm. Her fingers ached as they thawed out and she blew on them. He handed her a pair of thick sheepskin-lined gloves without further comment and she slipped them on as they drove towards her cabin.

It was almost five minutes later when he turned to her again, with that same gentle husky voice. Everything about him suggested the rugged strength of the mountains. 'Did you get hurt?'

She shook her head. 'No. Just cold. It would have taken me a couple of hours to get home.' She remembered to tell him where she lived then.

'That's the old Lancaster cabin, isn't it?' He seemed surprised.

'I'm not sure. I think so. I rented it from a woman named Dorsey, but we never met. I did it all by mail.'

He nodded. 'That's her daughter. Old Mrs Lancaster died last year. I don't think her daughter's been back in twenty years. She lives in Boston. Married to some social lawyer.' It was all so wonderfully small-town, the details that everyone knew so well. It made Daphne smile at the memory of her terror of being attacked. All this man wanted to do was tell her the local gossip. 'You from Boston too?'

'No. New York.'

'Came up for a rest?' It was idle chitchat as they drove along, but Daphne sighed softly. She wasn't really sure she wanted to tell him, and it was as though he instantly understood. He held up a hand, smiled at her apologetically, and then turned his eyes back to the road. 'Never mind. You don't have to answer. I've been here for so long, I forget my manners. Everyone in town asks questions like that, but it's none of my business what you're doing here. I'm sorry I asked.'

He was so kind about it that she smiled in return. 'It's all right. I came up here to be near my son. I just put him in the ... the Howarth School.' She had been about to say 'the school for the deaf' but the words stuck to her tongue and she couldn't. The man turned to her then, she might as well have said it, he knew what the Howarth School was. Everyone in town did. It was neither a disgrace, nor a secret.

'How old is your boy?' And then with a concerned glance, 'Or am I being nosy again?'

'Not at all. He's four.'

He frowned and looked at her as though he understood. 'Must be damn hard to leave him. He's awful young.'

It was strange, she wanted to ask him questions then. What was his name? Did he have children? They had suddenly become travelling companions on the dark country road. But a moment later he stopped in front of her house, and he hopped out to help her out. She almost forgot to give the gloves back, and she smiled up into his eyes. 'Thank you very much. I wouldn't have been home for hours, if it weren't for you.'

He smiled then, and she could see humour in his eyes that she hadn't guessed at before. 'Could have saved yourself at least a mile if you'd trusted me the first time.' Her face flushed in the dark and she laughed.

'I'm sorry – I almost came out – ' she stammered, feeling like a little girl beside this huge man. 'I was hiding behind a tree, and I almost did come out, but I felt like such a jerk for hiding in the first place.'

He grinned at the confession and walked her to her door. 'You were probably right. You never know who you'll meet, and there are some crazy kids in this town. There are everywhere these days, not just in New York. Anyway, I'm glad I found you and saved you the walk.'

'So am I.' She wondered for a moment if she should invite him in for coffee, but that didn't seem quite right. It was nine o'clock at night, she was alone, and she really didn't know him.

'Let me know if there's anything I can do for you while you're here.' He held out a sturdy hand and she felt its strong grasp on her own as they shook hands. 'My name is John Fowler.'

'I'm Daphne Fields.'

'Nice to meet you.' She opened her door with her key and he waved as he walked back to his truck, and a moment later he was gone, and Daphne stood in the empty cabin, wishing she had invited him in. At least he would have been someone to talk to.

Even her journal held no special interest that night. She kept thinking of the rugged face, the grey hair, the powerful hands, and she found herself oddly curious about him.

7

The morning after Thanksgiving, Daphne went to the Austrian Inn and exchanged the usual pleasantries with Mrs Obermeier. She ate bacon and eggs and croissants, and after breakfast she spoke to Franz and asked him what to do about her car. He directed her to one of the local garages, where she asked them to tow the car into town, and she set off in the truck to show the man where it was. But when they got there, the car was gone, and all that was left to show that it had even been there were the tyre tracks in the dirt by the side of the road, to evidence that it had been towed.

'Someone beat you to it, ma'am.' The boy who had driven her to the spot looked bemused. 'Did you call someone else to pick it up?'

'No.' Daphne looked startled as she stared at where her car had been. This was obviously the spot but the car was gone. 'I didn't. Do you think it would have been stolen?'

'Maybe. But you ought to check the other garages first. Someone might have hauled it into town for you.'

'They couldn't have. No one knew where it was.' And she didn't know anyone in town. Unless ... but that hardly seemed likely. She didn't know him after all. 'How many other garages are there?'

'Two.'

'All right, I guess I'd better check, and then I'll talk to the police.' She remembered what John Fowler had said the night before about 'crazy kids' in town. Maybe someone had stolen it, not that it was any kind of prize, especially with a broken axle.

The boy with the tow truck dropped her off at the first

of the two garages, and before she could walk inside to inquire, she saw her car, already being worked on by two boys in parkas, blue jeans, heavy boots, and greasy hands. 'This yours?'

'Yes.' She was still a little stunned. 'It is.'

'You got plenty of trouble under here.' He looked up at her with a boyish grin. 'But we'll get it fixed for you by tomorrow. Jack Fowler said you had to have it by noon, but we can't do it if you want us to fix the rest, too.'

'He did?' Then it was he after all. 'When did he bring it in?'

'About seven o'clock this morning. Hauled it in with his truck.'

'Do you know where I might find him?' The least she could do was thank him ... and then she flushed suddenly, remembering that only the night before, she had been afraid he might rape her. And what a decent human being he had turned out to be.

Both boys shook their heads in answer to her question. 'He works out at Anderson's logging camp, but I don't know where he lives,' the freckled redhead answered, and she thanked him as she dug her hands into the pockets of her coat and began to walk back towards her end of town. She was halfway there when she heard a sudden honking and saw his blue truck pull up beside her, and she looked up at him with a wide smile.

'I owe you an enormous thank you. You were awfully nice to – '

'Never mind. Want a ride?' She hesitated for only a fraction of a second and then nodded as he swung open the door. 'Hop in.' And then as she settled herself in the wide seat she glanced at him, and his eyes were laughing. 'Sure you wouldn't rather hide behind a tree?'

'That's not fair!' She looked embarrassed and his laughter was a deep chuckle. 'I was afraid that – '

'I know what you were afraid of, and actually what you did was very smart. Still' – he smiled broadly at her – 'it's a little bit insulting. Am I that fearsome-looking?'

But as he took in her size he answered for her. 'I suppose for a little mite like you, I am, aren't I?' His voice was suddenly gentle and his eyes kind. 'I didn't mean to frighten you.'

'I didn't even see you when I hid behind the tree.' She was still blushing faintly, but there was laughter in her eyes as well. And then as they drove towards her cabin she let out a small sigh. 'I think I've gotten a little quirky since ... since I've been alone with my son. It's an enormous responsibility. If anything ever happened to me...' Her voice trailed off and she turned her eyes back to his face, wondering why she had told him that, but there was something very comforting about him.

He was silent for a long moment and then at last he asked, 'You're divorced?'

She shook her head slowly. 'No. I'm a widow.' For five years she had hated the word. Widow. Like a spider.

'I'm sorry.'

'So am I.' She smiled so he wouldn't feel so bad, and they pulled up in front of her house. 'Would you like to come in for a cup of coffee?' She at least owed him that.

'Sure. I'd like that. I'm off till Monday, and I've got nothing on my hands but time.' He followed her inside, and they hung their coats on pegs beside the doorway, then she hurried into the kitchen to warm the coffee left over from that morning.

'The boys at the garage said that you work at the logging camp,' she said over her shoulder as she took out the cups.

'That's right, I do.' She turned to look at him and found him lounging in the doorway, watching her, and suddenly she felt very strange. He had picked her up on the road the night before, and suddenly here he was in her kitchen. A logger, a total stranger, and yet there was something about him that made her want him to stay. She was at the same time drawn to him, and yet frightened, but she realised as she turned away again that it wasn't he who frightened her, but herself. Almost as though he sensed her discomfort, he left the kitchen, and went to wait for her on the living room couch. 'Want me to start a fire?'

Her reaction was immediate and he saw something startling in her eyes. 'No!' And then as though she sensed that she had opened a part of herself to him that she hadn't intended, 'It gets too warm in here. I usually don't – '

'It's all right.' There was something extraordinary about him. It was as though he understood things before she said them, as though he saw things no one else could see. It made her faintly uncomfortable to realise that about him, and yet at the same time it was a relief. 'Are you afraid of fire?' The question was simply put and his voice was very gentle as she began to shake her head in rapid denial, and then stopping, she looked at him and nodded yes. She put the coffee cups down on the table and stood before him.

'I lost my husband and my daughter in a fire.' She had never said those words to anyone before, and he looked at her, almost as though he might reach out to her, his soft grey eyes boring into hers.

'Were you there too?' His voice was so soft and she nodded as tears filled her eyes. She looked away then, and handed him his cup of coffee. But there were still questions in his eyes. 'The little boy too?'

She sighed. 'I was pregnant then, but I didn't know it. They gave me so many drugs in the hospital during the next two months ... for the burns ... the infections ... sedation ... antibiotics ... by the time I knew I was pregnant, it was too late. That's why Andrew was born deaf.'

'You're both lucky to be alive.' He understood better now why she felt so responsible to Andrew, and how difficult it must be for her to leave him at the school. 'Life is strange sometimes.' He sat back against the couch, his coffee cup dwarfed in his hand. 'Things happen that don't make any sense at all sometimes, Daphne.' She was surprised that he remembered her name. 'I lost my wife fifteen years ago, in a car accident on an icy night. She was such a decent woman, everyone in town loved her.' His voice grew soft at the memory and his eyes looked like a morning sky. 'I never understood it. There are so many damn rotten people. Why her?'

'I felt that way about Jeff.' It was the first time she had spoken about him to anyone, but suddenly she needed to talk to this stranger about him, after five long, lonely years. 'We were so happy.' There were no tears in her eyes as she said it, only a dazed look that John watched carefully from where he sat.

'Were you married for a long time?'

'Four and a half years.'

He nodded. 'Sally and I were married for nineteen. We were both eighteen when we got married,' he smiled then, 'just kids. We worked hard together, starved for a while, did okay after that, got comfortable with each other. It was like she had become a part of me. I had a damn hard time of it when I lost her.'

This time Daphne's eyes consoled him. 'So did I, when I lost Jeff. I think I was in a stupor for about a year. Until after I had Andrew.' She smiled. 'He kept me so busy after that, I didn't think about it as much anymore . . . except sometimes . . . like at night.' She sighed softly. 'Did you have children, John?' There was something new and awkward about saying his name, and hearing her own on his lips.

'No. We never did. We didn't want to at first. We didn't want to be like the others, all the kids who married right out of high school and had four kids in three years, and then sat around complaining and hating each other. We made a point of not having any for the first few years, and then we decided we liked it like that. I never minded really . . . until after she died. You're lucky you have Andrew.'

'I know.' Her eyes glowed as she thought of the treasured child. 'Sometimes I think he means even more to me because . . . he's . . . the way he is.'

'Are you afraid to say the word?' His voice was so

kind, so gentle, it almost made her want to cry, or bury her face in his chest and let him hold her in his arms.

'Sometimes. I hate what it will mean to him.'

'It'll mean he has to try a little harder, that sliding by won't be good enough for him. It may make him better and stronger, I hope it does. I think what you've gone through has done that for you. Easy roads aren't always the best ones, Daphne. We think they are, but look at the people you respect in life, they're usually the people who've made it when the going wasn't easy, people who survived and grew from all the pain. The ones who have it easy don't have a hell of a lot going for them. It's the others, the ones who climb the mountains with their heads banged up, and their faces scratched, and their shins bleeding who're worth knowing. It's not easy to watch, but it may be that way for your child.'

'I didn't want it that way for him.'

'Of course not. Who does? But he'll make it. You have. And the going can't have been easy. It must have been damn rough for you.'

She looked at him pensively, their eyes holding from across the couch. 'Sometimes it still is.'

He nodded. 'What do you do with yourself when you're not living in a log cabin?'

She hesitated for a moment, looking back over the past five years. 'Take care of Andrew.'

'And now that he'll be at the school?'

'I don't know yet. I used to work for a magazine, but that was a long time ago.'

'Did you like it?'

She thought about it for a minute and nodded. 'Yes, I did. But I was a lot younger. I'm not sure I'd like it as much now. It was a fun job when I was married to Jeffrey, but that was so long ago...' She smiled at him, feeling ten thousand years old. 'I was all of twenty-four.'

'And now you're what?' He grinned, amused. 'Twenty-five? Twenty-six?'

'Twenty-nine.' She said it with solemnity and he laughed.

'Of course. I had no idea you were so old. I, my friend, am all of fifty-two. Twenty-nine looks like baby years to me.' He looked it, and yet he didn't. There was something very wise and old and rare about him. Like fine cognac.

They finished the rest of their coffee and he stood up and looked around the room. 'Are you happy here, Daphne? It's a cosy little place.'

'I like it. Sometimes I think I'll stay up here forever.' She smiled and watched him. He was a beautiful male animal, even at fifty-two.

'Why would you stay here? For yourself or for Andrew?'

She wanted to say that she wasn't sure, but she was. It was for him, and he saw the answer in her eyes. 'You ought to get yourself back to New York one of these days, pretty lady. Don't waste yourself up here, in a cabin, living life for your child. You ought to be back with your own people, your own kind, busy, working, seeing friends. I get the feeling you've been in hibernation all these years, and you know what? You'd damn well better not waste it. One of these days you'll wake up and you'll be as old as I am, and you'll wonder what in hell you've done with your life. There's more to you than that, I can see it.'

Her eyes met his and all the pain of loss and time was there. 'I'm not so sure. I don't have any remarkable goals, any urge to create anything memorable, no dreams of greatness. Why couldn't I be happy here?'

'Doing what? Visiting Andrew? Hanging on to him when you ought to set him free? Walking on dark country roads when your car breaks down? Going to the Austrian Inn for Saturday-night dinner? Come on, lady, I don't know where you've been in your life, but I can tell you from looking at you, you deserve more than that.'

'Do I? Why?'

74

'Because you're smart as a whip and damn pretty. Whether you want to remember that fact or not.' She blushed then and he smiled at her, reaching for his jacket. 'And having talked your ear off, and made a nuisance of myself, making speeches, I will now take myself off and see what those young 'uns at the garage are doing with your axle.'

'You don't have to do that.' For a crazy moment she didn't want him to leave her. She felt comfortable with him there, and safe and happy. And now she would be alone again. For five years it hadn't really bothered her, and now suddenly it did.

But he was smiling at her from the doorway. 'I know I don't have to do it, but I want to. I like you, Daphne Fields.' And then, almost as an afterthought, 'Will you have dinner with me some night over at the inn? I promise not to lecture or make speeches, it's just that watching pretty young girls waste their lives has always bothered me.'

'I'd love to have dinner with you, John.'

'Good. Then let's do that.' He looked pensive for a moment and then smiled at her. 'Is tomorrow night too soon?' She shook her head slowly, wondering what she was doing, who this man was, and why she felt such a need to know him better, to be with him.

'That would be fine.'

'I'll pick you up at six thirty. Country hours.' He nodded to her, smiled, and then ambled out the door, closing it softly behind him as she stood and watched him from the window. He waved once as he pulled his truck out of the driveway, and then in a splash of gravel, he was gone. She stood there for a long time, watching the empty roadway, wondering where her life was going, and who John Fowler really was.

8

On Saturday evening John arrived promptly at six thirty, wearing the same sheepskin coat, but this time over a pair of grey slacks, a blazer, and a shirt and tie. The clothes were neither well cut nor expensive, and yet on him they had a certain style. His extravagantly macho build had a way of making everything about him look handsome, and Daphne was touched that he had dressed for dinner with her. There was a certain old-fashioned chivalry about the man that she couldn't help but like.

'My, don't you look pretty, Daphne.' She was wearing a white skirt and a blue turtleneck sweater that almost perfectly matched her eyes, and over it she wore a short lamb's wool coat that made her look like a tiny French poodle. Everything about her seemed soft and small, and yet there was something so intrinsically powerful about the woman, that her tiny size sometimes seemed a lie. She had worn her hair in a simple chignon, and he looked at it with interest and a shy smile. 'Do you ever wear your hair down?'

She hesitated for a moment and then shook her head. 'Not lately.' She had worn it down a lot for Jeff, cascading past her shoulders. But that was all part of another time, another life, a woman she had been for another man.

'I'd love to see it that way sometime.' He chuckled softly to himself as he watched her eyes. 'I have a great weakness for blonde beauties, I have to warn you.' But despite the teasing, and the obvious interest in his eyes, she felt safe as she left the house at his side. It was a quality she had noticed before about him. Perhaps it was because of his size, or maybe it was his almost fatherly manner, but she always felt safe beside him, as though he would take care of her, no matter what. But there was something different about her now too. She knew she could take care of herself. She hadn't known that when she married Jeff. She didn't need this man. She liked him.

He drove her to the Austrian Inn for dinner, and the Obermeiers seemed surprised to see them together, and took special care of them both. They both happened to be among their favourite people, and in the kitchen when the frantic bustle of dinner slowed, Hilda looked at her husband with intrigue in her eyes and a victorious grin. 'How do you suppose she met him?'

'I don't know, Hilda. And it's none of our business.' He chided her gently, but her curiosity and amazement could not be stopped.

'Do you realise that I haven't seen him out to dinner since his wife died?'

'Do you realise that you shouldn't be talking like that, Hilda? They're grown people, what they do is their business. And if he wants to take a pretty woman to dinner, why not?'

'Did I say it was wrong? I think it's wonderful!'

'Good. Then take them their coffee and shut up.' He patted her gently on the behind and went back to see that all his guests had what they needed, and a moment later he saw John and Daphne talking over their coffee, he was telling her something funny and she was laughing like a little girl.

'And then what did you tell them?' Her eyes still looked amused.

'That if they couldn't run a logging camp, then they should run a ballet. And you know what, damned if six months later they didn't sell the business and wind up buying some kind of dance troupe in Chicago.' He shook his head, his eyes still laughing. 'Damn fools.' He had been telling her about the pair of New York phonies who had been thinking of buying a business a few years back,

77

and running it for a tax loss. 'Hell, I didn't get that place running like I did just for two jackasses from New York to come in and blow it. Not like that.'

'Do you like the work, John?' She was intrigued by him. He was obviously intelligent, well read, aware of what was happening in the world at large, and yet he had lived all his life in this tiny New England village, and worked with his strong back and his hands.

'Yes, I like it. It suits me. I'd never have been happy in an office. I could have. Sally's father ran a bank here and all he wanted was to get me to work with him, but it wasn't me. This suits me better, out in the air all day, dealing with the men, working with my hands.' He smiled at her. 'I'm a labourer at heart, Mrs Fields.' But it was obvious that there was a great deal more to him than that. But what the labouring had done was give him an earthiness, a strength, a sense of reality, and a chance to observe human nature. He was a wise man, and as the evening wore on she found that she liked that about him. It was over dessert that he looked at her for a long moment and then took one of her hands in his own. 'We've both lost a great deal, you and I, and yet here we are, strong and alive, we've survived it.'

'I wasn't always sure I would.' It was a relief to admit that to somebody.

'You always will. But you don't know that yet, do you?'

'Sometimes I have my doubts. Sometimes I think I won't make it another day.'

'You will.' He said it with quiet confidence. 'But maybe it's time you stopped fighting all your wars alone.' He had sensed instantly that there had been no one in her life for a very long time. She had the kind of silent sorrow of a woman who has almost forgotten the gentle touch of loving. 'Has there been anyone in your life since your husband died, Daphne, or shouldn't I ask?'

She smiled and looked shy, the huge cornflower eyes suddenly even bigger. 'You can ask. No, there hasn't. In

78

fact' – she blushed and he felt an almost irresistible urge to kiss her – 'this is the first date I've ever had ... since...' She didn't have to say the rest. He understood.

'What a waste of a beautiful woman.' But this time his words were too much, and she turned her eyes away from his.

'It was better that way. There was more of me to give to Andrew.'

'And now?'

'I don't know...' She looked troubled as she said the words. 'I don't know what I'll do without him.'

'I think' – he narrowed his eyes as he watched her – 'I think that you're going to do something very important.'

She laughed and shook her head, amused by what he said. 'Like what? Run for Congress?'

'Maybe, if that's what you want. But it isn't. There's something deep inside you, Daphne, that's aching to come out. And maybe one of these days you'll let it.' She was stunned by his words. She had often thought the same thing, and the only release that she had for what she felt was in her journals. For a moment she wanted to tell him about them, but then suddenly she felt silly. 'Would you like to go for a walk?' They stood up after dinner, and he followed her outside the inn as Mrs Obermeier watched with obvious pleasure. 'You've made friends in this town, little one.' He smiled down at her as they walked outside. 'Mrs Obermeier likes you.'

'I like her too.' They walked side by side in silence for some time, along the deserted streets, and then he tucked her gloved hand into his arm.

'When am I going to meet Andrew?' There seemed to be no question that he would, only when it would happen. It was as though in two days this man had become a part of her life, and she wasn't sure where they were going, but she knew that she liked it. She felt released suddenly from all the bonds that had chained her for years, and she felt a little bit adrift, but it was a pleasant feeling.

She turned her face up to his as they walked along and looked at the powerful profile beside her. She wasn't sure what he would be in her life, but she knew for certain that he would be her friend. 'How about tomorrow? I was going to visit him in the afternoon. Would you like to come?'

'I'd love it.'

They walked slowly back to his truck then, and he drove her home. He walked her to the door, and she didn't invite him in, and he didn't seem to expect it. She waved as she closed the door and he slipped into his truck and drove away, filled with his own thoughts of Daphne.

Andrew was waiting outside with two counsellors and some of the other children when Daphne and John arrived at the school, and she was quick to recognise a look of suspicion in her son's eyes. He wasn't sure who the man was, and perhaps he was threatened by John's size. But Daphne had the feeling that he wasn't sure if he liked seeing someone with his mother. He had an instinctive sense of possession about her, which she had allowed to flourish.

She folded him quickly into her arms and kissed his cheek and his neck, nestling her face beside his, feeling the familiar warmth of the child who was so much a part of her, and then she pulled away and signed to him that this was her friend, just as he had friends at the school. And his name was John. And John knelt on the ground beside him. He didn't know any of the signs Daphne had already learned, but he seemed to communicate with the little boy with his eyes and his huge, gentle hands, and in a few minutes Andrew came to him hesitantly, like a cautious puppy. Without saying a word to him, John stretched forth a hand and took Andrew's small hand in his own. He began to talk to him then, in his deep, soft voice, as Andrew watched him. The boy's eyes stayed riveted to John's and once or twice he nodded, as though he understood him. There seemed to be total acceptance between them as Daphne watched in fascination. And then, without a word to her, Andrew led John away to sit beneath a tree, and 'talk.' The child signed, and the man spoke, and they seemed to understand each other as though they had always been friends. Daphne stood in the distance, watching in total fascination as she felt

81

a surge of emotion within her, half sorrow to have lost another little piece of Andrew, half joy to see John reach out to this child she loved with her whole soul. And somewhere deep within there was resentment, too, to see the doors to Andrew's silent world swing open so easily for John, when she had struggled for so long to unlock them. But above all there was tenderness for both John and Andrew as they returned to her at last, hand in hand, and smiling. They began to play then, and a little while later all three of them were laughing. The hours until dinnertime flew like minutes, and Daphne showed John the school, suddenly proud that she had done the right thing for Andrew. And as they walked back downstairs from the room where Andrew slept, John looked at her with warmth that washed over her like a Mediterranean summer.

'Has anyone told you how terrific you are, little one?' She blushed and he put an arm around her shoulders and held her close. It was the first time she felt him near her, and it was a powerful feeling as she closed her eyes in his embrace. 'You're brave and you're wonderful. You did a beautiful thing for Andrew, and it's going to be good for both of you,' and then in a soft voice that took her completely by surprise, 'and I love you for it.' She stood staring at him for a moment, not sure what to say, and he smiled and bent to kiss her forehead. 'It's okay, Daphne, I'm not going to hurt you.'

'Thank you.' She wasn't sure why she said it, but she suddenly slipped her arms around his waist and held him. She had so desperately needed someone to tell her what he had just told her, that she hadn't deserted Andrew, that it was all right, that she had done the right thing. 'Thank you so much.'

He gave her a quick squeeze and then walked the rest of the way downstairs, where they found Andrew and the others ready to sit down to dinner. It was time for them to go, and this time Andrew whimpered for a minute before they left, and Daphne held him close to her with tears in her eyes, breathing softly on his cheek, 'I love

82

you.' She pulled him away from her then, so he could see her mouth the words, and he flung himself ferociously into her arms again and made a croak, which was his 'I love you.' Mrs Curtis came along then, and touched his cheek with a warm smile, signalling to him to ask if he was ready to come to dinner. He looked unsure for a minute, and then he nodded and smiled, signing yes, and then with a quick wave and a kiss, and a look of friendship towards John, he left them and joined the others.

'Ready to go, or do you want to wait awhile?' John didn't want to rush her. He could almost feel in his own gut the fresh pain she was feeling. But she nodded slowly, her eyes still riveted to her child, and then she turned and looked up at John, grateful that he was there. 'You okay?'

'Yes. Let's go.'

He followed her out, and she marvelled at how good it felt to have someone to take care of her for a change. And suddenly as the cold night air hit their faces outside, she wanted to run. The pain of leaving Andrew was already dim, and she felt more alive than she had in years. She laughed suddenly and skipped to the truck like a little girl, as John walked beside her.

'He's a terrific little kid, you know.' He looked at her almost with shared pride as he started the engine. 'You've done one hell of a fine job.'

'That's just the way he is. I'm not sure I had anything to do with it.'

'Yes, you did. And don't you forget it.' He sounded almost stern as they drove away from the school, and he saw with pleasure that she still looked happy. 'Want to go back to the inn for dinner? I feel like celebrating, and I'm not even sure what.' He glanced at her and their eyes met and held. There was a powerful bond forming between them, and she had just shared an important part of her life with him. He was touched and pleased that she had let him meet Andrew.

'How about if I make you dinner instead?'

'Can you cook?' He was teasing and they both laughed. 'I eat a lot.'

'How about spaghetti?'

'That's it?' He looked shocked and she laughed, feeling like a kid, and suddenly for no reason at all, she remembered the first time she had cooked dinner for Jeff at her apartment. That had been an eternity ago, and she was ashamed to realise that it all seemed dim now, long ago and far away and not entirely real. There were times now when she had the feeling that the memories of Jeffrey were fading. 'Just spaghetti?' John's voice brought her back to the present.

'Okay, how about a steak? And a salad.'

'I accept. With pleasure,' he added, and she laughed again.

'You must cost one hell of a lot to feed, John Fowler.'

He looked amused at the look on her face. 'Not to worry. I make a healthy wage logging.'

'Isn't it dangerous though?' Her brow creased in a small frown. And it pleased him that she was worried.

'Sometimes. Not very often. Most of us know what we're doing. It's the greenies you have to look out for. The young kids who sign on for a summer. They'll kill you, if you don't watch them.'

She nodded quietly and they pulled up in front of her house and walked inside, and for the next half hour she was busy cooking. He set the table and did the steaks. She did the spaghetti and the salad, and he looked longingly at the fireplace, and she knew instantly what he was thinking. 'It's all right, John. If you want to, go ahead. This room would be pretty with a fire.'

'We don't need that. It's pretty without it.' But suddenly she wanted him to. She wanted to leave the past behind. She was tired of the terrors and the fears and the agonies of the past.

'Go ahead. Light the fire.' There was something about him that made her feel brave.

'I don't want to upset you, Daphne.'

'You won't. I think it's time to leave the past.' It felt strange to say it, but at long last it did not feel like a betrayal.

He left the table to put on a log, and threw in some kindling. The fire took quickly and she sat staring at it for a long time, thinking not so much of that fateful Christmas night, but of the many times she and Jeff had sat at home on Sunday nights, reading the Sunday papers, and enjoying the fire. Without saying a word, John reached across the table and took her hand, and she found herself thinking of his arm around her shoulders at the school and how good it felt to stand beside him.

'What were you thinking just then? You looked so happy.'

Her eyes were aglow from the firelight, and he thought she had been thinking of Jeffrey.

'I was thinking about you. I'm glad you picked me up on the road the other night.'

He smiled at the memory too. 'I would have picked you up sooner if you hadn't been hiding.' They both laughed at the thought, and she brought out two cups of steaming coffee. 'You're a good cook.'

'Thank you. So are you. The steaks were just right.'

He smiled at her almost sadly. 'I've had a lot of practice. Fifteen years of doing my own cooking.'

'Why didn't you ever remarry?'

'I never wanted to. Never met anyone I cared about that much.' 'Until now,' he wanted to say, but he didn't want to scare her, and he knew it would have. 'I guess I didn't want to start over. But you're young enough to, little one. One of these days you should.'

She shook her head pensively, looking up at him. 'I don't think so. You can't do things "again" in life, you can't re-create what was. That only comes once in a lifetime.'

'That particular experience does. But other experiences come along, which matter just as much. They're just different.'

'Look who's talking. You're no different than I am.'

'Yes, I am. You're luckier.'

'Am I? Why?'

'You have Andrew.' They both smiled. 'Every once in a while I meet a kid who makes me sorry I didn't have any.'

'It's not too late.' But he laughed at that.

'I'm an old man, Daphne Fields. I'm fifty-two years old. Hell, I'm old enough to be your father.' But she only smiled at that. She didn't see him in that light, and he didn't feel that way towards her either. They were friends on a variety of levels. And she'd never had a friend like him before. Maybe because she'd never been the woman she now was. She had grown strong over the years, stronger than she had ever dreamed. She was an even match for any man. Even a man like John.

They sat on the couch looking into the fire for a while, and it was extraordinary how comfortable she felt beside him. There was something easy and unhurried about him, as though he had a lifetime ahead of him, and plenty of time to enjoy each precious moment. And the sharp sculpture of his face looked beautiful in the light of the fire.

'John . . .' She didn't quite know how to say what she felt. Maybe later she would be able to say it in her journal.

'Yes, little one?'

But she couldn't find the right words. At last, in a soft husky voice, she said what she could. 'I'm glad I met you.'

He nodded slowly, feeling all that she felt, and sensing the peace and understanding that flowed between them. He put an arm around her shoulders then, and she felt the same quiet strength that had felt so good to her earlier that evening. She liked the weight of his arm, the feel of his hand, and the scent of him beside her. It was a rich mixture of after shave and wool and fresh air and tobacco. He smelled the way he looked, like a strong, attractive man who had lived his whole life amid trees and mountains. And he looked down at her then, and

86

saw a tear creep down her cheek. It startled him and he pulled her closer. 'Are you sad, love?' His voice was so deep and tender, but she shook her head.

'No ... I'm so happy ... just here, like this...' She looked up at him then. 'You must think I'm crazy. But I'm alive again. I feel like I've been half dead for so long. I thought...' It was hard to say the words but she had to. 'I thought I should be dead because they were. I only stayed alive for Andrew. I only lived for him.' And now she was living for herself again. At last.

He seemed to pause for an endless time, his face very close to hers, watching her. 'You have a right to your own life now, Daphne. You've paid your dues.' He kissed her gently on the lips then, and it was as though an arrow shot through her. His touch went to her very core, and she felt breathless as their lips touched and he held her. He took her face in his hands then, and sat looking quietly at her. 'Where have you been all my life, Daphne Fields?' He kissed her again, and this time she slipped her arm around his neck and held him close to her. She felt as though she wanted to cling to him for a lifetime and never let go, and he held her as though he would like her to do that.

His hands began to travel slowly over her shoulders after a little while, and then they slipped gently on to her breasts, and at last under her sweater. She uttered a soft little moan, and he held her close, sensing the rising passion within her. He stopped and pulled away after a time, and looked into her eyes. 'I don't want to do anything you don't want, little one. I'm an old man. I don't want to take advantage of you.' But she shook her head and kissed him as he pulled the pins from her hair, and loosed it from its knot to cascade down her back and over her shoulders. He let his fingers run through it, and touched her face and breasts again, and then the huge hands moved gently to her legs and she couldn't keep herself from writhing with pleasure as he touched her.

'Daphne ... Daphne...' He whispered her name as they lay on the couch beside the fire, his whole body throbbing with desire for her, and then she stood up and took his hand, and led him towards the four-poster in her bedroom. 'Are you sure?' He knew how long it had been, and she scarcely knew him. Everything had happened so quickly between them and he didn't want her to do anything she'd regret in the morning. He wanted to know her for a long time, not just for a night, or a moment.

'It's all right.' Her voice was the merest whisper as he slowly undressed her, until at last she stood before him, tiny, perfectly formed, her flesh shining in the moonlight, her blonde hair almost silver. He picked her up then and slid her into the bed, and carefully took off his own clothes, dropped them to the floor, and slid in beside her. The feel of her satin skin was almost more than he could bear, and he had a hunger for her that was impossible to control as he lay beside her. But it was she who took his face in her hands, who held him close as she arched her body towards him, as slowly, like a forgotten memory come to life with a delicious vengeance, she felt him slip inside her, and she soared to heights that, even with Jeffrey, she had never known. John was an artful and extraordinary lover, and they lay spent at last, side by side, her tiny body intertwined with his as she whispered into his neck that she loved him.

'I love you too, little one. Oh, God, how I love you . . .' And as he said the words she looked up at him with a sleepy smile, pulled herself more tightly against him as her eyes closed and she drifted off to sleep in his arms, a woman again, a woman she had never been . . . his woman, and her own. He was right about her. The years had made her strong, stronger than she knew.

10

'What are these?' John was holding two of Daphne's leather-bound journals in his hands as he stood naked in her kitchen at six o'clock the next morning. She had got up to make him breakfast before he left for work, but they had got delayed by another intense bout of passion.

She looked over her own naked shoulder with a smile, still amazed at how comfortable she felt with him. 'Hm? Oh, those are my journals.'

'Can I read them sometime?'

'Sure.' She looked faintly embarrassed as she put fried eggs and bacon on the table. 'They may sound a little silly though. I've poured out my soul in them.'

'There's nothing silly about that.' And then he smiled at her naked bottom. 'You've got one hell of a great ass, do you know that?'

'Shut up and eat your eggs.'

'Talk about the end of a romance.' But the romance between them had just begun. They even managed to sneak in one more 'quickie' before he left for work an hour later. 'I'm not sure I'm strong enough to work today after all that good loving.'

'Good, then stay home. I'll take care of you.'

'I'll bet you would!' He laughed out loud, zipping up the heavy parka he kept in his truck for work. 'You sure do spoil a man, Daphne Fields.'

But as she held him tight before he left, she whispered softly, 'You're the one who's spoiling me. You make me happier than I've ever been, and I want you to know that.'

'I'll remember it all day. I'll pick up some groceries

on the way home, and we'll have a quiet dinner. Sound okay to you?'

'It sounds perfect.'

'What'll you do?'

Her eyes sparkled for a moment and she smiled. 'Maybe I'll make a new entry in my journal.'

'Good. I'll check it out when I come home. See you later, little one.' And then he was off, the truck whirring on the gravel as she waved, bare-breasted, from the kitchen window.

The day seemed endless after he left, and she wondered what she had done without him. She thought about going to visit Andrew to pass the time, but it was too soon for another visit. So she stayed home, and cleaned house, and began to write in her journal, but something different rattled around in her head all morning, and after lunch she found herself writing a short story. It came out all in one piece, with a flow of its own, and when it was finished, she sat staring with amazement at the dozen pages she had written. It was the first time she had ever done anything like it.

And when he came home, she was waiting dressed in grey slacks and a bright red sweater. 'Don't you look pretty, little one. How was your day?'

'Terrific. But I missed you.' It was as though he had always been part of her life and she had waited for him every evening. They cooked dinner together again, with the groceries he had bought, and he told her the anecdotes of the day from the logging camp. It was after that that she showed him her short story, and he read it with delight as they sat by the fire.

'This is marvellous, Daff.' He looked at her with obvious pride and pleasure.

'Come on, tell the truth. Is it hokey?'

'Hell, no. It's terrific.'

'It's the first one I ever wrote. I don't even know where it came from.'

He touched the silky blonde hair on her head with a smile. 'From here, little one. And I suspect there are lots

90

more stories in there like this one.' She had tapped into a resource she didn't even know she had, and she felt an even greater release than she had ever felt when writing her journals.

They made love that night in front of the fire, and again in the four-poster bed, and once again at five thirty the next morning. And he left for work with a song on his lips, and she didn't wait until afternoon this time. She sat down as soon as he left, and wrote another story. It was different from the one she had composed the day before, but when John read it that night, he thought it was better. 'You've got a damn powerful style to your writing, Daff.' And after that he spent weeks reading all of her journals.

By Christmas they had settled into a comfortable life. He had more or less moved into the cabin with her, Andrew was growing more and more independent at the school, and she had more time on her hands than she'd had in years. It allowed her to write short stories every day. Some were better than others, but they were all interesting, and all seemed to have the same distinctive style. It was as though she had discovered a facet of herself she 'had never known before, and she had to admit that she loved it.

'It feels so damn good, John. I don't know, it's hard to explain. It's like all of this stuff has always been there, and I never knew it.'

'Maybe you should write a book.' He looked very serious as he said it.

'Don't be silly. About what?'

'I don't know. See what comes. I know you've got it in you.'

'I'm not sure I do. Writing short stories is different.'

'That doesn't mean you can't write a book. Try it. Hell, why not? You've got the time. There's nothing else to do here in winter.' And there wasn't of course, except visit Andrew. She spent two afternoons with him a week, and John went with her once every weekend. By Christmas it was easy to see that Andrew was perfectly happy, and he accepted John now with ease, signing funny things to him, now that John had learned his language. And they roughhoused outside, and more often than not John ended up with Andrew on one shoulder, and one of his friends on the other. He had come to love the child, and Daphne watched them with pride, marvelling at the gifts life had brought her. It was as though all the pain of the past was swept away at last. It was easier now to live with Jeff's memory. It was only seeing little girls of Aimee's age that still hurt her so badly. But even that was better now, John had a way of soothing all hurts and making her feel peaceful and happy.

They even brought Andrew home with them for a few hours once in a while. John gave him a dozen small tasks to do around the house. They carried firewood in together, and John carved him little animals out of kindling. They baked cookies with Daphne, and once painted an old wicker rocking chair that John had found behind a deserted barn. It was obvious to all that Andrew was growing increasingly independent, and it was easier for him to communicate with them both. Daphne had grown more proficient at signing, and the tension between them had eased. Andrew was more patient with her when she made a mistake, and he giggled once or twice when she missigned a word, and then grinning, explained in sign language to John that his Mom had said she was going to cook a frog for dinner. But his silent communications with John still remained deeply touching. The two had become friends, as though they had always been part of the same life, walking side by side in silence in the fields, stopping to watch a rabbit or a deer, their eyes meeting, as though nothing needed to be said. And when it would come time to go back to the school, Andrew would sit on John's lap in the truck, and put his small hands on the steering wheel beside John's large ones, and Daphne would watch them with a smile as they drove along. He was always happy to get back to the school with the others. And leaving him was no longer as wrenching. She and John had their own little life, and she thought that she had never been as content in her entire life. And it showed in her writing.

In February she finally got up the courage to start a book, and she worked on it long and hard every day while John was at work, and at night he read the day's production, with comments and praise, and he never seemed to doubt for a moment that she could do it.

'You know, if it weren't for you, I couldn't do this.' She was lying sprawled on the couch in blue jeans and boots with a stack of work on her lap as he sliced some apples for them.

'Yes, you could. I have nothing to do with it, you know. It all comes from you. It's all there. And no one will ever be able to take that away from you.'

'I don't know ... I still don't understand where it all comes from.'

'That isn't important. Just know that it's there, within you. No one else can affect that.'

'Nope.' She took a slice of apple and leaned over to give him a kiss. She loved the feel of his face against her lips, especially at the end of a day when it felt rough from the beginnings of his beard. Everything about him was so masculine and wonderfully sexy. 'I still think it's all your fault. If it weren't for you, I'd never have written a damn thing.' They both remembered with a smile that she had written her first short story after the first time they had made love. She had sent it in to *Collins* after the first of the year, to see if they would publish it, and she was still waiting for an answer.

The answer came in March, from her old boss, Allison Baer. They wanted it for five hundred dollars. 'Do you see that? John, they bought my story! They're crazy!' She was waiting for him in the doorway that night with a bottle of champagne and the cheque, and Allison's letter.

'Congratulations!' He was as pleased as she, and they celebrated in bed until the wee hours of the morning. He teased her a lot that he never got any sleep anymore, but it was more than obvious that they both enjoyed it.

The sale of the short story to *Collins* spurred her on, and she worked harder on the book through the spring, and finished it at last in July. She sat staring at it, holding it in her hands, feeling the weight of the manuscript, and more than a little awed by what she had done, and at the same time saddened by the loss of the people who had become so real through the long months that she wrote it.

'Now what do I do?' It was a little bit like losing a job, and she was almost sorry it was over.

'That, my love, is an interesting question.' He looked at her, bursting with pride, his chest bare, his face and arms brown, drinking a beer after a long day's work. It had been a beautiful summer. 'I'm not sure, but I think you're supposed to find an agent. Why don't you ask your old boss at *Collins*? Give her a call tomorrow.' But Daphne always hated talking to her. She harped and harped on how unnatural Daphne's life was. Daphne had never told her about John, and she assumed that Daphne was staying in New Hampshire to be near to Andrew. She always insisted that Daphne should come back to New York and get a job, but Daphne always used the excuse that she had sublet her apartment until September. And after that she would find other reasons. She had no plans now to leave. She was happy with John, and she wanted to stay in New Hampshire forever. But even John occasionally argued with that, insisting that she belonged in New York, with 'her own kind' and an interesting job. He didn't think she ought to spend the rest of her life with a logger. But he didn't really want her to go, and she had no intention of leaving him, now or ever.

'How do you suppose one finds an agent?'

'Maybe you should take the book to New York and find out.'

'Only if you come with me.'

'That's silly, love. You don't need me for that.'

94

'Yes, I do.' She looked like a happy little girl as she sat beside him. 'I need you for everything. Haven't you figured that out by now?' He had, but they both knew how much she was capable of on her own, and she was capable of a great deal.

'What would I do in New York?' He hadn't been there in twenty years, and he had no real desire to go. He was happy in the mountains of New England. 'Anyway, why don't you call Allison tomorrow and see what she says.' But the next day Daphne didn't do it. She decided to wait until the fall. Somehow she wasn't ready to let the book go, and she claimed that she wanted to read it over a few times, to make some final changes. 'Chicken,' he teased. 'You can't hide forever, little one.'

'Why not?'

'Because I won't let you. You're better than that.' He always made her feel as though there were nothing she couldn't do. It was remarkable how much she had come into her own in the months with him.

And Andrew had changed too. He was almost five now, and no longer a baby. And in August, Daphne had plans to join him and some of the other children and parents on a camping trip, under the aegis of Mrs Curtis. It was a special event for everyone involved, and Daphne wanted John to go on the four-day trip, to share the experience with Andrew, but he couldn't get away. They had twenty college kids at the logging camp, and all of the senior men were needed to keep an eye on the 'greenies.'

'Can't you get away?' She was so disappointed.

'I really can't, love. I wish I could. You're going to have a great time.'

'Not without you.' She almost pouted and he laughed, he loved the child-woman in her.

On the third week of August they went, with sleeping bags and tents and horses. It was a new experience for the children to travel through the woods, and all around them were thrills and discoveries. Daphne had brought one of her journals along, so she could write everything down for John, all of the funny things Andrew did, and the little moments she was afraid she might not remember. But most of the time she found herself writing about John, and thinking of the night they had spent together before she left. This was the first time they had been apart in nine months, and she had ached at the prospect of being without him. Having lost someone she loved once, she had a wild fear of leaving John too. There were even nights when she had nightmares that one day she might lose him.

'You won't get rid of me that easy, little one.' He had whispered it into her neck as she shared her fears. 'I'm a tough old bird.'

'I couldn't live without you, John.'

'Yes, you could. But you won't have to try. Not for a very long time. So have a good time with the kids, and tell me all about it.'

She had lain beside him at dawn, after they made love, and had felt his smooth, cool male flesh touching her thigh. It always sent the same thrill through her.

'I may suffer withdrawal in four days.' In their lovemaking, he had spoiled her. He may have called himself an 'old man,' but there was nothing old about his passion. He had the ardour of a man half his age, blended with an experience that taught her things she had never known before. She wondered sometimes if it was so good simply because she really loved him. And it was about things like that that she wrote in her journal while she was away, whenever she wasn't playing with Andrew. She was relishing these special days with him, watching him with his friends, living together in the woods, and waking up in the morning to see that small sunny face she hadn't woken up to in so long.

They came home after four days, like any respectable bunch of campers, dirty and tired and relaxed, and pleased with what they'd done. The parents had enjoyed the trip at least as much as the children. She left Andrew at the school, and put her sleeping bag and her backpack in her car, and yawned as she slid behind the wheel. She could hardly wait to get home to John, but when she reached the cabin, she didn't find him. There were dishes in the sink, and the bed was unmade, and she smiled to herself as she stepped gratefully into the shower. She would have everything in order when he got home. But as she stood in the kitchen, washing dishes in her jeans, the knock on the door was unfamiliar. She went to open it with hands still covered with soap and she smiled when she saw one of John's friends, a man they seldom saw but whom she knew John was fond of.

'Hi, Harry, what's new?' She was tanned and relaxed and happy, but John's friend looked strained.

'When did you get back?' His face was grave and his eyes were sad, as they always were. John always teased him that he looked like his best friend had just died, but he had a fat wife and six kids, which would have been enough to depress anyone, John said. 'How's Gladys?'

'Daphne, can I talk to you for a minute?' This time he looked genuinely troubled. And suddenly somewhere behind her she heard the ticking of the kitchen clock.

'Sure.' She wiped her hands on her jeans, put down the towel, and came to where he stood. 'Is something wrong?' He nodded slowly, with no idea how to tell her. He couldn't begin to say the words, and there was an eerie silence between them.

'Let's sit down.' He moved nervously towards the couch, and she followed him as though in a dream.

'Harry? What is it? What's wrong?'

His eyes were like two sad black stones as they looked into hers. 'John's dead, Daphne. He died while you were gone.'

She felt the room spin around her as she saw Harry's face in the distance ... John's dead ... John's dead ... the words were from a bad dream, not reality, this hadn't happened, not to her ... again. And suddenly, in the stillness around them, she heard a woman laughing, hysterically, a raucous sound.

'No! No! No!' The shrill laughter turned to sobs as

Harry watched her, anxious to explain how he died, but she didn't want to hear it. It didn't matter. She'd been here before. But impervious to what she was feeling, Harry began talking. She wanted to put her fingers in her ears and scream and run. 'There was an accident at the camp the day you left. We called the school, but they said there was no way to reach you. Some of those damn college kids lost control of a winch, and a load of trees hit him...' Harry began to cry, and Daphne stared at him with wide eyes. '... broke his back and his neck. He never knew what hit him.'

Neither had Jeff. Or so they had said. What difference did it make? What did it matter now? She sat staring at Harry, and all she could think of was Andrew. What was she going to tell her son?

'We're all so damn sorry. The kids were sent home, and we had the funeral home keep the body. He has no family here, or anywhere, I think. They're all gone. And we didn't know what you'd want to do... Gladys thought – '

'It's all right.' She jumped up looking tense and white-faced. 'Never mind.' She had passed this way before. It was only when Harry left that the tears came, great rivers of silent, anguished tears. She looked around the room and sat down again. John Fowler would never be coming home again.

'You can make it on your own, little one.' She remembered his words from the past. But she didn't want to make it on her own. She wanted her life with him.

'Oh, John...' It was a soft, broken whisper in the silence of their cabin, and she remembered all that they had said before, he about losing his wife, and she about losing Jeff. This made no more sense than that had, and she understood it no better, and yet this was different, she knew the futility of hanging on. She walked out into the woods at sunset, and the tears came again as she looked into the summer sky and thought of him, the broad shoulders and big hands, the deep voice, the man who had loved her and Andrew.

'Damn you!' she shouted into the mauve and orange sky. 'Damn you! Why'd you have to do it?' She stood there for a long time, her tears flowing freely as the sky grew dark, and then wiping her cheeks on the sleeves of the logger's shirt she wore, she nodded. 'Okay, my friend. Okay. We'll make it. Just remember that I loved you.' And then, still crying, she looked at where the sun had been on the hills a little while before and whispered, 'Good-bye,' and then with her head bowed, she walked home.

11

Daphne woke before dawn the next morning, lying on the bed that suddenly seemed too large as she slept in it alone. She lay there, thinking about John and remembering their early mornings, side by side, and often their bodies joined as one before the dawn.

She lay there as the sun crept slowly through the windows, feeling leaden, wanting never to get up again. There was none of the horror and the panic she had felt when Jeff had died. There was only emptiness and loss, an abysmal kind of sorrow that weighed on her like her own tombstone as she ran the fingers of her mind over the wound again and again and again . . . the words ran rhythmically through her mind . . . *John is dead . . . is dead . . . is dead . . . I'll never see him again . . . never see him . . .* and the worst of it was that neither would Andrew. How would she tell him?

It was almost noon when she forced herself out of bed at last, and she was dizzy for a moment when she stood up. There was a sick, empty feeling, born of not having eaten anything at all since the previous morning, and she could eat nothing now as the same words continued to echo in her head . . . *John is dead . . . John is dead . . .*

She stood in the shower for half an hour, staring into space as the water beat down on her like angry rain, and it took her almost an hour after that to put on a pair of jeans, a shirt of John's, and a pair of shoes. She stared into their closet as though it held a lifetime of precious secrets, but she had been through this once before and could not let it demolish her again. When Jeff had died, the knowledge that she carried their unborn child had eventually pulled her through, but she wouldn't have that this time, the miracle of life to counterbalance death. What she had this time was Andrew himself. She knew she had to find her way to him now, for his sake and her own. She still had him.

She drove to the school, looking dazed and still feeling numb and strange, and it was only when she saw him happily playing with a ball that she began to cry again.

She stood watching him for a long time, trying to sift through her thoughts, and stop the tears, but they wouldn't stop now, and finally he turned and saw her, frowned, and dropped his ball, and walked slowly towards her, a worried frown in his eyes. She sat down on the grass and held out her arms towards him, smiling through her tears. He was the centre of her life now, as he had always been.

'Hi,' she signed to him, once he sat beside her.

'What's wrong?' All the love and protection they felt for each other was mirrored in his eyes.

There was an endless pause as she felt her hands shake. She couldn't bring herself to make the signs.

At last she did. 'I have something very sad to tell you.'

'What?' He looked surprised. She had sheltered him from all sorrows and disasters, and there had been none like this in his lifetime. But there was no way to keep this from him. The boy had grown very close to John. Daphne's chin trembled and her eyes filled as she put her arms around her son, and then released him to sign the words she dreaded. 'John died while we were away, sweetheart. He had an accident. I found out yesterday and we won't see him again.'

'Forever?' Andrew's eyes grew wide in disbelief.

She nodded and signed back. 'Forever. But we'll remember him forever, and love him, just like I do your Dad.'

'But I don't know my Dad.' The small hands trembled as they signed. 'And I love John.'

'So do I.' The tears rolled down Daphne's face again.

'So do I . . .' And then, 'And I love you too.' They clung to each other then as the small child began to sob, great gulping broken sounds that tore at her heart as they held each other close. It seemed hours before either of them was ready to let go. They took a walk then, in silence, hand in hand, and every now and then Andrew would sign something about John, the things they had done, the way he had been. It struck Daphne again how remarkable it had been that the big woodsman had so captivated her son without a single word. He hadn't been a man who needed words. There was some rare and powerful essence within that transcended all else, even Andrew's handicap and Daphne's fears.

It surprised her when Andrew asked her later, 'Will you stay here without him, Mom?'

'Yes. I'm here for you, you know.' But they both knew that for the past six months that hadn't been entirely true. Andrew had got more and more independent and Daphne had stayed in New Hampshire because of John. But she couldn't leave now. Andrew needed her, and more than ever, she needed him.

The remaining weeks of the summer crawled by, as Daphne ached silently for John. She stopped crying after a while, and she no longer wrote in her journals. She barely touched food, and she saw no one, except Andrew. It was Mrs Obermeier who finally stopped by, and was aghast at what she saw. Daphne had lost twelve pounds from her tiny frame, her face was anguished and drawn, and the old Austrian woman took her in her arms, but even then Daphne didn't cry, she simply stood there. She was beyond pain, she was simply hanging on to survival, and she wasn't even sure why, except for Andrew. Even he didn't really need her now. He had the school, and Mrs Curtis had suggested that she cut back her visits.

'Why don't you go back to New York?' Mrs Obermeier suggested over a cup of tea Daphne barely drank. 'To your friends. It is too hard for you here. I can see that.' Daphne knew it too, but she didn't want to go back. She wanted to stay in the cabin forever, with his clothes, with his boots, with his smell, with his aura around her. He had long since given up his own apartment before he died.

'I want to be here.'

'It's not good for you here, Daphne.' The wise old woman sounded firm. 'You can't hold on to the past.' Daphne wanted to ask her why not, but she already knew all those answers. She had been through it before. But it only made it that much worse this time.

Her story came out in *Collins* in October, and Allison sent her a complimentary copy with a note. 'When the hell are you coming back? Love, Allie.' In Daphne's mind, the answer was never. But at the end of the month she got a note from her landlord in Boston. Her lease was up, and the cabin had been sold. They wanted her out by the first of November.

She no longer had the excuse that there was someone in her apartment in New York. Her tenant had moved out on the first of October. Which left her nowhere to go except to New York. She could have found another cabin or apartment where she was, but it didn't make much sense. She was only seeing Andrew once a week, and he barely paid any attention to her. He was more and more self-reliant now and Mrs Curtis had recently pointed out that it was time he turn his full attention to the school. In some ways Daphne's visits held him back, allowing him to cling to her. But in truth, it was Daphne clinging to him.

She packed all her things, as well as John's, put them on a bus to New York, and stared around the cabin for a last time, feeling a terrible catch in her throat as a terrible sound finally escaped her. The sobs racked her for an hour as she sat on the couch, crying into the silence. She was alone. John was gone. Nothing would bring him back. He was gone forever. She closed the door softly behind her, and leaned her face against it for a moment, feeling its wood on her cheek, remembering all the moments they had shared, and then she walked slowly away to her car. She had given John's truck to Harry.

At the school Andrew was busy with activities and friends. She kissed him good-bye, and promised to come back in a few weeks for Thanksgiving. She would stay at the Austrian Inn now, like the other parents. Mrs Curtis made no mention of John as Daphne left, although she had known him and was very sorry.

The drive to New York took seven hours, and there was no thrill for Daphne as she drove into town and caught the first glimpse of the Empire State Building. It was a city she didn't want to see, a place she didn't want to come home to. There was no home left. There was only an empty apartment.

The apartment was in decent shape. The tenant had left it clean, and she sighed as she tossed her suitcase on to the bed. Even here there were ghosts. There was Andrew's empty room to contend with, the games he no longer played, the books he no longer read. He had taken all the treasures he loved most to the school with him, and the rest he had outgrown.

And Daphne felt as though she had outgrown the apartment too. It had a dreary city look to it, which depressed her after months of living in the cabin, looking out over the New Hampshire hills. Here there was only a view of other buildings, a tiny kitchen totally unlike the cosy one she had grown used to, a living room with curtains that had grown dingy, an old rug too well worn by Andrew's toys, and furniture that was beginning to show signs of nicks and chips. Once, she had cared so much about it, wanting to make it a happy, cheerful home for herself and her son. Now, without him, it had no meaning. She cleaned the rug the first weekend she was home, and changed the curtains, bought some new plants, but for the rest she simply didn't care. She spent most of her time out walking, getting used to New York again, and avoiding going home to the apartment.

It was actually a beautiful time of year, the best

possible in New York, but even the cool, golden sunny weather didn't cheer her. She didn't give a damn, and there was something dead in her eyes as she got up every morning and wondered what to do with herself. She knew she should go out and look for a job, but she didn't want to. She still had enough money to live for a while without working, and she told herself that after the first of the year she would think about it. She stuck her manuscript in a desk drawer and she didn't even bother to call her old boss, Allie. But she ran into her one day in a store downtown, where she was looking for pyjamas for Andrew. He had grown two full sizes in the past year, and Mrs Curtis had sent her a list of what he needed.

'What are you doing here, Daff?'

'Shopping for Andrew.' She sounded matter-of-fact, but she looked worse than she had the year before, and Allison Baer couldn't help wondering what in hell had happened to her.

'Is he all right?' There was worry in her eyes.

'He's fine.'

'Are you?'

'Pretty much.'

'Daphne' – her old friend touched her arm, concerned by what she saw – 'you can't hold on to the child forever.' Was it possible that she was grieving to that extent, from leaving the child at the school? It just wasn't healthy.

'I know. He's fine. He really loves it.'

'And you? When did you get back?'

'A couple of weeks ago. I meant to call, but I've been busy.'

'Writing?' Allie looked hopeful.

'Not really.' She didn't even want to think about that now. That was all part of her life with John, and it was over. As far as she was concerned, so was her writing.

'What ever happened to that book you said you were

writing, and promised to send me? Did you finish it yet?'

She wanted to say no, but somehow she didn't.

'Yes. I finished it this summer. But I didn't know what to do next. I meant to call you about finding an agent.'

'Well?' Everything about Allison rang out with the staccato of New York, and Daphne just didn't feel up to it. She was already exhausted after five minutes. 'Can I see it?'

'I suppose so. I'll drop it off.'

'How about lunch tomorrow?'

'I don't think I can ... I ...' She looked away, unnerved by the crowds in the store, and the pressure of Allie.

'Look, Daff.' She gently took hold of Daphne's arm. 'Speaking bluntly, you look worse than you did when you left last year. In fact, you look like shit. You have to pull yourself together. You can't avoid people for the rest of your life. You lost Jeff and Aimee, Andrew is all squared away in that school, for chrissake, you have to do something with yourself. Let's have lunch and we'll talk about it.' The prospect was truly appalling.

'I don't want to talk about it.' But as she tried to brush Allie off, it was as though she heard John's voice somewhere in the distance. 'Come on, little one, dammit ... you can make it ... you have to ...' All that faith he had had in her, all his excitement over her book. It was like denying him some final thrill to leave the book buried in her desk. 'All right, all right. We'll have lunch. But I don't want to talk about it. You can tell me how to find an agent.'

They met the next day at the Veau d'Or, and Allie was full of helpful suggestions. She seemed to keep searching Daphne's eyes, but Daphne kept strictly to the subject. Allie gave her a list of agents to call, took the manuscript in hand, and promised to return it to her after the weekend, and when she did, she was raving. She thought it was the best thing she had read in years, and in spite

106

of herself Daphne was pleased by her praise. She had always been damn tough with her criticism, and seldom generous with her applause. But for Daphne, she was applauding.

She told Daphne whom to call on the list, and on Monday she did, still feeling that she was doing it for John, but suddenly she was beginning to catch the fire of Allie's excitement. She dropped the manuscript off at the agent's office, expecting not to hear for several weeks, but four days later, as she was packing to go to see Andrew for Thanksgiving, the agent, Iris, called at four o'clock and asked if she could see her on Monday.

'What did you think of the book?' Suddenly she had to know. Slowly she was coming back to life, and the book was becoming important to her. It was her last link to John, and it was her only link to survival.

'What did I think? Honestly?' Daphne held her breath. 'I loved it. And Allison's right, she called me the day you dropped it off. It's the best thing I've read in years. You've got a sure winner there, Daphne.' For the first time in three months Daphne smiled a real smile and tears filled her eyes. Tears of excitement and relief, and that same old aching again, of wanting to share something with John, and realising once more that he wasn't there to share it. 'I thought maybe on Monday we could have lunch.'

'I'm going out of town...' She didn't want to have lunch, but she also knew that she would be back on Sunday. 'All right. Where?' Allison had warned Iris that Daphne wasn't easy, that she had been traumatised by her husband's and daughter's deaths years before, and she had a son who was in an 'institution' and she had never really recovered. Allison had always assumed that Andrew's being deaf meant he wasn't mentally quite 'normal.'

'Le Cygne at one o'clock?'

'I'll be there.'

'Good. And Daphne?'

'Yes?'

'Congratulations.'

She sat down on the bed after the call, her knees weak, her heart pounding. They liked her book ... the book she had written for John ... it was an amazing thought. More amazing yet if a publisher bought it.

12

Thanksgiving dinner with Andrew was its own special kind of joy, but that night, in her bed at the Austrian Inn, she lay awake and her mind roamed nervously from place to place. It was difficult to forget that a year before John had picked her up on a dark country road, and their life had begun, and now, only one year later, it was over. She had another holiday to hate now. Thanksgiving as well as Christmas. And she knew that this year Andrew had felt it too. Often she saw him looking dreamy, and once or twice with a wistful look in his eyes, he signed to her about John. They both had a lot of memories to live with. Too many, she thought to herself as she carefully avoided walking past their cabin. But she couldn't allow herself to think of John now, she had Andrew to think of, and his progress at the school.

When she left Andrew, this time it wasn't particularly traumatic. She was coming again during Christmas vacation.

She took a solitary walk in the hills where she had scattered John's ashes before she drove home. And she found herself speaking aloud to him, knowing that no one would hear her. She told him about the book and about Andrew, and then looking deep into the woods and up into the winter sky, she whispered, 'I sure miss you.' She could feel the echo of his thoughts and knew that he missed her, too. Perhaps, in a way, she was lucky to have loved him. Maybe that was all there was to know when it was over.

She got back in her car and drove to New York, and that night she fell into bed, exhausted. And the next day she got up and dressed in a white wool dress and heavy black coat and boots. It was freezing cold, and it seemed a thousand years since she had gone to one of those lunches. Now it seemed very strange to her to be meeting some woman to discuss her book. She remembered authors' lunches from *Collins*, but the funny thing now was that she was the author.

'Daphne? I'm Iris McCarthy.' The agent was red-headed and sleek, and a collection of elegant rings glittered on her well-manicured hands as they moved towards their table.

They spent the entire luncheon discussing her book, and over coffee and chocolate mousse Daphne began to talk about an idea she had for a second one. It was an idea she had discussed with John, and he had loved it. Iris did too, and Daphne smiled with pleasure. It was almost as though she could hear John whisper in her ear, 'That's it, little one . . . you can do it.' By the end of lunch they had settled on titles for both books, and Daphne was delighted. The first was *Autumn Years*, the one she had written in New Hampshire, about a woman who loses her husband at forty-five, and how she survives it. It was a subject she knew well, and Iris assured her that there would be a 'tremendous market for it.' The second was to be called simply *Agatha*, a story of a young woman in Paris after the war. It was a story she had written originally as a short story, but it had wanted to grow and now she would let it. She promised to get to work on an outline right away, and then to discuss it with Iris. And by that afternoon she was sitting at her desk staring at a blank sheet of paper. And when the ideas for the book began to come, she let them. By midnight that night she had the beginnings of a very solid outline and by the time she returned from her Christmas holiday with Andrew, it was not only finished but well polished. The outline was delivered to Iris in her office, and she gave Daphne the green light. For the next three months Daphne hid out in her apartment and worked night and day. It was not an easy book to write but she loved it. She was often so engrossed that she didn't even bother to answer the phone, but when it rang one day in April, she stood up and stretched with a groan and went to the kitchen to answer it.

'Daphne?'

'Yes.' No, Dracula, she was always tempted to answer. Who else would answer the phone? The upstairs maid in a two-room apartment? It was Iris.

'I have some news for you.' But Daphne was too tired to pay much attention. She had worked on the book until 4 a.m. the night before and she was exhausted. 'We just had a call from Harbor and Jones.'

'And?' Suddenly Daphne's heart began to race. In the past four months it had all begun to matter. For her sake, for John's, for Andrew's. She wanted it to happen, and it seemed as though it was taking a very long time. But Iris assured her that four months was nothing. 'Did they like it?'

'You could say that.' At her end, Iris was smiling. 'I'd say that an offer of twenty-five thousand dollars means they like it.' Daphne stood in her kitchen with her mouth open, staring at the phone.

'Do you mean it?'

'Of course I mean it.'

'Oh, my God . . . oh, my God! Iris!' Her face broke into a grin and she stared into the spring sunshine outside her kitchen window. 'Iris! Iris! Iris!' It had happened after all, John had been right. She *could* do it! 'Now what do I do?'

'You have lunch with your editor on Tuesday. At the Four Seasons. You've moved up in the world, Mrs Fields.'

'I sure as hell have.' She was almost thirty-one years old and she was about to publish her first book, and have lunch with an editor at the Four Seasons. Now that was a lunch she wouldn't miss for the world. And she didn't. She arrived on schedule at noon on Tuesday, in a new pink Chanel suit she had bought for the occasion. The editor was a dragonlike woman with a carnivorous smile, but by the end of the lunch Daphne knew they would work well together, and that she would learn a great deal from her. She began discussing her second book, as they sat at a table next to the pool in the centre of the white marble room with waiters scurrying around them. The editor from Harbor and Jones asked if she could see what Daphne had of the new book. A month later there was a second offer, and when she finished the book in late July, she went up to New Hampshire to spend a month with Andrew.

Her first book came out that Christmas, dedicated to John, and it enjoyed a modest success, but it was the second one that made her. It came out the following spring, and it hit *The New York Times* list almost at once. And the paperback rights sold for one hundred thousand dollars.

'How does it feel to be a success, Daff?' Allie took a maternal pride in her progress, and had invited her to lunch for her thirty-second birthday. 'Hell, I should make you pay for lunch.' But it was obvious that she didn't begrudge her what had happened. It had brought her back to the land of the living in a way Allison had never dreamed, and all of those who knew what she had been through in her life were thrilled for her. 'What are you working on now?' Her third book was well under way, already bought by Harbor and Jones before it was even finished, and scheduled for the following summer.

'Something called *Heartbeat*.'

'I like the title.'

'I hope you like the book.'

'I will, and so will all your readers.' Allie never doubted her for a moment.

'I'm a little nervous about this one. They're going to make me go on the road to promote it.'

'It's about time.'

'I'm glad *you* think so. What in hell do I talk about on talk shows in Cleveland?' Daphne still looked terribly young, and a little bit shy, and the prospect of television made her very nervous.

'Tell them about you. That's what people want to know. They always ask me.'

'And what do you say?' Allison stalled just long enough for Daphne to know the truth. 'That I've had a tragic life? That's exactly what I don't want to tell them.'

'So tell them how you write your books, all that kind of stuff.' She giggled then. 'Tell them who you're dating.' Daphne had looked so well for the past two years that she assumed there were a host of escorts. What she didn't know was that there had been no one in Daphne's life for two years, not since John died. And she was rapidly coming to the conclusion that she was going to keep it that way, for good. She couldn't have faced another loss, and she didn't plan to. 'Who is the man in your life, by the way?'

Daphne smiled. 'Andrew.'

'How is he?' But Allie was never really very interested. She liked grown-ups and careers and successful people. She had never married, and she didn't particularly like children.

'He's fine. Enormous and beautiful, and very, very busy.'

'He's still at the school?'

'He will be for a while.' Something sad came into Daphne's eyes, and Allison was sorry she had asked. 'I'm hoping that in a couple of years I can bring him home.'

'Is that a good idea?' Allison looked shocked. She still thought he was crazy. But Daphne knew that about her friend and didn't hold it against her.

'We'll see. There are conflicting theories on the subject. I'd like to put him in a regular school here at home, whenever he's ready.'

'Won't that interfere with your work?' Allison would never understand and Daphne knew it. How could a child she loved interfere with her work? Daphne knew that it could only enhance it. And it might complicate

113

things a little, but it was a complication she longed for. 'Well, tell me about the tour. Where are you going?'

'I don't know yet. The Midwest, California, Boston, Washington, DC. The usual insanity from what everyone tells me. Twenty cities in as many days, no sleep, no meals, and the terror that you won't remember where you are when you wake up in the morning.'

'Sounds great to me.'

'It would. To me, it sounds like a nightmare.' She still longed for the life she had once had in the cabin in New Hampshire, but that was long gone now, and it would never come again. She was thinking of buying an apartment in the East Sixties.

And after lunch she went home to work on the new book, as she did every day, every night, every hour that she wasn't visiting Andrew. She had found something to fill the void. A fantasy life conducted on paper, filled with people who lived and died in her head, and delighted hundreds of thousands of readers, and millions in paperback. There was nothing in her life except her work, but it paid off. Just before her thirty-third birthday, Daphne Fields's book *Apache* made it to the number one spot on the *The New York Times* Best Seller List. She had made it.

13

'How is she?' Barbara's eyes looked wearily at the nurse as she checked all the monitors again, but it was useless asking. There was obviously no change. It was incredible to think of her lying here, so still, so lifeless, so devoid of the energy she had so richly shared with those who needed her. Barbara knew better than anyone what mountains she was capable of moving. She had moved them for Andrew, and for herself, and for Barbara, over the years.

As the nurse left the room again Barbara closed her eyes for a minute, thinking back to the beginning, and the first time she had seen her, when Barbara was still living with her mother in those long-gone nightmare days. She had gone out to buy groceries, and had returned, exhausted and breathless after the long hike up the stairs to their dismal, dingy West Side apartment where Barbara had been trapped with her invalid mother for years.

Daphne had found her through her agent, who knew that Barbara took in typing at home, to supplement her meagre secretarial income, and also secretly to give herself an escape from the life she hated so desperately and the realities she almost couldn't bear. But the manuscripts added a touch of whimsy, a glimpse into other worlds, even if they were a lot of work.

Barbara had staggered through the door with groceries in both arms, assaulted as always by the smell of cabbage and decaying flesh. And there sat Daphne, serious, quiet, nicely dressed, and something about her so fresh. Looking at her was, for Barbara, like opening a window and taking gulps of clean air. The women's

115

eyes met almost instantly, and Barbara blushed. No one ever came here, she always went to the literary agency herself to pick up the work.

Barbara had been about to speak to Daphne as she heard the familiar plaintive wail. 'Did you buy me rice?' Barbara felt a sudden urge to scream as Daphne watched her, taking it all in. 'You always get the wrong kind.' Her mother's voice was, as usual, hideous and whiny, always angry and shrill.

'Yes, I got rice. Now, Mother, why don't you go inside and lie down while I – '

'What about coffee?'

'I got it.' The old woman began to dig through the two bags, making small clucking sounds, and Barbara's hands shook as she took off her jacket. 'Mother, please...' She looked apologetically at Daphne, who smiled, trying not to let the scene unnerve her. But there was something claustrophobic about just being there. She felt trapped just watching Barbara and her mother. Eventually the old woman had gone to a back room, and Daphne had been able to explain what she wanted. The manuscript had come back to her in two weeks, perfectly typed, without a single error. And Daphne said that she thought it remarkable that she had got it done at all with the old woman undoubtedly driving her crazy. It seemed like a ghastly life to her, and she wondered why Barbara had chosen to live with her mother.

She had brought her more work to do after that, typing rewrites and rough drafts and an occasional outline, and in time she had asked Barbara to come to her apartment and work with her there. And it was then that Barbara finally poured out her story. Her father had died when she was nine, and her mother had struggled to support her, put her through the best possible schools, and eventually helped put her through college. Barbara had gone to Smith, and had graduated with honours, but by then her mother had had a stroke and could no longer help her. Now it was Barbara's turn to struggle to support her, for two years the woman had been destitute.

116

Barbara took a job as a secretary to two attorneys, and at night she nursed her mother. There wasn't time for much else, and she told Daphne that she had been perennially exhausted. The romance that she'd had in college fell away, the young man couldn't stand the demands of her life, and when he proposed she tearfully refused to leave her mother. They couldn't afford to put her in a home, and her mother begged her not to. She just couldn't leave her, not after the years Eleanor Jarvis had spent standing on her feet night and day, working two jobs to put Barbara through school. The debt had to be repaid, and her mother constantly reminded her of it. 'After all I did, you would leave me . . .' She accused and she whined and she laid all the guilt at Barbara's feet. Barbara had no intention of leaving her. She simply couldn't. She spent two years nursing her mother back to health and working in the law firm. It was at the end of those two years that her boss left his wife and began to court Barbara. He knew about the life she led, and he felt very sorry for her. She was a bright girl with a good mind, and it irked him to see her waste her life. At twenty-five she was beginning to look and act and sound like an old woman.

It was he who urged her to get out whenever she could. He would come to pick her up, and chat with her mother. Her mother objected strenuously whenever she went out, but he was firm with Barbara about getting something out of life for herself, and she managed what time with him she could, while still trying to appease her mother. The affair lasted six months, and it was the only ray of sunshine she had, until Christmas, when he told her he was going back to his wife. She was going through change of life, and having a hard time, and the kids were giving her a lot of trouble.

'I have responsibilities, Barbara. I have to go back and give her a hand. I just can't let her go on struggling alone . . .' He was apologetic, and Barbara looked at him with a bitter little smile, tears bright in her eyes.

'What about your own life? What about the things you

117

said to me about getting what I need, and not just dancing to everyone else's music?'

'That's all true. I believe everything I said. But Barb, you have to understand. This is different. She's my wife. In your case, you're being strangled by an overbearing, demanding, unreasonable mother. You have a right to your own life. But my life is Georgia's too ... you just don't throw twenty-two years out the window.' And what was she supposed to do with her mother? Run out the door and never come back? He was full of shit and she knew it. He went back to his wife the next day, and the affair ended abruptly. She quit her job after the new year, and two weeks later she discovered she was pregnant. She deliberated for a week, locking herself in her room, and sobbing silently into her pillows. She had thought that she loved him, that he would be free, that he might marry her some day ... that she would be free of her mother. And what in hell was she going to do now? She couldn't take care of a child by herself, and having it aborted went against everything she believed. She didn't want to do it. In the end she decided to call him. He met her for lunch, looking very businesslike and a little distant.

'You're all right?' She nodded, looking grim and feeling desperately nauseous. 'And your mother?'

'She's all right. But the doctor is worried about her heart.' At least that was what she told Barbara, every time Barbara wanted even to go to a movie. Now she never went out. There was no point, and she didn't really feel up to it. She was constantly nauseous. 'I've got something to tell you.'

'Oh?' A wall instantly went up, as though deep in his gut he suspected. 'Didn't your last cheque arrive?' They had decided it would be better if she quit the firm and he had arranged a large severance pay for her to assuage his guilt. Yes, you son of a bitch, she thought to herself ... but this isn't about money. It's about my life. And your baby.

'I'm pregnant.' She couldn't think of a gentler way to

118

say it and she didn't really want to. Screw Georgia and her change of life. This was more important. At least to Barbara.

'That certainly presents a bit of a problem.' He tried to sound glib, but his eyes told her that he was nervous. 'Are you sure? Have you seen a doctor?'

'Yes.'

'Are you sure it's mine?' Even knowing her life, he didn't flinch as he said it, and her eyes filled with tears which spilled on to her cheeks.

'You know something, Stan? You're a real shit. Do you really think I was sleeping with someone else?'

'I'm sorry. I just thought – '

'No, you didn't. You just wanted to get out of it.'

For a moment he didn't answer. And then his voice was a little more gentle when he spoke again, but he didn't even reach out to touch her hand as she sat crying across the table. 'I know someone who...' She cringed at what he was about to say.

'I don't know if I can do it ... I just can't...' She began to sob and he looked nervously over his shoulder.

'Look, be realistic, Barb. You have no choice.' And without another word he scribbled a name on a piece of paper, wrote her a cheque for a thousand dollars, and handed them both to her. 'Call this number and tell him I sent you.'

'Why? Do you get a special deal?' Apparently this had happened to him before, and then with despair in her eyes she looked across at him, this wasn't the man she knew, this wasn't the man she had believed in ... the man she had thought would save her. 'Would you send Georgia to him?'

He looked stony-faced at her for a long moment. 'I sent him my daughter last year.'

She lowered her eyes and shook her head. 'I'm sorry.'

'So am I.' They were the last kind words he said as

he stood up and looked down at her. 'Barb, get it done fast. Get it over with. You'll feel a lot better.'

She looked up at him from where she sat. 'And if I don't?'

'What the hell do you mean?' He almost spat the words at her.

'I mean what if I decide to have the baby? I still have a choice, you know. I don't have to have an abortion.'

'If you don't, it's entirely your decision.'

'Meaning don't call you?' She hated him now.

'Meaning I don't even know if that's my child. And that thousand dollars is the last you'll see from me.'

'Is it?' She picked up the cheque, looked at it, and tore it in half before handing it back to him. 'Thank you, Stan. But I don't think I'll need it.' And with that, she stood up and walked past him out of the restaurant.

She had cried all the way home, and that night her mother had forced her way into her bedroom. 'He left you, didn't he? He went back to his wife.' She was so evil she almost gloated. 'I knew it ... I told you he was no good ... he probably never even left her in the first place.'

'Mother, leave me alone ... please...' She lay back on her bed and closed her eyes.

'What's wrong with you? Are you sick?' And then instantly she knew. 'Oh, my God ... you're pregnant... aren't you? Aren't you?' She advanced on her with a wicked look in her eye, and stood in front of Barbara.

Barbara sat up to face her mother with a look of grief in her eyes. 'Yes, I am.'

'Oh, my God ... an illegitimate baby ... do you know what people will say about you, you little whore?' Her mother reached out and slapped her and suddenly all the frustration and loneliness exploded within Barbara.

'Dammit, leave me alone. It happened to you with my father.'

'It didn't ... we were engaged ... he wasn't a married man. And he married me.'

'He married you because you were pregnant. And he

120

hated you for trapping him. I heard the things he said to you when you fought. He always hated you. He was engaged to someone else...' Her mother slapped her again, and Barbara sank back on to the bed sobbing.

For the next two weeks they barely spoke, except when her mother tormented her about the illegitimate baby. 'You'll be ruined ... disgraced ... you'll never find another job.' And the truth was that she was worried about the same thing. She hadn't been able to find a job since she left Stan's office. The unemployment rates had been soaring since the previous summer, and even with her summa cum laude degree from Smith, she couldn't find a thing. And now she was having a baby.

In the end there was nothing else she could do. Too proud to call Stan for the name of his doctor, she called a friend, got a name of a doctor, and had an illegal abortion in New Jersey. She rode all the way home on the subway in a daze, bleeding copiously on to the seat, and passed out cold on the subway platform. They called her mother from the emergency room at Roosevelt Hospital, and her mother refused to come. When she got home three days later, her mother stood in the living room and uttered two simple words. 'Baby killer.'

The hatred between them grew after that, and Barbara was going to move out. But her mother had another stroke, and she couldn't leave her. All she wanted was her own life and her own apartment. She got unemployment payments instead, since Stan allowed her to say she'd been fired, and her mother got a pension and they lived on that, but barely. She nursed her mother back to health for six months, and through it all her mother never let her forget about the abortion. She blamed the stroke on her, and her disappointment in Barbara as a human being. And without even realising that it had come, Barbara lived in a constant haze of depression. Eventually she got another job, working at another law firm. But this time there was no affair, there were no men, there was only her mother. She lost touch with all her friends from Smith, and when they called she didn't bother to return their calls. What could she tell them? They were all married or engaged or having babies. She had had an affair with a married man, had an abortion, worked as a secretary, and was a full-time nurse for her mother. And her mother was always carping at her that they needed more money. It was another secretary at the law firm where she worked who suggested that she call around to some literary agents. She could do extra typing at night, and the money was halfway decent. In fact, sometimes it was pretty good. So Barbara did, and it was thus that Daphne Fields found her, ten years after she had begun typing manuscripts at home in her spare time, a withered, lonely, nervous spinster at thirty-seven. The once handsome, well-built, athletic young girl who had been the president of the senior class at Smith and graduated summa cum laude in political science, was taking in typing in a fourth-floor walk-up on the West Side, nursing her ever more vicious mother. She hated everything Barbara was, hated her lack of spirit and fire. And yet it was she who had stamped it out. And in great part because of her, Barbara had never recovered from the tragic love affair and the abortion.

Barbara was fascinated by Daphne at first, but she didn't dare ask anything about her life. There was something very private and closed about Daphne, as though she were keeping a multitude of secrets. And it was only late one night when Barbara had delivered a manuscript to her apartment, a year after she'd begun typing for her, that the two women had begun to open up about themselves. Barbara had told her then about the abortion, and about being imprisoned by her invalid mother. Daphne had listened quietly to the long unhappy tale, and then told her about Jeff and Aimee, and Andrew. They had sat on the floor of her apartment, drinking wine and talking until the wee hours of the morning. It seemed like yesterday as Barbara watched her now, lifeless in her hospital bed, when only days before she had been so vibrant.

Daphne had been adamant, when she heard Barbara's tale, that Barbara had to leave her mother.

'Look, dammit, it's a matter of your survival.' They had both been a little drunk, and Daphne had pointed an emphatic finger at her.

'What can I do, Daff? She can hardly walk. She has a heart condition, she's had three strokes...'

'Put her in a home. Or can you afford to?'

'I could if I worked my ass off to do it, but she says she'd kill herself. And I owe her that much...' Barbara's thoughts drifted back to the past. 'She put me through school, she even put me through Smith.'

'And now she's ruining your life. You don't owe her that. What about you?'

'What about me? There's no me left.'

'Yes, there is.' Barbara had looked at her, wanting to believe her, but it had been years since she had dared to think of herself. Her mother had almost destroyed her. 'You can do anything you want to do.' It was what John had said to her in their cabin in New Hampshire. She told Barbara about him then. She was the first person she had told. There were no secrets left when the night was over. And again and again they went back to talking about Andrew. He was everything that mattered to Daphne, everything that counted, that brought life and fire to her eyes.

'You're lucky you have him.' Barbara looked at her with envy. Her own child would have been ten years old by then. And she still thought of it often.

'I know I am. But I don't "have" him in that sense.' A look of sorrow came across her face then. 'He's at the school. And I have my own life, such as it is.' Barbara suspected that in her own way Daphne was not so much better off than she was. She had her son and her work, but nothing else. There had been no man in her life since John died, and she was careful to see that there wasn't. Apparently several people had asked her out over the years, old friends of Jeff's, a writer she had met through her agent, people she met at publishing functions, but she had declined them all. In her own way she was as lonely as Barbara. And it formed a bond between the two. She confided in her more than anyone else, and after Barbara began coming to her house to work, they went to lunch now and then, or shopping on a Saturday afternoon together.

'You know something, Daphne? I think you're crazy.'

'That's not news.' She grinned up at her tall friend as they went through the racks at Saks. Barbara had actually managed to escape her mother for an entire afternoon and they had decided to spend it together.

'I mean it. You're young, you're gorgeous. You could have any man you want. What are you doing shopping with me?'

'You're my friend and I like you. And I don't want a man.'

'That's what's crazy.'

'Why? Some people never have what I've had.' She almost cringed as she said it, knowing the emptiness of Barbara's life.

'It's all right.' Barbara had looked down at her with a warm smile, looking suddenly younger. 'I know what you mean. But that's no reason to quit.'

'Yes, it is. I'll never have again what I had with Jeffrey, or John. Why settle for second best?'

'That's not a reasonable assumption.'

'In my case it is. You don't find men like that again in a lifetime.'

'Maybe not just like them. But someone else. Are you really going to give up on that for the next fifty years?' Barbara had been horrified at the thought. 'That really is goddamn crazy.' It didn't seem as crazy to her that she had given her life up to a mother she hated. But she didn't see herself in the same light. Daphne was beautiful and petite, and Barbara had sensed from the first that she was going to be very successful. Their lives were worlds apart to Barbara.

But it was Daphne who saw hope for her friend, and

she nagged her constantly to do something about it. 'Why the hell don't you move out?'

'To where? A tent in Central Park? And what do I do with my mother?'

'Put her in a home.' It became a familiar refrain between the two, but it wasn't until Daphne bought the apartment on East Sixty-ninth Street that she developed a plan, and she faced Barbara with it, her eyes filled with excitement.

'Christ, Daphne, I can't.'

'Yes, you can.' She wanted Barbara to move into her old apartment.

'I can't support us both.'

'Wait till you hear the rest of my idea.' She offered her a full-time job, at a handsome salary that she could well afford.

'Work for you? Are you serious?' Barbara's eyes had lit up like a summer sky. 'Do you mean it?'

'I do, but don't think I'm doing you a favour. I need you, dammit. You're the only thing that keeps my life running smoothly. And I'm not going to take no for an answer.' Barbara had felt her heart soar within her, but she was terrified, too. What about her mother?

'I don't know, Daff. I'll have to think it over.'

'I've already thought it out for you.' Daphne grinned at her. 'You can't have the job unless you move out from your mother. How's that for a stiff deal?' It was and they both knew it, but after a month of tormenting herself over what Daphne said, she got up the guts to do it. Daphne gave her two stiff drinks, and took her over in a cab to her apartment. She dropped her off with a hug and a kiss and told her she could do it. 'It's your life, Barbara. Don't blow it. She doesn't give a damn about you, and you've paid your debt. Don't forget that. How much more can you give? . . . How much more do you want to?' Barbara already knew the answer. For the first time in years she saw a light at the end of the tunnel, and she ran for it as hard and as fast as she could. She went upstairs and told her mother she was moving out, and she refused to accept the threats or the vengeance or the insults or the blackmail.

Her mother moved to a home the following month, and although she never admitted it to Barbara, she actually came to enjoy it. She was with people her own age, and she had a whole circle of cronies to whom she could complain about her selfish daughter. And when Daphne's new apartment was ready, Barbara took over her old place, and she felt as though she had finally been released from prison. She smiled now as she remembered the feeling. She woke up every morning with a light heart and a feeling of freedom, made coffee in the sunny little kitchen, stretched out on her bed, feeling as though she owned the world, and she used what had been Andrew's bedroom as an office whenever she brought work home, which was often. She worked for Daphne every day from ten in the morning until five o'clock, and when she went home she always took stacks of work with her.

'Don't you have anything else to do, for chrissake? Why don't you leave that here?' But as Daphne said it she was sitting at her own desk, preparing to work until the wee hours of the morning. The two were well matched, but neither of them had a normal life, and all that Barbara wanted out of life was to repay her for what she had done. She had helped her to free herself of her mother. But Daphne also realised that there was another danger, that Barbara would turn her habit for devotion and slavery towards Daphne.

'Just don't treat me like your mother!' she ranted teasingly when Barbara would appear with lunch on a tray when Daphne was working.

'Oh, shut up.'

'I mean it, Barb. You've been taking care of someone else all your life. Take care of yourself for a change. Make yourself happy.'

'I do. I enjoy my job, you know. In spite of what a pain in the ass you are to work for.' Daphne would grin at her distractedly and go back to work, working at her

126

typewriter from noon until three or four in the morning.

'How the hell can you work like that?' Barbara would watch her in amazement. She never stopped, except once in a great while for a cup of coffee, or to go to the bathroom. 'You'll destroy your health working like that.'

'No, I won't. It makes me happy.' But happy wasn't a word Barbara would ever have used to describe her. There was always something in Daphne's eyes that said she hadn't been happy in years, except right after she had seen Andrew. But the events of her life were etched deep into her eyes, and the ache she still felt over the people she had lost never really left her. She put the joy and satisfaction she felt from her work between her and the ghosts that she lived with, but they were always there, and it showed, although she seldom spoke of it to Barbara.

But when she was alone in her office sometimes, she would sit and look out the window, her mind far away ... in New Hampshire with John, or a place she had been to with Jeff ... or in spite of the iron control she kept over herself, her eyes would mist over with memories of Aimee. It was a side of her no one saw, and she was careful that they didn't, but she admitted her innermost feelings to Barbara, about what her life had been like at various times, and how much she missed it, the people she had lost, like John and Jeff and Aimee. And always, always, she would talk about Andrew and how much she missed him. But, she had a different life now than she had had when Andrew lived at home. A life filled with work and accomplishment and success, publishers and publicity people, and her agent. She had a good head for business, which she hadn't realised before, and she exercised her craft well, with a deft pen and a good sense for what her readers wanted. The only thing she hated about her work was the promotional appearances she occasionally had to do, because she didn't want anyone prying into her personal life, or asking about Andrew.

127

She wanted to protect him from all that. There was nothing about her personal life that Daphne wanted to share with the world, and she felt that her books spoke for themselves, but she recognised that her publishers felt the publicity was important. The issue came up again when she was asked to do *The Conroy Show* in Chicago and she hesitated, gnawing on a pencil.

'What do you want me to tell them, Daff? Do you want to go to Chicago tomorrow?' They had been bugging Barbara all morning and she had to give them an answer.

'In a word?' She grinned, rubbing her neck. She had worked late the night before on her new book and this morning she was tired. But it was a kind of tired she liked, the book was going well, and there was a sense of pleasure she always had with what she did. She didn't mind the ache in her back, or the inevitable pains in her shoulders. 'No, I don't want to go to Chicago. Call George Murdock at Harbor and ask him if he thinks it's important.' But she already knew the answer. Even though they were between books just then, publicity was always important, and the *The Conroy Show* in Chicago was a biggie.

Barbara came back five minutes later with a rueful smile. 'Do you really want to know what he said?'

'No, I don't.'

'I figured.' Barbara watched her sink into a comfortable chair with a sigh as she laid her head back against the soft white cushion. 'Why do you work so damn hard, Daff? You can't run away forever.' She still looked like a little girl as she sat there, but there was an undeniable aura of womanhood too, no matter how determined she was to deny it. She was kind to everyone who entered her life, her publishers, her agent, her secretary, her few well-chosen friends, her son, the people at the school, the other children. She was kind to everyone but herself. Of herself she demanded murderous goals, and almost unbearable standards. She worked fifteen hours a day, was always patient, interested, warm. The only warmth denied was to herself. She never really let anyone near her. There had been too much pain in her life, too much loss, and now the walls were around her forever. Barbara thought it again as she watched the still form in the hospital bed, and the echo of Daphne's words rang in her head.

'I'm not running away, Barb. I'm building a career, that's different.'

'It is? Looks the same to me.'

'Maybe so.' With Barbara she was usually honest. 'But it's for a good cause.' She was building up a fortune for Andrew. He would need it some day and she wanted his life to be easy. Everything she did seemed to centre around Andrew.

'I've heard that story before. But you've made enough for Andrew by now, Daff. Why don't you think of yourself for a change?'

'I do.'

'Oh, yeah? When?'

'For about ten seconds when I wash my face in the morning.' She smiled at her confidante and friend. There were some things Daphne didn't like to talk about. 'So they want me to go to Chicago, huh?'

'Can you get away from the book?'

'If I have to.'

'So we go?'

'I don't know.' She frowned and looked out the window before glancing back at Barbara. 'I'm worried about that show. I've never been on it, and I don't really want to.'

'Why?' But Barbara suspected the reason for her answer. Bob Conroy threw a lot of curves, and he was a prober. He had an extraordinary research team, and he had a knack for digging up bits and pieces of people's pasts, and confronting them with them on national television. She knew that Daphne was afraid that would happen. She had gone to great pains to keep her own story private. She never talked about Jeff, or Aimee, and she was violent on the subject of Andrew. She never wanted him subjected to idle curiosity or gossip. He lived a happy secluded life at the Howarth School in New Hampshire, and he had no idea that he had a famous mother. 'Are you afraid of Conroy, Daff?'

'Honestly? Yes. I don't want a lot of old stuff to come out.' Her eyes were huge and blue and sad as she looked at Barbara. 'It's nobody's business what happened in my life. You know how I feel about it.'

'Yes, but you can't keep everything a secret forever. What if it did come out, would that be so awful?'

'For me, yes. I don't want anyone's pity, and neither will Andrew. We don't need it.' She straightened her back and sat up in her chair, looking nervous and defiant.

'All it would probably do is make your readers love you more.' She knew better than anyone how much they already did. She answered all of Daphne's fan mail. Daphne had a way of pouring out her soul in her books, so that her readers felt they knew her. In fact, they knew her better than she liked to admit, the secrets of her soul were what made her books real, but she passed them off as fiction.

'I don't want them to love me more. I want them to love the books.'

'Maybe there's no difference.'

Daphne nodded silently from where she sat and then she stood up with a sigh. 'I guess I have no choice. If I don't go, I'll never hear the end of it from George Murdock. They've been trying to get me on that show for the last year.' She looked at Barbara then with a smile. 'Want to come? They have some nice shops in Chicago.'

'Do you want to spend the night?'

'Sure.' She had a favourite hotel now, as she did in almost every major city. They were always the quietest, most conservative and yet always the most elegant hotels in each city. Hotels where dowagers wore sable coats, and people spoke in hushed whispers. She ordered room service, and enjoyed the comforts of what her work

130

brought her. She had grown into it well, and she had to admit that there were aspects of her success that pleased her greatly. She no longer had to worry about money, she knew Andrew's future was secure. She had invested well, and she bought expensive clothes and antiques, and paintings she liked whenever she had the opportunity. But at the same time there was nothing showy about Daphne. She didn't use her money to flaunt her success, she didn't throw lavish parties, or try to impress her friends. It was all very quiet and simple and solid. And in a funny way, she knew that it was exactly what Jeffrey and John would have expected. She had grown up well, and knowing that pleased her.

'You're on the show at ten o'clock. Do you want to go in the morning or in the afternoon? You should rest for a while and have dinner before we go to the studio.'

'Yes, Mother.'

'Oh, shut up.' Barbara jotted some quick notes on her pad and disappeared as Daphne went back to her desk with a worried frown and stared at the keyboard. She had told Barbara that she had an odd feeling about doing the show, a strange, unhappy premonition. And Barbara had told her she was being silly. She remembered it now as she sat watching Daphne's face, so battered by the car that had hit her. It seemed a thousand years since they had been in Chicago.

14

Daphne and Barbara arrived at the studio at exactly nine thirty. Daphne was wearing a simple beige silk dress and her hair was coiffed in a quiet, elegant chignon. There were pearl earrings in her ears, and a large, handsome topaz ring she had bought earlier that year at Cartier's. She looked elegant and successful, but not opulent and showy. It was typical of Daphne. As usual, Barbara was wearing one of her navy blue suits. Daphne always teased her that she had fourteen that all looked alike, but she looked neat and trim and her straight black hair fell in a smooth, shiny sheet to her shoulders. She looked younger now that she had left her mother. And in the past year Daphne had noticed that she had become increasingly attractive. She looked more like the photographs of the girl who had been at Smith, and there was laughter in her eyes now as she looked at Daphne.

She leaned over and whispered as they were ushered into the standard waiting room, with comfortable chairs, a bar, and a maid to attend to their needs. 'Don't look so uptight. He's not going to bite you.'

'How do you know?' But she always got nervous before she went on talk shows. It was part of why she took Barbara with her. It was also nice to have a friend along, to chat with on planes, and help sort things out at hotels when things got loused up with their reservations. And Barbara had a marvellous ability for keeping everything in control. With Barbara around, the luggage never got lost, the meals arrived in Daphne's room on time, there were magazines and books and newspapers to read, the reporters were ushered to the door when she'd had enough, and her clothes were always pressed before she had an interview. She made everything seem miraculously easy.

'Do you want a drink?'

Daphne shook her head. 'That's all I need, to go on half bombed. Then I'll really tell him a thing or two.' They both grinned, and Daphne settled into a chair. Even at times like this she wasn't really a drinker.

'Miss Fields?' A production assistant stuck his head in the door. 'You're on first.'

'Oh, Christ.'

'Mr Conroy didn't want to keep you waiting.'

That was always the hardest spot, she didn't have time to relax about the show, and watch how the others handled themselves, but she also knew that tonight she had star billing. 'I wish he wouldn't do me such a big favour,' Daphne whispered to Barbara, feeling her palms begin to sweat, but Barbara whispered something reassuring.

'You'll be fine.'

'How long will I be on?' It was like setting an internal time clock for having a tooth filled at the dentist ... twenty minutes ... I can stand twenty minutes of pain ... or can I? And at least at the dentist they gave her Novocaine so she wouldn't feel the pain. This was cold turkey.

'They didn't tell me. I asked yesterday. The girl said he just wants to "let it flow." But I don't imagine it'll be more than fifteen minutes.' Daphne nodded, gearing herself up, and a moment later the production assistant reappeared and signalled for her to come with him.

'So long, kid.' She glanced over her shoulder at Barbara, thinking of the old saw 'We who are about to die salute you.'

'You'll be great.'

She rolled her eyes and disappeared and Barbara settled down with a glass of wine to watch her on the monitor.

The production assistant led Daphne to the set,

indicated which chair, and clipped a microphone to the neck of her dress, as a makeup artist ran up and dusted her face with powder. Her hair was perfectly in place, and the rest of her makeup was fine. The woman nodded and disappeared and the production assistant nodded and adjusted his headphones before whispering to Daphne. 'Mr Conroy is coming out now. He'll sit there.' He indicated a chair. 'He'll do the first ninety seconds alone, then he'll introduce you.' She nodded, noticing her last two books on the low table. Usually she was given some indication of what they'd talk about, but Conroy didn't work that way. It was precisely because of that that she was worried. 'Do you want a glass of water on the set?'

'Thank you.' Her eyes felt too large in her face, her mouth felt dry, and she could feel little rivers of perspiration rolling slowly down her sides as Bob Conroy appeared in a dark suit and a pale blue shirt and red tie. He was in his late forties and undeniably handsome. But there was something very cold and sharp in his eyes, something too glib and terribly plastic about him.

'Daphne?' No. Mata Hari.

'Yes.' She smiled, trying not to feel dizzy.

'Nice to have you on the show. How was the weather in New York?'

'Fine.'

He sat down and glanced out to see the angles on the camera. But before he could say anything more, the assistant producer began counting, a red light went on, and a camera moved in on Conroy's face as he smiled the sexy smile that turned American womanhood on, and told his viewers who they could expect on the show that evening. It was exactly like all of the other shows Daphne had been on. One was brought out like a dancing dog, asked to do one's act, and sent off the set with scarcely a thank you, while the host did his egocentric pirouettes to enchant his viewers.

'And our first guest this evening is a woman whose

134

books most of you have read, certainly you ladies' – he stopped to smile into the camera, and then picked a book up off the coffee table and then looked back into the camera – 'but I suspect that most of you have read very little about her. From all reports, Daphne Fields is a very private person.' He smiled again and turned slowly to Daphne as the camera included her and a second camera moved in slowly on casters. 'It's nice to have you here with us in Chicago.'

'It's nice to be here with you, Bob.' She smiled shyly at him, knowing the camera would cover her full front without her having to turn towards it. That was always the case except on shows in backwater towns where the only angle they ever shot was the host. She had spent an entire hour on a show in Santa Fe once, without realising that all the viewers saw was the back of her hairdo.

'You live in New York, don't you?' It was a typically innocuous question.

'I do.' She smiled.

'Are you working on a book now?'

'Yes, I am. It's called *Lovers*.'

'Now there's a title for you.' He looked deep into the eyes of his female viewers. 'Your readers will love that. How's the research going?' He gave a suggestive little laugh and Daphne blushed softly beneath her makeup.

'My work is generally fiction.' Her voice and smile were soft, and there was something wonderfully delicate about her, which made him look brash and sound harsh with his question. But he would get her for that, they always did. It was his show, and he planned to be on for a long time. Daphne was just a one-night stand. It was his ass on the line, not hers, and he never forgot it.

'Come, come, a pretty lady like you . . . you must have an army of lovers.'

'Not lately.' This time there was mischief in her eyes and she didn't blush. She was beginning to think she might survive it.

But the humour faded from Conroy's voice as he turned towards her. 'I understand, Daphne, that you're a widow.' It was a line she didn't expect, and for a moment she almost gasped. He had done his research well, and she nodded. 'That's a great pity. But' – his voice oozed sympathy and compassion – 'perhaps that's why you write so well. You write a great deal about surviving loss, and you certainly have. I'm told you lost a little girl, too.' Her eyes filled with tears at the shock of hearing him discuss Jeff and Aimee, and she sat there, with her guts on his cocktail table.

'I don't generally discuss my private life in association with my work, Bob.' She was struggling to regain her composure.

'Maybe you should.' The face was earnest, the voice helpful. 'It would make you more real to your readers.' Zap. He had got her.

'As long as my books are real – '

He cut her off. 'But how can they be, if they don't know who you are?' Before she could answer, he went on, 'Am I right in saying that your husband and daughter died in a fire?'

'Yes, you are.' She took a deep breath, and as Barbara watched on the monitor, tears filled her eyes. What a stinking thing to do. The son of a bitch . . . Daphne had been right to be afraid to come here.

'Was your husband the man you talked about in *Apache*?' She shook her head. It had been John. And with a sudden wave of panic she wondered if he knew about him, too, but there was no way he could have. 'What a striking character that was. I think every woman in America fell in love with him. You know, the book would make a marvellous movie.'

She began to recover then, praying for the interview to end. 'I'm awfully glad you think so.'

'Any prospects on the horizon?'

'Not yet, but my agent thinks they will come.'

'Daphne, tell us, how old are you?' Shit. There was no way around him, but she laughed softly.

'Do I have to tell the truth?' But she made no secret of her age. 'I'm working my way towards thirty-three.'

'Good Lord' – he looked her over appraisingly – 'you don't look it. I would easily guess you for twenty.' It was the charm that so delighted his female viewers. But as Daphne smiled he moved in on her again with that same sympathetic look she had come to distrust, and she was right again. 'And you've never remarried. How long have you been a widow?'

'Seven years.'

'It must have been a terrible blow.' With a look of innocence now, 'Is there a man currently in your life?' She wanted to scream or reach out and slap him. They never asked questions like that of male writers, but women were fair game, somehow it was assumed that a female writer's personal life was part of her work, and hence public property. A man would have told him to go to hell, but he would never have asked the question.

'Not at the moment, Bob,' with a gentle smile.

He smiled sweetly. 'I'm not sure I believe that. You're much too pretty to be alone. And then there's that book you're working on now ... what was it, *Lovers*?' She nodded. 'When will that be out? I'm sure all your readers are waiting breathlessly for it.'

'Not too breathlessly, I hope. The book won't be out until next year.'

'We'll be waiting.' They exchanged another plastic smile as Daphne waited for her reprieve, she knew it would come soon, and she could hardly wait to get off the set, and away from his questions. 'You know, there's something else I've been wanting to ask you.' She waited, almost expecting him to ask her bra size. 'Our next guest is also a writer, but not in your field. His book is nonfiction. He's written a marvellous book about autistic children.' Daphne felt herself grow pale as she saw him coming ... but surely he couldn't ... 'A good friend of mine in New York, at *Collins* where you used to work, tells me that you have an autistic child. Maybe, from a parent's point of view, you could shed some light on this subject for us.' She eyed him with open hatred, but she was thinking of Allie . . . how could she have told him a thing like that? How *could* she?

'My son is not autistic, Bob.'

'I see . . . perhaps I misunderstood . . .' She could almost envision his viewers panting. In ten short minutes they had learned that she had lost her husband and daughter in a fire, had worked at *Collins*, had no man in her life at the moment, and now they thought her only surviving child was autistic. 'Is he retarded?'

'No, he is not.' Her voice rose and her eyes blazed. Just how much did this man think he had a right to? 'My son is hard of hearing, he is in a school for the deaf, but other than his hearing impairment, he is a perfectly marvellous, normal child.'

'I'm glad for you, Daphne.' Son of a bitch. Daphne was seething inside. She felt as though she had been stripped naked. But worse than that, much worse, he had stripped Andrew. 'And I'm delighted to hear about *Lovers*, and I'm afraid that our time together is over. But we hope to see you again the next time you're in Chicago.'

'I'd like that very much.' She smiled through clenched teeth, smiled then for the benefit of the viewers, and they took a break for a collection of commercials. And with a look of barely veiled fury, she unclipped the microphone from her dress and handed it to him during the break. 'You know, I don't know how you can make excuses for yourself.'

'Why? Because I have a passion for the truth?' He wasn't smiling now. He didn't give a damn about her. He cared only about himself, his viewers, and his sponsors.

'What difference can any of that possibly make? What right do you have to ask anyone those kinds of questions?'

'Those are the things people want to know.'

'Those are the things people have no right to know. Aren't there things in your life that you don't want exposed? Is there nothing sacred to you?'

138

'I'm not at your end of the interview, Daphne.' He said it coolly as the next guest arrived to take her seat. She stood there for a moment looking down at him and she didn't extend her hand.

'Then you're very lucky.' And with that she turned on her heel and left the stage, walking quickly into the waiting room and signalling to Barbara to follow her.

They were on a plane bound for New York two hours later. It was the last flight out, and they reached La Guardia at two o'clock in the morning. At two thirty she was back in her apartment. Barbara had gone on in the cab. And on Sixty-ninth Street, Daphne closed her front door behind her, and walked straight to her bedroom without turning on the lights, threw herself on the bed, and broke into sobs as she lay there. She felt as though her whole life had been exposed that night, all her pain and her sorrow. The only thing he hadn't known about was John. It was a good thing she had never told Allie ... and tell us, Miss Fields, is it true you shacked up with a logger in New Hampshire? ... She turned over and lay staring at the ceiling in the dark, thinking of Andrew. Maybe it was just as well he was at the school. Maybe if he were at home with her in New York, his life would turn into a sideshow. People like Allie would treat him like a freak ... autistic ... retarded ... she cringed at the words, and lay there until she fell asleep on her bed, in the beige dress she had worn, with tearstains on her face, and her heart feeling like it had been beaten with rocks. She dreamed that night of Jeffrey and John, and she awoke the next morning, at the sound of the phone, feeling a wave of terror wash over her ... terrified that something had happened to Andrew.

15

'Daphne, are you all right?' It was Iris. She had seen the show.

'I'll live. But I won't do it again. You can tell Murdock that for me, or I will. Take your choice, but that's it. My publicity life is over.'

'I don't think you should feel that way, Daff. It was just one bad show.'

'Maybe to you. But I'm not going to go through that again, and I don't have to. My books sell just fine without my prostituting myself for assholes who want to hang my underwear on their clothesline.' But most of all, what still smarted was what they had done to Andrew. She tried to keep him so protected from that world, and in one brief moment they had torn away all her protection and exposed him as 'autistic.' She still shuddered at what they had said. And every time she thought of it, she wanted to kill Allie. She had to force her mind back to what Iris was saying. She was insisting they have lunch at the Four Seasons, but Daphne really didn't want to.

'Something wrong?'

'No. A very interesting offer, but I want to talk to you about it, hash it out for a while. Do you want to come to the office?'

'Why don't you come here? I don't feel like going out.' In truth, she wanted to go into hiding. Or go back to the school, to put her arms around Andrew.

'Fine. I'll be there at noon. All right with you?'

'Perfect. And don't forget to call Murdock.' But Iris planned to wait awhile on that. Publicity on Daphne's books was just too important to take a hasty stand, and it was possible that Daphne would back down. Although knowing Daphne, it was more likely that she wouldn't. She had a stubborn streak in her a mile wide, and the one thing that mattered to her most was her privacy. Having that violated on national TV had to have been a shattering experience for her.

'I'll see you in a little while.' It was already ten o'clock, and Daphne heard Barbara's key in the door as she walked into the kitchen in her stockinged feet and the dress she had worn the night before. She looked as though she had been to a very drunken party.

'My, don't you look lovely this morning.' Barbara was wearing grey slacks and a red sweater and a bright smile, and Daphne grinned at her as she put on a pot of coffee. She wandered into the kitchen and set down her bag. It was one of the rare times when she didn't have a notebook in her hand. 'Did you get any sleep last night?' Barbara had been very worried about her, but hadn't dared to call. She was hoping that Daphne was asleep, and suspected that her friend wanted to be left alone. But this morning Daphne was fair game and Barbara pulled no punches. 'If you'll pardon my saying so, you look like shit. Did you sleep?'

'Some.'

Barbara took a sip of the steaming coffee. 'I'm sorry that happened last night, Daff.'

'So am I. But it won't happen again. I just told Iris to call Murdock.'

'She won't.' She sounded matter-of-fact and Daphne smiled.

'You have everyone figured out, don't you? You may be right. But if she doesn't, I will.'

'What are you going to do about Allison Baer?'

An ugly look came into Daphne's eyes. 'Frankly, I'd like to kill her. But I'll settle for giving her a piece of my mind and then never speaking to her again.'

'It was a shitty thing for her to do.'

'I can forgive her almost anything, but not what she said about Andrew.' They both fell silent for a moment

141

and Daphne sighed as she slid into a chair, looking exhausted and rumpled. She looked as though she needed someone to undress her, and run a hot bath, and brush her hair, and Barbara was suddenly sorry that she didn't have a husband to do it. She was the kind of woman who would have made a man a good wife, and she needed someone to take care of her. She worked too hard, worried too much, carried all of the burdens on her frail shoulders. She needed a man, as Barbara did herself, but it wasn't likely that either of them would find one. And certainly not Daphne. She didn't let anyone near enough to her to hold her coat, let alone marry her.

'What does Iris want, by the way?'

'I don't know. She said something about an interesting offer. And if it's a publicity tour' – Daphne grinned ruefully and stood up – 'I'm going to tell her to shove it.'

'That I'd like to hear. Any calls you want me to make?' Daphne handed her a list and went to take a shower. And when her agent arrived five minutes before noon, she was wearing white gabardine slacks and a white cashmere sweater.

'My, don't you look pretty.' She had a quiet elegance about her that always impressed Iris. Most authors who made it eventually got showy, but Daphne never had. She had style, and there was something very distinguished about her. It made her seem older than her years at times, but that was the way she was, and it was no surprise after all she'd been through that she seemed somehow older. Dealing with life at its most painful had given her both wisdom and poise, and a great deal of compassion.

'So, what's new?' They sat down to lunch and Daphne poured her a glass of white wine as Iris looked at her long and hard. 'Something wrong?'

'You're working too hard.' She said it like a stern mother, but she had known Daphne for long enough now

142

to read her life through her eyes, as she did now. And she could see that Daphne was tired.

'What makes you say that?'

'You're getting too thin, and your eyes look like you're a hundred and fifty.'

'As a matter of fact, I am. A hundred and fifty-two to be exact. A hundred and fifty-three in September.'

'I'm serious, Daphne.'

'So am I.'

'All right, I'll mind my own business. How's the book coming?'

'Not bad. I should have it wrapped up in another month.'

'And then what? Any plans?'

'I thought I'd spend some time with Andrew. You know' – she looked bitterly at her agent – 'my autistic son.'

'Daphne, don't take that so hard. They say a lot of things like that on talk shows and in the papers.'

'Well, they're not going to say them about me, or my son. That's the way it is. Did you call Murdock?' Her eyes were hard as she looked at Iris.

'Not yet. But I will.' Barbara was right and she knew it. Iris was stalling.

'If you don't, I will. I meant what I said this morning.'

'All right, all right.' She held up a hand, as though begging for mercy. 'There's something else I want to discuss with you first. You've had a very interesting offer.'

'To do what?' Daphne didn't look impressed, more than anything she looked suspicious. The night before had burned her badly.

'To make a movie, on the West Coast.' Iris looked enormously pleased and Daphne watched her. 'They're interested in buying *Apache*. Comstock Studios called yesterday after you left. They want to buy the book, but they also want you to think about writing the screenplay.'

Daphne sat in silence for a long moment. 'Do you think I could? I've never done that.' Her eyes looked worried.

'There's nothing you can't do, if you want to.' It was once again an echo of John, and Daphne smiled.

'I wish I believed that.'

'Well, I do, and so do they. They offered you a very handsome fee for the package. You'd have to live out there and they'd also pay for your living expenses, within reason.'

'What does that mean?'

'A house, food, entertainment, maid, and a car and driver.'

She sat staring, looking into her plate, and then looked up at Iris. 'I can't do it.'

'Why not?' She looked shocked. 'Daphne, it's a fabulous offer.'

'I'm sure it is, and I'd like to sell them the book. But I can't write the screenplay.'

'Why not?'

'How long would I have to be out there for?'

'Probably about a year, to write it, and they want you to consult on the movie.'

'At least a year. Maybe more.' She sighed as she looked soberly at her agent. 'I can't leave Andrew for that long.'

'But he doesn't even live here.'

'Iris, I go up to see him at least once a week when I can. Sometimes I'm there for the weekend. I can't do that if I'm living in Los Angeles.'

'Then take him with you.'

'He's not ready to leave the school. I wish he were, but he's not.'

'Put him in a school there.'

'That would be too hard on him. It just wouldn't be fair.' She shook her head decisively. 'I can't. Maybe in a few years, but not now. I'm really very sorry. Maybe you can explain it to them.'

'I don't want to explain it to them, Daphne. From a

career standpoint you're dead wrong. Maybe this is a sacrifice you'll both have to make. I want you to think about it, at least until Monday.'

'I won't change my mind.' And knowing Daphne, Iris feared that she wouldn't.

'You'll be making a serious mistake if you don't do it. This really is the next important step in your career. You may always regret it if you don't take it.'

'And how do I explain that to a seven-year-old child? Tell him my work is more important to me than he is?'

'You can explain it to him, and you can fly back for a day or two whenever you have a break.'

'What if I can't get away? Then what? I can't call him on the phone and explain it.' That stopped Iris. Of course she couldn't call him. It was an aspect Iris had never thought of. 'I just can't, Iris.'

'Why don't you just wait to decide?' But Daphne knew already what her answer would have to be on Monday, and after Iris left, she discussed it with Barbara, sitting curled up in the big cosy white chair.

'Would you want to go if you could?'

'I'm not really sure, to tell you the truth. I'm not sure I could write a screenplay, and living in Hollywood for a year isn't really my style.' She looked around her pretty little apartment with a sigh and then shrugged. 'But it isn't worth thinking about anyway. I can't leave Andrew for that long, and it might not always be easy for me to get back.'

'Why not have him fly out to see you if you can't get away? I could fly back to get him if you want.' Although they had never met, she always felt as though she knew the child. And Daphne smiled at the generous offer.

'I love you for that. Thank you.'

'Why don't you talk to Mrs Curtis about it when you go up there this weekend, Daff?'

But what was there to think about? None of them understood. They just couldn't. They didn't know what it had been like to discover he was deaf when he was only a few months old, to struggle to communicate with him, to fight with every doctor she had seen about putting him in an institution. They didn't know what it had been like to pack his things and take him up to New Hampshire ... to tell him his friend John was dead. They didn't know what any of it felt like in her gut, or what it would mean to be three thousand miles away if something happened to him. They didn't know, and they never would. There was nothing for Daphne to think about, she realised again as she picked up her suitcase, put it in the car, and started the lonely trip to New Hampshire to see him.

16

Daphne made the trip in five hours, and pulled into the driveway of the Howarth School in the darkness of the winter evening. It always pulled at her heart to come back here, not only because of Andrew, but because of John. Her thoughts always drifted back to their days in the cabin. But the school was brightly lit, and she knew that in a moment she would see Andrew. She glanced at her watch and saw that she was just in time to join him for dinner.

Mrs Curtis was in the front hall when she walked in and looked instantly pleased and surprised to see her.

'I didn't know you were coming up this week, Daphne.' Over the years they had become friends, and she called Daphne by her first name, although due to her advanced years, Daphne never felt quite comfortable calling her Helen. She sent her all of her books though, and Helen Curtis admitted that she loved them.

'How's our boy?' Daphne took her coat off in the front hall and she felt as though she had come home. There was always something wonderfully warm and welcoming about Howarth. And the school was well endowed, so it was beautifully kept up. The whole place had been redone the summer before, and now there were murals in the halls that the children loved, and there were clouds painted on the ceiling.

'You won't recognise Andrew!'. Mrs Curtis was smiling at her.

'Did he cut off all his hair again?' The two women laughed, remembering how he had looked the winter before after he and two friends had had a spree with a pair of scissors. He hadn't come out of it quite as badly

147

as the two others. The little girls with the exquisite blonde braids had been almost bald and looked like little fuzzy ducklings when they were through with them.

'No, nothing like that.' Mrs Curtis shook her head with a smile. 'But he must have grown two inches this month. Suddenly he's enormous. You'll have to do some shopping again.'

'Thank God for my royalties!' And then with a hungry look in her eyes, 'Where is he?' Mrs Curtis answered her by pointing towards the stairs. He was coming down in a pair of beige corduroy pants and a little red flannel shirt, and he was wearing the new cowboy boots she had brought him the last time. Her face exploded in a wide smile and her eyes danced and she walked slowly towards him.

'Hi, sweetheart. How are you?' She said the words now as well as signing and he read her lips with a broad grin, and then he amazed her by speaking.

'I'm fine, Mommy ... how ... are you?' The words were clumsy and he still didn't speak clearly, but anyone would have understood what he had said. 'I missed you!' And then he flung himself into her arms and she held him, fighting back the tears that came so easily when she first saw him. They were used to their life now, and the days of their shared solitude in her old apartment seemed like a distant dream. He had seen the new place too, but he had signed to her that he liked the old one better. She assured him that he'd get used to this one too, and she showed him his room and told him that one day he would live there all the time, as he had in the old one. But now all she could think of was holding his warm, cuddly little body against her own as she swung him into her arms and he clung to her.

'I missed you too.' She pulled away a little so he could see her face as she said it. 'What have you been doing?'

'I'm growing a vegetable garden!' He looked thrilled. 'And I made two tomatoes.' He was signing to her, but when she spoke he read her lips, and he seemed to have no trouble doing it.

'In the middle of winter? How did you do that?'

'In a big box downstairs and it has special lights on it, and when spring comes, we're all going to plant flowers outside.'

'That sounds wonderful.'

They went into the dining room hand in hand then, and she sat with him and the other children as they ate fried chicken and corn on the cob and baked potatoes, and they laughed and told jokes, all of them signing.

She stayed until he went to bed, tucked him in, and then came downstairs to see Mrs Curtis before she left.

'Have you had a good week?' But there was something strange in her eyes as she asked the question, and Daphne instinctively knew she had seen the show. Who hadn't?

'Not really. I was in Chicago yesterday.' She hesitated to say anything more, but she didn't have to.

'I know. That was a rotten thing for him to do.'

'You saw the show?'

'I did. But I'll never watch him again. He's a bastard.' Daphne smiled at the uncharacteristic strong language.

'You're right. I told my agent I won't do any more publicity as a result. I've just had it. And what galls me is that they'd never ask a man those kinds of questions. But the worst of it of course was what he said about Andrew.'

'It doesn't really matter, you know. You and he know the truth, and the rest of the world will forget it.'

'They may' – Daphne didn't look so sure – 'and they may not. Muckrakers are amazing. Ten years from now someone will dig up a tape of that and come up with a story.'

'Yours is not an easy business, my dear. But it must be rewarding.'

'Sometimes.' She smiled but there was a troubled look in her eyes that the older woman saw.

'Is something wrong?'

'No ... not really ... but ... I need some advice. I thought maybe we'd talk later in the weekend.'

'Does it have to wait? We could talk now. Would you like to come in and sit down?' She waved towards her private quarters and Daphne nodded. It would be a relief to talk it over.

Mrs Curtis's apartment in the school was tidy and small, like the woman herself. It was filled with attractive Early American antiques she had bought herself, and there were paintings of the landscape of New Hampshire. There was a vase of fresh flowers on a low table, and a hooked rug she had bought in an antique shop in Boston. It looked like a school-teacher's house somehow, but it had an added warmth and some of her things were lovely. Most of all it was inviting. Daphne looked around, like everything else about the school, this was familiar to her. Helen Curtis looked around too this time, almost with nostalgia, but Daphne didn't notice.

She poured them each a cup of tea in her tiny separate kitchen, and she handed Daphne a delicate flowered Spode cup with a little lace napkin. 'Well, what's on your mind, my dear? Something about Andrew?'

'Yes, indirectly.' She decided to get right to the point. 'I've had an offer to do a movie. Comstock Studios want to buy *Apache*, which is very nice. It would mean my being in Los Angeles for about a year. And I just don't think I can do it.'

'Why not?' The older woman looked both pleased and surprised.

'What about Andrew?'

'What about him? Would you want to put him in a school there?' At this, Mrs Curtis looked troubled. She knew that for the moment, change would still be difficult for him. Howarth had been his home for a long time, and he would suffer.

'I think a school out there would be too much of a change for him. No, if I went, I'd leave him here. But he'd feel so deserted.'

'Not if you explained it to him properly. No more than any child his age. You could tell him that it's for your work, and that it's only for a while. He could fly out to see you, we could put him on the plane, or would you be coming back here?'

'Probably not very often. From what I understand, once a movie gets going it's almost impossible to get away. But do you really think he could come out?'

'I don't see why not.' She looked gentle and kind as she set down her cup of tea. 'He's getting older, Daphne, he's not a baby anymore, and he's acquired a great many skills that will help him. Has he ever been on a plane before?' Daphne shook her head. 'He'd probably love it.'

'You don't think the whole experience would be too hard for him? He wouldn't see me as often as he does now.'

'You know, most of the other parents don't visit as often as you do. You're fortunate that you can come up, most of the other parents can't, they have husbands and other children, jobs that tie them down ... you and Andrew are very lucky.'

'And if I go?'

'He'll adjust. He'll have to.'

It would be so damn hard leaving Andrew. She felt so terribly guilty. 'I know it won't be easy at first, but it might do you both good. It could be a marvellous experience for you. How soon would you leave?'

'Very soon. Within the month.'

'That still gives you plenty of time to prepare him.' And then she sighed and looked at her young friend. She had grown very fond of Daphne over the years, the girl had such guts and such a gentle way about her. Both of those qualities showed up in her books, it was a most appealing combination. 'I'm afraid I haven't had as much of a chance to prepare you.'

'Prepare me for what?' Daphne looked blank, her mind still full of the decision of whether or not to leave Andrew and go to Los Angeles.

'I'm leaving the school, Daphne. I'm retiring.'

'You are?' Daphne felt a rock fall through her heart. She had a hard time with change herself, and losing people she cared for. 'But why?' The silver-haired woman laughed softly.

'Thank you for asking. I would think the reason showed. I'm getting old, Daphne. It's time for me to go home, and leave Howarth to someone younger, more dynamic.'

'But how awful!'

'It won't be awful at all. It'll be better for the school. Daphne, I'm an old lady.'

'You are not!' She looked incensed.

'I am. I'm sixty-two. That's old enough. And I don't want to wait until I'm so old that you all have to shove me out of here in a wheelchair. Trust me, it's time.'

'But you haven't been sick...' Daphne looked like a child about to lose her mother... the way Andrew would feel when she told him. And how could she leave him now with Mrs Curtis leaving too? He would feel as though everyone he knew were deserting him. Daphne looked at her almost in despair. 'Who will take your place? As though anyone could.'

'Don't be so sure. The woman I succeeded thought she couldn't be replaced, and fifteen years later no one even remembers her. That's only right. The school is only as strong as the people who lead it, and you want those people to be young and strong and filled with new ideas. There's a wonderful man taking over for this year. He runs the New York School for the Deaf now, and he's taking leave for a year to see how we do things here. He's been running the New York School for eight years and feels he needs some fresh ideas so he doesn't get stale. In fact, you'll meet him. He'll be here tomorrow. He's been coming up during the week to get acquainted.'

'Won't that make too many changes for the children?'

'I don't think so. Our board of directors was comfortable with him. His tenure is for one year.

Matthew Dane is extremely well thought of in our field. In fact, last year I gave you a book written by him. He's written three. So you'll have that in common.' Daphne remembered the book, and she had thought it made a great deal of sense. But still . . . 'I'll introduce you to him tomorrow.' And then with a gentle smile she stood up. 'And if you'll forgive me for being overly maternal, I think you need a good night's sleep. You're looking awfully tired.'

With that Daphne walked towards her and did something she had never done before, she put her arms around her and hugged her. 'We'll miss you, Mrs Curtis.'

There were tears in her eyes as she stood back from Daphne's arms. 'I'll miss you too. But I'll come to visit often.'

Daphne left her then and drove to the familiar little inn, where Mrs Obermeier showed her her room and left her with a thermos of hot chocolate and a plate of cookies. People liked Daphne in the town, she was a celebrity they knew, and a woman they respected. There were those who remembered John, and they liked seeing her strolling along with Andrew. To them, she was extremely human.

She climbed into bed with a yawn, poured herself a cup of chocolate, and finished it with a dreamy look on her face. Suddenly so much was changing. She turned off the light and put her head down on the large fluffy pillow, and five minutes later she was asleep. She didn't even move in the bed until the sun streamed in the windows in the morning.

17

On Saturday morning, after breakfast at the inn, Daphne arrived at the school in time to watch the children play tag in the garden. Andrew was laughing and playing with his friends and he hardly noticed her arrive as she watched him. There was none of the clinging and desperation she had always envisioned there would be if she left him. He understood their lives now, as well as she did, sometimes better. She almost wondered sometimes what it would be like for him when he finally left the school. He would be so lonely without the constant companionship of other children. It was something that worried her at times, when she thought of the far-off day when he would be ready to come home. But by then he would be older, and life would be different. He would have his studies and new friends, hearing children, not just children like him.

She stood looking around for a while then, unconsciously waiting for Mrs Curtis, to continue their conversation of the night before. But when she saw her again, she was deeply engrossed in a conversation with a tall, lanky, good-looking man with a boyish smile, and she found herself staring at him. He looked vaguely familiar. Mrs Curtis turned then and caught her eye and motioned her towards them.

'Daphne, I'd like you to meet our new director, Matthew Dane. Matthew, this is Andrew's mother, Miss Fields.' In the years of her success, the Mrs had somehow become Miss, even here.

Daphne held out a hand to meet him, but the look in her eyes changed slightly, from welcome to questioning

154

glance. 'It's nice to meet you. I enjoyed your last book.'

He smiled at the compliment, a broad boyish grin that made him seem younger than his forty years. 'I've enjoyed all of yours.'

'You've read them?' She looked both pleased and surprised and he was amused.

'Along with about ten million other people, I imagine.' Somehow she always wondered who read her books, she sat at her desk for hours on end, creating characters and plots and outlines and working endless hours, and yet it was always difficult to imagine that out there somewhere were real people who read them. It always surprised her when people said they read her books. And most surprising of all was to see a stranger hurrying along the street with one of her books tucked under his or her arm. 'Hey ... wait ... I wrote that ... do you like it? ... Who are you? ...' She smiled at him again, their eyes meeting, filled with questions.

'Mrs Curtis tells me that you're coming to Howarth for a year. That's going to be a big change for the children.' There was concern in her eyes as she said it.

'It will be a big change for me, too.' There was something very reassuring about the man as he stood looking down at her from his long, lanky height. There was a boyish quality about him, yet at the same time, an aura of quiet strength. 'I imagine many of the parents will be concerned that my tenure here is only temporary, but Mrs Curtis will be around to help us' – he glanced at her briefly, smiling at her and then Daphne – 'and I think we'll all benefit from this experience. We have a lot to learn from each other' – Daphne nodded – 'and there are some new programmes we want to try out, some exchanges with the New York School.' It was the first Daphne had heard of it and she was intrigued.

'An exchange programme?'

'Of sorts. As you know, most of our children are older, and there are more younger ones here. But Mrs Curtis and I have been talking, and I think it might be very useful to some of the students from the New York School to come up for a week or two, to see what it's like living in the country, maybe to establish some kind of a big brother/big sister arrangement with the children here, and then bring some of the little ones down there for a week or two. They get very isolated up here, and that might make an interesting breakthrough for them, while still in an environment that's relatively familiar. We'll have to see how the idea develops.' And then the boyish smile appeared again. 'I have a few tricks up my sleeve, Miss Fields. The main thing is to keep our eye on our goals for the children, to get them back into the hearing world again. At the New York School we put a lot of emphasis on lipreading for that reason, more so than on signing, because if they're going to get out into the hearing world eventually, they have to be able to understand what's going on around them, and despite new awareness in recent years, the fact is that very few hearing people know anything about signing. We don't want to condemn these kids to living only among themselves.' It was something Daphne had thought of often and she looked at him now almost with relief. The quicker he taught Andrew the skills he needed, the quicker he could come home to her.

'I like your thinking, Mr Dane. That's why I liked your book so much. It made sense in terms of the realities, it wasn't filled with crazy dreams.'

'Oh' – his eyes sparkled – 'I have a few crazy dreams too. Like starting a boarding school one day for the hearing and nonhearing. But that's a long way off.'

'Maybe not.' They stood looking at each other for a moment, a kind of respect dawning between them, and then something softened in his eyes as he looked at her, almost forgetting Helen Curtis standing beside them.

He had seen Daphne two days before on *The Conroy Show* in Chicago and it explained a lot of things about her that he had sensed but hadn't known. The knowledge he had gained through the show seemed somehow a violation, and he didn't want to admit to her that he

156

had seen it. But she saw it all in his eyes as he hesitated, and her eyes were honest with him.

'Did you see me on *The Conroy Show* the other night, Mr Dane?' Her voice was soft and sad, her eyes wide open, and he nodded.

'Yes, I did. I thought you handled it very well.'

She sighed and shook her head. 'It was a nightmare?'

'They shouldn't have the right to do that.'

'But they do. That's why I won't do it again, as I told Mrs Curtis last night.'

'They're not all like that, are they?'

'Most are. They don't want to hear about your writing. They want to push themselves into something very private, your heart, your guts, your soul. And if they can get a little dirt in the bargain, they love it.'

'That wasn't dirt. That was pain, and life, and sorrow.' His voice was almost a warm embrace in the chill air. 'You know, in reading your books, one comes to know more than anything they could pull out of you, anyway. That's what I was going to tell you. I've learned something about you through your books, but more than that I've learned something about myself. I haven't had the kind of losses you have' – and he marvelled silently at how she had survived them and was still so whole – 'but we all suffer losses of our own, losses that matter to us, that seem the worst tragedies on earth to us. I read your first book when I got divorced a few years back, and it did something very special for me. It got me through it.' He looked embarrassed then. 'I read it twice and then I sent a copy to my wife.' His words touched her deeply. It was extraordinary to realise that her books mattered to anyone so much. And at that moment Andrew ran over to them, and she looked down at him happily and then at Matthew Dane, switching from spoken words to signing.

'Mr Dane, I'd like you to meet my son. Andrew, this is Mr Dane.'

But when Matthew Dane signed to him, he spoke in

157

a normal voice at the same time, moving his lips very distinctly, and making normal sounds. 'It's nice to meet you, Andrew. I like your school.'

'Are you a friend of my Mommy's?' Andrew signed to him with a look of open curiosity, and Matthew smiled, glancing quickly at her.

'I hope I will be. I came here to visit Mrs Curtis.' Again he signed and spoke at the same time. 'I'm going to be here every weekend.'

Andrew looked at him with amusement. 'You're too old to go to our school.'

'I know.'

'Are you a teacher?'

'I'm the director, just like Mrs Curtis, at a school in New York.' Andrew nodded, he had heard enough for the moment, and turned his attention to his mother, both arms around her, his blond hair blowing in the wind.

'Will you have lunch with us, Mommy?'

'I'd love that.' She said good-bye to Matthew and Mrs Curtis then and followed Andrew inside, as he leaped and skipped, waving and signing to his friends. But her thoughts were filled with the new director. He was an interesting man. She saw him again later, walking down the halls with a stack of papers in his arms. According to Mrs Curtis, he was reading everything he could lay his hands on, every letter, every file, every report and logbook, and observing the children. He was very thorough about his work.

'Did you have a nice day with Andrew?' The dark brown eyes were interested and kind.

'I did. Looks like you've got quite a load of home-work.' She smiled at him and he nodded.

'I have a lot to learn about this school.'

Her voice was very gentle as they stood in the hallway. 'I think we have a lot to learn from you.' She was intrigued by his emphasis on lipreading, and noticed that he spoke to all the children as he signed, and treated

158

them as though they could hear. 'How did you ever get into this, Mr Dane?'

'My sister was born deaf. We were twins. And I've always been especially close to her. The funny thing was that we made up our own language between us. It was a kind of a crazy sign language that worked. But then my parents put her away in a school' – he looked troubled as he spoke – 'not a school like this. The kind they had thirty years ago, the kind where you stayed for the rest of your life. And she never got the skills she needed, they never taught her a damn thing that would have helped her get back into the world.' Daphne was afraid to ask him what had happened to her as he paused, but then he looked at her with that boyish grin. 'Anyway, that's how I got into this. Thanks to my sister. I talked her into running away from the school when I graduated from college, and we went to live in Mexico for a year, on the money I had saved working in the summers on construction crews. I taught her how to speak, she learned to lip-read, and we came back and told our parents. She was of age then and legally she could do what she wanted. They tried to have her declared incompetent, once they even tried to have me arrested . . . it was a crazy time, but she made it.'

At last she dared to ask, 'Where is she now?'

His smile grew wide. 'She teaches at the New York School. She's going to take over for me while I'm gone this year. She's married and she has two children, both hearing, of course. Her husband is a doctor, and of course now our parents say that they always knew she'd make it. She's a terrific girl, you'd like her.'

'I'm sure I would.'

'She loves your books. Wait till I tell her I met you.'

Daphne blushed then, it seemed so silly, a woman who had conquered so much, impressed with Daphne's meagre works of fiction. It made Daphne feel very small in comparison. 'I'd like to meet her too.'

'You will. She'll be coming up here, and Mrs Curtis tells me that you come up here pretty often.'

Daphne looked suddenly troubled and he searched her eyes. 'I do ... I did ...' She sighed softly, and he waved towards two chairs in a corner.

'Do you want to sit down, Miss Fields?' They had been standing in the hallway for almost half an hour, and she nodded as they walked towards the chairs.

'Please call me Daphne.'

'I will, if you call me Matt.'

She smiled and they sat down.

'Something tells me that you have a problem. Is there anything I can do to help?'

'I don't know. Mrs Curtis and I talked about it last night.'

'Is it something to do with Andrew?'

She nodded. 'Yes. I've just had an offer to make a movie in Hollywood. It means moving out there for a year.'

'And you're taking him with you?' He looked suddenly disappointed but she shook her head.

'No, I really think I ought to leave him here. But that's the problem. He'll hardly ever see me ... I don't know if he could handle it, or more honestly, if I could ...' She looked up at him then, her enormous blue eyes reaching out to his brown. 'I just don't know what to do.'

'That's a tough one. For you, not so much for Andrew. He'd adjust.' And then gently, 'I'd help him. We all would. He might be angry for a little while, but he'd understand. And I'm going to keep them all pretty busy this year. I want to take a lot of field trips with them, get them back out into the world as much as possible. They're a little isolated here.' She nodded. He was right. 'What about having him fly out to see you during vacations?'

'Do you think he could do that?'

'With the right preparation. You know, eventually that's the kind of life you'd want him to lead. You want him to be able to get on planes, to go places, to be independent, to see more of the world than just this.'

She nodded slowly. 'But he's so young.'

'Daphne, he's seven. If he were a hearing child, you wouldn't hesitate to have him put on a plane, would you? Why treat him any differently? He's a very bright little boy.' As she listened to him she felt relief begin to flood over her, and walls she had built around Andrew in her mind slowly began to fall. 'And not only that but it's important for him that you're happy, that he see you leading a full life. You can't cling to him forever.' There was no reproach in his voice, only gentleness and understanding. 'You're no more than seven or eight hours away at any given moment. If we have a problem, we'll call you and you hop on a plane to Boston. I'll even pick you up at the airport, and in two hours you're here. It's hardly farther than New York if you look at it that way.' He had a marvellous way of solving problems, finding solutions, and making everything seem so simple. She could easily understand now how he had taken his sister out of her school and run off with her to Mexico. She smiled at the idea.

'You make it all sound so easy.'

'It can be. For you and Andrew, if you let it. What you have to base your decision on is what *you* want to *do*. One day he'll have to make decisions for himself too. Independent decisions, decisions to be free and strong and make choices for himself, not you. Teach him that early. Do *you* want to make a movie? Do *you* want to go to Hollywood for a year? Those are the issues. Not Andrew. You don't want to give up an important part of your life for him. Opportunities like that don't come along that often, or maybe they do for you. But if it's important to you, if it's what you want, then do it. Tell him, let him adjust to it. I'll help you.' And she knew he would.

'I'll have to think it over.'

'Do that, and we can talk about it again tomorrow. You'll have to brace yourself for a little anger from Andrew most likely. But you'd get that from any kid his age if you told him you were going away. Know that the anger and the reaction are normal. Being a parent isn't always easy.' He smiled at her again. 'I see what my sister has been through. She had twins also. Her girls are fourteen now. And if you think a seven-year-old boy is rough, you should try doubles that age, and girls!' He rolled his eyes. 'I'd never survive it!'

'You don't have children of your own?'

'No.' He looked sorry. 'Except for the hundred and forty-six I'm leaving at the New York School with Martha, my sister. My wife never really wanted children. She was not a hearing person' – Daphne nodded, accustomed to what would have been to someone else an unfamiliar term – 'and she was very different from my sister. She was terrified her own children wouldn't hear. She had a lot of hang-ups about her deafness. In the end' – he looked regretful – 'it's what did us in. She was a model in New York, and an incredibly bright girl. I had tutored her for a while, that's how I met her. But her parents always treated her like a china doll, and she hadn't had a crazy brother like me when she was growing up. She retreated into her deafness. She's a perfect example of why you shouldn't treat Andrew any differently than any other child. Don't do that to him, Daphne. If you do, you'll rob him of everything that will ever matter to him.' They sat quietly for a moment, each with his own thoughts. He had given her a lot to think about in the last hour. He had shared an important part of his life with her, and she knew she had made a friend.

'I think you're right, Matt. But it scares the hell out of me to leave him.'

'There are lots of things in life that are scary. All the good stuff usually is. Think of all the good things you've done in your life. How much of it was easy? Probably none of it was, but it was always worth the struggle, I'll bet. And I would imagine that making a movie is an important step in your career. Which book is it, by the way?'

'*Apache*.' She smiled at him, proud of herself and suddenly not ashamed to let him see it.

162

'That's my favourite.'

'Mine too.'

And then, picking up his stack of papers, he stood up. 'Are you staying for dinner?' She nodded. 'I'll join you for coffee afterwards. I'm going to take a sandwich upstairs in the meantime, so I can do my homework.' She thought again of what he had said. The good things in life weren't easy. They hadn't been for either of them.

'I'll see you later, Matt.' They parted company at the staircase and she watched him for a moment. Sensing it, he looked down at her as she looked up. 'And thank you.'

'Any time. You'll always get the truth from me, Daphne, about what I think and what I feel. Remember that when you're in California. I'll tell you how he is, and if he needs you I'll tell you. You can fly home, or I'll put him on the next plane.' She nodded, and he waved to her and then disappeared on to the upstairs landing. It seemed strange to her that he seemed to assume she was going. Had he read her mind? How could he know her decision before she did? Or was that what she had already secretly decided, and longed for. She wasn't sure as she went into the big playroom to find Andrew. And as she saw him she felt her heart sink. How could she leave him? He was so little and so dear.

But that night as she lay in bed at the inn she thought about it all again, pulled one way and then the other, by duty, obligation, love on one side, and fascination, curiosity, ambition, career on the other. It was a tough choice, and then suddenly the phone rang and it was Matthew. She was startled to hear him and wondered instantly if something was wrong.

'Of course not. If it were something like that, Mrs Curtis would call you. I'm not official yet, you know, at least not for a few more weeks. I was just thinking about your decision, and I had a crazy thought. If you get too tied up in Los Angeles at some point and you can't have him out to visit, I could take him home to stay with my sister and her kids. You'd have to give us special permission of course, but he might enjoy it. My sister is really quite something and her girls are terrific. How does that strike you?'

'I don't know what to say to you, Matthew. I'm overwhelmed.'

'Don't be. Last year I had forty-three of our students at my place for Christmas dinner. Martha cooked and her husband coached touch football in the park. It was super.' She wanted to tell him that she thought he was, but she didn't dare.

'I don't know how to thank you.'

'Don't. Just trust me with Andrew.'

She was silent for a moment, it was late, and he had been very open with her. She wanted to do the same with him. 'Matt, it's hard for me to leave him . . . he's all I've got.'

'I know that. Or at least, I suspected it.' His voice was very soft. 'He'll be all right, and so will you.' And as she listened to him she knew that, and the decision was finally made.

'I think I'm going to do it.'

'I think you should.' It made it easier for her that he said that, and it suddenly seemed amazing that she had only met him that morning and already she had come to rely on his judgement, and trust him with her son. 'When you go back to New York, I'll introduce you to my sister. Maybe you'd like to come to the school next week to meet her, if you have time.'

'I'll make time.'

'Great. I'll see you in the morning. And congratulations.'

'For what?'

'For making a tough decision. Besides, I have a selfish motive in all this. I want to see my favourite book made into a movie.' She laughed then and they hung up, and that night she slept peacefully at last.

164

18

'I know it seems like a long time, sweetheart, but you can come out to see me during vacations, and we can do fun things in California, and I promise I'll fly back...' She was signing desperately, but Andrew refused to watch her. His eyes were awash with tears. 'Andrew...darling ...please...' Her eyes filled too as she sat in the garden with him, fighting to keep from clutching him to her and sobbing. He stood with his back to her, his shoulders hunched over and shaking, his head bent, and when she gently pulled him towards her, he made terrible little gurgling sounds and her heart tore in half. 'Oh, Andrew ...sweetheart... I'm so sorry.' Oh, God, she couldn't do it. She couldn't, not to him. 'He'll adjust,' they said. Christ, it was like adjusting to double amputation, and why should he have to do that? Just because she wanted to make a film. She felt rotten and selfish as she sat beside him, hating herself for the decision she had made and what it was obviously doing to him. She couldn't do this to her child. He needed her too badly. After all... She tried to put her arms around him and he wouldn't let her, and she stood there in despair looking at him as Matthew Dane came outside. He watched them for a moment, saying nothing, and from the look on Andrew's face he knew instantly that she had told him. He walked slowly over to them, and looked at Daphne with a gentle smile.

'He'll be all right in a little while, Daphne. Remember what I told you. You'd have had this kind of reaction from any child, even a hearing one.'

'But he isn't a hearing child.' Her eyes blazed at him and her voice was sharp. 'He's special.' She wanted to add 'dammit,' but she didn't. She felt certain that he had misjudged the situation, he had given her bad advice about her son and she had let him. She was wrong to even consider going out west for a year. But Matt didn't look swayed from his earlier opinion, even now.

'Of course he's special, all children are. Special is all right, different isn't. What you're saying is that he's different. You don't have to cater to his handicap, Daphne. That won't help him. Any seven-year-old child would be upset by his mother going away. That's normal. Other parents have situations their children have to adjust to, siblings, divorces, deaths, moves, financial problems. You can't create a perfect world for him forever. It would be impossible for you to live up to, and in the end it would hurt him. Besides, can you really live up to that? Do you want to?'

She wanted to shout at him, he didn't understand anything, least of all her responsibilities to her child. He watched her eyes and knew what she was thinking, and he smiled.

'It's all right, go ahead, hate me. But I'm right. If you stick to your guns for a little while, he'll be okay.' They both saw then that Andrew was watching them, lip-reading, and Daphne turned towards her son with sorrow in her eyes. This time she spoke to him as well as signing.

'I'm not happy about going either, sweetheart. But I think it's important for me to do this. I want to go to Hollywood to make a movie out of one of my books.'

'Why?' He signed the word.

'Because it would be exciting, and it would help my work.' How do you explain lifetime career goals to a seven-year-old child? 'I promise you could come out to see me, and I'd come back here. I wouldn't see you every week, but it won't be forever . . .' Her voice drifted off and there was a distant spark of interest in his eyes.

'Could I come on an aeroplane?'

She nodded. 'Yes. A great big one.' This seemed to spark some further interest, and then he looked down and kicked the ground. When he looked up again, Daphne wasn't sure what he was thinking, but he looked less devastated than he had earlier.

'Could we go to Disneyland?'

'Yes.' Daphne smiled. 'We could do a lot of other things too, you could watch them make the movie when you visit.' And then, suddenly, she knelt beside him and took him in her arms for a moment before moving back so he could see her lips again. 'Oh, Andrew, I will miss you so much. I love you with all my heart, and as soon as I finish my work in California, I'll come back and stay here, I promise. And Mr Dane says that he'll take you to New York to visit his sister and her children ... maybe if we both keep as busy as we can, and learn as much as we can, the time will go very quickly ...' She wanted it to, she wanted it to be over right now. In her heart of hearts she didn't want to leave him, but she knew she had to. For herself. It was the first time in many years that she was doing something she knew she wanted to very badly, even though it wasn't easy, and suddenly she thought of all that Matt had said the night before. The good things in life weren't easy, either for her or Andrew. Something in Andrew's face told her then that even though he didn't like her going, he'd be all right. 'Andrew ... do you know how much I love you?' She watched him, wondering if he'd remember the game they'd played so often when he was younger.

'How much?' He signed it at her and her eyes shone with unshed tears. He did remember after all.

'As much as this.' She threw her arms wide and then threw them around him, and then whispered into his hair, 'As much as my whole life.'

Matthew left them to each other and they spent a quiet hour together, talking about things that were important to Andrew, about her trip, and how soon she would come back. She told him that she wouldn't be leaving for another month, and she'd come to visit often in the meantime, and then they talked about when he would come to California, the things they'd do, and what it would be like.

'Will you write to me?' His eyes turned to hers sadly, and her heart ached again. He was still so little and California seemed as though it were on another planet.

'Yes. I promise I'll write every day. Will you write to me?'

But this time he grinned at her. 'I'll try to remember.' He was teasing and her heart felt lighter.

When she got back to New York that night, she felt as though she had climbed a mountain. She unpacked her suitcase and walked around her apartment, and at last her thoughts turned from Andrew as she looked out the window at the brilliant lights of Manhattan. She was suddenly excited about what she was doing, and for the first time in three days the reality of it came home to her. She was going to California to make a movie of *Apache*! And suddenly she stood there, smiling to herself and laughing ... it was happening! She had really made it. 'Hallelujah!' she whispered softly, and then she walked into her bedroom, climbed into the bed, and turned off the lights.

19

'Well, kiddo,' Daphne smiled at Barbara as she came through the door the next morning. 'Hang on to your hat.'

'What's up?'

'We're going.'

Barbara looked startled. 'Where?'

'To California, dummy.'

'You're going to do it, Daff?' Barbara looked nothing less than astounded.

'I am.'

'What about Andrew?' She hated to ask, but she had to.

'I told him this weekend, and he wasn't too pleased at first, but I think we'll both survive it.' She told her then about all that Mrs Curtis had said, and about the new director at the school. 'I'm going to have Andrew fly out to see me, and I'll come back whenever I can. And Matthew says he'll bring him to New York, to visit the New York School and see his sister...' Her voice trailed off with a gust of laughter at the look of confusion on Barbara's face. 'He's the new director up at Howarth.'

'Matthew? How friendly!' Barbara's eyes were teasing. 'Do I sense the presence of an attractive man?'

'Very attractive, as a friend, Miss Jarvis, nothing more, I assure you.'

'Bullshit. You just quoted him like God, and he's bringing Andrew down to see his sister? Hell, you've never even let me meet the kid for chrissake and you're trusting him to a stranger? This guy must be pretty terrific, Daff, or you wouldn't let him do that.'

'You're right, he is terrific, and he's the smartest

human being I've ever known about the hard-of-hearing, but that doesn't mean I'm interested in him as a man for chrissake.' She was still laughing.

'Why not? Is he ugly?'

'No.' She was still chuckling. 'As a matter of fact he's very handsome. But that's not the point. Let's talk about us.'

'Us?' Barbara looked confused again. Everything was topsy-turvy this morning.

'I want you to come with me.'

'Are you kidding?' She sat down with a load of fan mail in her arms. 'What would I do there?'

'Run my life, the way you do here.' Daphne smiled.

'Is that what I do?' Barbara returned the smile. 'Run your life? I figured I had to be good for something other than answering fan mail.'

'You know damn well you are.' She knew that she was invaluable to Daphne and it meant a lot to her. And she never forgot that it was Daphne who had helped to free her from her old life. 'Now, will you come with me?'

'When do I pack? Is tomorrow soon enough?' She was beaming and Daphne laughed at her.

'I think you can wait a couple of weeks for that. First, we're going to have to get organised here, and I want you to come to Iris McCarthy's with me this afternoon, so you can hear what it's all about when I do. I think we leave next month sometime. That ought to give us plenty of time to get everything wrapped up.'

'What are you going to do with the apartment?'

'Let it sit here. I'll use it when I fly in to see Andrew, and Comstock is paying for me to rent a house out there, so I won't have double expenses. Besides, I don't want some stranger sleeping in my bed.' She made a face and Barbara laughed at her with a rueful smile.

'Listen, once in a while, I think that wouldn't be so bad . . .' The two women exchanged a smile.

They went to Daphne's agent together that afternoon, after Daphne took Barbara to the Plaza for lunch and they drank a toast to the West Coast and to Comstock.

It was all beginning to feel exciting, and by the time they left Iris's office at four thirty, Daphne could hardly wait to start. She turned to Barbara nervously in the cab going back to the apartment then, with a worried frown. 'Do you really think I can do it, Barb? I mean hell, I have no idea how to write a movie.'

'You'll figure it out. It can't be that much different from a book. Play it by ear, they'll tell you what they want.'

'I hope so.' There was a nervous flutter in the pit of her stomach as Barbara patted her hand.

'You can do it. It's going to be fabulous.'

'I hope so.' But whether it was or not, she knew she had to try.

She went back to see Andrew the following weekend, and he seemed by then perfectly adjusted to the idea of her going. He only complained about it once and that time only halfheartedly, the rest of the time he talked about Disneyland and her movie, and he seemed relaxed and happy and she marvelled at how quickly he had accepted it all. Children really were amazing, she decided, and she mentioned it all to Matthew when she saw him again, at dinner in the main dining room of Howarth on Saturday night.

'Will you kick me if I say I told you so, Daphne?' He smiled at her over the remains of dinner and she grinned. This week she looked relaxed and happy, and younger, with her blonde hair spilling over her shoulders, blue jeans, and a persimmon-coloured cowboy shirt.

'I may, so watch out.'

'You're scaring me to death.' But there was a pleasant banter between them. He told her about what had happened at the New York School that week, and she told him about the preliminary plans for the movie. Dinner seemed to fly as they chatted, and Helen Curtis left them alone after dinner, she said that she had work to do, and for once Matthew did not. 'I don't know how you manage to write those books the way you do, Daphne.' He stretched his long legs towards the fire after the children were in bed and they sat in the cosy living room of the school. She didn't feel like going back to the inn and it was still early. Besides, he was good company and she liked him.

He was nice to talk to, and she felt they had a lot in common. They shared Andrew, and interest in her book. 'I really don't know how you do it.' He was thinking about *Apache* and she looked at him with amusement.

'How can you say that? You've written three books yourself.'

'All of them nonfiction, about a subject I eat, sleep, and breathe. That's hardly very remarkable.' He smiled at her from where he sat.

'It's a lot harder than what I do. You have to be accurate, and you help an awful lot of people with those books, Matthew. Mine are all make-believe stories born out of nowhere, and they don't do a damn thing for anyone, except amuse them.' She was always modest about her work, and he liked that about her. One would never guess from talking to her that she was one of the nation's leading best-selling authors. She was bright and intelligent and amusing, and she did not show off.

'You're wrong about your books, Daphne, they do a lot more than just amuse. I told you, one of your books helped me a great deal, and they all taught me something' – he seemed pensive for a moment – 'about people ... relationships ... women.' He looked at her with interest. 'How do you know so much about that stuff, leading such a solitary life?'

'What makes you think I do ... lead a solitary life, I mean?' She was amused at the question.

'You told me so yourself last week.'

'Did I?' She shrugged and grinned. 'I talk too much. I suppose I don't have time for anything more than that. I work like a dog all week long, and then there's Andrew ...'

Matt looked disapproving for a moment and then his face softened in the firelight. 'Don't use him as an excuse.'

172

She gazed at him frankly. 'Usually, I don't.' And then she smiled, 'Only when someone puts me on the spot, like you did.'

'I'm sorry. I didn't mean to do that.'

'Yes, you did. What about you? Is your life so full?'

'Sometimes.' He was noncommittal. 'For a long time I was afraid to get involved again, after my wife.'

'And now?' It was strange questioning him this way, it was as though they were old friends, but he had that kind of quality about him, he was so warm and so open and so easy to talk to. She felt as though they had known each other for years, it was as though they were on a desert island, the rest of the world was unimportant. They just sat there by the fire, alone and comfortable with each other, and each one curious to know what made the other tick.

'I don't know ... I don't have much time for serious involvement these days. There's a lot going on in my life professionally.' And then he smiled at her again. 'And I don't suppose I'll find the woman of my life in the next year, up here.'

'You never know. Mrs Obermeier might decide to leave her husband.' They both laughed at the thought and Matthew looked at her more seriously for a moment. He had heard the story of John Fowler from Helen Curtis, but he wasn't sure if he could broach the subject with her, or if it was taboo.

'Don't you ever want to try again, Daphne?' He suspected that she was very lonely, and yet there was no sense of her reaching out towards a man, certainly not towards him. She had an easy, comfortable way about her that reminded him of his sister, and her warmth was in the same vein. But there was a sense about her that she had forgotten she was a woman, and didn't want to remember it ever again. She had obviously been very hurt.

But as she looked at him now in the glow from the embers, he saw sadness in her eyes beyond measure, and stories that he knew would never be told. 'No, I don't want to try again, Matt. I've had all I ever wanted. Twice in fact.' Daphne surprised herself with how easily her secret slipped out. 'It would be wrong of me to ask for more ... and stupid ... and greedy ... and very foolish. I thought I'd never find what I had once, with my husband, and yet I did find someone else. It was very different, very special. I've had two extraordinary men in my life, Matt. I couldn't ask for anything more.'

So she was ready to talk about Fowler.

'And so you've given up? What about the next fifty or sixty years?' The prospect of her solitude depressed him. She deserved more than that ... much more ... she deserved someone wonderful who would love her. She was too good and strong and young and wise to spend the rest of her life alone. But she smiled philosophically at him.

'I don't have any trouble keeping busy. And one of these days Andrew will come home ...'

'You're using him as an excuse again.' He sounded gentler this time, less disapproving. 'He's going to be terrific and totally independent when he gets older. So don't count on basing your life on him.'

'I don't really do that, but I must admit, I think a lot about his coming home.'

Matthew smiled at her in the soft light. 'That'll be a fine day for both of you, Daphne, and it won't be too long.'

She sighed softly then. 'I wish I knew that for sure. Sometimes all of this seems like forever.'

His eyes filled with a distant memory as he thought of the years without his sister when he was young. 'I used to feel that way about Martha. She was gone for fifteen years, and not in a place like Howarth. It was awful for her. Thank God they don't have places like that anymore.' Daphne nodded silent agreement and a little while later she stood up and decided that it was time to go home. 'I enjoy talking to you, Daphne.' His eyes were gentle as he walked her to the front door, and then he said something unexpected, which startled them both.

174

He hadn't really meant to say it to her, but he couldn't help it. 'Andrew's not the only one who's going to miss you in the next year.'

Had the hall light been brighter he would have seen her blushing, but it wasn't, and she held out a small, fragile hand. He took it in his own and held it for a moment. 'Thank you, Matthew. I'm just glad to know that you'll be here with Andrew. I'm going to call you a lot to see how he's doing.'

He nodded, feeling only slightly disappointed. But he had no right to expect more. He was only the director of the school where her son lived. Nothing more. And he knew how solitary her life was, and something told him that she wasn't going to change that. She was a strong-willed woman, and she hid behind solid walls. 'You do that. Call as often as you like. I'll be here.' She smiled at him then and left with only a whispered good night.

As she drove slowly back to the inn she found herself thinking of him. He was a lovely man and they were lucky to have him at Howarth. But she had to admit, even if only to herself, that she felt something more for him. Some vague, gnawing, deeper interest, as though she wanted to know everything about him and talk to him for endless hours. She hadn't felt that way since she had met John Fowler, but she also knew that she wasn't going to let herself feel that way again. Not about any man. Two losses were enough. Matthew Dane would be an important person to her, in the life of Andrew, and for all that he could teach her in helping Andrew back into the world of the hearing. But that was his only role in her life, and she knew it, no matter how much she liked him. Those things just didn't matter anymore. She wouldn't let them. It was enough to have loved and lost, she had no desire to love that way again. Ever. And it was easy to imagine loving Matthew Dane. He was a lovable, likable, admirable man. But for that reason she'd have to keep her guard up all the higher. Just to be certain she stayed safe. It was on Andrew that she showered all her love now, every feeling, every moment, every thought. She lived her life exclusively for him. And maybe a little bit for herself. The trip to California was the first sign of that.

20

Daphne all but closed the apartment on her last Friday in New York. She had done all her packing. Her suitcases for California stood waiting in the hallway, everything was ready, and all that was left was to spend one last weekend with Andrew. She would return on Sunday night, put her car in storage in the garage, and fly to Los Angeles with Barbara on Monday morning. They would stay at the Beverly Hills Hotel, in a cottage, until she found a suitable house there, and within a week of her arrival in LA, she would have to get to work on the screenplay. According to her contract she had only two months to write it, and it was beginning to give her sleepless nights.

She thought about it all the way up to New Hampshire, and made notes to herself late into the night once she got to the little inn. The next morning she spent with Andrew, and as usual joined him for lunch, and the afternoon and dinner, and it wasn't until then that she saw Matthew, and he looked almost as harassed as she felt by then.

'You look like you've had a tough week.' She smiled at him over coffee and he ran a hand through his thick brown hair and groaned.

'Oh, God, I have. Four major crises at the New York School since Monday, and this is my last weekend here as an observer. I start officially next Friday. Mrs Curtis leaves the following Monday morning for good, and if I don't have a nervous breakdown by then, I'll be doing fine.'

'Welcome to the club, I have two months to write my screenplay, and I'm beginning to panic. I have no idea

177

what I'm doing, and every time I sit down in front of a piece of paper, my mind goes blank.' He smiled in sympathy at the image.

'That used to happen to me every time I had a deadline on a book. But eventually, out of sheer desperation, I used to force myself to tackle the problem. You will too. Probably once you get there, everything will fall into place.'

'I have to go house hunting first.'

'Where will you be in the meantime?'

'I left Mrs Curtis all my numbers. I'll be at the Beverly Hills Hotel until I find a house.'

He rolled his eyes and attempted unsuccessfully to look sympathetic. 'Tough life you lead, lady.'

'Yeah, ain't it?' She grinned.

She only chatted with him for a few moments in the hall before she went back to the inn. He had to talk to Helen Curtis on this final weekend before he moved in for good, and Daphne was exhausted from a long week's work.

The next morning, as usual, she went to church with Andrew, and came back to the school to spend the day with him. And now each moment shared with him was precious. He clung to her more than usual this weekend, but that was to be expected. And she felt a need to be as close to him as she could, to touch him, to hold him, to feel his hair slip through her fingers so that she would remember its silky touch when she was so far away, to nuzzle his neck with her lips as she kissed him, to smell the last hint of soap on his childlike flesh as they hugged. Everything about him seemed more special to her now, and somehow dearer. It was the hardest weekend of all for her, and sensing that, Matthew stayed away. It wasn't until she was ready to leave that he approached her again, watching with silent understanding as she held Andrew, wanting to reach out to them both when he saw the first tears spring to her eyes. He knew that leaving wouldn't be easy for them. But Andrew would recover more quickly. It was Daphne who would suffer, worrying about the child, keeping him in her thoughts in every spare moment, wondering how he was, and longing for him from so far away.

'How are you two doing?' He said it to her over Andrew's head, pretending not to see her tears. 'He's going to be fine, you know, Daphne, in a few hours, no matter how hard he cries when you go.'

She nodded, a sob cluttering her throat, and then finally she took a deep breath. 'I know. He'll be okay. But will I make it?'

'Yes, you will. I promise.' He touched her arm gently then. 'And you call any time you like. I'll give you all the latest information and reports.'

'Thank you.' She smiled through her tears and touched her son's head with a gentle hand, and she bent then to tell Andrew that it was time to go to bed. She sat with him for a long time that night, talking to him about California, about all the fun they'd have, and how much she would miss him. And then, sadly, with the strange little sound he had always made when he was sad, he began to cry, and he held out his arms and held her tight, signing at last.

'I'm going to miss you so much.'

'Me too.' The tears ran down her cheeks. Maybe it was just as well he saw them after all. So he would know how much she would miss him too. 'But I'll see you soon.' She smiled at him through her tears and at last he smiled too. She stayed until he fell asleep, and she walked slowly downstairs as though she had lost her best friend, and she found Matthew waiting for her in a chair at the bottom of the stairs.

'Asleep?'

'Yes.' Her eyes were huge and sad, and she didn't even attempt a smile. And he said nothing at all but followed her to the front door. She had already said good-bye to Mrs Curtis before she took Andrew up to bed, she had checked out of the inn and her suitcase was in the car, there was nothing left to do but go. As though sensing her silent mood, Matthew walked her to her car, and

179

then watched as she unlocked the door. She turned to him then with those huge blue eyes, and he reached out and took both her shoulders in his hands.

'We love him too, and we'll take good care of him, I swear.' They always had before, but it was different now that she would be so far away. It all hurt more than it had in years and she felt ten thousand years old as she looked up into Matthew's dark brown eyes.

'I know.' She had seen so much loss in her life, so many people she had loved, and now all she had left was this one small boy. 'I'm not very good at this. I should be by now. I've had a lifetime of good-byes.' He nodded, it was all written in her eyes.

'This isn't the same, Daphne. Right now is the hardest part. And it won't be for long. A year seems like an eternity right now, but it's not.'

She smiled. Life was so strange. 'When I come back, you'll have done your year here, and you'll be ready to go.'

'And we'll all have learned so much. Think of that.'

The tears spilled over again as she shook her head. 'I can't . . . all I can think of is how he looked the first time I brought him here.'

'That was a long time ago, Daphne.' She nodded. That had been the beginning of her year with John. Why did everything always have to end in good-bye? But Matthew bent then and kissed her cheek. 'Godspeed. And call.'

'I will.' She looked up at him again and for a mad moment she wanted to fold herself into his arms, to feel the safety she had once felt, protected by a man. She longed silently for a time when she hadn't had to stand alone, when she hadn't had to be so brave all the time. 'Take care of yourself . . . and Andrew too.' And then she slid into her car, and looked up at him through the open window. 'Thanks for everything, Matt. And good luck.'

'I'll need it.' His face broke into a boyish grin. 'And

180

make me a great movie. I know you will.' She smiled and started the car, and as she drove away she waved and he waved back. And as she drove off into the night he stood there for a long, long time.

21

The plane touched down in Los Angeles with a small bump and seemed to soar along the runway before it stopped and taxied to the gate. Barbara was looking excitedly out the window, and Daphne smiled at her. Travelling with her had been like travelling with a little girl. Everything delighted her, and she had been excited from New York all the way to LA. Daphne had been quieter than usual and she had already written three postcards to Andrew. But now her mind was no longer on him. She was caught up in the realisation that a whole new life was about to begin.

They were met at the gate by the chauffeur Comstock had hired for her, a tall, seedy-looking man of indeterminate age in a black suit and cap, with a long, sorrowful-looking moustache. He stood holding a large card with her name written on it in red ink: 'Daphne Fields.'

'That's subtle.' She looked at Barbara with amusement, and her companion grinned.

'This is Hollywood, Daff. Nothing is subtle out here.'

It turned out to be a prophetic statement, as they discovered when they reached the Beverly Hills Hotel. It stood in pink stucco splendour surrounded by palm trees with its name splashed across the front in bright green. Inside the lobby everything was chaos, women hurried past wearing tight jeans, gold chains, silk shirts, blonde hair, and high-heeled sandals; men walked by in expensive Italian suits, or tight pants and shirts open to their waists. The aroma in the hotel was a veritable symphony of expensive perfumes, bellboys staggered

182

under the weight of enormous arrangements of flowers, or stacks of Gucci luggage, and the hotel roster read like the Academy Awards.

'Miss Fields? Of course. We have your cottage ready.' A bellboy solemnly wheeled her cartful of luggage past the starlets and would-be producers clustered around the swimming pool, and Daphne was fascinated by the array of bodies and more gold chains, everyone drinking white wine or martinis in the middle of the day. The 'cottage' turned out to have four bedrooms, three baths, an icebox stocked with caviar and champagne, and a view of still more palm trees, and there was a huge bouquet of roses and a box of chocolates from Comstock with a note that said 'See you tomorrow.' And suddenly she turned to Barbara with a look of terror.

'I can't do it.' Her voice was tense. The bellboy had just left them, and they stood in the enormous flowery living room of their cottage. Daphne's eyes were larger than Barbara had ever seen them. 'Barb, I can't.'

'What? Eat the chocolates?' Teasing was her only hope, it was obvious that Daphne was panicked.

'No. Look at all this. It's Hollywood. What the hell am I doing here? I'm a writer. I don't know anything about all this stuff.'

'You don't have to. All you have to do is sit down at your typewriter and do the same thing you do at home. Ignore all this bullshit. It's just window dressing.'

'No, it isn't. Did you see them out there? They all think it's real.'

'This is a hotel for chrissake. They're all from St Louis. Relax.' She poured her a glass of champagne, and Daphne sat on the pink-and-green-flowered couch, looking like an orphan.

'I want to go home.'

'Well, I won't let you. So shut up and enjoy it. Hell, I haven't even seen Rodeo Drive yet.' Daphne grinned at her, remembering the life Barbara had led with her mother. It was a far cry from all this. 'Do you want something to eat?'

'I'd throw up.'

'Christ, Daff. Why don't you just relax and enjoy it?'

'Enjoy what? The fact that I've signed a contract to do something I have no idea how to do, in a place that looks like life on another planet, three thousand miles from my only child . . . for God's sake, Barbara, what am I doing here?'

'Making money for your kid.' It was an answer Barbara knew would reach her if nothing else did. 'Get my point?'

'Yeah.' But it was small consolation. 'I feel like I've signed on for the foreign legion.'

'You have. And the faster you get to work, the faster we get out of here.' Not that Barbara wanted to, not by a long shot. She loved it already.

'Now there's a good idea.' She went to unpack then, and half an hour later she looked better. Barbara called Comstock and told them they had arrived safely, and after that they went out to the pool and swam. That night they shared a quiet dinner, took a look into the Polo Lounge filled with what looked like actors and models and businessmen and shady characters who might have been drug dealers, and by ten o'clock they were in bed, Barbara with a feeling of excitement and anticipation, and Daphne with a sense of awe at what lay ahead.

The next morning they went to a meeting at Comstock, and by the time they left at noon, back to the exotic splendour of the hotel, Daphne almost felt as though she might live. She had a better idea of what they wanted her to do with *Apache*, she had taken copious notes and she planned to get to work the same day. And Barbara's work was cut out too. She had the names of half a dozen real estate agents. She was going to look for a house for them to rent. She also placed a call to Daphne's agent, and got whatever messages Iris had for her. And by that afternoon things were beginning to roll smoothly. Daphne had brought her own typewriter from New

184

York, had shoved a table and chair into a corner, and had begun to work as Barbara went out to the pool.

When she came back an hour later, Daphne was still working, and Barbara turned the lights on for her. She was so engrossed in what she was doing that she hadn't even noticed the light grow dim.

'Mn?' She looked up with the distracted look she always wore when she was working, her hair was piled up on her head with a pen stuck through it, and she had put on a T-shirt and jeans. 'Oh, hi. Have a nice swim?'

'Very. Want something to eat?'

'Hm ... nah ... maybe later.' Barbara liked to watch her working, she got so totally involved in what she did. You could actually see the creative process at work. At eight o'clock she ordered room service for them both and when it arrived, she tapped Daphne on the shoulder. She never remembered to eat when she was working, and in New York Barbara would just set a tray on her desk and keep reminding her to eat.

'Chow time.'

'Okay. In a minute.' Which usually meant an hour, and in this case it did too.

'Come on, kiddo. You've got to eat.'

'I will.' At last she stopped pounding her typewriter and sat back with a sigh as she stretched and rubbed her shoulders. She smiled at Barbara then. 'Boy, that feels good.'

'How's it going?'

'Not bad. I feel like a virgin all over again.'

She went back to her typewriter after dinner, and stayed there until 2 a.m. And the next morning she got up at seven, and was pounding away again when Barbara got up.

'Didn't you go to bed last night?' She knew that sometimes Daphne didn't, but this time she had.

'Yeah. I think it was around two.'

'You're really smoking, huh?'

'I want to keep at it while what we talked about

yesterday is still fresh in my mind.' And she did keep at it all day. Barbara went out to see three houses, had lunch by herself, and sat at the pool. Then she came back to work in her own room answering fan mail, and they took dinner again that night on trays. In a funny way she was like a mother to Daphne, but she didn't mind it. She had had long years of training with her mother, and Daphne was a joy to work for. She was fun to be with, her work was exciting, and there was something marvellous about standing right next to that kind of genius. Daphne never saw it that way, but Barbara always did.

On the fourth day Daphne called Mrs Curtis to ask after Andrew, true to her promise she had sent him a letter every day. Mrs Curtis said he was well and happy, and had readjusted immediately after she left. She also reminded Daphne that she wouldn't be speaking to her again until Daphne returned to New Hampshire and came to visit her in her new home. The following day was her last day at Howarth. Daphne wished her luck again and hung up, thinking suddenly of Matthew, wondering how he was doing. She knew he was probably madly busy wrapping up at the New York School before he left.

'How's Andrew?' Barbara came in with a tray for Daphne, and she looked up with a smile.

'Mrs Curtis says he's fine. How are we doing on house hunting by the way?'

Barbara grinned. '"We" are doing fine. Except so far they're all lemons. Something ought to turn up soon though. Do you want a pool in the shape of a typewriter, or will one in the shape of a book do?'

'Very funny.'

'Listen, today I saw one heart shape, one oval, one in the shape of a key, and one crown.'

'Sounds very exotic.'

'It is, and it's tacky as hell, and the worst of it is that I love it. I'm discovering a whole other side to my personality.'

186

Daphne grinned at her, amused. 'Listen, if you walk in here with your shirt open to your waist, wearing gold chains, I'll know it's terminal.' And the next day, just for a laugh, she did, and Daphne roared.

'We've only been here five days and you've already been taken over.'

'I can't help it. It's in the air. It's stronger than I am.'

'Nothing is stronger than you are, Barbara Jarvis.' It was a compliment and she meant it, but Barbara shook her head.

'That's not true, Daff. You are. You're the strongest woman I know, and I mean that in a nice way.'

'Would that it were true.'

'It is.'

'You sound like Matthew Dane.'

'Him again.' Barbara watched her closely. 'I still think you missed the opportunity of a lifetime. I saw his picture on the back of his book, he's gorgeous.'

'So? What did I miss? An opportunity for a one-night stand before I left New York for a year? Come on, Barbara, what sense does that make? Besides, he didn't offer.'

'Maybe he would have if you'd given him half a chance. And you are going back after all.'

'He's the director of my son's school. That's indecent.'

'Think of him as another author.' But Daphne was trying not to think of him at all. He was a nice man and a good friend. And nothing more than that.

As usual she went back to work after dinner, and Barbara sat in her room, reading a book. It wasn't until the next day that she finally got antsy and took herself off to Rodeo Drive for a look around. She had done everything she had to do for Daphne and there were no houses that day, so she decided to play hooky.

The limousine dropped her off at the Beverly Wilshire and she stood looking around her with fascination. A long handsome street stretched ahead of her for several blocks, lined inch by inch with expensive boutiques selling clothes and jewellery and luggage and paintings for a grand total of at least several hundred million dollars. It was awesome and, she reminded herself with a feeling of amazement, a long way from the dingy West Side apartment she had shared with her mother.

Her first stop was at Giorgio's. When she wandered inside she was instantly accosted by a salesgirl wearing high-heeled lavender shoes, pearls, and a pink and mauve Norell suit that retailed for two thousand dollars. The price tags she saw on the clothes hanging on the racks were in the same league. She said she'd 'just wander around,' which she did, trying hard not to giggle. There was a men's department too in the store, offering mink trench coats and silver fox vests, beautiful suedes and leathers and silk shirts, and stacks and stacks of fabulous cashmeres. She tried on hats, looked at shoes, and at last bought herself an umbrella that said 'Giorgio's.' She knew Daphne would tease her unmercifully about it, but she hadn't brought one from New York, and she wanted to buy something. From there she wandered up the street, to Hermès and Celine and eventually to Gucci, which was an enormous store with a rich leather smell and wall after wall of the exquisite Italian leather goods in every design they made. She stood in awe in front of an entire case of handbags in black lizard. There was one particular bag that she couldn't take her eyes off. It was a large, simple, rectangular-shaped bag, with a plain gold clasp and a shoulder strap, and other than the fact that it was beautifully made in the expensive reptile, there was nothing pretentious about it. She liked it because it wasn't showy, and it was exactly the kind of bag she liked, but she didn't dare ask how much it was. She knew it had to be unbelievably expensive.

'Would you like to see the bag, madame?' A salesgirl in the simple black wool dress they all wore opened the case and handed it to Barbara. She was about to refuse, but as the bag danced beneath her eyes she couldn't resist the lure and took it from her. It had a wonderful feel to it, and glancing in the mirror, she slipped it on her shoulder. It was sheer heaven. 'For your height it has exactly the right proportions,' she lilted in her gentle Italian voice, and Barbara almost drooled, and then just for the hell of it she opened the bag and glanced at the price tag. It was seven hundred dollars.

'It's very pretty.' Regretfully she slipped it off her shoulder and handed it back. 'I'll look around some more.'

'Certainly, madame.' The pretty blonde girl smiled as Barbara began to walk away and saw that a tall, attractive man was watching her intently. She glanced at him, embarrassed that he had seen her give the bag back, and for a moment she wished that she could turn around and buy it. It was embarrassing somehow to be wandering through these gilded emporiums, totally unable to afford them. But his eyes never left her face as she walked away and looked at some scarves. She was thinking of buying one for Daphne. The woman had done so much for her, it would be fun to bring her a gift as she slaved away over her screenplay in the cottage. But as she handed a red and black scarf to one of the uniformed girls, she noticed that the man who had been watching her earlier had followed her. She turned her back and pretended not to notice, but she saw him slowly approach as she glanced in one of the long elegant mirrors. He stood behind her. He was wearing grey flannel slacks and a well-cut blue shirt, open at the neck, a dark blue cashmere sweater casually tied around his shoulders, and had she looked down she would have seen that his brown loafers were Gucci. But he didn't really have the look of LA about him, he looked more like New York, or Philadelphia, or Boston. He had sandy hair and blue eyes, she guessed he was in his late thirties or very early forties. And as Barbara glanced at his reflection again she had the feeling she had seen him somewhere before, but she didn't know who he was and she couldn't place him. He caught her eyes then in the mirror, and with an embarrassed smile he finally approached her.

'I'm awfully sorry ... I've been staring at you, but I thought...' Here it comes, she thought to herself, the old line, 'Haven't I met you somewhere before?' – a smooth line, his card pressed into her hand. Barbara's eyes were not as warm as he remembered as he walked towards her. But as he looked at her now, he was sure. She had changed a great deal, her frame was the same, but her face had a distant, almost distrustful, look. Life had apparently not been kind to Barbara Jarvis. 'Barbara?'

'Yes.' No invitation in her voice or eyes, but he smiled now, sure that it was she.

'I'm Tom Harrington. I don't think you remember me. We only met once, at my wedding... I married Sandy Mackenzie.' And then suddenly she knew, her eyes flew wide and she stared at him in amazement.

'Oh, my God ... how did you remember me? It's been...' She hated to think as she added it up. She hadn't seen him since she was twenty, almost exactly twenty years before. He had married her third-year roommate at Smith. She had dropped out because she was pregnant, and they'd gotten married in Philadelphia. Barbara had gone to the wedding and met him then. But she had never seen either of them after that. He had been a law student then, and after the baby was born they moved to California. 'How are you? How's Sandy?' They had sent Christmas cards to her for a dozen years and then finally stopped. She had always been too busy with her mother to answer, but she remembered Sandy distinctly, and Tom, too. She smiled at him warmly then. 'Is she here?' It would be fun to see her, especially now that she worked for Daphne. She hadn't wanted to write back to them then, because there was nothing she wanted to tell them. What? That she was living in a depressing little apartment with her mother, buying groceries and cooking, and working as a secretary in a law firm? What was there to be proud of then? But things were different now. 'How are the

190

children?' She remembered that they had had another four years later.

'They're great. Robert is at UCLA, as a drama major, which doesn't have us exactly thrilled, but he's good at it, and if it's what he wants...' He sighed with a smile. 'You know how kids are. And Alex is still at home with her mother, she'll be fifteen in April.'

'Good God.' Barbara looked genuinely shocked. UCLA and fifteen years old? How did that happen? Was it that long ago? But it was. She was so stunned that she didn't even notice the way he had phrased his answer.

'What about you? Are you living out here?' She saw him glance at her left hand, but there was nothing there.

'No, I'm out here for my job. The woman I work for is writing a screenplay, and we're out here for a year.'

'Sounds like a kick. Anyone I know?'

Barbara smiled with obvious pride. 'Daphne Fields.'

'That must be an interesting job. How long have you been here?'

She grinned. 'A week. We're at the Beverly Hills Hotel, it's a tough life.' They both laughed and then a shockingly beautiful redhead in white jeans and a white silk shirt joined them. She eyed Barbara with piercing green eyes. She couldn't have been a day over twenty-five, if that. She had creamy cameo skin and the red hair fell almost to her waist. She was quite something. 'Nothing fits.' She pouted at Tom, and decided that Barbara wasn't worth worrying about. 'Everything's too big.'

Barbara smiled in frank admiration of the couple they made, wondering who she was. 'I wish I had that problem.'

But there was something kind and intelligent in Tom's eyes as he looked at Barbara. 'You look marvellous, you've hardly changed in all these years.' It was a friendly lie, but she thought that it was nice of him to say so, and he didn't look particularly bowled over by the young beauty at his side. Barbara noticed then that he was already carrying a shopping bag filled with expensive goodies. She couldn't quite figure out the girl's role in his life with Sandy, but his introduction rapidly explained it. 'Eloise, I'd like you to meet Barbara.' He smiled at Barb, and then Eloise. 'Barbara is a friend of my ex-wife's.' And suddenly she understood. They were divorced. Then this was his girl friend.

'Barbara Jarvis,' she filled in for him and held out her hand, her eyes going quickly back to his, wanting to ask him more about Sandy, but this was not the time. 'It's very nice to meet you.' The young redhead didn't say much, but went off to look at a large beige lizard tote bag as Tom watched and then glanced back at Barbara with a look of amusement.

'I'll say one thing, she's got awfully good taste.' It didn't seem to bother him much, nor did he seem overly taken with her.

'I'm sorry to hear about you and Sandy.' Barbara looked genuinely sympathetic. It had been eight or nine years since the Christmas cards stopped. 'How long has it been?'

'Five years. She's remarried.' And then after a moment's hesitation, 'To Austin Weeks.' But that bit of news startled Barbara.

'The actor?' It was a stupid question, how many Austin Weekses could there be? He was a very well-known English actor, but he was at least twice her age, and had been a real Romeo in his day, but Barbara knew from his last movie that he was still breathtakingly handsome. 'How did that happen?'

'I handled a fairly large legal matter for him and we got to be friends...' He shrugged, but there was still something bitter in his eyes as he said it, and then he turned to Barbara with a forced smile. 'This is Hollywood, you know. It's all part of the game. Sandy loves it out here. It suits her to a tee.'

'And you?' Even twenty years before, Barbara had hardly known him, but she had liked him that day at the wedding. She had been the maid of honour and she had thought him intelligent and witty and decent, and she had told Sandy how lucky she was. Sandy had agreed, but there had always been something about her ... something dissatisfied, restless, greedy. She had been unhappy in college, and Barbara had always suspected that she had gotten pregnant just so she could get married. Tom had been from a Main Line family in Philadelphia, but there had been a lot more to him than just that even then. And when Barbara had driven back to school, she had thought of them both with envy.

'Do you like it out here, Tom?'

'Pretty much, but I have to admit, I've stayed out here because of the kids for the last five years. And I've been practising here for so long, it would be hard to go back.' He was in film law, Barbara remembered, and this was of course the place to be, but he didn't look as though he loved LA. 'It gets pretty plastic here after a while.' He flashed a warning smile and looked no older than he had at his wedding. 'Watch out that it doesn't get you. It's addictive.'

'I know.' Her smile answered his. 'I'm already getting to like it.'

'Oh oh, bad sign.' And with that Barbara's salesgirl returned with the gift-wrapped scarf, and Eloise returned to Tom's side; she had decided that the three thousand dollar lizard tote bag didn't suit her.

'It was nice to see you again, Tom.' Barbara held out a hand. 'And say hello to Sandy for me, if you see her.'

'I do. I see Alex a couple of times a week and I see them both then.' Again the flash of pain in his eyes. He had been betrayed by his wife and a man he had thought was his friend. It was a scar that would never leave him. 'I'll tell her you said hello. You ought to give her a call, if you have time.' But Barbara hesitated. Married to Austin Weeks, why would Sandy want to see her?

'Tell her I'm at the Beverly Hills Hotel with Daphne Fields, if she'd like, she can call me. I don't want to intrude.' He nodded, and after a moment Barbara left, thinking how interesting and strange life was.

'Well, did you conquer Rodeo Drive?' Daphne was sprawled out on the couch reading the day's work when Barbara wandered in, and she looked like she had put in a hard day's work. 'How was it?'

'Super.' She had lingered on for another two and a half hours, wandering in and out of Jourdan, Van Cleef & Arpels, Bijan, and a host of other shops, and at last she had stopped at a restaurant for a sandwich. That had been a whole other show to observe, and she was delighted with her afternoon. She had even bought herself a bathing suit, a hat, and two sweaters. 'I love this place, Daff.'

Daphne grinned. 'I always thought you were crazy. What did you buy?'

She showed her, and then tossed the small Gucci box on to her lap. 'And that's for you, Madam Boss. I would have bought you the white mink bathrobe I saw at Giorgio's but it wasn't your size.' She grinned happily at her.

'Oh, shit. Couldn't you order it?'

They both laughed and Daphne opened the box and was touched and pleased. Red and black were her favourite colours.

'You didn't have to do that, silly.' She looked at her friend with warmth in her eyes. 'You spoil me in so many other ways, Barb. Without you I couldn't get a damn thing done.'

'Bullshit, you'd do fine without me.'

'I'm glad I don't have to.'

'How's it coming, by the way?'

'Pretty good. But it really is a whole new skill to learn. I feel so damn clumsy most of the time.'

'You won't after a while, and I bet it reads as smoothly as your other stuff.'

'I hope they think so at Comstock.'

'They will.' They were interrupted then by the telephone, and Barbara went into her own room to answer. Daphne had the hotel switchboard answer the phone when Barbara was out, and when she was there

194

she took the endless calls from realtors in her own room not to disturb Daphne. She picked up the phone and sat down on her bed. At least she had had one day off from looking at houses. But she wanted to find something soon. She knew it would be easier for Daphne to work in more homelike surroundings. 'Hello?'

'May I please speak to Barbara Jarvis?'

'This is she.' Out of habit she grabbed a pad and picked up a pencil.

'This is Tom Harrington.' She was surprised and her heart skipped a beat. Why would he call her? But it was silly to get excited. He was just the ex-husband of an old friend and he wanted to be friendly.

'It's nice to hear from you, Tom.' She wanted to ask him then what she could do for him. Maybe, like most other people who called, he wanted access to Daphne.

'Did you have a nice afternoon?'

'Very. I covered every inch of Rodeo Drive.'

'That's an expensive pastime.' He glanced at his chequebook lying on the bed next to him. Eloise had done a fair amount of damage, but she was no different from all the rest. There had been dozens of Eloises in his life in the past five years, and no one like Barbara, ever. 'What did you buy?'

Barbara looked embarrassed and wondered what he was leading up to. Why would he call her? 'Just some silly stuff. Nothing in your league.'

'That was a nice bag you were looking at, at Gucci.' Then he had noticed. His eyes had seemed to take everything in, and he had watched her for a long time before finally coming over to speak to her.

'I'm afraid it's not in my league. Just a little rich for my blood.' Besides what would she do with a black lizard bag like that? Carry her pencils and notepad in it?

'Tell your boss you want a raise.' She bridled silently. She didn't need to tell Daphne anything of the sort. Daphne already spoiled her rotten. 'Or find some nice man to buy it for you.'

'I'm afraid that's not my style.' She sounded suddenly cool.

'I didn't think it was.' His voice was deep and gentle. If he did, he wouldn't be calling. He had Eloise for that. But Barbara was different. 'We didn't get much of a chance to talk this afternoon. Did you ever marry?'

'No. I never did. My mother got sick when I finished Smith, and I spent a long time taking care of her.' She said it matter-of-factly, without regret. It was what had been.

'That must have been rough for you.' But there was admiration in his voice. Sandy would never have done anything like that, and he wasn't sure he would either. In fact he was sure he wouldn't. 'When did you start working for Daphne Fields?'

'About four years ago part time, and then eventually it worked into a full-time job.'

'Do you like it?'

'I love it. She's the best friend I've got and she's a dream to work for.'

'That's unusual for a successful woman.' He had seen his share and most of them weren't easy.

'Not Daphne. She's the most unassuming woman I've ever met. She just does her work, and quietly goes about her life, she's really an incredible human being.'

'That's nice for you.' He didn't sound overly interested in Daphne. 'Listen, we didn't get much of a chance to talk. How about a drink later on? I have to meet one of my partners for a quick dinner to discuss a couple of contracts. But I should be free by nine o'clock. I could meet you at the Polo Lounge if that's convenient for you . . .' His voice drifted off and he sounded somewhat nervous. He correctly sensed that Barbara was well guarded. 'How does that sound to you?'

At her end there was a long silence. She didn't really want to go out, and she suspected that his dinner date was probably the young redhead. But on the other hand, she had nothing to do, Daphne would be working and wouldn't need her, and he was a nice man. Without letting herself think about it anymore, she suddenly nodded. 'Okay. Why not?'

'I'll meet you in the Lounge at nine. If I'm going to be late, I'll call. Will you be in your room until then?' He somehow suspected she would.

'Yes, I want to order Daphne's dinner.'

'Doesn't she go out?' The image he had of writers was one of carousing and drinking and parties.

'Very seldom, and never when she's working. She's working on the screenplay now and she hasn't left the room since we got here.'

'That doesn't sound like much fun.'

'It's not. It's hard work. She really works harder than anyone I know.'

'She sounds like she's up for early sainthood.' He said it with a smile.

'In my book, yes.' It was a warning to him not to malign Daphne, at this or any later date. Barbara defended her like a priestess at the altar of her private god, whether it was reasonable or not, it was simply the way she felt about Daphne. 'I'll see you later, Tom.'

'I'm looking forward to it.' And as he showered and shaved before meeting his partner at his house in Bel-Air, he was amazed at how true that was. She was attractive, but she was not a spectacular beauty. She looked more interesting than sexy, more intelligent than pretty, and yet there was something very alluring about her, something solid, something real. She looked like the kind of woman you could talk to, and hold on to and count on and laugh with. Tom Harrington had never even known a woman like that, but they were qualities that had struck him in Barbara twenty years before, in sharp contrast to Sandy. Sandy had been a pretty little blonde debutante from New York, with dazzling blue eyes and a smile that knocked him on his ass. But she had been spoiled rotten by her parents, and later by him, and she had always let him down, especially at the last when she had run off with Austin. She had taken both kids, and called him two weeks later. He had thought of fighting her for custody for a while after they got divorced, but it would have torn the kids apart, and he didn't have the heart to. And since then there had been no one important in his life. He didn't know why, but he suddenly felt an irresistible pull towards Barbara. He had known the moment he saw her that afternoon that he wanted to see her again, even if only to talk to her.

'Daff, did you eat?' Barbara walked into her room and glanced at the tray and saw instantly that she hadn't. But Daphne was frowning at the typewriter as she clattered along, and she barely heard her. 'Daff... hey, kiddo, food.' Daphne looked up with a vague smile.

'Huh? Oh. Yeah, okay. Soon. I want to finish this scene.' And then, with a glance over her shoulder, 'You going out?'

'Just for a little while. Can I do anything for you before I go?'

'No, I'm fine. I'm sorry I'm not much fun.'

'I can take care of myself.' She started to tell her then about Tom, but Daphne was already typing. 'I'll see you later. And don't forget to eat.' But Daphne didn't answer. She was already miles away, working on the scene, and Barbara closed the door softly behind her.

22

Tom gave Barbara the name of his own real estate agent, and the first afternoon that she went out with him to look at houses in Bel-Air and Beverly Hills they found exactly what she needed, in Bel-Air. It was a beautiful little house on Cielo Drive, with three bedrooms that looked out on a huge well-manicured garden. The house and grounds were surrounded by a tall brick wall, overgrown by hedges and vines, so it didn't look like a prison, but it was entirely private. There was a vast expanse of lawn and a simple rectangular pool, a sauna, a hot tub, and the house itself was really lovely. The floors were a pale beige marble, there were huge white couches everywhere, a collection of very valuable modern art, and a kitchen straight out of *House & Garden*. And throughout the house was a feeling of sunshine and peace. There was a library panelled in whitewashed pine that looked out on the pool, which was a perfect place for Daphne to write. It had everything that they wanted. And although the price was high, it wasn't something that Comstock would cringe at. It belonged to a very respected actor and his wife who were in Italy on location for a movie.

Barbara stood looking around her with an ecstatic smile as the real estate agent watched. She opened every closet, every drawer, and checked out each room with great care for her employer. 'Well, what do you think, Miss Jarvis?'

'I think we'll move in tomorrow, if that's okay with you.'

They exchanged a smile. 'My clients will be pleased. They've been gone for a month.' It was a miracle that the place hadn't already been rented, but they had placed some fairly stringent restrictions on the kind of tenant they wanted. 'Do you think your employer will want to see it first?'

'I don't think so.' And as hard as Daphne was working, she would have been in such a haze that she wouldn't have noticed if Barbara had rented a grass shack. 'She's very busy.'

'Then why don't we go back to my office and sign the papers?'

Barbara signed the lease for a year an hour later, and she and Daphne moved in the next day.

That night Daphne wandered around the house, adjusting to the new surroundings. Sometimes it was difficult to work right away in a new place, and she was trying to get settled. She had unpacked all her things, and her typewriter was set up in the pretty little den. Everything was ready and waiting, but Barbara had gone out, and it suddenly occured to Daphne that she didn't know where she had gone. Lately she seemed to have gotten very independent in Los Angeles. She seemed to have blossomed since they had arrived, and Daphne was glad. Barbara's life had never been very exciting, and if she was happy here in LA, then Daphne was happy for her. But as she sat in the kitchen now, by herself, eating scrambled eggs and thinking about her screenplay, suddenly she felt lonelier than she had in a long time. All she could think of as she sat there was Andrew, the meals they had shared long ago in their apartment, the moments and the days before she had put him in the school. And then she thought of him at Howarth, and ached just to hold him, touch him, see him. As she thought of it a sob broke from her and she pushed away the plate of scrambled eggs. And feeling like a child herself, she laid her head down on the counter and cried, keening for Andrew.

She promised herself, by way of consolation, as she blew her nose at last that she would send for him at the earliest possible moment, but in the meantime she just

200

had to tough it out. It was even worse to think about what he might be feeling, and the terror that he might be sitting alone in his room crying too reduced her to tears again. There was almost a sense of panic, of desperation, that filled her, a fear that she had failed him, that in coming to California she might have done the wrong thing. And suddenly she knew she needed reassurance, someone to tell her that her baby was all right, and there was only one person who could do that. Matthew. And without even looking at the clock to see what time it was in the East, she hurried to the telephone on the kitchen wall. With trembling fingers she dialled the familiar number, praying that he was awake. She had to talk to someone. Now.

She had dialled Mrs Curtis's old private number, and a moment later a deep, husky voice answered and just hearing him, she felt less alone.

'Matt? It's Daphne Fields.' Her throat felt tight as she heard his voice and her eyes filled with tears again as she tried to control them. 'I hope it's not too late to call.'

He laughed softly into the phone. 'Are you kidding? I'm sitting here looking at another two or three hours of work on my desk. It's nice to hear your voice. How's California?'

'I wouldn't know. I haven't seen it yet. All I've seen is my hotel room and now my house. We moved in today. I want to give you my new number.' She did and he jotted it down as she regained her composure, and she tried to sound less upset than she was as she asked him how Andrew was doing.

'He's fine. He learned to ride a bike today, a two-wheeler, Mom. He can hardly wait to tell you. He was going to write you a letter tonight.' It all sounded so healthy and so normal and suddenly the flood of guilt she had felt began to ebb. But her voice was sad as she answered. 'I wish I'd been there.'

There was a moment's silence as Matthew listened, empathising with what he suspected that she felt.

'You will.' There was a moment's comfortable silence between them. 'Are you okay, Daff?'

'I think so ... yes.' And then she sighed. 'Just lonely as hell.'

'Writing is lonely work.'

'So is leaving your only son.' She sighed deeply then, but there were no more tears. 'How are things at Howarth?'

'Hectic for me, but I'm starting to catch up. I thought I had a good grip on things before I got here, but somehow there's always another ton of files you haven't read, or a child you have to talk to. We're making some minor changes, but nothing earthshaking yet. I'll keep you informed.'

'I'd like that, Matt.' He could hear how tired she was, and she reminded him of a little girl who's been sent far from home, and is desperately homesick.

There was a moment's pause then and he tried to visualise her so far away in California. 'What's your house like?'

She told him about it and he sounded impressed, particularly when he heard who it belonged to. Their conversation was distracting her a little from her pain. He was good at that too. He was sensitive and wise and strong. But, she still felt the familiar ache for Andrew. 'I sure do miss you all.' He was touched to be included.

'We miss you too, Daphne.' His voice was warm in her ear, and she felt a stirring in her soul, and as she sat in the silent kitchen at eight o'clock at night, she reached out to this man she had known for such a brief time, yet who had become her friend before she left.

'I miss talking to you, Matt.'

'I know ... somehow I expected to see you here last weekend.'

'I wish I could have been. This seems like a million miles from home, no matter how pretty it is.'

'You'll be home soon.' But suddenly the year ahead stretched before her like a lifetime. She had to fight back her tears as he went on. 'And think of what a great opportunity this is for you. We both have a lot of important new lessons ahead of us.'

'Yes, I guess so . . . how is it for you at Howarth?' Little by little they were regaining the ease they had discovered with each other during their talks at the school, and she felt a little less lonely. 'Is it what you expected?'

'So far it is. But I have to admit . . . I feel about as far from New York as you do in California.' He smiled then and stretched back in his chair. 'New Hampshire is awfully quiet.'

She laughed softly from her seat at the counter in the kitchen. 'Don't I know that well! When I first moved up there, when I put Andrew in the school, I used to get nervous just listening to the silence.'

'What did you do to get used to it?' He was smiling, remembering the look in her eyes, and feeling the miles evaporate between them.

'I kept a journal. It became like a constant friend. I think in a funny way that that's how I started writing. The journal became essays, and then I started writing short stories, and then I wrote the first book, and now' – she looked around the streamlined white kitchen – 'and now look what's happened, I'm out on the West Coast writing a movie I have no idea how to write. On second thoughts, maybe you'd better get used to the silence and let it go at that.'

They both laughed. 'Miss Fields, are you complaining?'

'No.' She thought it over with a soft smile. 'I think I'm actually whining. I was lonely as hell tonight when I called you.'

'There's no shame in that. I called my sister the other night and I was practically in tears. I had one of my nieces relay all my complaints to her, in hope of getting a little sympathy from Martha.'

'What did she say?'

'That I was an ungrateful bastard and that I was getting paid twice what I make at the New York School

203

and I should bloody well shut up and enjoy it.' He laughed at the memory of the words his niece had relayed over the phone. 'That's my sister. She's right, of course, but I was mad as hell anyway. I wanted sympathy and I got a kick in the ass. I guess I had it coming. That's the kind of stuff I used to say to her before we ran away to Mexico.'

'What was that like?' She didn't feel like working anymore. She just wanted to hear Matt's voice as she sat in the kitchen.

'Oh, God, Daphne, Mexico was the craziest thing I've ever done, and I loved it. We lived in Mexico City for a while. We spent three months in Puerto Vallarta, which was a sleepy little town then with cobblestone streets, where no one spoke English. Martha not only learned to lip-read, she learned to lip-read in Spanish.' His voice filled with admiration and love again at the memory.

'She must be an amazing woman.'

'Yeah' – his voice was soft – 'she is. She's a lot like you, you know. She's got guts and heart at the same time, it's a rare combination. Most people who have survived tough moments in life become tough themselves. She never did, and you didn't either.' It made her wonder again just how much he knew, how much more than she had told him. But he had already decided to confess to her. 'Mrs Obermeier told me about your friend up here. The one you referred to last time we talked.' Matt was afraid to say his name, as though he had no right to. 'He must have been a wonderful man.'

'He was,' she sighed softly and tried not to feel the pain of loss again, but it was hard not to. 'I was wondering tonight how different my life would be now if he were still alive, or if Jeff were. I suppose I wouldn't be out here, beating my brains out over my type-writer.'

'You wouldn't be half the person you are now, Daphne. That's all a part of you now. It's part of what makes you so special.' She wondered if he was right. 'I don't know if I'd say you were lucky exactly, but maybe in a funny way you are. You've had some damn tough things happen to you in your life, but you've beaten them into tools you can use, and beautiful parts of yourself. That's quite a victory.' She had never really thought of herself as victorious, just as surviving, but she also knew that in other people's eyes that was how it looked. She had won: she was successful. But there was more to life than that, as she knew only too well. Much more. Even though now she no longer had that. But whatever she did or didn't have in her life anymore, Matthew Dane made her feel better about life and herself every time she talked to him.

'You're a hell of a good friend, Matthew Dane. You make me want to run out and conquer the world again.'

'It's an awfully nice world out there to conquer.'

'Who taught Andrew to ride the bike?' But she already knew without asking.

'I did. I had some spare time this afternoon, and he had nothing much to do. I'd seen him watching some of the older kids the other day and I saw the look in his eyes, so we went out and gave it a try, and he did great.' She smiled at the vision he conjured up.

'Thank you, Matt.'

'He's my friend too, you know.'

'He's a lucky boy.'

'No, Daff.' His eyes were gentle and wise as he sat in his chair. 'He's not the lucky one, I am. Kids like Andrew make my life worth living.'

There didn't seem much else to say. 'I guess I ought to let you go. We both have work to do.' It was a comforting feeling for some reason, knowing that when she went to her desk, he would be sitting at his, both of them working into the night for the next few hours.

'Give my love to Andrew tomorrow, and a big kiss from me.'

'I will. And Daphne' – he faltered for a moment,

always unsure of just how much to say – 'I'm glad you called.'

'So am I.' He had made her feel warm and happy and as though she had a friend somewhere. 'I'll call again soon.'

They each said goodbye and afterwards she could still feel his presence beside her in the kitchen. She went to her desk, and looked down at her work, and then she walked into her bedroom, took off her clothes, slipped into a black bathing suit, and walked out to the pool. The warm water was delicious on her skin and she swam a few laps, thinking of Matthew. When she got out, she felt refreshed and went back to her desk after she changed her clothes. And half an hour later she was a thousand miles away again, lost in her screenplay. But in New Hampshire, Matthew Dane put aside his files and turned off the lights and sat staring into the fire, thinking of Daphne.

23

'What's she like, Barb?' Barbara and Tom lay stretched out beside his pool. It had been two weeks since they'd moved into the new house, and she had barely seen Daphne. She was deep in her work and hardly knew what happened around her. Barbara completed whatever tasks she had to, and every evening now she came over to see Tom. Both their lives had changed radically in two weeks, since they had become lovers. He held lightly to her hand now as they watched the sunset and lay beside his pool. He was always fascinated by stories of Daphne.

'She's hardworking, loving, compassionate, sad.'

'She must be. She's had enough rotten stuff happen to her in one lifetime to kill ten people.'

'But it hasn't killed her. That's the amazing thing about her. She's warmer and gentler and more open than anyone I know.'

'I don't believe that.' He shook his head and looked into Barbara's eyes.

'Why not? It's true.'

'Because no one is more warm or gentle than you.' As he said it she realised again how lucky she was. In truth, luckier than Daphne. She was silent for a moment as Tom watched her and then leaned over and kissed her tenderly. He had never been as happy in his life and he had watched Barbara open up before him in the past two weeks like a summer flower. She was laughing and happy and her eyes were more alive than they had been when he met her when she was in college. 'Look at you, love. You were hurting too. Nobody can be that alone and be happy. I wasn't even alone and I was miserable.'

'You didn't look all that miserable to me that day at Gucci.' She loved to tease him about that. Eloise had disappeared two weeks before, and was already reported to be living with a young actor.

But Barbara also knew now that he had been desperately lonely while he was married. It was hearing him tell her about that that had opened her heart and allowed her to trust him. He had been so badly hurt, much more so than she had been by the lawyer who'd gotten her pregnant years before. She had told him about that too, and he had held her in his arms while she cried, spilling the guilt and the sorrow she had felt for thirteen years and kept bottled up inside. And then she had admitted that what she really grieved over was that she was now too old to have children.

'Don't be ridiculous, how old are you?'

'Forty.' He was forty-two, and he looked at her with gentle determination.

'Women today are having babies at forty-five and forty-seven and fifty, for chrissake. Forty isn't even remarkable anymore. Is there any medical reason why you couldn't?'

'Not that I know of.' Except that she had always secretly wondered if the abortion had damaged her in some way and would keep her from having children. For years she had no longer wondered. It was obvious that it was irrelevant. But Tom didn't agree. 'It really is too late. It's ridiculous to have children at my age.'

'If you want them, it's ridiculous not to. My children have been the greatest joy in my life. Don't ever deprive yourself of that, Barbara.'

He had introduced her to Alexandra, and she could see why his children brought him such joy. She was a beautiful, happy, easygoing young girl, with Sandy's striking blonde looks and her father's gentle disposition. She hadn't yet met his son, Bob, but from all that she

208

heard, he was much like his father and she was sure that she would like him too.

For six weeks Barbara kept her life secret from Daphne. Then one morning Barbara came home and found Daphne sitting in the living room with an almost drunken grin.

'What's with you?'

'I did it!'

'Did what?'

'I finished the screenplay!' She was exploding with energy and pride, her eyes alight with excitement. She had a sense of accomplishment second to none, and the secret bonus of knowing that the sooner she finished her work, the sooner she would see her son.

'Hurray!' Barbara had given her a huge hug, and had opened a bottle of champagne. It was on their third glass that Daphne looked at her with her eyes full of mischief.

'Well, aren't you ever going to tell me?'

'Tell you what?' Barbara's mind went momentarily blank.

'About where you go every night while I work my ass off.' Daphne grinned and Barbara blushed furiously. 'And don't tell me that you've been going to the movies.'

'I've been meaning to say something, but...' She looked up, with a dreamy expression in her eyes, and Daphne groaned.

'Oh, God, I knew it. You're in love.' She wagged a finger at her. 'Just don't tell me you're getting married. At least not until we finish the movie.' Barbara's heart sank, Tom had mentioned marriage for the first time that night, and her answer had been much like Daphne's admonition. He had been hurt by her loyalty to her employer, but he had agreed to wait until the propitious moment.

'I'm not getting married, Daff. But I must admit ... I'm crazy about him.' She smiled broadly and looked about fourteen years old instead of forty.

'Am I ever going to meet him? Is he respectable? Will I approve?'

'Yes, to all three questions. He's wonderful and I love him madly, and . . . he married my roommate in college, and I ran into him at Gucci, with this incredibly beautiful stupid redhead, and . . .' It all came rushing out at last and Daphne laughed at her.

'My, I've been missing a lot, haven't I? What does he do? And please don't tell me he's an actor.' She wanted the very best for Barbara, and didn't want her to get hurt again. She suddenly frowned, worried, thinking about what Barbara had said about his marrying her roommate. 'Is he still married?'

'Of course not. He's divorced, and he's a lawyer. He's with Baxter, Shagley, Harrington, and Row.' And at that Daphne suddenly grinned.

'You know them?'

'So do you, dummy, or you should have. We haven't had to deal with them yet, but Iris said something about them before we left New York. They're Comstock's lawyers for our movie. Didn't he know?'

'He's been all wrapped up in a tax case for one of his clients.'

'What happened to his wife?'

'She ran off with Austin Weeks.'

'The actor?' Daphne looked momentarily stunned and then realised, as Barbara had two months before, that it was a foolish thing to ask. 'Never mind, that was a dumb question. Christ, that must have been a blow to your friend. Austin Weeks must be two hundred years old.'

'At least, but he's rich as the devil, and twice as good-looking.' Daphne nodded.

'What's your friend's name, by the way?'

'Tom Harrington.'

They exchanged a slow smile and Daphne looked pleased. 'I'm happy for you, Barb.' She lifted her glass of champagne to her friend and toasted her happiness with Tom. 'I hope you both live happily ever after . . .'

210

And then she grinned. 'But not until we finish the movie.' There was the same feverish light in her eyes Barbara had seen ever since they'd come to California. All she wanted to do was work at breakneck speed, get it over with and get home. But now that almost frightened Barbara. She was in no hurry to leave California.

She introduced Tom to Daphne the next day. They had drinks beside the pool, and Barbara could tell when they left that Daphne had liked him. The conversation had been relaxed and she kissed him on the cheek as they left and told him to take good care of Barbara. Daphne waved as they got into his car, and then walked slowly back to the pool and picked up their glasses. She was happy for Barbara. And Daphne had an odd feeling of watching precious people set sail for a long journey. She felt somehow left behind on a lonely shore.

That night as she made herself a sandwich for dinner she decided to call Matthew. As a result of her two months of nonstop work, she still didn't know a soul in LA and she called Matt from time to time. He was becoming an even dearer friend, and her only real contact with Andrew. But when she called tonight, he was out, and she wondered where he was. He had never been out before, and she suddenly wondered if he had met a woman. It felt as though everyone in the world had someone except her, and all she had was her little boy, and he was three thousand miles away in a school for the deaf. It was a desperately lonely feeling, and even the victory of having finished the screenplay did not subdue her pain as she went to bed immediately after dinner, and lay there fighting back tears, her whole soul longing for Andrew.

24

The people at Comstock Studios were overwhelmed by Daphne's screenplay. It was more powerful than the book, they told her, and everyone could hardly wait to start. The actors had long since been lined up, the sets had been built. In three weeks they were to begin, and after a round of congratulations Daphne went back to the house, feeling pleased with herself, and very excited. They had hired Justin Wakefield for the starring role, and even though she thought he might be a little too handsome, she was extremely impressed by his talent.

'Well, madam, how does it feel?' Barbara smiled at her as they got back to the house together and wandered inside.

'I don't know. I think I'm in shock. I really expected them to tell me they hated it.' She sat down on the white couch and looked around, feeling a little disoriented.

But Barbara smiled at her friend. 'You're crazy, Daff. You always think Harbor's going to hate your books too, and they always love them.'

'So I'm crazy.' She shrugged with a grin. 'Maybe I'm entitled.'

'What are you going to do with yourself for three weeks?' They wouldn't start shooting until then. Daphne was barely able to keep herself from her desk for three days, let alone three weeks, but Barbara suspected what she had in mind as Daphne smiled at her.

'Are you kidding? I'm going to call Matt tonight and have him put Andrew on a plane.'

'You don't want to fly back to New York?'

Daphne shook her head and glanced at the pool. 'I

212

think he'd love it here, and maybe it's time he saw a little bit more of the world than just Howarth.' Barbara nodded silent agreement, wondering what he was like, she had still never met him. And then Daphne looked up at her with a warm smile. 'Do you want to come to Disneyland with us?'

'I'd love it.' Tom had a business trip to New York coming up, and she was already lonely just thinking about it. It made her dread how she would feel when she eventually went back to New York at the end of the year. She still hadn't accepted his proposal, on the grounds that she couldn't leave Daphne. Not yet.

Half an hour later Daphne got up and went to the phone, and called Matthew Dane at Howarth.

'Hi, Matt. How are you?'

'I'm fine. How's the screenplay coming?'

'Terrific. I'm all finished, and I found out today that they loved it. We start in three weeks. They had just been waiting for me to finish.'

'You must be excited as hell.' He sounded genuinely pleased for her.

'I am. And I want to spend the next two or three weeks with Andrew. How soon do you think you can get him on a plane?'

At his end, Matt looked down at the appointment calendar on his desk with a thoughtful look. 'I can take him into Boston on Saturday if you'd like. Is that soon enough?'

She smiled at her end. 'No, but it'll do. I can hardly wait to see him.'

'I know.' He knew better than she suspected how lonely she had been. He could tell by how often she called him. And it always amazed him that a woman with her looks and her mind and her success should be alone. There should have been flocks of people at her door, especially men, but he also knew that she didn't want them. 'How's life otherwise, Daff?'

'What otherwise? All I've done is work since I got here. Now suddenly I've finished and all I do is sleep.

213

I went out in the world today for the first time, to go to Comstock, and it was like having been dropped on to a new planet.'

'Welcome to earth, Miss Fields. What are you and Andrew going to do while he's out there?'

'Go to Disneyland for starters.'

'Lucky kid.' Matthew smiled, knowing how Andrew would lord it over the others, but not in a nasty way, he wasn't that kind of child.

'I'll have to see after that. Maybe we'll just hang out here at the pool, although to tell you the truth, that kills me. I keep feeling I should be working every minute so I can get out of here faster.'

'Don't you ever stop and just enjoy things?'

'Not if I can help it. I'm not here to have a good time. I'm here to work.' Sometimes she sounded as though she were driven by demons, and he knew what they were. She was always pushing herself so she could see Andrew. 'Matt...' She suddenly sounded worried and pensive. 'Do you really think he'll be all right on the flight? I could fly back to get him if I had to.' But she had to admit that she was bone tired from two months of incessant work. But nonetheless she'd have done it for Andrew.

'He'll be fine. Let him be, Daff. Let him try his own wings. This is a big step for him.' But what if something happened? 'Trust him. And trust me. He'll be fine.' There was something so comforting about him that she believed him.

He called her back the next day to tell her when Andrew was arriving. He was flying nonstop from Boston to Los Angeles the next day and due to arrive at three in the afternoon. She wondered for a moment how she would get through another twenty-four hours. Suddenly she ached to put her arms around him again, every moment would be too long. Matthew smiled, 'You sound as antsy as he does.'

'I am.' And then her face grew serious again. 'Is he scared about making the trip alone?'

'Not at all. He thinks it's going to be exciting.'

214

Daphne sighed into the phone. 'I'm not sure I'm ready for this, even if he is.' For years he had been so protected, and now at Matthew's urging he would be trying his own wings, even for something so simple as a plane trip to California; it scared her.

'What are you afraid of, Daff? That he'll get to be independent?' His voice was gentle but it was a low blow and suddenly there was anger in the cornflower-blue eyes.

'How can you say that? You know that's what I want for him.'

'Then let him have it. Don't make him feel different all his life. He doesn't have to be, unless you make him that way.'

'Okay, okay, I've heard the speech before. I get the message.' Their long talks on the phone had brought them the kind of friendship that allowed her to get angry, and she had before, but never for long. And usually, Matthew was right.

'Daphne, he's going to feel proud of himself, and you'll feel proud too.' She knew it was true. 'But I know that doesn't make it easy at this end of the flight. Tomorrow at this time you'll both be glowing. Don't forget to call me when he arrives.' Now it was Matthew who sounded like the worried mother hen.

'I won't. We'll call you from the airport.'

'I'll do the same tomorrow from Boston.'

And the moment he did, there began a six-hour vigil for Daphne, watching the clock, sitting by the phone, terrified that something would go wrong, that something would happen to the plane, or worse, that up in the air Andrew would be unable to communicate with anyone around him, or some child on the plane would torment him as they had in the playground so long ago. It seemed terribly wrong that he should face the world again now, all alone, and yet perhaps it was fitting. Perhaps Matthew really was right and it was Andrew's battle, to win on his own, and he had a right to that victory by himself, without anyone else sharing the glory or taking it from him.

'You okay?' Barbara stuck her head into Daphne's study, and saw the tension in her face. 'Any news?'

'Only that he's on the plane. Nothing since then.'

Barbara nodded. 'Want some lunch?' But Daphne shook her head. She couldn't eat, all she could think of was Andrew, winging his way towards her from Boston. She was going to the airport to meet him alone, and Barbara would meet him at the house. They had arranged a little party for him, with paper hats and a cake and balloons and a sign that said, 'We love you, Andrew. Welcome to California.'

When it was time to leave for the airport, Daphne showered and slipped into beige linen slacks and a white silk shirt, sandals, and a white silk blazer that Barbara had bought for her on Rodeo Drive. It was the perfect size and looked beautiful now as she picked up her handbag and walked out the door as Barbara watched her. She turned once in the doorway, and their eyes met and held, and then with a smile she was gone, and Barbara marvelled at what she had seen. There was a love in the woman's eyes that Barbara envied, a love for a child who was a piece of her own soul, whatever his problems, hearing or deaf he was her little boy and she loved him with all of her heart, with everything she had to give him.

At the airport Daphne looked up at the big board that listed the arrivals and heaved a sigh of relief. The plane was on time, and she hurried to the gate. She had another half hour to wait there, she had come early 'just in case,' and she stood watching at the window, watching planes land and take off, and feeling the minutes tick by like aeons. And finally, ten minutes before he was due to arrive, she walked into a phone booth and called Matthew.

'Safely arrived?' There was a smile in his voice, but Daphne still sounded tense.

'The plane's not due in for another ten minutes. But I can't stand it. I had to call you.'

'The last stretch, eh? He'll be fine, Daphne. I promise.'

'I know he will. But suddenly I realise that it's been two and a half months since I've seen him. What if he's different? What if he hates me because I'm out here?' She was terrified of seeing her own son, but Matthew knew it was normal.

'He doesn't hate you, Daff. He loves you. He can hardly wait to see you. That's all he's been talking about for the last two days.'

'Are you sure?' She felt like a nervous wreck.

'Positive. Come on, kid, hang in there. He's almost there.' He looked at his watch, and in the airport she saw people gathering at the gate. 'Another five minutes.'

And suddenly she grinned then, feeling silly. 'I'm sorry I called you, I just got so nervous...'

'Listen, I'd feel the same way. Just relax. Tell you what, don't bother to call me till you get home. If I don't hear from you, I'll assume he arrived safely. But don't louse up your first minutes with him by rushing for a phone.'

'Okay.' And then suddenly she saw the plane, taxiing slowly towards them. Tears filled her eyes and she couldn't talk anymore. 'Oh, Matt ... I see the plane ... he's here ... goodbye.' She hung up and he smiled, feeling the emotions rise within him, too.

Daphne stood very still as the plane pulled up to the gate, and she clutched a railing with one hand as it stopped. And a moment later people began to pour from it, tired-looking businessmen with briefcases, grandmothers with canes, models with portfolios, and no sight of Andrew. She stood there, saying nothing, her eyes combing the crowd, and then suddenly she saw him. He was smiling and laughing, holding a stewardess's hand, and then suddenly he pointed at Daphne, and said almost clearly, 'That's my Mommy!' With tears streaming down her face Daphne ran towards him and swept him into her arms, closing her eyes tight and holding him, and then she pulled away so he could read her lips. 'I love you so much!' And he laughed with delight and hugged her again and when he pulled away he moved his lips and spoke.

'I love you too, Mom.'

He was enthralled by the limousine waiting for them at the kerb, and the sign they had made at home, and the pool and the cake. He told Barbara all about the flight, moving his lips carefully and speaking awkwardly but nonetheless so that she could understand him. After dinner they all went for a swim, and at last he went to bed, Daphne tucking him in, stroking his fair hair, and kissing him softly on the forehead as he drifted off to sleep, and tonight she watched him for a long time as he lay there near her once more. Andrew was home. It was all she could think of as she stood there, and it was a long time before she left the room, and found Barbara putting the cake away in the kitchen.

'You've got one hell of a terrific kid, Daff.'

'I know.' There was little she could say, whatever happened tonight seemed to bring tears to her eyes and they came again as she smiled at Barbara. Then she went into her office to call Matt, and when he answered, she spoke in a tremulous voice. 'He made it, Matt ... he made it!' She tried to tell him about the trip, but halfway through she began to cry, in great gulping sobs of relief that he understood as he waited.

'It's all right, Daff ... it's okay ... it's okay.' His voice was gentle and soothing from three thousand miles away, and it was like being held in his arms as her sobs subsided. 'He's going to make it from now on. There will be ups and downs in his life, but he's going to be just fine. You gave him what he needed, and that's the most beautiful thing you could give him.' But she knew that Matthew and the others had given him something too, something she could never have given him. And she had only had the wisdom to let them.

'Thank you.' He knew what she meant, and for the first time in years he felt his own eyes fill with tears, and it was only with the greatest effort that he managed not to tell her that he loved her.

25

The trip to Disneyland was a huge success, and Barbara and Daphne enjoyed it as much as Andrew. They spent another day going to Knotts Berry Farm, went to the La Brea Tar Pits one afternoon, and Comstock Studios for a tour, and every afternoon they swam at their pool. The two weeks of his visit went all too quickly, and it seemed only moments later that their last day had come, and they sat at the pool, signing quietly. His eyes were grave as he told her all the things he had liked best, and how much he liked Barbara. Daphne smiled, told him she liked him a lot too, and then was startled at his next question.

'Are you ever going to be like her, Mom?'

'What do you mean?' She signed the answer slowly. It had never occurred to her to be 'like' Barbara.

'You know, with somebody who loves you.' He had met Tom and liked him too, 'almost as much as Matthew,' he had signed, which was the highest form of praise from Andrew. But he had just brought up a very tough question. It dawned on her too that not so long before they would never have been able to have this conversation. He was able to express himself now with extraordinary depth, by signing, and he accurately lip-read almost every conversation. There were no longer locked doors between her and her child, they had all been unlocked by the people who loved him at Howarth. But as she thought of them for a moment, Andrew repeated the question.

'I don't know, Andrew. You don't just find someone. It's a rare and special thing.'

'But it happened to you before.'

'Yes, it did.' There was a wistfulness in her eyes he had never seen as she answered. 'With your Dad.'

'And John.' He was still faithful to the memory of his friend, and she nodded.

'Yes.'

'I'd like to have a Daddy like Matthew.'

'Would you?' She smiled gently, half sad, half amused. No matter how hard she tried, there was always something she wasn't giving him, something she couldn't do. Now it was giving him a Daddy. 'Don't you think you could be happy with just me?' It was a serious question, and she watched his eyes and his hands as he signed the answer.

'Yes. But look how happy Barbara is with Tom.' She chuckled then, he was almost nagging, but he had made his point, and it was a tough one.

'What they have is very special, Andrew. You don't fall in love every day. Sometimes that happens only once in a lifetime.'

'You work too much.' He looked annoyed. 'You never go out.' How could he be so young and know so much?

'That's because I want to finish my work so I can come home to you.' He seemed appeased by that, but when they went inside for lunch, Daphne was still thinking with amazement of what he had said. He was beginning to see her as she was, with her fears and her flaws as well as her virtues. He was growing up, more than just to take an airplane alone. He was doing his own thinking. And she was even more proud of him for that.

'Maybe I don't need a man like Barbara does.' She brought the subject up again herself after lunch, as though to convince him.

'Why not?'

'I have you.' She grinned at him over dessert.

'That's silly. I'm just your little boy.' He looked at her as though she were really dumb and she laughed.

'You drive a hard bargain, don't you?'

He looked confused at the signed words, and she said, 'Never mind. We'd better get ready or we'll miss your plane.'

And this time the parting was far from easy. Neither of them knew for sure when they would see each other again, and he clung to her with tears rolling down his cheeks as Daphne fought to retain her composure.

'I promise, you'll come back soon, sweetheart. And if I can, I'll come to New York for a few days.'

'But you'll be too busy with your movie.' It was a sad little garbled wail. He had been speaking a lot since he had been there.

'I'll try though, I'll really try. And you try too ... not to be sad, and to have a good time with your friends at school. Think of all the terrific stuff you have to tell them.' But neither of them was thinking of that as the stewardess led him to the plane. He was suddenly only a seven-and-a-half-year-old boy aching for his mother, and she felt the most vital part of her being, being torn from her heart once again. How often she had known that pain, and yet each time it came again it seemed like the first time.

Barbara said nothing as Daphne cried, staring blindly at the plane, she simply put an arm around her shoulders and held her close. They waved frantically as the plane pulled away but they never knew if he saw them. And the trip back to the house was silent and sombre. Daphne went to her room when she got home and this time she didn't call Matthew, he called her. He could hear instantly from her voice how she was feeling, and he knew she would, which was why he had called her.

'I bet you feel like shit, huh, Daff?'

She smiled through her tears and nodded. 'Yeah. It was harder this time than it's ever been. It's different when I leave him at the school.'

'Look at it this way, even that isn't forever. One of these days he'll be home with you for good.'

She blew her nose and took a deep breath. 'It's hard to imagine that day will come.'

222

'It will. It won't be long. And for the next couple of months you're going to be awfully busy with your movie.'

'I wish I'd never signed the damn contract. I should be in New York, near Andrew.' But they both knew that she didn't entirely believe it. It was in part a reaction to his leaving.

'Well, then hurry up and finish the damned thing so you can come home. I wouldn't mind that either. Hell, you're the only parent I can complain to.' She laughed into the phone and lay back on her bed.

'Christ, Matt, sometimes life is so tough.'

'You've been through worse.'

'Thanks for reminding me.' But she was still smiling.

'My pleasure. Anytime.' They had a comfortable banter between them, and she seemed to tell him about all of her problems, all of which either centred around work or Andrew, there was nothing much else to tell him. 'When do you start the movie?'

'Day after tomorrow. The actors have been having fittings for costumes, "wardrobing," they call it, for the last two weeks. But they don't really start filming for another two days. I don't have to be on the set until then. I'll probably have to rewrite scenes and just watch how it's going. From here on out I'm basically just an adviser. The directors and the actors do all the work now.'

'Have you met the actors yet?'

'Yeah, all except for Justin Wakefield. He was in South America on location, and I don't think he got in until a couple of days ago.'

'You'll have to tell me what he's like.' There was something new in his voice, but she didn't recognise it.

'Probably an asshole, I suspect. Anyone that good-looking has to be spoiled rotten.'

'Maybe not. He may be a very nice man.'

'Just so he does a decent job with the movie, that's really all I care about.' It was a story about a modern-day man who was part Apache, what it meant to him, and the responsibilities and problems and joys it carried through his entire lifetime, as he turned his back on what he was and then eventually embraced it. It was a story about manhood and self-acceptance, independent of racial themes. It was a powerful story, and it surprised everyone that a woman had written it. But if Justin Wakefield did it right, it could win him an Academy Award, and Daphne suspected he knew it. He was a spectacular blond hero, idolised by almost every woman in the country, and he would bring something to it that should make *Apache* a sure hit. 'At least we know he can act.'

'If you have a minute, call and tell me how it's going.'

'I will, and I want to know how Andrew is, no matter how busy I am. I should have a number at the studio where you can reach me. I'll call you as soon as I know what it is.' Eventually they would go on location in Wyoming, but that wouldn't be for several months. First they would shoot the local scenes.

'I'll call you later too, when Andrew gets in.'

'Thanks, Matt.' As usual, he had brought her comfort, and she felt less distraught at the departure of her son. 'Matt?'

'Yeah?'

'Who does this for you?'

'What?' He didn't understand.

'Comfort you. You're always there for me, it's not really fair.' He was the only person she had leaned on in years, and sometimes she felt guilty.

'You pay a price for the people you love in life, Daff. I don't need to tell you that.' She nodded silently at her end. He was right. And she had. 'I'll call you later.'

'Thanks.' They hung up then and she wondered what she had done before there had been Matthew.

26

The making of the movie *Apache* began on an indoor set
on Sound Stage A of Comstock Studios at five fifteen on
a Tuesday morning. It should have started on Monday
but didn't because the female lead, Maureen Adams,
had the flu. According to the production manager's
computations, the delay cost the studio several thousand
dollars, but that was calculated into the budget, and it
gave Justin Wakefield an extra day he needed to study
the script and confer with the director, in this case
Howard Stern, an old Hollywood pro, given to cigars
and cowboy boots and fits of bellowing at his actors, but
also a genius recognised by his peers, and known for
making brilliant films. Daphne had been immensely
pleased to learn that he was the director.

Daphne got up at three thirty that morning,
showered, dressed, made scrambled eggs for herself and
Barbara, and was ready to leave the house at quarter to
five. The limousine was waiting, and they arrived on the
set at exactly the appointed hour to find most of the crew
gathered there, and the director already smoking cigars
and eating donuts with the cameramen. Maureen
Adams was having her makeup done. Justin Wakefield
was nowhere to be seen. Daphne said good morning to
the studio men who had shown up just to make sure that
everything was going smoothly and was introduced to
the director, who stuffed his donut in his shirt pocket and
looked at her piercingly for a moment before holding out
his hand with a broad grin.

'Awful little, aren't you? But good-looking, damn
good-looking.' And then he bent towards her, whispering to her with a smile, 'You ought to be in the movie.'

'Oh, God, no!' She held up a hand in protest, laughing. He was an amazing-looking man, well into his sixties with a face full of lines, hard won, hard earned, and somehow his face looked better for them. He wasn't a handsome man, and had been even less so in his early years, but Daphne instantly liked him. And she sensed that he liked her.

'Excited about your first film, Miss Fields?' He waved towards two chairs and they sat down together, his enormous frame filling his chair, and hers looking almost childlike as she looked at him and smiled again.

'Yes, very excited, Mr Stern.'

'So am I. I liked your book. In fact, I liked it a great deal. It's going to make one hell of a movie. And I like your script.' And then with a noncommittal look, 'Justin Wakefield does too. Have you met him before?' He eyed Daphne, thinking his own thoughts.

'No, I haven't met him yet.'

He nodded slowly. 'Interesting man. Intelligent, for an actor. But don't forget that's what he is.' He looked her over appraisingly. 'They're all the same. I know from years of working with them. There's a piece missing from them all, and something extra added, something childlike and free and wonderful. They're hard to resist. But they're selfish and spoiled and egocentric. They don't give a damn how you are, most of them, they only care how they are. It'll shock you when you first see it, but if you watch them closely, you'll see a similarity of character. After a while it's all very clear. There are exceptions of course' – he named a few, names she had heard of and seen on the screen – 'but they're rare. The rest are . . .' He hesitated and smiled, as though he knew a secret she did not, but would learn soon. 'Well . . . they're actors. Remember that, Miss Fields, it will help you to keep your sanity in the next months. They'll drive you crazy, and me too. But in the end we'll have a remarkable picture, and it will all be worthwhile, we'll all hold hands and cry and kiss good-bye. And the fights will be forgotten, the jealousies, the feuds. We'll

226

remember the jokes, the laughs, the extraordinary moments. There's a kind of magic to all this ... ' He waved an arm, taking in the entire stage with a majestic sweep. And then he stood up, and bowed, and his eyes laughed into hers, and off he went to confer with his cameramen again. Daphne felt more than a little in awe of him and the entire scene, and she sat watching silently as grips and extras and wardrobe people and sound men and lighting engineers came and went, performing mysterious tasks, until at last at seven thirty there was a sudden stir, a heightened sense of tension all around them, and she correctly sensed that they were about to begin.

Almost at the very moment that the flurry of activity seemed greatest, she noticed a man leave a dressing room in a T-shirt and a parka, sneakers and no socks, his thick blond hair falling across his forehead in a boyish way. He sauntered towards her looking tentative and shy, and then eventually sat down in the chair Howard Stern had sat in long before. He glanced at Daphne, at the set, and then back to her, looking taut and nervous, and she smiled at him, knowing just how he felt and wondering who he was.

'Exciting, isn't it?' It was the only thing she could think of to say and he looked amused as she gazed into deep sea-green eyes. There was something familiar about him and she wasn't sure what.

'Yeah, I guess it is. I always get sick to my stomach just before we start. Occupational hazard, I guess.' He shrugged and reached into his pocket for a piece of candy, popped it into his mouth, and then with a look of embarrassment for being rude, dug into his pocket again and held one out to her.

'Thank you.' Their eyes met again and she felt a blush creep into her cheeks at his appraising glance.

'Are you an extra in this one?'

'No.' She shook her head, not quite sure what to say. She didn't want to tell him she wrote it, it sounded so pompous, and he didn't pry. He seemed too busy watching the preparations on the set, and then nervously he got up and walked away.

When he reappeared, he looked down at her with a boyish smile. 'Can I get you something to drink?' She was touched. Barbara had disappeared twenty minutes before in search of two cups of coffee. They had momentarily run out on the set, and she felt useless standing there. But now Daphne nodded.

'Sure. Thanks. I'd give my right arm for a cup of coffee.' The set was cool and draughty and she was tired.

'I'll bring you one. Cream and sugar?' She nodded and he reappeared a moment later carrying two large steaming mugs. Nothing had ever looked so good. She took hers and sipped it slowly, wondering when they would begin, and when she glanced at her benefactor he was looking at her again with those startling green eyes. 'You're beautiful, do you know that?' She blushed again and he smiled. 'And shy. I love women like that.' And then he rolled his eyes and laughed at himself. 'That's a dumb thing to say, it sounds like I audition them by the hundred every day.'

'Doesn't everyone here?' They both laughed this time and he seemed intrigued by her. He could see in her eyes that she was bright and quick, not the kind of woman you could fool, or would want to. He liked her and wondered again who she was.

'No, not everyone here does that. There are still some decent people in this town, even in this business ... maybe.' He smiled, sipped his hot coffee, and then set the mug down. 'I'm curious about you, miss. What are you doing on this set?'

It was time to tell the truth. 'I wrote the screenplay, but this is the first one I've done. So it's all new to me.'

At that he looked even more intrigued. 'Then you're Daphne Fields.' He seemed impressed. 'I've read all your books, and like this one best of all.'

'Thank you.' She looked pleased. 'And now I get to

228

ask the same question. What are you doing here?' But at that he threw back his head and laughed, a wondrous golden sound, and then he looked at her again, and with one hand swept the blond mane back from his face and smiled and suddenly she knew and she was stunned. He was every bit as beautiful as he had been in all his films, but he looked so different here, so out of place, so unassuming in his old parka and worn jeans. 'Oh, my God . . .'

'No, not quite.' They both laughed then. He knew she knew. He was Justin Wakefield. He held out a hand to shake hers, and as their hands met, their eyes held, there was a kind of magic to the man, a childlike glee, a magnetism in his eyes that held one spellbound for a moment before letting go. 'I am performing in your movie, madam. And I hope very much that you'll be pleased with my performance.'

'I'm sure I will.' She smiled at him now. 'I was so happy when you took the part.'

'So was I,' he admitted frankly. 'It's the best damn part I've had in years.' She beamed. 'You write like a demon.'

'You're not half bad yourself.' Her eyes said that she was teasing him, and a little voice inside her whispered that she was playing with America's favourite movie idol. It was a heady feeling sitting here beside him. And for some reason she couldn't explain, for the first time in a long time she felt like a woman, not a work horse or just a writer, or even Andrew's mother. But a woman. She had caught his attention, she sensed it in the way he talked to her. But it had been so long since she had related to a man, except to discuss Andrew with Matthew, that she wasn't sure what to say. Feeling nervous, she fell back on her work. It made her feel safe. And she didn't feel entirely safe with this man. He was watching her too closely and she was afraid she'd say too much. Maybe he would see the loneliness she always camouflaged so well, or the aching void left in her soul when John died.

'What do you think of the script?'

'I like it, very much in fact. Howard and I had a meeting about it yesterday. There's only one scene so far that doesn't work for me.'

'Which one?' She looked suddenly worried but his eyes were kind as he reached into her chair and took the copy of the script that Barbara had left there.

'Not to worry. It's a small scene.' He flipped the pages, and obviously knew the script well, and pointed to the part he hadn't liked. She glanced at it, nodded, and was frowning when she looked up at him again.

'You may be right. I wasn't sure about that myself.'

'Well, let's wait and see what Howard says. We're both going to be making a lot of changes and adjustments before we're through. Have you ever seen him work?' She shook her head and he laughed. 'You're in for a treat. And don't let the old bastard scare you. He has a heart of gold' – he smiled impishly at her – 'and a mouth full of nails. You'll get used to it after a while. We all do. And it's worth it, the man is an absolute genius. You'll learn something from him. I've worked with him twice before, and each time he gave me something different. You're lucky that he's directing *Apache*. We all are.' And then, his eyes seeming to caress her face, he whispered to her, 'But we're even luckier to have you.' And with a smile that seemed almost a kiss, he left her then, to go into his dressing room to change, and at that moment Barbara reappeared.

'I can't find any goddamn coffee.'

'Never mind. Someone else got me some.' But Daphne still looked vague. Justin Wakefield was the most extraordinary man, and she wasn't sure if she liked him or not. He was obviously bright, extremely playful, handsome as hell, amusing at times, but she found it impossible to decide if he was real. How could anyone that beautiful be real?

'You look like you've just seen a vision.'

'I think I have. I've been talking to Justin Wakefield.'

'What's he like?' Barbara sat down in the empty chair, trying not to look impressed, but she was. She had been dying to meet him and hadn't as yet noticed him on the set. 'Is he as gorgeous as he looks on the screen?'

Daphne laughed. 'I'm not sure. He's awfully handsome, but I didn't even recognise him when he sat down next to me.'

'How come?'

'He just looked like some kid. I guess I was expecting something different.' Daphne smiled at her secretary and friend.

'Are you telling me I'm going to be disappointed?' She looked crushed.

'I wouldn't say that.' Hardly, with those looks. And as she sat lost in her own thoughts about him she saw him emerge from his dressing room in the soft caramel-coloured skintight suede pants the early moments of the movie demanded, with a white turtleneck sweater, and he looked like a young, blond Marlon Brando, and Daphne heard Barbara catch her breath.

'Oh, my God, he's gorgeous!' Barbara whispered and Daphne smiled as she looked at him. He certainly was in that outfit. He was breathtaking as his muscles rippled while he walked towards them, his hair was smoothed back now as Daphne had seen it before in movies, and he looked like Justin Wakefield, the actor, not the impish boy who had offered her a mug of coffee on the set.

He walked straight towards Daphne and stopped beside her chair with a warm smile. 'Hello, Daphne.' His mouth seemed to caress her name.

'Hello.' Daphne smiled, trying to look more composed than she felt. 'I'd like you to meet my assistant, Barbara Jarvis. Barbara, this is Justin Wakefield.' He shook Barbara's hand with a warm smile, and then turned and saluted Daphne before going off to join Howard Stern and begin shooting, as Barbara sat gaping at him and Daphne leaned towards her with a grin. 'Close your mouth, Barb. You're drooling.'

'Jesus Christ. He's unbelievable looking.' She couldn't stop staring at him, and Daphne first looked at him and then at Barbara's reaction. He certainly had an effect on women. That much she was sure of, and she had to admit that she was feeling it herself. It was hard not to.

'Yes, he is. But there's more to life than being pretty.' She sounded very old and wise and Barbara laughed at her.

'Oh, yeah. Like what?'

'Like Tom Harrington, or do I need to remind you?' Barbara blushed as she grinned.

'All right, all right.'

'How's that going, by the way?'

Barbara sighed and looked dreamy for a moment. 'He's the most wonderful man, Daff. I love him, and I love his children.' But there seemed to be more she wasn't saying.

'So? What's the problem?'

'There is none.' Barbara smiled at her. 'I've never been happier in my life, except when I remind myself that one of these days we'll be going back to New York.'

'Not for a while, so enjoy it while you have it. Don't spoil your fun by worrying about six months from now, for heaven's sake. Things like this don't happen every day.' She smiled at her gently. For Barbara it had never happened before. At forty, she was deeply in love with the right man for the first time in her life.

'That's what Tom said right from the beginning. Something like this only happens once in a lifetime, so we'd better grab it while we've got it.'

Daphne looked distant and sad for a moment. 'Jeff said that to me once, right after we first met...' Her mind drifted off as she thought about her husband and then she looked back at Barbara. 'He was right. Other things come your way, and each moment, each experience, is different. Each one only happens once. And if you let the moment pass you by, it's gone forever.' She

232

had almost let that happen with John, and had always been grateful that she hadn't. And then she forced her mind from the past back to the present. 'Even this, Barb. Even this crazy movie we're making. There will never be a first movie for me again, there will never be another first time in California for you . . . we might as well enjoy it, because it's all pretty damn special. You never know what's just around the corner, or who.' And for some reason she looked at Justin Wakefield as she said it, and he turned as though he felt her eyes on him. He stopped what he was doing and looked straight at her, and she felt an almost involuntary reaction run up her spine. His gaze bored into hers and she felt herself held by his magnetic gaze.

The making of the movie began at nine fifteen, and by noon the first scene had been shot twice. Howard Stern had roared at the grips and called Justin a flaming asshole, Maureen Adams had burst into tears and insisted she was still sick, and the studio men had disappeared as Daphne and Barbara watched the whole production in fascination. The hairdresser assured them that all of this was normal, and when lunchtime was called, everyone seemed to be friends again. Howard Stern put an arm around Justin, told him he was pleased, and pinched Maureen Adams's behind as she walked past. She didn't seem to mind. She blew Howard a kiss and handed a tightly rolled joint to Justin before going to her dressing room to lie down. Daphne was standing alone by then. Barbara had gone to call Tom.

'Well, what do you think about your first morning?' Justin came directly towards her and stood in his full, extravagant beauty just before her in his tight suede pants. She tried not to let herself be overwhelmed by the attraction she felt for him.

'I am beginning to strongly suspect that you're all crazy.' She grinned at him, trying to look aloof but not succeeding. There was something so damnably beautiful about the man.

233

'I could have told you that much before. How did you like the scene?'

'It looked fine to me the first time.' She was sincere as she said it. It had looked fine to her.

'It wasn't. Howard was right. I had to get angry and I wasn't. We're going to try it again at the end of the day and we're going to start off this afternoon with the scene with Maureen in her apartment.' It was a nude scene for both of them and Daphne looked startled even though she had written it. But it came much later in the film and seemed as though it would be difficult to do right after the opening scene, totally out of context. 'Don't look so shocked, kid. You wrote it.' He seemed amused.

'I know. But how does that work out of context?'

'The whole shoot is out of context. We just do it scene by scene, according to some masterful and insane plan in Howard's head, and then later they cut it all up like spaghetti and splice it all together and somehow it works. It's a crazy business.' But it didn't seem to bother him much. And he looked as though he was more interested in Daphne than his work.

'You did a hell of a good job, you know, Daff.'

His eyes caressed her again.

'Thank you.'

'Can I interest you in some rotten commissary lunch?'

She started to tell him that she was going to have lunch with her assistant and then she realised that Barbara would probably die to sit near Justin Wakefield for an entire meal.

'Yes, if I can bring my assistant.'

'Sure. I'll go change my clothes. I'll be back in a minute.' He disappeared into his dressing room, still carrying the joint Maureen had given him and she felt herself wondering if he was going to smoke it now or later, as Barbara returned from calling Tom.

'I just made us a lunch date.' Daphne looked as though she had mischief up her sleeve.

'With whom?'

'With Justin. All right with you?'

Barbara gasped and Daphne laughed out loud. 'Are you kidding?'

'Nope.' And just as she said the word Justin strode out of his dressing room, dressed in his blue jeans and sneakers. He was still wearing makeup and had his hair combed back. This time Daphne would have recognised him, unlike their first meeting that morning, and he looked almost as handsome as he had in the white sweater and suede pants.

'Ready, ladies?' Daphne nodded and Barbara simply stared and they followed him to the enormous commissary building, where they found themselves with cowboys and Indians, two southern belles and a whole army of German soldiers, as well as two midgets and a flock of little boys.

Barbara looked around and started laughing. 'You know what? This looks like the circus!' And suddenly Justin and Daphne were laughing too. They ate hamburgers that tasted like rocks and the ketchup looked like red paint, and then Justin brought them both apple pie and coffee. And it seemed only moments later when they were back on the set, and Justin had disappeared into his dressing room.

Barbara pulled up a chair beside Daphne, and as they waited for the action to begin, Barbara found herself thinking about Justin. It was easy to discern that he was attracted to Daphne, but despite his good looks, Barbara didn't think she liked him. There was something childlike and self-centred about the man, and she had noticed that every time they passed a mirror or window in which he could see himself, he ran a hand over his hair, or looked himself in the eye. It annoyed her, but she also had the unmistakable feeling that Daphne liked him.

Before she could say anything to Daphne, Justin had emerged from his dressing room in a long white terry cloth hooded bathrobe and Swedish clogs. There was something beautiful and mysterious about him, and almost monklike beneath the white terry cloth hood, which he slipped off his head with a toss of the blond mane and a smile. And then a moment later he shed the terry cloth robe entirely and strode on to the set wearing nothing but his lean, long, beautifully muscled flesh and limbs. Maureen Adams followed him on to the set a moment later, and dropped a pink satin bathrobe on the edge of the set, walking around, holding the script, and running a hand through her hair. But it wasn't Maureen who held everyone's attention. It was Justin. Aside from his obvious physical beauty there was an incredible electricity and excitement about the man. Daphne tried not to look impressed, but it was so long since she had seen a man naked that she found herself spellbound by his raw beauty and the long athletic-looking limbs. 'I hate to say it,' Barbara confessed at last, 'but he really is absolutely incredible looking.' But when she glanced at her employer, Daphne hadn't heard her. She was staring at Justin in a way that made Barbara nervous. But who could blame her? He simply was what he was. Justin Wakefield, king of the screen.

The scene as he played it was spellbinding, and after a time both Barbara and Daphne forgot that he was naked. Daphne sat riveted as she watched the scene she had written come to life. He twisted it and moved it and wove it around him like a rich brocade cloth, covering his nakedness with his genius, and several times he even brought tears to her eyes. The scene was spellbinding for everyone who watched. The man was not only beautiful, he was masterful with his craft. And then, as deftly as he had shed it, he picked up the white terry cloth robe and put it around him again, covering his head with the hood and slowly turning towards Daphne. He looked older than he had at lunch, and very tired, and very open, and his wide green eyes found her as though he had to know what she thought more than any other.

'I loved it. It was exactly what I meant when I wrote it, only more so. It was as though you took what I had

236

in mind and you went deeper and farther.' He looked enormously pleased that she was so impressed.

'That's what I am supposed to do, Daphne.' He sounded kind and wise, and she liked what she saw in his eyes now. 'That's what acting is all about.' She nodded, still impressed with his performance. He had actually brought her book to life.

'Thank you.' It was going to be a sensational movie. And he was a sensational man. And she felt something tingle deep within her just from the thrill of having watched him.

27

For the next week Daphne watched Justin Wakefield in total fascination, spinning his web of magic around them. She and Barbara ate lunch with him every day in the commissary, and once or twice some of the others joined them, but it was rapidly becoming obvious that Justin Wakefield wanted to get close to Daphne. They talked about her books and his movies, her deeper intentions for some of the characters, her philosophies about the plot. They talked a great deal about *Apache*, and he insisted that what she told him helped him each day on the set, that it was she who made the difference, who brought something out of him that he didn't know was there before.

'It really is you, Daff.' They were sitting on the set and sharing a can of strawberry soda, a disgusting concoction they agreed, but the only thing the machine still had in it, and they were both dying of thirst. It was a hot day and they had already spent long hours on the set. 'I couldn't do this without you here. It's my best performance. Ask Howard, he'll tell you. I've never been able to dredge up this much before, not day after day like this.' He looked at her then with those intense huge green eyes of his. 'I mean it. You do something wonderful to me, Daphne.' She wasn't quite sure what to say.

'You're doing something wonderful to my book.'

'Is that all?' He looked disappointed, as though he had wanted her to say something more. But he didn't know Daphne, how cautious she was, how high the walls were built around her. And then he surprised her. 'Tell me something about your little boy.' It was as though he

238

sensed that in talking about her son, perhaps she would let some of her guard down. And he wasn't wrong. She smiled, and thought of Andrew, so damnably far away.

'He's wonderful, and bright, and very special. He's about this tall' – she held up a hand to indicate his height and Justin smiled – 'and I took him to Disneyland a few weeks ago when he was here.'

'Where is he the rest of the time? With his dad?' He thought it unusual for a woman like Daphne to give up custody of her son, and his voice showed his surprise.

'No. His dad died before he was born.' It was easier to say that these days. 'He's in New Hampshire, in school.'

Justin nodded as though that made sense, and then he looked into Daphne's eyes again. 'You were alone when he was born?'

'Yes.' Something pulled at her gut as she said it, a lonely memory she had fled long ago.

'That must have been rough on you.'

'It was, and...' She didn't really want to tell him, about discovering that Andrew was deaf, and those ghastly lonely years. 'That was a pretty tough time.'

'Were you writing then?' It was the first time Justin had asked her questions about herself. They had talked about *Apache* and her other books, and his movies, all week.

'No, I didn't start writing until later. Until Andrew went away to school.'

'Yeah. I'll bet it's tough to be creative with kids around. You were smart to send him away to school.' Something pulled taut in her gut as he said that. He couldn't possibly know what she felt for the child or what it had been like to tear herself away from Andrew. And his comment reflected a selfishness that she abhorred.

'I sent him away to school because I had to.'

'Because you were alone?'

'For other reasons.' Something told her not to share the reasons with him. She still had a deep need to protect

Andrew. And she suddenly had the sense that Justin wouldn't understand. Maybe he wouldn't even try to, and she didn't want to find that out. 'I had no choice.' She suddenly felt very tired and old. What did this man know about that kind of heartbreak? 'You don't have children, Justin?'

'No. I never felt the need for that kind of extension of myself. I think that's an ego trip for most people.'

'Children?' She looked shocked.

'Yes, don't look so shocked. Most people want to see themselves reproduced and continued. I have my movies for that. I don't need to make kids.' It was an odd way to look at it, she thought, but maybe for him it made sense. She tried to understand his viewpoint. He wasn't an insensitive man, after all. He couldn't be, not the way he'd been living out *Apache* for the last week. And if he had different views from hers, she would listen. She at least owed him that.

'Have you ever been married?' She was curious about him now. Who was he? What made him the way he was, so able to interpret someone else's feelings, as he had hers in her book?

He shook his head. 'Not legally, at least. I've lived with two women. One for seven years, one for five. In a way, that was really no different from being married. We just didn't have the papers. It doesn't make much difference in the end. When someone wants out, they go, papers or no, and I wound up supporting them both after they left.' She nodded. After all, that was what she had had with John. But she suspected that eventually they would have got married. They might even have had children, although John had had no great need for children either. He had just wanted her. And Andrew, of course.

'Are you living with someone now?' She felt rude for probing, but they already knew so much about each other now. They had almost lived together, fifteen hours a day for the past week. It began to feel like being on a

240

desert island or a ship, thrown together in an intimate way.

But again Justin shook his head. 'I haven't lived with anyone for a while. I've been involved with someone on and off for the past year, but it's mostly off, she doesn't understand the rigours of this business, and God knows she should. She's an actress, but she's a twenty-two-year-old kid from Ohio, and she just doesn't understand where I'm at.'

'And where's that? Or am I prying?' Daphne's voice was cautious but he smiled, he didn't mind the questions, he liked them. He liked her, and he wanted her to know what he was about.

'You're not prying, Daff. By the time we finish this movie, we'll all know each other inside out.' He hesitated for a moment, thinking of her question. 'I don't know how to explain it to you, but I just don't want to tie myself down anymore to someone who doesn't understand this business. It's exhausting having to defend yourself all the time. She's insanely jealous, and I can't answer to anyone night and day. I need space. I need time to think about what I'm doing, where I'm going, what I am and think and feel. I'm better off alone than with someone who stifles that.' It was easy to agree with what he was saying and Daphne nodded, and then he laughed and shook his head. 'Loosely translated, I think that means "she doesn't understand me." You've heard that before?'

'Yup.' She took a drag on their shared soda and laughed. 'I have. I think that may be why I stay alone too. It would be damn hard to explain to anyone why I work eighteen hours a day, then crawl into bed at six in the morning feeling like I've been beaten. It gives me sustenance, but it's not likely it would do the same for someone else. I wouldn't have it any other way. Yet no sane man would put up with that.'

'I doubt it.' He smiled, feeling a certain kinship with her. 'Except someone with the same habits. Sometimes

I read all night, until the sun comes up. It's a great feeling.'

'Yes, it is.' She smiled too. 'I love that. You know, maybe one gets to a point in life when it's better to be alone. I didn't used to think that, but I do now. It works for me anyway.' She handed him the soda and he finished it and set it down.

'I don't think I agree with that. I don't want to be alone forever, but I don't want to be with the wrong person. I think I've finally gotten to the point where I'd rather be alone than with the wrong woman. Yet I still believe, must believe, that there's someone out there who would meet my needs and make me happy. I just haven't found her yet.'

Daphne saluted him with the empty can. 'Good luck.'

'You think it's impossible to find?' He was surprised. Certainly her writing didn't suggest that. She seemed to believe in love and happy unions. Yet she had a clear understanding of unhappiness and loss.

'I don't think it's impossible, Justin. I found it twice.'

'And? What happened?'

'They both died.'

'That's a bitch.' He looked sympathetic.

'Yes, it is. And I don't think you get more than two chances like that.'

'So you've given up?'

They were in the mood to be honest, so she was. 'More or less. I've had everything I wanted, now I have my work and my son. That's enough.'

'Is it really?'

'It is for me. For now. It has been for a long time. And I have no desire to change it.' That was not entirely the truth. There were times when she longed for someone to hold her, but she was too desperately afraid of an eventual loss.

'I don't believe you.' He was searching her eyes but not finding the answers he wanted.

242

'What don't you believe?'

'That you're happy like that.'

'I am. Most of the time. No one is happy all the time, not even if you're madly in love.'

'You can't be happy alone forever, Daff. It's not healthy. You lose touch with life.'

'Have I? Is that what you read in my books?'

'I read a lot of sorrow in those books, a lot of sadness, a lot of loneliness. Some part of you is crying out.'

She laughed softly then. 'You sound just like a man, Justin, unable to believe that a woman can survive alone. You told me that you're happy by yourself, why shouldn't I be?'

'For me, it's temporary.' He was being honest.

'For me, it's not.'

'You're crazy.' The whole idea annoyed him. She was a beautiful, vibrant, intelligent woman. What the hell was she doing, determined to be alone for the rest of her life? 'The whole thing is nuts.' And it was also a challenge. He couldn't stand thinking of what she had done to her life.

'Don't let it upset you. I'm perfectly happy.'

'It just pisses me off to think of you wasting your life. You're beautiful, dammit, Daphne, and warm and loving, and you have a brilliant mind. Why have you shut yourself off?'

'I'm sorry I told you.' But she didn't look particularly upset and she wasn't. She had accepted her life. And she was relatively happy.

And with that, Howard Stern called them all back to the set for another six hours of work, and when they left the set that day, Justin had to meet a friend for a drink, and Daphne left with Barbara without seeing him again. They went back to the house, and Daphne took a shower and then went out to swim in the pool in the balmy night air, and Barbara came out to tell her that she was going to see Tom.

'And I might be home later and I might not.'

243

'Good for you.' Daphne smiled as she floated in the pool. 'Say hi to Tom for me.'

'I will. And don't forget to eat dinner, you look bushed.'

'I am. But I'll grab something to eat before I go to bed.' And she wanted to call Matthew that night before it got too late. With their strange hours on the set and the time difference between California and New Hampshire, it was getting harder and harder to call. 'Have a good time, Barb!'

'Thanks, I will!' She called it over her shoulder as she left, and Daphne floated in the pool for a while before wrapping herself in a towel, and wandering into the kitchen to take something out of the refrigerator before she made her call. She dropped the towel on the counter after a minute, and stood in a tiny red bikini, dripping water on the kitchen floor. And just as she reached for the phone to call Matthew she heard the front doorbell ring, and wondered who it was. She wondered if Barbara had come back for something and had forgotten her key.

Daphne walked out to the front hallway, and tried to glimpse through a side window to see who it was. But whoever it was had his back turned and was standing too close to the front door for her to see him. She could only see part of one shoulder, so she stood at the front door and asked who it was.

'It's me. Justin. Can I come in?'

She opened the door in surprise and stood there looking at him. He was wearing white Levi jeans and a white shirt and sandals, and his golden tan looked darker at night as he stood there looking boyish as he smiled. 'Hi. How did you find me?'

'The studio gave me your address, is that okay?'

'What's up?' She never heard from him after hours and she was more than a little surprised. She was also tired and hungry and wet, and these were her off-hours, and she felt the need to have some solitude.

'Can I come in?'

244

'Sure. Do you want something to drink? Wait a sec, I'll go put something on.' She was suddenly conscious of wearing only the red bikini and it made her uncomfortable in front of him.

'You don't have to, you know. You've seen me in less.' He grinned at her boyishly and she laughed.

'That was different. That was business. This isn't.'

'Some business we're in, where you take all your clothes off to go to work.'

'I can think of others like it.'

He liked her sense of humour. 'Are you suggesting that acting is like prostitution?'

'Sometimes.' She said it over her shoulder as she disappeared into her bedroom and he resisted an urge to follow her.

'You happen to be right.'

When she returned she was wearing a bright blue caftan the same colour as her eyes, and she had combed her hair and put on sandals. He looked at her approvingly and nodded.

'You look lovely, Daff.'

'Thanks. Now what can I do for you? I'm pooped. I was about to eat dinner and go to bed.'

'That's what I figured and it sounds deadly. I was on my way to a party and thought you might want to join me. At Tony Tree's. You might like it.' Tony Tree had won five Grammies in five years, and he was easily the biggest singer in the country. Any other time she might have been intrigued enough to meet him, but not tonight.

'Sounds like fun, but honest, I just can't.'

'Why not?'

'Because I'm exhausted. Christ, you worked your ass off all day today. Aren't you tired?'

'No. I love my work, so I don't get tired.'

'I love my work too but it still knocks me out.' She smiled at him then, not wanting to sound harsh. 'I'd fall asleep on my feet.'

'That's okay. They'd just think you were stoned.

You'd fit right in.' She laughed at his quick answer and resisted an impulse to rumple his perfectly combed blond hair.

'Don't be stubborn. I'm pooped. You want a sandwich before you go? I'm going to make one for myself. I don't have any strawberry soda, but I might be able to find you a beer.'

'That sounds good. Where's Barbara?'

'Out with friends.' She handed him a beer from the icebox, and started to make herself a sandwich. Justin hopped up on a stool in the kitchen and watched her. He could see her naked silhouette through the caftan and he liked what he saw. He had liked the bikini better, but this would have to do.

'You mean Barbara actually goes out?'

'Yes. Believe it or not, she's human too.' The two had decided several days before that they didn't like each other. Barbara thought that underneath the charm he was a heartless bastard, and Justin thought she was an aging vestal virgin. 'You're like an old schoolmarm,' he had finally told her after she'd planted herself once too often between himself and Daphne. She sensed how vulnerable Daphne was to his charm, though Daphne denied it. Barbara saw something ugly in him, which Daphne did not.

'Does Barbara have a boyfriend?' Justin pretended surprise, speaking in the same bantering tone he always used with her now.

'Yes, a very nice one in fact.' She hopped up on a stool across the counter from him. Maybe it wasn't so bad that he had dropped by after all. It was pleasant to have company while she ate her sandwich, even though it meant that by the time he left, it would be too late to give Matthew a call. 'Her friend is an attorney.'

'That figures. Probably tax law.'

'Film law, I think.'

'Oh, Jesus. He probably wears a business suit and gold chains.'

'Come on, Justin. Be nice.'

246

'Why? I think she's an uptight bitch. I don't like her.'

'She's a wonderful woman and you don't know her.'

'I don't want to.'

'It's entirely mutual, which is no secret. And I think you're both behaving like children.'

'She hates me.' He sounded plaintive and Daphne smiled.

'She doesn't hate you. She disapproves of you, and she doesn't really know you. She was very badly hurt a long time ago and it made her suspicious of men.'

'You can say that again.' He had sensed her distrust of him, and it annoyed him. 'I can't offer her a cup of coffee without her getting on my back.' Daphne knew all about it, and she had already told Barbara to cool it. They didn't need feuds on the set. 'Anyway, I'm glad you're alone. She protects you like the Vatican Guard whenever I'm around.'

'She's possessive, that's all. We've been through a lot together.'

'She acts like she thinks she's your mother.'

Daphne smiled. 'Sometimes I could use one.' She had had so much on her shoulders, alone, for such a long time, and Barbara was the only person in aeons that had eased at least some of the burdens.

As she spoke he slid off the stool and came around the counter. He stood in front of her and took her face in his hands. 'Daphne. You're a beautiful, desirable woman and I want you.' She felt a wave of shock run through her and at the same time a long forgotten hunger between her legs.

'Justin, don't be foolish.' Her voice was soft and scared.

'I'm not foolish.' He looked hurt. 'I've fallen for you like a ton of bricks, and you're playing this stupid game, hiding behind your walls. Why? Why won't you let me love you, Daff?' His eyes almost misted over and hers were huge in her face.

'Justin, please ... we have to work together ... it would be a terrible mistake to – '

'To what? To fall in love? Is that what you're afraid of? Why? We're two strong, intelligent, talented people. I can't think of a better combination. I've never met anyone like you, and you've probably never known anyone like me. Why would you pass that up? Who's keeping track of how hard you are on yourself? In the end you'll wake up one day an old woman and it'll be all over, and you can tell yourself that you've been faithful to the memory of two dead men. Why, Daphne ... why?' And then he leaned towards her and kissed her, covering her mouth with his own and forcing her lips open with his tongue until he probed inside her and she felt her breath quicken as he folded her in his arms. And then breathlessly she pulled away and stood up. She was tiny beside him, but she looked at him with imploring eyes.

'Justin, please ... don't ...'

'I want you, Daff. And I'm not going to let you run away from this. I can't believe you don't feel anything for me. We understand each other too well. I understand every word you ever wrote, and I can see from the way you watch me work that you feel my work in your gut too.'

'What difference does that make?' She was still half angry, half frightened. He had shown up on her doorstep, kissed her, and now was trying to turn her life upside down. She wouldn't let him. It was dangerous. They were making a movie together, that was all. She didn't want to let her guard down. 'What do you want out of me for chrissake? A quick lay? An affair for six months? There are ten million starlets in this town, Justin. Go fuck one.' Her eyes filled with tears and she turned away. 'And leave me the hell alone.'

'Is that what you want?'

She nodded, her back still turned.

'All right. But think over what I said. I don't just want a quick piece of ass, Daff. I can get that anytime I want, anywhere I want. But I can't have another woman like

248

you. There is no one else like you. I know. I've looked around.'

She turned to face him then. 'Then keep looking. You'll find one.'

'No, I won't.' His eyes looked sad. He had finally found what he wanted, but she didn't want him. It wasn't fair, and he wanted her right there in her kitchen, but he wouldn't push her. He knew that that way he'd lose her forever. Maybe if he waited, there was a chance. 'I want you to think over what I've said to you tonight, Daphne. We'll talk about it again.'

'No, we won't.' She walked towards the front door with long strides and pulled it open for him. 'Good night, Justin. I'll see you tomorrow on the set and I don't want to discuss this. Ever. Is that clear?'

'You don't make all the rules, Daphne. Not for me.' His eyes blazed at her for an instant and then the boyish twinkle shone through the anger.

Daphne was not going to be swayed. 'I make my own rules. And you can either respect them or stay away from me. Because I won't deal with you at all if you won't respect how I feel.'

'What you feel is all wrong.'

'You can't tell me that. I've made my own choices in life, and I live by them. I made up my mind a long time ago.'

'And you were wrong.' He brushed her lips again with his then and he left, and as she shut the door behind him she leaned against it, her whole body trembling. And the most terrifying thing of all was that she believed in what she had told him, had for years, and yet her body had cried out for him each time he kissed her. But she didn't want to hurt again and love again and lose again. She wouldn't do it, no matter what he told her. But as she walked back into the kitchen she looked at where they had been sitting, and she felt her whole body begin to tremble again at the memory of his kiss, and with a moan of anguish she took his empty beer bottle and threw it against the wall.

28

'How was the party last night?' Daphne tried to look casual as they sat at the empty table at the commissary. Everyone else had finished early and gone back to the set and they were suddenly left alone. But Justin's eyes looked haunted as they met hers.

'I didn't go.'

'Oh. That's too bad.' She tried to change the subject. 'I thought the scene went pretty well today.'

'I didn't.' He pushed away his plate and looked at her. 'I couldn't think straight. You drove me nuts last night.' She didn't tell him that she had also lain awake half the night, fighting what she was feeling, and wondering if he would call. She had insanely mixed emotions about him, and it was the vehemence of them that upset her most. She didn't want to feel any of what she was feeling. She had never wanted to feel any of it ever again. 'How can you do this to us?' He looked like a small boy robbed of Christmas, but she put down her sandwich and glared at him.

'I'm not doing anything to "us," Justin. There is no "us," for chrissake. Don't create something that will only make life more complicated for both of us in the end.'

'What the hell are you talking about? What's so complicated? You're available, I'm searching. So what's your problem, lady? I'll tell you what it is.' He was speaking to her in a hoarse whisper and she hoped that no one overheard, but there was plenty of activity around them, and no one seemed to be watching, much to her relief. 'Your problem is that you're too fucking scared to let yourself feel again. You've got no balls left. You must have had them once, because I can see it in

250

your books. But now suddenly you don't have the courage to come out from behind your walls and be a woman. And you know what? It's going to show up in your writing sooner or later if you don't watch out. You can't lead the life you do and expect to remain human. You won't. Maybe you already aren't. Maybe I'm just in love with an illusion ... a fiction ... a dream ...'

'You don't even know me. How can you be in love with me?'

'You think I don't see you? You think I don't hear you in your books? You think I don't understand *Apache*? What do you think I'm doing up there every day? I'm living out the whispers of your soul. Baby, I know you. Oh, yes, I know you. It's you who don't know yourself. You don't want to. You don't want to remember who you are, or what you are, that you're a woman, and a damn fine one, with real needs, and a heart and a soul, and even a body, that's just as hungry for mine as mine is for yours. But at least I'm honest. I know what I want and who I am, and I'm not afraid to go after it. Thank God for that.' And with that he stood up and walked away from the table, slammed the door to the commissary, and stalked back to the set. And as Daphne followed him a few minutes later she had to smile to herself. Not many women in the country had the guts to turn down Justin Wakefield. It was funny and sad all at the same time.

She watched him work on the same scene over and over and over again that afternoon and evening and well into that night. Howard Stern was shouting at everyone; he even had her make several changes in the scene to see if it would work. But the problem was not with her writing, it was with Justin's mood. She could tell that he was desperately unhappy, and it was as though he wanted the whole world to know it.

And at last, at ten o'clock that night, seventeen hours after they'd all shown up for work that morning, Howard Stern threw down his hat with disgust. 'I don't know what's wrong with you bastards today, but this whole day has been shot. Wakefield, get over your snivelling moods and long face. I want everyone back here at five o'clock tomorrow morning, and whatever the problem is, you'd better fucking work it out.' It was the last they heard from him before he left, and Justin slammed into his dressing room without giving Daphne a second glance. But he made sure to walk directly past her, so that she could see how rotten he felt.

She walked silently back to the limo with Barbara and lay back against the seat with an exhausted sigh.

'Nice day, huh?' Barbara smiled as they wended their way home, but Daphne wasn't in the mood to talk. She was thinking about Justin, and wondering if she was wrong.

The next day was scarcely better, only this time she and Justin didn't speak at all. Howard let them off the set that night at seven thirty. He said he'd had enough of all of them to last him for a year.

But the next day it was as though there was magic in the air. When Justin arrived on the set, there was something hungry and angry and soulful burning in his eyes, and he tore everyone's guts out with his performance. At the end of a four-hour stretch with scarcely any retakes, Howard rushed over and kissed him on both cheeks, and the whole crew gave a cheer. For whatever reason, Justin had revived, and Daphne felt less guilty as she strolled over to the commissary for lunch. She was surprised when he sat down at her table, and she looked at him with a shy smile.

'You did a beautiful job today, Justin.' She didn't ask what had changed his mood, but whatever it was, she was glad it had happened.

'I had to. I felt I owed it to Howard. I was making everyone pay for what I felt.'

She nodded, looking first at her plate and then at him. 'I'm sorry I upset you.'

'So am I. But I happen to think you're worth it.' She wanted to cry as he said it. She had been hoping that he'd given up. 'But if this is the way you want it, Daff,

I guess I'll have just to accept it. May I be your friend?'
He said it with such humility and tenderness that tears
filled her eyes and she reached for his hand and held it
in one of her own.

'You already are my friend, Justin. And I know I'm
not easy to understand, but a lot of very painful things
have happened in my life. I can't help that. Just accept
me as I am. It will be easier for both of us.'

'That's hard for me to do, but I'll try.'

'Thank you.'

'I can't stop what I feel, though.' She still felt that he
didn't know her, and it made her unhappy that he was
being so tenacious, but maybe that was just the way he
was, and if they were truly going to be friends, then she
had to accept him, too.

'I'll try to respect that.'

'And I'll respect you.' And then he chuckled and
whispered, 'But I still think you're crazy.' She laughed
at the look on his face then and she couldn't help telling
him of what she had thought the other day.

'Do you realise that I'm probably the only woman in
America who would keep you out of her bed?'

'You want a presidential award for it?' He looked
amused and she laughed.

'Are you giving one out?'

'Hell, why not, if it'll make you happy.' And then they
went back to talking about the making of the movie, but
that night he showed up on her doorstep with a plaque
he'd had made by the guys in the prop room. It was a
bronze plaque, carefully mounted, and exquisitely
engraved. It was a presidential award to Miss Daphne
Fields, for bravery above and beyond the call of duty, in
keeping Justin Wakefield out of her bed. She roared with
laughter when she saw it, kissed him on the cheek, and
invited him in for a beer.

'You wanted a plaque, so I took you at your word.'

She propped it up on the kitchen counter and handed
him a glass and a beer. 'Have you eaten?'

'I had a hamburger after work. How about a swim in

253

your pool?' It was already eight o'clock, but it was a beautiful night and Daphne was tempted.

'Can I trust you?'

'What? Not to pee in your pool?' For a man of his age he was more like a boy than an adult, but she liked that about him. It was refreshing at times, and sometimes it drove her crazy.

'You know what I mean, Wakefield.' She looked at him sternly.

'Yes, I do, Fields.' He returned the look with mock grimness. And then he laughed. 'Yes, you can trust me. Christ, you're a twit, Daff. You put a hell of a lot of effort into stifling your feelings. Is anything worth that much trouble?'

'Yes.' She smiled at him. 'I think so.'

'Well, no one can say you're easy. At least I can't.' And then with a sad, lonely look on his face, 'Or is it just me?'

'Oh, Justin' – she didn't want him to believe that – 'of course not, you dummy. I've just lived this way for a long time, and I'm happy like this. I don't want to change that.'

'I got the message.'

'I got the plaque.' She smiled at him gently, and then waved towards her bedroom. 'I'll go put my bathing suit on.' She put on a modest navy blue bikini, and when she came out, he was already in the pool.

'The water is fabulous.' He dove deeper into the pool and she could vaguely glimpse that he had a white suit on, and she dove in neatly, and met him at the bottom of the pool. It was then that she realised that the white suit was only the small strip of flesh on his buttocks devoid of suntan, and when they came to the surface she looked at him in disapproval.

'Justin, it's about your suit...'

'I don't like to wear one. Do you mind?'

'Do I have a choice?'

'No.' He grinned happily and dove again, tickling her feet as he went, and then he came up like a dolphin and

254

he grabbed her and pulled her down with him. She resisted, pulling against him. He playfully pulled back. For ten minutes they played the game until finally Justin slowed down.

'Do you always have this much energy after work?'

'Only when I'm happy.'

'You know, for a grown man you act like a little kid.'

'Thank you.' No one would have guessed that he was over forty, but Daphne had to admit that in his company she felt younger too. 'You know, you look great in a bikini, Daff. But you'd look better without one.'

'Don't be a pest.' She swam a few laps then and slowly climbed the ladder and got out of the pool. And as she wrapped herself in a towel she turned her back, having noticed that he was getting out of the pool too. 'There's a towel on the chair.'

'Thanks.' But when she turned around, he hadn't used it. Instead, he stood before her in all his dripping naked beauty with the moonlight above them and a sky filled with stars. They said not a word for an endless moment, and he took one step forward and took her in his arms. He kissed her with all the gentleness of his childlike soul, and he held her, and she felt him tremble as she did, not sure if it was from desire or the cold. And for reasons she couldn't explain to herself as she stood there, she let him hold her, and felt her mouth respond to his as they kissed. It seemed hours before he turned away from her, and wrapped himself tightly in the towel she had provided, hoping to quell the ardour that had sprung to him. 'I'm sorry, Daff.' It was the voice of a small boy as he stood with his back turned to her, and she wasn't quite sure what to say. She had wanted him very badly for a moment, and she touched his back gently with her hand.

'Justin ... it's all right ... I ...' He turned to face her then and their eyes met.

'I want you, Daphne. I know you don't want to hear it. But I love you.'

'You're crazy. You're a wild, crazy boy in the body of a man.' And once again she remembered Howard's warning ... remember that actors are children. And Justin was. Or was he? He didn't look like one now as he took a step towards her and held her face in his hands.

'I love you. Can you really not believe that?'

'I don't want to believe it.'

'Why not?'

'Because if I do believe it' – she hesitated, her whole body trembling in the warm air – 'and I let myself love you too ... one day we'll get hurt and I don't want that.'

'I won't hurt you. Ever. I swear that.'

She sighed and leaned her head against his naked chest as he folded her into his arms. 'That's something no one can promise.'

'I'm not going to die like the others, Daff. You can't be afraid of that forever.'

'I'm not. I'm just afraid of losing what I love ... of hurting and getting hurt ...'

He pulled her away from him then and looked into her eyes so she could see his, just as she did with Andrew when she wanted him to read her lips.

'You won't get hurt, Daff. Trust me.' She wanted to ask him why but she could no longer fight it, the words didn't sound right anymore. Not even to her. She let him kiss her and hold her, and a little while later he carried her into her bedroom, and they lay on her bed and made love until dawn. They got up together the next morning, and he made her coffee and toast and they stood in the shower, kissing and laughing, and Daphne could no longer remember why she had fought so hard and so long to stay alone.

And when Barbara came home from Tom's at five o'clock to go to the studio with Daphne, there was shock in her eyes when she found Justin in the kitchen in his white jeans and bare feet.

'Have a good night, Barb?' His eyes locked into hers

as they stood there. She had a wild instinct to protect Daphne from him, but she knew it was too late for that now.

'Yes, very, thanks.' But her eyes said all that she thought and he understood her.

And at five fifteen they all got into Daphne's limo and rode to the studio. Justin put in a brilliant performance, and when everyone went to lunch, they snuck into his dressing room and made love until two o'clock in the afternoon, when everyone came back to the set to work on the movie.

29

Working on a movie set is like being trapped in an elevator for an entire summer, and there can be no secrets from the others. Within a week everyone on the set knew that Daphne and Justin were lovers, and only Howard dared to make comment, one morning over coffee and donuts.

'Don't say I didn't warn you. They're all children. Spoiled children.' But Daphne was already under Justin's spell.

He sent her flowers on the set, baked her cookies at midnight in her kitchen, bought her countless small, thoughtful gifts, and made love to her whenever and wherever they could. At night they lay beside her pool, and he recited love poems to her that he had learned as a child, and told her funny stories about the making of other movies that made her laugh until she cried.

The movie itself was going beautifully, well ahead of schedule, much to Howard's delight, and there were few problems on the set. Daphne had learned more about making a film in the last three weeks than she had hoped to in the entire year.

'And when we finish this one, my love, we'll make another, and another ... and another... We're an unbeatable team, kid.' And she was inclined to agree. The only trouble with their affair was that she knew that Barbara didn't like him and it was causing tension between them that was a constant strain. Barbara tried not to say anything about it, but it was obvious in all that she didn't say. At night, at Tom's place, she would talk to him about it and he would try to calm her, but it was useless.

'She's a grown woman, Barb. And she has decent judgement. You've said so yourself. Why not just stay out of it? We have our life, let her have hers.'

'Her judgement happens to stink in this instance. The guy is out to use her, Tom, I know it.'

'No, you don't, you suspect it. You have no evidence of that.'

'Stop sounding like a lawyer.'

'Then stop sounding like her mother.' He tried to kiss her into silence, but he couldn't quell her fears. She was terrified that Justin was using Daphne. There was something that made her not trust him and she was never quite sure what it was. He had all but moved in with Daphne, and he was constantly with her, at the set, in the house, out to dinner, at parties. It was a new life for Daphne and she seemed to enjoy it, but there still wasn't total bliss in her eyes. The years before had left their mark. And she was unhappy that she didn't have enough contact with Andrew. She still wrote to him every day, but there seemed to be no break scheduled in the shooting, when she could go back to see him, or have him come out to her. And there were long gaps between her phone calls to Matthew at the school. She never seemed to have enough time to call now. It seemed as though every time she told Justin she was going to call, he would distract her with a kiss, or a caress or a problem.

Finally one night Matthew caught her at home. 'Has Hollywood won your heart, Miss Fields, or are you just too busy to call?' She had felt guilty when he had called her, and for a moment she feared that something had happened to her son.

'Is Andrew all right?' Her heart was pounding but he put her mind quickly to rest.

'He's fine. But I have to admit that I was getting lonely. How's the movie coming?'

'Fine. Terrific, in fact.' But he also heard something else in her voice and he wasn't sure what it was. There was a distance between them that hadn't been there before, and he found himself anxious about what it was. Maybe it was just the movie, but he didn't really think so. And then the second time he had called her, Justin had answered the phone.

'What school?' Justin sounded vague. He was reading the next day's lines, and Daphne was in the tub. 'Ho – what?'

'Howarth. She'll know.' He was desperately sorry he had called her.

'Oh.' Justin suddenly remembered. 'Her kid. Well, she can't come to the phone. She's in the bathtub.' Matthew inwardly cringed. So that was the reason for her distance and her silence. There was a man in her life. It grieved him, but he hoped that at least he was a nice man. She deserved someone wonderful because she was wonderful. 'Should I give her a message?'

'Please tell her that her son is fine.'

'I will.' He hung up and looked at his watch then. It was eleven thirty in New Hampshire. It was a hell of a strange time for them to call. He wandered into the bathroom and told Daphne that someone had called her from her kid's school. 'He said to tell you that your son is fine.' And then he looked at her strangely. 'It's awfully late for him to call. Who is that?'

'Matthew Dane. The director.' But there was a look of regret in her eyes, as though she were sorry Justin had answered the phone. And suddenly he laughed at her and sat on the edge of the tub.

'Don't tell me that my little vestal virgin had an affair with the headmaster at her kid's school.' The idea seemed to amuse him and she looked annoyed.

'No, I won't tell you that, Justin, because it's not true. We happen to be friends.'

'What kind of friends?'

'Talking friends. Like you and I would have been if you had had any sense.' Her voice softened. 'He's a nice man and he's been a big help to Andrew.'

'Oh, Christ, all those guys in boarding school are

260

fruits, Daff. Don't you know that? He's probably in love with your kid's ass.'

There was suddenly fury in her eyes as she looked at him. 'That's a disgusting thing to say, and you don't know anything about this. This is a special school, and the people there are absolutely wonderful to those children.'

'I'll bet they are.' He did not look convinced, and then he glanced at her with an unspoken question. 'What do you mean it's a "special" school? Does he have some kind of a problem?' He remembered suddenly her saying that she had had to leave Andrew there, that she had no choice. A feeling of horror swept over him as he wondered if her son was retarded and she was watching his eyes, as though measuring how much she could trust him. There was a long pause and she nodded.

'Yes, he does. Andrew was born deaf. He's in a school for the deaf in New Hampshire.'

'Jesus Christ. You never told me that.'

'I don't usually talk about it.' She looked sad as she sat in the tub.

'Why not, Daff?'

'Because it's my business and no one else's.' She looked almost defiant as she sat there.

'That must be a bitch having a deaf kid.'

'It isn't,' and as she watched his eyes she knew that he didn't understand, but if he cared about her, he would learn to. 'He's a wonderful child, and he's learning all the things he needs to know to function in a normal world.'

'That's nice.' But he didn't seem to want to know more about it. He bent to kiss her, and then walked back into their bedroom to continue reading his lines.

Daphne got out of the tub, dried herself off, and went to call Matthew from the den. When he answered, he apologised profusely for having called.

'Don't be silly, Matt. I would have called myself, but I've been so damn busy.' She didn't explain Justin and she wasn't sure how to, but it was embarrassing to have him find out that he had been there. And Justin had told her that he had said she was in the tub, which she didn't consider an appropriate way of handling her phone calls. What if the press called? But Justin didn't seem to worry particularly about that. He was a lot more accustomed to their harassment than she was, and a lot less worried about his reputation. He already had tarnished that years before. 'How's Andrew?'

'He's fine.' Matthew gave her all the latest news, but there was a strange awkwardness between them, and the conversation gave neither of them what they had shared before. She wondered if she had talked to him so much because she was lonely, and she felt suddenly guilty for using him to fill her empty nights on the West Coast. And now there was Justin and things were different, but she felt a sense of loss when she hung up.

'Did you call your friend?' Justin teased her when she came back to the bedroom.

'Yes. Andrew's fine.' And her eyes told him not to pursue the subject further, and he very wisely did not. Instead he gently unravelled the towel she held around her, and ran a hand slowly up her leg and drifted it to her inner thigh. He pulled her gently towards him then, and they both forgot about her phone call as he pulled her slowly on top of his hungry body and they became one. But after they had made love, and he had gone to sleep, snoring softly beside her, she lay there and thought of Matthew.

30

The making of *Apache* moved relentlessly on for the next two months, with no break in sight, and at last Howard gave them all four days off to rest.

'Hallelujah, baby!' Justin was thrilled. 'Let's go to Mexico for a few days.' But Daphne had other plans.

'I can't. I have to see Andrew. I haven't seen him in almost three months.'

'Andrew? Oh, for chrissake. The kid can wait. Can't he?' Daphne looked shocked.

'No, he can't. I wanted him to come out here.' Her voice was both hurt and hard. Nothing was going to come between her and Andrew. Not even Justin. And by now she expected him to take an interest in her son, but he didn't. There were some things that mattered to him not at all, and children were one of them. He had no interest in anyone's kids, not even hers. And yet their loving was lavish and there were times when they would talk into the wee hours and she felt certain that she was in love. But she had the feeling sometimes that he was only in love with part of her, and there were other parts that he didn't know at all. Most especially Andrew, who was the major part of her life. 'Justin, what do you think? Would you like to meet him?' Maybe if she made him part of her plans he would begin to respond.

'Maybe. But to tell you the truth, babe, I need the rest and in my experience, kids aren't very restful.' He sounded neither apologetic or enthused. And she herself wasn't sure if it was wise to fly Andrew out. It was a big trip for four days. In the end she called Matt and asked him what he thought.

'Honestly, Daff. I think that's a long way for him to

come just for four days. For any kid his age.' Daphne had thought the same thing. She had just wanted him to meet Justin, but maybe it was too soon. Maybe neither he nor Justin was ready. Maybe it would be best to let Justin go his own way for the four days. They could live without each other for four days, and she could have Andrew to herself. The prospect of that didn't displease her, but she was still disappointed in Justin.

'I think you're right, Matt. I'll fly to New York and drive up.'

'That's dumb.' She was stunned. She hadn't seen him in almost three months. But he instantly understood her silence and laughed. 'I don't mean flying East. I mean flying to New York and driving up. Fly to Boston, and I'll pick you up.'

'I can't do that to you. You've got enough to do up there without chauffeuring me around.'

'And you've been working almost nonstop for the last five months. Can't I do a favour for a friend?' She had to admit that it would make life easier for her, but it didn't seem fair. Matthew was always thinking about her. 'I'm serious. It's no trouble at all.' She knew it was, but the offer touched her.

'Then I accept.' She checked the schedule she had got from the airline in advance, told him what flight she'd be on the next day, and went into the bedroom to pack. She was suddenly excited to see them both, and she could hardly wait to get her hands on Andrew again. She was smiling from ear to ear when she went into the bedroom, and Justin looked at her with his sexy boyish grin.

'You're really crazy about that kid, aren't you, Daff?'

'Yes, I am.' She sat down on the bed next to him and planted a soft kiss in the palm of his hand before looking up. 'I'd like you to meet him too.'

'One of these days,' and then after a pause, 'Can he talk?'

She nodded. 'Yes. Not always clearly, but most of the

time.' There was an expression in Justin's eyes that troubled her, but somehow she had to ask. 'Are you afraid of that? Of dealing with a deaf child, I mean?'

'Not afraid. I'm just not much into kids, normal or abnormal, I guess.'

'He's not abnormal. He's deaf.'

'Same thing.' She wanted to lash out at him then, but she restrained herself.

'I'm going to have him come out in the fall, when we finish the film. You'll meet him then.'

'That sounds fine.' Because it was three months off? She didn't like his reactions about her child, but there were so many other things about him she did like. And once he knew Andrew, she suspected that his reluctance would be overcome. Andrew was hard to resist, deaf or not.

'What are you going to do while I'm gone?' They all needed the rest, he most of all, and she looked at him with a warm smile.

'I don't know. I wanted to go to Mexico with you.' He touched the inside of her thigh. 'Sure I can't change your mind?' She smiled. He really didn't understand, and she shook her head.

'Nope, not a chance. Not even like that.'

'He must be some kid.'

'He is.'

'Well, tell him I'm crazy about his mom.'

'I will.' But she knew she wouldn't tell him about Justin yet. He wouldn't understand that. And in Andrew's eyes she belonged to him, always had and always would. 'Are you going to stay here, love?'

'I don't know. Maybe I'll go to San Francisco for a few days to stay with friends.'

'Well, let me know where you are, so I can call.' They hadn't been apart for a day or an hour in almost three months, and suddenly the thought of being so far away from him made her feel sad. 'I'm going to miss you, sir.'

'I'll miss you too, Daff.' He took her in his arms then

and they made love until almost dawn, and then she got a few hours' sleep before she had to get up and catch her plane.

Daphne went to the airport alone in the limousine, Barbara was with Tom and there was no reason for her to go, and Justin said he had things to do. Everyone in the cast and crew was using each precious hour of the four days. She boarded the plane at ten o'clock, and expected to arrive in Boston at seven o'clock in the evening, East Coast time.

The plane came in on schedule, and Daphne was among the first off, looking around for Matthew. She didn't see him at first, but then she spotted him standing twenty feet away, his dark eyes combing the crowd. Suddenly their eyes met and held, and she felt a strange little tug at her heart, which she didn't understand. In six short months he had become her friend, mostly over the phone, but she suddenly realised how happy she was to see him. A warm smile lit his eyes, and he walked slowly towards her.

'Hello, Daff. How was the flight?'

'Too long.' And then, without knowing why, she reached up and hugged him. 'Thanks for coming, Matt.' There was a moment of awkwardness between them.

'You look great.' He also noticed that she looked very thin. She'd been working too hard and it showed, but she also looked very happy. There was a smile in her eyes, and something more. Something that troubled him now. There was something different about her than there had been, more womanly perhaps, more overtly sexy. And his thoughts went at once to the male voice that had answered the phone. He tried to force it from his mind, but he couldn't as they went to pick up her luggage. 'What have you been doing out there, other than work?' She looked prettier than ever, and something inside him wanted to know why, even though he knew he had no right to. And as she looked at him she smiled, realising how isolated he was in New Hampshire, and how totally wrapped up in his work. There had been a number of

266

items about her and Justin in the paper, but he had apparently seen not a one. Knowing Matthew as well as she did, she knew he wasn't being facetious.

She smiled again as he picked up her bag. Her eyes teased him gently and he stopped and looked down into her face. 'You're looking awfully serious, Matt.' She didn't want to explain to him about Justin.

'I'm just happy to see you, Daff . . . I'm not quite sure what to say . . .' Her eyes gently touched his face and she nodded.

'Tell me about Andrew.' She felt the questions in his eyes, and she didn't want to answer them. Her life in California was totally separate from this. This was a different life for her. A life she shared with her son. The world of Justin Wakefield seemed ten thousand miles away, and in a way this felt like coming home. She had come home alone, and she wanted to enjoy it.

As they left the airport and made their way north, Matthew told her about the changes at the school, the two new people they had hired, the field trips they'd made, and the camping trip they were all going on in July. She desperately wished that she could be there.

She sighed as she sat beside him in the car. 'I feel like I've been there forever, Matt.' He wanted to tell her that he felt that way too, but it didn't seem right.

'How much longer do you think it will be?'

'I wish I knew. Three more months, maybe six. It's been going pretty smoothly till now. But everyone tells me that you have to expect it to stretch out. Howard doesn't like that to happen, no one does, but it can't be helped, and I guess that sooner or later there will be some kind of problem. I'll be home by Christmas for sure.'

He nodded, disappointment in his eyes. 'I'll be ready to leave by then. The new director from London is scheduled to take over on January first.'

'You don't think you'll stay, Matt?' She looked sad as she asked.

'No. Howarth is a wonderful place, but I want to get

267

back to the New York School' – he grinned at her then – 'I'm not sure I'm cut out for country life. Sometimes I think I'll go nuts up there.'

She laughed and watched his face. It was such a strong, handsome face, so different from Justin's golden beauty, but Matt had a beauty of his own, a kind of rugged, solid quality about him that made him more man than idol. 'I know what you mean. When I stayed up there for a year, there were times when I even missed the dirt and the noise of New York...' She thought of John then and her eyes grew vague.

'Well, I'll tell you.' He flashed his smile at her. 'I miss the resources we have for the kids in New York. The museums, the ballet...' His voice drifted off. 'My crazy sister.'

'How is she?'

'Martha? She's fine. The twins turned fifteen last week and they both got stereos for their birthdays. She says she's finally truly grateful that she's deaf. She can feel the furniture tremble when they play them and Jack says he's going nuts.' Daphne smiled, wishing it was a problem she would one day have with Andrew. 'I still want you to meet her when you have time.' They both silently wondered when that would be. For the moment it seemed like never.

He told her then that Mrs Curtis sometimes visited the school, she was well and always asked to be remembered to Daphne.

'I wish I had time to see her this time, but all I have is four days.' He felt his heart sink again.

The drive seemed to speed by as they talked and shortly after nine o'clock they reached the school. She knew that Andrew would be in bed, but she wanted to see him, just to cast her eyes on his face, kiss his cheek, touch his hair. She hurried inside, and ran upstairs. He was sound asleep in his bed, and she stood for a long time in his room, looking over him in his bed. It was a long time before she noticed Matt standing in the doorway. She smiled and bent to kiss Andrew's cheek. He stirred but didn't wake, and she went downstairs, with Matthew behind her.

'He looks so good. I think he's grown.'

'He has. And you should see him ride the bike you sent him.' She smiled and looked up at Matt.

'I feel like I'm missing so much.'

'It won't be long, Daff...' Their eyes met and held, and suddenly Justin Wakefield no longer seemed real. He seemed part of a distant dream. It was Matthew who seemed real now as he stood before her.

And suddenly in spite of all the promises he'd made himself, Matthew looked at her with searching eyes, and had to ask. 'There's someone important in your life out there, Daphne, isn't there?' She hesitated as he felt his heart pound and then, slowly she nodded.

'Yes. There is.'

A little child in him wanted to cry, but nothing showed in his eyes except concern for her. 'I'm glad for you. You needed that.'

'I guess I did.' But she wanted to tell him then about her concerns about Justin and Andrew. What if Justin couldn't accept a nonhearing child? But she was afraid to ask. Somehow it seemed out of place to ask him. And then she looked into Matthew's eyes again. 'It doesn't change anything here, Matt.' He wondered what that meant, but only nodded and opened the door to the little sitting room he had inherited from Mrs Curtis.

'Do you have time for a cup of coffee, or do you want me to drive you to the inn now?'

'No. I'm wide awake.' She glanced at her watch with a smile. 'It's only seven o'clock for me.' It was ten o'clock at night in New Hampshire though, and the school was very quiet, everyone had gone to bed. 'I'd love a cup of coffee with you. It's nice not to be just talking to you on the phone.' He smiled at her as he poured her a cup from his constantly brewing pot, and he wondered how serious the affair in California was, and if he was a good man. He hoped so, he hoped that very much, more than she would ever know. He handed her the cup of coffee and they sat down. He kept searching her face for unspoken answers.

She told him then about the making of the movie, the scenes they had already shot, the parts that remained to be made when they went back. 'I think next month we'll be going up to Wyoming.' The location they had chosen was Jackson Hole, a place Matthew had always longed to see.

'I envy you that.' He spoke with a slow, easy smile, his long legs stretched towards the fire. 'I hear it's a beautiful place.'

'So they tell me.' But she wasn't thinking of the movie as they talked, or even of Justin. She wondered if perhaps it was because now she was so close to Andrew. It was a relief not to be three thousand miles away, but right there, just beneath his bedroom. But maybe it wasn't Andrew at all. It was odd how Matthew pushed him from her head, she didn't really understand it, but there was a quality about this man that enveloped her with a sense of safety and well-being and comfort, and a kind of warmth that lulled her. She didn't feel tense or tired or overworked, she just felt peaceful and happy as they sat by the fire. Maybe that was why now she felt so content, and so happy. 'What about you, Matt? Will you get away this summer at all?'

'I doubt it. I may join Martha and Jack and the girls for a few days at Lake George. But I'm not sure I can get away from here.' He smiled ruefully at her, brushing back a lock of dark hair. 'I'm not even sure I want to. I always worry when I leave the kids. Mrs Curtis said she'd cover for me for a few days if I want to get away, but I don't want to impose on her.'

'You should. You need the rest too.' She noticed then that his eyes were more tired than when she'd left, and there were fresh lines that hadn't been there before. He looked young, but responsible and mature. It was something she liked about him. He didn't have the smooth, perfect beauty of Justin, but sometimes, constantly staring into that exquisite face grew tiresome. It

270

was staggering how gorgeous the man could look day after day. His physical appearance was like a country without rain or snow, only brilliant sunshine all the time. 'It's hard to believe that you've already been here for six months, Matt.' Harder still to believe all the things that had happened in her life since then.

But Matthew was laughing softly. 'Sometimes it feels more like six years.'

She laughed too. 'That's how I feel after fourteen hours on the set.'

'How's Barbara holding up?' They hadn't met, but he felt he knew her from all that Daphne said. She told him then about her romance with Tom. 'Is she liable to get married and stay out there? That would be rough on you.' He knew how much Daphne depended on her and had for years.

'I don't know if it's that serious yet.' But it was a possibility she had considered too.

And then suddenly he asked her, 'What about you?'

Daphne looked puzzled at the question, and then she understood, and she wasn't sure what to answer. She looked at Matthew thoughtfully. 'I don't know, Matt.' His heart trembled at her words. 'I ... it's difficult to explain.' She wasn't always sure what she felt for Justin. She loved him, to a certain point, but there was still a great deal she didn't know about him. Even though they were together every hour of every day, she sensed that there were unopened doors that she had yet to discover, and there was still the question of his lack of interest in Andrew. She decided to tell Matt, maybe he could help her handle it better. 'I'm not sure about him, Matt. He isn't very interested in getting to know Andrew.'

'Give him time. Does he know he's deaf?' She nodded, still looking pensive. 'How does he feel about that?'

'He won't admit it, but I think it scares him, and as a result he just pretends that Andrew doesn't exist, forgets his name, makes believe he isn't there...' Her voice drifted off and Matthew shook his head.

'That won't work, Daff. Andrew is too important to

you for the man in your life not to share him.' He wanted to be fair to her, to give her the best advice he could. 'Is that why you didn't bring him out this time and flew back here yourself instead?'

'Partly, and also I think it would have been too much of a trip for Andrew in only three or four days.' Matt had said that much himself on the phone. 'But it was because of Justin too.' Matthew looked suddenly shocked then. It couldn't be. But of course that made sense. He felt his heart sink as he asked her.

'Justin?'

She blushed, it was embarrassing to admit that she was having an affair with the actor starring in her movie. It sounded so Hollywood, so typical, so unreal, but it was more than that, she knew it. It just so happened that they had met there, and had had a chance to get to know each other because of the film, and the romance had grown as a result ... 'Justin Wakefield.' Her voice was soft, her eyes bright in the firelight.

'I see. That's quite a catch, Daff.' He took a long, slow, deep breath. He hadn't even thought of that. He had assumed it was some ordinary mortal, not the golden god of every woman's dreams. 'What's he like?'

She sat and stared into the fire, seeing Justin's face as though he were with them in the room. 'Beautiful, of course. Very beautiful, and bright, and funny, and sometimes very kind.' And then she looked back at Matthew again, she had to tell him the truth. 'And totally self-involved, and often very selfish and unaware of those around him. He's forty-two years old and sometimes he acts more like fifteen. I don't know, Matt, he's a lovely man and at times he makes me very happy ... and at other times it's like talking to someone who doesn't hear you. Like when I talk to him about Andrew, he's just not there.' It was why she still called from time to time for comfort, to talk about her son, or other things. It was something she had wondered about often, there were parts of her life that Justin simply didn't relate to. 'He's very understanding about my work, which is

272

important to me, he cares about that, but in other ways'
– she shook her head – 'he just isn't there. I sometimes
wonder if it would work.' She sighed softly. 'And I have
to admit that there are times when I'm not sure. It's
interesting, he and Barbara absolutely hate each other.
She sees a side of him I just don't see, a cold, empty,
calculating side she insists is there, but I think she's
misreading him. She doesn't know him as well as I do.
He isn't calculating, it's just that at times he's unthink-
ing. You can't hate a man for that.'

'No, but it could be mighty hard to live with.'

'Yes, it could.' She had to agree and then she smiled
dreamily into the fire. 'But sometimes he makes me so
happy. He takes away all those awful memories, all that
hurt and loneliness I lived with for so long.'

'Then maybe it's all worth it.'

'Right now I think it is.'

He nodded and sighed again. 'I figured that there was
someone when he answered the phone that time I
called.' It had only happened once, but he had had a
premonition, and she wasn't the kind of woman to
indulge in one-night stands. If he answered the phone
it was because he lived there and she wasn't afraid to let
the world know. 'I just didn't imagine that it was
him.'

'Justin?' He nodded, and she smiled. 'Fortunately, the
press hasn't devoted too much time to us, an item here
and there but not much. But we haven't been anywhere
because we've all been working so hard, but one of these
days they'll figure out that we're living together and it'll
be all over the papers.' She didn't look pleased.

'How do you feel about that?'

'Not very happy, and my readers will be shocked, but
I guess I'll have to face it sooner or later.' They both
thought of *The Conroy Show* she had done months before,
and their eyes met. 'I really don't want to have to explain
it, not until I'm sure.' Sure of what? He was terrified of
the answer to that one. Maybe she would marry Justin
and decide to stay in California. But he had to tell her

what he knew, for Andrew's sake, that was his role in her life after all, in spite of the friendship that had grown between them in the past six months.

'If you decide to stay out there, there's a terrific school for Andrew in LA.' He told her about it and she listened, but after a while she began to feel sleepy. She stood up.

'I'm not to that point yet, but if I get there, I'll talk to you about the school.' Somehow the thought depressed her. She wasn't ready to think about marrying Justin, and he hadn't mentioned it either, but sooner or later the subject would come up. Eventually she would have to decide if she was going back to New York, or staying in LA. 'Right now, all I have to do is finish the movie. Then I'll think about my own life.'

'Do what's best for you, Daff. And for Andrew.' His voice was so sad, so gentle, and she suddenly wondered about him. Once or twice she had called and he was out and she had wondered if he had met a woman that he liked, but this didn't seem the time to ask. He walked her to the car and drove her to the inn. They had left her key out on the desk with a note of welcome, and he left her there with a thoughtful smile in his eyes. 'I'm glad you flew back to see Andrew.'

'So am I, Matt.' They said good night and he left, and as she walked upstairs to her room she thought about their conversation and wondered why she felt suddenly so unhappy about Justin. Why couldn't he be more like Matt? Why couldn't he listen to her about Andrew? But maybe in time he would. It was Matt's business, after all, to care about children like Andrew. But there was more to him than that and she knew it. Much, much more.

31

The visit with Andrew passed all too quickly, he was ecstatic to have her near him, and he rode his bike for her, and showed her his garden, introduced her to his new friends, and bragged about her movie. They took long walks in the sunshine and went back outside after dinner. They were glorious June days, and she felt revived just being near him. It was as though the spirits of her soul had leaked out slowly in the past three months and she hadn't noticed. She had been so busy in California with Justin and the film. But now, once again, she knew how desperately she needed her son, and how important she was to him. He asked her again and again now when he would come back to California, when she was coming home, when they could be together.

He had just gone inside to take his bath after dinner, when Matthew found her, watching the sunset from the comfortable old-fashioned swing.

'May I join you, Daff?' She looked so peaceful and pensive, he hated to break into her thoughts. But he had seen her there and had been irresistibly pulled towards her.

'Sure, Matt.' She patted the seat beside her with a smile. 'Andrew just went in for his bath.'

'I know. I met him on the stairs and he told me you were out here.' They exchanged a long, slow smile and the sun disappeared behind a hill in a burst of flame. 'It's done him a lot of good to see you. He needs you more again these days. He's turning his attention to the world outside now, and you're a big part of it for him.'

'It's done me good too.' He could see that now. The worry was gone from her eyes, and her face was relaxed and happy. She looked like a little girl sitting in the swing, in blue jeans and an old sweat shirt, her long blonde hair fanned out down her back, and a pale blue ribbon the colour of her eyes keeping it off her face. And yet he saw concern in her eyes too, concern for Andrew. 'I feel as though I should be here with him, Matt.'

'You can't right now. He understands that.'

'Does he? I'm not sure I always do.' She fell silent and he watched her.

'You look like a little kid today.' His eyes were gentle. 'No one would suspect you of being a bestselling author.' Or the mistress of the movie star who lived in every woman's dreams.

She looked at Matthew happily. 'Up here I'm not anyone but me. And Andrew's Mommy.' It was an important facet of her life and they both knew it. 'I'm going to try and come back soon.'

'How soon is that?'

'Either right before or right after Wyoming, depending on what Howard says.'

'I hope it's before.' And then he had to be honest with her, he almost always was. 'Not so much for Andrew's sake, but for me.' She looked into his eyes then, and she felt something stir deep inside her. She was never quite sure what she felt for Matt, or if she should even let herself think it over. It was so comfortable the way things were. But it was strange how important he had become to her, how much she needed to know that he was there somewhere, that she could talk to him if she had to. She couldn't imagine life without him now, especially for Andrew's sake, but for her own, too. 'You mean a lot to me, Daphne.' His voice was husky in the twilight and she nodded, looking into his soft brown eyes.

'You mean a lot to me too.'

'It doesn't make much sense, does it? We've really never spent much time together. A bunch of talks at night in front of the fire, here at the school, and a lot of hours on the phone...' His voice drifted off.

'Maybe that's enough. I feel as though I know you

276

better than anyone else.' It was that that was so amazing about him. She did know him. And she knew that he also knew her, as she really was, with her scars and fears and private terrors, and all her victories and strengths as well. She had let him see more of her than anyone else she'd ever known, even Justin. Justin saw the funny side, the bright side, the solid, strong part of her being, but he didn't know what Matthew knew, and she wasn't sure she'd trust him to yet. But she knew that she trusted Matthew with all her secrets and her entire soul. And yet it was Justin she lived with, Justin who slept on the other side of the gigantic bed in Bel-Air.

'Maybe one day, Daff...' Matthew started to say something, and Daphne looked at him, startled, almost frightened. He changed his mind then. It wasn't time. 'We'll have more time to spend together.' It was a safe thing to say, yet nothing felt safe now. They were both treading on fresh ground and she sensed it. She watched him, and he leaned over and kissed her cheek. 'Be good to yourself in California, Daphne. Be happy. I hope things work out with your friend. And if you need me, I'm always here.'

'You don't know how comforting that is, Matt.' And she meant it. 'I always know that if I need you, I can call.' And then she smiled. 'And if you need me, you call too.'

'What does your friend think of that?' His eyes were only slightly worried.

'He teased me about it once.' She laughed, it seemed foolish now. 'He accused us of being lovers, but he didn't seem too upset by it. He's led kind of a...' She searched for the right words, she didn't want to be unkind to Justin. '...a liberated life, shall we say, until he met me. I don't think he's too concerned about the past.' Matthew felt a pang of something close to disappointment. 'Don't ever be afraid to call me, Matt.'

'I won't.' He smiled, feeling as though his heart had been torn out. They walked inside then and she went upstairs to Andrew, and when she came downstairs again an hour later, Matthew could see the tears in her eyes.

'Boy, it's tough to leave again.' She smiled at him bravely and he put an arm around her shoulders. 'I'll be back soon.'

'We're counting on it. And you know Andrew will be fine.' She nodded, and he drove her to the inn a few minutes later to change and pick up her bags to go back to the airport. She had insisted that she could take a taxi to Boston, but Matthew wouldn't hear of it. He drove her back, just as he had driven her to New Hampshire a few days before, and they stood at the gate for a long moment, her eyes holding him tight and his searching hers.

'Take care of my baby for me, Matt.' It was a lonely whisper as she tried not to cry, and then he threw caution to the winds and pulled her towards him, holding her for a long time like that as she drew on his strength and his friendship. She said nothing to him as she left, except as she stood in the doorway of the plane she signed to him, 'I love you.' He smiled broadly and signed back, and then she disappeared, back to LA and to Justin. And as Matthew walked back to his car he told himself he was crazy. Her life was too different from his, and always would be. He was nothing more than a teacher of deaf children, and she was Daphne Fields. For a moment he hated Justin Wakefield for everything he was, and everything Matt knew he wasn't, and then with a sigh he slipped into his car and went home, thinking every mile of the way of Daphne.

32

The plane touched down in LA at 1.30 in the morning LA time, and Daphne awoke with a start as they landed. For her it was 4.30 a.m. And she awoke with a heavy, lonely feeling, she had been dreaming of Matt and Andrew, playing in the garden with them at Howarth, and now she realised how far away she was again. For an instant she felt the same unbearable pain she had felt when she first left Andrew at Howarth. But as they landed she forced her mind back to Justin. She had to force her mind back to the present and what lay ahead, or she couldn't go on. But the memories of Andrew and Matthew seemed to stay with her. They were still too fresh in her head and she wasn't ready to let go. She didn't really want to be back yet. And yet, she reminded herself, she was coming home to Justin and all the thrills she felt in his arms. It was strange though, she felt as if she had been away not for three days, but for three months. Her two lives were so entirely separate that it was difficult to imagine leading both lives within the same week. And suddenly the thought of Justin was like thinking about a stranger.

She hadn't told the limousine to meet her at the airport, and she had told Barbara not to worry, that she would get home herself. She hadn't been able to reach Justin in three days because she didn't know the people he was staying with in San Francisco. But as she rode home in a cab she knew that in a few hours they'd all be back together. It was 2.00 a.m. by then, and they all had to be at the studio by 5.30. She realised as she walked in the front door that it wasn't even worth trying to go to sleep for two hours. She'd have to make do with the nap she'd taken on the plane.

The house was dark save for the lights that went on automatically each night to make the house look lived in even when it was deserted, and she walked inside thinking how strange it all looked. It seemed like someone else's house, not her own, and she realised again how far she'd flung herself. She walked into the living room and sat down, staring at the pool all lit up in the dark, and wondered how soon Justin would come home. And then she wandered slowly outside and thought of taking a swim. She looked down and saw a well-sculpted blue and white bikini top, two empty glasses, and a bottle of champagne. She wondered who might have left them there, and wondered if Barbara and Tom had used the pool while she was gone, but he had his own, and as she picked it up she saw that the brassiere was far too large for Barbara. She held it for a moment as her heart began to pound, and then she shook her head. It couldn't be. He wouldn't do a thing like that right here. She left it on a chair, trying not to think, and took the glasses and the champagne bottle into the kitchen and there she found a white lace blouse draped over one of the kitchen chairs. She smiled an ironic smile to herself, feeling like the Three Bears. 'Who's been using my pool? ... Who's been sleeping in my bed? ...' She wandered into her bedroom with the thought, and found him there, the golden god, sprawled out naked and beautiful in their bed. He looked less than half his age, and she marvelled at his looks again as she stood watching him and he didn't stir. Maybe he'd had a party before she came back and he'd been too tired to clean up the last of the debris. She felt suddenly guilty for what she'd thought, wondering if her confused feelings about Matthew made her want to think the worst of Justin. But that was wrong. She was in love with Justin, the golden god. As she took off her travelling clothes with a sigh, she felt an overwhelming longing for him. She lay down on the bed beside him for a time, but

280

she couldn't sleep, and she didn't want to wake him by tossing around. At last she got up, and put on coffee at four o'clock, and half an hour later Barbara came in.

'Welcome home.' She gave Daphne a hug with an enormous smile. 'How's our boy?'

'Absolutely wonderful. You should see him ride his bike, and he's grown again, and he sent you his love.' She looked sad for a moment as she sat down on the chair still draped with the lace blouse. 'It was so hard to leave, Barb. I wish we weren't working so damn hard so he could come out for a visit. And yet, I know that if I work my ass off, I can move back to New York sooner. It's a kind of Catch-22, isn't it?'

Barbara nodded, she felt what Daphne was going through. 'Maybe before or after Wyoming, Daff.'

'That's what I told Matt.'

'How was he?' Barbara searched her eyes, but there was nothing there she hadn't seen before, warmth, affection, interest, but nothing more. She was still in love with her Greek god, much to Barbara's chagrin.

'He's fine. As nice as ever.' She said nothing more, and Barbara poured them both coffee and when Daphne got up she glanced at the chair.

'Is that yours?' Her eyes were suddenly grim.

'No. Justin must have had friends in to swim.' The silence between them seemed to fill the room. 'Have you and Tom been around?'

Barbara shook her head. 'I came in every day to pick up the mail. You got two cheques from Iris yesterday, but other than that it was all junk and bills.'

'The new contract didn't come in yet?' She was signing with Harbor to do another book.

'No. They said not to expect it till next week.'

'No rush, I can't touch it till we finish the movie anyway.' Barbara nodded again and fought with herself for the hundredth time. Tom had told her to keep her mouth shut when Daphne got back, but every time she thought of Justin her stomach turned, and she had told Tom that she didn't owe the son of a bitch a thing.

'What made you ask if we'd been here?' Barbara averted her eyes and filled Daphne's cup again.

'Just curious. Someone used the pool. I found some wineglasses and an empty bottle of champagne.' She didn't mention the bra.

'Maybe you ought to ask Justin about that.' Her voice was unusually smooth and Daphne looked up at her. She was too tired to play games.

'Is there something I ought to know?' Her heart began to pound again. It wasn't a matter of Goldilocks this time. But Barbara said nothing at all, never taking her eyes from her friend's.

'I don't know.'

'Was he here? I thought he went away.'

'I think he stayed.' But she was too vague. Barbara would have known if he had stayed in LA, especially if she picked up the mail every day.

'Barb...'

She held up a hand, fighting back a rush of pent-up fury once again. 'Don't ask me, Daff.' And then through clenched teeth, 'Ask him.'

'What exactly should I ask?'

Barbara couldn't take it anymore. She held up the blouse. 'About this ... and the bra at the pool' – then Barbara had seen it too – 'and the underpants in the front hall...' She was prepared to go on but Daphne stood up, feeling her knees go weak.

'That's enough!'

'Is it? Just how much shit are you going to take from him, Daff? I wasn't going to say anything when you got back, Tom told me it was none of my business but it is' – her eyes filled with tears – 'because I love you, dammit. You're the best friend I've ever had.' She turned her back on Daphne for a moment and when she turned to face her again her eyes were bleak. 'Daphne, he had a woman staying here.' There was an interminable silence in the room as Daphne listened to her heart pound and the clock tick and then her eyes met Barbara's with an expression Barbara had never seen.

282

'I'll take care of this, but I want to make one thing clear. You were right to tell me, Barb. And I appreciate what you feel. But this is between Justin and me. I'll handle it myself. And whatever happens, I don't want to discuss this with you again. Do you understand?'

'Yes. I'm sorry, Daff...' Her tears spilled on to her cheeks, and Daphne went to her and hugged her for a moment.

'It's okay, Barb. Why don't you go on to the studio in your car.' It was almost five o'clock and Tom had been letting her use one of his cars. 'I'll meet you there in a while. And if I'm late, tell them that I just flew in from the East Coast.'

'Will you be all right?' She dried her eyes, frightened by Daphne's sudden calm.

'I'm fine.' Her eyes held Barbara's meaningfully, and then she walked out of the kitchen and closed the bedroom door. She walked over to where Justin lay and she touched him on the shoulder with a trembling hand. He stirred sleepily then, squinted his eyes, looked at the clock, and then realised she was in the room.

'Hi, babe. You're back.'

'I am.' She looked down at him and there was nothing friendly in her voice or face. She sat down in a chair across from the bed because she could no longer stand up and she stared at him. 'What exactly went on around here while I was gone?' She got right to the point and he sat up, barely rumpled by a night's sleep, with a look of innocence and curiosity in his eyes.

'What do you mean? How was your kid, by the way?'

'He was fine. But right now I'm more interested in you. What have you been up to around here?'

'Nothing. Why?' He stretched and yawned, and smiled invitingly as he reached out and touched her naked leg. 'I missed you, babe.'

'Did you? What about the woman who stayed here while I was gone? I'll say one thing, she's got big tits. Her bra would fit over my head.' But funny as she may have sounded, she was not amused, her eyes were hard as rocks and she pushed his hand away from her leg.

'I had some friends in, that's all. What's the big deal?' Suddenly she wondered if Barbara had been wrong. She would feel like a total jerk if he was telling the truth and had been falsely accused. Her eyes faltered for a moment and then she saw one of his discarded rubbers under the bed. She reached over, picked it up, and held it aloft like a trophy of sorts.

'What's this?'

'Beats me. Maybe someone slept here.'

'Are you telling me it's not yours?' Her eyes never left his.

'Oh, for chrissake.' He stood up in all his splendour and ran a hand through his golden hair. 'What's with you? I was here alone for four days and I had some friends in. What's the matter, Daff' – his eyes glittered nastily – 'don't I get pool privileges unless you're here?'

There was no other way to find out. 'Barbara tells me there was someone staying here.' But at her words he started, he hadn't known she was around.

'That bitch! How the fuck does she know anything? She wasn't here.'

'She picked up my mail every day.'

'She did?' His face grew pale. 'Oh, Christ.' He sat back down on the bed and dropped his face into his hands. He said nothing for a while and then he looked into Daphne's eyes. 'All right, all right. I got a little crazy. That happens to me sometimes after I work that hard. It doesn't mean anything to me, Daff ... for chrissake ... you have a lot to learn about this business ... it drives you nuts after a while.' But they were lame words and he knew it. There wasn't much he could say to her.

'Apparently it does. Nuts enough to sleep with someone else in my house, in my bed.' Tears filled her eyes. 'Does that seem right to you?' She felt betrayed and hurt. She had suffered loss before, but she had never suffered this ... brassieres left by the pool ... spots on the couch ... condoms under the bed ... and all in three lousy days. 'What the hell's the matter with you, dammit?' She got to her feet and paced the room. 'Can't you keep it in your pants for three days? Is that all I mean to you? A convenient piece of ass and when I'm not around you sleep with someone else?' She stood before him, her eyes blazing, and he looked sad.

'I'm so sorry, Daff ... I didn't mean – '

'How could you?' She began to sob. 'How *could* you? ...' She was beyond words and she lay facedown on the bed as she sobbed, and gently he stroked her back and hair. She wanted to tell him to go to hell, but she didn't have the strength. She couldn't believe what he had done, and the callousness of doing it in her own house and letting her find out made it even worse. This wasn't a quick screw he'd picked up at some bar, this was a girl he'd moved right into her house, her bed. The humiliation of it was almost more than she could bear. And what it told her about him was very painful.

'Oh, Daphne, baby ... please ... I got drunk, I snorted some coke. I just flipped out. I told you I didn't want you to go. I wanted to go to Mexico with you, but you insisted on flying East to see your kid. I just couldn't take it, I ...' He began to cry too, and turned her over gently to face him. She felt as though all her bones had melted into the bed. She didn't have the strength to fight. She almost wished that she were dead. 'I love you so damn much. This doesn't mean anything.' He wiped the tears from his eyes. 'I was crazy. It'll never happen again. I swear.' But her eyes said that she didn't believe a word as tears streamed down her face and she said not a single word to him. 'Daphne ...' He lay his head down on her slender thighs. 'Oh, God, baby ... please ... I don't want to lose you ...'

'You should have thought of that before your friend left her bra at my pool.' Her voice sounded defeated and she sat up slowly in the bed, feeling ten thousand years old, but not yet hating him. She was too hurt even to feel anger yet. All she felt was pain. 'Is this how you always behave during a shoot?' Or was this how he behaved in real life? She was beginning to wonder. And it made her feel like hell.

'This has been a rough shoot. You don't know how much of myself I've been pouring into this, Daff... how desperately I've wanted to please you ... to make this movie of yours a major hit ... Oh, Daff...' His eyes looked so childlike and so sad, he looked as though his best friend had died. The fact that he had killed her himself didn't seem to enter his mind as he grieved. 'Baby, can't we start fresh?'

'I don't know.' Her eyes went to the rubber she had tossed on to the bed and he picked it up and threw it in the john. When he came back, he looked at her.

'Maybe you'll never forgive me. But I swear I'll never do it again.'

'How do I know that? I can't sit on you for the rest of your life.' She sounded so tired and so sad and he smiled for the first time since he had seen her in the room.

'I wish you would.'

'I want to go back and see my son again. What happens then? I worry myself sick for three days while I'm gone that you're out screwing around again?' She was suddenly overwhelmed by a mindless, wordless, bottomless lonely feeling. Who in hell was he? And what did she mean to him? Did he care about her at all? It was hard to believe he did now.

'If you want, I'll come with you.' But suddenly she wasn't sure if that was what she wanted. She wanted him to meet Andrew, but there was more in New Hampshire than that. There was Matt. And suddenly she didn't want Justin to be part of that life, especially now. Suddenly, she didn't trust him. Not enough to expose Andrew to him.

'I don't know. I don't know what I want right now. I think I might want you to move out.' But she knew that

286

if he did, they would never work it out. He shook his head slowly and reached for her hands.

'Let's not do that yet. Please, Daff. Give me a chance.' It was like watching a little boy beg to get his privileges back, but this was a lot more important than that. 'I need you.'

'Why?' It seemed strange to hear him say that, she had thought that it was she who needed him. 'Why me and not someone else, like your friend with the big tits?'

'You know who she is? A twenty-two-year-old cocktail waitress from Ohio, Daff. That's all she is. She isn't you. No one is.' But Daphne narrowed her eyes. Something rang a bell.

'Isn't that the girl you were going out with before?' He hesitated at length and then nodded, dropping his head into his hands again.

'Yes. She heard through the grapevine that we were taking a break and she called.'

'Here? How did she know where you were?' The question struck fear in his heart, he was caught. Either he had let her know where he was before, or he had called her.

'All right, dammit, if you're so fucking smart, so I called her.'

'When? After I left or before?' She got out of bed and stood facing him. 'Just exactly what has been going on with you?'

'Nothing, dammit! I've been with you night and day for the last three months. You know I haven't seen anyone else. How could I? When?' It was true.

'You told me she was an actress.' It was a minor point, but everything mattered now.

'She is. She's out of work, so she's waiting on tables. Daphne, dammit, she's a nothing, a child. You're worth fifty thousand of her or any other woman in this town. I know that. But I'm human. I do crazy things sometimes. I did it, I confess, I am desperately sorry, it won't happen again. What more can I tell you? What do you want me to do to atone for my sins? Cut off my balls?'

'It's a thought.' She sat down in the chair again and looked around. Suddenly she hated this room, the whole house. He had poisoned it while she was gone. She looked up at him then, 'I don't know if I could ever trust you again.'

He sat down from her across the bed, trying to keep his voice calm. 'Daphne, every couple goes through these things. At some point or other, everyone screws up. Maybe one day you will too. We're all human, and at some moment in time, we all get weak. Maybe it's better to have it out now, to have some giant tear in hearts that we can sew up and make them stronger. We'll be better for all this if we make it through and we can, if you let us. Give me a chance. I'm telling you, it won't happen again.'

'How do I know?'

'Because I'll show you. And in time you'll come to trust me again. I know what you feel. But it doesn't have to mean the end. He reached out gently and touched her cheek with his fingers. She faltered for only a fraction of a second and he sensed it and moved in quick, reaching out and pulling her into his arms. 'I love you, Daff, more than you'll ever know. I want to marry you someday.' To him that was the ultimate statement – the beginning and the end – but Daphne still looked sad.

'This is a hell of a way to start out.' It had never happened to her with Jeff, or John. Maybe she had been right to hide behind her walls. Justin sensed her thoughts.

'You can't be half alive all your life, Daff. You have to be out here with the rest of us, get hurt, make mistakes, pick yourself up, and make it again. Otherwise you're only half a human being, and that's not you. You're a lot more than that. I'm sorry. I'm sorrier than you'll ever know.'

'So am I.' But she didn't look as vehement as before.

288

'Will you let it ride for a while? I swear to you, you won't be sorry.' She didn't answer. 'I love you. What more can I say?' There wasn't much. In the last hour and a half he had said it all, that he loved her, that he had been a fool, that he wanted to marry her someday. It was the first she'd heard of that, and she looked at him now, with a thousand questions still in her eyes.

'Were you serious about wanting to get married?'

'Yes. I've never said that to anyone before. But I've never met anyone like you.' His eyes were so gentle and her heart still felt as though it had been torn in half.

'You've never met my son.' It was out of context, but not really.

'I will. Maybe next time I'll fly East with you.' She didn't answer and he watched her. He didn't want to remind her that they were over an hour late for work. He knew what a crazy bastard he had been, and he knew also that he had to make it right with her before anything. He didn't want to give her more time to think. 'We have a lifetime ahead of us, my love.' It was an awesome thought. 'Will you give me another chance?'

Her eyes searched his but she didn't speak, and he leaned down and kissed her gently on the mouth, as he had so long ago when they came together in love. 'I love you, Daff. With all my heart.' And then the tears began to flow again and she held him tight, aching over what he had done while she was gone. Justin held her as she sobbed, cooing and soothing and comforting and stroking her hair. He knew he had won her back when she stopped crying at last. She was unable to say what she felt, but he knew that in time she would forgive him for what he had done, and he sighed softly to himself as he stood up and gently led her from their bed. 'I hate to say it, babe, but we have to get to work.' She groaned at the thought, it was the last thing on her mind. But she knew that he was right.

'What time is it?'

'Six fifteen.'

She winced. 'Howard's going to have a fit.'

'Yeah.' Justin smiled at last. 'But as long as he is anyway, let's make it worthwhile.' And then without another word he laid her on the bed again and began to make love to her.

She wanted to object, it wasn't what she had in mind, not after what he had done ... not so soon ... not yet ... but his skill was greater than her resolve and a moment later he plunged inside her and she gave a moan of sorrow and joy and knew herself to be his once again. And perhaps he was right, she told herself afterwards, maybe everyone suffers something like that. Maybe they'd be stronger for the pain.

33

When Justin and Daphne appeared on the set at eight fifteen, Howard was nearing an apoplectic fit. He turned to stare at them in disbelief as they walked in.

'I don't believe it . . . I don't believe it!' His voice rose to a crescendo and Daphne cringed. Justin looked unimpressed. 'What is it with you two? You can't get your goddamn asses out of bed to come to work? Doesn't anyone give a shit around here? *Three hours* late on the set and you walk in like you're coming to a tea party? The hell with you!' He grabbed a copy of the script and threw it as Justin went off to put his costume on and Daphne searched frantically for Barbara.

'You okay?' Barbara sat down next to her, looking at the tired little face, the ravaged eyes, but Daphne averted her gaze and nodded. Even now she had to fight back tears. Between the emotions and the lack of sleep, she was exhausted and overwrought.

'I'm fine.' She looked up at her friend with a tired smile. 'Everything's all right.' Or at least it was going to be. Barbara realised that Justin must have sold her a bill of goods.

'Do you want a cup of coffee?'

'Yes, if you're sure Howard didn't put arsenic in my cup.'

Barbara smiled, still watching her. She hated the sorrow she saw on her face, and hated Justin for putting it there. 'Don't feel so bad, Daff. Half of the crew came in late, that's why he's so pissed off. Apparently it always takes a couple of days to settle down after a break.'

'That's the understatement of the year.' For the first time since she had come home, Daphne grinned. And it was the only mention she made of the havoc she had found in her own house. Barbara brought her the coffee and slowly she began to revive, but between the long flight the night before, the lack of sleep, and the trauma she had had with Justin before work, she felt like a zombie all day long. They knocked off at six o'clock that day and Justin took her home and put her to bed. He brought her a cup of tea right away and dinner on a tray. It was like being an invalid, and she knew why he was doing it, but she had to admit she didn't mind. He was in the kitchen afterwards, putting things away, when Matthew called, and Daphne sank into the pillows with a sigh. It was a relief to hear his voice.

'Hi, Matt.' Her voice was small and she was glad that the bedroom door was closed.

'It must have been some day. You sound beat.'

'I am.' But he sensed instantly that there was more. 'Are you okay?'

'More or less.' She fought with herself not to tell him what had happened. She didn't want to. It had nothing to do with him. And yet she needed to reach out to him, she needed to know that there was still something solid left, somewhere, even if it was three thousand miles away. She didn't trust Justin yet, no matter how contrite he was. But she knew for certain that Matthew was her friend. 'How was Andrew today?'

'Not bad, considering that you only left yesterday How was the flight?'

'Okay. I slept.' For an instant she was reminded of her calls from Jeff when he went on business trips. There was comfort in the trivia of everyday life. It was all on a much smaller scale than what was happening to her, and that was a relief. What was happening in California was just too much. She fell silent then, and at his end Matthew frowned, he had known instantly when he heard her voice that something was wrong.

'Daff? What's the matter, little one?' No one had called her that since John and she felt her eyes fill with tears as she struggled with the emotions of the past eighteen hours. 'Can't I help?'

'I wish you could.' He could hear her crying now. 'It's just something that happened out here ... while I was gone...'

'Your friend?'

She nodded and choked on her tears. It was stupid to cry now, she told herself. They had made up. But it still hurt. It all hurt so damn much. And she wanted to tell it all to Matt, as though his comforting arms around her could change anything now. 'I found kind of a mess when I got back.' He waited and she went on. 'He had a woman staying here while I was gone.' It was shocking to be telling him about that, and yet she didn't feel shocked. She just felt sad. 'It's a long story, and he feels like hell about it now. But it was kind of a lousy homecoming.' She blew her nose and something within him began to burn.

'Did you throw the bastard out?'

'No. I was going to, but ... I don't know, Matt. I think he's sorry. I think he was just a little out of his head from the pressure of so much work for the past three months.'

'What about you? You've been working harder than he has, you wrote the screenplay first. Does that sound like a reasonable excuse to you?' He was mad as hell. And madder still that she wasn't, that she was willing to give the guy another chance.

'No. Nothing sounds like a reasonable excuse, but it happened. I'm just going to wait and see what happens now.' He wanted to shake her right out of her bed, but he knew he didn't have the right. He didn't want her to get hurt. But he was helpless. She was in love with someone else, and he was only her friend.

'Do you think he's worth it, Daff?'

'I do now. This morning I wasn't sure.' Matthew was sorry he hadn't called earlier then, but he knew it wouldn't have made any difference. She wasn't ready to give Justin Wakefield up, but Wakefield was a formidable opponent. Anyone in his right mind would have told him he was nuts even to hope that she'd give him up. 'I just don't know...' She sounded so fragile and so sad, it tore at his heart. '... I ... I've lost so much in the past, Matt...' He could hear her crying.

'Then don't cheapen what you had by accepting this.'

His reaction shocked her. 'You don't understand. Maybe he's right, maybe people do make mistakes. Maybe actors are different.' She was crying harder now. 'Dammit, how many times do you think I can start over?'

'As many times as you have to, you've got the guts, lady. Don't forget that.'

'Maybe I'm getting tired of having guts. Maybe they're all used up.'

'I don't believe that.'

'And besides, we have a commitment to each other. He said so.'

'Commitment? Was he thinking of that commitment while you were here?'

'I know, Matt, I know. I can't make excuses for him.' She was suddenly sorry she had told him at all. She didn't want to defend Justin to anyone, and yet she felt she should. 'I know it doesn't make sense, but I'm going to stick it out for a while.' She sighed and dried her eyes.

'It's all right, Daff, I understand. You have to do what's right for you. Just please, don't get hurt.' But she already was, and after she hung up, she began to cry again. Justin found her lying in bed, sobbing into her pillows, and not even sure why. She was still upset over the other girl, but there was something more. She was suddenly desperately lonely for Andrew and Matt and she wanted to go home.

'Oh, babe, don't ... everything's all right...' But it wasn't and she wasn't fooled. She lay in his arms and sobbed and at last fell asleep on his chest and he turned off the light. He lay looking at her as she slept, wondering if he had done the right thing. He cared about this woman more than he had cared about anyone else before, but he wasn't sure if he could live up to what she expected of him. He wanted to, he really did, but he felt a ripple of fear run through him as he looked down the years. She was so serious and so straight and she had been through so much. And his life was built on other things, excitement, and new people, and acting and having fun. He also knew he didn't have her knack for commitment.

And in New Hampshire, Matthew sat in the dark, staring at the fire, thinking himself a fool, and hating Justin Wakefield's guts, wondering if there was any hope at all as he ached for Daphne.

34

For the next month the making of *Apache* went smoothly and they were all scheduled to leave for Wyoming on the fourteenth of July. Howard had decided that they didn't have time off until they got back to LA before doing the final scenes on the Hollywood set. For Daphne, it meant that she wouldn't have time to fly back and see Andrew but Matt assured her that he was all right, he had his pack trip to look forward to, and as soon as she got back from Jackson Hole, she would fly back to see him. She was almost too busy to dwell on feeling guilty about it. There was a lot of material to rewrite for the scenes in Jackson Hole and she seemed to spend every waking hour on the set and all the rest of her time typing late into the night. And Justin had been marvellously supportive, he read over everything she wrote, told her when it was good and what didn't work and why. He was teaching more than she had ever hoped to learn about writing a screenplay and making it hold up for the characters involved. He sat up every night with her, bringing her sandwiches and coffee, rubbing her neck, and then they would fall into bed and make love. They were existing on almost no sleep, but she had never been happier in her life. She had a working relationship with him that she had never dreamed could happen, and she knew now that she had been right to stick it out with him after the fiasco in June. Even Barbara had to admit that he was behaving like an angel, but she still didn't trust him, as she told Tom often when they were alone.

'You never liked him from the first, Barb. But if he's good to her, what's wrong with that?'

'If he pulled a stunt like that on her once, then he'll do it again.'

'Maybe not. Maybe it was just a hangover from his old life, before he met her. He may have learned a lesson.' Tom didn't see anything wrong with him when he met him, and Barbara was so rabidly anti-Justin that he often suspected she was just jealous of someone else having that much influence over Daphne. The two women had been so close during their solitary lives at one time that maybe it was just hard for Barbara to let go, even though now she had Tom. He didn't really understand it, but he always urged her to keep her mouth shut if she valued her job. 'If she's serious about him, Barb, you'd better lay off.' He suspected, as the Hollywood press had finally come to do, that Justin and Daphne would get married.

'If she does, I'll throw rocks instead of rice,' Barbara snarled. 'That man is going to hurt her. I know it.'

'All right, Grandma, just relax. Hell, I hope he does marry her, then she'll have to stay out here.' It was now a frequent subject between them. He wanted Barbara to stay in LA and marry him, but she refused to decide until the making of *Apache* was over. 'But after that, my love, there are no more excuses. I'm not getting any younger and neither are you, and if you think I'm going to wait another twenty years to see you again, you're crazy. I want to marry you and get you pregnant, and watch you sit on your ass by the pool and spend my money for the next fifty years. How does that sound, Miss Jarvis?'

'Too good to be true.' But everything about him had been since the day she had met him at Gucci. It had been a storybook romance from the first. And he had long since surprised her with the handsome black lizard bag he had watched her covet that first day. And there had been other gifts too, a gold Piaget watch, a beautiful beige suede blazer, two jade bracelets, and countless other trinkets that amazed her. She still couldn't believe her good luck in having found Tom, and was constantly amazed to realise how much he loved her. And she loved him just as much. As the two parted, there were tears in her eyes when she left for Jackson Hole, but he was going to fly up every weekend while she was on location.

Daphne and Justin flew up in a chartered plane, the rest of the crew went in buses hired by the studio, and the shoot took on an aura of summer romance once they were up there. Couples formed in the romantic setting, people sat outside at night, looking at the mountains and singing songs they remembered from their childhoods from camp. Even Howard mellowed. Justin and Daphne's love flourished. On breaks from the set they went on long walks, picked wild flowers, and made love in the tall grass. It was all like a beautiful dream, and everyone was sad when it was over and they had to go back to LA. Only Daphne felt less regret than the others, because she knew she would see Andrew, she was flying to Boston again in a few days. Justin hadn't decided whether to come with her or not. It was the day before she was due to leave that he finally appeared in their bedroom doorway, a nervous look on his face as he sat down on the edge of the bed.

'I can't do it, Daff.'

'Can't do what?'

'I can't go to Boston with you.' He looked miserable and she was instantly suspicious.

'Why not? Did Miss Ohio call?' It was the first time she had made mention of it all summer and he looked crushed.

'Don't be like that. I told you. That will never happen again.'

'Then why won't you come?'

He sighed and looked desperately unhappy. 'I don't know how to explain it to you without sounding like a total asshole. Or maybe I should just accept the fact that I am, but ... Daff ... a whole school of deaf kids ... I ... I ... have this thing about handicaps, blindness, deafness, cripples ... I just can't handle it. It makes me physically sick.' She felt her heart sink as he said it. If it was true, they had a serious problem on their hands. Andrew was deaf. It had to be faced.

'Justin, Andrew isn't a cripple.'

'I know that. And I'd probably be fine with just him ... but all of them...' He actually looked pale and Daphne saw that he was trembling. 'I know that it's nuts for a grown man to feel like this, but I always have. Daphne, I'm sorry.' Tears filled his eyes and he hung his head. Now what in hell was she going to do, but then she had an idea. They had to meet each other. It was important. The affair with Justin looked as though it were going to last and he had to meet Andrew.

'All right, darling, look ... we'll fly him out here.'

'Do you think you could?' The colour began to come back to his cheeks and relief flooded his face. He had dreaded telling her for days, but he just knew he couldn't do it.

'Sure. I'll call Matthew and have him put on the plane. He did it last spring and Andrew loved it.'

'Great.'

But when Daphne called Matt, he told her that Andrew had had a slight ear infection the week before and he couldn't fly out to see her. She had no choice then. She had to fly East by herself, and leave Justin alone in California. When she told him, she looked unhappy and there was a vague look of suspicion in her eyes. She suddenly wondered if he had cooked up the story about his fear just so he could stay in LA and raise hell, as he had the last time, and just thinking about it made her angry.

'Daff, don't look like that. Nothing's going to happen this time.' But she didn't answer. 'I swear it. I'll call you five times a day.'

'What does that prove? Will Miss Ohio dial for you?' She sounded bitter and he looked genuinely hurt.

'That's not fair.'

'Neither was making love to her in my bedroom.'

'Look, dammit, can't we forget that?'

'I don't know, Justin. Have you?'

'Yes, as a matter of fact, I have. We've had three beautiful months since then. And I don't know about you, lady, but I've never been happier. Why do you have to keep throwing that shit in my face?' But they both knew the answer. She still didn't trust him, and going East was a painful reminder of what had happened when she was away in June.

She sighed then and sank into a chair as she looked at him bleakly. 'I'm sorry, Justin. I really wish you'd come with me.' That would solve the problem. But would it? All it would mean was that she could keep tabs on him, it didn't mean that she could trust him.

'I can't come with you, Daff. I just can't do it.'

'Then I guess I have no choice but to trust you, do I?' But now all the happiness of the past three months seemed suddenly dim.

'You won't be sorry, Daff. You'll see.' But she wondered as she packed her bags and they drove to the airport.

In New Hampshire the leaves were turning early, there had been a cold spell, and she had never seen the countryside more beautiful than this year. She and Matthew drove in silence for a time, and her thoughts drifted back to Justin, wondering what he was doing, and if he would be true to his word. Matt noticed that she was quieter than usual, and he glanced at her once or twice before she turned to him and smiled. She looked more peaceful than she had before, but she still looked tired. Even in Wyoming the shoot had been gruelling. Howard Stern worked harder than any other director in town.

'How's my favourite movie?' He was afraid to ask her about Justin. She seldom spoke of him lately and he wasn't quite sure what it meant. He knew that when she wanted to she would tell him. And he waited. But he also had other things on his mind.

'The movie's going fine. We're almost finished. Howard thinks it'll take another six or eight weeks of

300

studio work on the set and then that'll be it, we'll wrap it.' She had learned all the jargon in the last nine months, and he tried to tell himself that she wasn't different than she had been when they'd met. But in some subtle way, he knew that she had changed. There was a nervousness about her, a tension, that hadn't been there before, as though she was always watching, waiting, he wasn't sure for what. He wondered if living with Justin had done that to her, or just working on the film, or perhaps being away from Andrew. But she was different than she had been when her solitary life revolved around her books. Even here she seemed to have a hard time letting go of the frenzy, but he reminded himself that she had just got off the plane. 'I'm going to have Andrew come out for Thanksgiving.' She had already planned it. She would do an old-fashioned Thanksgiving dinner at the house in Bel-Air, and she wanted Barbara to bring Tom and his children. It was something she hadn't done in ten years, not since she was married to Jeffrey. But somehow, now she knew it was time to start again. Her years of solitude were over, for better or worse, and she wanted to make a real life with Justin. And it was definitely time he met Andrew. She was sorry he hadn't made it this time. But as she glanced over at Matthew she felt a small shaft of regret slice through her. She sensed now that things were different with him.

'What happens after Thanksgiving, Daff?' He looked at her as they drove through New England, and Daphne grew pensive.

'I'm not sure.' She wasn't yet, but she suspected that she and Justin would get married, if nothing ghastly happened in the meantime. In some ways, this trip was the test.

'Will you stay out there?' His eyes searched her face. He needed an answer. It was time for him, too.

'Maybe. I'll know more in the next couple of months.' And then she looked at him gently, she owed him some kind of explanation. She had told him the worst of it three months before, now she owed him the rest. It was

301

strange this friendship they had, it was platonic, and yet there was always just the faintest hint of something more. 'Things settled down a lot with Justin this summer. I think maybe I was wrong to tell you what happened while I was away last time.' Somehow, it didn't seem quite fair. Justin had never done it again and it coloured what Matthew thought of him, Daphne knew. Even now.

'There's no harm done.' He smiled as he drove. 'I won't tell the papers.'

She smiled in answer. 'I guess it was just an aberration.' She closed her eyes and sighed. 'But God, it was so awful. When I talked to you that time, I thought I would die.' He remembered and said nothing.

'Yeah ... I know. Have you looked at the school for Andrew?'

'Not yet. I suppose I should as soon as we finish the movie. I really haven't had time to do anything. I feel like I've been living in suspended animation for months.'

'Yeah.' He smiled again. 'I know the feeling. Me too.' It was strange to realise that in three months he would leave Howarth and go back to the New York School. It was difficult to remember a time when he hadn't been at Howarth, a time when she hadn't called him, when he hadn't been her friend.

There was something sad between them this time that Daphne couldn't quite put her finger on while she visited Andrew. She saw Matthew watching her from the window of his office, and then he would quickly turn away. It wasn't until he drove her back to the airport that she finally asked him.

'Matthew, is something wrong?'

'No, little one, nothing. I just had a birthday. I think maybe I'm just feeling old.'

'You need to get back to New York.'

His sister had said the same thing, but she knew more than Daphne, because she knew her brother was in love.

'Maybe.' He was strangely noncommittal.

'It's too lonely for you at Howarth. It was different for Helen Curtis. She's an old woman, she doesn't mind being locked up all alone.'

'You didn't mind it either when you did it, and you were half her age.'

'I wasn't alone the whole time I lived there.' As always, her voice was tinged with gentle memories of John.

'Neither am I, all the time.' It was the first time he had said anything like that. Daphne looked at him in surprise. He knew so much about her life that she had no hesitation about asking.

'Are you seeing someone up there, Matt?' Somehow she had always assumed that he was alone. And she was suddenly shocked to realise that she hadn't known more. Why hadn't he told her?

'Not really. From time to time.'

'Nothing serious?' She wasn't sure why, but it bothered her, which was ridiculous, she told herself. She was thinking of marrying Justin. Why shouldn't Matt have a woman in his life? He was just her friend after all.

He looked pensive. 'It could be serious if I wanted it to be. But I haven't wanted that.'

'Why not?' Her blue eyes were all innocence, and he turned towards her, marvelling at how blind she was.

'For a lot of foolish reasons, Daphne. Very foolish.'

'Don't be afraid, Matt. I was. And I was wrong.'

'Were you? Are you that happy now?' He sounded so sad.

'Not always, but some of the time. Maybe that's enough. At least I'm alive.'

'How do you know that's better? Is it good enough just to be alive?'

'You can't have perfection, Matt. I gave up after John died, because I knew I'd never find that again, but who's to say that we'd always have been that happy. Maybe even Jeffrey and I would have had our problems after a while. My career would be hard for any man to swallow. Look at this year, for instance. How would I have managed that if I were married, in a conventional marriage?' It was a question she had thought of often.

'You could swing it if that was what you wanted and your husband was understanding. You also didn't have to write the screenplay.' There was no reproach in his voice, he was just thinking aloud.

'I'm glad I did though.'

'Why? Because of Justin?'

'Partly. But mainly because I've learned a lot doing it. I don't think I'd do it again. It takes too much time away from my books, but it's been a marvellous experience. You were right to encourage me to go.'

'Did I do that?' He looked startled.

'You did.' She smiled. 'The first night I met you, and so did Mrs Curtis.'

Matt looked at her strangely. 'Maybe we were both fools.'

'What makes you say that?' She didn't understand what he was saying. Maybe because she didn't want to.

'Nothing. Martha tells me I'm getting soft in the head. She's probably right.' They exchanged a smile then as they drove on.

'So tell me about your new friend. Who is she?'

He might as well tell her. There was no harm now. 'A schoolteacher in town. She's from Texas, and she's very pretty and very young.' He smiled sheepishly at Daphne, this was a strange friendship that they shared. 'She's twenty-five years old, and frankly, I feel like a dirty old man.'

'Bullshit. It's good for you. Christ, there's nothing else to do up here except read. No wonder everyone here loves my books.'

'So does she. She's read them all.'

Daphne looked amused. 'What's her name?'

'Harriet. Harriet Bateau.'

'That sounds exotic.'

304

'I wouldn't call her that, but she's a nice girl, with a good mind, good values.'

Daphne looked at him then with a curious expression. 'Do you think you'll get married, Matt?' It was hard to think of him no longer there to take her phone calls, but he couldn't be forever. What they had had been a phenomenon of two lonely lives and kindred souls. The latter would always be the same, but her life had already changed and his was changing. The calls wouldn't go on forever. They both knew it. And they were facing it now.

But he shook his head. He wasn't ready to think of marriage. 'I haven't even thought of that yet. We've just been out a few times.' It was more than that, but in his mind it wasn't, though he knew how in love with him Harriet was. He didn't want to play with her heart, and he suspected that she knew what kept him distant from her. Sometimes he wondered if everyone did except Daphne.

She smiled at him now. 'Well, let me know.'

'I will. And you do the same.'

'About Justin?'

He nodded.

'I will.'

He stood looking down at her just before she got on the plane. 'Take care of yourself, little one.' More than ever before, this time his words had the ring of goodbye. She reached up and hugged him and he hugged her back, trying not to cling to her, and silently wishing her luck.

'I'll send Andrew out to you at Thanksgiving.'

'I'll be talking to you long before that.' But he wasn't so sure, and when he waved for the last time he had to turn away so she wouldn't see his eyes fill with tears at her going.

35

When Daphne stepped off the plane in Los Angeles, she found Justin waiting at the gate, and he swept her into his arms with a hungry look of glee. Four people recognised him before they reached the limousine, but as usual he denied who he was, and Daphne sat laughing with him in the backseat. He seemed ecstatic to see her, and when they got home, she found everything spotless and in order, and Justin looked very proud of himself.

'See! I told you I had reformed.'

'I apologise for all my evil thoughts.' She was beaming. Maybe he was for real after all. She felt relief sweep over her like a flood of cool, fresh water. Now she could let go again and trust him. She adored him, and everything was all right, but he looked down at her with serious eyes.

'No, Daphne. I apologise for my evil past.'

'Don't say that, darling ... it's all right.' She kissed him tenderly on the mouth and he picked her up in his arms and deposited her on the bed and they made love until morning without even going back to the car to get her luggage or turn off the living room lights, which, like their ardour, burned brightly until morning.

The movie got back to the usual grind the next morning and the next nine weeks flew by like magic. Daphne barely had time to call Matthew, and lately she felt reluctant to call him. It was beginning to feel like a betrayal of Justin to be pouring out her soul to Matt. He didn't seem to mind it, and he never seemed to notice when she called, but still it didn't feel right now, and several times when she did call, Matt was out. She assumed, correctly, with Harriet Bateau.

306

They wrapped up the last scene of *Apache* in the first week of November, and as Justin walked off the set for the last time there were tears in everyone's eyes. There were kisses and hugs, and Howard grabbed her and hugged her. Champagne flowed and they all left each other with regret, feeling like lost souls. It was impossible to imagine what they would all do without the filming of *Apache*. It had taken seven months, during which time they had become brothers and sisters and lovers. And now it was over, and the sense of loss was overwhelming. There was still plenty of work for Howard and the technical people. They would spend months on editing and cutting and splicing, the music and the sound would be worked on for a long time. But for Daphne and the actors it was all over, a dream come to an end, which had at times seemed like a nightmare, but now all the pains were forgotten. Like childbirth, it all seemed very dim, except the final burst of exhilaration at the end, and at the wrap party the next day everyone got roaring drunk and generally unruly. They didn't have to worry about being at work on time at five o'clock the next morning, or Howard screaming at them. It was over. *Finito*. Finished. Daphne stood, holding a glass of champagne and beaming at Justin, as Howard made a farewell speech and she felt tears fill her eyes.

'It's a beautiful movie, Daff. You're going to love it.' She had already seen rushes on a regular basis, but she had to admit that it would be the thrill of her life when she saw the finished film, and now she looked happily up at Justin.

'You did a great job.'

Everywhere, in every corner, were people congratulating each other and kissing. It was three in the morning before they went home.

And the next morning Daphne sat in her office with Barbara feeling lost and a little sad as she grinned. 'Christ, you know, I'm as bad as Justin. I don't know what to do now.'

'You'll figure out something.' Barbara smiled. 'Not to

mention the new book.' She had three months left to write it, and after Thanksgiving she had to get down to work. 'When's Andrew coming out?'

'The night before Thanksgiving. And that reminds me' – she handed Barbara a list – 'you and Tom and the kids are still coming, aren't you?' She looked suddenly worried. She knew that Barbara had never really made peace with Justin, and she was afraid that at the last minute they'd back out.

'We wouldn't miss it.'

'Good.'

She and Justin spent the next week doing the kinds of things film people do when they aren't working. They played tennis once or twice, went to a couple of parties, had dinner at Ma Maison and The Bistro and Morton's. The papers mentioned them several times, their romance was no longer a secret, and Daphne was feeling happy and relaxed. Justin seemed to look younger by the hour, and four days before Andrew was due to arrive he read the morning paper and smiled at Daphne.

'Guess what? There's snow in the Sierras.'

'Am I supposed to get excited about that?' She looked amused. Sometimes he still reminded her of a little boy.

'Hell, yes, kiddo. It's the first snow of the year. How about going skiing this week?'

'Justin' – at moments like this she spoke as though she were his extremely patient mother – 'I hate to remind you, my love, but Thanksgiving is next Thursday and we're having Barbara and Tom and his kids, and Andrew here for Thanksgiving dinner.'

'Tell them we can't make it.'

'I can't do that.'

'Why not?'

'Because for one thing Andrew is arriving on Wednesday, and this will be special for him. Come on, sweetheart, this is important to me. I haven't had a real at-home Thanksgiving in ten years.'

'We'll do it next year.' He looked petulant as he said it.

'Justin, please...' Her eyes pleaded with him and he threw down the paper and got up.

'Oh, shit. Who the hell cares about Thanksgiving dinner for chrissake? That's for preachers and their wives. It's the best snow they've had at Tahoe in thirty years and you want to sit here with a bunch of kids eating turkey. Christ.'

'Is that really so awful?' She was hurt by his words.

He looked down at her from his great height. 'It's extremely bourgeois.'

She laughed at the expression he had used, and took his hand in hers. 'I apologise for being so boring. But this is really important to all of us. Especially Andrew and me.'

'All right, all right. I give up. I'm obviously outnumbered by all you straight folks.' He kissed her then and didn't mention it again. She had promised him that as soon as Andrew went back to school, they would go skiing, even if it meant postponing her book. Justin wasn't starting a movie for several months, so they had plenty of time to go skiing. And Andrew was only staying for a week.

But on Tuesday night, as they lay in bed, Justin rolled over and kissed her and she saw that he was hemming and hawing about something. It was obvious that he had something to say.

'What's up, love?' She suspected that he wanted to ask her about Andrew. She knew that he was still nervous about his deafness. And she had tried to reassure him that Andrew was easy to talk to now, and she would be there to help. 'What's on your mind?'

He sat up in bed and looked down at her with a sheepish smile. 'You know me too well, Daff.'

'I try to.' But she didn't. She was in for a big surprise. 'So?'

'I'm leaving for Tahoe in the morning. I couldn't

309

resist, Daff. And to tell you the truth, I really need to get away.'

'Now?' She lay there and stared at him and then she sat up. He wasn't kidding. She couldn't believe it. 'Do you mean it?'

'Yes. I figured you'd understand.'

'What made you think that?'

'Well ... look ... I have to be honest. Family turkey dinners just aren't my style. I haven't done that kind of shit since I was in high school, and it's too late to start again now.'

'What about Andrew? I just can't believe you'd do this.' She got out of bed and walked around the room, torn between disbelief and fury.

'What's the big deal? I'll meet him at Christmas.'

'Will you? Or will you go skiing then, too?'

'Depends on how the snow is.' She stared at him then in total disbelief. The man who had pretended he loved her for the past eight months, and had finally convinced her, despite one aberration, was actually going skiing instead of staying home for Thanksgiving to meet her son. What in hell was in his head, or his heart? Again she found herself wondering 'Who is he?'

'Do you know how important this is to me?'

'I think it's stupid.' He didn't even look apologetic. He was totally comfortable about what he was about to do, and again Howard's warning that actors were all selfish children came to her mind. He had been right about everything, even the tears at the end of the movie. Maybe he was right about that, too.

'It's not stupid, dammit. And you want to get married one of these days and you haven't even taken the trouble to meet my only child. You didn't bother to come East with me in September and now this.' She stared at him in furious stupefaction, but beneath the fury was hurt beyond measure. He didn't want what she wanted in life, but more important than that, he didn't want Andrew. She was sure of that now, and that changed everything between them.

'I need time to think, Daff.' He looked suddenly very quiet.

'About what?' She was startled. It was the first time she'd heard that.

'About us.'

'Is something wrong?'

'No. But this is an enormous commitment. I've never gotten married, and before I tie myself down for good, I want some time alone.' It almost sounded right, but not quite, and she didn't really buy it.

'Well, your timing stinks. Couldn't you wait until next week?'

'I don't think so.'

'Why not?'

'Because I'm not sure I'm ready to meet your son.' It was painful, but honest. 'I don't know what to say to a deaf kid.'

'You start with hello.' Her eyes were cold and hurt and empty. She was sick and tired of his neurotic games about Andrew. And maybe Andrew was only the excuse. Maybe he didn't really want her. Maybe he didn't want anyone in his life except cocktail waitresses and starlets. Maybe that was all he was up to. He was suddenly diminishing in her eyes at a frightening rate, like a balloon with a hole the size of a fist in it.

'I just don't know how to talk to your kid. I've seen people like that, they make me nervous.'

'He lip-reads and he talks.'

'But not like a normal human being.' She suddenly hated him for what he was saying, and she turned her back on him and looked out the window. All she could think of now was Andrew. She didn't need this man. She needed her son, and no one else. She turned to him.

'All right, never mind, dammit, go.'

'I knew you'd understand.' He sounded perfectly happy and she shook her head in amazement. He understood nothing of what she felt. None of the disappointment or the hatred or the hurt he had just inflicted on her.

And then, suddenly, she wondered about something. 'Just when did you make these plans?'

At last he looked somewhat embarrassed, but not very. 'A couple of days ago.'

She stared at him for a long moment. 'And you didn't tell me?' He shook his head. 'You stink.' She slammed the bedroom door and slept that night in Barbara's bedroom, which she no longer used. She had moved in with Tom, and she came in every day, as she had in New York.

The next morning Daphne got up when she heard Justin making breakfast, and she walked into the kitchen to find him already dressed. She sat staring at him as he poured them each a cup of coffee. He looked relaxed and happy and she looked at him in open disbelief.

'You know, I just can't believe you'd do this.'

'Don't turn it into a major crisis, Daff. It's not such a big deal.'

'To me it is.' And she knew that to the others it would seem like one too. How was she going to explain his disappearance? Thanksgiving bored him so he'd gone skiing instead? She was suddenly grateful that she had said nothing at all to Andrew. She had been planning to have a talk with him on the way in from the airport. But now she wouldn't have to. Their meeting was going to have to wait until Christmas, if Justin didn't pull another disappearing act then. She was beginning to wonder about him, and as she watched him eat eggs and toast, she had an unpleasant thought.

'Are you going alone?'

'That's a strange question.' He kept his eyes on his eggs.

'Then it's appropriate, Justin. You're a strange man.' He looked up at her then and saw something unpleasant in her eyes. She was not only angry at him, she was livid. And she was looking for points against him. It startled him to realise that about her. But he didn't realise how deeply he had hurt her. In rejecting Andrew, he had

312

rejected her. In fact it was worse, but he didn't understand that.

'Yes, I'm going alone. I told you, I need some time to think up in the mountains.'

'I need some time to think too.'

'What about?' He actually looked surprised.

'You.' She sighed then. 'If you aren't going to make the effort to get to know Andrew, this isn't going to work out.' Not to mention the fact that if he ran off and did exactly what he pleased whenever he felt like it, it wouldn't suit her either. She hadn't a chance to see that side of him yet. They had been too busy working on the movie but now new sides of him were coming out. Sides that she suspected she couldn't live with. He disappeared for endless hours at times, never showed up when he said he was going to, and had a slapdash, easygoing way about him that he insisted was the only way he could balance the discipline and tension he felt when he was working. She had made excuses to herself, but suddenly she was no longer inclined to.

He tried to kiss her when he left, but she turned away and walked back into the house. And when Barbara arrived, she found Daphne in her study, lost in thought. Daphne looked a million miles away and Barbara had to speak to her twice before she heard her.

'I just picked up the turkey. Biggest mother you've ever seen.' She grinned. But there was no response at first and then Daphne seemed to force herself back to the present.

'Hi, Barb.'

'You seem far away. Already thinking about the new book?'

'Sort of.' But Barbara hadn't seen that vague, trancelike state in a long time.

'Where's Justin?'

'Out.' She didn't have the heart to tell her yet, but before she left for the airport to pick up Andrew, she decided she had to. She couldn't keep up the game forever, and why should she? She didn't owe it to him to make him look good. 'Barb, Justin's not coming to Thanksgiving dinner.' Daphne looked grim.

'He's not?' She looked as though she hadn't understood. 'Did you two have a fight?'

'Sort of. But not until after he told me he was going skiing for the next week instead of staying for Thanksgiving.'

'Are you kidding?'

'No. And I don't want to discuss it.' And the look on her face told Barbara that she meant it. She locked herself in her study then until it was time to go to the airport.

Daphne drove to the airport alone, her face set in a grim expression. She parked her car in the garage, and walked to the gate, her mind still reeling about Justin's behaviour. He had simply, flatly, walked out to do his own thing, as he pleased, without giving a damn about what mattered to her. And she was still running the exchange over again and again in her head as they announced Andrew's flight and she waited for the plane to pull into the gate. But when it did, suddenly all thoughts of Justin vanished. It was as though suddenly he no longer mattered, and everything came back into perspective. All that mattered was Andrew.

She felt her heart begin to beat faster as people came off the plane, and then in the midst of the crowd she saw him, holding a stewardess's hand, his eyes busily searching for her, and for an instant she was too stricken to move. This was the child Justin had rejected. This was the child she had built her whole life on. She began to move towards him then, no obstacle could stop her.

He saw her as she approached, and wrenched himself free from the flight attendant, running into her arms with the little sound he made when he was most pleased, and her whole life seemed to well up and spill from her eyes. He was all she had left from a lifetime of loss, and in truth he was the only human being who truly loved her. She clung to him like a life raft in the milling crowd,

314

and when he looked up at her face it was drenched with tears as she smiled at him.

'It's so good to have you back.' She mouthed carefully at him and he smiled in answer.

'It'll be gooder when you come home.'

'Much,' she agreed. And she suspected that that might come sooner than she had planned. They went to pick up his bags hand in hand and she seemed reluctant to let go of him even for a moment.

He had lots to tell her on the drive to her house, even a casual mention of Matthew's new girl friend, which, for some reason, cut her to the quick. She didn't want to hear about that now.

'She comes to see him at the school every Sunday. She's pretty and she laughs a lot. She has red hair and she brings us all candy.'

Daphne wanted to be pleased for Matthew, but somehow she wasn't. And she made no answer as they drove home, and the conversation moved on to other subjects. They had lots to do when they got to the house, they swam and talked and played cards, and Daphne began to feel herself return to the land of the living. They barbecued chicken in the backyard, and at last she put him to bed. He was yawning and could hardly stay awake, but he looked at her questioningly before she turned out the light.

'Mom, does someone else live here?'

'No. Why? Aunt Barbara used to.'

'I mean a man.'

'What makes you ask that?' She felt her heart skip a beat.

'I found some man's clothes in your closet.'

'They belong to the people who own the house.'

He nodded, seemingly satisfied, and then, 'Are you mad at Matt?'

'Of course not.' She looked surprised. 'Why would you ever think that?'

His eyes searched her face. Andrew was a very perceptive child. He was eight years old now, no longer

315

a baby. 'I thought you got mad when I talked about his girl friend.'

'Don't be silly. He's a nice man, he should have a nice lady.'

'I think he likes you.'

'We're good friends.' But she was suddenly dying to ask him what made him think so.

As though he read her mind, he answered with sleepy signs. 'He talks about you a lot, and he always looks happy when you call. Happier than when Harriet comes to visit on Sundays.'

'That's silly.' She smiled, brushing it off, but in some secret place in her heart she was pleased. 'Go to sleep now, sweetheart. We have a big day ahead tomorrow.' He nodded and his eyes were closed before she turned off the light, and went into her room, thinking of Matthew. She realised then that she still had to call him to tell him Andrew was all right. As usual, he answered his private line on the second ring.

'How's our friend? Safely arrived?'

'Very much so. And full of mischief.'

'That's nothing new.' Matthew smiled. 'He's just like his mother. And how are you?'

'Okay. Getting ready for Thanksgiving.' The conversations were always more impersonal now. Things were different since the advent of Justin and Harriet Bateau, particularly lately.

'Are you having a big turkey dinner at home?'

'I am.' There was a moment's hesitation in her voice, but she decided not to tell him. It wasn't his problem that Justin had skipped out, and maybe it didn't matter anymore that Justin refused to relate to Andrew. But she didn't want to drag Matthew into her decision, and she was beginning to think about going home. 'What about you, Matt?'

'I'll be here.'

'You won't be with your sister?'

'I didn't want to leave the kids.' And Harriet? But she didn't dare ask him that. If he wanted her to know more, he'd tell her. And he didn't. 'Are you coming to New York one of these days, Daff?' He sounded like the old Matt as he said it, and there was something lonely and gentle in his voice, but Daphne only sighed.

'I don't know. I've been thinking a lot about that.' It was time to make some decisions, and she knew it. 'I'm taking Andrew to visit the LA school next week.' At least that was what she'd been planning. But that was before Justin had shown his colours and gone to Tahoe.

'You'll love it. It's a great place.' But he sounded sad nonetheless. 'Everyone sure would miss him here.'

'You'll be gone anyway, won't you, Matt?'

But suddenly he sounded vague. 'I'm not sure.' Was he staying in New Hampshire then? Was it serious with Harriet Bateau after all? She felt a sinking sensation as she realised that was probably the case. What did Andrew know? He was only eight years old. Maybe Matthew was thinking of getting married.

'Let me know what you're going to do.'

'You too.'

She wished him a happy Thanksgiving then, and forcing herself not to think of Justin, she went to bed. The phone rang at midnight and woke her. It was Justin, happily ensconced in Squaw Valley, he told her, but the place where he was staying didn't have a phone. He started to tell her about the snow and how much he missed her, and then suddenly, in the middle of the conversation, he told her that he was freezing in an open phone booth, and had to hang up. And Daphne sat up in bed, staring at the phone, confused by the phone call. Why had he called her like that? And if he'd been freezing, why had he been so chatty before? She decided that she didn't understand anything about him, and forcing him from her mind once again, she went back to sleep, and oddly enough that night she dreamed of Matthew.

36

Thanks to Barbara and Tom's daughter, Alex, the Thanksgiving dinner turned out better than Daphne had dreamed. The three women worked together in the kitchen talking and laughing, and Tom and both boys putted golf balls around the lawn. He was amazed at how bright Andrew was and how funny he could be, even with his stilted speech. He discovered that he had a wonderful sense of humour, and when Daphne said grace before they began dinner, she felt more grateful than she had in years. Everyone ate tons of food, and sat by the fire after they were finished, and the Harrington troupe was sorry to leave when the time came. Both the teenagers kissed Daphne and hugged Andrew, and he promised to come visit them at their pool the next day, which they did. It was a comfortable, relaxed weekend, and other than missing Justin, Daphne was perfectly happy. The night before Andrew was to leave, Justin called her to check in, but hung up abruptly again, which annoyed Daphne. She didn't understand why he'd call, only to hang up a few minutes later. It didn't make any sense, at least not to her, but she thought about it at night after Andrew went to bed, and then suddenly it dawned on her. It was as though someone had approached him, and he'd hung up before he was found out. Suddenly she knew, and she sat up in bed livid. It was hours before she fell asleep. In the morning she was busy with Andrew. She put him on the plane and called Matt, and then went back to the house. For the next three days she tried to work on her new book, but nothing would come. All she could think about was Justin.

He drove in about two in the morning. He opened the front door with his key, propped his skis up in the hall, and then walked into the bedroom. He expected Daphne to be asleep, and was surprised when he saw her sitting up in bed with a book. She lifted her eyes to his without a word and looked at him.

'Hi, babe, what are you doing up?'

'I was waiting for you.' But there was no warmth in her voice.

'That's nice. Your kid get off okay?'

'Fine, thanks. And his name's Andrew.'

'Oh, Christ.' He knew then what he had in store. Another speech about Thanksgiving, but he was wrong. She had other things on her mind.

'Who were you with in Squaw Valley?'

'A mountain full of people I didn't know.' He sat down and pulled off his boots. After a twelve-hour drive he was in no mood for her interrogation. 'Could we just let it go until tomorrow?'

'No. I don't think we can.'

'Well, I'm going to bed.'

'Are you? Where?'

'Here. Last I heard I lived here.' He stared at her from across the room. 'Or has my address changed?'

'Not yet, but I think it might if you don't answer some questions. Honestly, for a change.'

'Look, Daff, I told you ... I needed to think...' But as he spoke the phone rang, and Daphne picked it up. She was instantly afraid that something was wrong with Andrew. Why else would anyone call at two thirty in the morning? But it wasn't Matt at the other end, it was a woman's voice, and she asked to speak to Justin. Without another word Daphne handed it to Justin.

'It's for you.'

Slamming the door, she left the room, and he found her in her study a few minutes later. 'Look, Daphne, please, I know how this looks but...'

And then, suddenly, as he stood there, tired from the trip, he realised that the pretence was too much trouble.

He was too tired for more lies. His voice was quiet as he sat down. 'All right, Daphne. You're right. I went skiing with Alice.'

'Who the hell is that?'

'The girl from Ohio.' He sounded desperately tired. 'It doesn't mean a hell of a lot, she likes to ski, so do I, I didn't want to stay here for your little family event, so I took her up there for a week. That's all there was to it.' To him it was normal.

There was no point fighting it anymore. It wasn't going to work. It was all over. She looked at him with tears in her eyes, and she felt so disillusioned that it was like a piece of her had been removed – the piece that loved him. 'Justin, I can't do this anymore.'

'I know. And I can't do it to you. I'm not made for this kind of thing, Daff.'

'I know.' She began to cry and he came to her.

'It's not that I don't love you. I do, but in my way, and my way is different from yours. Too different. I don't think I could ever be what you want. You want an honest-to-God regular husband. That's not me.' She nodded and turned her face away.

'It's all right. I understand. You don't have to explain.'

'Will you be okay?'

She nodded as the tears flowed, looking up at him, he was even more beautiful with his mountain tan, but that's all he was, all he had ever been, pretty to look at. Howard Stern had been right, he was a beautiful, spoiled child, who did exactly what he wanted in life, no matter who it hurt, or what it cost.

When she saw that he was going, for a mad instant she wanted to beg him not to go, to stay, that they could work it out, but she knew that they wouldn't. 'Justin?' The whole question was in the single word.

He nodded. 'Yes. I think I'll go.'

'Now?' Her voice trembled. She felt lonely and frightened. She had brought it to this, but there was no other way and she knew it.

320

'It's better like this. I'll pick up my stuff tomorrow.'

It had to end sometime and the time was now. He looked down at her with a sad smile. 'I love you, Daff.'

'Thanks.'

They were empty words coming from him, he was an empty man. And then the door closed and he was gone, and she sat alone in her study, crying. For the third time in her life she had lost, but this time for very different reasons. And she had lost someone who didn't really love her. He was capable of loving no one but himself. He had never loved Daphne. And as she grieved through the night she wondered if that was worse or better.

The next day she looked subdued when Barbara arrived and there were dark circles under her eyes as she sat in her study, working. 'You feeling okay?'

'More or less.' There was a long pause as Barbara searched her eyes. 'Justin moved out last night.'

She wasn't sure what to say in answer. 'Should I ask why, or should I mind my own business?'

Daphne smiled a tired smile. 'It doesn't matter. It had to be like this.' But she didn't sound convinced. She knew she would miss him. He had meant something to her for nine months and now it was over. It was bound to hurt for a while. Daphne knew that. She had lived with pain before. She'd live through it again.

Barbara nodded and sat down. 'I feel bad for you, Daff. But I can't say that I'm sorry. He would have screwed you over for the next hundred years. He's just like that.'

Daphne nodded. She couldn't disagree now. 'I don't think he even knows he's doing it.'

'I'm not sure if that's better or worse.' It was a hell of a statement about the man.

'Either way, it hurts.'

'I know.' Barbara walked towards her and patted her shoulder. 'What are you going to do now?'

'Go home. Andrew didn't like the school here anyway, and I don't belong here. I belong in New York, in my own place, writing my books, and being near Andrew.'

But it would all be different now. She had opened new doors since she'd left. Doors that would be hard to close, and she wasn't quite sure she remembered how to do it. It had been a lonely life for her in New York, and there had been a lot of joy at times with Justin.

'How soon do you want to leave?'

'It'll take me a couple of weeks to wrap up. I have some meetings at Comstock.' She smiled ruefully then. 'They want to talk to me about buying another book for a movie.'

Barbara held her breath. 'Will you write the screen-play?'

'Never again, my friend. Once is enough. I learned what I wanted to learn. But from now on, I write the books, they write the movies.' Barbara looked depressed. She had figured that. Even if Daphne had stayed with Justin on the West Coast, it was unlikely she would have done it again. She hadn't written a book in a year, and Daphne had complained about it often. 'So, we go home.' It was an assumption that Barbara didn't dare counter, and that night she told Tom as she fell apart in his arms, sobbing.

'For God's sake, Barb. You don't have to go with her.' He looked like he was going to cry too.

But she shook her head. 'Yes, I do. I can't leave her now. She's all broken up over Justin.'

'She'll survive. I need you more.'

'She has no one but me and Andrew.'

'And whose fault is that? Her own. Are you going to sacrifice our life for hers?'

'No.' She only cried harder as he held her, and then at last she quieted down. 'It's just that I can't leave her now.' It was in a way what she had gone through years before with her mother, and now Daphne wasn't there to help her gain her freedom. Her mother had died the year before in the home and now Barbara was tied to Daphne.

Tom looked unhappily at the woman he loved. 'Then how soon can you leave her?'

322

'I don't know.'

'That's not good enough, Barb. I can't live with that.' And then with a look of total despair he poured himself a stiff drink. 'I just don't believe you'd do this. After what we've had for the last year, you're going back to New York with her. For chrissake, dammit, that's crazy!' He was shouting at her and she started to cry again.

'I know it is. But she's done so much for me, and Christmas is coming and...' She knew how hard Christmas was every year for Daphne. And she also knew that Tom didn't understand. There was no reason why he should, but she didn't want to lose him. That was too high a price to pay, even for Daphne. 'Look, I promise, I'll come back. Just give me some time to get her settled in New York again and then I'll tell her.'

'When?' The word came at her like a shot. 'Tell me a day, and I'll hold you to it.'

'I'll tell her the week after Christmas. I promise.'

'How much notice will you give her?' He wasn't giving an inch.

She wanted to say a month, but she quailed at what she saw in his eyes. He looked like a wounded beast, and she hated to leave him more than she hated leaving Daphne. 'Two weeks.'

'All right. So you'll be back here six weeks after you leave?'

'Yes.'

'Will you marry me then?' His ferocious expression never changed.

'Yes.'

He smiled slowly then. 'All right, dammit. I'll let you go back to New York with her then, but don't ever do anything like this to me again. I can't take it.'

'Neither can I.' She folded herself into his arms.

'I'll come to New York on the weekends.'

'You will?' She looked up at him with wide happy eyes, and she looked half of forty.

'I will. And with any luck at all, I'll get you pregnant

before you even come back, and then I know you'll have to keep your word.' She laughed at the radical suggestion, but the idea didn't displease her. He had long since convinced her that she wasn't too old to have at least one or two babies.

'You don't have to do that, Tom.'

'Why not? I'd enjoy it.'

They spent every minute together that they could, and Tom came to the airport when they left. Daphne looked very New York in a black suit and a mink coat and hat, and Barbara was wearing the new mink jacket he had bought her. 'You two certainly look chic.' There was no trace of Los Angeles about them. And when he kissed Barbara, he whispered, 'See you on Friday.' She smiled and held him close and then they boarded the plane and took their seats and Daphne glanced at Barbara.

'You don't look too upset. Do I sense a plot afoot?' Barbara blushed and Daphne laughed at the truth. 'How soon is he coming to New York? On the next flight?'

'Friday.'

'Good for you. If I were halfway decent I'd can you right here and now and throw you off the plane.' Barbara watched her face but it was obvious that she didn't mean it. Daphne was looking very pale beneath her dark fur hat, and Barbara knew that she had seen Justin the night before. She suspected that it wasn't an easy meeting. Eventually, after lunch, Daphne told her about it.

'He's already living with that girl.'

'The one from Ohio?' Daphne nodded. 'Maybe he'll marry her.' And then she was instantly sorry she had said it. 'I'm sorry, Daff.'

'Don't be. You may be right, but I doubt it. I don't think men like Justin marry anyone at all. I just wasn't smart enough to know that.' They talked about Andrew then, and Daphne said she was going up to see him that weekend. 'I was going to ask you to come, but now that I know you've got better plans...' They exchanged a

324

smile, and then Barbara decided to tackle something she had thought of for a long time.

'What about Matthew?'

'What about him?' Daphne's eyes were instantly guarded.

'You know what I mean.' They had been together for too long to play games.

'Yes, I do. But he's just a friend, Barb. It's better that way.' And then she smiled. 'Besides, Andrew says he has a girl friend. And I happen to know he's right. Matt told me about her in September.'

'I have the feeling that if he knew you were free, he would dump her in about ten minutes.'

'I doubt that, and it's not important. Andrew and I have a lot of catching up to do when I get back, and I want to start the new book before Christmas.' Barbara wanted to tell her that that wasn't good enough, but she knew Daphne didn't want to discuss it. They each sat lost in her own thoughts. Barbara was relieved about the silence. She felt uncomfortable lying to Daphne about Tom and she wasn't ready to tell her they were getting married.

They arrived in New York, and Daphne grinned broadly as they drove into town. 'Welcome home.' But it no longer felt like that to Barbara. She already missed Tom. All Daphne could think of was Andrew. She talked about him nonstop for the next few days, and at the end of the week she took her car out of storage and drove up to see him. She could hardly wait as she drove along, singing and smiling. There was snow on the ground almost all the way up and it was a long tedious drive, but she didn't mind it. She had to stop and have chains put on her tyres, but never for a moment did she long for the balmy sunshine of California. All she wanted was to be near Andrew. She arrived in town well after nine, and she drove straight to the inn and called Matt to tell him that she had arrived and would be over in the morning. But one of the teachers answered his phone and told her he was out. So be it, she whispered to herself as she looked out the window. It was no longer time to think of him, he had his own life now, and she had Andrew. And the next morning when she got to the school, they had a grand reunion.

'And now we'll never be apart anymore.' It was amazing to think that the year was over. 'I'm going to come and get you in two weeks and we'll spend the whole Christmas vacation together at my apartment.' The visits to California had proven beyond any doubt that he was ready to leave the school for long periods of time, but he looked at her and shook his head.

'I can't, Mom.'

'You can't?' She looked shocked. 'Why not?'

'I'm going on a field trip.' Barbara was right. He had his own life, even now.

'Where?' Daphne felt her heart sink. She was going to spend Christmas alone.

'I'm going skiing.' And then he grinned. 'But I'm coming back before New Year's. Could I come then?'

'Sure you can.' She laughed softly. How life had changed in a year.

'Can we blow horns on New Year's Eve?'

'Yes.' But it struck her as a funny request, he wouldn't be able to hear them.

'I love the way they feel, they tickle my mouth, and everyone else will hear the noise.' There was definitely the eight-year-old inside him, despite his new independence.

And then Matthew joined them and Daphne smiled. 'Hi, Matt. I hear you're taking Andrew skiing.'

'I'm not. I'm staying here to finish up. But there's a whole bunch of them going to Vermont with some of the teachers.'

'That ought to be fun.' But he was watching the sadness he saw in her eyes.

'You wanted him in California for Christmas?' She hadn't yet told him that she'd moved back. She had just had Barbara call and tell them at the school that Daphne was in New York for the moment.

'No. I thought I'd stay in New York.' She searched his eyes but she saw nothing there. 'Andrew says he'll come down for New Year's.'

'That sounds great.' Their eyes met and held over the boy's head and a thousand thoughts went unspoken.

'When are you leaving, Matt?'

'On the twenty-ninth. For a while I thought I'd stay here, but they need me too much at the New York School.' He smiled. 'That doesn't sound very humble, but Martha says she'll quit if I don't come back, and they can't afford to lose us both. She's the one who's really valuable to them.'

'Don't be so modest. They're going to miss you like crazy up here.'

'No, they won't. The new director is arriving from London next week, and judging from her correspondence, she's terrific. And I'll be coming up pretty often, to visit the troops on weekends.' With that, Daphne understood that Harriet Bateau was still in the picture. It gave her her cue for the next moves, and she was careful with them. For a mad moment she had wondered if Barbara was right, that she should let him know she was free, but she had no right to do that to him now, and the fact was that there was no reason to think it would make any difference to him.

'Why aren't you going skiing with the kids?' But she assumed that she already knew.

'I want to stay here with the kids who can't go.' She nodded, but she understood the real reason. He went back to his work then and she only saw him in brief moments during her visit. He was desperately busy, getting things ready for the new director. And as had often happened before, it wasn't until her last night that they had time to sit down and talk after Andrew went to bed. She had decided to tackle the roads and drive home on Sunday night. For the first time in a long time, being in New Hampshire depressed her.

'So how's California these days, Daff?' He handed her a cup of coffee and sat down in his familiar chair.

327

'It was all right the last I saw of it. I've been in New York since Monday.'

'That's nice for Andrew that you're staying through Christmas. I gather your friend still isn't anxious to meet him. Or is he here with you?' It was the perfect opportunity to tell him, but she didn't.

'No, he's not. I have to get started on my next book.'

'Don't you ever relax?' His smile was gentle, but he was vaguely distant.

'No more than you do. From what I've seen in the last two days, you're entitled to a nervous breakdown.'

'I am. But I don't have time to collect it.'

'I know the feeling. The last few weeks of making *Apache* were absolutely nuts, but the wrap was great.' She told him about the last day and the wrap party, and he smiled as he listened. She had a nice way of weaving a tale and she was keeping the conversation from coming too close. She was still hurting too much to open up very much, even to him. It wasn't so much that she missed Justin. But she felt defeated. By Justin and the twenty-two-year-old girl from Ohio. Nothing like that had ever happened to her before. Or would again, she promised herself daily.

'What'll you do for Christmas with Andrew gone?' There was concern in his eyes, but maybe Justin would come in to be with her. The last time he had talked to her about him, she had said that they would probably get married.

'I'll have plenty to do.' It seemed an adequate answer and he nodded. There was a long pause then as they both sat lost in their own thoughts, and he found himself thinking of Harriet. She was a nice girl, but she wasn't for him, and they both knew it. She had started seeing someone else a few weeks before, and he suspected that any day he would hear of her engagement. She was ripe to get married, and there were plenty of people who would jump at the chance, but he wasn't one of them. He didn't love her. And she deserved better than that, he had told her that the last time he saw her. Daphne was watching him as he sat lost in thought. 'You look awfully serious, Matt.'

He glanced at the fire and then at her. 'I was thinking how times change.' Daphne wondered how deeply involved he was with that girl. Maybe he was getting married. But she didn't want to ask him now. She had enough with what she was going through, and when he wanted to, he would tell her.

'Yes, they do. I can't believe this year is over.'

'I told you it wouldn't be forever.' He looked quiet and wise, and she noticed that there was more grey in his hair now than there had been a year before. 'And Andrew did just fine.' He smiled at her then. 'You didn't do too badly either.'

'Andrew did well, thanks to you, Matt.'

'That's not true. Andrew did well because of Andrew.' She nodded then, and after a little while she stood up.

'I'd better go if I'm going to tackle those roads tonight.'

'Are you sure you should?' He worried and she smiled. He had given her so much comfort in the past year, it was difficult not to reach out to him now, but she knew it wouldn't be right for him. He seemed content, and he had said himself that times had changed. It was better left at that.

'I'll be fine. I'm indestructible, you know.'

'Possibly, but there's a hell of a lot of snow on those roads, Daff.' And then as he walked her to the door, 'Why don't you call me when you get home?'

'Don't be silly, Matt. It'll be three or four in the morning. That's my time of day, not any other normal human being's.'

'Never mind that, just call. I'll go right back to sleep. I want to know you're okay. If you don't call me, I'll stay up and keep calling you.' It was an offer above and beyond the call of duty, and reminiscent of their old friendship.

'All right, I'll call. But I hate to wake you.' She

329

thought about it again as she drove slowly south on the icy roads. It took her even longer than she thought and she didn't get home until five in the morning. It seemed a crime to call, and yet she had to admit that she wanted to. She dialled his number from her desk, and a moment later he picked up the phone, sounding sleepy.

'Matt? I'm home.' She spoke in a whisper.

'Are you okay?' He glanced at the clock as he asked. It was five fifteen in the morning.

'I'm fine. Now go back to sleep.'

'That's all right.' He rolled over in bed with a sleepy smile. 'This reminds me of when you used to call from California.' She smiled too, it was an odd sort of hour and it was easier to let one's guard down. 'I've missed you, you know. Sometimes it's strange when you pop in here. I'm busy and there are ten thousand people around.'

'I know. I feel awkward too.' They sat in silence for a moment and she thought she ought to let him go back to sleep. 'Are you happy these days, Matt?' She wanted to ask him about Harriet but she still didn't dare.

'Pretty much. I'm too busy to ask myself that most of the time. What about you?'

For a moment she faltered, then her guard went up again. 'I'm all right.'

'Getting married?' He had to ask.

'No.' But she didn't offer any further information. 'I think Barbara is, though.'

'The guy in LA?'

'Yes. He's just super. She deserves someone like that.'

'So do you ...' The words had sneaked out and he instantly regretted them. 'I'm sorry, Daff. That's none of my business.' Why not?

'It's okay. I've cried on your shoulder a lot in the last year.'

'You're not crying anymore, are you, Daff?' He sounded sad and Daphne knew he was asking about Justin.

330

'Not lately.'

'I'm glad. You deserve good things in your life.'

'So do you.' Her eyes filled with tears then and she felt stupid. He had a right to be happy with that girl, but she knew she was going to miss him. Once he left Howarth she would have no excuse to call him. They might have lunch once in a while, but that would be all, and maybe not even that if he was married. 'Go back to bed now, Matt. It's so late.'

He yawned and glanced back at the clock. It was almost six o'clock, and he had to get up. 'You get some sleep too. You must be bushed after that drive.'

'A little.'

'Good night, Daff. I'll talk to you soon.'

She had called to leave a message for Andrew when he left to ski, but Matt was out, and she was planning to call him on Christmas Day, but she never got to. The car hit her on Madison Avenue on Christmas Eve, and instead of calling Matt she was lying in Lenox Hill as Barbara watched her, with tears coursing silently down her face. She couldn't believe this had happened to Daphne. And what was she going to tell Andrew? Daphne had made her promise not to call, but sooner or later she knew she'd have to. And especially if ... she couldn't bear the thought as Liz Watkins signalled to her that it was time for her to go back out in the hall, and when she checked her pulse, she noticed that Daphne was running a fever.

'How is she now?'

Liz Watkins watched Barbara's eyes, wondering if she could take the truth, then they went out into the hallway. 'Not good, to be honest with you. The fever could mean a lot of things.' Barbara nodded, her eyes filling with tears again. She went to call Tom, he had waited all day in her apartment. It was a rotten way to spend Christmas, but she had to be here with Daphne.

'Oh, babe...' He thought that the worst had come, but Barbara was quick to reassure him. It was the tenth time she had called, and he worried when he heard her crying.

'She has a fever, and the nurse looks worried.'

He sat silently as his end for a long time. 'Is there anyone you should call, Barb?' It was an enormous responsibility for her to take on her own shoulders.

'The only family she has is Andrew.' She began crying softly then, thinking of him, it would kill him if he lost his mother. She knew that she would take him back to California with her to live with Tom, but that wouldn't be the same. He needed Daphne. They all did. 'And I can't call him. He's skiing. Besides, he's only eight years old. He shouldn't see this.'

'Does she look that bad?'

'No, but . . .' Barbara choked on the words. 'She may not make it.'

And then he had a thought. 'What about the guy at the school, that director who's her friend at Andrew's school?'

'What about him?'

'I don't know, Barb, but it may mean something to him. I've always had the feeling from what you've said that there was more going on than she admitted.' One thing was for sure, she wouldn't bother to call Justin.

'I don't think there was.' She thought about it for a while. 'But maybe I should call him.' Even Barbara didn't realise how close they had become, and maybe he would have some thoughts about whether or not they should contact Andrew on his ski trip. 'I'll call you back.'

'Do you want me to come over?' She was about to say no, and then suddenly she broke down again. She couldn't take it anymore. She needed him there. 'Never mind. I'll be there in ten minutes.' She told him what floor and he told her he'd bring something for her to eat. She wasn't hungry, but he knew that she needed some food to get her through the night, food and a lot of black coffee. He had a feeling that things weren't going to end

332

well for Daphne and Barbara was going to take it very hard if she died.

Barbara sat in the phone booth for a long time, trying to decide if it was right to call. In one of her few lucid moments Daphne had told her not to. But something even stronger told her to now. She had Daphne's handbag and she looked in the little address book she carried. The private number was there next to the name Matthew Dane.

He sounded distracted, as though he had been working.

'Mr Dane, this is Barbara Jarvis in New York.' She could feel her heart pound and her palms sweat. This wasn't going to be easy.

'Yes?' He sounded surprised. Daphne's official calls didn't usually come in at night, let alone on Christmas. He recognised the secretary's name at once. Maybe she was just calling to leave a message for Andrew.

'I ... Mr Dane, this is a difficult call. Miss Fields has had an accident. I'm at the hospital with her now ...'

'Did she ask you to call?' He sounded shocked and Barbara fought back tears as she shook her head.

'No, she didn't.' He could hear that she was crying. 'She was hit by a car last night, and ... Mr Dane, she's in intensive care and ...' The sobs broke from her then.

'Oh, my God. How bad is it?' She told him all she knew and she could hear that his voice was shaking when he answered.

'She didn't want me to tell you or Andrew, but I thought ...'

'Is she conscious?' He sounded relieved.

'She was for a little while, but she isn't now.' Barbara sighed deeply and told him what she had told Tom. 'She just started running a fever.' She also told him what it could mean, and he had to control his voice when he asked the next question. Suddenly he understood as he never had before, what it had been like when she had lost

Jeffrey and then John. And he didn't want to know more than he did now. He couldn't bear it.

'Is there anyone with her, Barbara, other than you?' He wasn't sure how else to ask her.

'No, but my ... my fiancé will be here any minute. He's here from LA...' And then she realised that she wasn't telling him what he wanted to know. She decided to take the bull by the horns. 'Mr Dane, she ended it with Justin a month ago.'

'Why didn't she tell me?' He sounded even more shocked than he had before.

'She thought you were in love with some girl up there, and she didn't think it would be fair to tell you about Justin.'

'Oh, my God.' And he had sat by the fire telling her how times had changed. He almost groaned as he remembered the conversation verbatim. He had been assuming that she and Justin were almost married.

'Do you think we should tell Andrew?'

'No, I don't. There's nothing he can do. And he's too young to deal with this, if he doesn't have to.' He looked at his watch then and stood up, beginning to pace the room with his phone in his hand. 'I'll be down in six hours.'

'You're coming?' She sounded stunned. She wasn't sure what she had expected.

'You didn't think I would?' He sounded hurt.

'I don't know. I don't know what I thought. I just knew I had to call you.'

'You were right. And I don't know if it matters now, but just for the record, I've been in love with her ever since I met her. And I was too stupid to get up the guts to say it.' He felt a lump rise in his throat and he could hear Barbara cry softly into the phone. 'I'm not going to lose her now, Barb.'

She nodded. 'I hope you never will.'

37

Matthew drove to New York as fast as he could, thinking every moment of Daphne. Every phone call, every meeting, seemed indelibly etched in his mind, and now it all ran through his head like a movie. Once in a while he smiled at remembered words, but most of the time his face was grim. He couldn't believe this had happened. Not to her. Not to Daphne. So much had already happened in her life, so much sorrow and pain, so many events that required unlimited courage. This couldn't happen to her now. It couldn't end like this, but he knew that it might, and the thought that she might die before he arrived made him drive even faster.

After driving to New York as fast as he could in the snow, Matthew arrived at Lenox Hill at two thirty in the morning. Most of the lights were out in the lobby and there was no one in the halls as he went upstairs. He went straight to the desk at intensive care, and then Barbara saw him. She had sent Tom home long before and insisted that she wanted to stay. The nurse had told them a little while before that the night would be decisive. Daphne couldn't hover much longer where she was, either she would start to improve, or she wouldn't make it.

'Matt?' He turned at the sound of Barbara's voice, wishing it were Daphne. She couldn't believe how quickly he had come. He must have flown over the icy roads. He was lucky he hadn't wound up in the same state as Daphne.

'How is she?'

'The same. She's putting up one hell of a fight.'

He nodded grimly, and there were deep grooves under

335

his eyes. He had been working like a demon, and now this. He was still wearing the old cords and heavy sweater he had been wearing when Barbara called him. He had left a hasty note for the night staff and run out the door, grabbing his coat and his keys and his wallet.

'Can I see her?' Barbara's eyes searched those of the familiar nurse and she looked at her watch.

'Why don't we wait a few minutes?'

'Nurse' – he turned to her and gripped the desk with powerful hands – 'I've just driven seven hours from New Hampshire to see her.'

'All right.' It didn't matter now. And maybe an hour later it would be too late. Liz Watkins led the way down the hallway to the open door, and there she lay, immobile, swathed in plaster and gauze, hooked up to all her machines in the bright light. Matthew felt an almost physical shock when he saw her. It had been only two weeks since her last visit to Howarth, and suddenly she looked so different. He walked slowly into the room and sat down in the empty chair at her side and gently stroked the pale hair as Barbara watched. She turned and left the room behind Liz. She didn't want to intrude, and the nurse searched her eyes. But she felt better now that she knew there was a man. It wasn't right for a woman like Daphne to be alone. And the man with the soft brown eyes looked perfect for her.

'Hello, little one.' He touched the delicate cheek with one hand, and then sat and looked at her for a long time, wondering again why she hadn't told him about Justin. Maybe he was even foolish to hope now, maybe she had never cared about him, and never could. But if she ever woke up again, he was going to tell her that he loved her. He sat there looking at her face for close to an hour and at last Liz returned to the room to check her. 'Any change?' She shook her head. The fever had gone up slightly. But he never left the room, and she didn't ask him to. He sat there until the shift changed at seven, and Liz told the morning nurse what was going on.

336

'Why don't you leave him in there, Anne? He's not doing any harm, and how do we know? Maybe it makes a difference. She's fighting for her life.'

The other nurse nodded. They both knew that at times people survived who originally seemed like they would never make it, and if having someone she knew in the room would help, they wouldn't stop it. Liz stopped in to say good-bye, and took a last look at Daphne. She thought she looked a trifle less pale, but it was hard to say. He certainly looked like hell, a shadow of beard had appeared on his face and the circles under his eyes were even darker than they had been.

'Can I get you anything?' she whispered to him. It was against the rules, but she could bring him a cup of coffee. But he only shook his head. And when she left, she saw Barbara asleep on the couch. She went home, wondering if Daphne would still be there when she got back. She hoped so. She thought about her all day, and found herself rereading parts of *Apache*, which was her favourite. And when she came back on at eleven o'clock that night, she was afraid to ask. But the nurse told her that he was still there, and so was Daphne. Barbara had finally gone home that afternoon to get some rest. And Daphne was still holding her own, but barely.

Liz walked silently down the hall until she reached her door and looked in, and she saw him standing over Daphne, looking into her face, almost begging her with his eyes not to let go.

'Would you like a cup of coffee, Mr Dane?' She whispered the name they had told her. Apparently he hadn't eaten all day, he had just drunk a steady stream of coffee.

'No, thanks.' He smiled at the door, the beard was thicker now, but his eyes were strong and alive and his smile was gentle. 'She's doing better, I think.' The fever was gone, but she hadn't stirred all day. He had watched them change her assorted tubes and he hadn't flinched. He had stood there and stroked her hair as he did now while Liz watched him.

She walked slowly to the bed. 'It's amazing, you know. Sometimes I think people like you make the difference.'

'I hope so.' They exchanged a smile and she left and after a while he sat down again, watching Daphne's face, and the sun was coming up over New York when she finally moved. He sat very tense in his chair and watched. He wasn't sure what kind of sign it was, but then she opened her eyes and looked around the room. She seemed puzzled when she saw him and then she drifted off again, but only for a few minutes. He wanted to ring for the nurse, but he was afraid to move, and for a moment he was afraid that he might have drifted off himself, and possibly dreamed it. But she opened her eyes again, and looked long and hard.

'Matt?' Her voice was barely more than a whisper.

'Good morning.'

'You're here?' Her voice was thin and thready and she didn't seem to understand, but she smiled and he took her hand.

'Yes, I am. You've been asleep for a long time.'

'How's Andrew?'

'He's fine.' He was speaking to her in a whisper. 'And you're going to be fine too. Do you know that?'

She smiled faintly at him. 'I don't feel so hot.' He chuckled at the understatement. He had kept his vigil for twenty-eight hours, fearing for her life. 'Not feeling so hot' was certainly one way to say it.

'Daphne . . .' He waited for her to open her eyes again. 'There's something I have to tell you.' He felt a lump in his throat and he stroked her free arm as she looked at him and nodded slightly.

'I already know.'

'Do you?' He seemed disappointed. Had she known all along and didn't want to hear?

'You're . . . getting . . . married . . .' Her eyes were big and blue and sad as she looked at him and he stared at her in amazement.

'Do you actually think I've been sitting here, waiting

338

for you to wake up, to tell you that I'm getting married?'

A small smile dawned on her face. 'You've always been very polite.'

'Not that polite, you dummy.' The small smile grew and she closed her eyes and rested for a minute. When she opened them again, he was watching intently. 'I love you, Daff. I always have and I always will. That's what I wanted to tell you.'

'No, you don't.' She tried to shake her head but winced instead. 'You love Harriet ... Boat ... or whatever her name is...'

'Harriet Boat, as you call her, doesn't mean shit to me. I stopped seeing her after I told her I didn't love her. She knew the truth. The only one who's never known it is you.'

She looked at him for a long time, taking it all in. 'I used to feel guilty for what I felt for you, Matt.'

'Why?'

'I don't know ... I thought it wasn't fair to ... to you ... or to Justin.' She looked at him again for a long time. 'I left him.'

'Why didn't you tell me?'

'I thought you were in love with someone else.' They were both still speaking in whispers. 'And you said...'

'I know what I said. I thought you and that Greek god of yours were getting married.'

She smiled at him then, a lifetime showing in her eyes. 'He's a jerk.'

'So were we. I'm in love with you, Daff. Will you marry me?'

Two huge tears crept from her eyes, and she coughed as she began to cry. He kissed her eyes then, and put his face next to hers. 'Don't cry, Daff ... please ... it's all right ... I didn't want to upset you ...' Then she didn't love him at all. He felt like crying too, but he only stroked her hair as she tried to regain her composure. 'I'm sorry ...' But then he heard her voice again and he froze where he stood.

'I love you too ... I think I fell in love with you the first day I met you ...' Her eyes looked into his, and the tears ran slowly down his cheeks.

'I love you more than I can tell you.'

Liz Watkins came in then, to say good-bye to him before she left, and she stopped as she stood in the doorway. She had heard Daphne's voice and she saw their heads close together. She knocked softly then and came into the room. She was going to ask how Daphne was, but she could see as she approached the bed. They were both crying, and Daphne was smiling.

'This looks like a happy group.'

'It is.' He answered for his future wife. 'We just got engaged.'

'Can I see the ring?' Her eyes glowed. She could tell instantly from looking at Daphne that she would make it. The crisis was past and the worst was over. 'Where's the ring?' she teased in her soft voice.

'She ate it. That's why she's here.' Liz laughed and left them alone again and Matthew looked down at Daphne with a smile. 'Is next week too soon?'

'Will I still have this headache by then?' She looked very tired but incredibly happy.

'I hope not.'

'Then next week is fine. Will Andrew be home?'

'Yes, and that's another thing I want to talk to you about. How about putting him in the New York School?'

'And have him live at home?'

'I think he's ready.'

She was still smiling as the morning nurse rolled in a cot, and opened it next to her bed with a determined smile. 'Doctor's orders. He said that if you don't get some sleep, Mr Dane, he's going to give you a general anaesthetic.'

When the nurse left the room, he stretched out on the cot, and reached up to hold Daphne's hand. She had gone back to sleep, but it was no longer an ominous sign. He knew she would be all right, and as he drifted off to sleep he smiled to himself. What fools they had been. He should have told her a year before, but it didn't matter now ... nothing did ... except Daphne.

You have been reading a novel published by Piatkus Books. We hope you have enjoyed it and that you would like to read more of our titles. Please ask for them in your local library or bookshop.

If you would like to be put on our mailing list to receive details of new publications, please send a large stamped addressed envelope (UK only) to:

Piatkus Books, 5 Windmill Street
London W1P 1HF

PIATKUS

The sign of a good book